Of Rags and Riches

and

Riches

ROMANCE COLLECTION

Nine Stories of Poverty and Opulence during the Gilded Age

Of Rags and Riches

ROMANCE COLLECTION

Michelle Griep, Erica Vetsch,
Susanne Dietze, Anne Love, Gabrielle Meyer,
Natalie Monk, Jennifer Uhlarik,
Jaime Jo Wright, Kathleen Y'Barbo

BARBOUR BOOKS
An Imprint of Barbour Publishing, Inc.

Print ISBN 978-1-68322-263-7

eBook Editions:
Adobe Digital Edition (.epub) 978-1-68322-265-1
Kindle and MobiPocket Edition (.prc) 978-1-68322-264-4

Published by Barbour Books, an imprint of Barbour Publishing, Inc., P.O. Box 719, Uhrichsville, Ohio 44683, www.barbourbooks.com

Our mission is to publish and distribute inspirational products offering exceptional value and biblical encouragement to the masses.

ecpa Member of the
Evangelical Christian
Publishers Association

Printed in Canada.

Contents

Union Pacific Princess

by Jennifer Uhlarik

Chapter One

D ara. . .are you coming?"

At her uncle's call, Dara Forsythe followed her cousin Becca onto the rear platform of their private railcar. The sky pressed in, cold, gray, and dreary, just like her mood. The town—if she could call it such—was a collection of dingy canvas tents of varying sizes, heavy-laden wagons, and muddy paths.

Her new home. No paved streets. No store windows. Goodness, not even a permanent building within sight. Her throat constricted.

This was *not* Boston.

People milled about, some waiting to meet the train, others scurrying between tents. She scanned every face. Nowhere did she see the one she longed for. Her heart sank.

Papa had begged her to come west after her mother's untimely death, and hoping to rekindle the bond they'd once shared, she agreed to leave the comfort of Boston and brave the journey west. Yet the niggling fear that things would never be the same was only perpetuated when she saw he wasn't there to meet them. They'd sent word of their expected arrival. The least he could have done was be on time.

A cool wind whipped around the passenger car, and Dara took the hand her uncle, Dr. William Chenoweth, offered, and descended to the mud below.

"Let me help you, Matilde." Uncle William assisted the pretty young freedwoman down the steps.

"So this is it?" Matilde stepped close and eyed the camp.

Becca looped her arm in Dara's. "I knew this would be an adventure, but I never imagined it would be so. . .primitive."

Primitive. Yes, quite.

"Don't you fret none, Miss Dara." Matilde smiled. "The dear Lord'll make this turn out right."

Mute, Dara nodded at her friend.

"I'll gather the trunks. Then we'll find Connor." Uncle William turned toward the baggage car.

"I'll help you, Doctor William." Matilde trotted after him.

Dara hoisted her skirt from the mud and followed. Thank goodness Uncle William had agreed to leave his Boston medical practice to become a frontier doctor. Having him and Becca here would help ease her transition, and she'd be lost without Matilde. *Thank You for them all, Lord.*

The one she missed most was Mama. How did one continue after such a crushing loss? Dara's aunt Mary had died when Becca was three, leaving Becca with almost no memories of her. Dara, on the other hand, had lost Mama to illness just four months earlier at seventeen.

"You look absolutely mortified." Becca's grip on her arm tightened. "Don't worry. This place *has to* get better."

"The place is only part of it. I miss Mama."

Grief was her near-constant companion, threatening to drag her into a dark pit and never let go. The only time it didn't plague her was when something triggered memories of her mother's fortitude and spirit. Always graceful. Always a lady. Yet never one to back away from what was right. Those characteristics had pushed Mama to join the abolition movement before the war, she and Dara both working for the cause. If only she could emulate Mama's traits, keep her character and spirit alive. But *how* in this backward place?

Uncle William and Matilde stopped beside the baggage car, calling to one of the handlers inside. Dara steered Becca to an out-of-the-way spot. The air sparked with chatter and busyness. Men bustled around the freight cars, unloading crates. Dara sighed as an empty ache stole through her. This might be busy for the Dakota Territory, but it was interminably slow compared with Boston.

The chug of a steam engine diverted her attention, and she watched as the hulking machine backed toward the caboose. Mr. Marston and Mr. Adgate, the two richly dressed, distinguished gentlemen whom she'd met on the train, called orders to a few baggage handlers. The dust-clad workers transferred several large wooden crates labeled BLANKETS from the last freight car into the backs of several wagons. Once finished, the workers drove the wagons away, and Mr. Marston released the coupling arm that joined the freight car and caboose to the train. As she and Becca watched the process, a stout, slovenly giant stepped in front of them.

"Ain't never seen the likes of you two before." He reeked of sweat and spirits.

Becca's cheeks paled. Dara made no response except to dart a glance toward Uncle William and Matilde. *Gone.*

Heart hammering, Dara turned them away from the man and searched for Uncle William. Of course, neither he—nor Papa—were anywhere to be found.

"I said. . ." He stepped in front of them again. "Ain't seen you two around these parts before."

Trembling, she turned. "You're being quite rude, sir."

"And you're right pretty. Where you from?"

How could Papa *not* have come to meet them? If he'd been here, this drunken scoundrel wouldn't have had the opportunity to approach them. She faced him. "I will thank you to leave us alone."

An average-height man ambled their way, half an apple in one hand, a large knife and an apple slice in the other. She barely breathed as he lifted the slice to his mouth then wiped the blade on his pants.

"You gonna answer me?" The drunken man's bawling barely registered as the other man sheathed the knife and smiled around the bite of fruit.

His warm brown eyes captivated her. "Pardon us." Hissing steam and grinding metal nearly drowned his words as he guided the belligerent fellow away.

Dara stared, slack-jawed, as the men exchanged words.

Becca giggled. "Dara, close your mouth. You'll draw flies."

Her cheeks warmed, and she clamped her mouth shut. The engine coupled to the caboose and freight car and chugged away from the makeshift train stop. When she focused again on their handsome rescuer, he patted the drunken man's shoulder and sent him on his way. The brown-eyed man, perhaps in his middle twenties, was simply dressed. His clothes were neat but patched and well-worn. He was fairly clean with dark brown hair and clean-shaven face. A tattered slouch hat topped his ensemble.

Maybe there was a bit of civilization to be found in this God-forsaken land after all.

Still trembling, she smiled. "Thank you, sir. That was very kind of you." Galloping hoofbeats pounded in the distance behind her.

A charming smile spread across his face. "My pleasure, ma'am. No self-respecting Georgia boy'd let that fella accost such a fine pair of ladies." He flicked a glance past her, eyes narrowing.

Her brow furrowed. A *Southerner?*

"Dara-girl!" The familiar voice boomed across the distance.

Papa.

He marched through the thinning crowd toward them. Dara grabbed Becca's hand and darted toward her father.

They'd barely gone five steps when something slammed into her, and she lurched face-first into the cold mud. With a startled cry, Dara reared back, trying to get up. Beside her, Becca also flailed in an attempt to rise. A weight crushed her farther into the goo.

"Stay down!" The Southerner's words twanged with urgency.

A light flashed, and an earth-shattering concussion rocked her surroundings, sucking the oxygen away. Dara clamped her hands against her ears, too late to block the deafening roar.

———— •◦• ————

Debris rained down around Gage Wells as he huddled over the two young ladies. Something sliced across his back, and he sucked down lungfuls of acrid air. Beneath him, the young ladies trembled, eyes shut and mouths agape. Their muffled cries barely registered over the ringing in his ears.

His heart pounded as he peeked at the empty boxcar where a horseman had thrown the lit bundle of dynamite. The remains of the wooden car sat cockeyed on its huge metal wheels, thick smoke billowing from its splintered shell. The caboose had fared little better. Gage's vision swam. Facing front, he dropped his throbbing head against one of the young ladies' shoulders.

Dynamite? He wouldn't grieve the loss of any train, but who in his ever-loving mind would light dynamite with folks so nearby? Especially to blow up an *empty* train car. . .

Muscles shaking, Gage sat back on his heels, fire racing down his back as he braced his hands against his thighs. Frigid mud soaked through his pant legs as he fought to regain his bearings. All around them, mayhem reigned. People ran, some away from the danger, some toward it. Riderless horses fled, reins trailing and stirrups flapping. Only feet away, other townsfolk lay bleeding—maybe dead. Not what two fine young ladies needed to see. He should get them up, away from here.

Gage stumbled to his feet, snatched his hat from the mud, and again settled his hands on his knees to steady quivering limbs. The world tilted. What was wrong with him? He touched the older girl's elbow first, and she snapped one large blue eye open. The other

11

young lady had a similar reaction.

Lightning surged down his spine. "Can you get up?"

Before either answered, a man crouched over the ladies. His voice was muffled as he helped the first girl from the mud. As he reached for the second, Gage really saw the fella. Muscular, blond, well dressed. Gage's eyes widened.

Connor Forsythe.

His throat constricted. He wasn't to be seen. Not by Forsythe nor anyone connected to the railroad. His self-assigned fact-finding mission depended on getting in, gathering his information, and slipping out before anyone grew wise.

Gage hoisted himself straight and walked away, only his body rebelled. He tottered sideways, went to one knee, pushed back to his feet. He must collect his horse and ride out before everything was ruined.

One more step, and both knees went soft. Gage crumpled into the cold, wet earth, blinked twice, and sank into velvety blackness.

Chapter Two

The scent of mud and—something sharp, bitter—filled Dara's nostrils. Her heart hammered as strong hands pulled her up, set her on her knees, and wiped away the mud covering one side of her face. She blinked.

"Papa?" She latched on to his coat with a talon-like grip.

He mouthed something, though all she heard was the ringing in her ears. He pried her fingers loose then turned to Becca.

Dara gaped. People ran in all directions. Chunks of wood and debris lay strewn around them. People—bodies—littered the ground. With legs as wobbly as a newborn foal's, she turned toward the nearest one. A man. Bloodied. Facedown on the ground. Dara's stomach dropped. Not just *any* man.

The Georgia boy.

"No." She stumbled toward him. "Please, no."

As she neared the man, Papa dragged Becca into her path and drew them into a crushing hug. A hiccuping sob boiled from deep in Dara's belly. She clung to Papa, though she peered past his shoulder to the man. The ringing faded, allowing distant shouts to filter into her consciousness. At the sound, she burrowed deeper into her father's embrace.

He finally drew back and spoke, his words far off, as if her ears were full of cotton.

"What?" She rubbed one ear to clear it.

"Are you injured?"

Understanding dawned, and Dara took mental stock then shook her head. "No, Papa, but the man who saved us is."

He turned to her cousin. "Are you?"

At Becca's stunned head shake, Papa clasped Dara's arm. "Where is William?"

She closed her eyes to order her thoughts. "I don't know. He and Matilde were gathering our luggage."

Glassy eyed, Becca looked toward the Southerner and clamped a hand over her mouth. "Papa, the man—"

"I must find William." He craned his neck, looking everywhere but at the body.

"The man, Papa. Please. . ." She tried to break free, but he held her arm.

After a moment, he called out to a man who ran by. "Vickers! Take my daughter and my niece to Morty's tent."

Vickers stopped short, gulped.

Surely he wouldn't leave her again. Heart in her throat, Dara slid up next to hi "Papa, we'll go with you."

"No." He drilled her with a glare then turned to the man. "Did you hear m

"You sure you want me to take 'em to *Morty's*?"

"Was I not clear enough?"

"Papa, please." Dara pulled at his sleeve. "Let us stay with you."

The man nodded. "Plenty clear, sir."

"Take them straight there, and don't leave their side. I'll be along as soon as I can." He disappeared into the fray.

He'd *actually* left. Just like seven years ago. Only this time, Mama wasn't here to pick up the pieces. What would Mama do at a time like this? Dara scanned the carnage around her.

"Didn't know Forsythe had any kin," Vickers mumbled.

The words pierced her like a well-aimed arrow. Just as she'd suspected—Papa had given no thought to Dara or her mother across these last seven years.

Vickers hooked her elbow. "This way."

Once more, her gaze fell on the injured man, and wrenching her arm free, she scurried to his side. She knew exactly what her mother would do. She would help.

"We'll see to this man before I go anywhere."

⚬⚬⚬

Floating somewhere between slumber and wakefulness, Gage slowly became aware as pain webbed through his back and skull. Minutes ticked by before he roused fully, prying one eye open. He lay on his belly in a bed softer than any he'd ever experienced. Limbs uncooperative, he struggled to roll onto his back, pain lancing him with every movement. Finally successful, he lay still until he'd caught his breath.

Ornately detailed wood tones enveloped the room. A richly upholstered chair sat beside the bed, and a costly looking crystal lamp shone softly from a small bedside table. Winter sunlight tried to penetrate heavy drapes lining the room's left wall. A single door with a shiny brass knob stood ajar, revealing a narrow hallway with more drape-covered windows.

Where was he?

He'd never set foot in such a fancy place, much less slept in one. Give him his unadorned soddy or the simplicity of the Cheyenne camp instead of all this finery. Gage fumbled to push off the heavy quilt but stalled. His clothes were missing, replaced by bandages that covered much of his torso. He tugged the quilt to his chest. Where were his pants?

Outside the room, a woman spoke, though too soft to make out her words. Laughter followed. Heart pounding, he strained to hear. Beth? *Lord, please let it be her. . . .* A moment later, a woman came into view, small tray in hand, giggling as she looked over her shoulder. His heart leapt with hope but fell when she faced him. She sobered quickly.

Not his Beth. He dragged the quilt higher.

"Good afternoon, sir."

A black woman peeked in the door. "Oh, thank You, Jesus," she whispered.

The woman with the tray turned to her. "Would you please get Uncle William?"

The black woman disappeared, a door closing somewhere down the hall.

"I'm glad you've finally returned to us," the first woman spoke.

"Finally?" What did that mean, and where had he seen her before?

She set the tray on the table. "You've been in and out of consciousness for three days. It's good to see some lucidity back in your eyes. That is, unless you plan to escape again."

"Escape?" What in heaven's name. . . "Am I a prisoner?"

"Goodness, no." She smiled, but it faded quickly. "You have no recollection, do you?"

She sat and laid a hand against his forehead. The gentleness of her touch soothed him in unexpected ways. Gage closed his eyes, and his muscles uncoiled.

"You saved my cousin and me from injury when a boxcar exploded."

The train. His eyes fluttered open again. He'd come to the hell-on-wheels camp to find some way to stop the railroad's progress and save his friends among the Cheyenne from further harm. And there this woman and her friend had stood in all their impractical mounds of expensive fabrics, looking quite lost.

She folded her hands. "Your back was laid open by flying debris. We took you to a tent for care, but after Uncle William treated you, you disappeared. We found you passed out in the mud."

Hazy images took shape. The explosion. Connor Forsythe approaching. His panic at being seen.

"Uncle William thought you'd rest better in a proper bed, so we moved you here." Glass in hand, she sat primly on the bed and cupped a gentle hand behind his head to help him drink. "Do you remember those things?"

"A little." Gage drank greedily then sank back. "Where am I, anyhow?"

She set the glass down, stood, and with a flounce of her costly blue skirt, seated herself on the edge of the chair. "For the moment, you're in my bed." Despite the sass in her tone, her cheeks flamed red.

So did his, from the feel of them. "I, uh. . .I'm real sorry, ma'am." He attempted to roll onto his elbow. "Just get me my clothes, and—"

"No." She pressed her hand to his shoulder. "You'll stay where you are until Uncle William says you may move. That won't be for a few days yet." She folded her hands. "So please rest, Mr.—"

"Gage Wells." He didn't have the gumption to argue. Not when the imprint of her palm nearly crackled with fire against his skin. He sank back, ignoring the awkward feeling, and looked around. "Where've you taken me?"

Her brow furrowed, but after an instant, she walked to the left side of the room and tugged the drapes aside. "We haven't taken you anywhere. You're in my father's Pullman Palace car."

Through the window, the sea of tents composing the moving railroad town was visible. A warning flashed in his thoughts. "Your father?"

"How rude of me. I haven't introduced myself. I am Dara Forsythe, Connor Forsythe's daughter."

His stomach clenched. He needed to go. *Now.* "Your pa's an important man around here. I surely don't want to impose, ma'am. Just bring me my clothes, and I'll be on my way."

"They're not here. Papa sent your pants to be cleaned, and your shirt and coat were beyond repair. He's having new ones made for you."

He swallowed the curse that rose on his tongue.

"And. . .your being here is no imposition, Mr. Wells. My family feels quite a debt, given your heroic actions to save Becca and me. We want to see you taken care of properly. However, even in your unconscious ramblings, you've been single-minded about leaving. Can you tell me why?"

"I talked in my sleep?" Hang it all. What had he said?

"You called out for Beth several times." Her gaze was almost probing. "I wondered if she might be waiting for you back home."

The comment struck like a punch to the gut. She'd waited all through the war. Only by the time it was over. . .

"Papa can send someone to tell her you're—"

"No." He winced, as much from the pain in his back as the pain in his heart. "Don't concern yourself about Beth." He scrubbed his face.

"Are you sure? I wouldn't want her to worry."

He looked away. "She's well beyond worrying about anything, ma'am."

Miss Forsythe's small hand curled into his. Startled, Gage looked her way.

"I'm very sorry." Her eyelids lowered. "I didn't mean to pry."

He swallowed the lump in his throat. "You were trying to be helpful, ma'am. Thank you."

She nodded as a door opened and closed in the outer room. "You should rest."

Her grip loosened, but before she could pull away, he latched on to her.

"Wait. Please."

Her blue eyes widened. "Yes, Mr. Wells?"

"What happened. . .to the train? Why'd they blow it up?"

She cocked her head. "I'm not entirely sure. Papa—"

"My superiors are investigating the matter," a man's voice broke into the conversation.

Connor Forsythe entered, followed by a dark-haired man. Dread skittered down Gage's spine. Not good. . .

"Papa. Uncle William." Miss Forsythe smiled at the newcomers. "I'd like you to meet Gage Wells. Mr. Wells, my father, Connor Forsythe, and my uncle, Doctor William Chenoweth."

"I can't thank you enough for saving my daughter and niece." Forsythe smiled. "I'd like to repay you the kindness, Mr. Wells. Once you've recuperated, we should talk. I'd like to offer you a position with the Union Pacific."

Gage stifled a derisive snort. Such an offer went against his intended purpose—to stop the railroad. "Thank you, sir, but I got plenty to keep me busy."

"Keep it in mind," Forsythe insisted.

He blinked heavily. "I'm real tired all of a sudden." Not a lie. The conversation with Miss Forsythe *had* sapped his strength.

The doctor stepped forward. "Dara, Connor, if you'll excuse us, I should change Mr. Wells's dressings so he can rest."

Miss Forsythe squeezed his hand as she stood. "Should you need anything, Mr. Wells, I won't be far away."

What he needed was to get out of Connor Forsythe's domain, though it was already too late. The man had seen him, knew his name. That would make it markedly harder to stop the railroad.

Chapter Three

One week later

P apa?" Dara called from across the Pullman car's parlor.

"Hmm?" He inclined his ear, though his gaze never left the paper he was reading. Her cousin shot her a grim expression at his distraction.

"Becca and I were wondering—"

A sharp knock interrupted her, and Papa immediately laid the paper aside and rose to answer the door. Upon seeing his superiors, Mr. Marston and Mr. Adgate, he slipped out onto the rear platform and shut the door partway.

"Good morning, gentlemen," Papa greeted.

"Morning, Forsythe. Any luck in finding that translator yet?" one of the men asked.

Through the window, Dara saw Papa shake his head. "As I told you last time we talked, it's my highest priority."

"I hope so. You've said you'll be moving the camp to Cheyenne in a few days, and we need to get these supplies delivered before that happens."

Dara sighed. Since her arrival, Papa hadn't taken a single hour to have a thorough conversation with her, but he routinely dropped everything to discuss business with the two bearded men. Was this what life would be like? If so, they should have stayed in Boston. She could've lived quite happily under Uncle William's roof.

A door down the hallway opened.

"Take it slowly." Uncle William's warm voice split the silence.

Eyes twinkling, Becca grasped Dara's hand and dragged her toward the far side of the room. Mr. Wells shuffled toward them, left hand braced against the wall for balance. Dara's heart beat a little faster at the sight of him out of bed and dressed in his new brown plaid shirt. The slight pallor to his skin and his seeming unsteadiness were the only immediate clues he'd been bed-bound for more than a week.

"Good morning, Mr. Wells," she and Becca called.

His rich brown eyes rose to meet hers, though he scanned the parlor before he smiled. "Morning, ladies."

Uncle William directed him to a nearby chair, and both Dara and Becca sat across from him.

"We'll be having breakfast shortly." Dara grinned. "Would you join us?"

"Oh. No, ma'am." Mr. Wells rubbed his stubbly jaw and glanced toward the door, looking like a caged animal. "Don't want to impose any longer, but thank you. For everything."

Uncle William took the remaining chair. "I hope you'll reconsider. I fear you're not strong enough yet to care for yourself."

"Thanks for the concern, Doctor. I have. . .friends. . .I can call on should I nee anything."

Uncle William looked displeased. "Connor and I would like to thank you for saving our daughters."

"You saved my life as well, sir. You don't owe me anything. Besides, I got to get home. . . ."

Dara's heart sank. With Uncle William and Becca tending the other injured, and Papa busy with his work for the railroad, she'd been Mr. Wells's main caregiver. The quiet gentleman had intrigued her, and she would miss the diversion of their frequent talks.

Papa reentered and paused at the door. "It's good to see you up and about, Mr. Wells."

His jaw clenched ever so slightly. "Thank you, sir."

"Connor," Uncle William called. "He says he needs to go home. Could you arrange a ride for him?"

Surprise registered in Papa's blue eyes. "Let's talk over breakfast, Mr. Wells. If you're still of the mind to go then, I'll arrange for a wagon." When Mr. Wells tried to protest, Papa cleared his throat. "I insist."

Few were bold enough to deny Papa.

Guilt settled over her at Mr. Wells's obvious annoyance. "Please, sir. It's only one meal. We'd like to get to know the heroic Southern gentleman that saved us from harm."

"There's nothing heroic about me, ma'am."

She lifted her chin. "The fact that Becca and I sit before you unscathed is proof to the contrary."

His cheeks flushed. "All right. I'll stay, but only for a meal."

They shifted to the dining table, Dara sitting across from Mr. Wells. As he settled in, his brown eyes widened at the collection of silverware adorning the table. She could have predicted the reaction. He was a man of simple pleasures, unrefined in etiquette, but charming in his own modest ways.

She cleared her throat softly. When he glanced her way, she fingered her napkin then retrieved it from under the forks, unfolded it deliberately, and placed it in her lap. After an uncomfortable second, he followed suit.

Matilde scurried out with several plates and served them all, then took a seat next to Dara. Astonishment crossed Mr. Wells's features, though he said nothing, only looked again at the silverware before him. Dara waited until he glanced her way and, yet again, touched the proper fork. When he reached for the corresponding utensil, she speared a dainty bite of her eggs.

"So, Mr. Wells. You're from Georgia?" Papa was the first to break the silence.

"Yes, sir." He forked a mound of scrambled eggs into his mouth and glanced around the table.

"What brings you to the Dakota Territory?"

Dara's muscles tensed. Her gentle probing of his background had always ended when he diverted the conversation elsewhere.

"The war." He spoke around the food he chewed.

"Did you serve?"

Mr. Wells rolled the food in his mouth and swallowed hard. "Yes, sir." His voice dripped distrust. "Did you?"

Papa nodded. "I did—for the Union."

He turned to Uncle William, who also nodded. "I was a Union doctor."

"Then we were on opposing sides."

"How could anyone fight a war to preserve slavery?" Becca asked.

Dara scowled at her cousin too late. Mr. Wells looked as if he'd been slapped.

"Begging your pardon, ma'am, but if you think every Southerner owned slaves and fought to keep 'em, you're sorely mistaken. My family lived on the same plot of land for three generations, and not once did we own a slave. Had no need, nor the desire—even if we'd had the money."

Dara mentally scrambled for a way to soothe the tension, though Mr. Wells pressed on. "Might we discuss another topic? This one turns my stomach."

"I'm certain my daughter meant no disrespect, Mr. Wells," Uncle William spoke softly.

Becca nodded, mortification staining her expression. "I didn't. Forgive me, please."

Dara's throat knotted. How might it feel to share a meal with a family who had, until only recently, been a sworn enemy? Surely that was the reason for his hesitance to share his past.

"I'm sorry," Papa whispered. "What do you do now, Mr. Wells?"

"I'm a man of simple means, sir. I grow a few crops. When I can, I plan to buy cattle."

Papa nodded slowly. "As I mentioned before, I could offer you a position with the Union Pacific Railroad. Consider it a means to earn money for your livestock."

Hope flickered in Dara's chest, but he shook his head. "I'm content doing what I do, sir. Not looking for a new job, thank you."

Whether or not Mr. Wells recognized Papa's irritation, Dara was quite aware of it. Fortunately, Papa didn't press him. The conversation moved to other topics, and finally Papa turned to their guest again.

"I'll find a wagon and team to drive you home, Mr. Wells."

Excitement fluttered in Dara's chest. "I'd like to ride with you both, Papa."

"I want to go as well." Becca looked to Uncle William. "May I, please?"

Becca's father grinned. "I don't mind, though I have patients to attend to. You'll have to go without me."

Papa scowled. "I didn't intend this to be a family affair."

The stern look added another deep nick to her already tender heart. "Please, Papa. Becca and I are both restless, and it would give us more time with our heroic guest."

After a pause, Papa turned to Mr. Wells. "Would you mind the company?"

The handsome stranger smiled at her. "No, sir. I'd welcome it."

"Then it's settled." At Papa's nod, she and Becca excused themselves to gather their coats.

Gage tugged the quilt draped around his shoulders a bit tighter and glanced at their surroundings. "Mr. Forsythe," he called from the wagon box. "You'll see a small path off to the right. Follow that about a mile, and you'll run straight into my yard."

Becca Chenoweth glanced back from the wagon seat toward him. "You walked all this way to the rail camp?"

He adjusted his new hat. If only his old one hadn't been lost in the confusion after the explosion. "No, ma'am. I rode my horse, but I left him ground tied on the far side of the train tracks." In fact, he'd left the mustang hidden some distance from the camp so no one would recognize the paint's distinctive markings. "He surely got spooked by the blast. If I know him, he ran home or went to my friends' place." He'd prayed so, anyway. His rifle was stowed in the scabbard, and while he'd hate to lose a good horse, the Whitworth rifle with the Davidson scope was irreplaceable.

"I wish you'd let us know sooner," Forsythe called over his shoulder. "I could have sent someone to search for him."

At the wagon's jarring movements, pain crackled through Gage's back. He stifled a grunt, though not before pretty Miss Forsythe slid nearer.

"How are you faring?" Her blue eyes reflected sincere concern.

He gritted his teeth. "Managing, thank you." His eyes strayed to the wagon seat. There was room enough for a third person between her father and cousin, yet she'd insisted on riding with him.

She moved her father's rifle from atop a folded quilt and drew the blanket nearer. "Lean forward." When he obeyed, she positioned the thicknesses of fabric between him and the wagon's side, protecting his still-tender back. "I wish you would consider staying a few more days."

He leaned back, thoughts warring. Dara Forsythe had been nothing but kind. In fact, her soft smile, gentle touch, and pleasant demeanor were a great comfort while he'd recuperated. She'd asked pointed questions but hadn't pressed for information he was unwilling to give, even steering their conversations to safer territory when he threatened to shut her out. He respected her ability to read and navigate the situation.

Blast it all. If she weren't Connor Forsythe's daughter, he'd consider her his friend. And goodness knew, he had few enough of those out here.

However, she *was* Forsythe's daughter, and that meant he never should've spoken to her, much less developed a fondness for her.

"I appreciate the kindness, ma'am, but I'll rest just as well in my own place as yours." Better. He'd be able to distance himself from Forsythe, and that way, the man—or his comely daughter—wouldn't discover Gage's intention to stop the railroad. Of course, to do that, he needed a plan, and now that he was known to Forsythe, it would become inordinately harder to concoct one.

"I understand. It's difficult to rest in unfamiliar surroundings." She lowered her voice to a whisper. "I dare say you and I both have had a difficult ten days."

Gage's cheeks burned. "I, uh. . .I apologize again, ma'am. Surely didn't mean to take over your be— I mean—"

"I wasn't referring to my room, Mr. Wells." Her cheeks pinked. "I'm referring to this place in general. I'm not familiar with any of my surroundings. Becca and I arrived only moments before the explosion."

That would explain why he'd never noticed the beautiful young woman when he'd spied on the hell-on-wheels camp in the previous weeks.

"Boston is my true home. . . ." The whispered admission dripped with longing and pain.

"Sounds like you miss it."

"Very much."

Dare he ask what brought her west? Probably better not to broach the subject, particularly if he wasn't willing to answer such questions himself.

"I'm real sorry to hear that. Truly."

"Thank you." She shivered.

At the full-body tremor, he extracted the quilt from his shoulders and turned to her. "Sit up a minute."

She shook her head. "You need that more than I do."

"Hogwash. I was getting too warm."

She did as he asked, and Gage draped the blanket around her shoulders.

She leaned back, smiling. "Thank you."

His heart pounded as memories washed over him. . .of draping a blanket around his and Beth's shoulders as they'd sat on their farmhouse porch on a cool fall evening. They used to cuddle under their blanket and talk as the sun set. On just such a night, she'd laid his hand on her belly and whispered that she was with child.

Gage shook away the memories. Dara Forsythe was not his Beth, and he'd be a fool to let himself imagine she was.

Yet when he realized her eyes brimmed with tears, his belly flip-flopped. He rubbed her arm with the back of his hand, hoping the small gesture might comfort her. Instead, a silent sob racked her small frame. Caving to his instincts, he circled her shoulders and tucked her close to his side. She leaned into him, head resting against his chest. Gage scrambled for some topic that might keep her from crumbling completely.

"Would you believe that before the war, I'd never been in a big city?"

After an instant, Miss Forsythe peered up at him and sniffled. "You hadn't?"

"It's true. Lived my whole life in the country."

She straightened, shrugging out of his grasp.

"Did you go to school, or. . . ?"

He chuckled. "Yes, ma'am. I went whenever Pa didn't need me on the farm, and Ma taught me at home when I couldn't get there."

"That's fascinating. I spent most of my life in the city. All this isolation is so foreign to me. I feel at loose ends. Mama and I spent our days helping others, but here, there's little to do but read books."

"What kinds of things did you do to help others?"

"Most recently, Mama and I would either visit with soldiers and other patients in the hospitals, or we've tried to help the men return to their families. Before and during the war, we. . ."

He shot her a sidelong glance. "You what?"

She lifted her chin. "We worked with the abolition movement."

Before Gage could react, Forsythe halted the wagon well outside the yard. Young Becca Chenoweth gasped.

"Someone grab my rifle." Forsythe spoke over his shoulder just loud enough to be heard.

Concerned, Gage reached over Miss Forsythe to lay hold of the gun. However, before he could, a distant, yet familiar call cut the stillness. All uneasiness fled. He rolled onto his knees to see the yard, pain rippling through his back with the movement.

A Cheyenne brave, dark hair shining in the morning sun, stood only feet from Gage's door. He tossed off the heavy buffalo hide wrapped around his lean frame and barged toward them. He spoke sharply and flailed his arms as if shooing birds from a field of freshly sown seed.

"Wells!" Forsythe hissed his name. "My rifle."

"You don't need the gun, sir. Spotted Hawk is a friend." Gage stood slowly and climbed down from the wagon, calling a greeting in Cheyenne as he did.

The brave softened his stance, though his demeanor still bespoke caution. "I have been looking for you, my friend," he called in his native tongue. "Your horse came to my tent many days ago without you. I was concerned."

"Thank you." Gage took several halting steps toward the brave. "There is much I have to tell you about these last days."

Spotted Hawk's eyes narrowed. "You are all right?"

"I was injured. These people took care of me." He nodded toward the wagon.

"Dara. . .stay!" At Forsythe's command, Gage turned to see Dara walking his way, though the railroad builder had latched on to her shoulder as she passed. "Wells, what's going on here?"

Gage shifted toward Forsythe.

"I promise you, sir. Spotted Hawk won't cause any trouble."

Forsythe eyed him. "How is it that you're friends with the Cheyenne?"

He shrugged. "Weeks after I came here, I found Spotted Hawk's daughter, Walks In Shadows, on the plains with a badly broken leg. I set it, cared for her until I could move her, then took her back to her people. A friendship grew out of that."

"And you speak their language. . ."

"I've learned some." He'd become fluent during their two years of friendship, and Spotted Hawk's broken English had improved as well, though Gage wouldn't volunteer that fact.

"I have need of a man with your language skills, Mr. Wells. My superiors have brought supplies—things to help the Cheyenne. Call them goodwill gifts, compliments of the Union Pacific Railroad. We've been unable to deliver them because we couldn't find a translator. If I'd known you were under my nose this whole time, it would have saved me a lot of searching. I'll pay you handsomely if you'd be willing to translate for us so we can deliver the items."

"Goodwill gifts."

"That's right. . . ."

Fatigue stole through Gage, and he braced a hand against the wagon. "Begging your pardon, sir, but since when has the railroad concerned itself with the goodwill of the tribes that make these plains their home?"

Forsythe's eyes widened, though he quickly schooled his expression. "Yes, the tensions have been high between us. We're doing this in hopes of creating peace."

How had he gone from trying to stop the railroad to being asked to translate for them? An odd twist. But his end goal was to help the Cheyenne, and since he'd lost the ability to use stealth to do it, perhaps this would provide another means to that end. Gage nodded toward his soddy. "Let's talk."

Chapter Four

Three days later

The Cheyenne camp was several miles beyond Mr. Wells's home, so Papa had agreed to take the promised supplies there, rather than Mr. Wells meeting them at the rail camp. As the supply wagons rumbled toward the meeting place, Dara studied the tumbledown house from her saddle. She'd always been aware that not everyone lived in the luxury she'd been afforded, but it had never struck home so sharply as when she'd set foot inside Mr. Wells's residence. The little house, built from stacked earthen squares with a stone chimney on one end, was a fourth the size of Papa's Pullman car. And that, in contrast, was miniscule compared with the Boston home where she'd lived. The soddy's interior was dark and shabby, the scant furnishings rickety at best. It flustered her, both then and now.

As the first of the wagons rumbled into Mr. Wells's yard, he stepped outside, tugging his hat on.

"Morning." He nodded to them.

She smiled, not wanting to acknowledge the flutter that ravaged her belly at his lingering, brown-eyed gaze. "Good morning."

Mr. Wells scanned the four wagons, each loaded with several wooden crates, followed by a herd of twenty cattle driven by several of the railroad workers. He pinned Papa with a sharp look. "This is all for the Cheyenne?"

Papa dismounted and handed his horse's reins to her. "You sound surprised."

"I am. My Cheyenne friends have told me the troubles between their people and the railroad."

One of Papa's superiors approached. "Rest assured, these gifts are meant to put an end to the tensions."

Suspicion etched Mr. Wells's gaze. "And you are?"

"Gage Wells, meet Pierce Marston." Papa made the introduction then shifted toward his other superior, who also approached. "And this is Thomas Adgate. They are my superiors."

Mr. Wells shook each man's hand, though the grim set to his mouth warned Dara he was uncomfortable. The four approached the nearest wagon, Mr. Marston motioning to the different crates as he spoke. After a moment more, the men headed back to their horses, and Mr. Wells strode into his tiny home.

He emerged with his rifle, mounted a spotted pony, and gave a call to follow him. Once the line of wagons and cattle moved out, Dara maneuvered her horse next to Papa's, though all his attention went to his conversation with Mr. Adgate. After several minutes of being ignored, she nudged her chestnut mare in Mr. Wells's direction.

The man grinned as she fell in beside him. "Morning. Your cousin and uncle didn't come today?"

A knot constricted her throat. "Becca wanted to come. Uncle William suggested I should spend time alone with Papa." Unfortunately, Papa had no desire to be alone with her.

"Not that I mind the company, but. . .if that's the case, why aren't you riding with him?"

"He's focused on business right now." *As always.* She couldn't recall such a driven nature when she was young. He'd been hardworking, but before the war he'd always made time for her.

His brown eyes clouded. "I'm sorry."

"Thank you." She forced a smile to her lips. "He'll be less preoccupied after we've met with the Cheyenne." She could hope. "You look like you're feeling better, Mr. Wells." The pallid tone had disappeared, and the stiffness that had plagued every movement seemed better as well.

"I am. Thanks again for looking after me."

"You're quite welcome."

"I, uh. . .I was thinking it might be easier if you'd call me by my given name. Gage." He hesitated an instant. "I'm not used to formalities."

"Oh." Dara nodded. "Of course, if that's what you'd prefer. You may call me Dara."

"Yes, ma'am." A lopsided smile curved his mouth. "It's a real pretty name."

An ache stole through her. "It was my mother's middle name."

"Was. . .not is?"

She faced front, willing herself to remain stoic. "She passed."

"I'm truly sorry." After several moments of silence, Gage finally spoke. "You were starting to tell me about the work you and your ma did in Boston. With the abolition movement?"

Dara tamped down the ache in her chest. "I wasn't sure how you'd feel about that."

"You want the truth?"

"I'd prefer it to the alternative." Or would she? She may not like his response.

"I'm none too sure how I feel, ma'am."

"You said over breakfast the other day that your family had never owned slaves. You never saw the need."

"True, but that doesn't mean I looked down on those who did. It was a different choice than mine. Before the war, I'd have told you the whole matter of abolition was off-putting."

Dara suppressed the anger threatening to flare across her features. "And now?"

He was quiet. "After befriending the Cheyenne, I've been rethinking the matter some. Maybe I'm able to see some similarities between that situation and what's happening to the Indians."

"I got the sense. . .Gage. . .that you aren't completely comfortable with what we're doing today. I'd like to understand why."

He exhaled heavily. "Have you ever seen a buffalo?"

"I've seen likenesses in the newspaper."

"The buffalo roam these plains in great numbers, so many that the herd stretches for miles."

"And?"

"The buffalo are sacred to the Indians. The men hunt them, then everyone feasts on the fresh kills. Their women make pemmican and jerky for winter stores. They use their skins for tepees, bedding, clothing, and winter robes. Buffalo bones become hand tools.

They drink from their horns, and use their stomachs and other innards as waterskins. They use the sinew for rope or sewing thread. Even buffalo dung gets used as fuel for their fires. They can't survive without these animals. But the Union Pacific has hired hunters to kill the herds."

"Why is that wrong? You just told me the Cheyenne kill the buffalo."

"My friends kill just enough to provide for their needs, and they use every part of the animal. The railroad's hunters shoot these animals by the *thousands*, skin 'em, cut their tongues out for the money they'll fetch back east, and leave everything else to rot on the plains."

The image turned her stomach. "Why would they do such a thing?"

"I don't know what Mr. Marston, Mr. Adgate, or your pa would tell you, but here's what I do know. The Indian tribes that live on these plains—they aren't like us white folk. We build homes and stay in one place. The Indians. . .they set up camp, stay for a while, then move on. I'm guessing the railroad doesn't like that much."

"Why?"

"The Union Pacific makes money bringing folks west on their trains. The Cheyenne want to roam. The whites want to settle in one place. The two lifestyles conflict. The whites will come by the thousands, building towns, homes, farms. . .and the Indians'll start feeling hemmed in. Then the government will shuffle the Indians onto reservations, expecting them to settle down and farm the land like white folks do. I think the railroad's killing the buffalo so it can hurt the Indians' way of life, make 'em desperate enough to move to those reservations." His brown eyes smoldered. "And that feels a whole lot like what I experienced during the war—someone from a long way off telling me I had to change the way I live. Also got me to thinking on how the slaves were treated—taken from their homes, brought to this country, and forced to work for someone else. None of it sits right."

No, it didn't. "But. . .Papa and the others intend to give the Cheyenne cattle and other supplies. How is that bad?"

Gage shook his head. "Maybe it's not. Let's just say I'm cautious."

———◆◆◆———

Gage smiled at the wonder on Dara's face as the Cheyenne camp came into view. Tepees dotted the landscape, and smoke curled from their tops. Around the perimeter, a sizable herd of horses grazed contentedly. Children played outside the camp, while the interior showed only moderate activity. As the wagons rumbled over a small rise behind them, a few of the older boys broke from the group of children and ran into the camp.

"Quite a view, isn't it?" He stopped well outside the camp's perimeter. Dara halted beside him.

"I've never seen anything like it."

Connor Forsythe rode up beside them. "Where do we go now, Wells?"

Gage adjusted his hat. "We wait until the elders welcome us."

"I thought you said you'd tell them we were coming."

Irritation crawled up his spine. "I did. Now we wait."

Within moments, the tribe's elders rode out dressed in ceremonial garb, among them Spotted Hawk. They stopped a good thirty feet from where Forsythe's wagons had lined up. Behind them, the younger braves watched. The women and children gathered at the back. When the chief, Little Wolf, signaled, Spotted Hawk rode forward alone.

"Stay here, please." Gage nudged his horse forward and met his friend between the two groups.

"You ride beside the pretty woman, just like the other day." Spotted Hawk spoke in his native tongue, eyes glinting as they stopped feet from each other. "You are drawn to her."

Heat crept up Gage's neck. He could tell Spotted Hawk otherwise, but anything he said would be riddled with half truths. The Cheyenne brave was too perceptive. "That is not what I have come to discuss."

Spotted Hawk's smile deepened. "But it is the truth."

Gage blew out a breath. "She has been kind to me while I healed. If things were different, I would call her my friend, but she is the daughter of the man who builds the iron horse."

"You do not trust this man?"

He cocked his head. "I do not know the man, but I know what men like him have done to your people. He and his chiefs say they bring gifts—food and supplies. I have tried to think how this could be harmful to you, but I see no danger in it unless they expect the Cheyenne to promise things in exchange for these gifts."

Spotted Hawk gave a thoughtful nod. "Little Wolf says we will talk with the iron horse men. He will not be fooled. Bring their chiefs to his tent. The rest should stay with the supplies." The man reined his horse around but paused. "Walks In Shadows wants to meet your woman. You can bring her to Little Wolf's tent also."

"She is not *my woman*!" He hissed under his breath.

Spotted Hawk answered with a low, knowing chuckle as he rode away.

No, Dara Forsythe was not *his* woman, but he was having an increasingly difficult time fighting the attraction.

Shaking the thought, Gage returned and explained their instructions. "They requested Dara come to Little Wolf's tent."

Forsythe shook his head. "This is business. She'll stay here."

Dara's eyes grew huge. "Papa, please take m—"

"Vickers." Forsythe turned to the man driving one of the wagons. "Take care of my daughter until I return." He turned to follow the Cheyenne elders.

The sheer panic in Dara's eyes wrenched Gage's heart. He rode after Forsythe, ready to give him a piece of his mind.

Chapter Five

Dara vacillated between anger and fear while watching the twenty Cheyenne braves stationed between the wagons and the Cheyenne camp. How could Papa leave her? She could sit silently while the railroad bosses and Cheyenne elders transacted their business. Instead, he'd left her with the railroad workers, many grumbling about the *savages* milling about. The demeanors of the braves ranged from boredom to vigilance to suspicion. Were they simply being watchful, or were they positioning themselves for attack? The fact that they carried weapons provided no comfort. She remained alert, praying no trouble would erupt.

More than a half hour later, the entourage emerged, a crowd of Cheyenne growing as they drew near. After a brief discussion, Mr. Marston and Mr. Adgate instructed the men who'd stayed with the wagons to off-load the crates and pry them open. Two smaller crates contained new knives with leather sheaths. The more plentiful larger crates contained folded trade blankets. Once the Cheyenne began filing up to collect their blankets and knives, Dara approached her father.

"Papa, may I have a word. . .please." She kept her voice soft and even.

He nodded to the brave who rather cautiously took items from each crate. "Now is not the best time, Dara-girl."

The childhood endearment had once made her feel so safe and loved. Now he used it to keep her at arm's length. "Please. I need you to understand."

"Understand what?"

"I've participated in meetings while Mama and I worked to free the slaves. I've organized hundreds of picnics and bazaars to raise money for that cause. I've helped soldiers find their loved ones after the war. I am not a child. Why wouldn't you let me sit with you while you spoke to the Cheyenne?"

"Now is neither the time nor the place for this discussion."

The words stung, but she tamped down her disappointment. "I know you're busy. When would be a better time?"

He focused only on the line of Cheyenne. "Perhaps tonight. At home."

"Tonight, then." Hopefully, he wouldn't dismiss her then also. She meandered away, putting distance between her and the camp.

"Dara." Gage hurried after her. "Where you headed?"

"I was in the way."

He fell in beside her. "I'm sorry. I tried to change his mind as we rode to Little Wolf's tent."

"Don't apologize. This isn't your fault."

He drew her to a halt. "I don't like what just happened."

"Thank you." At least he understood.

"Maybe this isn't the best time, but Spotted Hawk's daughter is asking to meet you." He nodded at a lone figure standing halfway between the camp and their solitary vantage point. "She's about your age."

"That sounds like a nice diversion."

At Gage's signal, the Cheyenne woman hurried their way.

"Dara, this is Walks In Shadows." He turned to the Cheyenne woman and spoke to her in her native tongue.

Smiling, Walks In Shadows stepped forward, spoke Dara's name, and held something out. Dara darted a glance Gage's way then back to the woman. When she didn't immediately take the item, Walks In Shadows nodded and held it nearer, spouting a flurry of words.

Gage shook his head. "I taught you the words." He spoke in English this time. "Tell Dara yourself."

Walks In Shadows scowled at Gage, first in confusion, then as if upset. However, she held out the object again. "You take my. . .friend?" She chewed her lip, waiting for Gage's confirmation.

"Friendship."

The Cheyenne woman nodded. "You take my friendship."

"She's offering you this gift of her friendship," Gage clarified.

Dara took the small leather medallion and ran her finger over the intricate and colorful decoration. "It's beautiful. Thank you."

The raven-haired woman nodded, braids dancing.

"She decorated that with dyed porcupine quills."

Dara's eyes rounded.

"You might think about giving her a gift in return."

"I have nothing to give," she whispered, "unless she'd like my hair ribbon."

"That'd be perfect."

She tugged the dark green bow from her blond braid and held it out to Walks In Shadows. "Please accept this symbol of my friendship."

Walks In Shadows's face lit up, and she attempted to poke her braid through the already-tied bow.

"Let me tie it for you." Dara retied the bow around her hair, and Walks In Shadows's smile deepened. She chattered happily in a combination of Cheyenne and English.

After a moment, Gage halted Walks In Shadows's words. "She's never seen something tied in a bow before."

"How?" Walks In Shadows plucked the ribbon from her hair and pushed it into Dara's hands.

"I'll teach you."

Gage chuckled. "I ought to get back in case they need my help. I'll leave you gals to your bow tying, but. . .do me a favor."

"What favor?"

"I don't mind you walking around some, but stay where I can see you."

"We will." She grinned. "Thank you. She's charming."

Gage shifted his attention between the railroad's gift giving and the largest hill in the distance where Dara and Walks In Shadows had wandered. Dara had stayed in sight, but they'd gone much farther than he preferred. He could trust Walks In Shadows to watch over the other woman, but he'd feel a heap better if they were nearer.

Forsythe was oblivious—both to the fact that his daughter had wandered out onto the plains and that he'd wounded her. Unaware, or unconcerned. Regardless, it stuck in Gage's craw.

Was the man blind? Dara's caring, intelligence, and loyalty were obvious the day he awoke in her bed. Women with such qualities deserved to be lavished with a man's attention. If Forsythe would put aside his work and listen to her, Dara would become one of his greatest allies. That's exactly what happened with his Beth. Her pa taught his girls about farming and livestock. In turn, she'd taught Gage plenty when he'd listened.

At seventeen, Dara was the same age Beth had been when they'd married. Both women had a spunk and a boldness he admired. But Beth had been simple and unassuming, content to be a farmer's wife. Dara oozed splendor and refinement, from her big, impractical dresses to her perfect manners and etiquette. To her credit, Dara had never made him feel like the man of humble means he was. He was grateful. Her unwavering acceptance stirred every ounce of protectiveness in him. Particularly where her thick-skulled father was concerned.

An older Indian boy approached, new blanket over his bony shoulder and knife in hand, grinning as he showed off the blade. Gage listened to his proud ramblings, commenting on the fine quality of the weapon. As the boy continued, Gage scanned the distance again.

His gaze stalled on Walks In Shadows, sitting alone on the distant hill. He watched a moment, then two. No Dara. Brow furrowing, he excused himself and approached his horse. Where had she gone?

Unfastening his saddlebag flap, Gage withdrew a cartridge and percussion cap for his rifle while scanning the surrounding countryside. She was nowhere to be seen. Despite Walks In Shadows's seeming lack of concern, apprehension climbed Gage's spine.

"Lord," he breathed. "Give me eyes to see the dangers. . . ." One half of the prayer he'd prayed each time he'd taken out a target during the war.

Eyes firmly on Walks In Shadows, Gage led his horse away from the crowd a good thirty feet then slid the Whitworth rifle from its scabbard. Settling the gun over his saddle for stability, he peered through the telescopic sight.

He finally found her, or rather, the top of her head. Her honey-blond hair—nothing more—was visible over the crest of the rise. Drawing back from the scope, he squinted at the distance then looked through the scope again. What was she doing?

"C'mon, Dara. . ."

As if on cue, her head and shoulders bobbed into view over the rise, though she halted again, her back to him. Gage's mouth turned to cotton. Something wasn't right. . . .

"Wells?" Forsythe called. "Everything all right?"

Dara backed up another step, and another, coming farther into view, her posture rigid, every movement slow and deliberate.

"What's got you spooked?" he whispered, searching the crest of the hill.

"Wells. Don't ignore me." Mr. Forsythe's footsteps rustled as he approached.

"Stay." He stalled the man with an upraised hand, focus never leaving Dara and the terrain around her. After an instant, she took one more backward step then turned sideways slowly. At the edge of the scope's view, a flash of movement. He shifted the gun to see Walks In Shadows stand and look at the crest of the hill.

By the time Gage shifted back to Dara, she'd started down the hill, running for all she was worth. At the top of the little rise, a sizable tawny splotch slinked into view. *Mountain lion.*

The cat crouched, ready to pounce.

Every nerve fired as he cocked the hammer and sighted in on the cougar. "Lord..." he whispered. "Give me true aim." He squeezed the trigger.

The gun bucked against his shoulder just as the big cat leapt. Heart hammering, he held steady, willing the cougar to drop. It did, but not before it took one mighty swipe at Dara's back, sending her to the ground also. Wasting no time, he reloaded, checked to see the cat wasn't moving, then swung into his saddle. Gage spurred his horse into a gallop, racing past Forsythe and several others who ran toward the distant hill.

By the time he reached them, Walks In Shadows had pulled Dara to her feet and led her away from the animal before her legs crumbled again. Dara sat upright, a distant, glassy look in her eyes.

"The ghost cat is still alive," Walks In Shadows panted, jutting her chin toward the cougar.

Gage dropped from his saddle and approached the beast. It lay on its side, laboring for breath, a low growl rumbling in its throat. With one more shot, he dispatched the animal, then dashed back to the women and sank to his knees.

"Are you all right?" he asked Dara.

She shifted a dazed glance his way, then to the others who had arrived, but said nothing.

"Your woman is hurt." Walks In Shadows held out a bloody palm before pressing it once more to Dara's shoulder.

Gage dragged Dara close, her head resting against him as he peeked over her shoulder. Her coat was shredded near the shoulder, dark fabric glistening with her blood. Probing beneath the fabric, he found several cuts stretching from her arm toward the center of her back. A chill ran through him.

"Give me your blanket," he barked at the nearest Cheyenne. When the brave did, Gage cut a wide patch from one corner then instructed the man to cut several narrow strips for him.

Forsythe dashed up, too winded to speak, though he sidled up to his daughter and brushed her hair back from her face.

"It clawed her pretty good." Gage pressed the folded patch against the wound and tied it in place with the strips the Cheyenne brave handed him.

Forsythe shook his head. "Take her to William," he panted. "I'll follow."

Gage stowed his rifle and mounted, Forsythe handing Dara up to him. The Cheyenne brave shoved the remnant of the blanket into Gage's hands, and after wrapping Dara in it, Gage spurred his horse into a lope.

Chapter Six

The ride came to a sudden halt, and Dara opened her eyes to find Papa's Pullman car.

"Can you hear me, Dara?" Gage spoke softly.

She bobbed her head.

"Good girl." He slid to the ground, lifted her down, and climbed the railcar steps. As he shifted her weight, she noted his mount was lathered and winded.

"Your horse..." She whispered the words.

"I'll see to him once you're taken care of." He barged through the door of the train car. "Where's William?"

"What happened?" Becca crossed the room to stand beside her.

"She got cornered by a mountain lion."

"Oh, sweet heaven above." Matilde crowded near also. "Miss Becca, go fetch your father. Quick, now."

Becca ran.

"Mr. Wells, take her to her room and get her out of that coat. I'll fetch some supplies."

In several long strides, Gage entered her room and sat her on the bed. He fumbled to unknot the strips of blanket tied around her. When that failed, he cut them free with his knife, then sheathed the blade, knelt, and unfastened the buttons.

He looked up at her. "You'll be just fine, Dara. You hear me?"

She gritted her teeth. "It hurts."

"Your uncle'll be here soon." He finished unbuttoning her coat and smiled. "You were real brave."

Her eyes slid shut. "I was terrified."

"That makes two of us, princess." He caressed her cheek as he straightened.

Her heart raced at the gentle touch and the soft endearment, but before it all sank in, he'd stripped the coat from her unaffected side and was gently peeling the material away from the injury. The coat removed, he pressed something to the wound again, and Matilde appeared with a tray full of bandages and supplies.

"Thank you, Mr. Wells. You got to go now." The young freedwoman put the tray down and lit the crystal lamp.

As Gage turned away, Dara caught his wrist. "Please stay."

"No, ma'am. I should go." She loosened her grip. "I'll be right outside, seeing to my horse."

He left quickly, the outer door slamming loudly.

"Where is that uncle of yours?" Matilde crossed to look out the window then closed the drapes. "Go on and unbutton that dress now, Miss Dara."

Weakness and cold made the task impossible. Matilde scooped the bloodied coat and blanket onto the floor then unfastened Dara's bodice herself. She carefully helped her strip off the shredded garments then sat next to her to see the wounds more clearly.

Dara crumpled against her, a sob wrenching free from her chest. "I was so scared."

"You're safe now, missy."

Matilde held her until clattering footsteps on the rear platform warned of someone's approach. Dara snatched the remnant of blanket and covered herself as both Papa and Uncle William shoved through the bedroom doorway. Matilde stepped out of the way.

"Uncle William." Her chin quivered as he gave her a once-over glance, then held her face and pulled one lower lid down, then the other.

"Can you tell me what happened?" He released her and reached for a rag on the bedside table.

"I was talking to Walks In Shadows, and I had to. . ."

He sat and pressed the rag against the wound. "To what?"

Her cheeks flamed. "Answer the call of nature. I walked over the hill for some privacy." She inhaled sharply as he probed at her shoulder. "I didn't realize until I was halfway to the bottom that it was there."

"Matilde, I'll need plenty of hot water."

"Already heating, sir. I'll check on it." She produced a quilt from the far side of the room and shook the folds from it. "You cover yourself in this, missy, and I'll take that dusty ol' scrap."

Matilde wrapped her in the quilt, and with a disgusted look, the woman collected the bloodied items and left.

Will probed her shoulder again. "I'll need to clean this very well, stitch up the cuts. I'm concerned about infection. If we can keep that at bay, you'll be up and about in a few days."

"Thank God Mr. Wells made that shot," Papa breathed from the doorway.

Dara looked at him as if noticing him for the first time. "Papa, please don't let Gage leave."

He nodded. "I assure you, he won't."

———•◦•———

Gage led both his and Forsythe's horse beside the tracks to cool them. The little he'd been able to see of Dara's wound didn't look critical. Deep, but a flesh wound. The fact that she'd been sitting up and talking eased his mind, but he'd be a whole lot happier once her uncle gave his professional opinion.

Lord, please. Please let her be all right. He raised a hand to mop his face but stopped when he saw her blood staining his coat sleeve. He fisted his hand, dropped it back to his side. *Lord, I've come to care for this woman—far more than I care to admit. What happened today scared me. Bad.*

"Wells!"

He spun to see Forsythe hurrying his way. "She gonna be all right?"

"Unless infection sets in, William says she'll be fine in a few days."

Gage pressed his eyes closed. *Thank You, Lord.*

Forsythe took his horse's reins and continued to walk. "How common is an attack like this?"

Gage shook his head. "It's not. Those cats are mostly night dwellers. They prefer the higher elevations but sometimes come to the flats to hunt or when a young male is searching for new territory."

Forsythe nodded. "What'd you do in the war, son?"

His nerves jangled. "Sharpshooter."

"A mighty fine one, if that shot you took is any indication. How far was it?"

"A mile, maybe." He'd made many that were longer, thanks to the Whitworth's precision.

Forsythe nodded as they turned. "Where'd you learn to shoot?"

"I grew up so poor, I learned not to miss when hunting. It cost too much to load our guns."

"Humble beginnings do teach us a specific set of skills, don't they?"

Gage nodded, though what Forsythe might know of humble beginnings, he couldn't fathom. "That skill translated real neatly into the war." Upon learning of his accuracy, his superiors elevated him to sharpshooter. He'd done all they'd asked, but taking lives, especially like that—at a great distance and from hiding—was nothing he was proud of.

"I owe you a tremendous debt."

"You don't owe me anything, sir."

"That's the second time you've saved my daughter. A simple thank-you hardly seems sufficient."

"Knowing she's safe is thanks enough."

Forsythe grinned. "That's why I wanted to talk to you. You have a keen eye and a knack for sensing danger. You know this territory far better than William or I. Because of that, I want to hire you to protect our girls."

"Protect them?"

He waved at the sea of tents. "This camp is full of soiled doves, saloons, and sin—hardly the place to bring two impressionable young ladies. Most residing here wouldn't knowingly bother the girls, given their connection to me, but there's always that chance. Both William and I prefer they never know of the vices that happen here, but work keeps us busy enough we can't protect them from the unprincipled and immoral elements every moment."

Had the man not thought about such things before Dara arrived?

"Also, we're a few days from moving this camp twenty miles down the track to Cheyenne. Four thousand people have flocked to the town already. I won't have the control there that I do here. I'm left with a dilemma. Either demand the girls stay cooped up in our home—a decision neither would be happy with—or find a way to let them have their freedom."

"So you want me to look after them. . . ."

"Exactly. You've proven you can protect Becca and Dara, and having you around would give William and me peace of mind."

The man had to be soft in the head, offering an almost-stranger the responsibility of protecting his kin.

Or maybe *he* was soft in the head. His farm chores were done for the winter, so taking this position would keep him busy, allow him to listen for any underhanded dealings the railroad planned for the Cheyenne. . .and let him spend time with the spunky woman he was growing to love. That alone was payment enough.

Chapter Seven

Cheyenne, Dakota Territory
Eight days later

How severe is the scarring?" Dara looked over her shoulder as Uncle William removed her stitches.

"It could have been far worse. That beast could've killed you if not for Mr. Wells."

The mention of Gage's name set her belly aflutter as memories of his fervent prayers, his kind reassurances, and the strong safety of his arms on that ride enveloped her again. That night, after they'd tucked her into bed, Gage had peeked in at her as she drowsed. Thinking her asleep, he'd tiptoed into her room, held her hand for a moment, and kissed her fingers ever so gently. He'd caressed her cheek. "Feel better, princess," he'd whispered as he rose. In that moment, her heart became his, though how she would explain her love of a poor Southerner to Papa was another matter entirely.

"The scarring will fade." Uncle William's words jarred her from her thoughts.

"It gives you character." Becca grinned from the corner.

"Character?"

"Certainly," Becca continued. "How many women can say they've been attacked by a wild animal and lived to tell about it?"

They all laughed. As Uncle William retrieved something from his medical bag, Dara threw a pillow at her. It thunked Becca in the face, and they both laughed harder.

"So will you *finally* release me to ride my horse again, Uncle William?"

"I've already had this discussion with Mr. Wells. I see no reason why you can't. But please. Take it slowly, and. . .watch for wild animals."

Her face warmed, whether because of the teasing or the mention of the handsome Southern gentleman, she wasn't sure. "Yes, sir."

The pillow, thrown by Becca, slammed into her head. Uncle William glared at his daughter, though Dara guffawed.

"Finished." Uncle William laid aside his instruments. "It's good to see your sense of humor returning. I've missed it."

She tugged her chemise back into proper position, rose, and gave him a quick hug. "I've missed it, too, Uncle."

He kissed the crown of her head. "Make yourself presentable. I'm sure Mr. Wells will be here soon." He collected his things and slipped from the room.

Becca flashed her a toothy grin. "You're smitten with him."

"Who?"

"Don't be coy. You know precisely who." She retrieved Dara's clothing, her voice a mere whisper. "You blush every time his name is mentioned."

As if on cue, Dara's face warmed. "He's quite gallant."

"And handsome. And kind, and attentive, and a gentleman, and I think he's just as smitten with you."

"He is not."

"No man would pack his things, close up his home, and follow a moving rail camp unless there was a very important reason. Like a beautiful, intelligent, charming woman."

"Stop yammering and help me dress!" Giggling, she snatched her corset from the pile.

Once she'd slipped into the garment, Becca tightened the lacing. "What will Uncle Connor say if Mr. Wells asks to court you?"

All mirth fled. "I would hope he'd agree, but Papa's so hard to understand. For all I know, he'll look as far as the fact that Gage is a poor Southerner and dismiss any such advances out of hand."

Becca tied the corset then stepped in front of Dara. "You were laughing more than I've seen in a long while. . .until I asked you that question. Forgive me. I feel like I just put a fly in the punch bowl at the grandest cotillion of the Boston social season."

After an instant, Dara pushed a smile to her lips. "Then we'll drink tea, my dear." She pantomimed sipping from an imaginary teacup.

They sank into laughter again, and Dara finished dressing, the pair emerging into the living quarters a few moments later. The room was empty, Papa's early-morning breakfast dishes still cluttering the table. Very unlike Matilde, who normally had the dishes washed, dried, and put away within minutes after each meal.

"Matilde? Uncle William?"

"Papa's bag is still here." Becca waved at the medical case in the seat of a nearby chair. "He wouldn't have gone far."

A quick search of Matilde's quarters revealed her bed unmade—another abnormality. She and Becca stepped into the chill November air and found Matilde sitting on one of the platform steps, Uncle William and Gage staring intently at her.

All eyes turned to them. "What's wrong? Matilde?"

The freedwoman turned glassy brown eyes her way. "Feeling a mite poorly this morning, Miss Dara. That's all." She reached for the railing. "I'll be in directly to prepare your breakfasts."

Uncle William shook his head. "No, you won't. You're weak and feverish. I'm prescribing bed rest."

"No, sir." She rose but clutched the handrail as she teetered on the edge of the step.

Dara looped her arm around Matilde's thin waist as heat radiated from her body. "You heard the doctor. . . ."

She led Matilde inside, guiding her toward her quarters.

"No, missy," Matilde protested. "Who's gonna take care of you and Miss Becca? Doctor Will—"

"We'll care for ourselves until you're well."

The woman shook her head as they reached her small quarters. "I been sicker than this and still worked. Don't want to upset Mr. Connor."

Dara's belly knotted. She faced Matilde and cupped her friend's face in her hands. "You're not a slave anymore. You're a free woman. None of us, Papa included, expect you to work when you're ill."

Fat tears welled in Matilde's eyes, and Dara pulled her into a huge hug. "You're safe here."

Matilde nodded her head against Dara's shoulder. "I know. You always did tell me that, missy. I'm trying to believe it."

"Good." She led her to the bed. "I'll send Becca to help you change clothes, and Uncle William will want to look in on you. I need just a moment with Mr. Wells, and then I'll return to sit with you."

Matilde sank to the edge of the bed, her cheeks tear streaked. "Yes, Miss Dara."

She trotted down the hall to where Becca, Gage, and Uncle William waited in the parlor. "Becca, would you help her change clothes?"

"Certainly." Becca departed.

"How is she?" Uncle William asked.

"Fearful." Dara willed her uncle to understand.

"Of being sick?" Gage asked, confusion lacing his words.

"Indirectly." She heaved a breath. "Matilde was a slave in North Carolina, owned by a particularly vile piece of—"

"Dara." Uncle William's cautioning tone stopped her long enough to suppress the venom that threatened to erupt.

"Her owner beat her for the smallest infractions—or no reason at all—and. . .did *worse* things to her for the more serious ones. There's a deeply ingrained fear of the consequences of failing to do her work."

Gage cleared his throat roughly. "I knew of men like that in Georgia." He shook his head, inhaled deeply as if he would speak again, but walked out the door instead.

"Papa?" Becca called from down the hall. "You can come in now."

Uncle William excused himself, and Dara stepped onto the rear platform where Gage stood. He stared over the fledgling town of Cheyenne, a deep scowl marring his handsome features.

"Did I upset you?" she whispered.

"If she was a slave in North Carolina, how'd she end up in Boston with you?"

"She found her way to the Underground Railroad."

Gage looked at her. "You hid runaway slaves?"

"Not regularly, no, but at times. She was the last of seven that Mama and I hid during the war. She ran away in winter, and by the time she reached us, she was heavy with her owner's child and on death's doorstep with pneumonia. The conductor knew Mama's brother—Uncle William—was a doctor, so he hoped we might have the medical knowledge to help her." Dara shook her head. "We applied mustard plasters and other remedies, prayed for days that she'd pull through. By the time she finally did, Mama and I had grown to care about her so much, we offered to keep her with us. She agreed but said she wouldn't take charity. She'd stay only if we'd pay her as a servant."

"Where is her child?" Gage asked.

"Her little girl was stillborn. Perhaps that was God's providence, given the circumstances, though Matilde grieved for her."

Gage removed his hat and turned toward the town again.

"What's wrong?"

He eventually shook his head. "In the South, slaves weren't people. They were property.

Their dreams and their hopes were of no importance. I never gave that a lick of thought until the war, until Sherman marched through Georgia and killed my pa, set my home and barn on fire."

Dara stared. "I'm so sorry."

"My three-year-old son, Braden, was asleep inside. Ma and Beth rushed in to get him, but the flames spread too fast. They all died in the fire. I never even got to see my boy. He was born after the war began."

Unable to find adequate words, Dara took his work-roughened hand in hers.

"To Sherman's men, my family was just a bunch of filthy Southerners standing between them and their goals. Doubt it ever occurred to them that all we wanted was to live a peaceful life on a little plot of land in nowhere, Georgia. Just like it never occurred to me that those slaves were people with their own ideas and dreams, or like white settlers trying to force the Cheyenne to give up the life they've always lived. God's challenging the things I always thought I knew, things I took as gospel truth. It turns my stomach that I never saw how wrong they were before."

She slid nearer. "I'm so sorry about your family. Your *son*."

He tugged his hat on and faced her, slid his hand from her arm to her shoulder and on to her cheek. The pad of his thumb brushed across her lips, and her heart beat a little faster. As his gaze locked with hers, his fingers curled around the nape of her neck, and he pulled her gently to him.

"Dara?" Becca called from inside.

Dara drew back, putting a foot of daylight between them. Breathless, she dropped her gaze. "I need to attend to Matilde. I won't be able to ride with you today."

She darted inside before he could stop her.

"How's the patient this afternoon?" Gage grinned at Matilde from the doorway of her small quarters.

"Better, sir." She winced, pushing sweat-dampened curls away from her face.

"Most of her symptoms have gone," Dara spoke from beside the bed. "She's keeping food down. Her fever broke within the last hour. Her achiness is subsiding. But now her throat is hurting."

"Glad to hear you're improving, ma'am."

Matilde nodded but didn't speak.

He turned to Dara. "And how's the nurse faring?"

"I'm well. Thank you."

Gage turned again toward Matilde. "Would you mind if I borrowed her for a bit?"

Dara tried to protest, but Matilde shook her head. "No, sir. Go on."

"Thank you kindly, ma'am." He pulled Dara from her chair.

"What do you think you're doing?" she grumbled as he led her into the hall. "I told you I need to stay with Matilde."

"You've been with her the last two and a half days. Your uncle says Matilde's improving. Becca's willing to stay in case she needs anything. So you and I are going for that ride we've been talking about."

"Gage, I shouldn't."

He pushed her out into the parlor. "Some time outdoors will do you good."

"Yes, it will," Becca chirped from an upholstered chair. "Go have some fun."

She eyed them. "You two are conspiring against me."

"Only because you've been cooped up in this train car since you got here. Nursing me, then recuperating from your own wounds, and now Matilde's illness. You deserve to get away from all this seriousness." He held out his arm in an invitation. "What d'ya say?"

"Won't it be getting dark fairly soon?"

"That it will." He nudged her with his elbow.

"Perhaps we should wait until tomorrow. It hardly seems appropriate for us to be out alone after dark."

"Quit fussing, Dara," Becca chided. "He asked my papa for permission to take you out. He's sworn on his life and the lives of his future children that he'll protect your honor."

"Thank you, ma'am." He grinned at Becca then turned again to Dara. "We won't go far. I promise."

She finally looped her hand into the crook of his elbow. "All right. But only a short while."

They donned their coats and gloves and stepped outside, where their horses waited.

"So where are you taking me?" She mounted easily.

Gage motioned to the western sky, already streaked with myriad shades of blue, lavender, and pink. "The sunsets are beautiful. Thought we'd sit on the plains and take one in."

Understanding lit her expression. "That's why you were being so persistent."

"Yes, ma'am."

"I'd like that." Her eyes glinted. "As long as I won't be attacked by a bear or another wild creature."

He chuckled. "That won't happen so long as it's my job to protect you."

Her smile faltered for an instant but reasserted itself. "Then let's go."

Gage swung into his saddle and led her away.

They rode for a couple of miles, Dara chattering on about Matilde's condition until Gage turned to her. "I brought you out here so you could forget about all that for a while."

Her cheeks flushed. "I'm sorry. I suppose I've been rather consumed."

"Just a little. So what were you like as a child?" He searched the landscape for dangers, gaze lingering on the colorful sky.

"I suppose like I am now. I cared for those less fortunate, only then, it was animals. A bird with a broken wing, a friend's cat that had just had kittens."

Gage grinned. "I can't imagine you scooping up a wild bird and carrying it home."

A sweet giggle escaped her lips. "*I* didn't. *Papa* scooped it up and brought it home." She paused. "Mama and I marveled at his gentleness while he bound the bird's wing and tried to keep it warm. He even went so far as to dig worms from the yard and hand-feed the little thing."

"Your pa. . . ?"

Dara sobered a little. "Hard to believe, isn't it? But once, long ago, he was a doting father who would do anything for his only child. Back then, I never sensed his work was more important than Mama or me. All I remember was how loved I felt."

She fell silent, a distant look glassing her eyes.

"What happened?"

"I wish I knew. About a year after that incident, he left. He and Mama never told me why or where he went. Mama would only say that he was working and promised he would return. But then the war began, and he joined without coming home. At the end of the conflict, we received notice that he'd taken a job with the Union Pacific. He didn't return then either. It broke my heart."

He drew up and dismounted, scanning the plains as he did. "So the day you arrived here you hadn't seen him in years."

She halted but didn't dismount. "Seven, to be exact."

Seven years. She'd have been ten years old at that time. Far too young to be without her pa's guidance. He circled around and lifted her from the saddle, her hands settling on his shoulders as he did. "You have no idea why?"

"No."

Gage retrieved the blanket he'd tied behind his saddle and spread it on the ground, and they sat.

"When Mama passed a few months ago, I had to make a choice. Move in with my grandparents or Uncle William and stay in Boston where everything was known and comfortable—and risk losing my father forever. Or come west and try to rekindle the closeness we once shared. My grandfather cautioned me to stay, but Uncle William offered to move west with me if I wanted to go." A wistful expression crossed her fine features. "I didn't want to regret not trying, but it's hard when he pushes me aside for his work."

"I'm sorry." He slid nearer. "It angers me the way he treats you." The way Forsythe dismissed her at the Cheyenne camp, or how he repeatedly focused on paperwork, taking his dinner across the room, away from his family. Dara had put her life aside to become a part of his, and Forsythe was too self-absorbed to care.

"Thank you." She rested her head against his shoulder. "You have quite the penchant for making me feel safe."

"That's the goal." If he could, he'd protect her from every danger, be it a cougar or her own pa's neglect.

They sat in silence for long minutes, watching as the sky changed colors and the shades deepened. The yellow-orange rays of winter sun shone from behind a single line of large clouds.

The sun dipped, coming into view below the clouds. Across the next few minutes, the full orange orb descended into view and slipped out of sight. The horizon lit with a golden glow, blazing upward into fiery orange and cooling again into deep blue.

Despite the beauty in the heavens, the wonder in her face was far more fascinating to watch.

In the waning light of day, she leaned against him again. "Thank you. This was beautiful."

Suddenly taken by her nearness, his tongue stuck fast to the roof of his mouth and refused to form a single word. No sunset could possibly hold a candle to this woman. *His* woman. Gage rocked to his feet as Spotted Hawk's words struck home. Yes, he wanted her to be *his*.

"Gage?" She scrambled after him.

He hadn't been this near to a pretty woman in a very long time. He planted a gentle kiss on the crown of her head. "Glad you enjoyed it, princess." His hand strayed to her cheek, fingertips skimming the downy softness of her skin.

Her eyes rounded, and her pouted lips parted slightly. As he continued to caress the curve of her face, her breath grew rapid and shallow. She didn't resist, only stared back at him.

Gracious, but her eyes were an unusual shade of blue. Pale as ice toward the center, but warming to a deeper shade on the outer edge. A man could get lost searching her gaze.

Warmth flooded through him, and he leaned in ever so slowly to claim her lips. She stiffened in his arms for an instant then melted against him, trembling just a little. He cupped her cheek and drank in her sweetness. She responded, her arms circling his waist. A tiny moan escaped her, and its effect was almost like a siren call. He pulled her nearer and deepened the kiss.

At the plaintive howl of a distant wolf, Dara pulled back, her eyes huge. "What was that?"

Blast it all. Even nature was conspiring against him. He looped his arm around her. "You got nothing to worry about." Several wolves answered their pack mate's call. "A wolf's howl can travel miles. They're no threat to us."

Dara wedged her hands firmly against his chest. "Let go." She squirmed hard to free herself.

He released her. "Why?"

"Take me back. *Now.*" Panic laced the words. She paced to her horse.

"Wait, Dara." He caught her arm. "I'm telling you, you have nothing to fear."

She shook her head. "The scars on my back and shoulder say otherwise."

"I've been watching this whole time. There's nothing near enough to harm you. Please trust me. Your pa does. . . ."

Her brow furrowed, and her panicky fidgeting stilled. "What does that mean—*my pa does?*"

Gage shook his head. "If he didn't trust me, he wouldn't have hired me to protect you and Becca."

"Hired you?" Her jaw went slack. "That's why you came along when we moved the camp? He's *paying* you to look after me?"

His gut clenched. "No. It's not like that. I'm here because I'm fallin—"

Without warning, her palm landed a stinging blow against his left cheek. "Don't you *ever* toy with my affections like that. In fact, don't you come around me again."

Before he could respond, she scrambled into her saddle and, spurring her horse, galloped toward home.

Chapter Eight

By morning, anger and hurt still bubbled deep in the pit of Dara's stomach. Fortunately, Uncle William had turned Mr. Wells away from the door without too much of a scene the previous night, and he hadn't returned so far that morning. Good thing. She had far more important things to consider than the dallying, traitorous Mr. Wells—or his self-centered employer. She gritted her teeth. If Papa was so very concerned for her safety, why couldn't he be bothered to look after her himself, rather than hiring a handsome nanny to oversee her daily activities?

Dara peered through the windows on both sides of the Pullman car. Seeing neither Papa nor Mr. Wells, she stepped out to the platform, and her breath puffed white in the November air. "Lord, please. . ." she whispered. "I need Uncle William." She'd sent a passerby to fetch him more than thirty minutes earlier, and he'd still not answered the summons. "Quickly."

She scanned the faces moving about. What could be taking him so long?

Matilde's symptoms had all but dissipated the previous evening—except for the newest symptom of a sore throat. However, when she awoke that morning, the ache and difficulty swallowing had turned to spots and several open sores dotting her tongue, and a rash spreading across her cheeks.

When she still saw no sign of William, she strode back to Matilde's quarters. Fortunately, her friend slept, though fitfully, as Becca watched over her.

Father, I feel utterly helpless. What can we do to ease her discomfort?

Several moments later, the outer door opened, and Dara hurried down the hall to see Uncle William enter.

"Thank God you're here. She's developed sores in her mouth and some sort of strange bumps on her face."

His footsteps faltered before he nearly ran to her quarters.

Fear sparked as she followed.

Uncle William knelt beside the bed. He turned her head one way then the other, the patient rousing. "Matilde, open your mouth, please."

The freedwoman blinked away sleep. "Hurts, Doctor William."

He nodded. "Open, please." She complied, and he directed her mouth toward the lamplight. "Now stick out your tongue."

Her tongue, splotched with tiny red dots, had even more open sores than when Dara had looked earlier.

Uncle William released her chin and stood. "You rest, Matilde."

He exited the room, Dara and Becca following.

"Papa, what is it?" Becca whispered.

Once he reached the parlor, he faced them both. "My initial assessment was wrong."

He pressed his eyes shut. "It's not influenza. It's smallpox."

"Smallpox?" Becca breathed. "How do we treat that?"

"No." Dara shook her head, her eyes stinging. *No, no, no. Lord, please. Don't do this to Matilde. She's been through so much already.*

"There is no course of treatment, other than to quarantine the patient, make sure she drinks plenty of water, and keep her as comfortable as possible."

"Quarantine?" Becca's face blanched. "Are we all at risk?"

"No. I vaccinated you both when you were children. You can't contract this. Connor and I are also protected. I'll need to check with Mr. Wells." He looked Dara's way. "I don't know what happened between you last night, Dara, but if he's ill, I'll be bringing him here for quarantine."

Her stomach clenched. She would attend to him if needed, but she wouldn't like it. "I understand, Uncle."

"Good. Has anyone else been in this train car since Matilde became sick?"

She closed her eyes, pushing away the fear that descended over her. "I don't think so. Misters Marston and Adgate have come to the door, but they haven't come inside."

"Make sure no one does. Once the lesions form in the mouth, she's at her most contagious."

Both she and Becca nodded.

"The rash will spread. First the mouth and throat, then the face, followed by the arms and legs, and lastly the palms and soles of the feet. Only after the rash has scabbed over and the scabs have fallen off will she be beyond the contagious period. That will take several weeks. It's of utmost importance that no unvaccinated people come through that door unless they're already infected."

"You *are* going to help us care for Matilde, aren't you?" Becca asked.

"I'll need to find Connor, let him know, then assess anyone who's been in the camp this week. You'll have to handle Matilde's care without me, at least for now."

Becca tried to look brave. "We'll do our best, Papa."

Uncle William crushed them both in a huge hug. "I know you will. Now go see to Matilde."

"Becca, I'll be right there." While her cousin headed back to the sickroom, she followed William to the door.

He turned. "What's on your mind?"

"What chance does Matilde have to survive?"

"She's young and strong. She's survived difficult things before."

"Uncle William, please."

He hung his head. "If memory serves, one in three people die from smallpox. Those that survive often experience horrible scarring, particularly on the face."

Dara covered her mouth and nodded. "Thank you for being honest."

"We'll all feel very helpless in these next few days. Remember to pray. The Lord still works miracles."

She nodded. *Yes, Lord, we'll need handfuls of them. Please.*

Uncle William patted her shoulder and stepped outside, turning to descend the steps. "Are you missing a hair ribbon?"

"No. . . ?" She peeked out after him to see the familiar green strip she'd gifted to Walks

In Shadows tied in a perfect bow around the platform railing.

"Someone must've thought it was yours."

Once he was gone, Dara looked across the plains. As taken with the gift as the Cheyenne woman had been, she wouldn't have returned it. Not without good reason. So how had it ended up here, and where was its owner?

As she headed inside again, something beneath her feet hissed. Dara spun toward the railing to find Walks In Shadows lying between the metal train tracks, peering up from under the platform.

"What are you doing here?" She cast a discreet glance to be sure no one was watching. Should anyone see a Cheyenne this near town, there could be conflict.

"I. . .need. . .find. . .Wells."

Dara's brows arched then fell. Of course she would need Gage Wells—one of the two men she had no desire to speak to. "Is something wrong?"

Confusion masked the other woman's features.

"Why do you need Wells?"

She understood that better. "My people. . .big. . .no." She scowled. "Uh. Mmmm. . . many. My people. . .many sick."

Ice filled her veins. "How? How are they sick?"

"Fire. . .in—" She pinched her cheek then her neck.

"They've been burned?"

"No. Fire in. . ." She held her hands where Dara could see and pinched the skin on one hand.

"Fire in their skin. Fever."

"Yes." Across the next several minutes, Walks In Shadows spoke and pantomimed several other symptoms, every one a symptom Matilde had experienced.

"Help me. . .find Wells?"

Even if she could find Gage, would he know what to do? For all she knew, he'd ridden back to his soddy. If they'd somehow carried smallpox to the Cheyenne, there was no time to waste. Someone with knowledge of quarantine protocols needed to get to them immediately.

"You don't need Wells. I'll help you."

⸺⸺•◦•⸺⸺

As the railroad crews would soon return from laying track, Gage stalked through the well-trampled lanes of the hell-on-wheels camp. He'd avoided the inevitable too long already. As much as he distrusted—disliked—Forsythe, the man was Gage's boss, and Gage had somehow compromised his mission to protect Dara. High time he quit skirting the issue and come clean. Tell him he could keep his blasted money if it meant Gage might be able to win Dara's heart once and for all.

He shook his head. What had happened? He'd spent his day hunched over a small campfire on the plains trying to decipher why Dara had grown so upset. The only conclusion was Forsythe hadn't told her about their arrangement. But why not?

Rifle in hand, he walked to the sad little tent Forsythe now called an office. He'd watched long enough to know that, prior to Dara and Becca's arrival, Forsythe had used the Pullman car for both personal quarters and office. The little tent was quite a step down from the warmth and opulence of the Pullman car made to his specifications.

At least Forsythe had the decency to give the girls his large bedroom and move himself and William into what had been his office, rather than forcing the girls to sleep in the tent in the dead of winter. He snorted. Gage wouldn't have put such a selfish act past the railroad man.

He reached the tent. Knowing Forsythe wouldn't have returned yet, Gage took up station near the corner. A conversation hummed inside.

"Tell me you can do this without messing things up like last time."

"I did what you told me," another man spoke. "I destroyed it."

"Wrong. We said haul it down the tracks and *burn* it." A third voice. "Not toss a lit bundle of dynamite inside when it was near enough to injure anyone."

Gage's ears perked.

"That was an unfortunate miscalculation." Spoken by the second man. "When I tossed the dynamite in the boxcar, the long fuse I put on it musta touched the fuse much closer to the bundle, so it blew too soon."

"I don't care what you call it, Vickers. Two men died, another lost a leg, many more were injured, and you nearly took out Forsythe's daughter and niece. If you'd just burned the thing like we told you. . ."

"Yeah, I got the idea."

Gage clenched his jaw. He recalled Vickers from the Cheyenne camp, but he couldn't place the other voices. He'd heard them before. . . . Silently, he stalked down the side of the tent, angled to the back side, and sprawled in the frigid grass. He lifted the canvas gingerly and squinted, one-eyed, through the opening he'd created.

"The question remains. . .can you do this without another catastrophic mistake?"

His eyesight adjusted to the lower light. Mr. Marston faced Vickers directly, and a few feet away, Mr. Adgate.

"That'll all depend on whether you got your information right. Has it been long enough? Am I gonna walk into that camp and find a bunch of Injuns dead from smallpox, or am I gonna go in there and find 'em none the worse for wear? Ain't in the mood to get myself scalped."

Gage dropped the canvas, thoughts firing in a thousand directions at once.

"Consider that your incentive to pay close attention before you steal into their camp. You've got two jobs while you're there. Burn those blankets so no one else gets infected and collect all those knives we gave out. We aren't here to outfit our enemies with weapons they can turn on us."

Gage snatched up his rifle and slipped away.

Smallpox. . .unleashed through infected blankets. . .and given as a *goodwill gift* to his friends.

Chapter Nine

B y the time the Cheyenne camp came into view, Dara was nearly frozen from the cold and exhausted from the twenty-mile ride, yet there was no time to rest or get warm. She must get to work. . .and pray the Cheyenne would obey her orders after only one prior introduction.

"Walks In Shadows"—she slowed her pace—"until I see what's happening to your people, you must stay outside the camp." From what she'd gathered, Walks In Shadows had been away from the camp several days and returned to find many sick.

She shook her head, obviously not understanding.

"You. . .stay here."

She shook her head more emphatically. "I go. Help my people."

"No. The smallpox will make you sick."

At her obvious confusion, Dara stumbled through two easier explanations before the woman understood.

Her brow furrowed. "How you. . .talk my people?"

Her belly lurched. How *would* she communicate with the Cheyenne? She must convey that she'd come to help, then set up quarantine areas for the infected patients. She hadn't even considered she might not be able to use Walks In Shadows as a translator when she'd chosen to tell no one, particularly Gage, where she was going.

Oh, Lord Jesus, I've made a terrible mistake, and I'm too far away from anywhere to ask for help.

———◦◦◦———

Gage barged into William's medical tent, praying he'd be in.

"Wells! Thank God." William shot up from his desk. "I've been looking for you all day."

Gage halted. "You have?" Surprising, given how firmly the man had turned him away from the Pullman car the previous evening. "Why?"

William dropped his voice to a confidential tone. "Have you ever been vaccinated for smallpox?"

Everything stilled. "Why?"

"I wrongly diagnosed Matilde. She developed the smallpox rash overnight, and you've been around her since she's gotten sick. I must quarantine any unvaccinated persons who've come in contact with the illness."

How had Matilde contracted smallpox? Marston and Adgate had infected the blankets they'd given to the Cheyenne, but Matilde was nowhere near the Indian camp that day. Mind scrambling, he reviewed the events of the visit.

"By all that's holy. . ." He'd bound Dara's wounds with scraps of the infected pieces.

He'd wrapped her in the remnant. They'd carried it straight to her.

"Wells, have you been vaccinated or not?"

He stared at the ground, mind still chewing on the details. "When I joined the Confederacy."

"You're sure?"

He finally met the doctor's eyes. "Yes, sir. What about Becca and Dara?"

"We've all had the vaccine. Now if I could just figure out where she contracted it so I can prevent others from getting sick."

As Gage relayed the details of the overheard conversation, shock filled William's face. "You don't think Connor is involved, do you?"

"What am I supposed to think? I had my doubts about Forsythe long before you all arrived. He's the one that asked me to translate that meeting. Now today, his bosses and the lackey he put in charge of his daughter discuss what they did. Seems like proof enough to me. They're all involved."

William shook his head. "I know my brother-in-law. There's a *lot* he does that I don't agree with, but he's no murderer."

"Right now, he's the least of my worries. We gotta get to that camp and see if we can't help them."

"I have one confirmed smallpox patient here, and the men who delivered those blankets could be infected without showing symptoms yet. This could turn into a full-blown epidemic."

Gage's muscles knotted with a mixture of frustration, anger, and fear. "And what about the epidemic that's surely tearing through the Cheyenne camp right now?"

"Wells, I'd go with you in an instant if I didn't have duties to attend to here. As soon as I'm certain we're safe, I'll join you at their camp. For now, you'll have to go without me. Take one of the girls. I've instructed both in what to expect with Matilde's illness."

"I'd rather take Dara, sir. The Cheyenne can be distrustful of outsiders."

"Then go with my blessing, and Godspeed."

He gathered his horse then went to the makeshift stable to saddle Dara's mount. However, as he looked over the horses, hers was nowhere to be found.

"Hey." He strode up to the stable hand. "Where's the chestnut mare you keep for Mr. Forsythe?"

"That handsome woman living in Mr. Forsythe's quarters asked me to saddle it for her this morning."

Every nerve sparked. "What time?"

The fella shrugged. "Ain't rightly sure. Hours ago."

Gage swung into the saddle, walked his horse to the Pullman car, and dismounting, tied the mustang to the railing. He ran into the Pullman car.

"Dara, that better be you!" Becca called from the hallway. An instant later, she trotted into the parlor, eyes widening. "You're not supposed to be here."

"I'm looking for Dara."

"That makes two of us." She hurried toward him. Palms firm against his chest, she tried to push him toward the door. "You still can't be in here. Matilde's got smallpox."

Gage stood his ground. "I can't get it. Do you know where Dara is?"

Her eyes clamped shut, and she shook her head. "No. I haven't seen her since Papa was here this morning."

"Any idea where she might've gone?"

"No." Her blue eyes brimmed with tears. "She was going to tend to Matilde, and I was supposed to help. This isn't like Dara. I'm frightened."

As was he. Could she have been so angry at him that she'd ride off alone? "Was she upset?"

"We both are. I love Matilde as much as she does."

"I mean about anything else. . ."

The girl nodded sheepishly. "She was quite angry last night. At you. She shut herself in our room when she returned, but she sat again with Matilde later. Neither Papa nor I could coax any information from her as to what happened."

"A misunderstanding is all. Was she still upset this morning?"

"Quiet, not openly angry."

No information that helped. "Thanks. Get back to Matilde. I'll see if I can't find Dara."

She hugged him tight and drew back, red cheeked.

He grinned then scrambled outside and back down the steps, but he paused when his hand skimmed over something soft on the railing. Something dark and thin knotted around the metal fencing, ends fluttering in the cold winter wind. Standing on the lowest step, Gage found a dark green ribbon tied in a bow.

The one Dara had given Walks In Shadows.

Chapter Ten

Exhaustion pulled at Dara as she stepped from Spotted Hawk's tent and shielded her eyes to look over the Cheyenne camp. She'd survived the first night. It hadn't been easy. After some talk, she and Walks In Shadows had finally ridden to Spotted Hawk's tent, where Walks In Shadows called to her father from horseback. When he'd stepped out, bundled in a buffalo robe and shivering with fever, the Cheyenne woman rode to the outskirts of camp.

To Dara's surprise, Spotted Hawk's English was pristine. Together, they'd circulated among the tents, and Dara was eventually able to quarantine the sick—or rather, separate out the few who weren't displaying symptoms yet.

Dara walked to the riverbank, waterskins in hand, mind clicking through the myriad tasks she must accomplish. With more than one hundred sick, her tasks outweighed her strength to complete them.

She squatted beside the water and broke the thin layer of ice with a stone, then dunked first one waterskin, then the other, into the icy water.

Lord, I don't know what I was thinking. I knew the numbers of Cheyenne that live here. How could I have dreamed I'd be able to care for all of them myself? I need help. I need You.

As the second skin filled, Dara looked across the camp. Early morning sunlight glinted against the frosted grass, almost blinding her as a silhouetted figure stepped from inside Spotted Hawk's tent. Dara stood, shading her eyes to see who was moving about. The figure took a few steps her way, blocking the glinting sunlight just enough that she could see.

"Gage."

The waterskin only half full, she plucked it from the stream, snatched up the full one, and dashed back into the camp. "Gage!" Dara fell into his arms.

"You all right, princess?" he whispered against her hair as he held her.

"Yes." *Now.* She nodded against his shoulder. "Just tired." *Very* tired. "Where did you come from? It's barely past dawn."

"Once I guessed where you'd gone, I set out. I'd have been here sooner, but it got too cold last night. Had to make camp and build a fire." He pushed her back to arm's length. "What in the name of Pete were you thinking, coming by yourself?"

Dara heaved a sigh. "I was trying to help." Just what Mama would've done.

"By yourself?"

"Walks In Shadows found me, said there was a great sickness here. When she described the symptoms, I realized it was smallpox. I admit, I didn't think it through like I should have. I was upset at the news about Matil—"

Her heart stalled for an instant as realization struck. "Gage, Matilde has smallpox. So do the Cheyenne. If you haven't been vaccinated, you could be infe—"

"Your uncle told me." As if seeing the waterskins for the first time, he took them from her. "I was vaccinated during the war. I'll be fine."

"Thank the Lord." Relief washed through her. "I'm so glad you came. There's too many for one person to attend to. I need help."

Gage's expression clouded. "I can't. Not yet."

"Why?"

"Dara, they were infected by the blankets. I overheard a conversation between Marston, Adgate, and Vickers. The railroad conspired to hurt the Cheyenne, somehow laced the blankets with smallpox and gave 'em out. Vickers is the one that blew up the boxcar."

"On purpose?" Her own *father* had done this?

Gage hung his head. "I need to burn those blankets. Once that's done, I can help with whatever else you need."

Dara nodded, trying not to let emotion and exhaustion get the better of her. "All right."

He carried the waterskins to Spotted Hawk's tent, and each set about their tasks. Dara moved from one patient to the next, offering water and checking symptoms. As she ducked out of a tent, a lone figure on horseback rode over the hill toward the camp.

"Gage?" she called as he appeared, carrying several blankets. Her belly knotted as she recognized her father.

They walked in his direction, and her father dismounted. Strangely, he crammed his hands deep in his trouser pockets.

"Papa." Every nerve flared warning.

"William told me what happened." He shifted a glance past her to Gage and then toward the Cheyenne camp.

Dara glared. "How dare you show up here after what you did to these people." Her hand arced toward his particularly pale cheek.

<hr/>

Gage caught Dara's wrist as a line of riders crested the hill behind Forsythe. "Wait."

All the fire she'd directed at her pa suddenly turned his way. She jerked free, gave him one mighty shove, and stormed past him, racing toward the stream.

Gage turned back to Forsythe. "Why are you here?"

The other man's Adam's apple bobbed repeatedly. "I brought help."

"That so?" The same anger from Dara's gaze boiled in his belly. "How do I know you didn't bring them to clean up the mess you made?"

"I swear to you, Wells." Forsythe shifted uncomfortably. "I didn't know what Marston and Adgate's true intentions were. The Cheyenne and the railroad have had their conflicts, but I would never have been party to such actions."

Silence prevailed as Gage sized up the other man. Always before, Forsythe had been the picture of control. A man who wielded power like a weapon. Yet, now there was only remorse in his gaze, a penitence Gage had doubted Forsythe might possess. This had rocked him in a way little else could.

"Just so you know, I called the US Marshals in. They'll be arresting Marston and Adgate."

A good start. Gage glanced to the odd assortment of people he'd brought—several muscled track layers, a couple of soiled doves who worked the rail camp, and numerous new faces.

"You sure they can't catch smallpox?"

"They're all immune."

"Good. We need the help." Gage stationed the ragtag bunch among the various tents. When only Forsythe remained, Gage stalked toward the stream, leaving him in the dust.

"Wells, what do you want me to do?"

Gage faced him. "Wait there while I fetch Dara. You two need to talk."

He hurried down the shallow incline of the bank, Dara turning as he approached.

"I'm sorry," she whispered, diving into his embrace. "I shouldn't have pushed you. I was just so angry at Papa, and you stopped me fr—"

"Shhh." Gage cupped her face in his hands and kissed her—soundly. She stiffened, but almost instantly her turmoil seemed to drain away, and her fingers wound into the thick fabric of his coat. Only when the trembling in her limbs subsided did he come up for air. Still cradling her face, he rested his forehead against hers and looked into her ice-blue eyes. "I love you, Dara Forsythe."

She stared back at him. "I love you, too."

"I'm real glad to hear that. You had me worried the other night." He stole another quick kiss before he pulled away and took her hands in his. "Do you trust me?"

Dara nodded.

"Then I want you to walk over there and talk to your pa."

Blue eyes rounding, she glanced around him and shook her head. "I have nothing to say to him."

"I beg to differ, princess. You've been asking to talk since the day that cougar attacked you. If what I'm seeing is right, now'd be a perfect time."

"Truly, I don't know what to say, Gage. Not after what he's done."

"I don't think he did anything. Not knowingly, anyway. He swore to me it was all Marston and Adgate's doing, and I believe him." He let that sink in. "Please go talk to him, darlin'."

"Only if you'll come with me."

At her reluctant consent, Gage led her back to her father. Uncomfortable seconds ticked by before Forsythe spoke.

"Dara, I'm sorry."

"For what, Papa?"

"For everything."

"That's not good enough," she hissed. "What are you sorry for—which part? Show me you know how you've hurt me."

Her raw words, the anguish in Forsythe's eyes drove a stake through Gage's heart. *Lord, help them work this out, please.*

"I'm sorry"—Forsythe gulped but met her eyes, tears pooling in his own—"for the man I've become. I'm sorry I left you and your mother all those years ago, and I'm sorry I wasn't there when she died."

A sob tore from Dara's small frame, and she launched herself into her father's arms. "Why, Papa? Why did you go?"

When Forsythe's tears also began to fall, Gage attempted to brush past, give them time to work through their wounds, but Forsythe caught his arm and mouthed two words. *Stay. Please.*

Hesitantly Gage nodded and stood a few feet away.

"I've let you believe I'm something I'm not."

"What does that mean?" Dara tried to look up at him, though he held her fast to his chest.

"I was born to the poorest of the poor, with no hope of ever making anything of my life." Forsythe looked straight at Gage as he spoke the words, then dropped his focus to the ground. "By the grace of God, I met your mother and grandmother. They helped me get a job in your grandfather's factory, and over the years your mother and I fell deeply in love. However, your grandfather wouldn't consent to our marriage. In his eyes, I wasn't worthy of his daughter, so we eloped. Your grandfather never let me live it down."

When Dara held him tighter, Forsythe pressed his eyes closed.

"After years of his badgering, your mother and I felt it best for me to leave, prove myself once and for all. It was never meant to be seven years, Dara-girl. We'd planned on two at the most. But then the war started, and I joined the Union. Somewhere along the way, I lost sight of what was most important. I let pride and greed rule my heart. It wasn't until you came that I've been able to see what I've become. To my shame, I don't like that man. I wish I had stayed. I missed out on so much."

"I wish you had, too, Papa. Mama and I missed you terribly."

"Mr. Forsythe!" a woman's panicked shriek split the air. They all jerked to face the camp as one of the soiled doves raced toward them. "Come quick. That Vickers fella's here!"

Both Gage and Forsythe ran toward the heart of the camp.

"He come barging into the tepee I was in and started digging around amongst their things," the woman panted. "When he saw me, he ducked back out, jumped on his horse, and rode off."

Forsythe ran to his horse at the far end of the camp, and Gage darted between Spotted Hawk's tent and the one next to it. Grabbing his Whitworth and his saddlebags, Gage swung onto the paint's bare back and raced to the edge of the camp. In the distance, Vickers galloped his horse full speed. Forsythe trailed far behind him.

Gage slipped from his mount's back and, with practiced precision, loaded his rifle. He leveled the gun over the paint's back and sighted in on his target. After careful aim, he blew out half a breath and squeezed the trigger. The Whitworth kicked against his shoulder, and he waited the extra instant to see Vickers tumble from his horse. Gage reloaded, sighted in on Vickers again. The distant figure lay prone, though moving. Forsythe reached him a moment later and hauled the man to his feet. Satisfied, Gage gently lowered the rifle's hammer and turned.

Dara stood only feet away, a half smile lighting her tear-streaked face.

"You all right?"

Her smile widened as she nodded. "There's a whole lot more Papa and I have to discuss, but I think I will be."

"Yeah, there's a rather important matter I need to discuss with your pa myself, princess."

Epilogue

Cheyenne, Dakota Territory
Three months later

Dara, are you coming?"

At her husband's call, Dara Wells pulled free of her papa's lingering embrace and pecked him on the cheek one last time.

"I'll miss you."

"Not near as much as I'll miss you, Dara-girl. I'll send word as soon as I've reached Washington, DC, and I'm already making plans to return for Christmas."

"You'd better."

When the train whistle blew, Dara turned, took Gage's hand, and descended from the train car's platform before it chugged into motion.

Papa stood on the lowest step and waved until the train rounded a bend in the track just outside town.

Dara turned to face Gage and Becca.

"How you doing, princess?" Gage asked.

She mustered a brave smile. "I'll be fine."

Becca's eyes misted. "I'm not. I was coming to really enjoy Uncle Connor again."

Gage looped his arm around the girl's shoulders. "C'mon, squirt, I told you. The work he'll be doing with the Bureau of Indian Affairs is important."

"But you're working with the bureau, and you're not going to Washington."

"No, but I'm the territorial agent. I handle things here locally. Your uncle will be setting policies in place that'll care for the Indian tribes in the whole country."

Uncle William dashed up, out of breath, and peered down the tracks. "I missed him," he panted. "I'm sorry. I spent all night tending a patient and couldn't get away."

"It's all right, Uncle William. He knew you wanted to be here."

He loosed a frustrated sigh.

"Reckon we ought to get home." Gage started walking toward their horses. "Matilde's going to have breakfast ready soon. You're both welcome to join us."

William looked at Becca. "Don't mind if we do."

Arm in arm with Gage, Dara looked around the street at several new buildings being constructed as two supply wagons hauled wood to the work sites along muddy, snow-dusted lanes.

Cheyenne. No paved streets. Primitive stores by Boston's standards. But it was growing. It was *home*.

Jennifer Uhlarik discovered the western genre as a preteen, when she swiped the only "horse" book she found on her older brother's bookshelf. A new love was born. Across the next ten years, she devoured Louis L'Amour westerns and fell in love with the genre. In college at the University of Tampa, she began penning her own story of the Old West. Armed with a BA in writing, she has won five writing competitions and was a finalist in two others. In addition to writing, she has held jobs as a private business owner, a schoolteacher, a marketing director, and her favorite—a full-time homemaker. Jennifer is active in American Christian Fiction Writers and is a lifetime member of the Florida Writers Association. She lives near Tampa, Florida, with her husband, teenage son, and four fur children.

The Right Pitch

by Susanne Dietze

Dedication

For Tamela, with thanks.

Author's Note

Baseball has changed a bit since its inception (some scholars say the 1780s!), so some of the rules described in *The Right Pitch* might be strange to us in the twenty-first century. Umpires (called judges) were culled from the stands, pitchers stood in a box instead of on a mound, and the national anthem wasn't played at ball games until the 1918 World Series. For flavor, I used the 1876 terms for player positions except for one: a catcher was called a "behind" back then, but I used our modern name for clarity's sake.

There were no official women's teams until 1866 when students at Vassar College created two. For the most part, female squads were temporary and made up of leisure-class players with ample spare time. They wore everyday clothes but not gloves. Players, male and female, caught the ball with their bare hands.

Philadelphia hosted the Centennial International Exhibition in 1876, held from May to November to celebrate the 100th anniversary of the signing of the Declaration of Independence.

It was also the fictional home of the Beale family, Winnie's neighbors. Little Penelope is the heroine of her own story, *In for a Penny*, in *The American Heiress Brides Collection*.

Love is the most important thing in the world,
but baseball is pretty good, too.
Yogi Berra

Walk worthy of the vocation wherewith ye are called, with all lowliness and meekness,
with longsuffering, forbearing one another in love; endeavouring
to keep the unity of the Spirit in the bond of peace.
Ephesians 4:1–3

Chapter One

Philadelphia, Pennsylvania
June, 1876

rack! Winifred Myles dropped the willow bat and darted straight to first base. When none of the outfielders caught the ball, she gestured at her teammate Drusilla Connor, who vacillated at second base, to keep running. "Go!"

Winnie hoisted her skirt above her ankles and sprinted after Dru—to second base then third, her peripheral vision fixed on the ball, and kept running until she reached home, almost tripping over Dru, who'd fallen across the flour sack marking home base.

Two runs! Not that the score counted—this was practice, after all, and half of the team's eight players couldn't cover the diamond they'd marked off in chalk in a local park. However, they'd all given their best, and every last woman on the field panted or flushed pink with exertion. A few of them even smiled.

Winnie clapped her hands, causing the fresh blisters on her palms to sting, but she didn't mind. They were badges of honor to a baseball player—if not to the proper lady Papa wished his daughter to be. "Splendid effort, ladies!"

"Ugh." Curly-headed Dru propped on her elbows.

Winnie tugged her dearest friend to her feet. "You, too, Dru."

"I'll have a splendid bruise to match my effort." Dru stood tall—a full six inches taller than Winnie—and tenderly rubbed her hip through the dirt-smeared gray wool of her skirt, grimacing at the contact. Then her gaze shifted somewhere past Winnie's ear. Her eyes widened, her jaw gaped, and her hand fell at once.

Winnie spun around. A well-dressed couple strode toward them over the grass, right through center field.

Gawkers, come to marvel at the ladies playing baseball? It wouldn't be the first time. It was also possible these folks were ignorant that their afternoon stroll interrupted a baseball game.

Taking a long, deep breath, Winnie tramped across the rough grass to intercept them. The gentleman's stride seemed purposeful, his broad shoulders relaxed. The chestnut-haired young woman on his arm didn't look happy, however. One of her hands clenched in a fist at the waist of her bronze polonaise walking suit, like she was upset with something he'd said.

Well, she might not like Winnie asking them to step aside, either. She forced a smile. "Good afternoon."

"How do you do?" The gentleman tipped his hat, revealing a thick shock of light brown hair.

Winnie didn't have time for small talk, but she knew her manners. "Well, and you?"

Twin dimples appeared in the man's fresh-shaven cheeks. "Fine, thank you."

"Fine," the lady on his arm echoed, but her tone implied the opposite.

Now that they were a mere three feet from each other, it was obvious the lady was young, still in the schoolroom if not barely out of it, and the gentleman was some ten or twelve years older than his companion. An odd pairing, not that it was any of Winnie's business. In fact, her business was baseball, and she'd best get back to it.

She gestured behind her, where the ladies of her team waited among the flour sack bases and the chalk-drawn pitcher's box. "I beg your pardon, but we're in the middle of baseball practice. I wouldn't wish for you to be struck by a stray ball."

"I wouldn't want that, either." Releasing the lady's arm, the man reached into the breast pocket of his coat and withdrew a sheet of paper. "But surely the Liberty Belles take excellent care with their aim."

Ah! She didn't need to see the paper to know precisely what it said:

Ladies, Take a Swing at the Bat.
Join the Liberty Belles All-Female Baseball Team
as we Prepare for an Independence Day Exhibition Game vs. The Patriots.
All Proceeds Benefit Charity of the Winner's Choice.
Liberty Belles will Donate to the Children's Hospital.
Francis Field, Sunny Afternoons at Three.
See Miss Myles, Captain.

Winnie's hands clasped under her chin. "You found one of my flyers."

"You're Miss Myles?" His blue eyes flashed.

"I am."

"I'm Beck Emerson. This is my sister, Louise. She's interested in joining the Liberty Belles."

Beckett Emerson? Just this morning, Papa saw his name in the newspaper and said how he respected his business sense but called him something of a recluse. Winnie had imagined the elusive Mr. Emerson to be an ancient fellow, peering down at Philadelphia from the upstairs rooms of his closed-up mansion. The man before her, however, was young, hale, and definitely too toned and ruddy-cheeked to closet himself up in his rooms all day.

And he'd brought his sister to play baseball!

"Perfect. We're one player short." Winnie thrust her hand at Louise. "You've played before?"

"A time or two. Beck's mad for it." The young lady's handshake was as halfhearted as her tone. Winnie bit her lip. A gal couldn't hold a bat with a grip like that.

The gentleman shook Winnie's hand next, his strong clasp much more suitable to catching a ball than his sister's. Much warmer, too, sending a prickle of heat up to her elbow. She rubbed her arm when he let go and turned back to his sister. "What's your favorite position, Louise? I hope you don't mind me calling you that, but we go by our Christian names here on the field."

"I go by Lulu, actually."

"Most of us go by nicknames, too. I'm Winnie. Dru Connor plays catcher, and these three gals are Irene Huntoon, Gladys Franks, and Rowena Quaid, who most often play as first, second, and third basetenders, respectively." As Winnie spoke, the ladies waved.

"Colleen Yancy's our short scout, and Fannie Quaid and Nora Huntoon are scouts in the outfield."

Lulu nodded but didn't look excited at the prospect of joining in.

Maybe she was nervous. Winnie gathered the willow bat from the ground, extending it with a smile. "Would you like to try a turn as striker?"

Beck Emerson nudged his sister. "Give it a go."

"Fine."

There was that word again, uttered with not-at-all-fine irritation. Oh dear.

Winnie gestured to the others to take their positions and she moved to the pitcher's box. Colleen tossed her the lemon-peel ball and Winnie squared to face Lulu.

Lulu knew how to hold a bat, at least. Winnie gently tossed the ball underhanded, forty-five feet toward home base.

Lulu swung at the easy pitch. And missed. Dru caught the ball and tossed it to Winnie.

"Let's try again." Winnie held it up. "Ready?"

Lulu nodded.

Winnie pitched. Lulu hit it this time and sent it bouncing toward Winnie's feet. Winnie sent her a few more pitches, and Lulu had similar success—or lack of it—but it didn't matter. Not everyone was a strong striker, and practice would help.

"Shall we try throwing and catching?"

"I just buffed my fingernails, so I'd rather not, ma'am."

Ma'am? Winnie wasn't *that* old. Dru hid her mouth behind her hand, but it was obvious she snickered. So did Gladys. Winnie cast them a quick glare, reminding them they were mere weeks younger than her twenty-two. Papa reminded her often of her age, anyway, and that she and his protégé Victor would make a lovely married couple. Smothering the irritating thought, she turned back to Lulu. "Call me Winnie. And I hate to say it, but all of our fingernails will be in sorry shape until the exhibition game."

Lulu peeked at her brother and then rolled her eyes. "Fine."

But this was not fine. Not at all. The Liberty Belles needed one more player, but clearly Lulu Emerson was not interested in being that woman.

"Lulu, if this isn't of interest to you—"

"Miss Myles?" Beck Emerson marched toward her over the grass. "A word, please?"

<hr/>

Beck Emerson walked beside the pretty pitcher out of the others' hearing, their steps muffled in the damp clusters of grass underfoot. Wait—had he thought her pretty?

He had no business thinking such a thing about anyone. But gazing down at her warm brown eyes and the pert tilt to her nose, he allowed himself to find her objectively attractive.

Even though the feeling was far more subjective. He even liked the frayed cuffs of her rust-hued jacket and the fact that dirt smeared her matching skirt with a thin spot above her knees, testifying to the fact that she'd slid into a base a time or two. A woman who liked baseball this much was a rare treasure. She might even like it as much as he did.

And she *was* pretty—

He brushed the traitorous thoughts aside. "Your team looks quite good."

"Thank you, Mr. Emerson, but pardon my bluntness. This seems to be more your idea than your sister's."

He couldn't deny it. "It is."

"She shouldn't be forced to do something she doesn't want to do."

"I'm not forcing her. I'm strongly encouraging it, but she's here of her own volition." This was coming out wrong. "She enjoys baseball, or at least she did until recently. But right now she *needs* baseball."

"I don't understand."

"Lulu is seventeen years old and thinks herself madly in love. I told her I'd be more amenable to her marriage if she devoted herself this summer to some sort of service, like playing on your team to benefit charity."

"She can do charity work in other ways."

"But not like this, learning cooperation and teamwork—skills she'll need if she's to enter into the partnership of marriage."

Miss Myles nodded. "That makes sense. Baseball is a cooperative effort, but she's not that interested—"

"She agreed to this. I wouldn't have brought her otherwise." It was true. Lulu was motivated to do anything to get Beck's blessing on her marriage. Beck was equally motivated to get Lulu occupied with something that wasn't her beloved Alonzo, so he determined to entice Miss Myles. "You're playing for the Children's Hospital, I see. Is anyone sponsoring the team?"

Her jaw went slack. "No."

Ah, he'd piqued her interest at last. "Emerson Works will sponsor you, then, and I'll make a significant donation to the Children's Hospital."

Her temptation to accept was evident in her wide eyes. Then, back on the field, Lulu fumbled a ball and refused to chase after it. More than one of the teammates crossed her arms or rolled her eyes.

Despite his insistence that Lulu agreed to be here, she wasn't demonstrating it. No doubt Miss Myles weighed her desire for sponsorship against having Lulu on the team.

He'd spare her from saying no. "I see I can't convince you to let Lulu on the team. I'll make the donation to the hospital anyway, but before I go, one suggestion: You're a good pitcher, but you're rushing. That makes your body bend, and your arm is too low."

Her brows lifted into perfect little arches. "Lulu said you enjoy the game. Are you a pitcher?"

"Once. I played every spare moment I had before the war. During the war, too, until I couldn't play anymore." He glanced down at his left hand.

She looked at it then, as if she hadn't noticed it hanging lifeless at his side until this moment. When she said nothing, he grinned, as he always did to set people at ease.

"War injury."

"The war between the states?" Her eyes crinkled in disbelief.

"I was sixteen when I joined the army, too young, but my father didn't stop me." Father had wished he had prohibited it, though, when a minie ball struck Beck's left shoulder, damaging the nerves and bones.

"You're a brave fellow, Mr. Emerson."

At least she wasn't repulsed by him, like other women of his acquaintance. "I appreciate your time. Lulu and I won't keep you any longer." He nodded and turned.

"Nonsense. Lulu should finish practice if she's to be on the Liberty Belles."

He turned back. "She's on the team?"

"Of course. Every lady wishing to play may join. It's only that I am not convinced *she* wishes to play."

"Thank you."

"No thanks necessary. Neither is your sponsorship, but any donations are joyfully accepted." She grinned, a pleasing sight. So pleasing he almost didn't catch her next words.

"Why not share your expertise with the whole team? Help us train."

"Me?" Surely he'd heard wrong.

"Yes."

No. He had a full schedule. And one arm. "I'm not suited for it."

"I thought your advice for me to be quite sound." She pretended to pitch, taking her time, her eyes crinkled in amusement.

But this wasn't funny. "I have a business."

She nodded, as if she knew. "It would be for but a few weeks, and it's for a good cause. Besides, I've heard you're a fair, knowledgeable man."

She had? "Where?"

Her eyes twinkled. "My father is Hector Myles. He invited you to a soiree at our home tonight benefitting the hospital, but you haven't responded. Did you misplace the invitation?"

His collar suddenly pinched his neck. "No. It's on my desk."

"Perhaps you have other plans relating to the Centennial celebration."

There were dozens, since Philadelphia's Centennial Exhibition celebrating the hundredth anniversary of the Declaration of Independence lasted from May to November and had inspired dozens of social events, but he couldn't lie and claim he had a conflict. "No."

"Good. We can discuss baseball tonight, then. See you at eight?" She smiled and walked backward so she could still look at him while she rejoined her teammates.

"You're persistent, Miss Myles."

"I'm my father's daughter." Her smile widened into a mischievous grin. "I don't like to hear 'no' very often."

Beck believed it, but she'd be hearing it from him very soon. Tonight, in fact. He was stuck going to the soiree, but he would not be coaching the Liberty Belles.

What a ridiculous notion, indeed.

Chapter Two

Beck's molars ground together. He stood before the looking glass in the parlor of his townhouse on the edge of Rittenhouse Square that evening, ruining yet another white tie. With an exasperated tug, he yanked the offensive strip of snowy cloth from his neck.

Gilby Gresham, his closest friend and business partner, shook his blond head from his spot at the desk in the corner. "Lulu will insist you need a valet, if she sees you."

"I'll what?" Lulu peeked in the doorway. "Oh, Beck, really. You need a valet for these types of events."

Gil laughed, of course, so Beck grimaced at his friend's reflection. "I never attend these types of events, so I don't require a valet, do I? Say, Gil, why don't you attend for me?"

Gil stood, packing up the last of the papers that required discussion before Beck left for the evening. "Because I was not invited by Mr. Myles. I am not the one with money. I am the poor friend you took pity on and hired."

"Emerson Works would be nothing without you, Gil."

"Emerson Works is solidly in the black, and the latest safety precautions are installed." Gil clapped Beck's shoulder. "So relax and enjoy your evening. Maybe meet a few ladies."

Beck did not attend social events, nor did he court ladies. He was twenty-eight and perfectly satisfied with his bachelorhood. "I am fine with my sister, friend, business, and church, thank you very much."

"That's why people call you reclusive." Lulu took up the tie and looped it around his neck. "I should like to strangle you with this, forcing me to join that baseball team."

"Encouragement isn't the same thing as forcing. You agreed, remember?"

She shrugged in acknowledgement. God willing, baseball would give her something nothing else could, something he'd missed since being on a team of his own. A healthy, wholesome distraction. Camaraderie with peers, something she'd sorely ignored since falling for the supposed charms of that dandy Alonzo Gunderson.

Gil nicked Lulu under the chin. "You'll have fun on the team."

Lulu rolled her eyes. "Did I tell you she asked Beck to coach, Gil?"

As they continued speaking about it, a thought occurred to Beck. If he helped with the team, Beck and Lulu could spend more time together. He hadn't thought of that particular benefit when he urged her to join the Liberty Belles—

Except he was not coaching. Absolutely not.

"There." Lulu stepped back, allowing him to admire the neat knot at his throat. "A valet could have done a better job."

"Doubtful." He kissed her cheek and then reached for his silk top hat. "Are you certain there's no more business that needs going over, Gil?"

"Go," Gil ordered. "In fact, I'll walk out with you." Beck had no choice but to bid Lulu good night and quit the house with Gil, parting on the stoop to venture in separate directions.

He mulled his attitude on the short walk to the Myles's home on the opposite end of the Rittenhouse Square neighborhood. *Lord, it's been so long since I've done anything like this.* The prayer calmed him, and a whistle formed on his lips. Perhaps tonight would surprise him.

It did, the moment he crossed the threshold into the grand, emerald-papered foyer and met the gaze of Jocelyn Jones.

Ten years hadn't changed her. Same golden hair, same green eyes, same uncomfortable expression when she looked at him.

When he'd finished handing his hat and gloves to the manservant at the door, she'd left the foyer. At least he didn't need to make small talk with her. He passed through a wide door flanked by twin Ionic marble columns and joined a crowd in a high-ceilinged chamber papered in white and gold, trimmed in deep blue—an elegant home befitting an oil magnate like Hector Myles.

Before he could accept a glass of punch from a passing servant's tray, Winnie Myles was at his side, fresh as a peach in a honey-orange gown that suited her dark hair and eyes. "Mr. Emerson, how good of you to come."

"You were most persuasive."

Her lashes batted in a teasing gesture. "Papa has long wanted to meet you, and now that you're coaching our team, I thought this the perfect opportunity."

"About that—"

"Here he is." She waggled her fingers at a gentleman with graying brown locks and a thick mustache. "Papa, meet Mr. Emerson."

"At long last." Mr. Myles pumped Beck's hand. "So glad you could attend."

"I was happy to make a donation to such a worthy cause as the Children's Hospital, sir."

"And you'll see that the Liberty Belles win the exhibition, so there will be even more donations to the cause, eh? Winnie told me all about it. Said you know a fair bit about the game." Mr. Myles gripped Beck's lifeless arm around the bicep.

Beck stiffened, awaiting Mr. Myles's inevitable look of pity, but his attention was drawn away by an approaching gentleman with dark hair and catlike eyes. "Ah, Victor Van Cleef, my protégé at Myles Oil, meet Beckett Emerson."

"So you're the elusive Emerson." Victor Van Cleef's thin lips quirked underneath his waxed black mustache.

Beck preferred to think of himself as discriminating about where he spent his time, not elusive or reclusive. "Business keeps me occupied."

Miss Myles rapped her father's sleeve with her feathery fan. "And you've been most eager to talk business with Mr. Emerson, haven't you, Papa?"

"Indeed." Mr. Myles rubbed his hands together. "I'm curious about the safety precautions it's said you've set in place at Emerson Works."

"Safety precautions?" Miss Myles looked up at him, as if she was truly interested.

But she couldn't possibly be. She was a good hostess, was all. "Fire walls, additional exits in case of emergency, that sort of thing."

Victor chortled. "Unnecessary expense, if you ask me."

Miss Myles's brow furrowed. "I think it wise."

"I'm undecided," her father said. "I should appreciate a lengthier discussion on the subject, good sir, but my late wife would never have approved of me discussing business at a party—ah, I will make one exception, however. Victor, I see Archie Quaid. We must take advantage of his attendance to convince him to allow the merger to go through. Excuse us, Mr. Emerson, Winifred."

Miss Myles shook her head, an indulgent gleam in her eye as her father and Victor disappeared into the throng.

This was as good a time as any to refuse to coach her team. But first, a little gratitude. "Thank you for taking Lulu on the team, Miss Myles."

With a flick of her wrist, she waved her cheeks with her fan. "If you are coaching us, I insist you call me Winnie, else I may not respond to your commands in the heat of a practice session, Beck—may I call you that? It will be so much easier on the field." She didn't wait for his nod before continuing on. "And I told you, every lady who wishes to play may join."

"She may not be enthusiastic at this moment, Winnie." He grinned at the use of her Christian name. "But as I said, she needs the structure and distraction."

"Ah, yes, diversion from the object of her affection. I imagine he is a ne'er-do-well, to have earned your disapproval?"

"That's not quite it." At her surprised look, he shrugged. "I don't care that he has little in terms of worldly goods. I'm more concerned that he sees her as an heiress, not a wife. Time will tell, and while they have spoken of marriage multiple times in their six-week acquaintance, I wish her to have more time before making such a monumental decision."

"And she's seventeen, correct? Not the youngest bride in Philadelphia, but you said you were sixteen when you went to war. I imagine you are concerned for Lulu because you know youth can be impetuous."

"On the contrary, I know well how strong youthful determination can be. I would never underestimate it, nor would I take too lightly the power of love at any age." Jocelyn Jones strode behind Winnie, watching him from the corners of her eyes. Beck tugged his gaze away and met Winnie's squarely.

"Oh, I see." And it was clear from her breathy tone that she did.

Beck inwardly groaned. Now Winnie knew he had toppled head-over-boots in love as a young man—and had not quite gotten over it.

———— •◦• ————

Winnie snapped shut her fan. She was not accustomed to the sensation clumping in her stomach like old, uneaten oatmeal, but the direction of her thoughts made it clear what she felt: jealousy.

She'd never loved anyone before, not like that. It had never bothered her, either, but for the first time, she wanted to have that sort of love. She was two-and-twenty and marriageable, as Papa reminded her daily. How much easier would marrying be if she was actually in love?

But love didn't always end happily, as Beck's set jaw made clear. Whomever he'd cared for had broken his heart.

A change of subject might be best. She grappled for words, finding them slippery as a muddy baseball and just as awkward to do anything with. At last she settled on the obvious. "Punch?"

"None for me, but I shall fetch you some if you like."

"Thank you, no, but oh, here are our neighbors. I must introduce you." She greeted the elegantly dressed couple in their early thirties. "Mr. Beckett Emerson, meet Mr. and Mrs. Edwin Beale."

After the how-do-you-dos, Winnie tipped her head to Beck. "Their daughter, Penny, is my particular friend. How is she this evening?"

"Impish," Marjorie Beale uttered.

"Asleep," her husband said at the same time.

At Beck's lifted brow, Winnie laughed. "Penny is four."

"She is determined not to trade the baseball you gave her for a croquet mallet." Marjorie sniffed.

When the talk shifted to Emerson Works and its manufacture of horse-drawn street cars and freight cars, Winnie left them to greet other guests. She kept an eye on Beck, however. Half the Liberty Belles attended, and Beck spoke to them all. He socialized with businessmen, politicians, and representatives from the Children's Hospital alike, not behaving at all like the recluse Papa and Victor said he was. What a mystery Beck Emerson was turning out to be.

Victor came alongside her. "Emerson is your new friend, I take it."

"Didn't Papa tell you? He's coaching the Liberty Belles."

"He mentioned it, but honestly, I shouldn't expect too much."

"Because of his business obligations?"

"Not that. His arm doesn't work." Victor whispered it like it was a secret.

"A wound sustained in service to our country. And what has his arm to do with anything, anyway?"

"I suppose you're right. One doesn't need two arms to merely coach."

"*Merely*? 'Tis a vital role."

"For a girls' exhibition." Victor smiled indulgently. "Do not look at me like that. I find your enthusiasm for the game charming."

Her mood swung from defensive to horrified. Charming? Oh, dear. Had Papa spoken to Victor about his idea that Winnie marry him? It was one thing for Papa to encourage her in that direction, but it was another altogether to tell Victor about it. Especially since the idea of marrying her father's protégé struck her like a rogue baseball to the gut.

"Speaking of the game, will you attend?"

"Indubitably." He bowed. "I'll allow you to see to your guests."

Her hand pressed her fluttering stomach. She'd put off speaking to Papa about his ridiculous idea that she marry Victor, since it was far easier to dismiss it from her mind and hope it would go away. However, she hadn't expected Victor to call her charming.

Nor had she expected to see Beck engaged in a conversation with one of the loveliest women in Philadelphia, Jocelyn Jones. Neither smiled, but then Jocelyn's fingers landed on Beck's forearm in a familiar gesture. Even from across the room, Winnie could see his jaw clench.

The minute they finished, Winnie hastened to him. "Beck, do you know who that is?"

"Mrs. Jones?"

"Her sister is the pitcher of the Patriots, our competition at the exhibition. No doubt she learned you are our coach."

"Paulette plays?"

"You know Paulette Perry?" Winnie's breath stopped somewhere on its way out. "Oh, you were not discussing baseball, were you?"

"I knew the family when I was younger, but it has been over ten years since I saw them last. Paulette had bird legs and long braids down her back at the time."

Paulette was precisely Winnie's age. Jocelyn was six years older—and Beck watched after her while a muscle worked in his cheek. Suddenly, Winnie's stomach did that strange, cold-oatmeal thing again, but this time, it sent chilly tendrils down her legs, accompanied by a sudden dislike for Jocelyn Jones. How ridiculous. She didn't even know the woman.

But she nevertheless distrusted her. "The Patriots' charity isn't even a real group. If they win the game, the proceeds will pay for tea luncheons at the Women's Club Auxiliary's aid meetings."

Her hand flew to her mouth. It may have been true, and she may not approve, but it was not her place to say it with such unkindness and in that superior tone. Heat suffused her neck and face as she prayed for God's forgiveness. Then she turned to Beck. "I'm sorry. What I meant to say was—they're a good team."

He laughed, a deep hearty sound that pleased her. "What you meant to say was you want to win. I cannot blame you."

She couldn't quite smile, but her heart lightened. "With your coaching, I'm sure we will."

His head tipped to the side. "I came tonight intent on refusing you, you know."

But she'd not given him the chance. And much as she wanted him to coach the team, he had a business. "Forgive me, then. I fear I'm quite good at charging ahead, ignoring what I don't want to see. I've been selfish."

"I don't know about that." His eyes twinkled. "But as for baseball, I have a few ideas to help the team improve."

"What are they?"

"I'll tell you tomorrow at three."

She gasped. "You're coaching us, then?"

"I'll make arrangements to leave my friend Gil in charge at Emerson Works each day."

"Huzzah!" Her voice was too loud, but she didn't care. His smile and dimples said he didn't care, either.

Oh my, he was handsome. And generous.

And now that they had a coach, the Liberty Belles were bound to beat the Patriots.

Chapter Three

A week later, Winnie wasn't certain having a coach made much of a difference after all. Standing in her pitcher's square in the park, she gripped the ball and wished for an end to the worst practice they'd had since Beck agreed to coach.

It wasn't that he wasn't a good instructor. On the contrary, he had been patient, informative, and encouraging. The Liberty Belles had experienced a sense of invigoration and excitement under his guidance—at least, until today.

The ball slipped repeatedly from Dru's hands, Colleen's throws went everywhere but their intended targets, Winnie herself batted foul ticks, and Lulu hadn't arrived yet. The weather probably didn't help. Clouds all but obscured a colorless sky, baking the earth below with humid heat, and the team's moods reflected the heavy atmosphere. Irene's feet dragged over the limp grass as she took her turn at the bat. From her position in the outfield, Irene's sister Nora, the right scout, tugged her cap from atop her thin, mouse-brown hair and waved it like a fan over her face. Her counterpart in left field, tiny, dark-haired Fannie, shoved her cuffs as high on her arms as she could while still maintaining her propriety.

Beck had stripped his coat and rolled up his shirtsleeves, too. The crisp white cotton of his tailored shirt emphasized the broadness of his shoulders and chest—not that Winnie should be noticing such things. Just that he was no doubt as hot as the rest of them. Other than beads of sweat on his brow, however, he didn't show any signs of being overheated, only focused, standing several feet to the side of the home plate, his eyes narrowed.

Winnie wouldn't complain, either. Practice was too important. She couldn't do anything about the way her clothes stuck to her sweat-damp skin, other than pray for a breeze and determine to do her best, despite her discomfort.

As Winnie's arm pulled back to pitch to Irene, Colleen strode past her, stopping her short. Colleen's position as short scout enabled her to move freely about the field, but she trod right out of the diamond. "It's too hot, Beck. Why don't we call it a day?"

Beck shook his head. "Tomorrow's our lone practice game against the Patriots, and we've only been out here twenty minutes. Not everyone is even here yet." Meaning Lulu. Every other day this week she'd arrived with Beck, so she must be with her beau.

A small figure emerged from the willow oak near third base and dashed behind the red maple near home plate. Winnie grinned. "We have a visitor."

"Ralph, go home!" Colleen stomped forward. "You don't belong here."

"I can be at the park if I want," a high voice shouted back. "You don't own it!"

With brows raised, Beck sauntered over toward Winnie. "Who's our guest?"

"Ralph, Colleen's brother. He's our unofficial mascot."

A small head donned in a tweed cap peered around the tree. "What's a mascot?"

"A nuisance." Colleen rolled her eyes.

"Ah, sisters," Beck muttered. "Come on out, Ralph."

Grinning, the boy leaped out, his freckled cheeks round as young apples. "I get to play?"

"No," Colleen said.

"Yes and no," Beck amended. "It's a ladies' exhibition, so we fellas can't be on the team. But we can help, and I need a special assistant."

Ralph's face screwed up like he'd been presented with cod liver oil. "What's that?"

"A batboy. Someone to make sure the striker has a bat, chase balls, that sort of thing. Do you know how to hit?"

"Sure do, mister."

"Call me Beck."

Winnie's chest warmed with affection. Ralph couldn't be more than eight or nine, but Beck had found a way to include him. She grinned until Gladys, the dishwater-blond basetender, held out her hand for Beck's inspection. "Blisters, see? Aren't you proud?"

"I am." Beck chuckled. "They prove how hard you've been working."

Gladys wiggled her fingers for him and giggled. *Blech*. Winnie squeezed the ball. "Striker to the line!"

"Oh, that's me!" Gladys gave Beck a saucy smile. "I'm not sure I'm holding the bat right. Could you show me again?"

"Let's see." He sauntered with her to home base while a fresh rivulet of perspiration snaked down Winnie's back, along with a wave of irritation. Gladys didn't need help holding the bat any more than Winnie needed help lacing her boots.

But he was happy to help. In the past week, he'd taught them a few tricks, like how to aim where the opposing team was weak. The team had also started additional exercises, such as taking vigorous constitutionals each day to strengthen their bodies.

He'd also taught them how to better hold the bat. Now he wrapped his arm around Gladys to correct the position of her elbows. "Try a swing. Does it feel better?"

"Oh, yes."

Winnie's gaze caught Dru's—until Dru crossed her eyes. Biting back a laugh, Winnie squeezed the ball. "Ready, Gladys?"

She was ready to bat, all right—her eyelashes, not the ball. "Thanks, Beck."

"Happy to help."

Winnie snorted and pitched the ball. Gladys squealed. "Not so fast!"

"Sorry." Winnie didn't mean to throw that hard.

Beck rubbed the back of his neck. "Actually, it's a good reminder that the pitcher for the Patriots, Paulette, may throw harder than you're used to. We should all practice batting different types of balls. Try again, ladies."

He looked at Winnie when he spoke, and the corners of his mouth lifted in a small smile. Winnie couldn't help but smile back. Despite his initial reservations, Beck was a good coach. *Thanks, God, for bringing him here to help us.*

Gladys hit the next pitch high over Winnie's head.

"Got it!" Colleen called out, forestalling Fannie, who was rushing in from the outfield. Colleen caught it on the second bounce.

Beck pumped his fist in the air. "Excellent. Colleen called the play, and Fannie was there to assist if necessary. Well done." In the past week, he'd coached them not just on technique and strategy, but communication as well. Now when they played, the person with the best chance of catching the ball announced her intention, preventing multiple players from rushing toward the ball at the same time.

Every player smiled at his praise.

"Sorry I'm late!"

At the frantic voice, Winnie turned. Lulu scurried over the grass, followed by a square-jawed young man with slick-backed blond hair. A glance at Beck's mulish expression confirmed that he was Lulu's beau, Alonzo.

"Forty minutes late, Lu." Beck shook his head.

"I said I'm sorry." Lulu hadn't changed into appropriate practice garb. Instead, she wore an almond-colored confection of a dress that would be dusty in moments. "What position should I play?"

"You're up as striker."

His tone didn't sound harsh to Winnie, but Lulu, as his sister, must have interpreted something in it because she glared at him and snatched the bat Ralph offered.

Ignore it and practice. Winnie tossed the ball.

Lulu's hit sent the ball flying foul. It struck an oak tree beyond third base.

Beck shook his head. "Concentrate, Lu."

"I am." But she glanced at Alonzo, who stood in the shade of the tree.

"I'm serious." Beck stepped closer. "One week from tomorrow is our exhibition game, and tomorrow is our practice game against the Patriots. We're not ready."

Gladys chuckled. "We will be in a week. Tomorrow's only our practice game."

Only? Winnie's stomach tightened. She was competitive, true, but this wasn't just about winning for winning sake. "It's more than that."

Gladys balked, but Beck held up his hand. "No, Winnie's right. This is our chance to see what sort of team they are, and they'll gain insight into our team, as well."

Which, right now, didn't look cohesive or threatening.

Dru nodded. "Then let's show them what we're made of, Liberty Belles."

Before Winnie could pitch, Beck held up his hand to her. "Colleen, take over as pitcher. Winnie, come over here for a minute."

He scooped a ball from Ralph's bucket and held out his arm, as if to guide her off the field. For some inexplicable reason, it sent her insides aflutter, like she was nervous. How ridiculous. What was there to be nervous about? He was her coach. Wiping sweat from her brow, she accompanied him to the tree the ball had bounced off of a few minutes ago. He pointed. "See this knot right here?"

Belly high and scarred grayish brown, the knot was hard to miss. Some years ago, the tree had lost a limb, producing a saucer-sized wound on the trunk that scratched her fingertips when she touched it. "What of it?"

"I want you to hit it." He held out the ball.

"Target practice." Their fingers brushed as she took the ball, sending a jolt up her spine.

"Precisely. Try this—here." He sidled alongside her, taking her right hand with his and drawing it back a little farther from her body than she usually did. "I'm sure this feels strange, but sometimes your elbow stays tucked into your side."

It felt strange all right but not because of her arm's motions. His words tickled her ear, his breath warmed her cheek, and the faint, rich scent of his cologne filled her senses and sent her pulse ticking. It was strange, unfamiliar, and even a little frightening. At the same time, she wanted to drop the ball and grip Beck's fingers and—

Oh! She was as bad as Gladys, swooning because her coach had to get close to her to help her.

Maybe *bad* wasn't the right word. It wasn't a bad thing to be drawn to Beck. Who wouldn't be? He was kind and brave and generous and handsome. She might as well admit to herself how much she liked everything about him, from his concern for his employees to his love for his sister, his deep voice to his broad chest. Oh no, did she really just think about his chest? *Stop it, Winifred. It's one thing to be drawn to him, but it's another thing altogether to behave like a ninny.*

She swallowed hard. "I'll hold my elbow farther from my body."

"Let's see." He stepped back, leaving the right side of her body afire with heat that had nothing to do with the sultry weather.

Deep breath. Don't rush. She untucked her elbow and swung her arm back. The ball released from her fingers and hit the oak trunk just south of the knot.

"Well done." Beck scooped up the ball and tossed it to her. "Still in the strike zone."

"I'll hit that knot." It would give her something to focus on other than the strange things Beck's proximity did to her pulse.

"I know you will." He continued to scoop up the ball and return it to her after every pitch. She'd hit the knot twice when he paused before tossing the ball back to her. "I should make sure the others are ready for the practice game tomorrow. I'll send Ralph over to fetch the ball for you if you'd like to keep hitting the target."

Nodding, she stepped to take the ball from him. "Thank you, Beck."

His brow scrunched in a confused expression before he grinned. "It's nothing. You're a good pitcher, but trying to hit a target is an easy way to clarify your aim."

"Not that." Although yes, his knowledge about baseball and his gentle coaching to help the team were just two more of the many things she liked about Beck. "Thank you for coaching us."

His smile turned shy, and almost conspiratorial. "I'm happy to do it, really. Your friend Victor is right. I have a tendency to stay in sometimes. It's good to be part of a team again. I hope you know I'm here for you."

That was another thing she liked about Beck. He didn't say things he didn't mean. And she was starting to become aware that she wanted him to be there for her—and not just as her coach.

<hr />

The next afternoon, Beck paced behind Dru as the practice game against the Patriots neared its dreadful conclusion. Despite their best attempts, the Liberty Belles floundered, and by the ninth inning, the score was 8 to 2 in the Patriots' favor.

It probably didn't help that the umpire chosen from among the spectators was Jocelyn's husband, a biased observer if ever there was one since his sister-in-law pitched for the Patriots, and the blond-haired lawyer seemed to know as much about baseball as a turnip.

Rowena slid into home plate a fraction of a moment before their team's catcher caught the ball. Jocelyn's husband squinted at Paulette. "Is that an out?"

"Yep," Paulette said.

"No," Beck and the entire Liberty Belles shouted.

"It's out, dear." Jocelyn's sweet tone held a hint of iron.

"Out," Mr. Jones determined.

Jocelyn clapped. What had Beck ever seen in her?

The two of them had been children back then, but he'd hoped they'd grow up together. Her rejection damaged him worse than the bullet he took in the shoulder. Now, though, all he felt when he looked at her was cool relief that God had spared him from marrying her. This was a practice game for an upcoming charity exhibition. Why did she need her sister's team to win even if it meant bending the rules? To trounce Beck once again?

Despite the bent rules in the opposing team's favor, the Liberty Belles weren't playing well. Before the bottom of the ninth, Beck waved the team over. "Nora, Lulu, are you hurt?"

Both women rubbed their shoulders, no doubt still smarting from their outfield collision. Nora shook her head. "I should've called the ball, like you taught us, instead of thinking I'd get it instead of Lulu."

But neither of them had caught it. Instead they'd bumped into each other and the ball tangled in Lulu's skirts. Nora and Lulu both knew better. Frankly, the entire team seemed to have forgotten some basic skills, but this wasn't the time to scold. Their faces revealed they knew well how they fared.

"Colleen, you're first up to bat. Paulette knows you're a strong striker so she'll send you unfair balls to prevent you from making a solid hit."

"Coward." Rowena sneered.

"It's strategy." Beck shrugged. "You're good players. Don't take unnecessary risks; just try to get on base."

"Will do, Beck." Winnie, as ever, was all business when it came to baseball. "You heard him, gals, let's get on base."

Paulette pitched a laughably low ball that skirted Colleen's shins.

"Foul tick," Jocelyn's husband called.

"That wasn't foul, it was *unfair*." Winnie's tone was kind but firm. "A foul tick goes out of bounds. Three unfair balls are termed a *ball*. Three balls and Colleen *walks* to first base."

"So she needs eight more of those low ones?"

"Yes." Winnie sounded far more patient than Beck would have if he'd responded. It was all he could do not to rub his face and groan.

Once Colleen endured nine deliberately horrid pitches and planted atop first base, Lulu hit the first pitch Paulette sent, but it was caught before it hit the ground. Gladys hit next and got to first, but the cost was Colleen being called out before she reached second base. Dru's hit sent the Patriots scurrying in a blur of gray skirts, but the small victory was short-lived. Irene's ball was caught just as Lulu's had been, and even the baseball-deficient Mr. Jones could count to three.

"Three outs. That's the game!"

Beck shook his hand as his grim-faced team shook the hands of the Patriots. Even Ralph extended a hand, at least until Paulette laughed. The sound sent a chill over Beck's skin. "A little Liberty Belle boy, how adorable. Half a man, like their coach."

Not even a bird chirped to break the silence that followed. Beck had heard worse and wouldn't dignify the remark with a response, but Ralph's face scrunched, like he knew he was being mocked but wasn't sure how. And that made Beck's ears burn hot. "Ralph is an invaluable member of the team—"

"And my brother," Colleen intruded, her face pink.

"And Beck is my brother." Lulu stomped forward, her defense surprising him.

"And an amazing, remarkable man." Winnie stepped toe-to-toe with Paulette. Where Lulu's defense warmed him, Winnie's words almost knocked Beck flat. Remarkable? She wasn't finished, though, and her knuckles popped as she curled her fingers, as if she just might hit Paulette. "I find it inexcusable that you would denigrate the sacrifice he made serving our country—"

"My, this Centennial celebration has you in a patriotic lather. Beck knows I'm teasing." Paulette blanched, but her smile was as sweet as Jocelyn's used to be. "Right, Beck? We used to tease when you were at the house practically every day."

She'd been like his little sister then. Now he didn't know her at all. He could say a million things to her, and some would be quite satisfying, but most of them would be sinful. He shook his head instead. "Good day, Paulette."

Beck beckoned the Liberty Belles to their bench. "Ladies?" He walked ahead of them, offering a brief prayer for the best words to say to the team despite what just happened with Paulette, a distraction if ever there was one.

"Poor form, that Paulette," Dru said.

"I'd like to rub her face in the outfield," Rowena muttered.

Beck reached their bench. "Circle up." When the Belles had gathered, Beck glanced back. The other team was dispersing fast. Good. They didn't need to overhear this. "Ladies, and Ralph, Paulette's intention was to upset us because it gives her team power over ours. We're better off ignoring her."

Ralph tapped Colleen's elbow. "Why are Beck and me half men?"

Colleen bent down, but everyone was listening in. "Because you're nine years old, and Beck only has use of one arm."

Ralph made his cod-liver oil face again. "That's stupid. Being short or not having an arm doesn't make you half."

Beck chuckled. "Thanks, Ralph. Thanks to all of you for coming to my defense, truly. You've touched me with your protective natures, but now we need to talk about today's game. If the point of it was to learn about them while they learned about us, they'll have a happy evening, because we revealed ourselves to be a disorganized mess while they worked like an oiled machine in my iron works."

Beside him, Winnie shook her head. "You're right."

"We tried." Gladys offered a cheerful smile.

"Did we?" Rowena glared at Lulu.

"I'm sorry I struck out." Irene hung her head.

"At least you caught the ball," Fannie said. "I couldn't seem to do that today."

Dru nodded at Beck. "We didn't work together as a team."

"They looked like one, though." Colleen gestured to her green plaid skirt. "We don't match."

Beck was responsible for that error. "The team caps I ordered are coming soon. Sorry about the delay. They would've helped us look more like a team today."

"It was more than that." Colleen looked at him pityingly. "The Patriots wore gray. It made them look more uniform. Maybe we could all wear ensembles that are the same color, too."

Dru snapped. "Something patriotic. Red?"

Fannie's head shook. "The only red in my wardrobe is evening wear, nothing suitable for baseball."

"Nora and I don't have anything red at all," Irene said. "Mama frowns on crimson."

Colleen's brows rose. "Pity, it's in vogue this season."

Beck's eyeballs started to ache. This was worse than waiting for Lulu at the milliner. "You can discuss clothes when I'm gone, but first—"

"Why don't we wear brown?" Gladys clapped.

Rowena snorted. "Why brown?"

Gladys tipped her head to the side. "Because we're the Liberty Belles. We could be the same color as the actual Liberty Bell."

"The bell isn't brown. It's metal," Rowena protested.

Beck stepped backward. Maybe none of the ladies would notice if he slipped out of the circle and gathered his coat. He could address their strategy issues tomorrow.

"It's brownish, and the yoke is elm. *Brown*." Gladys's voice raised in pitch.

Colleen held up a hand. "I'm not wearing brown. It's not flattering on me."

Beck was almost to his coat, and once there he could call Lulu and tell everyone he'd see them tomorrow—

"Blue, then. It's patriotic, and everyone should own something blue. Don't you think, Beck?" Dru's query drew him up short.

Caught. "Blue is. . .nice."

Nora's head shook. "I don't have anything plain blue. Just my blue-and-gray plaid wool."

Beck rubbed the bridge of his nose. How many colors were left?

"Wear that, Nora." Winnie spoke at last, her tone flat. "We don't have to match exactly."

Lulu sighed. "It doesn't matter what we wear. We won't win, anyway. We're horrible."

Beck's gaze rose, catching on Winnie's. Her gaze fixed on him, but her words were for the others. "This isn't about what we wear or how well we play. It's about what we're playing for."

Ralph's hand shot up. "I remember. The love of the game and Colleen's last chance to run in public before she marries Ives."

Colleen's jaw went so wide she could swallow a baseball. "I ought to box your ears."

Ralph's hands covered his ears in protection. "It's what Father said."

Beck chuckled as he ruffled Ralph's hair.

Winnie's head tipped to the side. "I can't blame her, Ralph. I like running in public, too. We all do, I think." Her glance skittered over Lulu. "But we had another goal in mind. A reason to do our best."

"The hospital." Dru's arm went around Winnie.

"Oh, yeah," Ralph marveled.

Winnie hugged Dru back. "Tomorrow I think we should cut practice short and visit it."

Beck had always liked Winnie, from the minute he saw her. The way she defended him from Paulette touched him, and he couldn't help wondering what she would have said before Paulette cut her off.

Winnie was lovely, kind, caring, generous, and at this moment especially, a far better coach than he was.

He straightened his cap as well as his shoulders. "I'll make arrangements."

Chapter Four

By the end of their shortened practice the next afternoon, Winnie's muscles ached. So did her pride. Despite her best attempts to remember her lessons about aiming, her pitches went afield.

"What's wrong?" Dru came alongside her during a break.

"Paulette Perry. How dare that woman say such a vile thing about Beck, even as a joke?"

"I don't know, but it didn't seem to bother him. Or if it did, he turned the other cheek." Dru nudged her arm. "Want to visit the art gallery at the Centennial Exhibition with me and Xavier tomorrow? You and I missed it on our jaunt, and you might enjoy it."

It was kind of Dru to invite Winnie out with her and her beau, but Winnie wasn't in the mood. She needed to pray and think. "I think I need a quiet evening."

"Sure." Dru took her turn at bat with Colleen pitching.

Was that why Beck hadn't spoken up? He'd turned the other cheek? Winnie respected and admired it even as she wasn't sure she wanted to follow his example.

"Forgive, as I have forgiven you."

Winnie sighed. *Help me want to, Lord.* That might be the logical first step.

She was still praying and mulling during the ride to the Children's Hospital in one of the carriages Beck had rented. Colleen, Nora, and Dru shared her coach, chatting about Colleen's upcoming wedding. Dru nudged Winnie's shoulder.

"I don't expect it'll be long before Rowena and Fannie's beaus propose. What about you?"

Winnie's throat dried. "Me?"

Rowena bent forward. "Do you think Victor will ask for your hand?"

The others watched Winnie with expectation, but Winnie shook her head. "He's not my beau. He's. . ." She searched for a word. "Papa's protégé."

"I didn't necessarily mean Victor, Winnie." Dru grinned. "Surely another gentleman has caught your eye?"

Winnie's eyes widened in warning at Dru. "I don't have a beau."

"But there's someone," Rowena persisted.

Nora giggled. "I think it's Beck. She gets all moon-eyed when she looks at him."

"He's our coach, that's all." Winnie's arms folded. "We were talking about betrothals. What about you, Dru? Don't you think Xavier will propose?"

"I hope so." Dru chuckled. "It's long past time. But let's talk more about Beck."

"Or his friend Gilby," Nora said with a sigh. "Every time he comes to the field with a paper or question for Beck, my knees wobble."

Dru stared Winnie down. "Do your knees wobble for Beck?"

The carriage lurched to a halt in front of the Children's Hospital and there was, thankfully, no time for anyone to press her further.

But there was nothing to tell, honestly. True, she was drawn to Beck and just thinking of him made her insides spongy as a trifle dessert, but she and Beck were nothing but a team member and coach. Descending from the carriage to Beck's waiting smile made her wish it was something more, though.

"Welcome, ladies and gentleman—pardon me, *gentlemen*." Smiling down at Ralph, one of the physicians, a balding, thin fellow named Dr. Post, greeted them on the hospital stoop. "We are so grateful you are playing an exhibition game on our behalf."

"We appreciate your work, Doctor." Beck shook his hand. "Are you certain a tour won't interfere?"

"Not at all. Some of our patients are eager for visitors and would like to meet you."

Beck grabbed a bucket of pale-brown baseballs and brought them inside—oh, as gifts. How thoughtful! He caught her smiling at him and she flushed hot.

On the brief tour, Winnie attempted to view the hospital through the others' eyes. She'd been here countless times, reading to patients and rolling bandages. Dru had come a few times, as well. But what did the others think, passing bed after bed of tiny ones too ill to be treated at home? Beck offered each child a ball, and Dr. Post laughingly warned them not to throw them at the nurses.

Dr. Post led them to a larger chamber full of cots. On one bed, two nightclothes-clad boys younger than Ralph sat cross legged, a pouch of spilled marbles between them.

"Are you playin'?" Ralph leaned to look.

"Just lookin'."

Beck squatted beside the bed. "Those are some fine marbles."

The freckled boy coughed. Dr. Post patted the boy's head. "Kenny, Zechariah, greet our guests, the Liberty Belles baseball team."

"Baseball? I can't wait to play again once I go home," Kenny said.

The curly-headed lad, Zechariah, didn't respond when Beck offered them each a baseball. He just flicked a marble with his forefinger.

Dr. Post moved on, introducing other children, but Winnie held back when Beck didn't rise from his position on the floor. He peered up at the lad. "Do you like baseball, Zechariah?"

"Sure. But I can't play no more."

His right sleeve was pinned closed where the boy's elbow should be. She hadn't noticed, but Beck had. Slowly, Beck's hand pulled his left arm up to rest on the bed. "This arm of mine doesn't work. It's still here, but I can't use it. It's floppy as a dead fish." He pulled a face, which made the boys chuckle. "I play a little baseball anyway."

"You do?" Zechariah's brows shot under his curly fringe.

"Sure. Not well, maybe. What do you think, Miss Myles?" He looked up at Winnie.

"You throw better than I do, Mr. Emerson."

"Catching isn't always easy, but the thing is, I can do most of the same things I did before I got shot in the war. Just a little differently, is all."

"I reached for the firewood, and my brother wasn't done with the ax." Zechariah's voice was soft. Winnie's stomach lurched. What a tragic accident.

Beck's swallow was audible. "But we persevere, don't we?"

Feeling a little like an interloper, Winnie stepped back. Beck was ministering to

Zechariah, and even Kenny's attention was fixed on him. His care was its own sort of medicine, a lesson that might make a difference in the way they lived their lives. To persevere, even when it was difficult. She dabbed a tear from her eye.

The tear became several as Winnie glimpsed her team with the children. Gladys read to a girl with a bandage over her eye. Ralph, Irene, and Nora engaged in a game of jacks on the floor with three boys. Rowena and Colleen chatted with patients, and Lulu perched on the bed of a young woman with bandaged hands, perhaps twelve years of age, to comb her hair for her.

Maybe like Winnie, they would be blessed by the visit, even though they'd been the ones who'd come to learn and be a blessing.

After thanking Dr. Post and promising to return, the Liberty Belles sauntered out to the carriages, chattering about the children. Beck and Winnie followed, their pace slower. One ball remained in his bucket, and he pocketed it. "How's that for planning?"

She looked up at him. "You were wonderful with those boys. Especially Zechariah."

"I'll keep him in my prayers. He has a rough adjustment ahead."

"But it will be a little easier, now that he's met someone who's been through it."

"He made a few things easier for me, too, although he has no idea of it. He reminded me of how far God brought me through my experience. That, and there's always hope." He assisted her into one of the carriages—not the one she'd ridden over in. This one contained Lulu and Gladys, who chattered the entire way to Gladys' grand manse at one end of Rittenhouse Square. Beck saw her to the door, then returned, smiling at Winnie.

"Would you mind if we leave Lulu and the carriage at our house, and I'll walk you home? I'd like to ask you something."

Winnie startled. A walk alone with Beck? "Of course."

If Lulu thought Beck's request strange, she didn't show it, hurrying inside mumbling something about Alonzo calling soon. Beck offered his arm and Winnie took it, starting down the street until they reached the green of the square. "Shall we cut through? I don't think you mind walking on grass."

She laughed. Her hem was stained with it, as well as mud, since they hadn't changed after practice. "Not at all."

Birdsong among the green leaves overhead and the fresh scent of scythed grass filled her senses. Her house was in sight, but she didn't want to stop walking on Beck's arm—although she couldn't ignore the trepidation in her chest. "Is anything wrong?"

"Of course not." He stopped walking. "Why?

"Because you said you had a question for me."

"I do." Beck's brow furrowed. "About yesterday, when Paulette said what she did to me and Ralph. Why did you defend me?"

<hr />

Beck shouldn't have asked so bluntly, if at all. It had sounded like he was begging her to state how she felt about him, and while he'd love to know, he wasn't in any sort of position to court a woman.

Although he couldn't remember why at present, when she looked up at him through those thick dark lashes.

But that was neither here nor there. He shouldn't have asked because he already knew the answer. Winnie had defended him because she was the sort of woman who didn't tolerate injustice. How to take the question back? "I appreciate you stepping up for me, I do. It touched me that you cared—you and Lulu. So, I don't have a question after all. Just—thank you."

He sounded like an idiot.

She flushed. "So you saw my hand fisted. I didn't think I was a violent person, but I was so angry, I didn't even realize what I was doing." Her head shook. "What she said to Ralph was unkind. He's a child. But what she said to you—well, you were there. Even now, thinking of it, my stomach is as tight as my fist was yesterday. I don't think I would have struck at her—I've never hit anyone—but I'm capable of things I never thought I could be, I suppose."

"We all are." He nudged her with his shoulder. "But thanks for coming to my defense."

"The Liberty Belles care about you."

"I care about them, too." Some more than others, though. Maybe it was time to revisit his decision not to court anyone.

"Winnie!" A high, childish voice carried across the green. A dark-haired little girl in a pink dress and straw hat dashed toward them, followed by a woman whose gray gown all but shouted "governess."

"Good afternoon, Penny." Winnie smiled at the governess. "Miss Foster, good day."

"Good day, Miss Myles, sir." Miss Foster's clear eyes curved with her smile.

Winnie performed introductions, sharing that Penelope Beale was her next-door neighbor. Little Penny curtsied. She hadn't risen to her full height, however, when she scowled up at Winnie. "You're dirty."

"We've been playing baseball."

Her mouth formed an O. "I want to play."

Miss Foster touched the child's shoulder. "They aren't playing anymore, Penny."

Beck pulled out the ball that he'd pocketed at the Children's Hospital. "We could play for a few minutes, if that's well with you, Miss Foster."

She nodded, so Beck held up the ball. "Hold out your arms and catch."

Penny held her arms stiff in front of her. Winnie molded Penny's hands so they cupped open, as if they were about to receive water for washing. He sent the ball the short distance between them, and it hit Penny's forearms and bounced to the grass.

She scrambled for the ball before he could bend to pick it up. "Again!"

"As you wish, madam." He tossed. It hit her cupped hands and bounced off. She retrieved it and threw it directly at his stomach. "Ooph."

Winnie's mouth moved. *Are you hurt?*

No, he mouthed back. "Nice throw, Penny."

This time, the little girl caught the ball. Beck, Winnie, and Miss Foster clapped, and Penny bounced, making the ruffles on her pink dress wobble. She was a darling little—

Oomph. Now *that* ball to the gut hurt.

Winnie's hand flew to her mouth. Oblivious, Penny hopped up and down and clapped. "Again!"

"I think it's enough for today." Miss Foster took her charge's hand. "Are you injured, sir?"

"No. I'd not be much of a coach if I didn't get hit now and again." He managed what he hoped was a genuine smile. "Perhaps we'll see you at the exhibition."

"I shall ask Mr. and Mrs. Beale," Miss Foster said.

Penny waved. "I hope you win, Winnie. *Win Winnie.* That's funny."

"It's hilarious," Beck agreed.

Miss Foster nudged her charge along.

Beck tossed the ball to Winnie.

Winnie caught it and, absently, sent it back, an easy catch for his one hand. "Are you hurt, really?"

"I'm fine. She's got a good arm, though."

Winnie chuckled, but her eyes were sad. "I was only a little older than she is when my mother died. I missed her so much—I still do—but even though I had a lovely nanny, she wasn't my mother. Does that make sense? Penny's mother travels often. I suspect Mr. and Mrs. Beale are only here now because of the Centennial. Miss Foster is a wonderful governess, but I think Penny misses her parents. There is a certain loneliness about her sometimes. I don't wish it to always be so for her, so I pray for her."

"God will care for her."

"And for the rest of us." She waggled her fingers, expecting him to return the ball, so he complied. Their gentle game of catch continued. "I'm trying to remember that for myself."

"What do you mean?"

"Papa wants me to marry." She caught the ball and tossed it back. "He doesn't want me to be alone when he passes on."

"So you'll marry soon, then?" The thought didn't sit well on his stomach.

"I told Papa I'd consider the matter. I'm confident the exhibition game will be my last. Female squads are temporary things, and the domain of the young and unwed."

It was clear how much Winnie would miss it. He clutched the ball tight in his fingers. "I know a little what it's like to not play baseball anymore."

Her cheeks reddened. "Forgive me, I didn't think."

"That isn't what I meant. Just that. . .I understand."

Her gaze softened. "Thank you. But unlike your circumstance, I know when my last game will be. That's why I am trying to squeeze all the fun I can out of it before it is too late."

"I haven't had fun like this in a long time."

"It's difficult to resist Penny." Winnie laughed, the sound pleasing and musical as a carillon of bells.

Penny was fun, all right, but that wasn't what he'd meant. Winnie had reminded him life could be enjoyable. He threw the ball to her, but it slipped through her hands like water.

She burst into laughter. "I am a butterfingers all of a sudden."

"Please tell me you plan to wipe your buttery hands before the game, then."

"You are incorrigible." She lobbed the ball at him, laughing too hard to aim.

It landed at his feet. "Aren't you supposed to be a pitcher?"

Her laughter paused so she could mock gasp. "Incorrigible!" She dashed for the ball and threw it at him, but she started laughing again and the ball sailed so high and far to his left that he didn't even try to catch it. Not that he could have, because all of a sudden he was laughing so hard he couldn't move.

His stomach hurt, and not just from Penny chucking the ball into his midsection. When he managed to catch his breath, an inelegant snort escaped Winnie's nose.

Her eyes widened.

So did Beck's. "Was that you or a horse?"

They burst out laughing again. After a moment, she staggered to where she'd thrown the ball so far from him. "I've a mind to throw this at you, like a snowball—"

Her words cut off. She straightened, staring at her house. While they'd been teasing, a coach arrived, and her father's protégé Victor stood watching them, his mouth set in a disapproving line.

Winnie rubbed her mouth, as if wiping off any trace of a smile.

Regret soured Beck's stomach. Laughing with her in the square was not criminal or indecent, but it was unconventional. "I should have taken more care with your reputation, Winnie. I'm sorry."

She looked up at him, blinking. "Don't be a goose, Beck. We did nothing wrong. Papa is accustomed to me causing a scene. I do play baseball, after all."

But Victor's presence certainly dampened Winnie's mood. He clearly didn't like that Winnie laughed with Beck. Maybe he was more than her father's protégé. "Is he your beau?"

"He accompanies us socially, like to the charity ball next week at the Exhibition, but a beau? I've never—that is, no." Her words came out in a rush. "Will you be there? At the ball?"

"Yes." He decided that instant. "Lulu wants to go."

"Wonderful. We will see you there."

"And tomorrow at practice."

Her cheeks reddened again. "Well, yes."

Beck rocked back on his heels, feeling lighter in his chest. "Thank you for today. For the hospital. And for this." Whatever it was.

"Thank you, too, Beck." Her smile warmed him to his toes.

Chapter Five

A week of baseball practices, visits to the hospital, and household matters didn't leave much time for a dress fitting for the Centennial charity ball. Tonight, however, standing before the looking glass in her bedchamber, Winnie was glad she'd kept the appointment.

The bright blue faille suited her coloring, as did the gown's cut, with its square neck and narrow skirt. Trimmed with chenille scarlet poppies, the gown's colors reflected the spirit of 1776. Would Beck like it?

Her cold fingers pressed against her warm cheeks. It didn't matter if Beck liked it or even noticed what she wore. She might be drawn to him, but he'd disappear from her life in just over a week after the game. He'd probably be relieved to no longer be coaching the Liberty Belles, so he could return his full attention to his business. Clearly he was busy, since his blond friend, Gilby Gresham, jaunted over to the practice field with files in hand for Beck's perusal almost every day this week.

He'd been so busy, she hadn't tried to be alone with him, much less sidle up to him. They'd had fun together in the park, but she shouldn't read anything more into it.

"Ready, Winifred? Victor's here." Papa paused in the threshold.

She nodded, and in less than an hour, they arrived at the Exhibition grounds and the site of the charity ball: a specially constructed, wood-framed pavilion with walls fashioned of glass. Music and light spilled out the windows and open door, and in the twilight, the glass building seemed like something from a fairy tale.

"How delightful." Winnie squeezed Papa's arm.

"Almost as pretty as my daughter."

"Flatterer." But she was pleased by Papa's kindness. Once inside, he excused himself to speak to friends, leaving her and Victor to saunter into the main room, where gold upholstered seats surrounded a dance floor. A gilt screen hid musicians—a string quartet, by Winnie's guess. Many of Philadelphia's elite wandered past, and Winnie nodded hello to several acquaintances. Then she grinned.

Lulu paused in the threshold in a vision of pink, dazzling at her first ball, but it was the gentleman beside her who stole Winnie's breath. Beck, dashing in white tie and a black coat, stared at her, a tiny smile pulling at his lips.

"He's smitten, you know."

"What?" Winnie startled, her gaze tearing from Beck's.

"Emerson." Victor gestured to where Beck and Lulu now engaged in a conversation with the local congressman. "He has eyes for you."

"He's simply my coach."

"If you say so, but I don't think you're immune to him, either."

She almost denied it, but the lie stopped at the fence of her teeth. She was still sorting her feelings when Lulu found her later. "Beck is talking safety regulations with politicians—he thinks there should be laws protecting workplace safety—and I add nothing to the conversation, so I hope you do not mind my company. Actually, that's not true. I must speak to you."

About Beck? Winnie's muscles seized. Were her emotions that obvious? "Of course."

"'Tis about Alonzo."

Winnie almost smiled in relief, but Lulu's frown stifled it in a heartbeat. "Did he hurt you?"

"On the contrary, he is wonderful. But even though I joined the Liberty Belles, Beck still won't grant his permission for me to marry Alonzo."

"Why do you suppose that is?" Winnie tipped her head, indicating that they should take a turn about the ballroom. Arm in arm, they strolled past chattering groups.

"He says it is because Alonzo might want our money, but Alonzo didn't know who my brother is when we met at a church function."

"Are you certain? He might have gleaned your identity prior to that day, much as I hate to say it, or judged your wealth by your clothing."

Lulu's head shook violently. "Alonzo had just arrived from New York to care for his uncle. When we met, we were packing missionary barrels, and I wore something two years out of fashion."

Two whole years. Winnie bit back a smile. Still, it did seem the couple's first meeting began innocently enough. "Alonzo sounds like a decent fellow, but I understand you've not known him long. Perhaps if Beck had more time to get to know him, it would help?"

"I've told him Alonzo and I are willing to wait a year, but he still resists. I don't know how to convince him Alonzo doesn't care about my inheritance. Or money at all."

"That makes him a rare gentleman, indeed."

"He's the real reason I joined the Liberty Belles. When I told him Beck blathered on about how I should better understand cooperation and teamwork, Alonzo agreed with him!"

"Did he? I thought the opposite, since he kept you late from practice."

"That was me. I dragged my feet that day. But something has changed. I am enjoying being among new friends, and last week at the hospital, I saw the world is much bigger than the home I wish to start with Alonzo. I shouldn't neglect helping others."

Winnie squeezed Lulu's arm. "I am so glad to hear this. I'm certain Beck is, too."

"Poor Beck." Lulu sighed. "The biggest reason Beck refuses his blessing, I fear, has nothing to do with my maturity or even Alonzo. Years ago, his heart was smashed like a saucer. No matter how many pieces one recovers and attempts to glue back together, there are always tiny shards missing, and the poor plate never looks quite right again."

Winnie's heart ached for Beck. At the same time, she could understand what love did to a person. After knowing Beck, she would never be the same again. When the exhibition ended and they parted as friends, the china saucer of her heart would bear a chip.

Winnie's steps faltered. Love? She was drawn to Beck. . .but love?

Lulu pulled her around a potted palm. "See, he is speaking with her now. I do not know how he manages to be so cordial."

Beck and Jocelyn Jones exchanged polite smiles before he bowed and scanned the room for someone—Lulu, because the instant he saw her and Winnie, he grinned and strode toward them. At the same moment, Dru and her beau, Xavier, drew alongside.

Blond-haired Xavier stood a full half-foot taller than Dru, and Winnie had to crane her neck to smile up at him. Xavier and Beck shook hands—apparently they had met at some sort of club meeting, but in his profession as a banker, Xavier seemed to know everyone, anyway. "Seems several of your teammates have arrived."

"Irene and Nora," Dru welcomed. Colleen and her fiancé, a mustachioed art dealer Winnie had met several times, followed behind. Other Liberty Belles attended, too. Gladys chatted with Victor near the door, and over in the corner, Fannie and Rowena greeted an older couple.

Winnie's heart still thumped in her ears over Beck once caring for Jocelyn Jones, but he was looking at her quizzically, so she fumbled for something to say. "Isn't this pavilion enchanting?"

"I was just saying the same thing to Xavier." Dru shook her head at Winnie. "I'm amazed we missed this when we were looking about the grounds a few weeks ago."

"We must come back to see everything, Ives." Colleen smiled at her fiancé.

"You've not viewed the exhibitions?" Beck asked. When their heads shook, he turned to the Huntoon sisters. "How about you?"

Nora smiled. "The Main Exhibition Building only."

Dru tutted. "You must visit the ancillary buildings before the Exhibition closes in November."

Irene's mouth twisted. "I'm not much interested in agriculture."

"There's so much more than that. What of the foreign pavilions?" Winnie had enjoyed their exhibits. "The Japanese dwelling was fascinating."

Dru nodded. "We also tried root beer from Mr. Hines."

"Oh, it was delicious. We had some, too." Lulu nudged her brother. "Beck enjoyed the Machinery Hall most, of course."

Everyone chuckled except for Winnie. "That makes perfect sense. You don't just own Emerson Works. You're invested in *every* aspect of it."

Lulu rolled her eyes. "Indeed. We barely made it on time tonight. He and Gilby were poring over plans and papers."

Beck shrugged, unapologetic. "A few employees are staying tonight to finish a project. They are my responsibility. I had to ensure it was well for me to leave tonight."

Winnie liked his meticulousness.

She liked so many things about him that it took her a few moments to realize the conversation had gone on without her, and Dru was extolling the delights of the Women's Pavilion. ". . .engineering, art, and a sculpture made of butter, *Dreaming Iolanthe*. Winnie and I joked about returning to it with yeast rolls in our bags."

"You wouldn't!" Lulu laughed.

"Of course not," Winnie said, smiling. "But it was funny."

Beck's rich laugh drew her gaze, and oh if she didn't almost blurt out how handsome he looked. She could stare at him forever. Maybe it was a good thing the music changed and everyone shifted.

Xavier inclined his head. "I hear a waltz, Dru. Will you do me the honor?"

She pretended to consider, making them all laugh, before nodding. "I should be delighted."

They moved to the dance floor, followed by Colleen and Ives, and gentlemen appeared asking for the other ladies' hands, leaving Winnie and Beck alone on the perimeter of the dance floor. He didn't ask. She didn't look at him.

But she couldn't deny her feelings for him. She wished to spend as much time with him as she could before the exhibition game, so she prayed for boldness and faced Beck, her heart ramming at her ribcage.

———◆◆◆———

Beck didn't usually feel sorry for himself, but the nagging bites of self-pity and jealousy nipped at his gut as he watched the couples twirl about the floor. Tonight, he'd pay all he had for five minutes to hold Winnie in both his arms and lead her in a dance.

To feel whole, not just outside but inside, too. To feel new.

The way she faced him, smiling, he almost did feel it.

Winnie tipped her head toward the dance floor. "You should dance."

He wished he could. "I cannot."

"Yes, you can." She swallowed. Hard. "It is poor form for me to ask you, but should you like to, I will say yes."

"I truly cannot."

"Because you don't know how, or because of your arm?"

"My mother ensured I took lessons. But my arm—"

"You do not need it. Ask me to dance, and I will show you."

"Winnie—"

"Ask me."

He felt a corner of his lip twitch. "You already said yes."

"Incorrigible," she muttered—her favorite word for him.

A more accurate term for him would be coward. He just didn't like to look a fool, which is precisely what Jocelyn had said would happen if he attempted a dance with her at her debut ball, weeks before she ended things between them.

But Jocelyn had never looked at him the way Winnie did now, with warm, trusting eyes and a smile of genuine delight.

He'd played it safe for so long. Maybe, just this once, he shouldn't. And Winnie looked so very beautiful tonight. How could he resist her?

"Will you do me the honor, Winifred?"

"The honor is mine, Beckett."

She nodded at his right hand and glanced at her left side. With no small amount of hesitation, he placed his hand above her waist, at the small of her back. Instead of placing her left hand on his right shoulder, as was expected, she rested her right hand on his left shoulder and held her left hand to the side in a graceful pose. "See? We do not need your left hand. We are balanced like this."

It didn't look a thing like proper waltz posture, nor was it conducive to dancing. "How shall I lead you, hmm?"

"I think we will manage."

Beck wasn't so sure, but he didn't much care anymore if he looked foolish or their dancing was lopsided.

They stood two feet apart, but it was closer than he'd been to anyone in a long time, except when Lulu took his arm. Or, come to think of it, when Gladys needed help with batting practice.

This was different, though. He couldn't look away from her. Winnie's dark eyes crinkled into happy crescents, the way they always did when she smiled, and it made him smile, too.

He couldn't help but tease. "Is this the most awkward dance of your life?"

"Oh no, that was with Dru's brother Aloysius at her debut ball. He didn't speak, shuddered from time to time, and bore a pinched expression. I thought I was doing a horrid job, which made me stiff and nervous, but it turned out that he had a burr in his stocking, and every time he stepped on it, he wanted to cry out in pain."

"If only he'd said something. Poor Aloysius."

"Poor Aloysius." She laughed, tipping back her head and exposing her neck. The delicate fragrance of her perfume wafted about him, filling his senses with blossoms and spring. For a moment, he felt like a boy again, that same liveliness and hope and yearning for the future all tangling in his gut. Like he was falling in love again.

He stumbled, causing her to misstep and clutch his shoulder. Beck gripped her waist to support her, but she righted at once. "Do you have a burr in your stocking?"

"No, I'm just clumsy." And addlepated, thinking he could fall in love again.

She swayed with the music, never losing time. "You aren't clumsy. You have excellent aim on the baseball diamond."

"I was not much of a dancer before the war."

"You were a boy before the war. You had little opportunity to dance."

"Precisely."

She laughed, which was what he wanted. Winnie's laughter was the best thing in the world. Better, even, than baseball.

"I'm glad you asked me to dance."

Her eyes widened with mock dismay. "I did no such thing. It would have been indecorous of me to ask a gentleman to dance."

"Terribly so. But I'm glad all the same."

"Me, too."

He would dance with her again. She was right. He hadn't needed two hale arms. All he'd needed was the openness to try. Maybe he should follow suit when it came to his feelings, too. He was more than halfway to being in love with Winnie, anyway. Love wasn't safe, though. It came with the frightening possibility of getting hurt, or being used, like Lulu probably was by Alonzo. Like he had been twelve years ago by Jocelyn.

But exchanging the briefest of pleasantries with Jocelyn tonight didn't hurt a whit. How sad, because he'd taken so few risks in the past twelve years because of her, but as Winnie had pointed out, risk was necessary to gain something greater, sometimes.

Winnie was so many things he admired. She cared for the children at the hospital, her little neighbor Penny, and her father. Her intelligence charmed him as much as her smile did. She was a loving friend, a dutiful daughter, and an amazing pitcher.

He was wrong. He wasn't halfway to being in love with her. He loved her. No dispute.

"Winnie?"

The music ended and she lowered her hand. "Yes?"

"Sir?" A lanky, uniformed manservant appeared at Beck's elbow. "Are you Beckett Emerson?"

"I am." A sense of dread unspooled in his stomach.

"This arrived for you. I was told it's urgent."

Beck took the folded sheet of paper from him and flicked it open with his thumb. Gil's scrawl covered the page, its message brief and calm in tone, but the words dried Beck's mouth. "I must go."

Winnie's fingers landed on his forearm. "What has happened? May I help?"

"Ensure Lulu gets home, please. I must leave without her. At once." It was hard to look Winnie in the eye as he spoke. He'd started to lose control of his feelings, but this was the perfect reminder that he must take caution in every aspect of life in order to prevent disaster. "There's trouble at Emerson Works."

Chapter Six

Trouble could mean a thousand things, but Beck's stricken look told Winnie that whatever happened at Emerson Works was a serious matter. She found Papa, and they gathered Lulu and culled Victor from a conversation with Gladys, piling everyone into the carriage and returning to Rittenhouse Square. Lulu waited with Winnie in the parlor while Papa made inquiries, and within the hour he told them there had been a fire at Emerson Works.

"A small one," he clarified, "but it could have been worse, if Beckett hadn't put so many precautions in place."

"Was anyone—" The words stuck in Winnie's throat.

"No. And the building stands. Louise, you're welcome to stay, if you wish."

Lulu's head shook. "I should be home when Beck returns."

Papa delivered her there personally, and when he returned, Winnie was standing where he'd left her. "What's this? It's well, poppet." Papa patted her cheek with his cold hand. "But you may not see your coach at practice tomorrow."

Winnie sank into a chair in an unladylike slump. "I don't care about practice. It's Beck and his workers I'm worried about."

"Hmm." Papa eyed her funny. "I'm off to bed."

It was a happy surprise when Beck and Lulu arrived at practice the following afternoon. Beck carried a bag over his shoulder, his head bowed so she couldn't read his expression. Lulu, however, looked grim.

Oh dear. Things at Emerson Works must have been worse than Papa thought. Winnie hastened toward them just as Beck lifted his head. "Ralph, come pass these out."

Colleen's brother dashed past her, reaching for the bag. Winnie wished she could run, too, but running toward a gentleman was not as acceptable as running base to base on the diamond, so she walked as fast as she could.

Ralph dropped the pack to the ground and bent inside, pulling out white baseball caps embroidered with royal blue letters: *LB*.

"Liberty Belle caps!"

Lulu showed the players one of several professional, eye-catching flyers Beck had printed up announcing next week's exhibition game between the Liberty Belles and the Patriots to be held on Jefferson Grounds, on the corner of Master and 25th Streets. The flyers included the ticket price of twenty-five cents, stating that all proceeds would benefit the winner's charity of choice, the Children's Hospital or the Women's Club Auxiliary.

As the team ambled back to the field, Winnie stepped closer to Beck. "These are wonderful. Thank you." She traded her worn cap for the team cap. "How does it look?"

"Fine." He didn't look at her.

He must be terribly busy, after the fire. He shouldn't be here. Her hand landed lightly on his forearm. "Beck, if you need to get back to work, you must."

"I will. Thanks for understanding. There's a lot to be done today. And tomorrow." His gaze met hers at last, his expression stony. "And after that, Winnie. I can no longer coach the Liberty Belles."

———◦••◦———

"What?" Winnie's jaw gaped, but Beck couldn't be moved by the shock and hurt blanching her face. He had to stay firm.

"I can't coach the team anymore." His arm went cold when her hand fell from it. "I'm sorry, but the fire reminded me how much I have to attend to at Emerson Works."

Her head dipped. "I never meant to take away from your business."

This wasn't just about Emerson Works, though. It was about his traitorous heart. "You didn't. I just. . .need to focus on things I can control."

"Papa said a spark flew where it shouldn't have. You couldn't have controlled that. We can be cautious and things still go wrong."

"I'm a perfect example of that." He pointed to his arm. "I was shot by a fellow in my own regiment when a skirmish broke out. I thought one of my friends fell into me, until I landed in the dust and couldn't get up again."

"Oh, Beck."

"The corps medical director stemmed the hemorrhage and I was taken to a field hospital. They closed the wound and told me if I didn't succumb to infection that my arm might come back to life. But it hasn't."

"You lived, though. That's all that mattered to the people who love you."

One would think so. "My sweetheart pitied me, but she couldn't quite hide her revulsion. I was still her beau when she made her debut that spring, but a few days later she said she needed time. Not much, as it turned out. She married someone with two working arms before we were Lulu's age."

"Jocelyn Jones."

"How'd you guess that?"

"You and Paulette both mentioned knowing each other in your youth, and then Lulu all but confirmed them last night." Winnie looked at her toes. "I'm sorry you're still hurt over her."

"I'm not, but I learned that while some problems can't be avoided, I was going to be as careful as I could be in every other aspect of my life, to avoid another. . .loss."

His gaze fixed on Lulu, who modeled her cap for a giggling Gladys. Winnie sighed. "Like your expectation that Alonzo will break Lulu's heart? I know she's young, but she's willing to wait to wed, she told me. So is Alonzo."

That wasn't the point. "She's going to get hurt. That's one problem I don't want her to have."

"Love isn't a problem to avoid."

But it was. He had almost succumbed to romance last night—the glass pavilion, the lights, the music, holding Winnie close. He let himself feel everything he'd held at bay, and he'd been about to ask Winnie outdoors to view the lights with him. It was the first time he'd have taken an emotional risk since Jocelyn abandoned him, and although the events weren't correlated, he'd been about to pin his heart to his sleeve when he learned his business had almost burned down. It was a firm reminder that love came with pain, every single time.

"Maybe not, but love isn't the answer to everything. You out of everyone should know that."

"I assure you, I don't."

"Victor Van Cleef. You don't love him, but you marrying him would be the answer to your father's hopes, wouldn't it?"

She wanted to deny it, but she couldn't. "He hasn't mentioned it in a while, but yes."

"Have you told your father you're not interested?"

"No. I've avoided the subject as best I could—"

"Speak up. Every day you don't, you string them along in the hopes of a Myles and Van Cleef union."

Her skin went pale. "You're right. I hoped he'd notice I don't love him so I wouldn't have to tell him. I hoped he'd notice I—"

"What?"

She glanced at the other ladies, tossing balls back and forth while they waited. "I don't want to keep you from Emerson Works, but I hate to part like this."

Neither did Beck, but it was probably for the best. If she was hurt and angry with him, he would know he had no hope with her—something he knew in his head but not in his traitorous heart. But he couldn't break things altogether. "We're friends, Winnie."

She nodded, clearly disbelieving him. She was right. They wouldn't see much of each other, especially once he retreated to his old way of solitary living and she married.

"You'll be fine without a coach." He turned away from her. "Goodbye, Winnie."

"Thank you, Beck." Her words pulled him back. "You've been a wonderful coach."

He waved and left the field. Maybe someday God would heal his inability to take a risk. At least he was the only one hurt by his foolishness. Winnie would forget him in a fortnight.

Chapter Seven

Independence Day arrived warm and dry, the sky clear and blue. Winnie couldn't have asked for a better afternoon for a baseball game.

She stood in the pitcher's box in the center of the diamond at the Jefferson Grounds, brushing the dirt underfoot with her broken-in boot. The act might be small, but it was grand, too: she, Winifred Myles, might well be the first woman to pitch here, at the home of the Athletics, Philadelphia's professional team.

Unlike their practice plot at the edge of the park, this was no weedy field harboring animal burrows and mud puddles. The diamond and outfield were as neat and well tended as a garden, its five-year-old sod protected from outsiders by a ten-foot fence. Benches bordering the outfield provided seating for five thousand people. When the Athletics played here, each seat was taken, and spectators lined the fence, climbed trees, and even perched on neighboring rooftops to watch the games.

Winnie had no such expectations for attendance today, but she was grateful for every person who trickled into the grounds. Either the Women's Club Auxiliary or the Children's Hospital would benefit from the sales, but the game would also provide wholesome entertainment for families and show young women that they, too, could play baseball.

What would Susan B. Anthony, in town for the National Woman Suffrage Association meeting, think of that?

Voting was not the same as baseball, but Winnie smiled nonetheless.

She was the only one on her team to do so, though. At their bench between third base and home plate, the Liberty Belles waited for the game to start. Determined to look more uniform for the game, they had all donned dark blue jackets, coordinating skirts, and the team caps, but no one looked any more confident. Irene paced. Ralph clutched a bat as if frightened he might forget to hand it to the first striker. Colleen's pat on his back was too hard. Rowena's arms folded, Nora mumbled, and Fannie's skin tinged the strange yellowish-green of pond algae, like she was about to retch. Dru's arm wrapped around Gladys—oh, dear, was Gladys crying?

Winnie was at her side in a moment. "What's wrong?"

Dru mouthed *I don't know.*

Nora frowned. "Lulu's not even here yet."

One problem at a time. Winnie gently cupped Fannie's forehead, finding it cool. "Is it something you ate?"

"I haven't been able to eat anything since yesterday. I'm afraid I'll drop the ball again."

Poor dear. "You won't—"

"If anyone drops it, it'll be me," Nora insisted. "Every time it comes to right field—"

"At least you can hit the ball." Irene interrupted. "I won't be able to, I just know it."

Gladys lifted her head. "I don't remember how to hold the bat without Beck."

Ah. Gladys was pining over Beck. He would have had just the right thing to say, but he wasn't here. He didn't even gather Lulu after practice anymore. He'd quit them completely a week ago.

He hadn't quit Winnie's thoughts, though—practical thoughts about whether or not the team should take a long walk this morning or rest in anticipation of the game. There were impractical thoughts, too, recalling his smile, his voice, and the fact that she loved him. . .but he'd made his choice.

She was left to gather the broken pieces of her heart and lead this team. She tugged her hankie from her sleeve and thrust it at Gladys, next on her list of priorities. "You don't need Beck. You can bat just fine."

"I'll help you, Gladys." Ralph offered the bat. "I'm the only man left on the team, and I'm a good striker."

Winnie patted the top of his cap. "That's sweet of you, Ralph, but—"

"Land sakes!" Rowena's outburst made her jump. "Look at them!"

The Patriots entered the field as one, their ensembles worthy of a full page spread in *Harper's Bazaar*. Navy blue *paleot* jackets trimmed with white star appliqués emphasized their trim figures, and their candy-cane striped skirts swayed like bells. Red ball caps were set just-so atop fashionable coiffures of frizzled fringes and thick coiled chignons at the nape.

"Look at those jackets," Fannie whispered.

"And their hair." Awe tinged fine-haired Nora's tone.

"It's artificial. Those are *frizzettes* and *scalpettes*; I'm sure of it." Rowena scowled.

"We look dowdy in comparison," Gladys moaned.

She was right. "But we dressed for a ball game, not a promenade."

Dru nodded at Winnie. "They'll be worrying about their hairpieces falling off in front of half of Philadelphia."

At least Dru didn't seem nervous. It must have something to do with the way she kept exchanging smiles with Xavier, who perched in the front row. They'd probably be engaged before the fireworks finished over Independence Hall later tonight.

The Liberty Belles had a game to win first, however, and fancy outfits weren't going to intimidate her team. Winnie clapped her hands, praying for words of inspiration. "It doesn't matter what we're wearing, what matters is our hearts! We are among the first women to play an exhibition baseball game for charity in the United States, and we mustn't forget how privileged we are to even play. Few women have the freedom to do what we've done this summer. As for the game, Beck said—"

Her voice broke. *Lord, I miss Beck.*

She cleared her throat as her teammates watched and waited, except for Gladys, who still hid her face in Dru's shoulder. Winnie smiled. "Beck told us to do our best and not take risks. It's sound advice. Let's win, and show the world baseball can be enjoyed on any afternoon, by anyone. And we will have fun doing it, and maybe bless the Children's Hospital, too. What say you?"

"I say aye," Dru said with a grin.

"Aye," Ralph chirped.

"Aye." Colleen's voice was strong.

The rest of the team joined in, even Gladys. The rest of the team seemed calmer now, but Winnie's stomach knotted as if she'd absorbed their anxiety. The game would start soon, and if last week's practice game was any indication, there was a good chance they wouldn't win. She'd done her best to encourage her teammates, but their opponents were formidable.

And Lulu still wasn't here. They were a player short.

Winnie beckoned Nora, Fannie, and Colleen. "Without Lulu, there's a hole in the outfield. Colleen, you'll need to run back to assist if necessary."

"I will." She nodded, but walked off mumbling about thinking Lulu had changed.

That was the thing: Lulu had changed since the visit to the hospital. This past week, especially, she'd been cheery, timely, and helpful. Where was she? Beck might still be angry with Winnie, but he'd wanted Lulu to learn responsibility and teamwork. Playing the game was an essential part of that commitment.

Lord, care for Lulu, wherever she is.

And Beck, too.

She'd prayed for him, his business, and his well-being all week. He may not return her love, but she'd keep on praying for him and thanking God for him. He'd been right to challenge her about Victor and Papa. She'd not had an opportunity to talk to either of them, but she would today, after the game. It might be a short one, without Lulu.

The stands had filled in the time her back had been turned. Many of the faces belonged to people she knew, neighbors and friends and oh, there was Papa, wearing a patriotic ribbon on his lapel. Beside him, Victor chatted with Gladys's mother. A row ahead of them, a little girl with dark hair danced at her seat—Penny! Winnie waved at her and Miss Foster.

Penny cupped her tiny hands around her mouth. "Win, Winnie!"

"I shall try, Penny!"

To the left, she spied Dr. Post from the Children's Hospital and two patients who must have been deemed well enough to attend. Winnie rushed over to greet them. "Kenny! Zechariah! How pleased I am to see you!"

Kenny's face was flush with color. "I'm better, Miss Myles."

"You cannot imagine how glad I am to hear it, Kenny."

Zechariah squinted past her. "Where's Mr. Emerson?"

"I'm not sure," she answered honestly.

"They're busy." Kenny nudged Zechariah's stump. "The game starts in five minutes."

It was later than she thought. "I'd best rejoin the team, boys. Cheer for us."

They responded with rousing huzzahs.

Winnie marched past the Patriots and their fancy uniforms. Dru held out her hand. "Shall we pray?"

Winnie took Fannie's hand in her empty one and they bowed their heads. "Lord, for the freedoms we celebrate on this day, for this game we are to play, and for our many blessings, we thank Thee. Guide and protect both teams, we ask in Jesus' name. Amen."

The ladies broke apart as the stout field manager called for an umpire from among the spectators. A bearded, middle-aged gentleman in the front row stood. "I've judged baseball before."

"Suitable." The manager spun around. "Patriots up first. Striker to the line!"

Ralph handed Winnie a ball. She jogged to the pitcher's box, even as her belly fluttered with nerves. The memory of Beck's voice filled her ears. *Take your time. Don't rush. Stand tall.*

She took a deep breath and pitched.

Crack! The ball flew midfield, right where Lulu would have been standing. By the time Nora captured the ball, the striker was at second base.

Irene fumbled the next hit, resulting in the first run scored by the Patriots. Winnie's attempts to pitch strikes failed, as each one connected with the ball and sent it just out of the Liberty Belles' reach.

Twenty minutes in, the Patriots had scored four runs. Winnie rubbed her aching forehead. There was a lot of game left to play, but the Liberty Belles were already losing.

"Sorry!" A slender woman in a dark blue jacket rushed toward the umpire, panting from exertion. "I'm on the Liberty Belles. Carriage accident...."

Lulu!

"Get on the field." The judge pointed to the gaping hole in the outfield. The Patriots protested, but the judge waved them off. "They're a man down. I mean a woman. Aw, just play."

Winnie met her halfway. "Are you well, Lulu?"

"Yes. Extremely so." Her smile was bright and her words intriguing.

Winnie didn't have time to press Lulu on the mystery, however. She spun back to pitch—

Lulu hadn't come alone. Alonzo and Gilby Gresham hurried to find seats. Parting from them, donned in a blue suit to match the team and a Liberty Belles cap, Beck jogged to the bench to join Ralph. His smile melted the bones in her shins.

Despite the sudden weakness in her knees, her arm and shoulder didn't falter. She tossed the ball so hard the striker swung and missed.

———•◦•———

Adjusting the bill of his cap to better block the July sun, Beck grimaced at the scoreboard. "The Patriots scored four runs already?"

"Yep." Ralph adjusted his bill, too. "Them fancy girls kept hitting the ball to Lulu's spot."

"Can't blame 'em. It's good strategy." Beck bent forward as Winnie tossed the ball and the striker missed for the third time.

"Yer out, missy." The judge pointed. The Patriots striker threw down the bat.

"Two more to go!" Beck wished he could clap. "Don't rush it, Winnie!"

She didn't. The next striker had two strikes against her when she sent the ball to the outfield, allowing her to take first base. With a pat to Ralph's head, Beck rose and moved closer to Irene, silently communicating with a nod that the next up to bat had a tendency to hit down the line.

She did. Irene was ready, scooping up the ball, tapping her base, and tossing the ball efficiently to Gladys on second base. That made three outs! "Well done, Liberty Belles!"

The team rushed in, surrounding him with eager, smiling expressions.

"Good to see you, Coach." Dru smiled.

Gladys beamed. "Are you really back?"

"I am. Sorry we're late." He spoke to the team, but his eyes were on Winnie. She hadn't said anything to him, but her smile told him how glad she was to see him.

Lulu took Winnie's arm. "There was a carriage accident. No one was hurt, but the roads were blocked."

"Why are you grinning like that, if there was an accident?" Fannie asked.

"Oh, something else happened. I'll tell you later," Lulu promised.

"Striker to the line!" The judge's order was sharp.

Beck nodded. Time for business. "We have a long game to play."

"I don't like that girl." Ralph glared at Paulette, waiting in the pitcher's box.

"Me neither." Rowena's default expression was a scowl that didn't budge.

"I don't like what she said, and it's not been easy to forgive her." Winnie's jaw clenched.

But her words implied she was trying, and Beck thanked God for it. He patted her shoulder—a coach-like thump of approval that wouldn't look like anything affectionate to anyone observing, but it sent a shock up his arm. "Winnie's right. Paulette isn't our enemy. She's our opponent, and her remarks were meant to upset us. You Liberty Belles are as strong as your namesake, so go prove it. Play smart and clean, no risks. Irene, you're up first. Aim low between first and second base, if you can. That's their weak spot."

Winnie's eyes were wide when she looked up at him. Oh, his hand was still on her shoulder. Uh-oh.

She stood with him rather than taking a seat on the bench. "I'm glad you came back."

"I couldn't leave my team." Then, even though this wasn't the time or place, even though he'd left her at the ball and quit the team, even though his actions had hurt her, ever-so-slightly, he nudged her arm. Just a brush of fabric from his sleeve against hers.

Two seconds later, she did the same, and Beck didn't believe for an instant it was an accident. A grin tugged at his lips.

Much as he would have liked to stand by her side for the rest of the afternoon, he had a game to coach. Irene made a solid hit, and so did Gladys. Dru batted third and sent the ball flying, so the bases were loaded. Winnie, batting fourth, took the bat from Ralph and approached the plate. He didn't need to remind her that if she got a base hit, the Liberty Belles would score a run.

It would be a much-needed boost to the team, and a start toward evening the score.

Paulette tossed the ball. Winnie jumped back. If she hadn't, the ball would have battered her hip.

The judge shook his head. "Unfair ball."

"Sorry," Paulette called.

Winnie nodded but no more. She wasn't about to let anything break her concentration.

Paulette's next pitch was so low and close it brushed Winnie's skirt. The judge called it unfair. Beck groaned.

So did Ralph. "Is that lady really going to throw nine unfair balls so Winnie walks to first?"

"No." She wouldn't sacrifice a run like that. "She's trying to anger Winnie and then strike her out."

"That's mean."

"It's strategy." Beck glanced down at Ralph. "But yeah, it's not in the spirit of the game, is it?"

The crowd booed and cheered, depending on which side they supported, as Paulette continued to pitch balls aimed at Winnie's body rather than the strike zone. Beck cupped his hand over his mouth. "Stay calm, Winnie."

Her tiny nod told him she'd heard, but she didn't break her focus on Paulette as she threw and Winnie dodged. Then Paulette threw right into the strike zone. Winnie swung and missed.

"Strike one," the judge called. The Patriots hooted. The Liberty Belles muttered.

Come on, sweetheart. Don't let her bully you.

She didn't. Winnie swung and connected with the ball. The ground ball was caught and Winnie was out at first base, but her sacrifice enabled Irene to score a run. The two hugged as they made their way back to the bench.

Their smiles died when they met Beck's serious gaze. Winnie licked her lips. "Did I do wrong?"

"No, I did." Beck eyed each player. "I told you not to take risks. Well, I've changed my mind."

"Take risks?" Winnie's brows rose.

"Yep."

"But you said it's not good strategy," Lulu said.

"We'll never know if we don't try. The children at the hospital deserve our all, and you deserve to have fun. So go steal bases, whatever you want."

Winnie boggled at him. "Beck Emerson, encouraging us to take risks? I never thought I'd see the day."

He nudged her shoulder. "Just wait. The day's not over yet."

He was about to take a risk of his own where Winnie was concerned. After all, like he'd just told the team, he'd never know if he didn't try.

Chapter Eight

By the top of the ninth inning, the crowd was so loud and exuberant that everyone's nerves ran high, but in a good way like nothing Winnie had ever experienced before. The cheers resounding through the ball field seemed to feed her ability to pitch, to hit, to run. And oh, did the Liberty Belles hit and run.

Nora's jacket was caked in dirt from sliding headfirst into bases. Rowena's hem tore from all the lunges she executed to tag out the Patriots, and Dru's brown curls frizzed out the back of her cap from her similar efforts at home plate. Sweat ran like tears down Colleen's cheeks, and sweet, quiet Fannie argued with the judge that she was safe after sliding into home. Gladys hit two home runs and her mad dashes around the bases left her face red as a boiled lobster. Lulu took a tumble in center field that left her limping—but she'd caught the ball.

Winnie's shoulder ached, but she didn't care. They were not playing it safe, and they'd managed to score seven runs to the Patriots' six.

Winnie scratched the soil in the pitcher's box with her boot, a habit that enabled her to peek at the loaded bases out of the corners of her eyes. If the Patriots scored a run—or four—now, the Liberty Belles would have the rest of the inning to attempt to change the score.

But if Winnie struck out Paulette right now, with two outs against the Patriots, the Liberty Belles would win.

Winnie glanced at Beck. His hand rested on Ralph's shoulder as they watched, too tense to sit on the bench. Beck's jaw was set, but the corner of his mouth lifted in a twitch. It was as if his body told her to *win* and *have fun* at the same time, two opposing messages.

Paulette's smug smile sent Winnie an altogether different message, one that made Winnie's blood pound in her ears. She threw the ball. Hard.

Paulette swung and missed, just as Winnie had hoped, but the victory felt hollow when the judge yelled "Strrrrike!" Because she was angry at Paulette, unforgiving and oh, whatever this feeling was in her chest that made her want to protect Beck like a mother lion defending her cub, Winnie's throw hadn't been controlled, and Paulette might have hit it out of the field, enabling her teammates to score.

Some risks were worth taking. This one might not be.

Lord, help me want to forgive her. I know I've asked countless times, but now that she's in front of me, I—

Paulette's boots shuffled, a nervous gesture. Suddenly Winnie's emotions shifted. Paulette was a person with weaknesses and hopes. Winnie wasn't certain she'd forgiven her, just like that, but she wasn't angry anymore.

Her second pitch reflected it. It was well aimed but too fast for Paulette to hit.

"Strrrike two!" The judge bounced on his toes.

Paulette pinked.

The crowd cheered, feet stomped, and her teammates hollered, but she heard one deep voice above all others. "That's right, Winnie!"

She glanced at Beck, whose wide grin made her chest expand with love.

One last pitch—in the game, and in her career as a baseball player. *Thank You, Lord, for the opportunity to play today.*

Winnie threw the ball.

Paulette swung.

And missed.

"Strrrike three! Yer out, missy!"

The crowd was silent for half a second, and then cheers erupted throughout the field. With a score of 7 to 6, there was no need to play the second half of the inning. The Liberty Belles had won.

The team embraced in a large huddle near third base, Ralph at their center, and then broke to hug Beck with words of thanks.

Winnie held back, shy, but before she could take her turn hugging Beck, the Patriots arrived to shake hands. Winnie took Paulette's hand. "Good game. You're a terrific pitcher."

Paulette grunted.

Stifling a laugh, Winnie turned back to her team. The field manager stood in their midst, calling for silence. "I've informed both charities represented today that Beckett Emerson of Emerson Works will match the game proceeds, so the Children's Hospital and the Women's Club Auxiliary will both receive donations."

All eyes went wide, except for Lulu's. "I have an announcement, too. Before the game, Beck gave his blessing. In a year, Alonzo and I will be married."

Winnie cheered. Congratulations and kisses followed, and soon the families ambled onto the field, including Papa. Gathering her courage, Winnie met him halfway.

"Exciting game, Winifred."

"I'm glad you enjoyed it, Papa." She prayed for words. "I have something important to tell you, something I should have told you from the start. I know you want me to marry Victor, but I don't care for him."

"I have eyes, daughter. I can see where your affections lie, and fear not, I approve."

He did? There was nothing to approve of, though. Beck didn't want her. "I'm not disappointing you?"

"Oh, 'twas an old man's folly, thinking I could keep the business in the family, seeing you safe and cared for."

"God will manage that some other way."

"I suppose you're right." His eyes narrowed at something over her shoulder. "It seems Victor has other plans, anyway."

Winnie spun. Gladys clung to Victor's arm, and they stared at her and Papa with guilty expressions.

Bustling toward them, Victor frowned. "Gladys and I are courting. I hope you aren't upset."

"No, I just. . . Not at all." Winnie saw now that he would have made some sort of overture long ago, had he intended to court her. "When did this happen?" Gladys had been asking Beck for all those batting lessons.

Gladys beamed. "I met Victor at your house, and I didn't want to look like an idiot when he saw me at the game, so I asked Beck for help. I'm glad I did, because I hit well today."

"I'm truly happy for you both."

She meant it.

They strolled away, as did Papa, leaving a clear path between Winnie and Beck. He didn't smile, but his eyes were soft as he strode toward her, only to be intercepted by Dru and Xavier. "Coming to the fireworks at Independence Hall, you two?"

Winnie nodded. "I wouldn't miss it."

Beck nodded. "We'll find you there."

We?

Beck smiled. "I asked your father if I could accompany you two to view the fireworks tonight. Well, me, Lulu, and Alonzo. If you don't mind too much."

"I don't mind." A grand understatement.

With a flash of his handsome smile, Beck bid them all farewell and met his friend Gilby by the entrance, all calm and normal. But Winnie's heart was beating so fast, it was a wonder it didn't puncture through her ribcage.

<hr />

After a bath and an early supper with Papa, Winnie donned a patriotic blue ensemble. True to his word, Beck arrived at dusk, hat in hand. Alonzo and Lulu waited in the carriage, and after a lively ride spent discussing the baseball game, their little party arrived at Independence Hall to find a huge throng already gathered. Torches illuminated the dimming sky, and a brass band performed patriotic tunes.

It was indescribable, being in this place one hundred years after the Declaration of Independence was signed. Winnie gave thanks for her country as they found a viewing area, but before they could get comfortable, Beck turned to Papa. "May I borrow Winnie for a moment?"

"I think you'll need more than one, lad." Papa grinned.

Beck offered his arm. When Winnie took it, her hand fit just right in the crook of his elbow, even if her limbs trembled a little. What would Beck say, now that they were alone?

He led her through the crowd. "Thank you for coming tonight."

"Thanks for inviting me. I didn't like how we parted. Is everything well at Emerson Works?"

"How kind of you to ask. Yes, my employees and my equipment are safe."

"Taking precautions paid off."

"Not where you're concerned." He smiled at the confused expression that must be contorting her face, despite her trying to hide her response. "I was upset after the fire—with myself, not you. I'm sorry I took it out on you. I had a lot of thinking to do, because you challenged me. But you were right. I've missed a lot, holed up in my office and fretting over possible troubles. You reminded me that while the world may not be the safest of places all the time, it's also beautiful."

"Precautions are wise, though. You showed me I need to take more. Pretending trouble doesn't exist is inconsiderate."

"There will always be trouble. Didn't Jesus say that? But you make my troubles lighter."

"I do?"

"I want to do the same for you." His deep voice softened. "I love you, Winifred Myles. So much that it terrifies me. But you're worth the risk."

"So are you." She swallowed hard. "I love you too, Beckett Emerson."

Overhead, a large firework boomed, followed by a blast of golden light and a shower of sparks, but the glory of it couldn't compare to the look of adoration on Beck's face as he bent his head and lowered his lips to hers. His kiss was gentle but full of promise.

Her arms clasped about his broad shoulders, holding tight to him and what he offered. His heart. His love.

There, under the shower of a thousand sparks of light and the songs of celebration, Winnie knew love.

She might be a good pitcher, but this was one thing she would never toss away.

Epilogue

The late October wind bit into Winnie's cheeks, but she snuggled closer to Beck as they strolled through the Independence Exhibition grounds before it closed next month. "Do you think Mr. Hires will sell his root beer? I'd like more than that small sample cup he's offering."

"I'm sure he will, and I'll buy you bottles and bottles of it." Beck chuckled. "Say, look where we are."

The glass pavilion looked different in the autumn daylight than it had that June night when torches and lamps blazed golden light through it, but it was beautiful all the same. "I'm rather fond of this place."

"Me too." Beck cleared his throat, which sounded pinched all of a sudden. "I was thinking, Winnie. You had the right pitch, asking me to coach the Liberty Belles. But now I have a pitch for you."

"Oh?" She grinned. "Creating another baseball team?"

"That wasn't the sort of team I had in mind." He peeked at her. "Remember our dance here, the night of the charity ball?"

His abrupt change of topics made her blink, but then her thoughts filled with the memory of being held by him while they moved in time to the music and how perfect the moment had been. "I'll never forget it. I could have danced with you forever."

"Your feet would have tired out eventually," he teased.

"You're not very romantic," she teased back.

"I'm trying, believe it or not. This team I mentioned? Actually, I didn't say *team*. You did. I said *pitch*, but—" He broke off, laughing.

Winnie didn't catch the joke, but it was fun watching him laugh. Then her smile froze. Pitch. Team. Their dance.

This had nothing to do with baseball.

"Beck?" Her voice squeaked.

He took her hand and pulled her gently around the back of the pavilion, hidden from the view of others strolling the grounds, although anyone inside the glass building could see them if they happened to be watching—but the grounds were quiet this autumn afternoon, and the pavilion was probably empty. Beck cupped her cheek, rubbing his thumb over her lips and sending a trail of fire down to her stomach. For a moment, she thought he'd kiss her, until he lowered to one knee.

Oh!

"The pitch I mentioned?"

She nodded.

"I'll love you for all our days if you'll forge a team with me. I love you with all that

I am, sweet Winnie."

"Beck." His name came out as a whisper, an endearment, as emotion filled her throat. "Yes, oh yes."

He was standing and kissing her before she could take another breath, but too quickly he pulled back. "Are you certain? I have but one arm to escort you, one arm to work for you." He paused. "One arm to hold a baby."

"You hold *me* just fine." She bit her lip. "More than fine—"

Her words were lost to his kiss. Then kisses. She was as breathless and weak kneed as if she'd run around the bases, but she wouldn't stop for anything—

A loud thump tugged her out of bliss back to the autumn world. And she gasped.

"There are people in the pavilion?"

"The rest of our team." Beck didn't sound the least bit embarrassed as he tucked her into his chest. Through the glass, happy faces looked out at them: Lulu and Alonzo, Dru and Xavier, Nora and her new beau Gilby, and Papa, nodding his approval.

"I asked his blessing." Beck kissed Winnie's temple.

"Thank you." She waved at her loved ones and then they disappeared, hurrying outside to join them. In moments, she and Beck were surrounded by embraces.

Her pitch to Beck those weeks ago had been the right one, indeed.

But his pitch to her was even better.

She popped to her toes and told him so with a kiss.

Susanne Dietze began writing love stories in high school, casting her friends in the starring roles. Today, she's the award-winning author of a dozen new and upcoming historical romances who's seen her work on the ECPA and *Publisher's Weekly* Bestseller Lists for Inspirational Fiction. Married to a pastor and the mom of two, Susanne lives in California and enjoys fancy-schmancy tea parties, the beach, and curling up on the couch with a costume drama and a plate of nachos. You can visit her online at www.susannedietze.com and subscribe to her newsletters at http://eepurl.com/bieza5.

A Gift in Secret

by Kathleen Y'Barbo

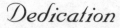
Dedication

To "The Girls":
Linda Kozar,
Janice Thompson,
Sharen Watson, and
Dannelle Woody

You are my source of strength, inspiration, and entertainment.
Your prayers sustain me, and your texts kept me anchored to
Home and you when I needed it most.
Thank you for the love and laughter!
May we grow old together—in Texas!

A gift in secret pacifieth anger. . . .
PROVERBS 21:14

Chapter One

"A bsolutely not."

Samuel Austin III rose and headed for the door. Allowing his father to convince him to attend this ridiculous meeting was his first mistake. Staying to hear anything else the late Thomas Bolen's attorney planned to say would not be his second.

The old man had died a year ago, by his recollection. And while the funeral for the owner of Bolen Shipping had been elaborate according to the lengthy article in the *Picayune*, there were no Austins in attendance that day.

But then none were expected. Nor was his daughter, May, or her mother, Bolen's wife, in the chapel to grieve him.

Heavy velvet curtains on the wall behind Mr. Breaux stood open, allowing the mid-morning sunlight that slanted through the crystal vases arranged on a rosewood sideboard to cast pinpoints of color across the polished wood.

A chair scraped against the floor behind him, but Sam kept walking.

"I assure you that Mr. Bolen was quite intent on having you take the reins of Bolen Shipping. In fact, he made it abundantly clear that the stakes should be raised to the point where you could not refuse."

With his hand on the polished silver doorknob, Sam considered a response that would let the lawyer know he was talking to the wrong Austin. Sam Jr. would have accepted the offer to take back the company that was stolen from him without caring the terms.

"I feel it my duty to advise you," Mr. Breaux said as Sam turned the knob. "Should you refuse Mr. Bolen's most generous gift, you will be effectively putting his daughter in an untenable position."

Sam yanked the door open. "I'm sure Miss Bolen will survive," he said over his shoulder. "Bolens always do."

"Without you at the helm, the company will be sold and the proceeds donated. Miss Bolen will have nothing. Are you certain she will survive that?"

He froze.

"I thought that might get your attention," Mr. Breaux said. "Mr. Bolen thought so as well. Now if you'll just return to your chair and give me a few more minutes of your time."

"You assume I care what happens to a Bolen," Sam snapped as he turned to face the attorney. "I assure you, no Bolen ever stopped to consider what happened to the Austins when our business was stolen from us."

Mr. Breaux settled back on his chair and gave Sam a pointed look. "I assume you are a man given to actually caring what happens to a young lady who is soon to be destitute."

"She can have whatever the old man left to me. I don't want it."

"I'm afraid that's not possible," Mr. Breaux said as he peered at Sam over his spectacles. "The will is very clear in this. You may go from rags to riches, as it were, or Miss Bolen may go from riches to rags. It is all up to you."

Everything in him wanted to tell the smug lawyer he was wrong. That he truly did not care what happened to Miss Bolen.

But that was a lie. And there had been enough lies between the Bolens and the Austins.

So instead, Sam retraced his steps and returned to the chair and sat. "I'm listening."

"Very well. In light of the guilt Mr. Bolen felt over the reduced circumstances of the Austin family—"

"Spare the sentiment, please."

The lawyer's bushy brows rose. "Yes, of course." With slow and precise movements, he straightened the corners of the pages in front of him, removed his spectacles, and then folded his hands. "In precisely one hour I will meet with Miss Bolen to inform her of the terms of her father's will. She will understandably be distraught."

Sam allowed the lawyer's statement to go without comment. After a moment, Mr. Breaux's expression softened.

"It is my understanding that your father is still living. Am I correct?"

"You are."

"Your younger brother, Joseph, is a professor at Tulane, and you are a captain of certain vessels of trade that ply the Orient routes. You are a close family who lives by modest means."

Sam shifted positions. "I prefer not to discuss anything other than the terms of this will."

"Fair enough," he said. "I mention these things merely to remind you that a great loss of fortune does not necessarily mean a loss in the quality of life."

"Mr. Breaux, I am confused. You've just warned me that I could be committing Miss Bolen to poverty while reminding me that the poverty her father committed us to wasn't so bad after all. Are you now saying that the Bolen woman losing her fortune is not so awful?"

"I am saying that I believe Mr. Bolen saw something in the Austin family that he did not have in his own family. He and his daughter were, to put it mildly, not particularly close."

Again Sam let the silence fall between them.

Finally the lawyer cleared his throat. "This brings me to my next point: should you accept Mr. Bolen's gift of Bolen Shipping, you are expressly forbidden from using any of the funds associated with the company to assist May Bolen in any way."

So Bolen had been every bit the heartless man Father claimed he was. Sam opened his mouth to respond, but the lawyer held his hand up to silence him.

"Should you feel compelled to assist Miss Bolen, there is one important exception to this clause in the will."

Sam inhaled deeply then let out a long breath. "All right. What is it?"

"She must become your wife."

He laughed. "Not likely, sir."

Mr. Breaux shrugged. "I do understand, but should you change your mind, I must inform you that Miss Bolen can never be told of the terms of her father's will."

"Then you're going to have an awfully short meeting with her in an hour."

The lawyer sat back in his chair and toyed with the edges of his stack of papers. "What

I tell Miss Bolen is scripted entirely from what her father wishes her to know. She will be informed that the fortune will be going elsewhere pending certain conditions. Only you and I will know whether it goes to you or to charity. It will not be an easy meeting for either of us."

"Let me get this straight," he said as he leaned forward. "I either accept ownership of Bolen Shipping or I allow it to be sold for charity. Also, I either marry May Bolen or I allow her to become a charity case, and I cannot tell Miss Bolen any of this."

"That is correct," he said. "Of course, once you're married, should you choose that option, you are free to inform her that you're Bolen Shipping's new owner."

Married to a Bolen. He couldn't even imagine it.

And yet he knew what poverty did to a person.

Sam rose. "You've given me plenty to think about. My first inclination is to walk out of this office and forget any part of this conversation ever happened."

"I would not blame you, sir. The Austin family has been treated most unfairly by Mr. Bolen in the past." He paused. "There's just one more thing, though."

"What is that?"

"You have thirty days to decide whether to accept the terms of the will. On the thirty-first day from today, liquidation of Bolen Shipping will begin and Miss Bolen will become a pauper."

"What is stopping me from striking a deal with Miss Bolen? Who will know?"

Mr. Breaux smiled. "You will know, Mr. Austin, and I suspect your conscience would not allow it." He paused. "However, marriages have been built on far less."

<hr />

One hour later

"Miss Bolen, thank you for coming. I know you've made a long journey from New York City, and I do appreciate that you've made yourself available today."

May offered her father's attorney her most polite smile. "I was made to understand this was a matter of the utmost importance, as was the requirement that I see you today rather than delay."

Though this airless room with its hideous drapes and old-fashioned furniture was not where she wished to be at the moment, she nevertheless did not indicate her displeasure to the older man seated across the desk. It simply was not done.

A lady was gracious at all times—this she learned at her mother's knee. At the thought of her mother, May sat up a bit straighter. Good deportment as well as good posture were the guiding principles of her childhood, and the string of governesses and finishing schools that followed only served to reinforce these teachings.

Mr. Breaux lifted his spectacles to his rather narrow face and turned his attention to the stack of papers before him. These were fresh papers, crisp and white and not at all like the yellowed and curled-at-the-edges documents her father kept in his library at the home on Chartres Street.

Though he appeared about to begin reading, the attorney lifted his attention to catch her gaze over his spectacles. "First allow me to offer condolences on the loss of your father on this, the first anniversary of his death."

May fixed her attention on the oversized painting of the Battle of New Orleans above the fireplace behind him. Though several responses occurred to her, she settled for a simple word of thanks. Anything else might have ventured into the area of untruth. For as much as she was flesh and blood of the man, she knew very little of who he had been, for they'd neither lived under the same roof nor spoken more than a few words since he'd paid a visit to Mama in New York City more than a decade ago.

This she believed was intentional on her father's part, for she'd heard enough from the few others willing to speak of Thomas Bolen to know he was a difficult man at best and a terrible one at worst. Mama remained silent on the subject, though it was the only subject upon which she held her tongue.

"I know it must be difficult contemplating life without your father," May heard him say, drawing her attention back to this room, to this conversation. "I do hope you will call on me should you find yourself in need of any advice or assistance that might have once come from your father."

A lady must remain unruffled and kind despite any unpleasant situation, she recalled as she punctuated Mr. Breaux's statement with a slight lift of the corners of her mouth. To call it a smile would be unfair, but she did make the attempt.

"Mr. Breaux," she said evenly, "I do appreciate your offer, but considering I never called on my father for anything during his lifetime, I doubt I will be availing myself of your generous offer."

"Yes, well, I suppose we should get on with it, then. I should tell you before we begin that your father has been quite specific in what I am to tell you. He does allow in his instructions that I can either read this word for word or I can summarize his wishes in more understandable terms. Which do you prefer?"

Best not to prolong this visit. The sooner her father's affairs were put in order, the sooner she could return home to New York City. "Summarize please."

"Yes, of course." He returned his attention to the document in front of him, shifting a page from the bottom of the stack to the top. "Apparently Mr. Bolen anticipated you would say that, because he has provided a summary, and it is this: Bolen Shipping will be liquidated and its proceeds given to charity unless you take steps to prevent this."

"What?" she managed with the last of her breath. "But that will render my mother and me..."

She could not say it.

Could not imagine it.

In a breath, she went numb.

"Penniless?" Mr. Breaux supplied. At her nod, he said, "Yes, quite, although there is another option that might mitigate the problem."

"Do explain then." May blinked back tears she refused to allow.

He sat back in his chair and steepled his hands. "You could marry."

May shook her head, and with that action some of the numbness fell away. "Marry?"

"Yes, you know. Wed?" He leaned forward again and his chair creaked, the only sound in the room louder than the pounding of May's heart. "Miss Bolen, I have been instructed to tell you that your father's will allows that you will regain access to your father's accounts if you have a husband."

"Well then," she said upon an exhale of breath as hope dawned. This time her smile was quite genuine. "That's quite different than being disinherited altogether. I merely must wed."

She'd certainly had her share of offers, so accepting one of them would not be the worst thing to happen. Given time, May knew she could decide upon a groom who might suit her purpose.

"You have thirty days," the attorney added. "Thirty-one days from today, the process of selling off the company assets will begin and all financial accounts will be frozen."

"Thirty days? That is ridiculous. No woman of quality could be married in such a short time. There would be questions. Society would shun me, not to mention what my mother would do. It simply isn't done."

"I do understand," he said gently, "and might I suggest that a quiet civil marriage might suffice to complete the requirements of your father's will? A more fitting public ceremony could be planned for a later date and no one in society would be any wiser. I'm sure your mother would prefer that to. . ." He paused and seemed to consider his words. "Well, to the alternative."

"Yes," she said slowly as she began to consider her options. Teddy Vanderwellen certainly might be convinced to go along with such a plan, as would either of the Campbell twins.

In any case, Mama would never fare well should either of them be forced to live by their wits.

"Miss Bolen, might I interrupt your thoughts to interject one more important piece of information before I end our time together?"

"Yes, of course," she said as she made a mental note to add that handsome viscount who'd pursued her with a string of ardent letters over the past few years to her list of options. If he were to agree to some sort of marriage by proxy, her problems might be solved.

"There is one important condition attached to the identity of your husband." He paused. "You must have Samuel Austin III's permission in writing in order to marry."

"I'm sorry." She leaned forward, palms on her knees. "Exactly who is Samuel Austin III?"

Chapter Two

One week later

The New Orleans docks at the Mississippi River smelled every bit as awful as May had been warned. A brisk north wind swept down the levee at Canal Street, carrying not only the chill warning of an unseasonably cool day but also the putrid scent of overripe produce, rotting fish, and unwashed bodies.

May tucked her reticule closer to her and picked up her pace as she shrugged closer into her woolen wrap. Though anyone who knew her back home in New York City would be shocked at her unseemly display of haste, there was little chance of recognition here as she hurried toward her destination.

She'd tried this walk just yesterday and had turned around before she reached her destination. Today, however, telegrams offering marriage from Teddy Vanderwellen and both Campbell twins were tucked into her reticule along with a letter of approval for one of them—which he chose did not matter—that Mr. Austin merely had to sign. With just over three weeks left to find a solution, May could not afford to allow her disgust of this vile place to keep her from reaching the man who could set her free from it all.

Stepping over a thick rope, she pointedly ignored the stares of a group of ruffians, who ought to have been minding their work, by returning her attention to the line of vessels tied to the ramshackle docks. Here stacks of cotton, barrels, and crates were lined up higher than May's head, and more just like them were being unloaded all down the docks.

All around her, throngs of persons of questionable background scurried off and on these ships, making for a chaotic walk down the narrow boards that passed for a sidewalk. To make matters worse, black clouds had begun to gather overhead and a rumble of thunder rolled past.

She had paid the detective well for the information, so Mr. Austin's vessel had better be where he claimed. Things would have been much easier if Mr. Breaux had simply answered her question regarding the identity of the man Father put in charge of determining her future.

But no. The attorney could only tell her what Father allowed him to say. And apparently Father had anticipated with great glee the difficulty it would take to acquaint herself with Samuel Austin III.

However, he had not anticipated May's ability to achieve whatever goal she set after. Just another example of how her father hadn't known her at all. She was just as at fault, for had she taken the time to be a proper daughter to him, she might have anticipated this debacle and somehow prevented it.

She stepped into a smear of something slimy and skidded toward a wall of cotton bales. A man stepped in between her and the bales, allowing her to slam into his generously broad shoulders rather than the wall of cotton.

Arms that felt more like bands of steel caught her and held her upright. May looked up into a pair of sea-green eyes fringed by thick black lashes. He wore a workingman's shirt and trousers and had bound his dark hair back with a length of leather, reminding May of the pirates in children's storybooks.

This was no pirate, of course. Their ilk was long gone from the Louisiana waters. And this man, though rugged, bore only a small crescent-shaped scar on his right cheek. Her gaze lifted from the scar back up to his eyes.

Slowly one dark brow lifted. He then released her without a word, though his eyes still held her.

May knew she should return to an errand much more important than anything else, but she remained still. Took just a moment longer to study the curve of his jaw beneath the stubble of a beard and the fullness of his lips as they formed a smile.

"Mademoiselle, you have found me."

She matched his smile and then realized how foolish she must seem. "I must be going," she muttered then made her escape.

A few minutes later, May came to a stuttering halt. There it was, the battered wooden hull of the *Vengeance* wedged between a more elegantly sleek sailing ship and an overloaded merchant vessel that looked as if it would sink under the weight of its cargo.

This was the home of the man who held her destiny—and the purse strings to her father's accounts—in his hands. What had Father been thinking?

She knew the answer to that question, of course. He'd been thinking that he would take one last opportunity from beyond the grave to voice his displeasure by saddling her with an impossible situation. And not just her, but her mother.

A lady does not dwell on the unpleasant. May straightened her backbone even as she felt the eyes of nearby dockworkers on her.

Though she had been informed the vessel was not the most luxurious, she had not been prepared for its current state of dishabille. Like its owner, the detective had warned.

The down-on-its-luck *Vengeance* bore traces of a former glory in the ornately carved woman decorating the prow and the glints of gold paint on the masts. Three masts pointed skyward, though the centermost of the trio appeared to have been recently repaired.

May paused to consider whether the boat was seaworthy. While it wasn't the most unpleasant ship rocking at anchor, it was by no means a vessel she would willingly board under any other circumstance. But she boarded it now, striding up the makeshift gangplank as if she owned the miserable thing.

Bolen Shipping likely owned a number of the ships surrounding this one and all down the river, though May never cared to step aboard any of them. If her mission here went well, perhaps she never would have to.

If she failed. . .

"No," she said under her breath as she held tight to the reticule that held her key to a future outside of this wretched city. "I simply cannot fail."

Glancing around the deck, May thought the vessel unattended until she spied something moving beneath a mildewing pile of burlap.

May reached over to pick up a length of wood off a stack near the burlap. Wielding the stick, she poked at the burlap, and the movement ceased.

Then she spied the fingers reaching out from beneath the fabric.

————•◆•————

She hadn't recognized him. That was the only explanation for the Bolen woman's behavior.

From his vantage point on the docks, Sam had spied May Bolen heading toward him well before she nearly landed in the cotton bales. Thanks to her father's will, at the top of the list of trouble Sam inherited along with the family name was the slip of a woman boarding his ship as if she owned it and the entire Canal Street docks.

Of course, rich girls like her were taught from the cradle how to walk like that. How to assume the world and everything in it were theirs for the taking.

After the Bolen woman's first attempt to walk the length of the docks yesterday, something a woman of her quality should never have done, he had made it known the striking brunette was not to be accosted. The warning served to reduce the usual abuse a female might have endured to something akin to lecherous stares.

She wore yellow that day. Today she had chosen a gown of pale blue, and given the fact her nose was in the air, she was likely oblivious to the smears of mud decorating her hemline.

Sam gave her another long look and thought of how she felt in his arms. If she weren't a Bolen, she might have been worthy of more than just a second look. But she was a Bolen, and she must know that he held her future in his hands.

"What is she doing?"

Sam glanced over his shoulder as his brother, Joseph, approached from the opposite direction. He frowned. As much as possible, he tried to shield Joe from the unseemly world of the docks. Protecting the younger Austin was a cause he'd taken up at a young age. While he was meant for this wild and ugly place, gently raised Joe, the mama's boy, was much more suited to his chosen life as a college professor.

"Her?" he asked with a nod toward the Bolen woman. "I believe she's looking for me."

Joe ran his hand through his hair, a gesture so reminiscent of their father that it hurt. "Who is that?"

Sam gave a moment's thought to telling his brother the story of the will and what this soon-to-be poor little rich girl likely wanted from him. But to repeat the story was to bring Joe into something he had no business knowing about yet.

Not until Sam decided what he was going to do about all of it.

"No one you'd know."

"Whoever she is, she's sure not suited for the docks." Joe shifted his attention away from the woman to slide him a sideways look. "What business would she have with us?"

"I suspect her business is with me, but I think I'll just wait and see."

"Why's she poking that pile of sails? Wharf rats?" Joe said.

"Not on my vessel, though it could be a stray dog or cat." He shrugged. "Or worse."

"Worse?"

Sam nodded. "More likely one of those deckhands I hired on last week."

They watched in silence as the lady in question made a circular trip around the pile and then raised the stick only to lower it again. If, indeed, there were cats or dogs hiding there, she'd get a nasty surprise when they scattered. If a lazy crewman was sleeping, which was the more likely possibility, the surprise would be worse.

Once again the woman raised the stick. Something caught her attention.

"Shouldn't you stop her?" Joe demanded.

"I'm sorely tempted not to," he said. "But I have far too much trouble keeping good deckhands."

"You know you can always call on me," Joe said, his eyes narrowed. "I'm as much an Austin as you are, and as such am fully capable of doing any work on an Austin vessel that needs done."

Sam clamped his hand on Joe's shoulder. "Stick to the classroom, Professor. You're not suited for that sort of work, and even if you were, I made a promise to our mother and I won't break it."

"You know how I feel about that promise you made not to—oh no!" Joe gestured toward May Bolen, who held the stick poised over her head like a warrior about to go to battle.

"Woman, drop your weapon," Sam called, but as soon as he said the words, he knew they were too late. The Bolen woman slammed the stick against the sails hard enough to be heard over the noise of the docks.

Sam scrambled forward, colliding with a workman and his load of barrels. The barrels went rolling in all directions, and the workman came up swinging.

As Sam ducked the smaller man's right fist, he spied his formerly sleeping deckhand emerge from the sails to tackle the source of his pain. "Let her go," Sam shouted, taking his attention off the workman.

Something cracked against his skull, sending him down onto the slime that coated the docks. A second later, the fellow landed with a thud beside him.

"Need a hand?" Joe asked as he reached down to help him to his feet.

"Where'd you learn to do that?" he demanded as he rubbed the back of his head.

Before Joe could respond, a scream split the air. Though the deckhand was still fighting the sailcloth wrapped around him, he had managed to knock the Bolen woman off her feet and was holding her in place with his free hand.

As Miss Bolen scrambled to try and get away, Sam bolted toward the gangplank. Snatching up the edge of the sail, he gave it a yank. The deckhand fell backward, releasing Miss Bolen, who spun around and slammed into Sam.

He caught her. "Mademoiselle, we meet again," he said to her.

"Release me," she demanded as she pressed her palms against his chest.

Sam let her go then grabbed her elbow once again when she nearly tumbled. "Easy now. You'll need time to adapt to standing on a deck."

"I do not intend to take any more time than necessary." Her eyes flashed anger. "Do stop following me."

"Mademoiselle, I believe it is you who are following me," he said. "And perhaps you're trying to find me?"

"Only if you are Samuel Austin III, though I would seriously doubt you if you made the claim that you are he."

He slid a sideways glance at Joe, who had come to stand beside him. With his brother's grin broadening, Sam shrugged.

"Well then, I suppose you've got a better idea of who Samuel Austin III is and where he might be?"

For the first time since she marched aboard the *Vengeance*, Miss Bolen looked less than sure of herself. "My source says he owns this vessel and often stays aboard."

"Your source?" Sam said. "Might he have a name?"

"He does indeed, and a very prominent name at that." She paused. "However I'll not be revealing anything to a man of your sort."

"And what sort is that?"

"Well, the sort who would follow me and. . .oh, I don't know," she said, clearly flustered. "I am not looking for trouble, only just to find Samuel Austin III."

"If you were not looking for trouble, you should not have taken a stick to an innocent man," he said as he nodded toward the deckhand now glowering at them from a safe distance. "A man who will apologize and then leave us."

At his subtle command, the deckhand moved a few steps forward to mutter words that might have been a request for forgiveness. As soon as the request was out, the man had disappeared below deck.

"There," Sam said. "Now tell me about this Austin character."

Joe chuckled under his breath, causing Sam to elbow him in the ribs. Miss Bolen's nervous attention skittered between Joe and Sam, finally settling on Sam.

"I believe you are toying with me, sir," she said as she straightened her backbone and squared her shoulders.

"For what purpose?"

"I cannot say, though I merely wish to deliver a. . ." She looked down and then back up at Sam, her expression now distraught. "Oh no. My reticule. I've lost it." Ignoring the conversation at hand, she wandered away with her attention now on the deck.

He nudged Joe. "Help her find whatever she's looking for."

Leaning against the mainsail with his arms crossed, Sam watched the pretty lady scour the deck while Joe walked the perimeter of the vessel. "I think I see it," Joe shouted a few minutes later as he gestured to the water on the leeward side.

Miss Bolen stood beside him and then seemed to crumple. Sam hurried over in case he needed to catch her for the third time. There, floating in the river between the *Vengeance* and the next vessel was a beaded bag with strings flowing out of one end.

He fetched a net and scooped up the bag, depositing it onto the deck along with three dead fish, a rotting piece of fruit, and a length of rope. When he lifted the bag from the soggy, stinking mess, a lump of pale-colored pulp fell out.

"Oh no," she said as she dove for the pulp, and then moaned when it disintegrated in her hands. For the first time since May Bolen came aboard the *Vengeance*, she appeared to be at a loss as to what to say or do.

"Something important?" Sam asked.

"More than that," she said, her voice barely above a whisper against the noise of the riverfront docks. "I thought with these documents I might have. . ."

A tear slid down her cheek, and Sam reached up to swipe it away.

"Mademoiselle"—he said gently as he wrapped his arm around her shoulder and led her toward the gangplank—"I see you are in distress. Perhaps I can help. This Samuel Austin III. What if I were able to deliver him to you? Or you to him?"

Eyes the color of café au lait lifted to meet his gaze. "It's him, isn't it?" she said as she nodded toward Joe.

Sam laughed.

"I knew it was," she said as she whirled around and ducked under his arm to march over to where Joe stood. "Good sir," she said. "Am I correct in my guess? Are you Samuel Austin III?"

Joe opened his mouth to respond, but Sam shook his head. Until he had more time to consider his next move, he intended to use her disbelief to his advantage.

Joe closed his mouth and then began again. "I am not," he said. "However, he is my brother. Would you like me to arrange a meeting?"

"I would like that very much," she said sweetly. "Mr. . . . Austin, isn't it?"

"It is. Joseph Austin at your service."

Her eyes narrowed. "I hope you'll understand my reluctance to rely on your word alone," she said. "You see, this is a matter of extreme urgency and I must be certain to whom I am speaking."

Though Sam shook his head again, Joe ignored him. "In that case, meet me at my office at Tulane University tomorrow morning at ten. I am a professor in the mathematics department. Would the plaque with my name on my office door convince you of my identity?"

"Possibly," she said, "although I will have to check the notes from my source to be certain a brother is listed in Mr. Austin's dossier. Might I bring my detective with me?"

"I insist," Joe said as he shot Sam a grin. "After all, I would hate to think of you traveling unaccompanied. As a matter of fact, I am concerned as to where your escort might be. Surely you did not come down to the docks alone."

While Joe made a big show of looking around for the Bolen woman's escort, May Bolen's expression told Sam she was enjoying the attention. Before Sam could convey a warning to his brother, Joe had talked May Bolen into allowing him to escort her off the docks.

By the time Joe returned, Sam had worked up a powerful irritation. "What were you thinking, Joseph?" he demanded as soon as his brother boarded the *Vengeance*.

"I was thinking that a pretty lady needed an escort, and she certainly wasn't going to allow you to be the man to do that. Besides, she made it plain she didn't want to spend time with you."

"And yet tomorrow you're going to tell her how to find me."

"Well, yes, that's the purpose for the meeting," he admitted. "Don't act like it's my fault. You could have tried harder to convince her of your identity."

"I'll speak with her on my own terms when I'm ready."

"Now that's an odd statement, Sam," his brother said. "She's quite pleasant. I enjoyed chatting with her."

"In all the chatting you did on your way up the docks, did you happen to ask that pretty lady her name?" Before Joe could respond, Sam continued. "I know you did not. How did I know, you might ask?" He paused. "Because that woman you just spent time flirting with is May Bolen."

"As in Bolen Shipping?" Joe shook his head. "Why would a Bolen be looking for you?"

"That, Joseph, is a much longer conversation that I don't want to have out here on this boat. Let's go back to your office, and I'll tell you all about it."

"All right"—he said as he fell into step beside Sam—"but tell me one thing. Is Miss Bolen single or spoken for? I find her fascinating."

"The answer to that question, little brother," he said with a grin, "is up to me."

Chapter Three

May Bolen never allowed nerves to interfere with anything she wished to accomplish. Nor did she fidget.

As she waited for Samuel Austin III's arrival, however, she did both. Finally, she settled her attention on Mr. Breaux.

"Remind me, sir," she said as evenly as she could manage. "The man who walks through that door is the man who will determine whom I marry and whether I am to remain within reach of my father's accounts or out on the street."

The attorney had the good sense to look away. "Much as I dislike it, Miss Bolen, the answer is yes. That is exactly what Mr. Austin will be deciding."

"I met his brother, as you know." She waited until Mr. Breaux was looking at her again. "He's a very nice man. A professor of mathematics at Tulane. I do hope the elder brother is as pleasant as the younger one."

"I have been told I am not," a decidedly masculine voice said. "Although it was quite kind of Joe to see that you believed him enough to call on Mr. Breaux and agree to this meeting."

May turned to see a familiar face at the door. "You again." She looked over at Mr. Breaux. "I do apologize. Apparently this man has decided to once again interject himself into my life. I suggest you call for assistance in removing him."

"I cannot do that, Miss Bolen, but I can make proper introductions," the attorney said. "May Bolen, may I present Samuel Austin III. Mr. Austin, it appears you have already met Miss Bolen."

"I have," he said as he fixed a smile on her.

"What?" she managed. "But you cannot be. . ." She paused to shake her head and then gave up speaking in favor of merely staring.

The pirate was the man who would decide her fate? Surely not.

In contrast to yesterday's workingman's clothing, Samuel Austin III wore a gentleman's suit of decent but slightly worn construction and had replaced his boots with a pair of proper men's shoes. He'd also shaved since their encounters on the dock and aboard the *Vengeance*, though his hair was still overlong and in need of a trim.

And somehow, he still looked like a pirate.

"You are Joseph's brother?" She shook her head. "I don't believe it."

"My dear departed mother often voiced the same thought," he said. "It is a source of pride that my brother has made better of himself and is now associated with a university. However, it is also a source of pride that I have made my own way in the world. I'll not apologize for the calluses on my hands or the fact that I did not inherit the money that pays my bills."

"Well said"—she snapped as her anger rose—"although I doubt you'll also apologize for whatever influence you used over my father to cause him to put you in charge of such an important decision in my life. Was it blackmail, sir, or did you use those callused hands to threaten bodily harm?"

Ignoring her question, Samuel Austin III returned his attention to Mr. Breaux. "Thank you for facilitating our meeting," he told him as he crossed the room.

The attorney greeted Mr. Austin with a formal shake of hands and then spared May a quick glance before hurrying out and shutting the door behind him. Suddenly the air seemed to go out of the room. May rose and went to the window, turning her back on Mr. Austin.

What an arrogant man. And yet she must somehow find a way to charm him into doing her bidding. Until she could secure his permission to accept one of her offers of marriage, she was at the wrong end of a situation that could end in disaster.

A lady is pleasant, even to the unpleasant. She mustered a smile, though it took several attempts. When May turned around, fully prepared to offer that smile to the ruffian, she found him sitting behind Mr. Breaux's desk watching her.

"Please sit." He indicated the chair she'd just left. "I do not believe in wasting time or words, so I would like to get on with this."

"Yes, of course," she said sweetly. "Though I do wonder if you'll enlighten me as to how you came to have the upper hand over me in my father's will. Perhaps we can begin our meeting with the answer to that question."

"The answer is, I have no idea."

She sat back and gave up on trying to charm him. "Forgive me if I don't believe you. This whole thing sounds preposterous."

"Might I interrupt?" Mr. Breaux peered around the partially open door. "You see, I couldn't help but overhear your conversation and, well, I may be able to shed some light on the subject."

"Please do," May said.

"With the understanding that I am legally obliged to keep Mr. Bolen's secrets unless he has expressly allowed me to speak of them, I can tell you, Miss Bolen, that your father was of sound mind when he chose Mr. Austin. And, Mr. Austin, you should know that he was specific in his choices and that he had very good reasons for them, even to choosing the first anniversary of his death to reveal the terms of his will."

May looked away. She knew the reasons, and they all amounted to the fact that she'd been a terrible daughter and was now reaping what she had sown. While she may deserve this, however, Mama did not.

"Just one more thing," Mr. Breaux said, his voice rising. "For better or worse, the two of you are inextricably tied together for the time being. As you've both been told, on the thirty-first day, the company begins to be dismantled and your time to work together for a mutually beneficial outcome will be gone. Considering you have less than three weeks until the deadline, I suggest the two of you put aside your suspicions and differences and figure out a way to solve the problem that Mr. Bolen has saddled you with."

"I had a perfectly good solution," May said. "In fact, had I not been accosted on this man's boat and lost my reticule and its contents to the river, I would have proof of three excellent offers of marriage to discuss with Mr. Austin."

"Without proof there are no offers, Miss Bolen," Mr. Austin said.

"I assure you I can obtain proof. I will just need time."

"Time is something neither of us has," he said.

The attorney exchanged an odd look with Mr. Austin. "That is regretful," he said when he returned his attention to May. "However I am certain you and Mr. Austin will come to some sort of agreement. Now if you don't mind, I did allow for an introduction at my office, but I am afraid my time is also short. I have another appointment waiting, so perhaps you will take this conversation elsewhere?"

"I was under the assumption we could use your office. I do not know this man. How can I be seen alone with him?"

Mr. Austin rose abruptly to walk around the desk. "Miss Bolen, at the moment your reputation is the least of your concerns. Let's give the man his office back."

✦

Sam wasn't sure the Bolen woman would cooperate, so when she did, he didn't waste any time getting her out of the building. They'd reached the street before she did as he expected and stalled.

He placed his palm at the small of her back and urged her gently forward. "Miss Bolen, I do not care if you decline or accept my invitation to relocate our meeting. It's not me who stands to lose everything."

"Point taken," she said in a voice that made him regret his harsh tone. "Where do you propose we go?"

Waving away the liveried driver with the Bolen Shipping crest on his lapel, Sam offered Miss Bolen his arm. "Not far."

After a short walk, he halted in front of the Bolen Shipping offices. "After you," he said as he held open one of the ornate double doors with the company emblem carved into them.

This time she seemed more frozen in place than reluctant.

"You'll have to lead the way," he told her. "I've never been here."

She looked up at him, tears shimmering. "Neither have I."

The pain in her voice threatened to stall him right there in the fancy lobby. Instead, he took hold of her elbow and led her across the marble floor to an ornate staircase trimmed in gold. Though he'd spent his life in much less grand circumstances, it didn't take a rich man to figure out the boss's office was most likely on the topmost floor.

So he kept walking up those stairs, his grip on the Bolen woman's elbow just firm enough to keep her moving, until he ran out of stairs. From there, he followed the fancy carpet all the way to the end of the hall where it stopped at a pair of double doors that were a scaled-down version of the ones they'd come through to enter the building.

The Bolen woman shrugged out of his grip to step closer to the doors. Reaching up to rest her palm on the doorknob, she closed her eyes.

"Miss Bolen," he said. "I rarely ask this question of a woman, but I wonder what you're thinking."

"I'm trying not to," was her whispered reply.

Sam gently moved her aside and opened the double doors. Though he had few memories of the mansion on Royal Street where he'd been born, he could recollect his father's office at the shipping company. In comparison, this room—which took up fully half of the upper floor of the building—looked as if it belonged to European royalty rather than a man of commerce.

Anything that could be covered in gold or intricately carved had been, from the chairs scattered around the room to the chandeliers overhead. The walls were so crowded with framed paintings that appeared to be Old Masters that the gilded wallpaper beneath could barely be seen. Swags of crimson velvet drapes trimmed with golden fringe blocked out the sunshine and cast the room in a gloomy light.

Without a word, Miss Bolen walked over to that window and pulled the drapes back to flood the office with sunlight. After turning to face him, she gasped.

"What?" he demanded.

Rather than respond, she continued to look at something behind him. Turning slowly, Sam let out a low whistle.

Filling the wall was a larger-than-life portrait, predictably framed in the same gold-painted wood as the others in the room. Unlike the Old Masters paintings elsewhere in the office, judging from the subject matter, this one was painted recently.

"It's me," Miss Bolen whispered.

And it was, although Miss Bolen was only one of the dozen figures that appeared to be frozen in time while attending some sort of fancy ball. However, while everyone else was captured from a distance and appearing to be in motion, the Bolen woman stood perfectly still, her smiling face peering around her dancing partner to look directly at the artist.

Her hair was elaborately done up with what looked like pearl combs, and she wore strands of pearls around her neck and encircling the arm that reached around to grasp her escort's shoulder. Very little of her dress was visible, but what could be seen was white.

The subject of the painting brushed past him to stand before her image. Slowly she reached out to press her palm against the canvas.

"I don't understand," she said to Sam when he moved to stand beside her. "I haven't seen my father since I was a child. How could he. . . ?" Her voice faded away as her hand dropped to her side.

Sam shrugged. "Perhaps a gift from your mother?"

Her laugh held no humor. "I doubt that. There was little love left between them when they parted. I doubt she would consider doing this or, for that matter, allow it to be done."

"So you did not pose for this?"

Miss Bolen looked up at him, unshed tears shimmering in her eyes. "I've never seen that ballroom in my life nor worn those pearls or that dress, so no, I can safely say I did not."

Just as he'd done at the attorney's office, Sam grasped her elbow and led her away from the painting and toward a pair of chairs situated in front of her father's desk. Once she'd settled there, Sam considered the chair behind the desk but chose the place across from Miss Bolen instead.

"So here we are," he said.

"Yes," she responded, her voice shaky. "Here we are."

"I know you have questions about the situation we're in, and so do I," Sam said. "But I don't think either of us—"

The door flew open and an older woman, willowy thin and nearly as tall as Sam, stepped inside. "Who are you?" she demanded as she crossed the room at a surprisingly swift pace. "Oh," came out as a soft cry when she stopped in front of Miss Bolen. "It's you."

"I'm sorry," Sam said as he stood. "Who are you?"

"I'm Roselyn Gallier, Miss Bolen, your father's business partner."

Sam's surprise must have shown, because the older woman turned to him. "I am left to assume you are Mr. Austin."

"I am," he said as he shook her hand. "Breaux did not mention he had a business partner."

"Well, no, I don't suppose he would have. Thomas bought out my part of the business a few months before he died with the request that I stay on until the transition was complete."

"Transition," Miss Bolen said. "That's an interesting way to put it."

"An accurate one, I do believe; but in any case, I'm going to be your new best friend," she said with a chuckle, "because I know where all his important papers are as well as where he kept the key to the safe and the home on Chartres Street. But if you're here, well, you probably already know all of these things."

"I know none of these," Miss Bolen admitted. "I've been staying at a hotel. I wasn't certain what the arrangements would be so. . ."

She reached over to pat Miss Bolen on the shoulder. "You let those tears out now," she said. "Losing a papa, it doesn't ever come easy no matter the situation. Just know that he loved you very much."

"I don't know that at all," she snapped. "In fact, I am appalled at his treatment of me in his will and completely confused as to why he has a portrait of me that I never posed for. I am also appalled that you would think you knew how he felt about someone with whom he never made the attempt to know."

"Your father was a complicated man. Stubborn as a man could be and yet the Lord got hold of him anyway. He told me before he died that his greatest wish was to go back in time and fix what he'd broken in his life."

"A convenient response considering," Miss Bolen said.

Her eyes narrowed. "I'd say it was most inconvenient, what with the two biggest regrets in his life being how he conducted his business and how little time he spent with his only child."

"Yes, well, I have your word to take for it because I certainly heard nothing of the kind from him. However, I will have that key to my father's home. As I am apparently going to be destitute soon, staying at the Hotel Monteleone seems like an unnecessary expense."

"Yes, of course. You'll find the staff is paid through next month, so there shouldn't be any inconveniences for you staying there. I'll see that a key is delivered to the Monteleone for you within the hour."

"Wasn't that nice of him?" she said in a most sarcastic tone before turning her attention to Sam. "I think our attempt at conversation is over for today."

To punctuate her statement, Miss Bolen turned her back on them both and walked toward the door.

"Then I will call on you tomorrow," Sam said. "At your father's home."

She stopped short and whirled around, likely unaware that the expression on her face mirrored the one on her image in the painting. "Mr. Austin, my father may have appointed you guardian of my future, but you are not guardian of my present. I shall meet you when and where I wish and if I wish. Do you understand that?"

"You have less than three weeks left before any arrangement between us means nothing. Are you sure you want to be so difficult?"

She looked away. "All right, then. Half past ten tomorrow. I'm sure Miss Gallier can provide the address."

"That's Mrs. Gallier, and yes, I can do that." When the door shut behind Miss Bolen, the older woman reached over to touch his sleeve. "Now don't you mind her. From what I know about all this, she's not had an easy go of things despite the fact she was born in luxury. Having more money than love is not good for anyone."

"I'll have to trust you on that," he told her. "My father was a lousy businessman, but we never had to wonder how he felt about us or our mother, rest her soul."

Mrs. Gallier gave him an appraising look. "Yes, you're Samuel's son. How is he?"

"You knew him?" At her nod, Sam shrugged. "Determined to outlive us all but failing miserably."

Her smile was broad and quick. "Well, I do like to hear that he has lived a good life. I wondered given, well. . ." She paused. "Water under the bridge, all that. Look, I do not know the particulars of whatever it is that will requires you to do, but I do know one thing. That painting over there, Thomas commissioned it exactly as you see it. He gave that poor artist such grief until every detail was just right."

Sam walked over to the painting as he listened to Mrs. Gallier. Up close the brushstrokes and colors showed the artist was possessed of a unique talent.

"Do you know what the title of this painting is, Mr. Austin?" When he shook his head, she continued. "May's Wedding."

He let that thought settle as he said his goodbyes.

Chapter Four

May stifled a yawn. Perhaps tomorrow she would actually climb the stairs and seek out a proper bedchamber, but last night she'd barely managed to find a soft chair to rest for a few hours.

While sleep had evaded her, regrets and memories had not. Those had chased her through the rooms she'd managed to walk and swirled around her even after she'd given up trying to ascend the staircase.

Mama and her friends in New York would be aghast to see her now. Even as she had the thought, May couldn't think of a single one of them she expected would still call her a friend once word got out that she had married in haste.

Or worse, that she was penniless.

The benefit to all her sleepless hours, however, was the time she had to consider how to best remedy her situation. Though several plans had occurred to her, each of them was tripped up by one thing. By one person.

And that person was Samuel Austin III.

If her father's servants thought it odd that she chose to sleep in a chair in her father's library and to wash and dress in an empty room tucked off in a remote corner of the first floor, they were too discreet to say so. Even the girl who brought her morning meal had kept her eyes downcast and avoided looking anywhere but at the tray overflowing with food May would eventually ignore.

She wanted to tell them all that it wasn't fear that kept her from climbing those stairs but guilt. Guilt and a profound sadness.

Her father's butler appeared at the door. "Mr. Austin is here to see you, Miss Bolen."

"Please send him in," she said as she rose to pinch her cheeks and smooth her hair back into place. After exchanging a greeting with Samuel Austin, she returned to her chair and indicated that he should take a seat.

"You're prompt," she said as the grandfather clock in the hallway chimed half past ten.

"I work for a living, Miss Bolen. Being prompt is generally required of a man like me." He paused. "But we're not here to talk about me, are we?"

"Aren't we?" May let that question settle between them before she continued. "After all, I have no power in this odd situation we've both been put into. You're the one who will be making the choice, so in that case, I think that talking about you is exactly why we are here."

Mr. Austin acknowledged her statement with a dip of his head but remained silent. Finally he shrugged. "Then help me make the choice," he said.

"And how do I do that?"

"Tell me about those alleged offers you've had," he said. "The ones you've purported to have brought me aboard the *Vengeance*."

"The telegrams I delivered to you were real indeed, Mr. Austin," she snapped. Oh, how this man irritated her. "And if I had not been treated so poorly while aboard your vessel, I would still have them to offer as evidence. As such, I have sent responses asking for another telegram from each of them."

"If you had not come aboard my vessel uninvited, and had you not prodded my deck-hand with a stick, you would indeed still have them." Mr. Austin shifted positions. "Look," he said as he leaned forward and rested his elbows on his knees. "I am no more happy about any of this than you are, so can we agree to work together to solve our mutual problem?"

"Of course," she said as sweetly as she could manage. "And how do you propose we go about this?"

"Tell me about these three offers. Who are these gallant men who are willing to marry you on such short notice?"

May searched his face for signs that he might be teasing her. When she saw none, she nodded. "I realize it may be difficult for you to understand that I could find three men to make offers of marriage so quickly, but truly all three of them—and several more—have been making offers regularly for quite some time. You see"—she said as she paused to consider her words— "when a woman lives at a certain level of comfort and ease, gentlemen tend to gravitate toward her."

"So what you're saying is rich girls get marriage proposals pretty regularly?" Mr. Austin sat back in his chair and seemed to be pondering his own question. "If these three men are making offers to you due to your 'level of comfort and ease,' then that does not speak highly of them, does it?"

"I disagree. All three of them are well thought of in the community and among our set. Why, I can name a dozen charities that have benefitted from each of them. And many more likely that I do not know about. Each has his own high level of financial comfort as well."

He crossed his arms over his chest. The expression on his face told her he was completely unconvinced.

"All right," she said as she held her hands up. "You tell me what you want to know about them."

"Nothing you could say would give me good reason to say yes to any man I have not met."

May's breath caught. "Are you serious?"

"Quite."

"You'd ask three men to drop everything and hurry to New Orleans so that you can look them over like prize racehorses?" She paused for effect. "Truly?"

"No," Mr. Austin said. "I would not."

"Well, that's more like it."

He shifted positions but held her gaze. "You would. After all, it is up to you to bring the offers to me. I merely make the choice."

Several responses came to mind, but none of them would be beneficial to achieve what she wanted from this man. So she smiled. And then she offered a slight nod of her head.

"You know, this does not have to be so difficult, Mr. Austin. Wouldn't it be easier to simply take my word for it that these are men whose reputations are sterling and with whom I am willing to spend my life? Must everything be so difficult?"

"The easy way is rarely the best." Mr. Austin's gaze swept the length of her, and then he shook his head. "Miss Bolen, do you believe in a loving God?"

What an odd question. "Of course I believe in God."

"That isn't what I asked. I want to know if you view your heavenly Father in the same way you apparently saw your earthly father. If you think He is good and loves you." He paused. "Because I don't believe you thought the same of Thomas Bolen."

"Thomas Bolen was content to live without me. I would hope that God did not wish to abandon me, although there were times. . ."

"Times when what?" he urged.

May shook her head. What was it about this man that made her want to unburden her thoughts on him? "Times when I felt that my heavenly Father might be as far away as my earthly one. Or, at least it felt that way."

"I do understand," he said.

"So you are estranged from your father, too?"

"Quite the opposite," he said. "I see him almost every day when I am in port and write him daily when I am not."

"Oh," she said as she felt the slightest twinge of jealousy. What might it feel like to have that sort of relationship with a parent? Sadly, she would never know.

"But I digress. I asked for your thoughts on God because I want to understand whether you believe the Lord can have your best interests in mind when plans are interrupted or life changes abruptly. A good father always protects his children, even when the children do not always understand they are being protected."

"So you believe I am being protected from something by being cast into this untenable situation?"

"I would rather know whether you believe that."

May rose to walk over to the window. Though there was a lovely garden just beyond the glass, she looked beyond the beauty to the brick wall that protected her from the world outside. That sort of protection she understood. The kind this man was claiming for her made no sense at all.

Finally she turned around to lean against the windowsill. "I confess I cannot reconcile the situation."

"Meaning?"

"Meaning if my father truly cared what happened to me, why did he not leave me cared for? Why didn't he provide a roof over my head and an allowance on which to live?" She straightened but remained by the window. "And why wouldn't a loving God intervene to cause my father to do that?"

"So you want God to make you safe and happy?" he said. "To see that you do not experience any discomfort or have any questions as to how your life will turn out. That is your definition of a loving God and a loving father?"

"It is," she said as she focused on the tiny scar on his cheek rather than the man himself.

"Then you and I will have to agree to disagree."

May crossed her arms over her chest. "I fail to see why. Do you have children, Mr. Austin?"

"I've never been married, Miss Bolen, so no, I do not."

She smiled. "So all of this is based on what? Theory? Some sort of significant study of biblical texts? Perhaps a sermon you once heard?"

Mr. Austin rose to come and stand in front of her. "All of this is based on experience, Miss Bolen. You see, my earthly father's greatest failure was in the area of making life comfortable and easy for his children. Despite his best efforts, he lost his company, his home, and eventually his wife. And yet my brother and I never doubted his love."

"Oh," she managed, as much in response to the intensity of his words as to the nearness of him. She slipped past him to return to her chair though she stood behind it rather than sitting once more. "Your father sounds like a wonderful man. Congratulations on that."

"This is not a contest, Miss Bolen."

"But it is, if you think about it. I either win or I lose, and in either case, you—a complete stranger—are the one who decides." She met his even gaze. "You'll forgive me if I remain skeptical that a loving God would allow something like that."

"Let's just see what God does," he said. "And in the meantime, let's talk about the issue of my meeting your prospective suitors. Why don't you just see who is willing to make the trip and then we'll go from there?"

May opened her mouth to protest, but he held up his hand to silence her. Her fingers gripped the back of the chair as she bit back words she might regret.

"In the meantime, I've brought a list of questions I would like to have answered." He retrieved an envelope from his pocket and held it out in her direction. "Just some basic information so that I can learn more about you."

She accepted the envelope and then dropped it onto the chair. "This is highly irregular."

"So is our situation, don't you think?"

May retrieved the envelope and opened it, pulling out the pages. The first few questions concerned her likes and dislikes. "Broccoli and a warm bath," she said, answering the first two.

"Please write them in the spaces provided," he told her.

As she continued to scan the questions, her irritation rose. "On which side of the bed do I sleep? Do I prefer my toast buttered or with jam?" Again she dropped the papers onto the chair. "This is ridiculous."

"This is valuable information," he told her. "Although it is just part of the information I need in order to make a decision. I do hope you'll cooperate. We only have a few weeks until the deadline."

He'd bested her with that statement, and his expression told her he knew it. May, however, was not prepared to give in so easily. "Fine," she said with a polite nod. "I shall endeavor to answer each of these questions with the care this document deserves."

"Good." Mr. Austin's voice held a tone of wariness. "When can I expect your answers?"

She upped her smile. "Oh, I shall begin work on these just as soon as you and I return from our errand."

"An errand? I don't recall mentioning any such thing."

"You haven't," she said. "But what you've just said has me thinking. How can I possibly know you well enough to present a man who meets your approval if I do not find out more about you?"

Mr. Austin's grin began as a slight rise at the corners of his mouth. As he appeared to consider her question, the smile grew. "Yes, all right," he said with the hint of a chuckle. "I suppose that's fair."

"Oh, it's more than fair, as is the list of questions you'll be presented with as soon as I find the time to write them out." She paused and gave him an appraising look. "A few have already come to mind, such as have you ever sustained a significant blow to the head? I suspect you will answer that in the affirmative."

Now the laughter sounded genuine. "Fair enough. And I shall endeavor to answer each of those questions with the care the document deserves," he said, echoing her words to him.

"Fair enough indeed. Now if you'll excuse me, I'll just get my things and we will be off."

May stepped into the foyer to find the butler wearing a worried look. "Miss Bolen," he stammered, "I fear there's a problem."

"What is it?"

He nodded toward the stairs. "There's been a delivery for you. Mrs. Gallier says she must personally see that you receive it. I tried to stop her, really I did, but she just went on past me of her own accord. I am sorry, Miss Bolen."

"Mrs. Gallier from my father's office?" At his nod, she added, "Where is she?"

Diverting his eyes, he replied, "Up in your bedchamber, I'm afraid."

"Do see to Mr. Austin. Let him know I may be a minute longer than anticipated and offer him refreshments."

May turned toward the staircase, an imposing matched set of stairs that curved around to meet in the center halfway to the second floor. She paused on the landing with her heart slamming against her chest, not from exertion, but from dread of reaching the second floor.

Of stepping into a bedchamber she'd last left as a small child.

"There you are," Mrs. Gallier called from the top of the stairs. "Do forgive the imposition, but a thought occurred after you left yesterday and I realized I had a situation in need of a remedy."

"That seems to be happening to me quite frequently since I arrived in New Orleans," May muttered as she joined Mrs. Gallier in the second-floor hallway. "So what is this situation in need of remedy, exactly?"

"Come with me, child, and I will show you."

She led May down the hall to the last bedchamber on the right—the room across from the one that had once been May's—and gestured for her to step inside. To her recollection, this bedchamber had been saved for visitors. Nothing seemed to have changed, as the canopy bed and both south-facing windows were still hung in white lace and the walls were still covered with wallpaper depicting pink roses climbing trellises.

In the midst of all this, an ugly black garment lay draped across the bed. Mrs. Gallier gestured toward it.

"Do you know what this is?"

She did. "It is a mourning gown," she said as she fingered the jet buttons that traveled down the front of the bodice.

"Then you know why I've brought it." Mrs. Gallier moved to stand beside her. "I know you and your father weren't close, but here in New Orleans it is a sign of respect to our loved ones that we wear mourning attire."

She noticed for the first time that the older woman was also clad in black. "Was my father a loved one to you?"

"He was," she said with a wistful smile. "But not in the sense you're probably thinking. He was a good man, May, though I doubt you got to see that side of him."

"And you did?"

"Oh yes, as did my husband. You see, your father was a fixer. Do you know what that is?" She waited for May to indicate that she did not before continuing. "A fixer is a person who comes into a situation and believes he's got to make it right. Now before you scoff, listen. He wasn't always that way. When I first started to work for him, well, let's just say he was not an easy man to spend time with. But then neither was I, so we developed an understanding. I was a war widow with little children who needed feeding and clothing, and your father was. . .well, he was a man who had just found out his wife and daughter were moving up north and leaving him here to fend for himself."

"So you stepped in to take my mother's place."

"I did nothing of the sort," she snapped, "and shame on you for suggesting it. No, on the day I came in for my job interview he told me he didn't hire women, and I stood right up to him and told him that I would earn him more money in one day than any man could earn him in a week. Of course he had a good laugh, until I told him I had a special skill. You see, I can read something one time and remember every word of it. Same goes for hearing it. Once your papa realized I was a walking encyclopedia of information, he decided I was probably right. Now here I am shedding a tear because he's gone, when he only kept me around for what he could get from me, at least until he changed there at the end."

"I guess that's why he never bothered with me," May said. "I had nothing to offer. Nor did my mother, apparently."

"Oh honey, I wish you knew how wrong you are," she said.

"As do I." May pasted on a smile. "So while I truly am grateful you thought to bring this to me, I feel hypocritical wearing this for him."

"Then do it for yourself when you're ready," she said. "Forgiveness is a powerful thing. Even if it is to put that dress on and never leave this house. Of course, it's just a suggestion."

May took a deep breath and chose her words carefully as she gripped the bedpost with her right hand. "My father died one year ago. I was not informed about this until approximately four weeks ago. In the time since I arrived in New Orleans, I have been informed that my father thought so little of me that he gave the responsibility of choosing a husband to someone else and then required me to marry within thirty days of the reading of his will or lose everything."

Mrs. Gallier reached over to grasp May's free hand then placed her other hand atop it. "That's hurt talking. It's pain pure and deep that's guiding you right now. Let it for now if you must," she said. "But I'm going to warn you that if you let it forever, you'll be the one to pay for it and no one else. See, hurt is skin deep, but bitter goes straight to the bone."

May released her grip on the bedpost and pressed her hand atop Mrs. Gallier's. "Thank you," she said. "Truly."

"Sweet girl, I wish I could do more, but just know that here I am if you need me." She nodded toward the dress. "It's past the required mourning period, so do with that dress what you will. The Lord, He knows your heart. He doesn't have to look at what you're wearing to know when you're finally mourning your father."

"Yes, I believe that."

"And whatever you do while you're here in New Orleans, make sure it's not coming from bitter, yes?"

Once Mrs. Gallier said her goodbyes and left, May sank onto the bed beside the awful black dress and tried not to cry. She failed.

Finally, she rose to summon a maid to deliver a message offering her regrets to Mr. Austin and providing details and a request to complete their errand tomorrow at the same time. Then she stepped out into the hallway to face the door that led to her childhood bedroom, and opened it.

To her surprise, it looked exactly as it had in her youth. It was as if she walked out at a young age and then time stopped once the door closed. Without stepping inside, she shut the door and returned to the guest room, where she once again summoned the maid.

"Do something with this, please," she said, gesturing toward the hideous ensemble. "And then have someone bring up an envelope and papers I left in the parlor."

When she was alone again, May went to the desk and retrieved several sheets of writing paper. If Samuel Austin III could require her to answer a list of questions, then she would most certainly do the same.

Chapter Five

S o you decided not to abandon our plans today."

Sam offered a lopsided grin as he helped Miss Bolen into the buggy he'd hired for the occasion. Whatever sudden malady she'd developed yesterday had apparently disappeared.

"I do apologize for the abrupt cancellation. I had an unexpected. . ."

"Visitor?" he supplied. "I saw Mrs. Gallier leaving. Did she say something to upset you?"

"I prefer not to discuss it," she said as she smoothed out nonexistent wrinkles on her skirt with a gloved hand and avoided his gaze. "I have brought the answers to the questions you asked."

She reached into her reticule and retrieved the documents he'd left with her. Then she offered a broad smile as she handed him a second stack of folded papers. "I took the liberty of asking a few questions of my own. I'm sure you'll oblige."

He laughed. "Of course," he said as he tucked the documents away in his jacket.

"I am looking forward to meeting your father."

"About that," Sam said as he climbed up beside her and took up the reins. "Please understand my father is an old man who is not always well but is always truthful." He paused. "Even when the truth is best left unsaid."

Miss Bolen gave him a sideways look. "So he might say things to me that I will not wish to hear?"

"That is quite possible," he said as the buggy lurched forward. "Which is why we will not be paying him a visit today."

"Is he not in the mood to receive visitors?"

"My father has not been in the mood to receive visitors since the Yankees blockaded the river back in '62." Sam grinned. "But you will meet him. Eventually. However, I have another plan for today."

She gave him a skeptical look. "I'm not sure I approve of a change in plans."

He shrugged. "I didn't ask for your approval, although should you decline, I will be glad to take you back to your father's home."

"Fine then. Do proceed." Miss Bolen looked away then. "Where do you live, Mr. Austin?" she asked in an odd change of topic.

"I'll show you soon," he said as he brought the buggy to a halt. "It's a short walk in that direction."

A few minutes later, he had helped her down from the carriage and led her around to the shortest route to both their venue for today's outing and his current home: the *Vengeance*.

"I don't understand," she said as she rounded the corner and saw that they were now on the docks. "Why are you taking me here?"

"In an interesting coincidence, I had already planned to bring you here as an invited guest to the *Vengeance*. However, since you've asked where I live, it is also the *Vengeance*, at least most of the time."

She glanced around and then back at him. "You live here? On this?"

"I've sailed in worse," he said as he nodded toward his current vessel. "She's been good enough to get me to the Orient and back twice, and she'll do it again soon. So, with those credentials, I figure she's good enough for me to find a comfortable bunk here in port."

"But your father and your nice brother Joseph. . ." She hesitated. "Do they. . ."

"Live here with me?" Sam laughed. "No, although my father would probably enjoy it much more than his current residence."

"And Joseph?"

Sam paused to take her by the elbow and help her aboard. "My nice brother Joseph would probably like it better here than living with my father, but unfortunately, neither of them have been invited to join me here." He spied his boatswain moving toward them across the deck and motioned for him to wait. "Joe and our father share a house near Tulane. It suits them better than my father is willing to admit."

"But you?"

"Suffice it to say it does not suit me at all."

The Bolen woman gave him an appraising look.

"I know this is a dangerous question, but what are you thinking, Miss Bolen?" he asked as she continued to study him.

With a tilt of her head, she met his gaze. "I am trying to decide exactly what does suit you."

"Oh, so you believe you can decide that, do you?"

She paused as if considering his question and then smiled sweetly. "Given time, perhaps. But I have decided one thing: You are a puzzle, Mr. Austin, and deliberately so. First you're a pirate, then a gentleman. Now you're a captain aboard his Orient-bound vessel."

"And you're looking to solve that puzzle, are you?"

"In three weeks?" She shook her head. "Hardly. Not without your cooperation, which I am not foolish enough to believe you'll allow me."

"And that I am not foolish enough to allow." He nodded toward the center of the vessel. "So instead I will offer a tour. Welcome aboard, Miss Bolen."

Around them deckhands were busy prepping the vessel for its next voyage, a trip to the Orient that would take him away from New Orleans for an extended period. Given the current trouble and the potential results from whatever happened three weeks from now, being at sea once again for a year or more had sounded like a good idea.

However, as he slanted a look down at his companion and watched her take in everything around her, he felt an odd surge of protectiveness that did not bode well for a long absence. Perhaps he would have Joe look in on her while he was away.

The question that remained was would Joe be looking in on a penniless woman or Sam's wife?

Giving the men working on the sails a wide berth, Miss Bolen stayed close to his side. One of the deckhands spied him and called out a warning that the captain was aboard.

Sam guided his guest to the spot where the wheel awaited and settled her on a crate nearby. "Stay put and try not to poke anyone with a stick," he said with a wink. "I'll be back as soon as I see to a few things."

"That's not funny," she called after him, though he couldn't help but notice she spoke those words with laughter in her voice.

May watched him go and did not care if any of the rough characters around her knew it. Samuel Austin III was certainly an enigma. With his long legs he crossed the deck easily, leaving the crewman to hurry to keep up.

Today he was a curious mix of pirate and gentleman. As he barked orders to the laborers on deck and conferred with several men who appeared to hold a higher office than deckhand, he was definitely a man in command of his surroundings. Yet, when he sat in her father's parlor, he'd seemed just as comfortable.

Of the two places, he belonged here. May hardly knew this man, but it was easy to see this was where he was meant to be.

A pang of jealousy hit her. She'd never felt such a kinship as to know she belonged somewhere. True, she was quite comfortable in New York, but did she belong there?

She'd never had a deep certainty that she did.

The man in question spied her watching him and held her gaze across the distance between them. Though she thought to offer a smile, May decided to look away instead. When she braved another look, he was still watching. This time she allowed a grin, and he did the same before hoisting a coil of rope on his broad shoulder and walking away.

Indeed Mr. Austin was a puzzle. Oh, but he was going to be an interesting puzzle to solve in the brief time they had together, she decided as she swiveled on the crate to get a better look at her surroundings.

In contrast to the hurry and chaos on the Canal Street docks, the Mississippi River flowed slowly downriver, lapping against the sides of the vessels with hardly a sound. Today the sun shone, but despite the brightness of the morning, the river remained deep brown.

A few vessels slid by, each with sails trimmed and crew members hurrying about. What would it be like confined to a vessel of this size for months on end? It would certainly be nothing like her life back in New York.

How was Mama faring there? The question came to mind as she spied an older woman on a passenger vessel as it sailed by. The gray-haired matron lifted a gloved hand to wave, and May returned the gesture. For all her faults, Mama was good company.

And right now she ached for good company.

After a few minutes, Mr. Austin returned to her side. "Feeling unwell?"

"No," she said as she turned back toward the wheel, where he had moved. "Just thinking."

"Ah, well, we've had a slight change in plans. What would you say to spending a few hours sailing?" He held up his hands as if to delay her response. "Two or three hours at the most, I promise, and I've already sent over to Tujague's Restaurant for box lunches for the two of us, but I am willing to deliver you and your lunch back to your father's home before I sail if that is your preference."

May hesitated only a moment. Though she had her trepidations as to whether the *Vengeance* was seaworthy, apparently Mr. Austin did not, or he'd not put himself in danger. Or at least she comforted herself with that thought as she said, "It sounds lovely."

"I don't know if anyone has called any voyage this ship has taken lovely, but I'm glad you've decided to stay."

Two hours later, with the city of New Orleans long behind them, she and Mr. Austin had enjoyed the last bites of their box lunches at a table made from wooden crates. Thus far their discussion had consisted of Mr. Austin showing her around the vessel and then pointing out landmarks along the river as they sailed past.

Now they had turned and were once again headed upriver to New Orleans. A companionable silence had fallen between them. May watched as the pillars of one massive riverside plantation home gave way to the spires and gardens of the next.

"Must be a lovely place to live," she mused. "Though I warrant there are enough mosquitoes and heat down here to ruin such a beautiful place."

"Oh, I don't know," he said. "If you're raised here, you barely notice the heat and mosquitoes."

May laughed. "I may not have been raised here, but I was born here and stayed long enough to know you are sadly mistaken."

Mr. Austin's expression went pensive. "Other than your admiration for the River Road plantation homes, you don't like Louisiana much, do you?"

"That's not true," she protested. "I like Tujague's. And you're not as awful as I originally thought."

"Nor are you," he said with a decidedly wicked grin. As he leaned back and stretched out his long legs. "As long as we are speaking of things we like, tell me about these three men who are contenders for your hand. Do you like them?"

Unprepared for the question, she straightened her spine and pretended to consider her answer. In truth, she had no answer, at least no good one. *When a question is not one that should have been posed, a lady will respond with an answer that should have been given.*

"They are likable men," she said. "Each of them."

"Likable men," Mr. Austin echoed. "So you are willing to spend the rest of your life married to a likable man?"

"Given the alternative, yes."

"The alternative being that you lose your father's fortune?"

"Yes, although it does sound rather predatory when you put it that way." She paused. "Just as you have your father to care for, so I have my mother. Given the sacrifices she has made for me during her life, I find it difficult not to make a similar sacrifice to bring her comfort in her final years."

"I see." Mr. Austin looked away and then slowly returned his gaze to her. "Miss Bolen," he said slowly, "these men, are they able to provide for you and your mother?"

"Yes, of course," she said.

"You're certain? And I should clarify that I am asking if any of these gentlemen have enough personal wealth to. . ." His voice faded, and his expression showed he was having difficulty completing the sentence.

"You're wondering if any of my potential grooms are rich enough to keep Mama and me comfortable in our current lifestyle?" At his nod, she continued. "Then the answer is yes."

"Even if theirs was the only income?"

May's breath caught. "But it will not be. Not if I marry one of them." When Mr.

Austin did not immediately reply, she tried again. "I was led to understand I must marry to keep my father's money. Are you saying that even if I marry one of these men, I could lose it?"

<hr>

Sam was well and truly stuck for an answer. If he told her the truth, he would be betraying a confidence and breaking the rules. If he did not tell her, he was allowing Miss Bolen to believe she could solve her problem with a marriage that would only increase her troubles.

"I am merely asking questions." He retrieved the two sets of papers from his pocket. "Speaking of questions, let's see what we have here. You did take particular care to answer these, didn't you?"

"Oh, most certainly," she said, apparently accepting the diversion in their conversation. "You can see by the answers that I put deep thought into each of them, especially question seven."

"Question seven," he echoed as he turned the page. "Here it is. Do you prefer beignets or calas? And you said—"

"Neither since I cannot get either of these in New York City," she supplied.

"Oh, Miss Bolen, you are not playing fair." He returned his attention to the page to scan the answers she'd given then looked back up at her. "Every response in some way relates back to New York City. Look at question fourteen. Where do you prefer to eat steak?"

"And my response was Delmonico's."

He shook his head though he had to laugh. "You did not take this seriously at all. So just expect that I will do the same when I attempt to respond to yours."

"Why wait?" she said as she snatched the second set of papers from his hand. "We've got time before we dock. Why not answer mine now?"

"Fair enough," he said as he tucked her answers into his pocket and prepared to be quizzed.

"You are marooned on a desert island. What one thing will you bring with you?" She lifted her gaze from the page and offered an expectant look. "Do take your time in answering."

"Don't have to take my time," he said. "I would bring a boat with me so I could leave that island anytime I wanted. Next question, please."

Miss Bolen looked as if she might protest then shrugged. "All right. Well, if you were to somehow be granted three wishes, what three things would you wish for?"

"I only need one wish, and that would be for unlimited wishes." He winked. "However, I am a generous man, so I would be happy to give you the other two."

Her eyes narrowed. "You are not taking these seriously."

He shrugged. "Just because you do not like my answers, that does not mean I am not being serious. Ask another."

"All right," she said as she returned her attention to the page. "Tell the truth or break the rules?"

Sam's heart thudded against his chest. "I, um, that is. . ."

"It is a simple question, Mr. Austin. Tell the truth or break the rules?"

"It is never that simple," he snapped as he stood and walked away.

The Bolen woman caught up to him as he reached the rail. He'd not been sure whether she was one of those persistent women, but now he had his answer.

She touched his sleeve. When he looked down at her, she said, "It is that simple."

"If it's that simple, then you answer the question, Miss Bolen. Which would you choose?"

To her credit, May Bolen seemed to give considerable thought to the question. Finally she nodded. "I do concede perhaps this is not as simple as I claimed." She swung her gaze up to meet his. "Do you believe in God, Mr. Austin?"

"Of course I do," he managed. "Are we answering questions with questions now?"

"You just did," she said with a grin. "But bear with me. When I have trouble with an answer, I ask myself what is right biblically. What would the Lord say if I asked Him?"

"And?"

"And I think He would say that the truth would set you free." She paused to grip the rails, her attention now focused on the water lapping against the ship.

"He did say that, actually," Sam admitted.

"So what is your answer?"

He looked down at her and tried to voice the words he wanted to say. "My answer is I will have to think about my answer."

"I see," she responded as she thrust the paper back in his direction. "Then perhaps you should think about the other answers, too, and we can discuss them another time."

He accepted the papers and returned them to his pocket. "You're disappointed," he said.

"No, but I reserve the right to be disappointed another time," she said. "For now I'm thinking you're buying time in order to wrestle with your conscience some more. I'm just curious as to what the issue is you will be wrestling over."

"Ah, I see," he said gently. "You know I cannot tell you that. It would break the rules."

She seemed to search his face for a moment and then began to giggle. He joined her laughter though he knew there would be a time very soon when she would not want to laugh with him.

And that would be the day he told her the truth.

"I very much am enjoying sailing with you, Mr. Austin. I have vague recollections of being aboard a vessel like this one. Perhaps when I was a child."

"My father had me aboard a ship before I could walk. You could say I grew up with first the river and then the ocean beneath me." His attention drifted past her to a spot upriver. "Had our fathers not parted ways, you and I might have been raised very much the same. As it is, I don't think any two people could be more different."

"I disagree," she said.

"Well, of course you would," he responded. "And in disagreeing, you have proved my point. What do you do in New York, Miss Bolen?"

She shook her head. "Are you trying to change the subject, Mr. Austin?"

"I am not trying," he said. "I have succeeded. So what fills your days?"

"I don't know. The usual things, I suppose. Charity events, balls, visiting, and of course, caring for my mother. What about you? What fills your days?"

"This," he said as he gestured around him. "We sail in a few weeks. I'll have much to do to get ready, and then we will all stay busy making sure we arrive safely to all the ports of call on our itinerary."

"I see," she said. Dare he assume she looked disappointed that he might be leaving soon? "And how long will you be gone?"

"Twelve, maybe eighteen months."

"But that's a whole year. Or longer."

"Very good, Miss Bolen. It is."

"But why so long?" Her eyes widened. "It doesn't take nearly as long to sail to Europe. Are you taking the long way?"

He chuckled. "No, but we are making a number of stops. In each port we will stay for however long we need and then move on. Eventually we will return." He paused. "Why? Will you miss me?"

"I would say I don't even know you, but I assume you'll be remedying that once you answer those questions." She shook her head. "Still, how can you bear it?"

"Bear what?"

"Bear being away from those you love for so long?"

Sam shrugged. "If I'm lucky, there are only two people who will miss me, and that's my brother and my father. However, I think they'll both manage just fine. And so will I."

Her brow furrowed. "You won't leave until everything has been settled with the terms of the will, will you? It is imperative that you stay and see this through."

"I'll stay just long enough to see you're situated," he said as a thought occurred. A solution to the worry in his gut at turning this soon-to-be penniless woman and her elderly mother over to a husband with sole control of the purse strings. "Miss Bolen, I have a question, and it is not on the list I gave you."

"Go ahead and ask," she said, "but understand I may not answer." Her pretty lips lifted in a smile. "Or I may find other questions to ask you. So ask at your peril."

"Duly noted." Sam turned to face her. "Would you consider marriage to a man who had no intentions of living with you if it meant that you and your mother would gain permanent access to your father's fortune with no possibility of it being taken away again?"

Without pausing even for a second, May Bolen looked him in the eye and said, "Absolutely. In fact, it would be my preference."

"Then in that case, Miss Bolen," he said as he moved closer. "Would you marry me?"

Chapter Six

"Marry you?" May managed through her rising anger. "Do not tease me, Mr. Austin."

He leveled one of those pirate looks in her direction. "I assure you, Miss Bolen, I am completely serious."

She thought a moment. What would cause such a sudden change in this man? Then it came to her.

"Oh, I see. You've been thinking about this and decided why allow another man to have the Bolen fortune when you can have it for yourself." She clapped. "Well, bravo, sir. It's a plan I would never have considered."

His expression tight, he looked away. "I suggest you consider it now."

"Well, at least you do not deny it," she said on an exhale of breath. "I fear my other three options would not be so honest."

That admission caused him to turn back to her. "Honesty is one of the few things I can offer you, Miss Bolen."

A sweeping glance of the ship's captain, and her decision seemed a bit easier. A life tied to this man was not what she had planned, but there were certainly worse options.

Still, she did have her pride. "I will consider your offer, Mr. Austin. After I have received the answers to your questions, that is."

"Then consider this as well," he said, his expression unreadable. "If we do marry, I want it to be understood that I will provide for my family. Bolen Shipping is yours by rights, and it will remain yours. So, if you think I am marrying you for your money, you are mistaken. I am marrying you because it is the right thing to do under the circumstances."

"I see. But you will benefit from a marriage to me," she said. "I would not require my husband to live here on this ship. What is mine is yours." May paused. "If we were to marry, that is."

"That is a generous offer," he said, "but I will respectfully decline. You get my name and keep Bolen Shipping. I will not profit from Thomas Bolen's will. Those are my terms."

"Then answer the questions honestly and we will take up this conversation at another time."

Later that afternoon as she sat beside him on the trip back to Chartres Street, she could think of nothing but what her answer must be. To distract herself, May studied her future husband, covertly of course, as open staring just was not done.

He had workingman's hands, strong and tanned from the sun, and he handled the reins expertly as he negotiated the narrow crowded streets. His features were pleasant, more than pleasant, actually, and when he smiled he looked much less fierce than he did now.

From her observations, May had deduced several things. Samuel Austin was a good son and brother, and he was a great respecter of honesty. Her father had seen fit to give him more power than his own daughter in determining what would happen to Bolen Shipping and the Bolen heir, so apparently he had other redeeming qualities as well.

Had the situation been different, she could easily imagine falling in love with such a man. "When do you set sail for the Orient?" she asked to chase the thought away.

"Several weeks. My investors know I have responsibilities here that will keep me in port until they are handled." He paused to give her a sideways look. "So unless you were hoping for a lengthy honeymoon at sea, you should plan for your husband to absent himself from New Orleans within a day or two of the wedding."

The idea of marrying a man who would never live under her roof had a certain appeal. Even so, a tiny slice of her heart broke at the thought that she would be forced into such an arrangement.

"Do you make this journey often, Mr. Austin?"

"As often as I can so as to provide for my family." He paused. "Miss Bolen, under the circumstances, please call me Sam."

May nodded. "As you wish. And I suppose it wouldn't be improper to use May now that we are. . ." She couldn't say it. Not yet.

"Friends?" he supplied.

"Yes," she said on an exhale of breath. "I believe I would like to be your friend."

A short while later, Sam helped her down from the buggy and escorted her inside her father's home. "Might I offer tea?" she asked.

"Thank you but I need to get back. There's much still left to do to prepare for the trip, but perhaps another time."

She nodded, and an invitation left atop the stack on the table in the hallway caught her eye. "I wonder," she said slowly, "would you consider a favor if I asked nicely and agreed to allow you to not answer the last three questions on the list?"

"It depends on the favor."

"I have a stack of invitations to events and I have not accepted a single one. Perhaps you could attend something with me—a ball or lecture perhaps—just to see if we were a good fit. What do you think?"

"Knock off the last five questions and let me pick which event and we have a deal."

She reached out her hand to shake. "Deal. Go ahead and choose so I will know which hostess to send my acceptance."

Sam picked up the invitations and sorted through them. "You're a popular woman," he said as he discarded three and went back to his search.

"Not really. My guess is New Orleans hostesses are curious as to what I might be like. They knew the father but do not know the daughter. That sort of thing. But if they realized I could be penniless by next month, I doubt there would be invitations at all."

He leveled an even gaze. "You won't be penniless."

"Because I will marry?"

"Because you will marry me." He halted his search and lifted a card from the pile. "Madame Gallier's costume ball is my choice. I will call on you three days hence. Should you decide to marry me in the meantime, do save the news until then."

"Very well," she said with a chuckle. "But I would like to review your responses to my questions before then. Perhaps you can send them by messenger." She paused. "Or deliver them. Your choice, of course."

"Of course. My choice." He stepped out the door and then paused to look back at her. "Allow two days for my responses."

Two days later, the butler delivered Sam's answers on a silver platter. "Is he here?" May asked as she retrieved the folded document.

"Mr. Austin sends his regrets and asks that you accept his apology for not paying you a proper visit."

"I see." She dismissed the butler and then crossed the room to settle on a settee beside the fireplace to read Sam's responses.

In response to a question about his childhood, Sam had written about the loss of his mother, Maribelle, and his baby sister at a young age to yellow fever. When asked about his favorite toy, he told her about the pony cart he and his brother had fashioned from discarded lumber and wagon parts and had used as their means of transportation when they sold eggs to neighbors to help their father make ends meet.

The list went on, each answer more honest and touching than the next. By the time she reached the last one, or rather the sixth from the end, May was in tears. The picture of a man whose life and work ethic were so foreign to hers had emerged. She placed the pages beside her as she swiped at tears.

Collecting them once again, the whole stack slid onto the floor. When she retrieved the pages, she realized Sam had gone on to answer one more question—the last one.

Why should I marry you?

" 'Because I am the man your father chose for you,' " she read aloud.

May was still contemplating the meaning of those words when Sam arrived to collect her for the costume ball. She smiled when she saw his choice of costume.

"A pirate," she said. "How fitting."

"I thought so." He gave her a sweeping glance, his eyes seeming to take note of every detail of the mourning dress she'd chosen to wear. "Interesting costume. What are you?"

"Forgiving my father," she said as she allowed Sam to lead her out into the evening air.

"Interesting," was his only comment.

"Freeing, actually," she said. "Mrs. Gallier was right."

Sam helped her up into the buggy and then walked around to join her. If he had any questions about her sanity or her choice of costume, he kept them to himself. At the door to the ball, each of them were handed masks, white for May and black for Sam, and instructed not to divulge their names until the proper time in the evening.

A few minutes later, May discovered that despite his rather antisocial lifestyle, Sam Austin III was quite a good dancer. Though he was careful not to monopolize her on the dance floor, he did play the attentive escort and kept watch over her while she danced with others.

The few times she found him in the ballroom with another dancer, May felt an odd pang of jealousy. She barely knew this man. Why should she be jealous of a nameless dancer in a mask?

And yet after reading his sometimes brutally honest responses to her questions, May felt as if she did know him quite well.

She moved toward the table where refreshments were being served only to find Sam waiting for her there. He handed her a glass of punch and then escorted her away from the ballroom and toward the doors leading to the balcony.

Compared to the ballroom, it was quiet here, quieter still when Sam led her out the doors and onto the balcony. She took a sip of punch, grateful for something to quench her thirst.

"Are you enjoying yourself?" he asked as he set his punch aside and turned to face her.

"I am. Are you?"

"I am," was his soft reply.

Moonlight slanted over his features, giving credence to his look as a pirate. May took another sip of punch and allowed the sound of the fountain splashing in the courtyard below to punctuate the comfortable silence between them.

"Sam," she finally said. "Your responses to my questions were. . ." She paused. "Well, they caught me off guard."

He moved slightly closer. "Too much honesty?"

"Not at all. You told me you were an honest man, and I can see that you are." She paused to look up into his eyes. "But there's one thing I do not understand. How do you know that you are the one my father chose for me?"

"Because he told me. Indirectly, of course," Sam added.

"Through his will?" At his nod, she continued. "I forgave him for not caring enough for me to provide for me in his will." May looked down at her dress then back up at Sam. "That's what this is about."

"You didn't have to explain," he said. "And I disagree. Your father did provide for you in his will."

She shook her head. "How so? By appointing a stranger to control who I marry? I fail to see. . ." May took a deep breath and let it out slowly. "I'm sorry. It's not worth getting upset over. It's my father's choice how he distributes his estate, and we are left to honor that choice."

"May," Sam whispered as he moved closer again, this time to catch May's tears with the back of his hand. "Much as the truth sets us free, so honor binds me to what I can tell you. Please know your father loved you enough to provide more than just money to secure your future. Perhaps someday I can tell you exactly how he managed it, but for now I cannot."

More tears threatened. "Someday will you tell me, then?"

His thumb traced her jawline. "Someday. I promise."

"So Sam," she said softly, "when might we wed?"

He flashed her that pirate smile once again. "So you're beyond just considering it then?"

"I am merely asking," was her quick reply.

"We do have a time limit of approximately two weeks by my count," he said. "So should you accept my offer, we would need to make arrangements as soon as possible." His hand wrapped around the back of May's neck and drew her closer. "Have my answers to your questions done anything to sway you?"

Once again, she blinked back tears. "They have. But there's just one more mystery that remains."

"A question I failed to answer?" he said.

"Of a sort," she replied as she lifted up on tiptoe. "Will you kiss me, Sam?"

"Honestly," he replied. "I will."

And so he did.

"May," Sam whispered against her ear when the kiss ended. "I have two questions, and I want honest answers."

"All right," she managed though she found breathing most difficult.

"First, will you marry me?"

"I am still considering it," she said. "Perhaps we could go and see Mr. Breaux tomorrow and discuss it further."

"Fair enough. And second," he added. "Do you want me to kiss you again?"

"Yes, very much."

———— ••• ————

The next morning, Sam pulled the buggy to a stop in front of Mr. Breaux's building. "I doubt he will mind that we do not have an appointment when he hears what we have to tell him," Sam said as he helped her down.

"I have not agreed to your proposal," she said, stopping just short of the building's front doors.

"Then I will be sure to inform Mr. Breaux of that." He reached out to grasp her hand then stopped short and stole a quick kiss. "Consider this an informational visit. You cannot make an informed decision if you do not know all the facts."

May allowed Sam to lead her back up to Mr. Breaux's office door. Before Mr. Austin could reach up to knock, the sound of laughter, both masculine and feminine, drifted toward them.

Her companion looked down at May and then knocked. A moment later, the door swung open and Mr. Breaux appeared. "Well, look who we have here," he declared as he stepped back to reveal he had guests in his office.

"Mama?" May said a moment before Mr. Austin said, "Father?"

"Do come in," Mr. Breaux urged. "We were actually just talking about you two."

"Why are you here, Mama? The better question is how did you get here?"

Her mother spared only the briefest smile. "The usual way, darling. By ship."

"Yes but. . ."

Mama waved away any further questions with a sweep of her bejeweled hand. "Truly, May, I am here now and that is what matters. I understand there's been a few developments with your father's will that you had not yet written to me about."

Mr. Breaux gave May a sheepish look. "What I was not able to tell you at our first meeting is that there were also letters sent out to certain parties before your arrival here. Those letters went to Mrs. Bolen and Mr. Austin."

At the sound of his name, the elder Austin rose to offer his hand. Cut from the same cloth as his son, Samuel Austin Jr. was tall with broad shoulders and a military man's posture. His grip was firm, and his eyes seemed to study her with a mixture of amusement and curiosity.

"She's pretty like you, Rebecca." He turned to Mama. "Good thing. I feared she might turn out favoring her daddy. Now wouldn't that have been a shame?"

Mama giggled, and May could only gape. Never once in all her twenty-two years had she ever heard her mother giggle.

"Would any of you like to enlighten us as to the contents of these letters?" Sam asked. "And as to why you are gathered here in this office?"

"T'ain't none of your business, son," his father said.

"Samuel," Mama said. "You were always so hard on the boy. Don't you think these two young people deserve to know about the plotting that has happened on their behalf?"

"And you were always far too softhearted for your own good." He paused and then shrugged. "But if you want to spill the beans on what's been going on, then you go right ahead. Me, I prefer to stay out of such things."

"Since when?" Mama and Sam said together.

"Point taken," he said, though his gaze was aimed at Mama. "But I'm still going to sit here quietly and let you tell the story."

"All right then," Mama said as she focused on May. "It all started almost two years ago when your father learned he was very ill. He spent his remaining time making things right."

"Well, it would have been nice for him to make things right with me," she snapped. "I received no letter, nor did he bother to see me."

"He wanted to see you," Mama said as she rose to draw May close. "In person. But, well, he misinterpreted how ill he truly was, and he never got to take that voyage to New York that he had Mrs. Gallier book for him."

"I'm not sure I believe you."

Mama looked over at Mr. Breaux and nodded. The lawyer went to his desk and produced a small envelope tucked into a leather Bible and handed them both to May.

"Open it," Mama said as she gestured to the Bible. There Proverbs 21:14 had been underlined.

" 'A gift in secret pacifieth anger,' " May read aloud.

Inside the envelope were three tickets to New York aboard a vessel set to leave just a week before he died. "Why three?"

"He intended to bring Sam and his father."

Sam shook his head. "Why wasn't I told about this?"

"Because you're stubborn as I am," the elder Austin said. "Thomas and I thought it best once we patched up our feud that we keep quiet until the time was right. Sadly, that day never came." He paused. "But we planned to introduce the two of you. Thomas even had that painting commissioned in the hopes that it would be your wedding gift."

"It still can be," Mama said.

"Sure can," Sam's father said. "See, we both agreed that ever since you were little tykes you were meant to be together. Why, you marked him up good, Miss May. He still bears the scar of the time you poked him with a stick when you were playing pirates."

"I poked him with a stick?"

Sam came up behind her to envelop her in an embrace. "It seems she still has trouble with that."

"Oh stop," she said although she was laughing.

Sam shook his head. "Let me get this straight. All of this was done just to see that May and I were married?"

"All of what?" May asked.

"It's a long story, and I cannot tell you until after we're properly wed. However, I want it known to everyone in this room that Mr. Breaux will be drawing up papers to show that a certain wedding gift is given to my wife upon our marriage. Not a gift in secret like Mr. Bolen noted in the Bible, but a very public gift of Bolen Shipping to my wife, May."

Mr. Breaux grinned. "Mr. Bolen anticipated this and had me draw something up. It does give the company to Miss Bolen but stipulates a certain person to be in charge of the business as long as he lives."

"No," Sam said. "I want no part of Bolen Shipping. I will take care of my wife and any children we might have with my own two hands."

"I'm sorry, Mr. Austin," the lawyer said. "You are not the man Mr. Bolen suggested to run Bolen Shipping."

"Oh," he said. "Then who is?"

"Your father, Samuel Austin Jr." He shrugged. "Although he does suggest a change of company name to Austin-Bolen Shipping."

"I like that very much," May said as she turned to whisper in Sam's ear. "And I find I like you very much. If the offer still stands, then my answer is yes. I will marry you."

Epilogue

A nd that is the story of how your mama and your papa came to fall in love," Sam said as he smoothed back the hair of their youngest daughter, an exact copy of her mother. The twins had fallen asleep once the story turned from adventure aboard the *Vengeance* to the deep bond of love that had developed between him and May over the years.

While his sons much preferred stories of Sam's sails to the Orient—all taken before May became his wife because he found he just couldn't leave her once they wed—little Maribelle wanted all the details of the love story that had surprised both him and May.

"Tell us the story again, Papa. Start at the beginning, and don't forget the part about how Mama poked that man under the sails with a stick."

May left her post in the hall where, as always, she had been eavesdropping on Sam's nightly bedtime ritual with the children and stepped into the nursery. "That is quite enough storytelling for tonight," she told them in the mock-serious voice she attempted each evening. "Tomorrow is a big day and I want your papa well rested. He's taking me dancing, you know."

Maribelle scooted over to make room for her mama on the bed and then climbed into her lap with her favorite toy. "Does this mean Papa is going to have a new story to tell me tomorrow night?"

"This means you are up far too late, my dumpling, and you are to close your eyes right now."

May kissed their daughter on the top of the head and held her tight as Sam's heart squeezed. Painfully aware he had done nothing to deserve the life God had given him, he gave thanks right then and there for it anyway.

Minutes later, Maribelle was sound asleep, her little arms cuddling the black sheep May had made from that wonderful and awful mourning dress she'd been wearing when Sam first kissed her. The boys had matching sheep, and to May's count, there was plenty of fabric for an army of Austin children to each have his or her own.

What Sam did not yet know was that there would soon be a need to place an order with the seamstress for one more little sheep. Or perhaps, should she get another surprise set of twins as she had with the boys, two sheep.

———◆◆◆———

Sam lifted Maribelle from her mother's arms and settled the five-year-old beneath her covers. Taking May's hand, they walked toward the door. As always, May stopped to turn around and take one last look at the children before she closed the nursery door for the night.

"Can you believe they're ours?" she murmured against his ear.

"I cannot believe you are mine, May Austin," he said as he gathered her to him and lifted her chin to look into her eyes. The boys had her eyes while Maribelle had his. It was a fair trade, for if their daughter had been possessed of all this woman's traits, there would be no man safe once she reached marriageable age.

And while Sam was determined that Maribelle May Austin would marry the man she loved at the time she wished, there was nothing in his life with May that he would change, except perhaps that she had been in his life all along.

Bestselling author **Kathleen Y'Barbo** is a multiple Carol Award and RITA nominee of more than sixty novels with almost two million copies of her books in print in the United States and abroad. A tenth-generation Texan and certified paralegal, she has been nominated for a Career Achievement Award as well as a Reader's Choice Award and several Top Picks by *Romantic Times* magazine. She is celebrating her fifteenth year as a published author by receiving the *Romantic Times* Inspirational Romance Book of the Year Award for her historical romantic suspense *Sadie's Secret*, a novel from The Secret Lives of Will Tucker series. To find out more about Kathleen or connect with her through social media, check out her website at www.kathleenybarbo.com.

For Richer or Poorer

by Natalie Monk

Dedication

To my generous Redeemer.
And to Momma, my first cheerleader, who filled my head with publishing
dreams and whose homeschooling gave me more time to read.
You kind of started something.

Acknowledgments

I thank God for allowing me this ministry. And I thank you, Daddy, Momma, Tony, and Bethany. Your endless love and sacrifice inspires me and gives me hours in the writing cave.

Special thanks to:
My agent Tamela Hancock Murray of the Steve Laube Agency, Gabrielle Meyer and the ladies in this collection, and the editors at Barbour—you all made my dream reality
My critique partner Janette Foreman—your beautifying fingerprints are all over this story, and the world lacks sufficient chocolate for proper thanks
Granny, for asking when my next book will be ready
My youngest beta reader, Annalisa Laudadio, who loved my writing when I lacked the courage—miss you, sweet girl
My ever-supportive C. P. Courtney Ballinger, my VIP Book Launch Team, Aunt Linda and other friends and family who prayed for and encouraged me, and my writer-hero Karen Witemeyer, for sharing wisdom and making me feel like one of the gals
ACFW, Seekerville, and Tina Radcliffe, who mentored me and saw the writer I could be
Finally, Ms. Caroline Wallmark, whose parents' immigration story sparked this tale.

Historical note: needing a confessional for one scene's antics, I took creative license and changed the Old First Presbyterian Church on Broad Street to a "cathedral."

Chapter One

I f you get caught in this dress"—Ella whispered to herself—"there'll be the devil to pay."
But the consequences didn't scare her as much as losing her loved ones to star-vation. If she, Marcella Elena Lipski, had to don her employer's discarded gowns and search tourist locations for a husband—a rich husband who would bring her family to America—so be it.

Her first target area: Walsh's ice cream parlor.

Breathless, Ella leaned forward in the wire-frame chair beside the window as a rich-looking couple approached on the sidewalk outside. When the frowning woman glanced up and confirmed she was not Mistress Theodore, a sigh escaped Ella, her heart beating at double speed.

The couple did stop in for ice cream, however. Three scoops each.

The parlor's sugary scents—unlike anything Ella had ever smelled before—commenced her stomach to growling, and she licked her lips before she caught herself. What a wonderful thing, to be so rich.

Carrying their desserts, the man led his companion from the long counter to the table across from Ella's. Her pulse clogged her throat as she attempted a graceful smile.

They didn't spare her a glance, consumed in their clipped discussion.

Of all the ill-mannered. . . Ella rearranged the unfamiliar metal hoops under her skirt and sat straighter. Hiding her chafed face behind a menu, she sneaked glimpses of the couple. While their English conversation tripped and stumbled on her Polish-born ears, the few hissed words she interpreted revealed nothing. But their scowls and untouched dessert spoke a universal language.

Finally, the gentleman—the suave sort Mama intended for her to meet and marry—threw his napkin on his ice cream and stood. Storming from his companion, he approached Ella, who clutched her collar. Mumbling something in bitter tones, the man tossed a small card onto her table before heading out the door. Ella's eyes stretched wide.

As the lady companion left in a huff, heading a different direction than the man, Ella flipped over the card and caught her breath.

A ticket to Mrs. Theodore's spring ball.

One of the two hundred tickets she and her fellow housemaids had stuffed into invi-tations this very morning.

Floating to her feet, Ella tucked the slip of paper inside the tight cuff of her gossamer sleeve, which she pressed against her waist until she reached the walkway outside.

God bless that miserable, beautiful couple. Their fight must have been significant for the gentleman to chuck such a valuable ticket.

She crossed the street in the twilight air, weaving through the masses, peddlers, and newsboys calling out on every corner. People milled by on foot, drove past in carriages, some glancing her way. Did they suspect? Did it show on her face—that she'd come by a coveted treasure she had no business possessing?

Wait until she wrote Mama of her good fortune—the poor thing would faint, right there in the wicked Baron Zimmer's potato fields. Ella's lips curved upward.

When *Tata*—father—discovered the husband-hunting plan, though. . .he would explode. Mama's hand had trembled when slipping Ella her orders in a letter before Ella left for America.

Clattering wheels and a dog's barks drew Ella's attention to a horse and cart thundering around the corner toward her.

The drayman laid his weight against the horses' pull of the reins, roaring something in English.

Ella lurched forward. Her narrow hoopskirt minced her stride, and when the cart's wheel caught her skirt tail, she twisted, cried out, and fell to her hands and knees on the unforgiving cobblestones. Deep pinching warned of coming bruises, but she wasn't run over, thank heavens.

Propped on one palm, Ella checked her sleeve for the ticket, reassured when the stiff card brushed her fingertips. She gingerly gathered her skirt in preparation to stand, incidentally promoting her back end—oh dear.

The slow clop of horse hooves stopped near her. A breath later, strong hands helped her rise and face the drayman, whose fine dark eyes made her lungs ache just looking at him. The same drayman who doffed his low top hat to her every morning as she walked to work.

Now, he swiped off the curvy brimmed hat and checked her over for injuries, a frown rumpling his forehead. His dark hair, brim-creased and soft-looking at his temples, set off those keen eyes. Well-trimmed whiskers blended down past his cheekbones and grew darker in the center of his chin, lending a dangerous air.

Not that she was looking. She couldn't afford to stand and admire a humble drayman while an invisible dumpling stuck in her throat. No. She was just being. . .observant.

His voice rustled over several English words. He took in her dumbstruck silence and tried again, "*Przepraszam*—I'm sorry. You all right, miss? Dog scared the horse."

While his heavily accented *Polski* words sunk in, his grip warmed her upper arms and logical thought flew from her head like so many ill-fated lovebirds. He smelled of fresh straw—no doubt from his wagon crates—and leather. . .and lemon drops? She tried to put space between them, but the pain in her knees forced her to grasp his elbows—she must wrap these bruises and put her feet up tonight to survive work tomorrow.

"Please, I will take you to my home." His stubborn-little-boy expression might have been endearing had his words not shocked her cold.

"No, you will not!" Heat blazed from her collar to her ears.

He drew back. "*Nie rozumiem*—I don't understand."

Was the man an abductor. . .or bungling her language? "You will take me to *my* home."

When understanding dawned in his gaze, he chuffed a laugh. "I beg your pardon. My Polish customers, they are always chiding me for pronoun errors."

She chuckled and massaged her temples then slid her fingers into her poufy, American-style pompadour—a fashion she'd modeled to resemble one of Mrs. Theodore's uppity coiffures. This morning, after the woman instructed her to discard a pile of perfectly good dresses, Ella envisioned herself wearing the gowns to seize conversations with dapper *gentlemen*—not a scruffy, too-handsome cart driver.

"What address, please?" he asked.

Puffing a red-blond strand from her view, she straightened. "Harper Street—number 219?"

After a quick nod, he lifted her onto the high wagon seat with more grace than she'd thought possible for a drayman, then vaulted up next to her. His proud, easy bearing didn't belong to a cart driver. Had he been a butler, perhaps? No, too young for that.

He offered his hand. "Woody Harris, cart driver and deliveryman, at your service. Free conveyance for a week for the trouble I bring you."

While her traitorous heart fluttered at the prospect of riding alongside this man every day for a whole week, she placed her hand in his. The world tilted, then righted under his candid appraisal. "I'm Ella. Thank you, Mr. Harris, that would be helpful."

"Call me Woody." Mr. Harris sat there, painted by evening shadows, studying her until her blush heated up again—were Americans always so bold?—then he urged the horse forward. "Good then, Miss Ella. I'm late for one stop on the way, please." He winked. "No dogs, this time."

Down by Morris Canal, the scents of rotting wood and rust lay heavy on the wind while a dark alley loomed to the left. Chills skittered over Ella's arms. She clutched her collar and swallowed hard. Despite this man's endearing qualities, she didn't know him from anyone. He could be some murderer luring her who knows where.

Jumping off and gimping away might be the most prudent choice.

Her companion stopped the horse outside the alley, where blackened silhouettes approached. This "Woody" turned toward her, and Ella's throat closed until he reached past her to lift a crate from the loaded cart, engulfing her with homey scents of yeast and crust. The alley figures grew closer in the darkness, but never taller. . . . Children? With smudged faces, they crowded the wagon and pinned expectant stares on Mr. Harris—er, Woody. Balancing the box on one knee, he took out a giant loaf of *chlebem*, or bread, and broke off chunks into their waiting hands, then did the same with a block of cheese.

Where did all these kids come from?

As each received their bread, Ella recognized the German *danke* and English, "Thanks, Woody." But most spoke the Polski word *dziękuję*.

When the banter rose, she grasped the rhythm of Woody's broken Polski and worked to make more sense of his word combinations. Still amazed he spoke her language, she at last untangled his hodgepodge of accents. With the recent deportation of Poles from much of Europe, thousands to America, he would have encountered many dialects on his freight route no doubt.

"Where's Musty?" Woody asked.

"It's Marciszewski!"

All the boys laughed, then two youngsters the drayman called "Newsie" and "Shoe Shine" pushed forward the runt—a chubby-cheeked thing dressed in short pants and shoes, but nothing else. Why, he was just a baby.

"Yeah, yeah. . .Musty." Woody helped the child scamper up into his lap and roughed his hair, earning a begrudging grin. "Listen, fellas, I can't stay long. I need to take Miss. . . Miss Ella home."

A hush fell over the rowdy group as all eyes turned to her. She waved.

"What're you doing with some ole girl, anyway?" This, in perfect Polski, came from an oil-spattered boy.

"Freckles." Voicing his surprise, the drayman thumbed his hat back from his forehead. "Is that any way to talk to a lady?"

Vulnerability lurked beneath the kid's stubborn features. After the boy shuffled his feet, Woody dipped in his coat pocket and pulled out a paper cone of candy—the lemon drops she'd smelled? "Here. Make sure everyone gets some."

Freckles caught the candy with a nod, then Woody jounced the little tyke slumped in his lap. "Where's your shirt, buddy?"

Musty shrugged and mumbled in Polish, "Almost summertime."

When Woody passed the reeking child to Ella, she covered her wince—both from the odor and knee pain—and shifted the boy's weight from her bruises to her upper legs.

"Musty" lifted worried eyes, and her heart trembled at the familiar signs of poverty. The same empty gaze as Eryk. Her lungs seized as she remembered her brother's desperate coughs the night he succumbed to fever and malnutrition.

Musty blinked at her. How long since this poor child bathed? Since he satisfied his stomach? Since his mama held him?

Was his mother living?

Beside Ella, Woody shrugged out of his coat, vest—good heavens, and his shirt-sleeves—leaving his undershirt. His new state of dress did nothing for her recent blushing malady. Though her brows rose, so did her regard for the man as he buttoned Musty into the too-big shirtwaist and retrieved a small length of rope from his cart to cinch the middle. "Every boy needs a shirt, no matter the season. There. Down you go."

His movements drew her attention to a leather string at his throat, bearing a small ring. At her stare, he replaced his outerwear and tucked the necklace away.

With a few parting words, they left the boys and the alley behind, a tiny piece of Ella's heart staying with them. There was much more to this Woody Harris than first met the eye.

"So, Ella of 219 Harper Street. . ." Her driver continued to speak in Polish as he studied her. "Just Ella?"

Pursing her lips, Ella folded her hands in her lap. Would he think less of her when she told him she wasn't rich? Then again, what did it matter? He'd drive her home tonight and maybe to work next week. End of story. "Marcella Lipski, Austrian-Polish immigrant and housemaid. I came to America two weeks ago."

His frank gaze skimmed her dress. Should she have given him her address? He'd been kind to the children, though. Surely he wouldn't harm—

"Fancy dress for a housemaid. Did you steal it?"

"What? Of course not," she huffed. Only borrowed. From the trash. Her eyebrow reared. "Did you steal the bread?"

"No." The serious line of his lips quirked, then he snickered before focusing on the road again and mumbling, "Touché." When he offered her a lemon drop, she refused.

"My employer told me to get rid of her old wardrobe, so I did. I needed dresses—other than my maid uniform." Ella had ceased worrying about her fancy garb, since chances were slim she'd be recognized on this side of town. Better conditions than her family endured, though. They needed relief soon. Her sister Ina especially, always sick and the most at risk. Ella was their sole hope.

"The children are lucky to have you to bring them food. It's kind of you."

He gave a humorless laugh. "Precious little kindness. I'm afraid sometimes it only delays the inevitable."

"Perhaps that's more of a kindness than you know." She silently dared him to contradict her.

After a sigh, he considered her, elbows on his knees. "Maybe."

She dropped her attention to the curious scars on his hands, hands that dealt gently with the boys. A pat here, a ruffling of hair there, all the while he assessed their well-being, missing nothing. Did he, too, feel guilt for being unable to do more for those he loved? "I suppose everyone wishes they were richer so they could help others in need."

His mouth pinched. "How many rich people you know are that generous?"

At the morose thought, she searched for a transition to happier subjects. "Surely, sometime in your life, you've wished to be someone you're not."

The startled frown he gave her killed the conversation. She stiffened, straightened her filmy skirts. Strange, the loss she felt at his silence. Had she stumbled onto a subject taboo for Americans? If he kept his promise and drove her to work tomorrow, she'd have to remember not to make the same mistake.

Escorting her to her door, Woody took one look at her closet of an apartment, then retrieved a half-loaf of bread from his cart and pressed it into her hands with the last of the cheese. Food he'd no doubt set aside for his own sustenance.

After he lit his guide-lantern and drove off into the night, she set the bread aside and plucked the ticket from her sleeve. So she had an inroad to society's most popular event of the season. Now what? She knew no English, nothing of American customs, and the evening gowns she possessed were the hostess's castoffs. Provided she could get into the ballroom at all, without alerting the head housekeeper who hired her.

Hungry and frazzled, Ella prepared her supper of bread, cheese, salad greens she'd gathered, and a hot cup of water—the best she could do without tea. She shoveled in the food before worry could steal her appetite.

If she were caught in one of Claudia Theodore's ball gowns. . .she'd be dismissed and left without references. Minus her income, her precious family was as good as left without hope.

———— ••• ————

With a fresh shirt on, Woody let himself in the service entrance of Pierce's sprawling three-story brownstone then nodded to Cook as he passed. His fingers eased off the loan payment in his pocket. He'd be too late for his usual Friday supper with the Pierces, but would feel better getting the funds into the right hands.

Thank God for a friend who trusted Woody enough to loan the money to start his livery. For three years, he'd made his bread and butter from the combined livestock, smithy, and freight business. Hauling the cart didn't pay much, since most businesses hired their own deliverymen, but the freight route made a good cover for his finding more street children to help. Lord willing, Pierce's trust had deepened enough for Woody to ask the question burning in his mind of late. His boys' reaction to Miss Lipski only stoked the flames.

Youthful giggles and whispers met him before he reached the upstairs family room, coaxing a grin.

Pierce's wife peeked up from her embroidery and smiled. "Woody."

"Good evening, Beth."

"Uncle Woody!" Lizzy and Laura abandoned a pile of puzzle pieces in the center of the floor and rushed him from both sides, leaving their baby brother to crawl after them. The scene warmed his heart and brought a twinge of envy as it had every Friday night for the past four years.

Pierce sat up from his place on the couch and folded his newspaper. "Girls. Give the man room to breathe."

After hugging the blond darlings pulling at his clothes, Woody made a show of "finding" lemon drops for each of them, then fell into the velvet-covered chair opposite Pierce. The girls popped the sweets into their mouths and skipped back to their puzzle before the fireplace.

"Would you like tea?" Beth scooped up little Gerald before he could gum the toe of Woody's boot. "Cook kept a plate in the warmer for you. Everything all right?"

Taking his "nephew" from her, he settled the lad on his knee. "Just a few delays. I'm sorry I didn't send word. I would take tea, thank you, but ask her to pack the dinner for later, please."

He couldn't eat right now with the question he wanted to ask Pierce weighing on his stomach. Besides, one never knew when a pretty foreigner might need his supper.

Upon Beth's exit, Pierce crossed his ankles and pinned him with a stare. "A few delays? You haven't missed our Friday dinners in a year at least. Nothing bad happened, I hope."

"Nope." Fishing the loan payment from his hip pocket, he transferred the bills to Pierce's hand. "Nothing bad. On the contrary. . . I met a girl."

As if waiting for a slap on the back and a "gotcha," Pierce squinted.

Gerald squirmed in Woody's hold, and when bouncing didn't suffice, Woody propped his boot on his knee and set the boy in the triangle he'd created. After several failed escape maneuvers, the Lilliputian grinned and squealed at the game. "I well-nigh ran her over."

Pierce's foot thumped the floor.

"Who'd you run over, Uncle Woody?" Lizzy asked, backlit by the fire.

"A lady in town, sweetheart. Don't worry, she's fine now." He hoped. She *had* limped back into her snuggery of an apartment. He'd have helped more, had propriety allowed.

Pierce frowned. "You're serious."

"Yes."

"Who was she? Did she involve the authorities?"

"No, nothing like that. She was a foreigner. Polish-speaking. I think she was bruised from the fall, but she didn't complain." In his line of work, he encountered many a socialite, prude, and fishwife. He'd braced for an outrage. Instead, she peered up at him with those kitten eyes. . . How could he not offer aid at that point? And when she'd expressed her thanks in deep-throated Polish. . . What a beautiful reward.

Gerald gnawed Woody's knuckle with his slippery little mouth, then made a face and looked toward the door—wishing his mother would return with tastier fare, no doubt.

The lad's sweet round cheeks and fuzzy head made Woody wonder, not for the first time, what his own child would look like if he had one. It was the atmosphere in this home—unlike anything he'd known growing up—that birthed a longing in a man for all things sweet and tender.

Pierce traced the bridge of his nose with one finger. "Maybe she was too afraid to complain. You're a bit of a dark wolf, you know."

Dark wolf? Really? "I hope not. I offered her free conveyance for a week."

Pierce's finger stilled.

Under the heat climbing his face, Woody cleared his throat once, twice, then untangled Gerald's fingers from his boot laces. His friend had never seen him show interest in a lady, and no wonder. If anyone had a right to avoid the altar, he did. His parents' miserable marriage ruined thoughts of wedlock for him. . .until he got to know Pierce and the sweet moments his family afforded him. Yes, he might consider matrimony now, a family of his own. A virtuous match might lend credibility for his orphanage idea. Except, none of the young ladies at church shared his passion for helping the hopeless.

A thin, determined face came to mind.

He first spotted Miss Lipski a week ago comforting a street child with a scraped knee. Every time he'd passed her since, her blond hair and resolute green eyes turned his head. More than that, something about her reminded him of Molly. Made him want to look out for her, help her. Perhaps because both women shared the same watchful bearing of housemaids.

After returning with tea, Beth retrieved her son, now standing with his hands buried in Woody's hair, then quieted the runt's fussing with a few crumbs of cookie. "What did I miss? You gentlemen look awfully suspicious."

Woody took an eternal sip of tea.

The twitch in Pierce's mustache didn't bode well. "Woody's getting married."

While Beth's eyes tripled in size, hot tea suctioned into Woody's lungs. He grabbed a napkin off the tea tray and coughed until Pierce pounded his back. Unsure if he'd rather enter the next life by choking or a beating, Woody waived the attention and managed a long pull of air.

Gerald frowned at him like he'd stolen the last cookie. Had the girls not fallen asleep on the floor, they might have jumped into the excitement.

Finally, Pierce sobered and recounted the tale to Beth, who speared Woody with a shrewd grin. "Was she pretty? Has she met your boys?"

"Yes. And yes." Woody chanced another draw of tea and swallowed. "I was on my way to deliver food when we had the accident."

"How are they?" Beth hugged Gerald tighter.

"Musty was shirtless again. I'm not sure if a bully steals his clothes or if he's figured out he can sell them for food." On his right, the fire crackled in the hearth. Were the boys warm enough? Unlikely. "They didn't know what to think of Miss Lipski. The ones who remember their mothers looked ready to weep. The small ones stared at her like she was some type of fairy."

Palming Molly's ring through his shirt, Woody remembered his purpose for coming.

Two years ago, he spotted Freckles and Oliver digging through the city trash heaps and offered to buy the boys a meal, never imagining he'd become so involved with so many children. But Molly's memory urged him on. Figuring they'd scatter if he reported their needs to the authorities, he doled out food often and helped some get jobs at Pierce's textile mill where they'd earn fair wages.

The more he provided for the boys, the more he cared, and they in turn accepted him into their close-knit pack as the big brother they never had. Still, they needed so much more. "The street's no place to grow up. The oldest boys are hardening to any kindness. They need homes, real families."

Beth's eyes glistened, and Pierce rested his cup against his mouth.

"I'm wondering. . ." Woody ground his palms together. Asking for help from a wealthy person still went against his grain. *Lord, we've discussed this, and time's ticking. Help me now.* "What if I got backing to start an orphanage? There's one on Bleeker Street, I know, but it's filled to overflowing. Besides, some people won't take in immigrant children, not knowing their language or background."

Slowly, Pierce placed his empty cup on the tray. "I've had that thought. Worthy cause. I've too many volatile investments to give serious ongoing support, but a donation in my name may help. Have you tried the church?"

Woody gave a hesitant nod. "I've talked to Pastor Bridges. He liked the idea. But. . ." When Pierce eyed Woody in the astute way he'd learned both to love and hate, a sigh pressed for release. "He suggested I make amends with my own. . .kin before thinking of running an orphanage."

"Hmm. . . I know you've thought long on this, but I'd have to agree with him. As a matter of ethics, I can't comfortably support the project until your pastor does."

Might have known. Woody grunted. "That door closed to me long ago. I don't foresee it opening anytime soon."

The silence stretched long and awkward. Pierce and the pastor would want the best for him in their own way, but they didn't know Woody's parents like he did. He stood with an old-man groan and gripped his friend's hand. "Thank you for listening, Pierce. I enjoyed the tea, Beth."

As he chucked Gerald under the chin and left with his warm supper, Woody couldn't shake the weight in his chest. If Pierce wouldn't support him, he'd have to proceed on his own. The boys would fare better over the summer, though, which gave him time to work on a plan.

Perhaps this was his cue to begin building a solid reputation in his pastor's eyes, settle down. Secure a wife.

Chapter Two

"Where would you like to go on this fine Saturday morning?" Woody asked in well-pronounced Polish, helping Ella onto his wagon. Someone had been practicing.

She situated her wire hoops and ruffled skirt while forming an easily translated reply. Where else in this country might she find a rich husband? "What sights are there to see in Newark? Free ones."

Despite his ducking around the front of the horse, she sensed his amusement.

Heat rose in her cheeks. He needn't know the other requirement: *frequented by wealthy, single gentlemen, preferably handsome and kind.* Doubtful he'd drive her if he did.

"There's an old cathedral on Broad Street." He climbed beside her and adjusted his coat. "Draws visitors from all over to gaze at its beauty. Granted, a building of ninety years isn't old compared to your European"—he struggled with the word—"castles. . .ones I've seen in paintings, I mean. But it's one of the oldest structures here."

Ella shrugged her consent. A tourist attraction was a tourist attraction, and if she was to obey Mama's instructions to provide for her family, she must go where the men were. Though dwelling on that thought hadn't helped much when Woody showed up at her door a few minutes ago with a picnic basket full of bread, cheese, sausages, and pickled beets—a barter from one of his clients, he said—and insisted on sharing the lunch later on. Now the spicy-buttery aroma tormented her for skipping breakfast again.

"Nice dress, by the way. Your employer has good taste. That. . .purple color becomes you." His squinted amusement bordered on smugness. Must he remind her she was but a servant putting on airs?

Her chin came up.

As they rattled along, shopkeepers greeted him and ladies followed him with their eyes.

When his shoulder brushed hers, Ella chuffed and made extra space on the seat between them. He might be helpful, well liked, and have ravishing good looks, but her sister Ina's life out-valued twenty handsome faces. He did make a striking figure, though, more a king enthroned than a cart driver. Silly thought. When were draymen ever regal?

"This is where you ask if I attend the grand old cathedral." He stared straight ahead, though his mouth curved.

Her traitorous cheeks warmed. "Oh?"

"Yes. And I answer, 'No. Sundays, I worship with a small congregation near the livery.'"

Was he flirting? Americans. . . Under normal circumstances, the shyness Ina teased Ella about would take over and save her from any intelligent response.

But *no*. Questions bobbed to mind pell-mell:

Did he attend church out of duty, or truly know God and talk to Him each day?

Was he a student of the scriptures?

Did he have access to a copy of the Bible?

Despite her curiosity, she pinched her mouth shut. She'd give her back teeth if he'd stop studying her like a freshly unearthed potato. Extra attention she did not need, from him or any passersby.

Ojej!—Oh dear! Might Mistress Theodore or one of Ella's fellow servants spot her here?—then she'd truly be in the rice. She shrank in her seat and fussed with her shiny sleeve buttons.

"How long have I attended there, you ask?" He leaned in a fraction, that smirk still in place as the wind assaulted his hat. "Why, it is three years now."

Biting her lip against his humor, she studied the passing buildings. If he was content conversing solo, could it hurt to listen?

"My friend Franklin Pierce found me in. . .much need of God's love," he said. "He also found the crack in my armor—a deep love for learning. I agreed to study the Bible with him, but when the Book told me my attempts to make up for my sins were. . .rotten in God's eyes, I grew angry."

Self-awareness tightened his smile and his ears reddened. "Many things I didn't understand. How could my good deeds be thought bad? How could the blood of Jesus Christ 'wash' me from sin when blood only stains?

"Somewhere between Pierce's kindness and prayers, I quit fighting and knew only one thing—I wanted a new life. I wanted to feel. . .clean again. So I gave myself to God—good, bad. . . All the other. Today, I can't think of life without Him."

His gaze held hers for a moment, the candor there quaking something inside her, stirring a desire to share her own story. Grappling new respect for his sincerity, she contemplated his profile as he slowed the wagon at an intersection then guided the horse in a turn.

"Are you a woman of faith, Miss Ella?" he asked above the hum of the passing marketplace.

When she found her voice, Ella relayed in simple terms her own salvation when as a young girl she'd gone to the local chapel to learn to read. The old bishop, an earnest student of the scriptures, taught her how Jesus' sacrifice paid for her sins and that, because He didn't stay dead but rose from the grave, she could repent, have her sins forgiven, and heaven for her future home.

"Thank you for telling me." He regarded her a moment. "You could join me for worship tomorrow. I'd be happy to drive you."

Longing to agree—she'd not settled on a church in America yet—she gave a noncommittal answer instead. Somehow their mutual faith and the common ground it created roused guilt about today's mission.

At Ella's request, Woody pulled up several yards from the old church. He held Ella's trembling hand as she climbed down, then he stored away his hat. On solid cobblestones, she fluffed her tiered skirt and smoothed her hair, taking in the cathedral's stoic grandeur. Would a rich man first stroll the gardens behind the church or start inside like others were doing?

Glancing sideways, she caught Woody's stare, and her heartbeats thickened. Having him along while she hunted a husband was proving a tad counterproductive. Yes, she should be grateful he agreed to drive her around Newark on his day off. But what would he say if he discovered her plans?

Why his opinion mattered in the least was a question for another time, when those warm brown eyes turned elsewhere.

He clipped an anchor of sorts onto his horse's bridle and chocked the wheels of his cart. "You sure this isn't too far? I could have driven you closer."

And have everyone see her ride up in a delivery wagon? No, thank you. She breathed the spring wind, appreciating the cherry trees shedding pink blossoms along the walk. This day was made for wooing. "I prefer to take the air. It's a beautiful day."

Woody fell into step alongside, his hands clasped behind his back. "I look forward to viewing the cathedral inside."

Ella's steps slowed. He was coming with her? "You've never been here?"

After striding ahead, Woody turned back and shrugged while the breeze took liberties with his hair. "Are there no interesting things in Austrian-Poland you've never seen, though you lived close by?"

Come to think of it, he was right. The fearsome, snowcapped mountains that rose behind Baron Zimmer's estate had beckoned to her all her life, but she never once ventured to explore them.

"We often overlook the things nearest us," he said, taking the walk's street-traffic side.

True. She determined then and there to not overlook any wealthy gentlemen in her husband search. If she paid attention, Lord willing, she'd find a courteous man of strong integrity, honorable and true, a man of faith.

Kind to needy children.

When she lengthened her pace to catch Woody, the stares they received climbing the steps together screamed a new dilemma. How did one attract a wealthy gentleman with another man—a common deliveryman what's more—at her side?

In a split-second decision, Ella held her thumbs for good luck and entered the cathedral's arched doorway alone.

Her progress slowed, however, as her eyes adjusted to the dim interior light. She'd stepped into another world, a world smelling of moist stone, tallow, and old parchment. The arched ceiling curved down into a balcony, while stained glass and a many-piped organ at the front drew her past several visitors—unfortunately, none of them young gentlemen.

Despite the surrounding beauty, her hopes fell. If she lingered a few minutes, might a likely target present himself?

She slid onto the front pew and stared at the ornate altar and accoutrements. Each carving and piece of ironwork—the best to be had—bespoke the crafter's devotion.

Was it wrong to seek the best, to grasp at it with all her might?

The faithful old bishop in her homeland taught her Jesus Christ already did the earning and the paying for her sins. But physical blessings? Provisions for her family? Wasn't she supposed to achieve those on her own, through the work of her hands and the strength God gave her? As the old saying went, if you pray for potatoes, you'd better have a hoe in your hand.

But securing a rich husband might bring unwelcome consequences as well. What if her husband wanted only heirs, not a lifelong love? Ania, her older sister, married for love.

Something in Ella rebelled at being denied the same privilege.

Lord, why have you not spared us the hunger, the harsh taskmaster in Baron Zimmer, my brother's death?

No answer.

No matter. She'd accepted her lot when she left the homeland. She couldn't back out now, not with Ina and the rest depending on her. How she missed that girl! Eyes all spark and vigor in a hunger-weary face. Homesickness reared and moistened Ella's eyes.

Loosening her purse strings, she sniffed, then drew out her new kerchief—Ina's good-bye gift. Ella's fingers trailed the crooked Polski words embroidered along the hem.

WALK BY FAITH, NOT BY SIGHT. THE JUST SHALL LIVE BY FAITH.

What did that mean, anyway?

"Beautiful, isn't it?"

She startled at the English words she understood.

At her left hovered a dapper gentleman, fair of hair and light of eyes. He smiled—at her!

Heart tripping over itself, she smiled and stood. An answer to her prayer so soon? *Thank you, Father.* She tried her tongue at an English greeting. "G—Good morning."

His reply included "here" and "church" and ended with a lilt. Oh bother, was he asking her a question? His gibberish was a Spanish village to her.

Attempting to form a response, she couldn't remember any phrases Anetka—her fellow housemaid—had taught her for pleasant conversation. Clasping her hands at her waist, she gave a nervous laugh. When she got home she was going to burn her emigrant guidebook—worthless thing, as useful as an overcoat for the dead.

He smiled his confusion before giving a slight bow and leaving her to study the stained glass.

Shame and defeat flooded through her. She must find a way to communicate better or her cause was lost.

Awash in sudden lonesomeness, Ella turned around. Where was Woody?

An older couple strolled the aisle. The only others in the room were the young man she'd made herself a fool to and another robed man tending the altar candles.

With a wistful glance at the fashionable young man, Ella made her way toward the exit, her footfalls loud in the cavernous room. When she reached the confessional cabinet, someone spoke.

"Miss?" Behind her, her almost-prince—she *must* learn his name—held up her kerchief.

"Oh," she breathed. When had she dropped it? She accepted the returned treasure and managed the English, "thank you."

Searching her face, he said something she couldn't interpret except the word "understand."

Drat.

<hr />

Inside the confessional, Woody debated whether to translate Jamieson Leech's words for Ella. He couldn't risk revealing himself to his rival from boarding school days—the whole reason he'd dashed into the confession box in the first place. What was Leech doing here? The fellow had uncanny connections with the gossip mill. No quicker way for Woody's name to go public again and resurrect the family scandal. He ran a hand over his hair and naked jaw. Going without his hat and whiskers today might not have been the best decision.

But if he expected to get to know Ella, he wanted her to see the real Woody...as much as he could afford.

He couldn't forget the sad longing in her eyes when she'd held Musty close yesterday and smiled at him, despite the boy's odor. She'd looked from boy to boy with a compassion that shook him to his boots. As if she knew their pain and wished for a way to help them, too.

Her earnestness when telling him how she met the Lord convinced him of her virtuous character. Could she be the ally he'd prayed for?

"Don't you have a translator?" Leech asked slowly, as if addressing a small child.

Ella smiled and shrugged but didn't turn to leave.

"You can't understand anything, can you?" Leech chuckled. "More's the pity."

Woody frowned. Miss Lipski might not know the English language, but she was no simpleton.

What a clod he'd been, leaving her without a tour guide. And now "Leech the Leech" thought he could speak to her like a child?

Not on Woody's watch. He tapped the confessional's latticed wall and whispered in Polish, "Ella, do you wish me to translate?"

She stiffened. "Woody? What are you doing in there?"

Woody's whispers were out of Leech's hearing range, but at Ella's string of words, the dandy shrugged and shook his head. Woody smiled. This could be a lot of fun. Besides, if he wanted to learn more about Ella...

"I ducked in here to avoid a..." What was the Polish word? No, he'd best be vague. "Someone I didn't wish to talk to. Now listen, I'll tell you what he says, then you can whisper what you wish to say back. He'll think you're translating in your head before you speak."

"*Efektowny*—Brilliant," she uttered in husky Polish.

Woody's chest expanded. That spark of appreciation in her eyes when he lifted her from the street hadn't lied. She liked him, whether she admitted it or not.

If she shied away, he'd simply have to draw her out. Once upon a time he'd been quite the smooth talker. Right now, though, she needed a translator. *At your service milady. Your knight in shining armor*—er, confessional box.

Rendering her desired response in English, he dropped prepositions and quoted incorrect verb tenses to authenticate Ella's farce. She echoed him, mispronouncing the "th" sounds with a hard "d" and rolling her *r*'s. Rather than mention herself, she inquired about the city and Leech. Questions Woody could have answered if she'd but asked.

Halfway into the conversation, her breathy whisper raced chills over his arms and shoulders. He cleared his throat, which helped nothing. Brushed a hand over his hair, his scalp heating up. The act of whispering was a blasted intimate thing.

His gaze trailed the determined set of her silk-clad spine and her beautifully coiffed hair. Like honey spilling from a honey dipper. She was something of a curiosity, not to mention darling, in that dress. A maid wearing hand-me-down finery about town. A riddle to unravel. And unaffected, which he admired most. Not oversweet or plying clever turns of phrase.

What would it be like, having such an honest someone to whisper aspirations to, sharing the soul's deep longings, during the lonely seasons? Someone who'd help you keep secrets, help you dream? He'd lost that in Molly and still missed—

Ella's hand darkened the lattice holes with a smack.

He shuffled for purchase on the bench. Straightened. Smoothed his collar. Thunder and lightning, how had he gotten so distracted?

Not a hard thing to do when her clean-cotton scent wafted to him on her whispers. Her graceful arm tapered into a slender wrist, the silhouette of her small hand against the lattice begging his attention. He covered it with his own, his chest warming along with the wood between their palms.

"I'm sorry, could you repeat that?" he muttered in English.

Aloud, Ella parroted him.

Leech took a step closer. The vulture. "Are you free a week from tomorrow? There will be a Grand Sacred Concert at Phoenix Hall by the Venetian Troubadours."

As Woody's brow fell, he straightened. Of all the preposterous. . .

Ella smacked the lattice again with a soft "ahem" to cover the sound. Sassy woman.

The Polish interpretation came stiff through Woody's clenched teeth as he pressed his head against the confessional wall behind him, trying not to growl and failing. "Say 'no' for *nie*. . .or 'yes' for *tak*."

Say no. Say no.

She bounced on her toes. "Yes."

"Dash it all," Woody groused under his breath. He would have invited her himself if he knew she wanted to go. The event was free of charge. Why hadn't he thought to ask? There's no way he'd let Leech steal Ella from under his nose when he hadn't had a hound's chance in a horse race to court her himself.

Yet.

She needed to learn English, and he possessed the skills to teach her. He wasn't about to let *that* opportunity slip by without asking.

The moment Leech left, Woody climbed from the box and rounded on Ella.

Her radiant smile caught his breath and wouldn't let go. "Dziękuję," she whispered. "Thank you so much."

He stuffed his hands in his pockets and almost forgot to use Polish. "You don't have to whisper anymore, he's gone."

As her joy faded, he wanted to snatch back the words and gulp them whole. From "brilliant" to smile-killer in ten minutes. Well, when you're neck-deep, you might as well swim.

"If you want to thrive in America, you need someone to teach you the language."

She nodded, pensive, and pivoted toward the door.

"Why not let me?"

Her green eyes met his, and that spark flared again. Small, work-roughened fingers worried her bottom lip while her cheeks pinked up. "I don't know."

Time to sweep her away with his signature rascal's grin. He pocketed his hands and leaned a shoulder against the confessional. "Where else will you get lessons from a native English speaker?" He raised his chin. "*Free* ones?"

The priest cleared his throat.

Woody straightened and coughed. All right, so maybe he'd lost the pretty-boy factor when he first learned to shave.

Ella quit pulling at her lip—a most distracting habit, by the way—and glanced at the robed man. When she cut her eyes at Woody, a shy smile peeked through before she turned to exit the building. "Fine. You will teach me."

Eureka.

Chapter Three

The sunset glinted pink off the waters of Randolph pond as Ella knelt outside a maple grove, sharing crumbs with the geese eyeing her supper—fried peach pies and lemonade, compliments of Woody. Her lungs deflated, and she massaged her temples. She'd come to Woody's "birthday party," along with several of the street boys, to practice the English she'd learned so far. And here she was battling admiration for him.

As if his crafting birthday favors—folded-paper animals unique to each child—wasn't endearing enough, his cathedral rescue last week brought a sigh each time she recalled him whispering *Polski* through the lattice. That voice. . .oh, so rich. Like the charred butter coating these fried pies he loved.

Every day since the confession box incident, he'd given her English lessons and shared food while driving her to work and back—he'd been studying, too, she could tell. A patient, affirming instructor, he taught her so much more than the language. In their "practice" conversations, she'd managed to glean information about the upper class, their speech, behavior, and customs.

Woody's unmistakable attraction to her became both a blessing and a curse. Without his tutelage, her date with Mr. Leech and the upcoming Theodore ball would prove disastrous. She understood that now. But Woody offered no quarter in the charm department. Plus, he had a way with people—the street children especially—that drew her, unwilling as she was.

Mostly.

A few yards from her, Woody swung Musty onto his shoulders to view a bird's nest. With the kids crowding around his legs—bashful Shoe Shine, take-charge Freckles, cheerful Newsie, and others—he switched from Polish to German, Italian to French, teaching them the English words for *egg*, *nest*, *sky*, and *fly*. Unashamed when he stumbled over a word and the boys corrected him, he learned as much as they. A born linguist.

He winked at her.

She flushed. Correction, a born flirt.

The smile fighting its way to her lips seemed enough to get him walking toward her through the dappled sunlight. Hefting Musty to the ground, he watched the boy hustle to his friends, then sank to the earth beside her.

Digging her fingers into the lawn, she kept her seat. Thus far, any kindness she'd shown he'd had to wheedle out of her—she treated him no better than a threat.

It was time she acted civil. After everything Woody had done for her, she could at least thank him with friendship. Besides, friendship might prove her best shield against his kindness. Forming an attachment with a poor man would result in heartbreak—or worse, distract her to the point she might consider abandoning her family for him.

She filled her lungs. Upon exhaling, she offered a friends-only smile.

After several moments returning her regard, he propped his wrist on his knee. "*Tęsknisz za swoją rodzinę?* Do you miss your family?"

Grief ricocheted through her. She shifted, the tears gathering too quickly to blink them away. She'd done well until now, not thinking of her kin until bedtime, when she could bathe in the sweet memories she left behind.

Before she reached her kerchief, Woody offered the one from his vest pocket.

"Dziękuję," she said, then gave the English translation as agreed. "Th—thank you."

Shaking his head, he said in Polski, "Don't worry about practicing right now. I'm sorry to bring you pain."

She breathed a "no" and waved away his apology, still dabbing her eyes. How mortifying, wilting in front of him like a squashed cabbage. "I haven't talked about them. . .since I left."

Anetka spoke little of the homeland and never about family, probably missing her own too much. No wonder Ella felt fond of Woody. He and Anetka were her sole friends in this country.

"My sister, brother, parents, and grandparents still live in Austrian-Poland. They plan to come here when. . .we earn the money." She swallowed, trying not to appreciate the way the wind ruffled his hair and spread his shirtsleeves against his skin. He'd grown handsomer since yesterday, the rogue. How was he still walking about, unattached? Someone had better marry the man, and soon, for the sake of all female hearts everywhere—hers included.

No. She couldn't think like that.

As his *friend*, she'd have to tell him about her mission, for both their sakes. Otherwise, one of them would get hurt.

She gathered her composure. "In my homeland, my family are starving tenant farmers. I had a brother die one winter when I was young." Her voice broke despite her raised brows. "Without proper nutrition and no money for a doctor, he suffered a miserable, pitiful death." She shut her eyes against Eryk's memory, and her breath left her in a rush. "My mother sent me to America. . .to find a wealthy husband, so I can pay for the rest of the family to come here."

At his low whistle, she looked at him. Rubbing a hand over his mouth, he blinked toward the lake. Was that disappointment lining his eyes? "You ah, have a candidate in mind?"

Why do you ask? "Mr. Leech is the only wealthy single man I've met so far."

Woody hummed. "I've had dealings with the man. Wouldn't advise it."

"Then who would you recommend?" she asked, exasperation weighting her brows.

His forced chuckle grated her nerves. "I don't want to meddle. But. . .you'd do well to. . .consider options other than Leech."

After a full minute of her nibbling at the last of her pie and his pulling at a snag on his pants leg, she pounced on a safe subject. "Is your family nearby?"

He squinted into the fading sun, ears reddening. "They shut me out, years ago."

Not so safe, then. "I'm sorry."

A slow nod. "The first year was. . .dark. I didn't come to know the Lord until later."

Sensing raw pain behind the words, her heart hurt for the lonesome young man he must have been. When he offered nothing more, Ella brushed a crumb from her lip and gestured to the outline of the necklace beneath his shirt. "May I ask about the ring?"

After considering the piece, then her for a long moment, he retrieved the leather string and drew his finger over the silver band where two hands held a crowned heart. "Belonged to a friend. Her name was Molly. She's passed away now."

"It's beautiful."

"I think so." He replaced the necklace, then smiled at the roaring and laughing going on behind her. The children charged a flock of geese, wielding sticks for swords and singing some type of battle march. Singing quite well, actually.

Smile fading, Woody said, "Thanks for your help today. They haven't known a"— meeting her eyes, he faltered, cleared his throat—"motherly touch in a long time. You're good with them."

She held back her smile but couldn't hold back her blush. She'd noticed he stumbled more when near her. "I'm only a student. Are there no girls?"

"I'm sorry?"

"On the streets. I never see girls with you."

"Sadly, the girls learn early not to trust a man. Few men give gifts to street children without. . .expecting some type of favor in return. For the boys, maybe a theft, pick-pocketing or housebreaking. For the girls. . .it's worse. The younger boys help me get food and blankets to them."

Ella's stomach rebelled at the circumstances he implied. She'd grown up safe from those kinds of dangers with *Tata i Dziadunio*, Father and Grandfather, there to guard her. These children had no one. Except Woody. "You're a Godsend to them."

After plucking a blade of grass, he twirled the shoot between his fingers. "I feel it's my calling from God. I want to build an orphanage for them, a refuge and learning center, to teach them how to survive in America, and of course facilitate adoptions to good homes. So far, I haven't gained much support." He stared over the pond in the twilight and whispered, "Maybe the time isn't right."

Her hand settled on his. "God will help you find a way."

His darkening gaze, his warmth, and the gentle lapping of the pond at their feet all descended on her heart in one fell swoop.

Before she could snatch her hand away, he folded it in his own. "Thank you, Ella Lipski. For having faith in me."

Every heartbeat bloomed soft and new, but pain sprouted alongside. She lowered her lashes. No matter how hard she fought, she was falling for a man she couldn't have.

<hr>

Two weeks later, lantern in hand, Woody poked around the makeshift shelter his boys called home and refused to panic. His knees prickled, and his head throbbed, but by George he would *not* panic.

The boys' once-cluttered shanty gaped bare and cold without the blankets he'd given them—no signs of life inside but the wallowed-out dirt.

Woody combed Morris Canal, tunneling fingers through his hair. The nearby swaying grasses and skeletal docks revealed nothing. They were kids. How far could they have gone?

After trudging back to his wagon, he drove by the usual hangouts and asked around town, but the boys hadn't mentioned their leaving to anyone. Exhaling a pent-up breath, Woody debated going to ask Ella if she'd heard anything, but he couldn't visit her apartment at this time of night without igniting gossip. He stopped his cart in an alley, his heart still galloping. Face-in-hand, he prayed, "You can see my boys, Lord. Help me find them."

When no miracle surfaced, he pushed himself up and started the wagon forward, determined to overturn every grate in the city until he recovered them.

On his third drive through the restaurant district, rustling noises lured him to check behind DiMaggio's Café. A boy dug through the ripe garbage barrels. Was that Oliver's red hair?

Woody climbed from the wagon. With light from the kitchen shining on the rubbish, he kept to the shadows until he got close enough to speak. "Oliver, it's Woody."

A trash barrel spilled in the kid's haste to get shed of him.

"Wait! Ollie."

At the pet name, the boy slowed. Turned. His emotionless glare forced a shaft of pain through Woody's heart.

They were back to this? Reeling inside, he managed one word. "Why?"

"We ain't going to any orphanage."

"What?"

"The lady and you talked at Randolph's Pond about putting us in a orphanage didn't you? So we voted to scram, soon as possible."

The boys heard that? They'd kept silent on the drive back that night, but he figured they were worn out from playing. "We talked about a refuge. . .for all children who find themselves on the street. A place they'd learn English and how to get jobs and make a good life here. And they could be adopted if they wanted a family of their own."

Oliver's eyes flickered, but he didn't move.

"Orphanages aren't all bad."

"You ever lived in one?"

"No, Ollie," Woody said, suddenly weary. "No, I haven't."

"Then how do you know this. . .refuge will be any better than a workhouse?"

God give him strength. "Because I'll operate it."

Oliver relaxed a bit. "How you gonna babysit a bunch of kids all the time? Miss Ella gonna help you?"

Ella. After their pond conversation and subsequent lessons, he hoped she might care enough to get involved. But she had courtship on her mind now—he never inquired about her outings with other men, but at least he knew what he was up against. She planned to attend the upcoming Theodore ball and had put off further lessons until afterward. He'd talk to her then. "I haven't asked. I hope so."

The boy chewed his lip. "Me too."

A deep place in Woody cracked and thawed. After much prayer, he'd had no divine revelation of a solution. He'd tried to dissuade Ella from pursuing wealth. Though if Ella was to be his, God would keep her from marrying anyone else and take care of the outcome. That's all there was to it. He couldn't picture Ella as high society. Candid and untouched by the elite's coy games, she had a way of getting straight to the heart. She certainly got to his. Would she consider helping him—maybe rescuing girls as well as boys?

Oliver turned to go.

"Ollie."

The small redhead stopped.

"Tell the other boys for me? I don't want the little ones going hungry because of this."

He shrugged. "I'll do what I can."

And so would Woody.

It was all Ella could do to keep from running away.

If someone had told her a month and a half ago she'd be in America wearing her employer's dress in the woman's own ballroom at the biggest social event of the season, she'd have doubted their sanity. Now, she doubted hers and resisted pinching herself on the grounds she might bruise—in this elegant ball gown, her arms showed. Thank goodness Anetka helped her alter the dress into something less recognizable.

Between two ferns and a vase, Ella crunched on a cucumber sandwich and took advantage of an enormous mirror she'd polished just this morning. Pretending to inspect her gloves for crumbs, she scouted the candlelit reflection for her employer, ever aware of jeopardizing her livelihood. Hundreds of guests floated about, offering witty comments and sipping punch while the orchestra played—a scene she thought she'd love—but the whole evening grew tedious.

Earlier a gaggle of socialites snubbed her when she couldn't comment on Who's Who and social politics, and her mind bugled a retreat.

But after the letter she received from Mama yesterday, failure wasn't an option.

Ina was coming early. Forced to work sick in Baron Zimmer's fields, she'd collapsed, and farmers of neighboring lands took pity, collectively loaning money for Ina's passage to America. Life and death weighed on Ella's success now, and she had trouble keeping her shoulders from bowing under the load.

The orchestra swelled into a familiar song, and her eyes slipped closed. Days ago, Woody guided her through the steps of this waltz, helping her brush up on the dance Grandfather—Dziadunio—taught her as a child. Ever the gentleman, Woody had laced his fingers with hers so she could feel the push and tug of his lead through his palms without his arms around her. Alone with him at the pond this time, she'd been most grateful for his consideration. But his eyes hadn't behaved. They shone dark and warm and no doubt spied her feelings for him.

Over the past weeks, his rugged charm and relentless spirit had drawn up deep things from her heart, threatening her mission. At the same time, he provided the tools she needed to transform from Ella, the immigrant, into Marcella Elaine Lipski, tourist and ball guest of the Theodores.

She would never forget the brown-eyed rogue who welcomed her into his makeshift family and gave her so much more than the gift of communication. He'd given her a place to belong.

But now she'd have to say goodbye.

The waltz ended, and a dark suit drew close in the mirror. Jamieson Leech. Despite Woody's warning, she'd seen nothing from Jamieson to make her reject his suit. Had

Woody denounced Jamieson out of sheer jealousy?

As a married woman, with her own family, she'd soon have no time to think of Woody and "what ifs."

"You look lovely this evening," Jamieson said.

Ella gave her best effort at a smile.

On their several outings since the concert date, she'd grown uncomfortable when Jamieson kept reaching for her hand—nothing inappropriate. After all, she'd held Woody's. Still. . .

Jamieson lifted his punch glass. "Care for some?"

"No, thank you."

"Would you like to dance, then?"

The room took on a suffocating air as couples moved onto the dance floor. Her pulse quickened, drawing her hand to her throat. She'd never danced with any man but Grandfather. And Woody. But if she became Jamieson's wife, what was a simple dance? He was handsome and considerate. And rich. What, then, set her on edge?

Were his eyes red-rimmed? He'd either lost sleep. . .or been drinking?

He hiccupped, pupils widening as he pressed a knuckle to his mouth. "Pardon."

Heavens. She hesitated. "May we walk. . .outside?"

On their way to the veranda, they passed wall sconces with lamps she'd cleaned and wicks she'd trimmed. Satisfaction ran through her at a job well done. With bronze ceiling tiles gleaming above, wall tapestries adorning the perimeter, and light illuminating every mirror, the ballroom radiated the beauty of a fairy tale.

Jamieson pulled her hand into the crook of his arm and caressed her fingers in a way that made her grateful for her gloves.

Maybe not a fairy tale, but a dream. A strange, luxurious dream where the atmosphere and her gown lifted her spirits, but her task took all her fortitude.

Her escort stumbled over the threshold to the garden. He scowled at the ground, his slurred words hard to interpret. "They should have that fixed. . .certainly rich enough. You'd think they'd take pride in the grounds."

Entering the garden on his elbow, Ella swallowed her last bit of hope. Would she marry a drunkard then? What choice had she? There was no time to "consider other options" with Ina arriving early.

Under a high rose trellis, she summoned her farm-girl grit and faced him with her best English—the question she'd been practicing. "Jamieson, have you never thought of taking a wife?"

"Perhaps I've never found a woman who captivates me as you do." He cupped her face. The contact raised gooseflesh on her arms, his sour-punch breath wafting over her. "You're so. . .exotic. Like a desert orchid."

Captivates? Exotic? Orchid? Woody did not teach her those words.

Jamieson blinked, then took her arms.

Sensing his impending kiss, Ella closed her eyes and tried to envision Woody, but felt doubly wicked. *This is what your family needs, Ella.*

She called to memory little Eryk. For her siblings' sake—

When Jamieson's ill-aimed kiss glanced off her chin, Ella's eyes flew open and she turned her head. Could she endure this as his wife, with a husband so inebriated he couldn't properly show affection? She pushed against him, but his grip held her firm.

"So beautiful," he slurred.

A chill raced down her spine as she struggled and stumbled backward. "You're hurting me."

Smattering her neck with kisses, he pressed her into the rose bush.

Thorns pierced her arm and back through her dress. "*Przestań proszę!*—Stop, please!"

Chapter Four

Woody drove by the Theodore residence alone, the loud orchestra music crashing through his tired muscles. He massaged his forehead.

Children couldn't vanish into the night mists—the boys had to be somewhere he'd overlooked. He'd found nothing since the night he spotted Ollie. Too dark for further searching, this evening would be better spent poring over his city map with a good strong cup of tea.

Light glimmered through the tall hedges surrounding the Theodore property. As he passed the gardens, the perfume of roses assailed him. Was Ella there now, dancing with someone else? He gritted his teeth. What he'd give for the chance to stroll through such a garden with her.

If things were different, he'd take her on a tour of the elaborate flora at his parents' home and. . . But things weren't different.

At the thought of telling her the boys had left, his stomach curdled. He'd hoped to surprise her with good news—two sponsors had taken on the orphanage project since they last talked. The boys had to turn up soon. They'd survived too much together—

A woman's cry rent the night.

Every cell in Woody's body answered—he knew that voice. He yanked the horse to a stop, jumped to the ground, then raced across the street and lawn foliage.

I'm coming, Ella.

Where was she? Rounding a rose arbor, he found her struggling in the clutches of Jamieson Leech.

Woody spun the fool around by his shoulder and connected a hard right to his jaw. Leech's spew showered the air, reeking of alcohol.

The scum.

Leech stumbled back, eyes glazed, a hand to his well-bloodied lip.

Breathing hard, Woody braced his legs and reassumed the offensive. Leech might be drunk, but he was no weakling—their self-defense lessons during the class of '77 proved that.

"Elwood Harrison?" A clumsy laugh spilled from Leech's gaping mouth. "I thought you'd have crawled into some alley and died by now. Spoiled rich kid like you."

A symphony of gasps echoed his name through the throng leaking from the ballroom.

Woody stiffened, shifted his feet. No more anonymity. Back to people thinking of him as a fallen icon instead of a human being. All those years trying to bury the past, down the sewer grate.

In his peripheral, Ella edged a safe distance toward the house. Her safety was worth his reputation and more. But how could she settle for a man like Leech? Didn't she know she was better than this?

Eyes widening, she clutched her neckline. "*Uważaj!*—Look out!"

The blow came from nowhere—pain exploded from his cheekbone, spread under his eye, through his teeth, and knocked him onto his back in a flowerbed.

Leech staggered over. "Get him out of here."

Two chucker-outs shuffled Woody backward over the underbrush to the pounding of his heart. Resisting, he pled, "Ella, you don't belong here. Don't let them make you into something you don't want to be."

Like Molly. She'd never have chosen a brothel if she'd had a choice. He had to believe that.

Tears plummeted to Ella's chin before she turned.

When his back slammed the ground once more, Woody rolled to gain his footing, resisting the urge to trip the gorillas who'd hauled him to the brick road.

Ella, still in view, ascended the path toward the house. Didn't once look back.

What an addlepated fool he'd been, nigh swooning over her, believing he'd found the one woman who adored the street children as much as he. A woman unselfish, candid, untouched by society's corruptive hand. A woman he could love.

As she disappeared into the crowd, he was struck with the night's sick irony. What a match they were, she, pretending to be rich, he, pretending to be poor. Well, not pretending, since his father *had* disinherited him from the family wealth.

Ella though, in all her ballroom finery, was a fearsome beauty to behold—a marvel to any eye. No doubt full of plans he couldn't begin to reason out.

And he'd created her.

He'd taught her how to walk like a duchess only to watch her glide away from him.

As he turned away, he cursed himself for worrying over her. She couldn't know—if she was at all who she said—the pain in store for her if she pursued the heights of riches and ambition.

———◆◦◆———

Ella entered the livery's dimness, last night's disaster weighting her steps. Spotting a man at the forge, she asked after Woody.

The smith jutted a smudged thumb toward a door in the back. "He's expecting you."

He'd heard, then. She had to explain.

When she knocked, Woody answered, eyes serious and tired. Had he slept as little as she?

Hating this new wall between them, she spoke in Polish, knowing she'd never be able to get the words out in English. "There was a fire at the Theodore mansion last night."

"I know."

So did the whole city, apparently.

"It was my fault." She massaged at the ache behind her eyes. "Before the ball, I noticed one wall lamp loose as I filled them, but the night's excitement distracted me. I forgot to alert anyone of the needed repair.

"I changed back into my uniform after you left, so I would not be recognized. Then Mister Theodore discovered the fire and dismissed me. My landlord put me out, too, when he heard I was responsible for starting a fire." Pausing for breath, her voice clogged. She closed her eyes. *Father in heaven, help me. I don't know what to do.* "Mistress Theodore kept this week's pay to cover damages. I can't find work anywhere. Even if I had money for rent, no one would take me as a tenant now."

Woody said nothing.

Helpless, Ella staggered backward. "I'm sorry. I don't know why I came here. I just don't know what to do."

He pushed off the doorjamb and grasped her arm. "Ella, the furnace."

Gasping, she turned to face the flames.

Woody released her arm then led her back to his quarters, past orderly grain bins and an immaculate wall of tack, so characteristic of him. Frown persisting, he took care to prop his door open. Typical Woody—ever mindful of others and her reputation, even when upset. Crossing the raised-brick threshold, he held a hand out for her.

Craving the safety of his strong grip when her heart felt so raw and vulnerable, she curled her fingers against the temptation. Then, stuffing wariness aside, she clasped his palm and let him pull her into the room.

Pungent tallow and lemon oil perfumed his living space, while light from one window revealed a desk, chair, kitchen area, and stove. He scooted the chair out for her then circled the room, straightening an already organized collection of maps then a pair of boxing gloves and a teacup.

Seated, she followed him with her eyes, brushing her hand against the fabric of her skirt, the feel of his palm lingering.

Two books he replaced on a shelf in the corner. Then he set a miniature pair of shoes atop a clothing-filled crate and slid the box behind a curtain, revealing a tidy bed and washstand. On the desk's far side, he placed his hands on his hips and rolled his lips inward. "I'm afraid I've some bad news as well. I had no chance to tell you earlier. . . The boys have run away."

Coolness pricked her nape. She clamped the upholstered chair arms. "What?"

"I scoured the city and found Ollie. He knows where the others are and is trying to bring them back. In the meantime, I managed to get a couple of sponsors for the orphanage project. Unfortunately, the biggest sponsor withdrew his pledge this morning, as soon as he heard of last night's spectacle." He rubbed a thumb across his bottom lip. "Yours isn't the only name feeding the gossips today."

Something fussed at the back of her mind. What Leech said—

"Good news is"—he spread his fingertips on the desktop—"knowing you'd be in a strait when I heard about the fire this morning, I sent word to Pierce, to inquire if he'd hire you. Provide you with lodging. The maid wouldn't let me in, because the house is taken with chicken pox, but she said you could come for an interview if you've had the disease before." His thumbs bounced. "Have you?"

He'd made provision for her, knowing she deserved the consequences of her decisions? She fidgeted, more uncomfortable than ever in her elegant dress—her only decent option with her uniform returned and her homespun dresses threadbare. "No."

He sighed, dragging a hand over his hair. "Right. . . Pierce will hire you eventually—he's a good man—but you'll have to live somewhere until the family recovers and. . ."

When light from the window fell across his features, revealing a bruised eye and several cuts, she lost the rest of his sentence. "Oh, Woody."

He turned, gaze softening. Bits of dried blood clung to his chin, tattling his unsuccessful attempt to wash away last night's fight and present himself as a gentleman.

Swallowing a wave of compassion, she forced herself to speak. "You don't have a mirror here, do you? You should see yourself."

"That charming, huh?" His voice lacked humor.

"That bruise under your eye is terrific. Do you have witch hazel and a cloth?"

He touched his eye. Boots echoing across the room, he pulled open a cabinet and took down the items.

Emboldened by his need, she snagged his arm and steered him to perch on the desk edge. "Let someone care for you for a change."

"I could see to them." The way he examined his swollen knuckles did strange things to her heart—brought sympathy for his suffering, pleasure at his caring enough to step in harm's way for her. Her conscience ached. She should have championed him at the ball after his rescue. Maybe left with him. She couldn't go back, though.

Strange she so often felt pained and cared for in the same moment when near him. Was that not a common symptom of love?

Love or not, she couldn't marry him.

She focused on opening the bottle of witch hazel.

"When I heard you cry out, then found Leech with you. . ." His breath stirred her hair—no lemon drop scent this time. Just Woody. "I wanted to hurt him like I haven't hurt anyone in a long time." Serious brown eyes met hers, scanned her face. There was no steeling herself against the fragile warmth there. His leatherworker scent, suggesting gentle strength, invited her to stay this close to him forever, made her wonder how his arms might feel around her.

Hands trembling, she folded and doused the cloth, then helped roll his sleeve up to his forearm. Their fingers brushed. She pulled away, her calluses snagging on his shirt fabric, mocking her chances of being anything but a farm girl. How could she marry Jamieson now, knowing he was as Woody warned? She could justify her actions with the motive of saving Ina all she wanted, but Woody would know she'd compromised her ideals, all for a chance at Leech's money. She couldn't face Woody's disappointment. Not when she'd. . .

Not when she'd come to love him.

Avoiding his gaze, she swabbed a scrape under his bruise and recounted Mother's letter. "I permitted Jamieson Leech's attentions because Ina is coming to America early. I thought if I convinced Leech to marry me, I could support her better."

Did he flinch from the sting. . .or the touch of a traitor? Swallowing the threat of tears, she breathed deep into her lungs. Taking his chin in her hand, she dabbed at his cheekbone, all too aware of the roughness scraping her palm and the way he studied her features, her hair.

She refolded the cloth and pressed a clean side to the abrasions on his right hand, but he laced his fingers with hers. His steady regard held her captive. "Ella, how can I make you understand?"

The simple question leeched her breath and raised her defenses. "You can start with 'Elwood Harrison.'"

Breaking eye contact, he pursed his lips and nodded. Releasing a deep breath but not her hand, he began. "Before I was born, my father, Wesley Harrison, foresaw the War Between the States and sold our Mississippi plantation to buy into the railroad. Father's investment proved profitable. Very. Profitable. The Harrisons are now among the wealthiest in New York."

She untangled her fingers from his, unable to reconcile the Woody she knew with this rich, powerful stranger before her. "Then why do you struggle to help the boys, seeking sponsors for the orphanage if you can pay for it yourself? Are you a gambler? A swindler?"

His brows rose and he huffed, touching his chest. "Ella, it's me, Woody, remember?"

"Elwood," she interrupted.

"No. Only my mother calls me that." Propping his hands on his hips again, he leaned back. "Don't make me a monster. I was disinherited five years ago. I don't own a penny of my family's wealth."

Engulfed in shame, she averted her gaze and moistened her lips. "Maybe I shouldn't have said that."

Grasping his necklace through his shirt, Woody rubbed his thumb over the material. "I was never close to my parents. Raised by a governess. Sent to boarding school. When I graduated and came home, I befriended an Irish maid in our house named Molly Gallagher." His words came slow. "Little slip of a thing, orange hair sticking out in every direction."

Ella dreaded the end of the tale, for it couldn't be good.

"With all my school buddies living far away, Molly and I became fast friends. Nothing romantic. I didn't want a miserable marriage like my parents'. My mother, an ambitious woman, never content. . ."

Shaking his head, he settled back on his palms, his vest rumpling between each button. His eyes narrowed, pleading with her to understand. . .something. "Mother disapproved of the friendship—had plans for me to marry a debutante from a powerful family. So when a servant suggested Molly wanted to lure me into elopement, Mother fired Molly without severance. Put her on the street. Worse, she spread the rumor among her society friends.

"Months passed before I received Molly's letter. Without references, she couldn't get work. . ." His mouth closed, pulled to one side. He inhaled and the next words came out in a rush. "She was starving. Sold herself for a piece of bread, started working in a brothel, then took her own life. The letter was a suicide note."

When his eyes reddened, Ella's watered as well. A twitch started in his cheek, and his voice grew hoarse. "She wrote to thank me. . .for being her friend. Sent this ring—her grandmother's. I made a cad of myself to get back at Mother, shamed my parents until they kicked me out." He flexed his doctored hand. "On the street for two years, I survived by my fists, using boxing skills I learned at school to fight illegally for money. Then Pierce found me beaten on a curbside. He recognized me as the son of a famous railroad tycoon, took me home, and patched me up like a Good Samaritan. Later, he led me to Christ. No one from my old life speaks to me but Pierce. So I settled here, hoping the state line would provide a buffer for my parents and my past."

She couldn't fathom having her parents close, but estranged. "Do you ever go back home, try to visit?"

"Couple times, but Mother would never allow me entrance. Especially not after this. . ." He lifted his fist. "I've resurrected the family scandal. People will remember my behavior, how it reflects on my parents—the last thing I wanted for them. . .or for the orphanage."

Lacing his fingers on his knee, he gave a bitter laugh. "Furthermore, seems I've given my heart to a woman both bent on seeking wealth like my mother and desperate enough to sell herself to the highest bidder, like Molly."

"Woody, that's not fair." Not when his confession chafed her conscience and summoned her affections at once. "It's not the same thing."

"Isn't it? When you're willing to settle for a scoundrel like Leech?"

"You know my reasons," she whispered.

"You're worth so much more than that."

Tears blurred his strong, familiar frame. "I must consider my family, my sister. I—I don't even know where I'll sleep tonight, much less how to support her, too."

"You'll stay here."

She jumped away and dropped the cloth. "What?"

With his fingers circling her wrists, he pulled her back. "I'll sleep at the boys' shelter down at the canal, in case they come back for something in the night. I've already told the livery hands I might lend the place to you and charged them to look after you."

Trembling beneath his gentle hold, she blinked at the way his thumb caressed her wrist.

His mouth tilted. "That, or you could marry me."

The words mule-kicked Ella, and Woody's grin froze, then faded into something infinitely more serious. The most somber, handsome, vulnerable, unfair look he'd ever given her.

"I've fallen in love with you, Ella." His voice rasped like fine velvet as he scanned her face, laying bare her vulnerable heart. He caressed her cheek with the backs of his knuckles. With the bridge of his nose. His breath. His lips.

Her eyes slid shut on a sigh, her insides twisting deep and long at the answer she had to give. She put a hand to his shoulder for support, and the words came hoarse. "Woody, you know I can't."

Stiffening, he pulled away.

Desperate, her words flowed unchecked. "Not yet. Maybe if you talked to your parents—"

Dragging a hand down his face, Woody stood and laughed. "So you're only interested if I'm rich."

"It's not just about my family, Woody. You talk like wealth is evil, but you refuse to acknowledge the good it can do. Funds to help the boys lie at your fingertips and you in your pride won't reach for them."

"I told you, Ella, I tried."

"In the last year? Month? How can you talk about doing great things for the street children if you won't cross the state line and apply your own resources to help them? I don't understand." She raised her hands. "I don't understand you Americans!"

Bending low, he gathered a bag from beside the desk, a fat bag with furled maps sticking out the side. After settling his hat on his head, he slung his suit coat over his shoulder and paused at the door. "Double-check the front door at night. The lock's finicky."

Chapter Five

Woody mounted the steps to his family home and tapped the door knocker. Pity he couldn't bring the boys here. They'd love playing hide-and-seek in the cubbyholes he and Molly had discovered.

He tugged her necklace into his palm. Though she was outspoken and Ella reserved, they matched in kindness, honesty, and resilient spirits.

He'd give his life to keep Ella from Molly's fate.

Thank God he could keep Ella off the street for now, though maybe he couldn't change her choice to pursue wealth and the certain disaster to follow. As far as the boys were concerned, he could still do so much. Ella was right. He had one last resort, and he intended to use it. He'd be hanged if he let his plans for the orphanage go without a fight.

Letting the ring fall against his heart, he shoved his fists in his pockets. That offhanded proposal had slipped off his tongue so blasted easily. He'd meant to lighten the moment. Had no idea he'd feel the words to his core. The mix of anguish and longing in her features dubbed him the lowest man in New England. Reminded him he had no rights to her when he'd nothing to offer. But in his deepest heart, her rejection still stung.

If his parents could just loan him enough to bring her family to America—

The massive door opened and Steele answered. The old butler schooled his shock into a sedate expression. "You know I'm not to allow you entrance, sir."

"It's a matter of life and death." When a sliver of sympathy entered the man's tired eyes, Woody blinked against sudden emotion. "Please, Steele."

The butler's wrinkles deepened. There was no denying the irony of Elwood Harrison, once-heir to a railroad empire, pleading with a servant. "Very well, sir. Eh. This way, sir."

Where family portraits once hung from the woodwork, oil paintings and Asian statues now decorated the hall. A vast improvement over the gloomy expressions marked by lonely dinners with strained conversation. For years, he'd felt in everyone's way, always homesick for the even colder boarding school.

Steele showed Woody to the lower parlor, where he paced the carpets. Strange, being back, less welcome than ever. If a plea for the orphanage didn't reconcile him with his parents, what would? Who didn't want to help the hurting and hungry?

As he silently rehearsed his case, arguments hotfooted across his mind.

Steele returned. "Sorry, sir. The lady of the house won't come down."

Heart rate sluggish, Woody ran a hand over his hair. "What did Father say?"

"Nothing, sir."

So that was the way of it.

Woody straightened. So be it. He'd come back every day for a month, a year, if that's what it took. "Thank you, Steele. I'll see myself out."

Passing the stairs cascading from the family rooms, his ears picked up his mother's strident voice, her Southern-belle accent strong. "You will *not* see him, Wesley. Remember the shame he put us through! I've forced myself to forget we had a son, and I won't go through that pain again."

"He's my son, too, Lavinia. You can't keep me from him forever. After the debacle at that ball, it's curious he would show up here at all. I'm eager to hear why." Father descended the stair, tucking a shirtfront beneath his morning coat.

Trailing him in an elaborate day dress was Mother, pale and taut. "Why can't we leave things be? He'll only drag us down—"

"Hello, Father, Mother."

Father slowed on the steps, his visage unchanged except for his graying hair. Same military bearing, his right sleeve pinned up from the amputation.

When Mother reached the landing, she gasped. "My lands, his face."

Woody fought the itch to reach for his bruised eye.

"It's true, then," Father said, his mustache bunching. "What've you done, boy? Exposing yourself, participating in vulgar fisticuffs before all of society. Why can't you abide our living in peace?"

"I told you this wasn't a good—"

"Quiet, Lavinia."

Shame over Woody's rebellious youth poured through him. If he hadn't made a rake of himself to avenge Molly, they'd believe him now. Might have had a better marriage without quarrelling over his constant misbehavior.

"I'm here to apologize, Father. Yes, I came to blows with Jamieson Leech at the Theodore ball, but it was in defense of a lady."

"That's not what I heard," Mother murmured.

"With all due respect, Mother, there's no telling what you heard. Half the gossip circulating is pure falsehood."

"Watch your tone, boy."

With his tongue pressed against his teeth, Woody counted to ten. "I wanted to tell you how much I regret the shame I brought upon you in the past. I retaliated. . .out of hurt. I hope you'll forgive me."

Father's brows rose. He rested his hand behind his back.

"You want something." Mother squinted.

Pegged, Woody pulled at his ear. "On my first attempts to visit, I admit, I came for financial reasons alone. But I met someone recently who cannot visit her parents. Today, I came hoping we might at least speak on friendly terms again."

Shifting to his good leg, Father weighed the situation, radiating indecision. Mother's mouth firmed. "Pretty sentiments won't get you your father's money."

Woody presented his palms. "What else can I say?"

"What's this talk I've heard about you and an orphanage?" Father asked.

With prayers for their understanding, Woody laid out his ideas and their necessity.

After a long silence, Father stepped forward, reluctance etched in the lines around his eyes. "I'm torn, Son. Part of me hopes you've changed, wants to help you." Mother's face blanched. "Based on your behavior in the past, however, I can't allow myself to trust you. Until you can enter our home without bringing a trail of scandal, I think it's best you leave."

"Father, consider the children. The orphanage is a worthy—"

"Goodbye, Son."

Back rigid, Woody left with nothing but his integrity, and that he couldn't prove. They'd never had time for him when he was a youth; why should they now? He'd gone back for Ella, knowing they'd reject him beforehand, but that didn't lessen the pain of knowing he was unwanted, denied a place to belong.

At the canal, grasshoppers hummed through the tall grasses and birds sang a too-cheery song. With the sun warming his head, Woody leaned a hand against the boys' shelter, then smacked the wood with his palm, snatched off his tie. Crumpled the ribbon.

"What are you doing, God?" he asked, anchoring his fist on his thigh. "'Cause I sure can't see it now. Nothing is right. My parents are a lost cause. Even if the boys return, I can't provide for them like I want. And Ella..." How had it come to this? Woody massaged the bridge of his nose, eyes watering. "I thought she was the one."

With a grunt, he blinked. He'd survived rejection before. He'd do it again.

"I will never leave thee, nor forsake thee."

Woody swallowed hard, stared at nothing in particular. The inaudible words radiated in his mind with pulsing clarity. He must have read them in his Bible a hundred times or more, but did he let them change the way he lived?

"Forgive me, Lord." Foreboding circumstances didn't mean God was far off. The Lord was there when Pierce had found him and told him the good news of Jesus. When he received Molly's letter. When Ella crossed his path.

And here, now.

"The Lord is at hand," Woody whispered toward the sky. Not far away, but within his reach. *When my father and my mother forsake me, then the Lord will take me up.* He wasn't unwanted. He had a Father who'd paid the ultimate price for him.

A quiet conviction overcame Woody, quickening his heartbeats. Though he'd failed to retrieve funds for Ella's family, though he'd nothing to give her, he could still offer the comfort of these verses, assure her God cared.

But would seeing her again so soon make things harder for her?

Blowing out a deep breath, Woody replaced his tie. No. If the Holy Spirit wanted him to speak to Ella, he'd do so and leave the outcome to God.

What had he told the boys in their last Bible lesson? "Faith is trust in action."

Well, then. It was time to start living by faith.

◄──•◦•──►

At the soot-fogged train station, Ella examined the disembarking passengers for the third day straight.

When Woody met Ina, he'd understand why Ella couldn't stop fighting for her family.

Thunder clapped, and Ella trembled. Had Ina enjoyed the voyage or taken seasick? Was she any recovered from her usual illness?

A half hour later the sky opened in a deluge and forced Ella under the depot roof. The crowd thinned with no sign of a short, aproned girl with brownish-reddish braids wrapped in a kerchief. Fear gripped Ella's throat. What could have gone wrong?

A strange woman approached. She spoke in Polski, "Are you waiting on two women?"

Two? Ella tucked a windblown strand behind her ear. Perhaps Mother had asked another immigrant to chaperone Ina. "Maybe. My family name is Lipski."

"Mmm. Yes. One of them sickly."

Prickles crawled over Ella's shoulders and nested in the pit of her stomach. "That's my sister, Ina."

"Ah, I'm sorry. I met them on the boat." The woman's face wrinkled up before Ella's vision blurred her out.

Lord, please. "What happened?"

Old chin atremble, the woman grabbed her wrist with a bony hand. "She didn't make it, lamb."

"No." Hot tears plopped onto Ella's cheeks. It couldn't be.

But Ina should have arrived by now.

The woman patted her hand and mumbled something in a sad tone before limping off to join a young couple in a carriage.

When Ella could no longer bear up under their sympathetic stares, she sloshed away from the station. Numbness overtook her as the frigid downpour washed away her tears. She put one foot in front of the other until she entered Woody's quarters and shut the door behind her.

"Dear God, why?" she whispered into her trembling palm. She and Ina had such plans. Talked of raising their families together. "I thought You said You'd never forsake your own. Ina's always trusted You. Where is *Your* plan in this?"

Choking back a sob, Ella tossed her belongings in a crate. She'd failed her family. But then, she'd always been helpless to fix things.

Knowing that, she should never have involved Woody. She'd used him to learn the skills she needed to get Jamieson's attention. Woody deserved better. Her family deserved better than a failure for a daughter, a sister. She pressed her hand to her mouth and wept.

There was nothing left but to throw herself on Jamieson's mercy. Drunkard or not, she would propose to the man for the rest of her family's sake and never look back. *Lord in heaven, I can't do this without You. Show me what to do.*

Scavenging the room for items she'd missed, her eyes burned with new tears—everything bore traces of Woody. After smoothing the bedcovers, she wormed Ina's kerchief from under the pillow. Tracing the *Polski* words, she whispered them. "Walk by faith, not by sight. The just shall live by faith." Numerous scripture references followed. If God recorded the command so many times, He must have meant His children to take heed. Did—

"Where's Woody?"

Ella spun, wiping her face.

Freckles stood in the doorway, Newsie and Shoe Shine behind him supporting Musty, who glistened with tears and shuddered between hiccups. Freckles scanned her with a harried glance. "Musty broke his shoulder, I think. Why're *you* crying?"

Stuffing aside her grief, she brushed past him and set Musty upon the bed. "Let me see."

The lantern's glow revealed the odd tilt of the boy's shoulder. Ella gently probed the area, noticing he didn't cry out. "Woody's not here. He's living at the shelter you boys made by the canal—in case you came back. I'm. . .taking care of his house while he's gone."

Having grown up with three rough and tumble brothers, Ella easily diagnosed Musty's arm. "It's out of joint, not broken. Relax for me, and I'll put it back in place, all right?"

With a whine, Musty shook his head, inching away from her.

Freckles shook the boy's leg. "She's trying to help. You want to be better, don't you?"

Wiping his eyes, Musty nodded.

"Here, squeeze my hand." Freckles offered a dirty palm, and the little fellow gripped it with all his might.

Ella counted to two in her head, then shoved the bone into its joint.

Musty panted and whimpered, then his face cleared as he moved his little arm this way and that, as one might move a doll's arm. He hugged his tummy and smiled at her around the finger he stuck in his mouth. "Dziękuję."

"You're welcome, sweet one."

"Now, what's your problem?" Freckles put his hands on his hips. "You helped Musty. Maybe we can help you."

She sat down beside Musty with a sigh, a fresh wave of tears threatening. No one could help. But the need to share her burden with another human being overwhelmed her. She explained Ina's absence at the train station.

"But she might not be dead." Newsie scratched underneath his oversized cap, and for the first time she glimpsed more than his wide mouth. His eyes were blue.

"Yeah, that old lady could be wrong." Freckles said. "There's lots of people that don't show up at the trains 'cause they get held behind at Castle Garden.'Specially if they're sick like your sister, 'cause then they send 'em to the hospital to get well before they find jobs."

"Yeah," Newsie chimed in.

"Yeah." Musty, too.

Ella held her breath against rising hope. Could Ina simply be delayed? Could the old mother with failing ears have gotten the name wrong?

"We could pray for her." All eyes turned to Shoe Shine, with his impossibly long lashes and button-sized ears. It was the first he'd spoken since she met him. He blushed. "That's what Woody would do."

Ella exhaled, reached out to him, and brought him into the circle where he knelt beside the bed. "You're right."With Musty's little paw in one palm and Shoe Shine's rough one in the other, she closed her eyes, but struggled for a place to begin.

After a peek at each bowed head, warmth filled her heart. Though orphaned and unrelated, they still had faith for tomorrow. Had their own special brand of family, right here. And they were at peace. Something riches couldn't buy. Certainly not with Jamieson Leech.

Her own discontent over the last two months. . . How ugly and selfish it shone in the light of their behavior. She hadn't sought to please the Lord or know His will on how to find help for her family, but rather asked Him to bless her own plans. *I'm so sorry, Lord. I've been unwilling to put my trust in You to work. Even before Mama tasked me with marrying money, I've always wanted more than what You've given. I should be grateful You've allowed me to come to America at all.*

When Shoe Shine peeped at her, she prayed.

"Dear Father in heaven, thank You for these sweet boys. Thank You that they are safe and that You know where my sister is. Get her safely to me, Lord. . .if—if that's Your plan. If not, I know I'll see her in heaven one day." Her throat swelled to aching. "And the lady who died, please comfort her family. No matter what comes of this, help me obey You and trust You with the outcome. Thank You. Help Musty's arm, I pray. Amen."

"You said thank you a lot," Newsie observed.

Ella gave up restraining her smile. For the first time, her burden lightened. "I did, didn't I?" One by one, she hugged them, from Musty, who snuggled close, to Shoe Shine, who patted her shoulder and stepped away. "Thank you for suggesting we pray."

"Boys?" Woody stepped through the open doorway and approached. Caution, disbelief, then affection, lightened his gaze to molasses brown. He mussed Freckles's hair and left his hand there, taking in the vestiges of hers and Musty's tears. "What's going on?"

Freckles spoke up. "Ella fixed Musty's shoulder, and we told her her sister's not dead. Then we prayed."

"Oh?" Woody's dark eyes met hers, peaceful with tempered hope. The world slowed for a moment, warmed. As if she'd been wrapped in a blanket.

When Shoe Shine pressed the corners into her hands, she realized she had. In her grief, she'd forgotten her soggy state. "Thank you."

Woody came to kneel before her. "Ina wasn't at the station?"

"No," she whispered, eyes filling once more.

"Oh, Ella. I'm sorry." The grip of his hand conformed to hers like the most comfortable pair of shoes.

Drinking in his presence, she managed a nod, unwilling to release the connection though tears poured down her face. "I've given the situation to God." *Woody, too, Lord. You've given me a great gift in this man.* If he asked again, she'd be hard tempted not to say yes.

<hr />

"I've given the situation to God."

As Woody erased Ella's tears with his thumbs, his heart pounded at her words. She meant her sister's situation, of course, but what if she'd also given her marriage plans to God?

His gaze dropped to her full lips, and he swallowed the question slugging his ribcage. Selfish of him to think of his own heart when she didn't know if her sister was safe.

"God is a present help in times of trouble, Ella," Woody said, appreciating her smooth skin and the complete trust resting in her green eyes. "He's faithful. Remember that."

Covering his hand with her palm, she closed her eyes.

When something brushed his shoulder, he startled to find Musty leaning into him. Woody pulled the boy close, his heart still raw at seeing them all here, hale and whole. "I missed you boys. Every one."

"Sorry we ran off," Freckles said. "We thought Miss Ella would make you put us in a orphanage. Lots of ladies talk such, and we don't wanna go someplace we won't feel like family."

Ella finger-combed Freckles's hair. "I never want to make you go where you're scared or mistreated."

Amazed at the love creasing her brow, Woody addressed the boys. "I think you should get an education, though, so you can get good jobs when you become men. The place I want to build would help with that. Plus, you'd have beds and hot meals and someone to care for you if you got sick. I thought, too, we could hire folks from your home countries to help in the project."

The little ragamuffins perked up, and Woody's heart swelled. Ella's, too, judging by the way she watched him. "Miss Ella and I want you safe and well cared for."

"We know now, since she fixed Musty's arm." Newsie's proclamation brought nods all around and a twitch to Ella's lips.

"Good." Woody winked. "I'm working on a plan, fellas. All this is up to God, so help me pray hard, but don't get disappointed if He says no, right?"

"Right." A big nod from Musty. "He love and care of us."

The lisped words, sincerely spoken, made Woody's tear ducts burn. "You got it."

"Woody!" Ella breathed.

"What?" He jerked to his feet, wobbled, and grabbed Ella's arms. At her wide-eyed stare, he checked behind him, made sure the boys were safe, then looked back at her. "What's wrong?" She was obviously fine—or gone stark mad. That slow smile, however, could drive any red-blooded man mad along with her. Such a smile would fit his perfectly if he tilted his head just so. He blinked and dragged his thoughts to the matter at hand.

Ella gripped his elbows. "Woody, I have an idea."

Chapter Six

Ella licked her pencil point and scratched items off her list while she rocked down the street in the Pierce family carriage.

Have Woody ask Mr. Pierce to consider hosting a charity ball for the orphanage.
Check.

Woody had assured her Mr. Pierce would not support the orphanage until Pastor Bridges did. But on faith, Woody went to his friend anyway and found him in conversation with the pastor. The pastor mentioned the Harrison's butler, Steele, had told him how Woody visited the Harrison House several times a week now, reaching out to his family in love though never allowed entrance. The pastor and Pierce agreed then to help Woody with the orphanage project. Mrs. Pierce, after hiring Ella as part-time nanny, took over planning for the ball, which held every indication of becoming a smashing success.

Have tickets printed with "Elwood Harrison" as the guest of honor.
Call on New York City's richest gossipmongers to sell them ball tickets (dressed as a fine lady, of course!).

Woody achieved permanent hero status in Ella's heart when he volunteered to expose himself and resurrect his family scandal for the orphans' sakes. Intrigued as to why Mr. Pierce would honor such a "rogue" at his charity ball, the gossips bought tickets by the hundreds.

Convince the most influential to buy name spaces on a monument to donors.
Reserve twenty prominent name spaces for ball guests to bid upon during festivities.

The monument was her idea. And what a success! With Mr. Pierce handling the orphanage funds and his good name driving the event, status-seekers purchased name spaces at exorbitant prices.

Ella closed her eyes. Besides saving orphans from unmentionable dooms, this orphanage would secure her and Ina a future as staff members—Ella had to believe they'd find her sister soon.

Next item?

Organize boys' practice times so Woody won't find out.

After her fateful refusal of his proposal, she'd wanted to bless him somehow. The boys snapped up the idea. She just needed to keep the secret tucked away a few more hours.

"Have we forgotten anything?" Woody asked from the opposite seat.

Ella slapped her tiny notebook shut and laid a hand over her heart. "No, I think everything is accounted for."

"Sorry, I startled you." He took her hand.

At his continued perusal, she grew fidgety. Was her hair still in place? She smoothed her skirts—probably wrinkling horribly sitting this way. Did she appear the pretentious fool she felt?

"You look beautiful." In the glow of the carriage lamps, Woody's eyes shone warm and inviting. Entering the carriage on his arm earlier, it was all too easy to imagine herself as his wife and he as a millionaire, though she'd love him no matter his financial status.

"Thank you, Woody." Her cheeks radiated as she touched her borrowed pearls. Mrs. Pierce insisted Ella wear a new gown and lent her hairdresser.

Releasing her hand, he stretched his arm along the carriage cushion behind him. Not for the first time this evening, his slicked hair and tailored suit drew her eye. With that brooding gaze, square jaw, and kingly air, he must have broken many hearts during his reign as Elwood Harrison the Rake.

Each day she fell for him a little more. The way he loved the Pierce children with the same affection as the orphans melted her heart into mushy little bits and spiked her respect for the man he was.

She'd vowed to let God handle their future and not interfere, but nobody said faith came easy. Over the last weeks, Woody had limited himself to friendliness and hadn't mentioned his proposal again. Had he made up his mind to move on?

"Something wrong?" Woody asked.

She schooled her features. "No, just hoping tonight goes well."

Had she given the boys the right instructions about which entrance to use? Lord willing, the staff would let them in. House servants could be snobbier than the elite—especially to their own kind. And children seemed to reap the worst of any circumstance.

Woody toyed with the cushion seam. "Me too. Thank you for all you've done to make this possible."

Surely he knew she'd worked not only for herself but for his sake. "I would do it all over again if it would help you. . .help the boys."

His keen look intensified. Then he blinked and adjusted his lapel. "I know we've prayed for success all along, but. . .shall we pray together now?"

As Ella rested her hands in his and the unique tones of his voice flowed around them, she prayed for grace to accept the outcome of this night, whatever God chose to do. And He'd do it without hindrance from her, of this she was determined.

———— •◦• ————

As the orchestra hummed, Woody meandered through the ballroom, schmoozing potential donors. Ladies tittered behind their fans as he passed, no doubt giddy to see a former rogue in the flesh.

What he wouldn't give to wear Ella on his arm, showing her off to New York society. She should be sharing in the glory of the evening—her plan was working splendidly so far. But she'd disappeared five minutes ago—to the ladies' refreshment rooms perhaps?

Pierce proved selfless once again, renting Oration Hall to hold the massive number of people. Upon introducing Woody at the beginning of the ball, Pierce explained Woody's absence from polite society, reasoning he'd spent years living among the children, gaining their trust. Good ole Pierce simply left out the disinheritance part. Amazing how forgiving society became when someone of status and wealth endorsed you.

The chuckle rumbling his chest brought a curious glance from one matron drizzled with diamonds and lace.

Gasps quieted the room behind him.

He turned as Ella ushered in twenty or so street children, lining them up on the stage that held the orphanage monument.

No. Lord, please. Ella couldn't know the harm this would cause.

Already, judgment creased the donors' faces. It was bad enough society incriminated all street orphans as pickpockets. If the children paraded in front of these people, whose slander could destroy them beyond hope of good futures. . .

He had to help Ella get them out of here.

Halfway to the front he halted as his boys—and the new girls—harmonized the American national anthem in perfect choir formation.

Spellbound, he listened as the expressions of his peers became enraptured. Ella led the children through several foreign songs, French, German, Polish, then ended with the redemptive hymn, "Amazing Grace." Tears gathered in his eyes when they reached the lyrics, "I once was lost, but now am found."

Lord, let it be true of them. Physically and spiritually.

Several ladies—and gentlemen—dabbed their noses with embroidered handkerchiefs.

With a wink in his direction, Ella filed the children through the same door they'd entered.

When had this come about? The little sneak. He dabbed his eyes and wiped a hand over his mouth to cover his smile. What a woman.

If only. . . In his experience, charity balls performed well enough but wouldn't completely underwrite the orphanage cost. He'd wait to invite Ella to share his life until he could afford to hand her her dreams. He wouldn't have her wondering "what if" she'd married wealth. But earning enough to bring all her family to America could take years at the livery.

"Your attention, please," Pierce announced from the platform. "Bidding will now begin for the remaining name spaces on the Bright Hope Orphanage Monument. To encourage your donations, Mr. Harrison has agreed to match all funds up to fifty thousand dollars."

Between rounds of applause, the audience peppered the auctioneer with bids.

Woody's heart dropped, then rivaled the fireworks Pierce had ordered for the evening's finale. He exploded into action, meeting his friend coming off the stage. "You know I don't have that kind of money."

"I do." Father emerged from the crowd.

With a clap on Woody's back, Pierce exited.

"Father, what are you doing here?" Dumbfounded, Woody stared at the man whose features so closely resembled his own. "What changed your mind? And. . .thank you."

"Thank Franklin Pierce." Father led them to the room's edge. "When I heard you were to be guest of honor for this charity ball, I thought it a mockery. I called on Pierce and demanded a reason. His explanation, your persistent visits, and the fact you never turned vindictive when I refused your request for orphanage funds. . . Those are the reasons I'm here. Pierce relayed how you'd changed. Something of a religious nature, I believe? I'd like to hear more. For now. . .I think you ought to know your mother is here, too."

Though English, the words were difficult to comprehend. Could she finally forgive him. . .and he her? Woody spread his hand against his vest. "And?"

"All is not as it seems with her. She lost her brothers in the War." Father touched his limp sleeve. "And part of her husband. She also. . .lost several children before she birthed you."

"During your growing-up years, she was protecting you, in her own way." He motioned to where Mother stood aloof from a group of women. "Everyone bears a burden. Some are just more visible than others."

Woody studied his mother's proud posture. Yes, she'd been hard, cruel. But had he judged her heartless when she was only reacting to pain? "I had no idea. I'll talk to her before the night's over."

"I can't say whether she'll receive you."

After a moment, Woody nodded. "That's fine."

Father's meaty hand clasped his shoulder. "I'm proud of you, Son. You've got a place in the railroad business anytime you want. Oh, and the shares in your name. . .I never changed them. They're yours."

Woody's head came up. At the kindness in his father's eyes, the approval he'd craved for years, his limbs began to shake. He'd prayed, but never dreamed. . . Why was he surprised when God came through for him?

"Thank you." His voice closed off, so he tried again. "Thank you, sir."

"Seems there's a young lady to whom you'd like to tell the news." Father nodded across the room to where Ella watched the bidding, hands clasped at her bosom.

"Go on, now. Don't forget I want to meet her soon." With one last shoulder squeeze, Father left.

Exhaling disbelief and gratitude in the same breath, Woody crossed the ballroom toward the object of his affection, a beautiful vision in a blush-pink gown, the style of which he couldn't begin to name.

How would she react to the news? If she let him, he'd give her the world, whether she loved him or not. A man who'd lost his heart couldn't be choosy.

The crowd moved to obscure her, and he wove his way through. The grand ballroom was perfect for proposing. Perhaps for announcing their engagement as well, once she met his parents.

If she said yes.

God, grant me the right words this time.

<hr>

"You've been avoiding me."

Ella turned to find Jamieson Leech serving himself a glass of punch. Why was he here? Not to get back at Woody, she hoped. Whatever the reason, Leech's presence would save her a trip to break things off with him. She began her rehearsed English speech. "Mr. Leech, I must apologize. I've—"

"Mr. Leech?" He chuckled. "I thought we had an understanding."

"This is what I am try to tell you. I only court you for your money. I'm sorry."

Leech shrugged and looked her over while taking a sip. "Then marry me."

Ella's brows sank in a scowl. Was the man obtuse?

"I'm rich." He continued to leer. "I've got what you want. . .and you've got what I want."

Engulfed in hot indignation, she spun and started toward the tall French doors leading to the veranda. She needed some air. Very cool, very breezy, and very quick. Lest she do something rash and jeopardize the whole night—like empty the punch bowl on him.

He caught her hand. "Sweetheart, it's obvious we belong together."

Forcing a smile so as not to cause a scene, she pried her hand from his. Her anger made translating to English difficult. "*Mister* Leech, I cannot do this 'understanding.' I am no longer needing for to marry money. No. . . . I will follow God. He will guide for who I marry. Not you. Not me. If you come to this ball only for to proposing to me, you should be leaving. Goodnight, sir!"

"Listen, doll. . ." He grabbed her arm. Icy shivers chilled her spine.

Woody clamped the back of Leech's neck. "You've worn out your welcome, old pal. Don't force me to toss you out."

When released, the vulture ground his jaw and left with his coattails flapping, the crowd parting to let him pass.

Woody brushed her arm and led her toward the French doors. "You okay?"

"Yes." Ella regained her breath, but her heart still thrummed—what if she'd married that scoundrel? Good riddance. Ella touched her lips, suppressing sudden mirth before lapsing into Polski. "Ooh, Woody, that was magnificent."

Straightening his lapels over the tall, confident frame Ella had come to love, he stepped close, eyes turning to molten chocolate while his mussed hair begged her smoothing touch. "Funny, I was thinking the same of a beautiful woman I know. First with the choir—very sneaky, by the way—then with telling off Leech. . . Did you mean what you told him?" His warm regard soothed her frazzled nerves.

"Every word. I'm trusting God to make a way for my family while I pray daily."

"Let me pay their way to America."

She shook her head. "I can't accept what will take years for you to earn. I know you don't have the money—"

"I do now." The joy defining his eyes and cheekbones thickened her pulse.

"Woody, what are you saying?"

"Because of what you've done to make tonight possible, my father has welcomed me back to the family business."

"I don't understand." She placed a hand to her bosom, afraid to hope.

"We can build ten orphanages if you want. And have your family here within the year."

Her mouth fell open, and breathing became difficult. But. . .she'd turned him down. How could he be willing to—

"Keep looking at me like that, sweetheart," he groaned, "and I'm going to kiss you in front of all these people."

With a shocked laugh, she covered her scalding cheeks, but when he took her gloved hands in his, her heart responded to everything his eyes promised.

"Ella. . . I never thought I'd open my heart to love like this. Then I met you. Never dreamed I'd find someone who loves the kids like you do. You've challenged me to reach beyond myself to do what's best for the boys—and girls. And you encouraged me to repair the breach in my family, which in turn healed me of a deep wound." Woody kneaded her palms and leaned in, like he'd lost something precious in her gaze. "I love you, Ella. Your honesty and compassion have completely captured my affections. . . Plus, you're the most beautiful woman in this room, and I feel privileged you've put up with me this long. So please, when I ask to fund your family's trip to America, let me?"

Tears spilling down her cheeks by now, she laughed. "I love you, too, Woody. But I vow I'll earn the money myself unless you say you want to marry me."

A slow smile. "Marry me, darling. I want to spend the rest of my life loving you."

"Yes," she sighed.

Gathering her against his chest, Woody rested his cheek atop her head, his warmth overwhelming her. A lump rose in her throat as she hugged him back. How wonderful, the first time she'd been held after months without hugs from her family. Did he know what he was doing to her heart? "Oh, love, thank you." She melted into his embrace.

The orchestra quieted in preparation for the first dance, signaling Woody's duty as guest of honor to take a turn with the most prominent ladies attending. Oh, bother.

He eased back, smile twitching. "You know, that was the most beautiful proposal I've ever received from a lady."

Her ears caught fire.

Quick as a candle's flicker, he swooped in for a soft peck on her lips. Gasping, she swayed toward him and caught a hint of lemon drops, but he gently set her back. "I've got to go, but this conversation's nowhere near finished."

The diverted glances he sent her way as he gained the front of the ballroom promised a proper engagement kiss would be hers before the night's end.

A bit disappointed he didn't ask her for the first dance, Ella gathered her heavy skirts and edged toward the refreshment table where Musty and Shoe Shine drained their punch cups, sandwiches in their free hands. Hadn't she told them to remain in the playroom with the games and snacks she'd prepared? They'd develop stomachaches if they kept this up.

Murmurs drew her gaze to where Woody stood before his mother, expression shielded. Ella's breath stagnated in her lungs while Mrs. Harrison stared back, spine rigid.

If he'd wanted an opportunity to humiliate his mother for years of neglect and ill will, this was it.

After a slight hesitation, he lifted his chin and extended a gloved hand.

Ella's heart swelled nigh to painful. Oh, that man. She laced her gloved fingers together and felt pressure from her left ring finger. Flipping her palm, she caught a silver glimmer. Two hands holding a crowned heart.

"Woody," she breathed, flicking the moisture from her tear-blurred eyes. Stealthy as a pickpocket, he must have slipped it on her finger while holding her hands.

What had it cost him to give her such a dear piece of his past?

She made a fist and cradled the treasure against her chest. *You knew all along, didn't You, Lord? You sent Woody, not only to look after me but after my heart as well.*

After several aching moments, Mrs. Harrison glanced about, then slipped her hand into Woody's grasp. He made a broad, dashing figure as he drew her into his arms for a waltz. All eyes followed their whirling figures, the unheard exchange of mother and son softening their features from hesitant to hopeful.

Ella thumbed his ring—*her* ring. Had this New York prince just proposed to her, a humble Polish farm girl, or was she dreaming?

That kiss, though. . . Tender, but powerful. Not a dream.

Woody, her Woody, who loved street kids and peach pies and maps and tea, who lived and breathed languages and boxing and compulsive organizing—now a millionaire, wanted to share his life with her, his aspirations, his possessions. . .and the greatest prize of all, his heart.

Epilogue

Kiss me like you did the night we became engaged."

In the downstairs parlor of the orphanage, Woody grinned at his wife's heavy Polish accent and settled her more securely on his knee. In the eight months since their engagement and seven months since they married, she'd requested he do this twenty times at least.

Maybe thirty. "You never tire of that, do you?"

She touched her nose to his. "Mmm."

Good. Neither did he.

And right now, he'd do whatever it took to keep her distracted until her family arrived—a surprise he'd hidden for weeks now. Not the fact they were coming to America, but that they would land today, in time to celebrate her birthday tomorrow.

"Well, all right, then. I had no *idea* I made such an impression." He swooped in for a quick peck on the lips.

Rolling those vibrant eyes, she crossed her arms, a delicious pink stealing over her neck and face.

He bit his lip and tried to appear innocent. "What?"

"You know that's not the one I meant."

"Yes, but now you're blushing like you did the moment I took you in my arms under the fireworks." So what if his smile was smug—he couldn't help it. She was too beautiful tinted red not to tease her once in a while. "The moment wouldn't be the same without it. Careful, darlin', if your chin rises anymore I fear it'll hit the ceiling."

With a glare, she edged her lovely pregnant bulk off his lap. "If I blushed it was because the boys were staring from the ballroom, watching us."

He gathered her right back, resting his palm over the side where his son or daughter always kicked. *God, I'm a blessed man. Thank You.* "Mmm—no, sweetheart. I faced the ballroom, remember? I clued you in on the boys' watching *after* I finished kissing you."

She squinted, then nibbled her lip. "Really?"

His smile stretched wide, the heel of his hand absently kneading her back muscles. If he'd known how adorably forgetful she'd be with this pregnancy, he'd have told her much earlier how he'd sent for her family. Each morning she woke to the remembrance—she even had to reorient herself after naps—they got to celebrate all over again.

One thing she'd likely never forget was her reunion with Ina. The girl's ship had docked for repairs, hence her late arrival. Ina took to Freckles, Newsie, Shoe Shine, and Musty right off. Now she and the foursome waited in the foyer, watching for the carriage he'd sent for her parents. His parents agreed to come, too, but Mother begged off until tomorrow. He'd make their relationship better, if it took him the rest of his life.

Now where was he? Oh yes, the boys.

"Yes," he said. "So I think you first blushed simply because my nearness makes you weak." This he whispered against her neck, unable to keep his lips away—or the husky laughter from his voice. What flowery perfume was this?

"Nonsense." Her breathless laughter belied her words.

"Then why did you blush when our gazes first met with no one else watching?"

She drew back. "Because you'd run me over with your wagon and I was embarrassed from falling on my face."

He frowned. "That's not when our eyes first met."

"It's not?" Her brows dipped.

"No. . ." He patiently recounted how he'd noticed her long before the wagon incident and couldn't wait to find a reason to talk to her.

"Oh, Woody." She leaned in, and he closed his eyes.

<hr />

"Woody?" Couldn't the man remember anything?

His eyes peeped open in the most adorably sheepish way. "I thought you were about to kiss me," he confessed.

Ella chuckled. "No, *you* were going to kiss *me*."

"Oh?" The backs of his fingers stroked her lips. "Yes. I was, wasn't I?" Gifting her with his softest smile, the handsome young orphanage master gathered her close—their child nestled between them—and directed his beautiful brown gaze to hers, the intense possessive gleam there setting her pulse to jumping. Sliding his thumbs to her temples, he angled her face, kissing first the right corner of her mouth, then the left. With a sigh, he murmured in Polski, "I love you, Marcella Elena Lipski Harrison, with all that's in me."

Her eyes moistened, and her heart smiled, but she refused to let pregnancy tears ruin this moment. "I love you, too, Elwood Joseph Harrison," she whispered. "For richer or poorer. . ." At her words, he claimed her lips, the scrape of his whiskers drawing her fingertips to the soft hair at his temples, his breath bringing the familiar smell of leather and lemon and Woody. He smelled like home. She sighed and burrowed her hand into his hair. His heart thundering under her other palm, Woody tightened his hold and deepened his kiss while he plucked the pins from her hair. After eight months of marriage, the cherished feeling of being held in her husband's arms still overwhelmed her with newness.

"Oh!" Ina stood in the doorway, then turned around.

Ella startled, then stared at Woody. His dark locks jutted every which way, and hers, freed from its pins, now pooled at her collarbone. She tucked her brow against his shoulder to hide a giggle—and her hot face. Between selling the livery and getting the children and employees settled at the new orphanage, she suffered a twinge of jealousy at having to share her husband all the time.

"Remind me"—his words rustled against ear—"to tell my contractor to hurry up and add our wing to the orphanage."

Before Ella could ask what Ina needed, the doorbell rang, and the girl ran to answer.

Ella hopped off Woody's lap—something she hadn't thought possible in her current walrus phase—and began fixing her hair. Woody ran his right hand over his own hair, then his left—she loved when he did that—then commenced brushing the wrinkles from her dress. They possibly could've gone on like that for some time—wrinkles, wrinkles everywhere—but Steele appeared.

"Announcing Mr. and Mrs. Tabor, Mr. and Mrs. Lipski, and young master Lipski."

"What?" Searching Woody's innocent expression, then fixating on the empty doorway, Ella fought for each breath, her heartbeat thumping her ears. She flexed her fingers toward Woody's hand and found him already reaching to take hers. Once again tears overtook her, but she didn't stop them. Why try when she'd be drowning before the day's end? "You arranged this didn't you, so they'd arrive for my birthday?"

He simply pressed a kiss to her hair.

Her grip tightened. So long she'd waited—would have waited longer if not for him. She brought his wrist to her lips.

When little Feliks stepped into the archway, followed by Mama, Tata, Grandma, and Grandpa, Ella gave a cry and rushed into their circle of kisses and mingled tears. Then one by one she hugged them, Mama crowing as Ella's belly impeded their embrace. When they calmed enough for Ella to remember, she crossed to where Woody stood back a respectful distance and took his hand to introduce him.

After sedate greetings, Grandpa yanked him into a mammoth hug and Woody exploded into laughter. Her family congratulated and teased the new "tata," and Woody gave and received in kind.

Pride expanded her lungs, knowing her beloved made this possible. He, who often woke up on the floor, insisting he wasn't yet used to a soft bed after sleeping at the boys' shack. When all along she knew he'd gotten on his knees sometime in the night and fallen asleep praying for orphan children across the city still sleeping in cobblestoned alleyways.

While Ina presented the boys to her family, Woody gathered Ella against him with a wink. "*Kocham Cię kochanie.*"

She pressed a kiss to his jaw, replying in English, "I love you, too." How blessed she was to have a man who put his faith into action. Her thumb traced his knuckles. Maybe it wasn't possible for them to rescue all the lost boys and girls in New York and New Jersey, but. . .

Or was it? *With God, nothing shall be impossible. . . .*

Natalie Monk is a member of the American Christian Fiction Writers and is represented by Tamela Hancock Murray of the Steve Laube Agency. A country girl from the time she could shimmy under a string of barbed wire, Natalie makes her home in south Mississippi, where she proudly wears the label "preacher's kid." She is a homeschool graduate, piano instructor, and former post hole digger. She loves porch swings, old-fashioned camp meetings, and traveling with her family's singing group. Her goal in writing, and in living, is to bring glory to her Savior, Jesus Christ. Come chat with her on her website: www. nataliemonk.com.

A House of
Secrets

by Michelle Griep

Dedication

To the One who knows the secrets of my soul.

Acknowledgments

Thank you to those who polish my stories to a fine sheen:

Elizabeth Ludwig, Ane Mulligan, Julie Klassen, MaryLu Tyndall, Shannon McNear & Chawna Schroeder.

And a huge shout out to you, readers, who make this all worthwhile.

Chapter One

St. Paul, Minnesota
1890

"He's late. Are you worried?"

The question floated across the sitting room like an unmoored specter, haunting Amanda Carston about the constancy of her fiancé. A smile quirked her lips. Good thing she didn't believe in ghosts.

"Come away from the window, Mags. Watching for Joseph won't make him appear any sooner." She rose from the settee, smoothing wrinkles from her gown. "He'll be here."

Maggie turned from the glass, letting the sheer fall back into place. "But it's your engagement dinner. And the *Pioneer Press* photographer will be there. How can you possibly be so calm?" She drew near and pressed her fingers against Amanda's forehead. "Are you feeling ill?"

"Don't be silly." Amanda batted her hand away, frowning. Being late for a dinner party was the least of her concerns this weekend. Coming up with a service project idea by Monday—her first as the new Ladies' Aide Society chairwoman—vexed her more.

Maggie's brow creased. "You *are* worried. Don't pretend."

Slamming the lid on her chairwoman woes, she smiled at her friend. "I am sure Joseph's aunt is used to delaying a meal even with important guests in attendance. A city attorney's schedule is rarely predictable."

"Ahh, but it's not his aunt who alarms me." Light from the gas lamps glistened on the pity filling Maggie's eyes. "What of your father, dearest?"

This time doubt didn't float in. It fell heavy on her spirit like a tempest, and her smile faded. Father would be disappointed at her tardiness. But truly, they all would have been late if he'd had to swing by from the office to pick up her and Mags. Must something always thwart her efforts to please her father?

She whirled and strode from the sitting room. "Let's bundle up so we may leave for Aunt Blake's as soon as Joseph arrives."

Maggie's footsteps echoed into the foyer, and by the time they slipped into their cloaks and secured their hats with a final pinning in front of the big mirror, the knocker pounded against the door.

"No need to trouble yourself, Grayson." Her words halted the butler's trek down the grand staircase. "I'm certain it's Mr. Blake. Don't expect us until late."

Ignoring his scowl and his "highly improper," she swung open the door to the man of her dreams—

And a police officer.

"Joseph?" she murmured.

A smile flashed across his face, brilliant in the dark of the October eve. He reached for her hand and pressed a kiss against the back of her glove, the heat of his mouth warming the fabric. "Don't panic, my love. Just a bit of business left over from the office. Please allow me to introduce Officer Keeley. Officer, my fiancée, Miss Amanda Carston." He leaned in scandalously close, breathing warmth into her ear. "Soon to be Mrs. Joseph Blake."

She arched a brow, unsure if she ought to censure him or wrap her arms around him. Instead, she nodded at Keeley. "Pleased to meet you, Officer."

He tugged the brim of his hat. "The pleasure is mine, Miss Carston."

Behind her, Maggie cleared her throat.

"My apologies, Miss Turner." A sheepish grin curved Joseph's mouth. "May I introduce you as well? Miss Turner, meet Officer Keeley. Officer Keeley, Miss Turner, my fiancée's confidante and partner in crime."

Amanda stepped closer to Joseph, speaking for his ears alone. "Does your aunt know to set another place?"

He winked down at her. "The officer won't be joining us for dinner. He's along to help me attend to an unfinished matter beforehand. Now shall we?"

He offered his arm and Amanda wrapped her fingers around his sleeve. Unfinished business? Whatever it was must be important, but tonight of all nights? She puzzled over the mystery until the feel of his muscles riding hard beneath her touch drove her to distraction. Inhaling his familiar fragrance of sandalwood and ink, she was hard-pressed to figure out which made her more weak-kneed—the intimacy of knowing his scent, or his husky voice caressing her ear.

"You look lovely tonight," he whispered.

Her cheeks heated. Good thing Maggie and the officer walked ahead—and what a pair they made. Him tall. Her short. A canyon of difference between a suit of blue and the golden gown of a railroad tycoon's daughter.

Joseph helped her into the carriage, and she settled next to Maggie, the men on the opposite seat. The driver urged the horses from the circular drive on to Summit Avenue, and just as she opened her mouth to ask Joseph about his unfinished business, the carriage turned left.

Left?

She peered out the window. Indeed, they headed east, not west, rolling past the old Grigg place. Despite being in the company of a strapping fiancé and a lawman, she shuddered at the eerie sight. At the front of the lot, half-burned timbers reached into the night sky, dark on dark, like blackened bones trying to escape from a grave. Beyond the remnants of the gatehouse stood the ruins of a once-grand home, bricks holding in secrets like a jealous lover, guarding rumors of foul play. If the city were going to do nothing about this blight, then maybe. . .perhaps. . .

The seed of a glorious idea took root. This just may be the service project she'd been looking for. Indeed, the more she thought on it, the larger the idea grew.

Until the carriage turned left yet again. She squinted into the darkness as they traveled farther from their engagement announcement. "This isn't the way to your aunt's."

"No, it isn't. As I've said, a small bit of business first. Merely a short detour."

Joseph's words pulled her gaze to him. "Where are we going?"

"To Hannah Crow's."

Amanda's jaw dropped. Maggie gasped, her fingers fluttering to her chest. Officer

Keeley took a sudden interest in looking out the window. Clearly he was in on this—whatever *this* was.

"Joseph Blake!" she scolded. "Why on earth are you taking us to a brothel?"

⸺ ❖ ⸺

Like an arc of lightning, blue-tinged and life threatening, the flash in his fiancée's eyes struck Joseph—with humor. The little firebrand. He stifled a grin. He could get used to such passion, but he sure hoped not. Her fiery spirit was what attracted him to her in the first place.

"I thought you might like to see the culmination of a year's worth of work," he said.

"Mr. Blake." Amanda's friend clutched her hands to her chest, eyes wide. "Surely you've never set foot in such a place?"

Amanda studied him a moment more, then leaned sideways, lips twisted into a smirk. "Don't fall for his dramatics, Mags. He's playing us with as much finesse as his violin."

Keeley elbowed him. "You've met your match in that one, sir."

Indeed. Why was God so good to him? He folded his arms and relaxed against the seat, memorizing how the passing streetlights bathed half of Amanda's face in golden light, the other dark. The contrast was a perfect picture of what lay beneath. . .pluck and humility. Softness and steel.

"I suppose she'll suit," he drawled.

She swatted his knee. "You, sir, are a scoundrel."

He caught her hand before she could pull it away and kissed her fingertips. "Ahh, but I am your scoundrel, hmm?"

Color deepened on her cheeks. "Not if we never make it to our betrothal dinner. Father could always change his mind, you know."

Joseph rapped the carriage wall, urging the driver to up his pace, then faced Miss Turner. "My soon-to-be wife is somewhat used to my unorthodox ways, but I can see you are not. In answer to your question, Miss Turner, while I am well versed in Hannah Crow's business, I have never entered her establishment. My aim is to shut her down, and I've finally found a way. That's why Officer Keeley is with us tonight."

"Wonderful news!" Amanda beamed at him—a smile of which he'd never tire.

Miss Turner frowned, eyeing the policeman. "Are you expecting trouble?"

"Don't fret, miss." Keeley tipped his head at her. "I'm merely a formality, a witness to the delivery of a document."

The grind of cobbles beneath the wheels changed to a gravelly crunch as the carriage eased off Summit and onto Washington Street. Miss Turner balanced a hand against the side of the carriage as they lurched around a corner, or did she clutch it for courage? Amanda's gaze found his, and he searched the blue depths. Was she afraid as well?

Nothing but clear admiration blinked back. "I am so proud of you, even if your timing is a bit off."

Law and order! With regard such as this, he could conquer more than a brothel—he could take on the world. He leapt out of the carriage before it stopped and patted his coat to make sure the injunction still rode inside his pocket. This was it. Finally. A night he wouldn't soon forget.

He and Keeley climbed the stairs to Crow's House of Hair. Hair products, of all things. The sign, the business, the audacity fooled no one. More went on behind those velvet drapes than the production and distribution of supposed growth elixirs—and everyone knew it. Sorrow punched him hard in the gut for the women trapped inside, chained by desperation and lost hope. He bit back a wince. The thought that Elizabeth had died as such nearly drove him to his knees.

He swallowed against the tightness in his throat and reached to ring the bell, but his finger hovered over the button. Something wasn't right. Lifting his face, he narrowed his eyes above the doorframe. The House of Hair sign was gone.

Keeley nudged him. "What are you waiting for?"

Exactly. So what if the sign was missing? He shook off a foreboding twinge and punched the button.

No answer.

He stabbed his finger on it again.

And. . .nothing.

Keeley shouldered past him and pounded the door so that it rattled in the frame. "Open up! We know yer in there. Don't make me bust down this—"

The door swung open. A glass chandelier rained beams of light onto a woman buttoned tight from toe to neck. Hannah Crow could be anyone's saintly aunt. Prim and proper on the outside—but that gray silk encased wickedness and greed.

Joseph stared at her angular face, refusing to look past her. One glimpse of a young girl tangled in her web would undo him, despite standing on the brink of this victory. Even so, loss clenched his jaw.

Oh, Elizabeth. Would that you'd been able to escape such a fate.

"Mr. Blake." Mrs. Crow dipped her head, a nod toward respectability—the closest she'd ever get. Then her dark gaze glittered, little lines spidering out at the creases of her eyes. "Bit late for you to be calling. Is this business or pleasure?"

"Entirely my pleasure." He handed over the injunction.

Hannah's eyes scanned back and forth, top to bottom, and in case she didn't understand all the legal jargon, Joseph added, "According to a recent addition to ordinance 245.1, your conditional use variance is null and void. In essence and practicality, madam, this is the end of your business."

"Well, well. . ." She lifted the paper high and released the document to the October breeze.

Keeley growled. "Even if that paper blows to kingdom come, Mrs. Crow, I seen you take it. I seen you read it. I'll swear to that in court."

She smiled at him as she might a mark with no money, her chipped eyetooth reminding Joseph of a sharpened fang. "No need, Officer. There will be no hearing. That ordinance means nothing to me. My home is no longer a business, just a humble abode."

A genuine smile tugged at Joseph's lips. "Nice try, Mrs. Crow, but that won't help you. This property is zoned for business, so either way, you're finished."

Her hand disappeared inside a pocket, and she pulled out a folded document, offering it to him with a feline stretch.

What sorcery was this? He yanked the paper open. Snippets of phrases pummeled him back a step. Emergency city council meeting. Dated the previous day. Zoning changed to residential. Signed by Willard Craven.

A slow burn ignited, from stomach to throat. Craven! He should've known.

Wheeling about, he stalked toward the carriage and called over his shoulder, "We'll see about this."

And he'd have to—or he'd be out of a job by month's end, his sister's death still unavenged.

Chapter Two

Most of the shameless maples had already disrobed for their coming marriage to winter, but a few discreet maidens refused to shed their orange and red leaves. Amanda lifted her face and relished the spot of colorful brilliance in front of the ruined Grigg house. Surely if God created such beauty in the midst of ashes, He could do anything. . .like help her—for surely it would take heavenly assistance to accomplish the plan she was about to undertake.

A small flame of guilt kindled in her heart, and she closed her eyes. *Forgive me, Lord.* For indeed, He already had helped her at dinner last Friday night. Not a miracle of Red Sea proportions—for Father had been snappish over her tardiness. But at least he'd not made too big of a scene, especially when Joseph took full responsibility for their lack of punctuality.

Behind her, carriage wheels rolled to a stop, and her eyes popped open, pulling her back to the present. Was she ready for this?

"This is an interesting venue for our Ladies' Aide Society meeting." Maggie's voice turned her around.

Her friend's glance drifted to the burnt gatehouse. She crossed the boulevard and stopped on the drive next to Amanda. "What are you up to?"

Direct as always—which is what she loved most about Mags. No guile. No secrets. Amanda smiled. "I had a wonderful idea."

Maggie's lips pulled into a pout. "If it involves the Grigg house, then it might be your last idea as chairwoman. The place is positively haunted."

A parade of lacquered carriages rolled up the street, one by one stopping to let out an array of colorful gowns. One in particular was more stunning than the rest.

Maggie shook her head. "I'm surprised Lillian agreed to meet here."

"She didn't. . .exactly."

Maggie pulled her gaze from the women swarming their way. "How did you manage that?"

She shrugged. "I sent a note to her driver, along with a little incentive."

Maggie's brows drew together. "I hope you know what you're doing, dearest."

Her breath caught in her throat. So did she.

Lillian Warnbrough, one part peacock, the other lioness, led the remaining nine members of the Ladies' Aide Society to a standstill in front of Amanda. Without so much as a '*good afternoon,*' she started right in. "I demand to know why we are meeting outdoors like common laborers."

This was it. *Lord, give me strength.* Amanda stiffened her shoulders—and her resolve—then flashed a smile. "Ladies, I have a surprise for you."

Lillian faced Amanda with a thundercloud of a scowl. "Do *not* tell me you're thinking of holding the fall festival here."

"No, of course not." It was a struggle, but she held onto her smile, albeit tightly. "I've found our next project, the Grigg home."

Lillian sniffed, the closest she ever came to an outright snort. "I hardly think removing a blight in our neighborhood would be looked kindly upon by the"—she waved her hand toward downtown—"less fortunate."

Her smile slipped. The only type of aid Lillian liked to supply was that which benefited her. Amanda bit the inside of her cheek lest unkind words slide out with her proposition.

Counting to ten, she smoothed her skirts before she spoke. "I suggest we renovate, not remove. While it's true we've helped the poverty stricken with their housing, I feel there is more work to be done. And aid is what our society is all about, is it not?"

Some ladies huddled closer, clearly interested. The rest looked to Lillian for her response.

But Amanda charged ahead before anyone could object. "We shall restore the old Grigg house into a school for the downtrodden."

Lillian's head shook before Amanda even finished. "Ridiculous. There are already schools. Many, in fact. This is a waste of time." She turned away.

"You're right on that account, but children of the poor do not attend those schools. Did you know there is an ordinance excusing the absences of those unable to dress properly?"

Lillian whirled back, a gleam of victory shining in her eyes. "Opening another school will not change that."

Amanda sucked in a breath. If she could pull this off, not only would the poor of St. Paul receive an education, but her father might finally see that she—a woman—could do something of value. She clasped both hands at her waist and stood taller. "True, yet we will not only provide the institution, but the uniforms, as well. It's a victory for us in that there will no longer be a decrepit piece of property driving down costs of the adjoining lots, and an even bigger triumph for the poor children who will receive an education. And in the grand scheme of things, you must agree, Lillian, this would be a huge conquest against ignorance and destitution."

A few birds chirped. What leaves remained rustled in the breeze. But no one said a word. Not even Lillian.

Amanda lifted a helpless gaze to Maggie.

She smiled back. "I think it's a wonderful idea."

Lillian huffed. "I suppose it has its merits." She stepped so close, the sparks in her eyes burnt holes in Amanda's confidence. "But know this: I will not have your little scheme interfering with our fall festival. It's tradition, something you seem to have a hard time grasping." She retreated a step to stare down her elegant nose. "There is no possible way we can arrange a respectable dinner and ball by mid-November if we do not begin plans by the first. So, I counter your proposal. If, as chairwoman of the society, you produce the deed to the Grigg house, then we parcel out the renovation to the lowest bidders."

For the first time since the meeting began, the tension pounding in Amanda's temples began to slip away. Success was at hand.

Lillian narrowed her eyes. "If you cannot secure the deed by the end of October, however, this little endeavor is over. In the meantime, the rest of us will begin working on the festival."

What? She threw out her hands. "How am I to purchase a lot on my own in less than one month? How am I to even find the owner?"

Lillian quirked a perfectly arched brow. "You concede, then. Good." She spun, her hat ribbons hitting Amanda on the cheek. "Come along, ladies. We have a festival to plan."

"No!"

Lillian spun back. "What did you say?"

For a second, her knees trembled. She glanced over her shoulder, picturing the many lives that would be changed from this renovation. This *had* to work.

She lifted her chin. "I shall have the deed in my hands by the thirty-first."

A wicked grin pulled up the sides of Lillian's pouty little mouth. "A fitting deadline to purchase a haunted house, is it not?"

Striding through the front door of the Minnesota Club, Joseph swept off his hat. He gave a brief tip of his head at the coat check as he draped his topcoat over his arm. He wouldn't be here long enough for that. Hopefully.

"Mr. Blake! What a pleasure." The maître d', Pierre François, rushed from his podium. He greeted Joseph with a firm handshake and an accent that was no more French than Joseph was a Shetland pony.

"I suppose it has been awhile, eh, François?" He patted the man on the back. "How goes it?"

"Ahh, you know. A little intrigue, a lot of tips." He waggled his eyebrows. "And good thing you've kept hold of your topcoat. *Ze* club is a little brisk tonight, despite the hearth fires."

"Don't tell me you still haven't replaced the boiler man?"

"Oh-ho-ho...'*zen* I will not." François chuckled. "Though I hear tell a new one is soon to be hired. Let us hope he is not *très incompetent,* or it will be a long winter. Now then, how can I be of service to you tonight, monsieur?"

Joseph peered past François's shoulder, into the lounge area of the gentlemen's club. From this angle it was impossible to see much. He cut his gaze back to François. "I'm looking for Mr. Craven. Is he here?"

"He is." François nodded. "Shall I direct you?"

He held up a hand. "No need, thank you."

As he slipped past the maître d', he pressed a coin into the fellow's hand. He strode through the grand pillars standing tall on either side of the entrance and entered the ornate receiving room of the Minnesota Club, the haunt of movers and shakers. The room reeked of bourbon, smoke, and far too much power. A chill snaked up his pants leg. François wasn't kidding about the sorry state of warmth in here. It would be a *very* long winter if they didn't get that boiler going.

Ahead, a few senators huddled at a table, playing a game of five-card draw. Near the hearth, a tycoon and a judge warmed their backsides while engaging in an even hotter debate. How many deals were struck in this room? How many underhanded schemes?

Across the room, near the servants' door, Willard Craven sat ensconced at a table between two gas lamps. The brilliance illuminated splotches of red on his fat cheeks, a skin problem he'd acquired from too much malt liquor. In fact, everyth . . . too much. The white satin bow tie and winged collar. The jewele . . . fingers. His ego. He watched Joseph approach, the cigar in his mo . . . color as he puffed away.

Joseph stopped two paces from him. "A word, if you please, Cra . . .

"Well, well. . ." Willard punctuated the air with his cigar, pull . . . nabes into his orbit. "Witness, my dear fellows, a rare sighting of the . . . a creature who generally hides in a cloister of righteousness and justi . . . and who seldom partakes of company carrying the faintest whiff of debauchery. Tell me, Blake"—he rolled the cigar between forefinger and thumb as he spoke—"have you finally stepped down from your pedestal to rub shoulders with us wretches?" With his free hand, he snapped his fingers. "Porter! Another chair, please."

Joseph halted the porter with a shake of his head. "No need. This won't take long."

"So, you've not come to drink or game?" Craven took a drag on his cigar and blew out a puff of smoke. "I thought not."

Such dramatics. It was a struggle to keep his eyes from rolling. "You know why I'm here, Craven."

The big man shrugged, the shoulders of his tuxedo rolling with the movement. "Can't imagine."

"Your little meeting of the zoning commission doesn't fool me. There's a rat at city hall, a pack of them, and you're the leader."

"Pish! It's always a conspiracy with you." Craven chuckled then tamped out his cigar in a crystal ashtray. "There was nothing more devious about that meeting than astute revenue generation. Profits were down on business, and residential property taxes are on the rise. Changing the zoning will be a boon to the city."

Of all the bald-faced lies. Joseph clenched his hands into fists, fighting to keep them at his side. "Hours before I was to sign and deliver an injunction? You expect me to believe that?"

"Come, come, Blake. Why don't you trade your sour grapes for a glass of Bordeaux?" He lifted his hand to once again snap his fingers. "Porter—"

Joseph grabbed Craven's wrist, squeezing until the bones ground beneath his grip. "I don't know how you discovered what my next move was going to be, but I'll save you the trouble of wondering what I shall do next. I'm coming for you, Craven. Mark my words, I *will* uncover the real reason you protect Hannah Crow."

Wincing, Craven jerked his hand away and shot to his feet. Red crept up his neck, matching the splotches on his face. "Back off, Blake, or I'll see your name linked to the brothel in a way you won't like. I wonder what your pretty fiancée will have to say about that."

The threat cut deep, exposing a raw nerve he did his best to always keep hidden. If Amanda or—God help him—her father knew of his family's history with brothels, his aunt's dire prediction would come true: *"No respectable woman will have you if the truth is known."*

He sucked in a breath, nearly choking on Craven's leftover cigar smoke. Any show of weakness would be blood in the water. His lips pulled into a sneer. "She'll never believe your lies."

y, my dear fellow, I'll be so convincing that even you will doubt yourself. And a
attached to the great city attorney will not bode well for the mayor's reelection
w, will it?"

Joseph gritted his teeth, hating the way Craven's words burrowed under his skin.

Craven leaned forward, the stink of tobacco and whiskey fouling the air. "The loss of
your job, the loss of your love. . . Tell me, is shutting down one house of ill repute worth
so much?"

Chapter Three

Grabbing her hat with one hand, Amanda leaned over the side of Joseph's phaeton, closing her eyes against the thrill of speed. A completely brazen act, the breeze teasing out bits of her hair, but so irresistible. How could one pass up facing a glorious Sunday afternoon when winter would soon squeeze the life out of everything?

She glanced back, expecting a raised-eyebrow reprimand from Maggie. But her friend was a small dot, blocks behind, riding in Mr. Rafferty's lumbering coach.

"Chicken *and* an apple pie?" A low whistle traveled on the wind.

She snapped her attention back to Joseph and caught him in the act of lifting the lid on the picnic basket at their feet. She batted his arm with a fake scowl. "No peeking, sir."

A mischievous grin stretched across his face, highlighting a single dimple on his cheek. "Be thankful that's all I've peeked at." He aimed a finger at the hem of her gown.

Her gaze followed to where he pointed and—great heavens! She bent and snatched the fabric from where it had snagged up near the railing, exposing the lace of her petticoat and far too much of her stockinged leg.

Tucking the fabric between her calves and carriage, she straightened out her gown and her dignity—then promptly changed the subject. "I met with the Ladies' Aide Society on Monday."

"Oh? And how does it involve me?" He winked—and a thrill charged through her.

Even so, she pursed her lips into a sulk. "You make me sound like a criminal."

His eyes twinkled, the lift of his brow altogether too handsome. "And you are skirting the question."

"I was merely conversing. Any fiancé would take interest in the matters of his betrothed."

"Ahh, but you forget I am used to divining truth from felons. So judging by the contents of that basket"—he leaned close and nuzzled her neck—"the smell of wild rose perfume, your gown of blue, all of which are my favorites, you are about to ask me for a favor. You needn't go to so much trouble, though, love. I would grant you anything." He swept out his free hand as they rumbled down the hill, into the innermost part of the city. "Even up to half my kingdom."

"Well. . ." She nibbled her lower lip. Maybe now was as good a time as any. "It's not exactly a kingdom that I want."

"But you do want something, hmm?"

"Yes." She flashed him a grin. "And you're the man to help me get it."

She darted a glance from road to sidewalk, building to building, and when satisfied no pedestrians looked their way, she stretched up on her seat and kissed his cheek.

"Well now." His gaze smoldered down at her. "How can I refuse that? What is it you want?"

"The title to the Grigg house."

The gleam in his eyes faded, and he faced the road. "Why would you want that?"

She frowned. Would he need as much convincing as Lillian? "I've had the most wonderful idea. What if the decrepit Grigg house was made into a school for the poor? With uniforms and hot lunches and the chance to leave poverty behind? Think of the possibility."

Perhaps he was thinking of it, for a muscle tightened and loosened on his jaw. But he said nothing, just kept a firm hold on the reins as they wove their way through the innards of St. Paul.

She touched his sleeve. "You will help me, won't you?"

"Whoa, now." He spoke to the horse—or did he?

"Joseph?" She stared at him. For the first time in their relationship, an alarm bell rang.

"Look at that." He pulled the horse to a stop and angled his head.

Leaning forward, she followed his gaze. They'd stopped at a crossroads. On the corner nearest them, a young boy, more dirt than skin, held out a torn newspaper, equally as filthy. His cries to sell it competed with a much larger and louder boy on the opposite corner. At the younger lad's feet, a babe in a basket whimpered, lusty enough to be heard in the phaeton. Want and need haunted the caverns of their hollowed cheeks. Their clothes, rags really, hung off their bones like garments pegged to a clothesline.

Amanda's heart broke. These were exactly the kind of children she wanted to help. She turned to Joseph. "Is there not a law you can enforce to keep little ones at home with their mother?"

He shook his head. "It's very likely their mother is off working, as is their father." His tone lowered to a growl. "If there even be a father in the home."

"Surely something can be done."

"I cannot right all the wrongs of the world." He gazed down at her and tapped her on the nose. "But I can right this one."

Tying off the reins, he hopped down from the carriage.

What was he up to?

◆━◆●◆━◆

Joseph strode from the carriage, pleased for the diversion. If Amanda knew who really owned the Grigg title, his card-house of helping brothel girls would collapse. He squatted in front of the younger boy, who was four, possibly five years old. The purple beginnings of a shiner darkened one of the lad's eyes. The other was swollen from tears, salty tracks yet visible on his dirty cheek.

"Buy a paper, mister?"

Pity welled in his throat, and he swallowed. "Tell me true, lad, did that boy"—he hitched his thumb over his shoulder, denoting the news seller on the opposite corner—"steal your papers?"

Without warning, the lad kicked him in the shin. Pain shot up to his knee. Little urchin! He stifled a grimace and avoided glancing back at Amanda, who surely hid a smile beneath her gloved fingers. Well, so much for donning his gallant-knight armor.

But the battle wasn't over.

He straightened and wheeled about. Dodging a passing omnibus, he stalked over to the lad's competition. A large, freckle-faced boy held out a handful of ripped and dirty newspapers. Calculating eyes weighed and measured him, glinting with far too much knowledge for one not yet a man. No wonder the other lad hadn't ratted on this boy. Were he ten years older, Joseph would think twice about crossing the bully without Officer Keeley at his side.

"Buy a paper, mister?" His tone was gravel, hardened by life on the streets.

"No." Joseph pulled out his wallet. "I'll take them all."

"Caw!" The bully's freckles rode a wave of astonishment. "All right. That'll be fifty cents." He held out his hand, palm up, shirtsleeve riding high enough to reveal a small *s* tattooed on his inner wrist.

The mark confirmed Joseph's suspicions. He pulled out a nickel and flipped it in the air. The coin landed in the dirt.

Though he towered at least two hand spans above the bully, the glower the boy aimed at him punched like a right hook. "I ain't stupid. That ain't a fifty-cent piece." Even so, his foot stomped on the money, trapping it beneath his shoe.

"If I were you, I'd take what's being offered, then run far and fast."

A foul curse belched out of the bully's mouth. "Shove off!"

He widened his stance and impaled the boy with a piercing stare, one he'd perfected when confronting a defendant. "I'm the city attorney. I could have you arrested."

The bully turned aside and spit, then swiped his hand across his mouth. "I ain't doin' nothing wrong. You ain't got nothing on me."

Joseph chuckled. "I don't need a valid reason. Any charge will detain you in jail for a few days."

A smirk smeared across the bully's face. Were he born on top of the hill instead of below, this kid would give Craven a run for his position. "No matter. I'll come back out here, takin' what I want, when I want."

"I think not." Joseph grabbed the boy's wrist and turned it over. "By the look of this mark, you're one of Stinger's boys."

The bully wrenched from his grasp. "So what if I am?"

"Haven't you heard? Stinger is in jail. If he finds you've taken money without giving him a cut—and trust me lad, rumors abound in prison—well, I don't think you'll be back on this corner anymore." He bent, leveling his own scowl at the boy. "Or anywhere else, for that matter."

The bully's face blanched, freckles standing out like warning beacons. Papers landed in heap on Joseph's shoes. All that remained of the boy was the stink of both an unwashed body and fear as he tore down the street.

Scooping up the papers, Joseph strolled back to the other corner, two sets of eyeballs watching his every move—the lad and Amanda's. He dropped the newspapers at the boy's feet and took out a fifty-cent piece, pressing it into the boy's grubby hand. "That ought to be enough for you to go on home now, eh?"

The boy stared up at him, mouth agape. He didn't say anything. He didn't have to. Gratitude poured off him in waves.

With a tussle of the boy's hair, Joseph pivoted and rejoined Amanda in the carriage.

The same hero-worshipping sparkle lit her gaze. Hopefully this meant she'd forgotten about the Grigg house, as well.

"That's exactly what I love about you, Mr. Blake."

He grinned. This little venture had been a victory in more ways than one. "What's that?"

"You always do the right thing."

Chapter Four

Amanda's shoes tapped on the marble floor of city hall's lobby. This early on a Monday, suits in various shades of navy and black darted in and out, the smell of bay rum aftershave and determination thick in the air.

Skirting the large information desk at center, she proceeded up the grand staircase that opened onto a gallery of offices. The heart of the city beat here. She sped past the mayor's door, cringing at the raised voices inside, bypassed the next two doors, and finally stopped in front of the fourth, Joseph's name painted in golden ink on the frosted-glass pane. Twisting the knob, she entered a small reception room. After a fruitless week of trying to find out who held the Grigg title, she couldn't wait any longer to enlist Joseph's help.

"Why, Miss Carston!" Joseph's secretary, Mary Garber, more mouse than woman, twitched her lips into a smile. "Good morning."

"Morning, Mary." She smiled back. "Is Mr. Blake in?"

"He is, but. . ." If the woman had whiskers, they'd be quivering. She ran a slim finger down a column on a sheet of paper. "Your name isn't on the schedule. Is he expecting you?"

"No." She leaned over the desk, cupped a hand to her mouth, and lowered her voice. "This is a secret ambush."

"Such intrigue. Perfect for a Monday morning." Mary popped up from her chair and scurried to the door leading into Joseph's office.

"Mary? What's. . ." Joseph's question stalled as Amanda stepped over the threshold.

For a moment, her breath hitched. She'd never tire of the way he looked at her. More than love simmered in that gaze. More than desire. The warmth of his brown eyes reached out and held her, cherishing her as the most valuable of God's creations. Her. The sole focus of such tenderness. She wished she could package it up and carry it around with her all day.

In four long strides, he wove around his desk and pulled her into his arms. "This is a nice surprise." His lips pressed against her cheek, then slid like a whisper across her jaw toward her ear. "Would that I could kiss more than propriety allows."

A tingle settled low in her tummy. If she turned her face, his mouth would be on hers. But if Mary were to walk in and find them so entwined—

She pulled from his embrace. "Soon."

"Not soon enough." He cocked his head to a rakish angle. "You know there'll be no stopping me once you're my wife."

She glanced over her shoulder at the open door leading to the reception room then frowned back at him.

He grinned. "Don't worry. If nothing else, Mary is discreet." He swept out his arm.

"Have a seat. I'm pleased you're here, but surely you've not taken a sudden interest in legal briefings?"

She sank onto the leather chair while he leaned back against his desk in front of her.

"No, not briefings," she began, "but I do have a legal matter with which I could use your help."

"Oh?" He folded his arms, one of his professional stances. Good. Hopefully he'd take her seriously.

"I mentioned my interest in the Grigg house yesterday, but then there was the matter with the newsboys, and Mr. Rafferty's incessant chattering." She averted her gaze. Her words would be embarrassing enough. "Nor did you make conversation easy on the drive home with the way you. . ." Her face heated.

"The way I what?" His sultry tone, edged with laughter, challenged her to look at him.

She refused, but it was hard to fight down a small smile. "You know I cannot think when you hold my hand and rub little circles on my wrist."

He said nothing.

She dared a peek. La! What a mistake. The heat in his gaze was enough to singe her modesty—which was likely the exact effect he hoped for. She squared her shoulders. "Regardless, I am here now, making my request today. I need to acquire the title to the old Grigg house by the end of the month, yet I've been shuffled from office to office with no success. I thought you might be able to get it for me."

Unfolding his arms, he retreated to the other side of his desk. For a while, he didn't say anything, just tapped a finger on the mahogany.

"You'll need to go to the deed's office," he finally answered.

"I've been there. No luck." She leaned forward in her seat. "Surely you can hasten the process."

He shook his head, his brown gaze completely unreadable. "I am sorry, Amanda. I cannot help with this project of yours."

"Cannot?" She sank against the cushion. The word made no sense. Without his help to speed along her search for the title, she'd never make Lillian's appointed deadline. Her first project proposal would be a dismal failure—one that wouldn't improve her father's opinion of her, either. No, she simply couldn't accept either outcome.

She straightened, folding her hands in her lap. "I am sure it won't take long."

He sighed. "With the mayor's upcoming election, I don't have the time."

The rejection stung—but only for a heartbeat. She'd learned long ago that determination fed off rejection and grew the larger for it.

She stood. "I understand. I should get busy as well, then. Good day, Joseph."

She strode to the door, but a strong hand on her shoulder turned her back.

"Please, Amanda, don't take this personally." He wrapped his arms around her, drawing her close, the nearness of him melting some of her resolve. "You know I'd do anything for you, but not this. Not now. Save the Grigg project for another time."

She couldn't help but run her hands up and down his back, loving the feel of strength beneath his suit coat. "I do understand, and I should not add to your burdens."

He crooked a finger, lifting her chin with his knuckle. "Then we are agreed?"

"Of course." She quirked her lips into a saucy smirk.

Of course she wouldn't add to his burdens—but that didn't mean she'd give up getting that deed on her own.

⸺•◉•⸺

Joseph waited until the outer office door closed behind Amanda before letting his smile slide off. Tenacious woman! A trait he admired—but not this time.

He strode to his secretary's desk, flexing out the tension in his fingers. "A telegram, if you please, Mary."

"Yes, sir." She pulled out the form, pencil poised.

"To the Rev. Robert Bond, Chicago, Morse Park, Number Twelve." He paused as her fingers flew. "Urgent, *Stop.* Transfer title, *Stop.* Must be your name, *Stop.* Only yours, *Stop.*"

Just as her pencil caught up to his words, the outer door opened once again, followed by a booming voice. "Hey Blake, the mayor wants to see you, and he's in one devilish mood."

Joseph turned. His friend and fellow attorney Henry Wainwright stood on the threshold. Waggling his eyebrows, he mocked, "Devilish. Devilish. Devilish."

A smirk twisted his lips. "Been prodding you with his pitchfork so early in the week, has he?"

Henry opened the lapels of his suit coat, revealing the vest beneath. "Got the holes to prove it."

"I best not keep him waiting, then." He glanced back at Mary as he headed for the corridor. "Send that telegram immediately, please. And thank you."

"Yes, sir." Mary's voice followed him out into the hall.

Henry already was striding off in the opposite direction. "Good luck, Blake."

Blowing out a long breath, Joseph advanced down the corridor. Was this a death march? Not that he hadn't expected it. Still, a man on his way to the gallows couldn't help but have his throat burn.

Both of the mayor's office doors were open, outer and inner. A bad omen. The old lion likely sat on his haunches, ready to strike as soon as Joseph entered his lair. He nodded at the matron manning the secretary desk, a drill-sergeant compared to his mousy Mary.

"Good morning, Miss Strafing. Mayor Smith is expecting me?"

Her lips puckered, a perpetual look for her. Either the woman sucked on lemons to keep in practice or the sourness inside her refused to be held in. "He is."

"Thank you." He stalked into the mayor's den and stood at attention. Better to be on the offensive, for weak prey attracted rather than repelled. "Good morning, Mayor Smith."

"Blake. Blake. Blake." The man shoved back in his chair and stood, planting his hands on his desk. A strategic position to launch an attack—one Joseph often employed on the accused.

"Do you know what day it is, Blake?" the mayor asked.

He'd learned long ago never to look directly at the man. To do so jumbled his thoughts. One could not help but stare at the collection of tiny growths dotting the mayor's face. Oh, the fellow tried to hide the things with whiskers, but the sparse, white hairs only magnified the darkened moles. Truly, only a mother could love that face, which explained why Mrs. Smith's portrait hung on the wall behind the man's desk—and that's exactly where Joseph pinned his gaze. "Today is October thirteenth, sir."

"Not the date, man. The day."

He hesitated. What kind of trickery was this? "It is Monday, sir."

"Ah. . .Monday. Monday. Monday. Yet you told me Hannah Crow's brothel would be shut down by Friday." The mayor's voice sharpened. "A week ago Friday. I've since heard otherwise. Is that true?"

The turn of conversation and the mayor's annoying quirk of repetition left a nasty taste at the back of Joseph's throat. He swallowed. "True, sir. The zoning commission—"

"Enough!" The mayor's eyes narrowed. "Do I need to remind you the general election is less than a month away?"

So that was to be the man's game, eh? Wielding his future employment as a scythe to his neck. He gritted his teeth, then finally ground out, "No, sir."

"What's my slogan?"

Rage burned a trail up from his gut. Pandering to the pompous fellow never came easy—but for now, with only three months until the wedding, he'd have to take it for Amanda's sake. After New Year's, though, all bets were off. He'd find a different position, maybe even open up his own practice.

"I'm waiting, Blake."

"'A clean city is a strong city,' sir." He clipped out the slogan, direct and sharp.

"Clean. Clean. Clean." The man stepped away from his desk and crossed to the front of it, emphasizing the rest of his words with an index finger on Joseph's chest. "Do you think a brothel in the center of St. Paul upholds the image of cleanliness?"

He stifled the urge to shove the man back a step. "No, sir."

"My reelection hinges on this." His tone lowered to a growl. "So does your job."

The muscles in his legs hardened, the restraint of lunging forward almost unbearable. Bullies came in all sizes, from the ragged, young news-seller, to this well-dressed power broker. He forced a calm tone to his voice—barely. "Trust me. I want to see Crow shut down as much, if not more, than you. I assure you I am working on it."

"Working. Working. Working." A chuckle rumbled in the mayor's chest. "See that you are, or you'll be lucky to be working as the city dog catcher. Dismissed!"

He wheeled about and strode from the office—and there sat Willard Craven. Judging by the man's leer, he'd heard everything. Joseph's hands curled into fists. Ah, but he'd love to punch that smug look off Craven's face.

Ignoring the man, he stomped back to his office. What a day. Lifting his gaze to the ceiling, he silently prayed—for truly, what else could he do?

Help me find a way to shut down that brothel, Lord, and thwart Craven. And soon.

Chapter Five

F or the record, I think this is a terrible idea."

Amanda frowned at her friend. "You've said that. Repeatedly. Come on."

Crouching low, Amanda darted from the cover of an overgrown hedge and sprinted across the open expanse of the Grigg backyard. Amazing how fast one could move without skirts. If Joseph or—God forbid—her father saw her racing about in trousers belonging to Maggie's brother, well. . .a wicked smile curved her mouth as she motioned for her friend to follow. She'd just have to make sure no one saw them.

This late in the day, dusk cast a shadow from the remains of a porch roof to the door, large enough to hide in. She charged forward, wrapping herself in darkness as she might a cloak.

Maggie pulled up breathless beside her. "Remind me again. . .why we are doing this?"

Reaching for the doorknob, she shot her friend a sideways glance, then tried not to giggle. Though she likely looked as ridiculous herself, Miss Margaret Turner garbed in britches was a sight to behold. "I already told you, Mags. Father and Joseph are too busy. The registrar at the deeds office refuses to deal with a woman unless a man is present. I've spent the last week since I spoke to Joseph about it, trying to find an answer, but there's no way for me to get a look at that deed to find out who owns this place. So here we are. There's got to be a clue, a book left behind with an inscribed name, maybe even an old family Bible. Something. Someone I could contact."

She shoved open the door.

Maggie's hand pulled her back. "No, that's not what I mean. Why are you going to such trouble to find out who owns *this* house in particular? There are other buildings in which to create a school, others easier to renovate. Some that Lillian might not frown upon."

"I know. You're right. It's just that. . ."

That what?

She blew away an errant hair tickling her nose and stared up at the house. A bat swooped out a broken third-story window. The corner of the roof bled tiles, which had long since given up on clinging to the rafters. For years the place had been abandoned. Unloved. Forgotten.

A tangible picture of her life before Joseph Blake.

She pulled her gaze from the house and hiked up her trousers, riding low from the jaunt across the yard. Fitting that Mr. Charles Carston's daughter now wore the pants of the son he'd never had.

And there it was—the truth.

She turned and faced Maggie. "I fear you know me too well, my friend. I suppose this is my last attempt to do something grand in my father's estimation before I leave his home."

"Is it that important to you?"

"It is." Tears stung her eyes, and she blinked them away. "I would have a happy ending to this chapter in my life." Her chin rose. "Now, are we going to do this before it gets too dark?"

"Very well." Maggie stepped forward and linked arms with her. "But I still think it's a terrible idea."

They crept together into a back room. Dirt coated the floors. Empty pegs poked out from a wall, save for one, where a stiff, mildewed canvas hung like a piece of meat on a hook. An upturned bucket lay in one corner. Amanda stared harder. Wait a minute. That was no bucket. The dark shape darted for the open door.

Maggie shrieked, her nails digging into Amanda's arm. Together they sprinted blindly down a corridor and into another room.

Panting, Maggie slapped her hands to her chest. "This. . .is. . .a. . ."

"Terrible idea," Amanda finished. Her own heart beat loud in her ears. That had been a scare, but a raccoon or stray dog or whatever that had been was not going to get the best of her.

She caught her breath and scanned the room, what she could see of it anyway. Hard to tell with the last of day's light hovering near the windows. This might've been a grand room, once. Large. Stately. But now wallpaper blistered on the walls, blackened plaster lay in piles on the floor, where sporadic floorboards yet remained. What a ruin.

Ignoring the rubble, Amanda picked her way over to an old desk tipped sideways, nearly tipping sideways herself as her toe caught in a hole in the floor.

Maggie groaned. "This isn't safe. I'm leaving."

"Hold on, Mags. I feel sure we'll find something." Yanking out drawer after empty drawer, Amanda rummaged faster. "If it makes you feel better, go stand by the front door and wait for me there."

Maggie's footsteps padded off. Then stopped. "Did you hear that?" Her friend's voice squeaked.

Amanda straightened and listened, having turned up nothing but an empty inkwell and broken pen nibs. "What?"

"The floorboards upstairs. They creaked." Maggie's words choked into a whisper. "We are not alone."

"Of course we're not." She flicked her fingers toward the ceiling. "There are probably squirrels racing around up there. Wait outside if you like."

Maggie scooted one way, Amanda the other. In a smaller room across the hall, a few old books lay riffled open on the floor.

She snatched one up, paper crumbling as she paged through it. No names. Just a lot of dust that tickled her nose. Fighting a sneeze, she grabbed the other book and—paused. Plaster bits rained down on her head. Was something heavier than squirrels upstairs?

Straining hard to listen, she held her breath and glanced up. Another poof of ceiling sprinkles dropped. Then another. And another. Paces apart. Traveling in a straight line.

As if a person were walking.

Maybe this *had* been a terrible idea. Her stomach twisted and her mouth dried to bones. She couldn't shriek if she wanted to—nor did she need to.

Maggie's scream ripped the silence.

Autumn evenings generally fell hard and fast. So did the lad who'd sprinted down the Grigg front driveway and sprawled in the gravel. Another boy disappeared through a hole in the side gate. Joseph narrowed his eyes. What mischief was this?

He jerked his gaze to the third-floor window. The drapery was wide open—and the timing couldn't have been worse.

Anger ignited a slow burn in his gut. If those boys had discovered what he'd so carefully kept hidden this past year, the whole operation could grind to a halt. Well, then. . . he'd just have to put the fear of God and man into the remaining lad.

He took off at a dead run and hauled the hoodlum up by his collar. "What are you doing—?"

His words, his rebuke, his very thoughts vanished with the last light of day. Wide blue eyes stared into his. Blond curls escaped a tweed flat cap, framing a cherub face. A fresh scrape bloomed on one cheek, set below a tiny, crescent scar. Recognition punched him hard.

"Amanda?" He'd experienced many a surprise in twisted legal cases, but this? His hand fell away, and he retreated a step, shaking his head to clear it. "What are you doing here? And dressed like a boy, no less?"

Tears sprouted at the corners of her eyes, rolling out one after another. "Joseph. . . I—I can explain."

"You'd better." His voice came out harsher than intended. But sweet mercy! She had no idea what she might've seen. The hard work she might've undone. The women's lives she might've ended—

The danger she'd been in.

He clenched his jaw so hard it crackled in his ears. "You could've fallen down a loose stair and broken your neck! What were you thinking?"

She cringed. "I didn't. . .think."

Choppy little breaths strangled whatever explanation she attempted. He'd get nowhere trying to bully an answer out of her.

Sighing, he wrapped his arm around her shoulder and led her to a boulder, away from the drive and far from the street. It wouldn't do for the city attorney to be seen embracing a boy.

"Just breathe." He pressed her down onto the rock and dug into his pocket, retrieving a handkerchief. Dropping to one knee, he dabbed the blood on her cheek and dried her tears. As much as he'd love to throttle this woman, his anger slowly seeped away with each quiver of her lip.

When her chest finally rose and fell with regularity, he started over. "Now then, let's try this again. What are you doing here, dressed like this?"

She sucked in a last, shaky breath. "Trying to find a name."

"A name." Even repeating it, the reason made no sense. "I don't understand."

She blinked as if she were the one perplexed. "I told you I wanted to acquire the deed to this place. I need the name of the owner."

He frowned. "You also told me you'd wait until after the election."

"I never said that."

"What?" Crickets chirped a singsong beat as he revisited their last conversation in his mind. "You stood there, in my office, and agreed to give up this project of yours until later."

She wrinkled her pert little nose. "I agreed I wouldn't burden you, not that I'd give up my quest."

"Of all the absurd, irrational. . ." Stuffing the handkerchief away, he pressed the heel of his palm to the bridge of his nose and the ache spreading there. Would married life be this confusing?

"Joseph, you don't understand. If I fail at my first project, Lillian will never let me live it down. And Father. . ." She heaved a great sigh, as mournful as the breeze whistling through the barren branches. "All my life I've tried to be the son he never had. I thought that this time, as a chairwoman, he'd see me as a success."

The hurt in her voice sobered him, and he turned to her. "But the only good opinion you need is God's, my love. And that you have. His and mine."

She blinked, eyes once again filling with tears—and the vulnerability he saw there broke his heart.

He skimmed his fingers over her cheeks. "You *are* loved. Trust in that. Believe in that."

Pulling her into his arms, he lowered his mouth to hers. A kiss wouldn't solve everything, not a hurt so deep, but that wouldn't stop him from trying anyway. Slowly, she leaned into him, hopefully surrendering some of the pain she harbored.

By the time he released her, she gazed up with luminous eyes—but this time not from weeping.

"I love you, Joseph Blake."

"I love you, too, soon-to-be Mrs. Blake." He tapped her on the nose.

She smiled. Slowly, her brows drew together beneath the rakish boy's cap. "Wait a minute. . .what are you doing here?"

He glanced up at the darkened house. As much as he yearned to be completely honest with her, he yet owed it to his aunt for the promise she'd wrenched from him years ago. Of course he'd reveal the truth eventually, but now? Breathing in the scent of Amanda's sweet lilac cologne, feeling the warmth of her next to him in the cool of the eve? The thought of her possible rejection punched him in the gut.

No, not yet. Soon, but not yet.

Donning his attorney mask, he gazed back at her. "I decided to walk home from the office tonight and heard a scream. And a good thing I came upon you instead of someone else. Now, shall I walk you home and sneak you in before your father sees your attire? Hey. . .where did you get those clothes anyway?"

"My secret." She grinned.

Leaning close, he kissed her forehead and whispered against her soft skin, "Fine, hold onto your secrets. For now."

He stood and offered his hand—for he would hold onto his, for now, as well.

Chapter Six

Yawning away the last bit of sleep, Amanda stretched her neck one way and another, then entered the dining room. She might need more than one cup of coffee this morning. Was Maggie this weary after last night's intrigue at the Grigg house?

But as soon as her foot crossed the threshold, her step faltered. Ensconced in a chair at the far end of the big table, her father gripped an open newspaper as if it kept him afloat. Which it did. He could no more navigate life without his precious business section than a ship without a rudder. Strange, though. He usually took breakfast hours before her.

"Good morning, Father." She crossed the room and pecked him on the cheek, his whiskers as prickly as his usual disposition.

He mumbled something, more a rumble than a greeting, without pulling his eyes from the newsprint.

She retreated to the sideboard and reached for the silver urn, steam yet curling out the spout. Good. Nice and hot. After pouring coffee into her cup and stirring in some cream, she seated herself opposite her father. "I am surprised to find you at home this late in the morning."

The paper lowered slowly, revealing Charles Carston's face inch by inch, from the white hair crowning his balding head to the frown folding his mouth nearly to his necktie. "Indeed. I should be at the office, but I need to speak with you, Amanda."

His gaze pierced like a flaming arrow. She swallowed a mouthful of coffee for fortification, heedless of the burn. Had he found out about last night? "Sounds ominous."

"It is." He folded his paper, crease after crease, using the methodical movement and the tick-tock of the mantle clock to batter her nerves.

Finally, he laid the *Pioneer Press* beside his plate. "I've heard rumors, Amanda."

She set down her cup, sickeningly awake without having finished it. "Oh? What rumors?"

"A tale of inappropriate behavior. . .by my daughter."

Her stomach twisted, and she shoved her cup away. How had he found out about her escapade of the previous evening? Maggie couldn't have told, for she'd be censured as well. And certainly not Joseph. She pressed her napkin to her mouth, hiding her trembling lips. Who else could've seen her?

She lowered the napkin to her lap, clutching onto it as tightly as he had the paper. "I don't know what you're talking about, Father."

"Mr. Warnbrough saw you traipsing about city hall the other day, unaccompanied I might add. Do you know what kind of women frequent city hall alone?" His fist slammed the table, rattling the water glasses. "Harlots!"

She stifled a flinch. Barely.

"Betrothed or otherwise, it is not seemly for you to be seen chasing after Joseph Blake in public." His eyes narrowed, pinning her to the chair. "I am ashamed of you."

Her stomach rebelled, queasiness rising up to her throat. Could he never think the best of her? "But I did nothing of the sort."

"You deny an eyewitness?" Red crept up his neck, like a rising thermometer about to explode. "One of my esteemed friends?"

"No. I deny your conjecture." She shoved back her chair. Breakfast now was out of the question. "I was not 'chasing after' Mr. Blake. Honestly, Father, what kind of daughter do you think you raised?"

"Then what were you doing?"

She turned from his awful glower and stared out the window. How dare the sun shine so merrily on this horrible morning? She'd have to tell him about the Grigg project, but it was too soon. Too uncertain. Not yet a conquest she could offer him to gain his regard.

"I asked you a question, Amanda."

He left her no choice. Inhaling until her bodice pinched, she slowly faced him. "As chairwoman of the Ladies' Aide Society, it is my assigned duty to acquire the deed to the old Grigg estate by the end of the month."

"The Grigg house?" His brows met in a single line. "What on earth for?"

"I had an idea to turn it into a school. An institution." The more she spoke, the deeper his scowl—and the stronger her determination to change his disapproval to admiration. "The Grigg home will provide a safe place where children of need can receive an education without wilting beneath the scrutiny of those who deem them unfit to be taught."

He shot to his feet, his chair rearing back from the sudden movement. "Why this obsession with the poor? Surely you know the Warnbroughs and others frown upon such associations. We must play by society's rules. Furthermore. . ."

His voice droned on while he paced the length of the table. Her eyes followed the movement, and she gave the appearance of listening, but truly there was no need. She'd heard this tirade so often she could stand at a podium and present it with as much gusto as he.

". . . Or find ourselves counted among the outcasts. You are a lady of upstanding circumstance. Why can you not be happy with dinners and dances?"

Disgust choked her as much as the aftertaste of her coffee. She stood and tipped her face to frown up into his, despite her being shorter than him by a good six inches. "And why can you not soften your heart toward those less fortunate? Life is more than entertainment, a fact the privileged have a hard time understanding."

"That *privilege*, Daughter, I have worked long and hard to achieve." His words bled out as if from a deep, jagged cut. "Yet you dare undermine all that I've accomplished, knowing from where I've come. I do help the poor, more than you're aware, but I will never—*ever*—live amongst them again."

Her vision swam, and she forced back tears. It was a sharp blow, one that stung. Not only was she not the son he'd always wanted, but she was an ungrateful, spiteful daughter, as well. She padded over to him and placed a hand on his sleeve. "I didn't mean that, Father. I know you've worked hard. Please—" Her voice broke, and she swallowed. "Forgive me."

He pulled from her grasp and stalked to the door without so much as a backward glance.

Swinging down from the carriage in front of city hall, Joseph closed the door behind him. Too bad it wasn't as easy to shut out the ruckus of itinerant merchants, hawking their goods like carnival barkers on State Street. Strange that Craven didn't change the zoning around here, for his office faced the busiest side of the road.

He retrieved a coin and paid off the cab driver just as his friend Henry Wainwright charged toward him.

"The hero of the day!" Henry's meaty hand slapped him on the back. "Congratulations on finally breaking that Hofford case."

Joseph shot him a sideways glance. "A little premature, don't you think?"

"Hah!" He shoved a newspaper into his hands. "Don't play coy with me, Blake."

What the devil? Shaking open the front page, he focused on a bold headline: Financier Charged with Extortion.

Scanning further, he read: "Last night in a swift move by City Attorney Joseph Blake, the underhanded dealings of the Hofford Financial Group were finally brought to an end as Phillip Hofford was taken into custody."

What? The words were like rocks cast into a pond, sending out ripple after ripple. How could that be? He was still waiting on a deposition from his informant, Hofford's brother-in-law. This made no sense, especially since he'd spent the evening secreting Amanda home from the Grigg house, then dining with her.

He continued. "Blake cast a wide net to entrap the unscrupulous Hofford, enlisting the aid of other departments and even that of the city council, chaired by Mr. Willard Craven."

The newspaper drooped in his hand. Craven. He should've known. But why would Willard help him with this when the man did nothing but thwart every effort to shut down the brothel? He scrubbed his jaw with his free hand. Could it possibly be a peace offering?

He rejected the idea immediately. Men like Craven didn't go out of their way to help anyone for such a trivial ideal as peace. Something smelled as rank about this as the fresh pile of horse droppings landing on the cobbles behind him.

"Drink tonight at the club?"

Henry's voice derailed his train of thought. "Sorry. What?"

"I said, meet me at the club for a celebratory drink tonight?"

Club. Craven. Their last meeting barreled back. Craven hadn't linked his name to the brothel, as promised, but instead dished it to the press by tying him to an extortion case. A very public way of sending him a message. Bribery in the open, for all to see. Leave it to a degenerate like Craven to come up with the idea of hush publicity.

"Did you even hear me?" Henry asked.

He shoved past his friend and wove his way through businessmen and legal aides. Darting into the lobby, he took the stairs two at a time. This early in the day, the scent of coffee and aftershave clung to the men he passed, until he neared Craven's office. There cigar smoke tainted the hall like a yellow stain. Joseph shoved the door open. No secretary graced this single room. Craven wasn't important enough, which almost made Joseph smile.

He strode from door to desk and slapped the paper onto the mahogany. "I'm only going to say this once, Craven, so listen up. I cannot be bought."

The man's waistcoat jiggled as he chuckled. "My dear Blake, think of it as one colleague helping another. You were stuck. I merely gave you a push—or rather, I pushed Hofford's brother-in-law. I should think you'd be grateful for the positive publicity."

He clenched every muscle to keep from leaping over the desk and grabbing the man by his collar. "I don't need your help," he choked out. "I need you to get out of my way."

"That shouldn't be a problem." Willard stabbed out his ever-present cigar into an overflowing ashtray, little poofs of gray exploding past the edge. His smile flattened into a straight line. "I'll stay out of your way, as long as you stay out of mine."

"Are you threatening me?" His voice cracked, but it couldn't be helped. Who in their right mind threatened a prosecuting attorney?

Willard tented his fingertips, tapping them together in a systematic rhythm. "I prefer to think of it more like a promise."

"Well I have a promise for you, Craven." The muscles in his hands shook with the force of keeping his fists at his sides. "I will find out what it is you're hiding. There are no secrets that time will not reveal."

Leaning forward, Willard jabbed his fat finger onto the date of the newspaper. October 21st. Just two weeks from the election. "Too bad time isn't on your side."

Chapter Seven

Joseph stormed down the corridor until he hit a brick wall—a man-sized slab of muscle and bone. Henry Wainwright angled his head toward the alcove of a bay window, and Joseph had no choice but to retreat into the recess. Wainwright was possibly the most easygoing man he'd ever known—yet the most dogged in the rare instance an ambition overtook him. Apparently Joseph was that ambition today.

Henry folded his arms. "You can't run off, disappear into Craven's office, then try to breeze past me without a word. What's going on?"

Glancing past Henry's broad shoulders, Joseph scanned the hallway. Empty. Even so, he tempered his voice. "You know that Hofford case? I had nothing to do with it. Craven got the man to talk, not me."

"What?" Joseph's scowl lowered his friend's volume. Henry shuffled closer. "Why would he do that?"

"He wants me to back off from shutting down the brothel." Saying it aloud stoked the fire in his belly. Never. He'd never back off. Craven or not.

Henry slowly nodded. "I think I know why. I was going to tell you at the club tonight, but now's as good a time as any."

"What do you have?"

"It's not hard evidence, mind you, but. . ." This time Henry glanced over his own shoulder, waiting until a delivery man scuttled past with a stack of boxes before he spoke again. "I overheard Tam Nadder—you know, the errand boy—boasting with the other runners about his exploits at Hannah Crow's. How he'd saved all his money for one night of pleasure. . .yet he's sporting new clothes and shoes today."

"So a runner spent all his money and is wearing new clothes." Joseph raked fingers through his hair, a desperate attempt to comb through Henry's information. "Sorry, but what has this to do with Craven?"

"I'm getting to that. Tam said some gent paid him not to mention he'd bumped into him at the brothel. The boy didn't name any names, but he gave a pretty accurate description of your friend Craven, bragging to his friends how he could turn this into a regular payment to stay quiet."

Joseph's lips twisted. How ironic. The exploiter being exploited. God certainly had a sense of humor.

"I knew Craven was involved, but I didn't know it was that personal." He blew out a long breath, mind abuzz. "If I can get Tam to talk, it would expose Craven's corruption. And if I could get him to go back to Hannah's—document she's still in business—it would shut her down." Humor rumbled in his throat. "All this time I've been using my legal bravado to end that brothel, and God laughs at my pride by sending an errand boy."

Henry's big hand landed on his shoulder, fingers squeezing encouragement. "Well, what are you waiting for? Go close that brothel. For Elizabeth."

His heart constricted in response, and he nodded, holding Henry's gaze. "Thank you, my friend."

"Yeah, well it's on you to buy me one at the club." Henry cuffed him on the arm, then sauntered away.

"Tonight, Wainwright," Joseph called after him before speeding off to his own office.

He swung through the door with a grin. "Cancel my morning appointments, Mary. I'll be out for a bit."

"Yes, sir." She held up a paper, waving it like a flag. "Want to take this telegram with you?"

He shot forward. Indeed. This was shaping up to be a banner day. Snatching it from her grasp, he read:

DEED TRANSFER IS A GO *Stop* PAPERWORK FILED ON MY END *Stop* ROBERT BOND

Balling up the paper, he dashed into his office with a bounce in his step and yanked out the bottom desk drawer. He removed a stack of files and deposited the pile onto his desk, then pulled out a penknife and pried up the false bottom of the drawer. A single document lay beneath—one more piece in a puzzle finally coming together. He pulled it out as Mary peeked her head in the door.

"The mayor wants to see you. Says it's urgent."

A sigh deflated his chest. Now of all times? He set down the document and faced his secretary. "I'm on it. See that no one enters this office while I'm out."

<hr />

Amanda forced dignity into each step as she exited the Ladies' Aide Society meeting, smiling goodbyes and see-you-soons. But the instant she set foot in the hallway, she fled from the building and hailed a cab, huddling on the seat until Maggie caught up. Tears burned her eyes, but she refused to let them spill. Not even one. Not on account of that she-devil in a dress, Lillian Warnbrough.

The carriage lilted to the side as Maggie climbed up. She gathered one of Amanda's hands in hers and patted it as the cab jerked into motion. "That was horrible. Simply awful. Lillian had no right to question your competency with such scathing remarks. She's jealous that you got elected chair and she didn't." Her patting stalled, and she leaned close, peering at her with a puckered brow. "Are you all right, dearest?"

For a moment, the compassion in Maggie's green gaze almost unstopped her tears. She sucked in a shaky breath. "I admit it has been quite a day. First my father, then Lillian."

"Poor pet. How to make this afternoon better?" Maggie released her hand and leaned back against the cushion. Grinding wheels and street sellers competed for attention, until Maggie shot forward and turned toward her. "I know! How about we stop by Delia's Delights for a pastry? That ought to set you to rights."

Just then the cab lurched around a corner, swaying back and forth. Back and forth. Like the tea in her stomach. Amanda pressed her fingers against her tummy. "Nice try, but I don't think so."

"All right. Then let's drive to Lake Como and feed what geese remain." Maggie nudged her shoulder. "That always makes you smile."

"Not in the mood." She sighed.

"I see. This calls for something drastic." Grasping the edge of the cab door, Maggie craned her neck out the window. "Driver, city hall, please."

"City hall!" Amanda grabbed a handful of her friend's cape and tugged her back. "You know my father doesn't want me seen there."

A Cheshire cat couldn't have grinned with more teeth. "Then we shan't be seen, darling."

"For once, I think you're the one with a terrible idea. Even if we're not seen, Joseph told me in no uncertain terms that he's too busy to help with the Grigg project."

"He told *you* that. He never told me." Lacing her fingers, Maggie perched her chin upon them like a practiced coquette. "With two of us batting our eyelashes, he can't help but spare ten minutes to escort us to the deeds office, hmm? I'm certain this will work."

Despite the awful day, a half-smile lifted her lips. "Since when did you get so devious?"

"La!" Maggie rolled her eyes. "Years of being your friend have taught me a trick or two."

The cab pulled up to city hall, and Maggie climbed out first, making sure no one they knew strolled about. Before they attempted a dash to the door, a small group of dignitaries and their wives departed from a line of carriages behind them.

"Here's our chance," Maggie whispered. "I told you this would work."

As the group passed by, they matched pace at the rear, blending in. By the time they cleared the foyer and gained the stairs, Amanda breathed easier. Perhaps this day truly was improving. They swung into Joseph's office as if a guardian angel had ushered them all the way.

Mary looked up from her desk, her little nose twitching. "Good afternoon, Miss Carston, Miss Turner."

"Good afternoon, Mary." Amanda pushed the door shut behind them and advanced. "Is Mr. Blake in?"

"I'm afraid he's not here, though he said he'd be gone only the morning." She glanced at the big clock on the wall. "I expect he'll return shortly, but I can't promise anything."

Outside in the hall, men's voices grew louder. Amanda edged toward Joseph's office door as the footsteps stopped in the corridor. Suit shadows blocked the frosted window, and panic hitched her breath. What if those men came in here? What if one of them knew her—or worse—her father?

"We shall wait in Mr. Blake's office, Mary."

"I'm sorry, miss, but Mr. Blake said no one was to enter his office until he returned."

"Surely I'm not *no one*." She grabbed Maggie's sleeve and fled to the safety of Joseph's sanctuary before Mary objected any further. The smell of him lingered in the room, sandalwood and ink, all masculine and strength, which did much to calm her nerves.

Leaning back against the door, she shot a glance at Maggie. "What if someone comes in and sees us before Joseph arrives?"

Maggie whirled toward the desk, her skirts coiling around her ankles. "Have a little faith, my friend." She grinned. "Is that not what you always tell me? Oh! Look here. How sweet."

Sweeping up a silver frame perched on the corner of Joseph's desk, Maggie handed over a photograph—and all Amanda's angst melted away. How could it not? Joseph, smiling down at her, their fingers entwined. Tenderness in his gaze. Love in hers. Marking them as one though it was but an engagement photo. How sweet that he'd taken the time to frame and keep it where he could see it at all times. The man was positively romantic.

The first genuine smile of the day bloomed on her face, and she crossed the small office to set it back on his desk. Her sleeve riffled the top paper on a pile of documents next to it, and she straightened the stack. She turned to Maggie—then spun back. Surely she hadn't seen. . .Joseph's name would be on lots of documents, of course.

She picked up the top paper, scanning the contents, and the world shifted on its axis.

A deed. Joseph Blake's signature on the owner's line.

For the Grigg house.

Chapter Eight

J oseph raked a hand though his hair as he strode down the corridor, then worked to straighten his necktie. Were mayors of other cities as insecure as this one? Three hours— *three*—of going over the past four years' worth of cases that could be exploited for good press. If he'd known the position of city attorney involved this much hand-holding and politics, he'd have taken up horse training instead. He smirked. Maybe he ought to invest in a good horsewhip anyway to prod along the next inevitable reelection meeting.

He breezed through his office door, counting the days until the election was over. "That took longer than I expected. Clear my schedule for the rest of the day, if you please, Mary."

His secretary glanced up. "I can clear all but one, sir."

He cocked his head, waiting for an explanation.

Mary's lips quirked into a smile. "Your fiancée and Miss Turner are in your office."

His gaze shot to the clock. Half past two. Dinner wasn't until eight. That's all he'd promised her for today. . .wasn't it?

He looked back at his secretary. "Am I forgetting something?"

One of her thin shoulders twitched. "Not that I know of."

"Hmm. Thanks, Mary."

He strode into his office, then froze. At his entrance, two sets of eyeballs skewered him through the heart.

Amanda glowered, cheeks aflame. Her friend stood near the window, wringing her hands, then without a word, dashed past him. The door slammed, sharp as a gunshot.

He stared at the paper in Amanda's hand and then at her. Alarm ramped up his heart rate, making a whooshing sound in his ears.

Her lips pinched. No, her whole body did. Like a gigantic, clenched fist. Ready to strike.

"You!" Her voice tightened to a shrill point. "You lied to me!" Her hand shot out, the deed to the Grigg estate quivering in her grasp. Good thing it wasn't a gun.

His heart stopped. His breaths. Time and sound and life itself ground to a halt.

"I—" He swallowed and tried again. "I never lied to you, I swear. I just never told you."

Amanda splayed her fingers, the document fluttering to the floor like a lost dream. "You weren't too busy to help me. You were too deceitful."

He edged closer. Carefully. Walking on glass. One wrong step and they'd both shatter. "Now hold on, love. I can explain."

"Do not think to call me your love!" The temperature in the room plummeted, so cold, so chilling her anger.

"Amanda, please, calm down." He reached for her. If he could but hold her, maybe he could right this wrong.

"No!" She shrugged off his hand, recoiling from his touch. "I cannot calm down. I will not."

Rage sparked in her terrible gaze. Without warning, tears sprouted. Her mouth trembled, and she pressed her fingers to her lips. A sob overflowed. Followed by more. Until shaky little cries and gasps for breath took over.

There wasn't one thing he could do about it.

He was a beast. A cad. What kind of man did this to a woman?

God, what do I do?

Powerless, he snatched a chair and dragged it to her side. "Please, sit. You're overwrought."

She didn't look at the chair. Or at him. She stood there, staring at the floor, shaking her head. Would she ever look at him again?

"How?" Her voice came out ragged. "How could you have let me go on about renovating the Grigg estate if you had no intention of ever letting it happen?"

"It's not like that. I only asked you to wait."

An iron rod couldn't have stiffened any more rigid than her spine, and when she finally did lift her face, he wished she'd still stared at the floor, so dead-eyed was her gaze.

"Why do you own that house, and why didn't you tell me?"

"It's. . ." His shoulders sank. He'd talked his way past hung juries and determined judges, but this? Impossible. The jaws of a trap snapped into his very bones. He couldn't reveal the Grigg home as a safe house, not yet. Not until Hannah Crow's brothel was shut down, for where would the girls go who wanted to escape?

He pinched the bridge of his nose, avoiding her eyes. "It's a secret. For now. But I promise you, all will be made clear to you soon. Very soon. You must trust me on this."

"Trust?" The word pinged around the room like a bullet. "Oh that's a very pretty word coming from your mouth. How is one to trust a deceiver?"

Deceiver? His jaw clenched from the direct hit. He'd been nothing but honest! Guarded, yes, but truthful. He stiffened. "Did you not say that I always do the right thing?"

"The right thing is to transfer over that deed and renovate the place into a school. Immediately."

"I can't. Not yet." Each word cost him. Strength. Faith. Hope. Until he was gutted and empty.

Her blue eyes, shimmery and red-rimmed from weeping, sought his. "Why?"

He swallowed. *Oh God, what is the lesser sin here? Breaking or keeping a promise? Either way I fail a woman I love.*

"I. . ." He pressed his lips tight and shook his head. "I'm sorry, Amanda."

"So am I." Clutching handfuls of her gown, she stormed to the door. "Don't bother calling on me, for I won't see you. Ever again."

⋯ ◆ ⋯

Air. She needed air. But even that might not be enough. How was one to breathe with a heart that wouldn't beat? Blood that refused to flow? How could she possibly face the future, her friends, her father?

Amanda fled from the unbearable questions, tearing out of Joseph's office and into the hallway—and crashed headlong into a big chest. And why not? The rest of her life was one big train wreck.

She bounced back a step and bumped into Maggie, who'd caught up from behind, sandwiching her between friend and possible foe. Willard Craven smiled down at her, a toothy grin, yellowed by age and cigars. Did he know her father? Would he tell that he'd seen her exiting Joseph's office?

Did it even matter anymore?

"Someone's in quite a hurry." He leaned closer, searching her face. "Are you all right, Miss Carston?"

"I. . .I. . ." She stammered, but it was not to be helped. Too much anger and far too much hurt choked her.

"We are sorry, Mr. Craven." Maggie stepped to her side. "Forgive our haste. We must be leaving."

"Of course." He tipped his hat toward Maggie but then wrinkled his brow at her. "Why, you're pale as a sheet, Miss Carston. Are you feeling faint? Perhaps you ought to sit until the spell passes. My office is just down the hall." Stepping aside, he swept out his hand.

"No. I am—" She was what? Devastated? Undone? Barely able to stand? She clutched Maggie's arm for support. "We would not trouble you, Mr. Craven. Good afternoon."

She turned.

But coming down the opposite end of the corridor, Lillian's father, Mr. Warnbrough, strode toward them.

She whirled back. "On second thought, I should like to sit."

"Amanda!" Maggie whispered under her breath.

"This way, ladies." He crooked both arms.

Maggie shot her a sideways glance with a small shake of her head.

Footsteps thudded on the tiles at her back, growing more distinct with each passing second.

What to do?

Placing her hand on Mr. Craven's sleeve, she pled with Maggie via a gaze. Her friend had no choice but to take his other arm. The three of them moved down the hallway as one, leaving behind Mr. Warnbrough, Joseph's office—and Joseph. The betrayer. The master of secrets. . .

Oh, Joseph.

Her heart fluttered, and by the time Mr. Craven ushered them into his office and pulled out a chair, she folded into it, fighting sniffles and a fresh flood of tears. Maggie swooped in next to her, patting her back.

"Oh my dear, Miss Carston." Mr. Craven yanked out a handkerchief and handed it over, then pulled the only remaining chair in the cramped office to face hers and Maggie's. "You are distraught. I may not have a daughter of my own, but I hope you will think of me as a father figure. Is there anything I can do to help?"

Dabbing her eyes, she tried to speak past the little squeaks in her throat. "I think not."

"I have learned that sometimes merely unloading the weight on one's soul is enough to get you back on your feet, especially to impartial ears." He reached for her hand and patted it. Gently. Tenderly. Nothing at all like her father had ever done.

He leaned nearer. "You are amongst friends, Miss Carston. Miss Turner and I have strong shoulders, should you like to lessen your burden."

She glanced at Maggie. Worried green eyes stared back. Ought she share everything here and now? Get it over with? Find release? "I don't know what to say."

Mr. Craven gave her hand a little squeeze, comforting, lending strength. "I find it's best to start at the beginning. Tell us everything that's happened."

She sucked in a breath. It would feel good to shed all this emotion. Slowly, she deflated. "Very well."

Chapter Nine

W hat am I going to do, Henry?" Joseph dropped his forehead onto his hands, ignoring the banter filling the Minnesota Club. How dare the world continue in such a merry fashion when all the happiness in his life had been wrung out?

A whining moan drifted out of the heat register, as haunting as Amanda's last words. . . "*I won't see you. Ever again.*" Glass scraped across wood, and a bottle slipped into his circle of vision on the table.

"Have a drink, man. You'll feel better."

"No." He shoved the whiskey back at Henry. "I deserve to feel this way. I never should have kept secrets from Amanda in the first place."

Henry chuckled. "Ain't a man alive who don't hold a few cards close to his chest."

A bitter taste filled his mouth. "Yeah? Well, look where that got me."

"She'll come around."

"I don't know. I hurt her pretty bad." The memory of Amanda's tears, the shock, the pain pooling in her eyes was an image forever seared into his heart. He shook his head. "She has every right to hate me."

Henry's gray eyes sought his, probing deep. "You still want her?"

"More than anything." Did that ragged voice belong to him? He swallowed.

Henry reached for the bottle and refilled his glass. "Then go after her."

Joseph spread his hands wide. "How? She said she'd never see me again."

"Find a way." He tipped back his head and the glass in one swift movement. "You'll only have one shot at this, so make it count. Tell her everything. If she's the woman for you, and I think she is"—he slammed the glass onto the tabletop— "like I said, she'll come around. But she needs to be told, despite your aunt's wishes."

Joseph nodded in agreement. His heart, not so much. How could he break a promise he'd made to the woman who'd raised him since a lad?

Drained, he hung his head. Would that Henry's words might come true, but there was no guarantee. "I don't know. Happy endings are for fairy tales, not real life."

Another squeal screeched from the heat register, higher in pitch. Henry snorted and jabbed his thumb toward the register. "You've still got a shot at a happy ending, but if that boiler man keeps this up, he's sunk."

The scent of gin and tobacco hit Joseph's nose an instant before Willard Craven swaggered to a stop alongside his chair. "Join me at my table, Blake."

He scrubbed a hand over his face. Could this day seriously get any worse? "Not tonight."

Craven hitched both thumbs in his waistcoat. A strutting rooster couldn't have posed with more bravado. "I think you'll want to hear what I have to say."

"I'm not in the mood." His voice sharpened to a fine edge, drawing the looks of a few senators sitting nearby.

"You heard the man," Henry added, shooting Craven a scowl.

Craven eyed them both. "Two words: Grigg house."

Exhaling in disgust, Joseph shoved back his chair and followed Craven over to his little piece of the kingdom near the back door.

Craven sat.

Joseph folded his arms, refusing to comply. "Let's have it."

Willard pulled out a cigar from an inside pocket while nodding his head toward the empty chair across from him. "Is there nothing civilized about you?"

"Not when it comes to you." Nearby, brows rose. If he didn't want this turned into a dog-and-pony show, he'd have to sit.

But it took all his strength to ignore Craven's smirk as he sank into the chair.

Pulling out a pocketknife, Craven flipped it open and carved precise little cuts into his cigar, whittling the end into a V-shape. Each slice rubbed Joseph raw.

"I just came from a council meeting. Thought you might be interested in the results." Craven held up the cigar for inspection. Apparently pleased, he slapped shut the knife and tucked it away. "A certain property on Summit Avenue was brought to my attention earlier today. Something had to be done."

"What's your point?"

Retrieving a silver box from his pocket, Willard removed a match and struck it against the rough edge on one side. He waited until the flame caught, then worked to light the outside edge of the cigar, rotating it for an even burn.

Sweet mercy! This was more than a man could take. Joseph ground his teeth and waited.

Finally the man laid the match on the ashtray. "The Grigg house has been condemned and is in the process of being appropriated for public use. Whoever owned that property will take a big loss in more ways than one."

"You got something to tell me, man, now's the time."

Craven wrapped his lips around the cigar, drawing in puffs of air, then exhaled in a single stream—right at Joseph. "Looks like the city attorney may be facing manslaughter charges. Oh. . .that'd be you, wouldn't it?"

Joseph shot to his feet. If he stayed any longer, he'd be guilty of first-degree murder. He pivoted to return to Henry's table—until Willard's words stopped him cold.

"Apparently you haven't heard about Tam Nadder, then. Poor lad. I sent him on an errand over to the Grigg house this afternoon, right before the committee met."

His hands curled into fists, nails digging into his palms, the sharp sting a welcome sensation.

"The young fellow nearly broke his neck falling down the stairs. Even now he's fighting for his life over at St. Joe's."

Joseph wheeled about, rage as keening as the next squeal from the heat register. "If this is your handiwork, I'll have you locked up so tight, you won't be able to breathe!"

Gaslight painted Willard's face a pasty hue. "Don't blame me for your negligence. If you'd taken better care of your property, such an accident wouldn't have happened in the first place."

In two strides, he closed the gap between them, towering over Craven's chair. "How did you find out?"

Craven exhaled smoke like a dragon. "Seems you're not only negligent about property, but women as well."

A roar rumbled in his chest. He grabbed the man by the lapels and yanked him to his feet. "Leave Amanda out of this!"

The banter in the room stopped. The swoosh of heads and chairs turning their way circled like autumn leaves caught in an eddy.

Craven clucked his tongue. "Why, the poor little lamb ran straight into my arms for comfort after your betrayal."

The words ripped through him. The thought of Amanda anywhere near Craven punched him in the gut, the sickening feeling spreading like a wound. Amanda would never willingly plot with Craven against him. The blackguard had likely manipulated her.

He rocked onto the balls of his feet, ready to spring forward—

And at the same time an ear-shattering explosion shook the building, throwing him to the floor.

What on earth? Hard to tell with the buzzing inside his head and chaos erupting around him on every side. Tables tipped. Bottles broke. Men and servants scrambled to get out the front door. Joseph staggered to his feet and coughed, an acrid stink thickening the air.

Craven shot up from his chair, their eyes locking as the back door burst open. Servants poured out. So did super-heated air, smoldering white clouds, and a shout for help from belowstairs.

Willard stared at the smoke-belching door—then bolted. Away from the cry.

Coward!

Ducking, Joseph charged toward the sound and into hell. *God, help me. Help us all.*

The next cry was more faint, yet still audible. He pitched forward on the stairs, catching his hand on an exposed timber to keep from plummeting head first. "Where are you?"

"Here." The word traveled on a spate of coughing near the bottom of the stairs.

Joseph pressed on, horrified at what he might find. How had the boiler man even survived the explosion?

The stairs ended, opening onto a hallway, the top half clouded with smoke. To his left, a door hung crooked from one hinge, barely concealing a black maw gaping like an open grave. The smell of dirt and fear added to the stench of fire.

"Hurry!" A ragged voice called from the hole.

Joseph shoved the door aside and dove into what appeared to be a tunnel of some sort, but he didn't go far. A fallen beam pinned the man's leg just inside. The fellow didn't stand a chance of moving it. Still, he struggled to free himself.

Edging past him, Joseph angled for the best position to lift the thing.

The man peered up at him, the whites of his eyes a stark contrast to the darkness. This was no boiler man, not in a ruined suit and tie. "Thank God Craven sent you."

Craven? No time to think on that now. Straddling the fallen end of the beam, he squatted, praying for the strength of Samson. "I won't be able to lift this much, but at the slightest movement, pull away for all you're worth."

He yanked the wood upward, straining every muscle and grunting from the effort. Sweat dripped down his forehead, stinging his eyes.

The man yelled, "Free!"

He dropped the beam, chest heaving.

A bright flash erupted from the hallway, followed by another explosion. They had to get out of here. Now.

"I think my leg's broken." The fellow groaned.

Blast! Joseph grabbed the man beneath the arms and hefted him up, supporting him on the side of his injured leg. He lugged the fellow to the stairway, until a horrific thought stopped him cold. "Are there any others trapped in there?"

"No," the man hacked out. "I left Hannah's alone."

The man's revelation was as dazing as the awful heat licking their backs. He half-dragged, half-shoved the man up the stairs. No wonder Craven always sat near the back door, gatekeeper to a terrible secret, likely getting a cut of the money. When he got out of here—*if* he got out of here—he would finally have all the evidence he needed to shut down the brothel and go after Craven.

At the top of the stairs, smoke erupted in black swirls, darkening the top half of the club. Crouching, Joseph ignored the man's screams as he forced them toward the front door.

He cleared the pillars, charged into the foyer, freedom and air yards away.

Something hard and dull cracked against his skull—and the world went black.

———◆●◆———

The downstairs clock chimed midnight. The last toll struck the final nail into the coffin of the worst day of Amanda's life. Though she was fully dressed, she shivered from the ghostly echo leaching through her bedchamber door. Standing at the window, she stared into a night as black and endless as her thoughts. Outside, wind gusted, rattling tree limbs like bones. A storm would break soon. A tempest. And why not? If nature mimicked her life, then the world ought to be ravaged.

From the recesses of the downstairs foyer, the front door knocker hammered out a loud report. She stiffened. Only tragedy or terror called at such an hour. Dreading both, she snatched her shawl off the end of her bed and cracked open her door. Down the hall, her father did the same, only he held an oil lamp, the circle of light casting macabre shadows against the wallpaper.

"Go to bed, Amanda," he grumbled as he swept past.

She fell into step behind him. "Sleep is out of the question."

The words trailed her down the stairs. Indeed. She may never sleep again, so tormented was her heart. Oh, the silly thing still beat, but merely from habit. Joseph's betrayal had seen to that.

Grayson reached the door before them, and at Father's nod, the butler swung it open.

A dark shape entered, smelling of smoke. When Father raised his lamp, Henry Wainwright removed his hat, a fine sprinkle of ash falling to the floor. He tipped his head toward them both, his gray eyes devoid of their usual sparkle. "Mr. Carston, Miss Amanda, I come with hard news."

Father's gaze shot to Grayson. "Light the lamps in the sitting room."

Henry shook his head, hair spilling onto his brow from the movement. "There's no time."

Amanda swayed, or maybe the floor did. Whatever Mr. Wainwright had to say couldn't be good. She rushed out of the shadows toward the light and clutched her father's arm. "What's happened?"

"There was a boiler explosion at the club. I escaped, but Joseph. . ." Henry's mouth twisted. "A pillar caught him on the head. The doctors aren't sure if he'll make it."

Aren't sure. The words taunted like demons. Trembling started in her knees and worked its way up her legs, until she gripped Father's arm tighter in a vain attempt to stop it. When she'd told Joseph she'd never see him again, she'd never meant anything this final. Her heart lurched. What if he left this world without peace between them?

Oh, God. Not death.

Henry stepped closer, pity etching creases at his eyes. "I'll take you to him, if you like, with your father's permission, of course."

She lifted her face to her father, seeking his approval without words. Her voice wouldn't move past the lump in her throat even if she tried.

Father's jaw worked, harsh lines furrowing the sides of his mouth. Then, surprisingly, the movement stopped. The lines softened. So did his tone. "Go. You have my blessing."

She froze. For the first time, he looked past convention, what others might think, and stared straight into her heart.

"Thank you," she whispered.

Grayson held out her cloak, and she moved from the house to Henry's carriage like swimming through a murky pond. Gloom painted the night sky with a black brush, air cold and damp as a cellar. By the time Henry seated her and clicked his tongue for the horse to walk on, thunder rolled a bass warning.

This late at night, no other carriages traveled on Summit. Just her and Henry and the awful knowledge sitting in her soul that even now Joseph might be dying.

Henry glanced at her. "I, uh, I suppose there's no easy way to say this, but Joseph told me what happened between you and him today."

She stifled a gasp, but truly, should she be so astonished? This man had been friends with Joseph since their days of rock skipping and knickers. "You know?"

Henry nodded. "I think there's something you should know, too. That man of yours is faithful to a fault."

Faithful? Neglecting to tell her that he owned the very property she'd been trying to acquire was faithful? She cleared her throat to keep from scoffing.

"Joseph's too pig-headed to tell you, so I will." Henry sighed, as blustery as the next gust of wind. "He was using the Grigg estate as a safe house. You know how big he is on closing down Hannah Crow's brothel, right?"

A safe house? What did that even mean? Her hat lifted, and she righted it with a quick grab, ruefully wishing everything could be as easily set straight. "I fail to understand how the two are connected."

"I'm getting to that." A flash of light and a crack of thunder interrupted him, and he paused to rein in the horse, which shied toward the curb. "When the Grigg house, dilapidated as it was, came on the market, Joseph snatched it up on the sly, allowing and even spreading the rumors that it was haunted. That way no one would go snooping around and possibly discover his operation."

"What operation?"

"Blast it! Joseph should be the one telling you this. Not me." Henry clicked his tongue and snapped the reins. "Pardon the delicacy of the topic, Miss Amanda, but allow me to be blunt. It's near to impossible for a woman to leave behind a tawdry lifestyle on her own. Besides the haunted house rumor, Joseph also let word spread, woman to woman, that if any wanted to escape the brothel, all they had to do was make their way to the Grigg house and hide upstairs. When he saw the drapes opened in the third-floor window, then he knew a woman wanted out. He'd go at night and escort her to the train station, where he'd pay her fare to Chicago. From there, his reverend friend, Robert Bond, helped the woman find a new life."

"Joseph? My Joseph did this?" Though it was hard to believe, everything Henry said rang as true and clear as the next arc of lightning. Perhaps she and Maggie had not been imagining things when they'd heard footsteps, and this would explain why Joseph had been so close at hand when they'd run from the house.

She looked up at Henry, the next strobe of light harsh on his face—as severe as the single question girding up what remained of her anger. "Why did he not tell me?"

"Because he was hoping to be done with this by now. He kept trying to shut down the brothel, and once that happened, he'd sell the Grigg house. End of story—and not really a story for a proper lady's ears to hear. He was trying to protect you." Henry gazed down at her, gray eyes hard to see in the dark, but the steadiness in his voice was pure and true. "There are things in this world that are ugly. Evil. Things no one should have to know."

Rain broke then, pattering on the roof like tears. A whimper caught in her throat. She'd gotten so caught up in her own schemes to right this world that she'd failed to think others might be doing the same.

The wind shifted. Rain needled her cheek from the open side of the carriage, as stinging as her misguided pride. The closer they drew to the hospital, the more carriages and pandemonium crowded the streets, despite the late hour. Henry wove through undaunted, shouting bold threats to clear the way.

She hated to distract him, but the need to know flew past her lips. "Why did Joseph want to help the brothel girls in the first place?"

He slowed the horse to a halt and tied off the reins. "The rest is for Joseph to say." He hopped from the carriage and rounded the back of it to her side, reaching to help her down.

She grasped his big hand—and didn't let go even when her feet hit the ground. Gas lamps burned on each side of the hospital entrance. A man, leaning heavily on another, staggered out the front door, sorrow etching his face. But at least he was walking. Unlike Joseph. What would she find when she went through those doors?

"I'm afraid, Mr. Wainwright." Her voice shook. So did her legs.

He squeezed her hand. "So am I.

Chapter Ten

Amanda paused in the doorway leading to Joseph's ward, trying hard not to breathe too deeply of disease and despair, a trick she'd learned to master over the past couple of days. Mortality lived here as insidious as the stains on the white walls. Though scrubbed clean, years of blood and toil marred the plaster with a sickly gray.

Dr. Beemish, frocked in a knee-length lab coat, strode down the center aisle toward her. "Good day, Miss Carston. I hope you know what a welcome sight you are. Your care for Mr. Blake and the others is commendable."

"All I have to offer is a listening ear or a hand to hold. Not much for those who were so horribly injured." She shuddered thinking of the disfigured gentlemen she'd comforted, then searched the doctor's face, pleading for a morsel of good news. "How is he?"

The doctor clasped his hands behind his back. "I shall be frank with you, my dear. If Mr. Blake doesn't wake soon, I fear he might not at all."

She stared at him, dry-eyed. She'd cry if she had any tears left. But nothing remained. She was a shell, a husk. Held together by skin alone, for her emotions had checked out that first night she'd seen Joseph lying on white sheets, bloodied bandages swaddled around his skull. Deathly still.

"But take heart in this." Dr. Beemish reached out and gripped her arm, imparting strength. Or maybe courage. Hard to tell, for despite his action, she felt none.

"The rest of Mr. Blake is sound and whole. Body functions are normal. Reflexes without flaw. Should he regain consciousness, recovery will be swift."

"Thank you, Doctor." She used her confident voice, but it was fake. Everything about the last forty-eight hours had been a ruse of backbone and pluck on her part. Lies, all. Though she'd labeled Joseph as such, she was the liar.

Once Dr. Beemish swept past her, she let her shoulders sag. Walking the aisle to Joseph's bed, she trembled from the coldness inside her soul—then froze, jaw dropping.

Two beds over, dark brown eyes stared into hers.

"Joseph!" She darted ahead and sank to his side, afraid to hope. What if this wasn't real? "You're awake?"

"Apparently." Voice raspy, he cleared his throat. "Water?"

She grabbed a pitcher from the bed stand and poured a glass, hands shaking. *Oh, God. Oh, please. Oh, thank You!* Cradling Joseph's bandaged head, she lifted the water to his mouth. Most dribbled down his chin, darkened by two days' worth of stubble, but even so he offered a weak smile when he finished. "So good."

Replacing the glass, she leaned closer to study him. Purple bruised the skin near one temple. A cut on his chin scabbed over in a jagged line. But he was alert. Aware. And all the more handsome because of it.

"How are you feeling?" she asked.

"Been better." He reached to finger his bandages, and did such a poor job of concealing a wince, she couldn't help but smile.

He reached for her. "You're here."

"I am. I—" Her voice cracked, and the dam broke. Elation, gratitude, sorrow, grief—too many emotions bubbled up and flooded her eyes, running down her cheeks and over his fingers.

"I was so afraid!" she cried.

"Shh." He fumbled his thumb across her cheek, wiping away tears. "Help me sit."

She sucked in a shaky breath. For his sake, she had to pull herself together. Swallowing the lump in her throat, she took his hand in both of hers, lowering it to his side. "You've only just awakened. Do you think it wise?"

"Wise or not"—he grunted as he tried to push up on his elbows—"I must."

Stubborn man. Beautiful, stubborn man whom she could not live without. Fighting a fresh round of tears, she tugged up the pillow behind him and helped him settle upright. Seeing his gaze, soaking in all the love she read in those brown depths, she blurted out everything that'd been bottled up inside.

"Oh, Joseph, I'm so sorry I jumped to conclusions. I didn't expect the best out of you, but instead ascribed the worst." She pressed her knuckles against her mouth, stopping a cry.

"All's forgiven, love." Battered and beaten, likely in pain, he used such tenderness that it hurt deep inside her. "You didn't know."

"But neither did I trust! I let self-pity blind me. I couldn't see that you weren't trying to thwart me. You were merely working on a more urgent plan than mine. I treated you abominably, without waiting like you asked—" She froze as a stunning realization hit her. Hard. Her mouth twisted into a rueful pinch. "Just like I do to God."

"God knows I've done the same, yet He's always there to pick up the pieces."

She shook her head. How could such goodness, such kindness be understood? "I don't deserve it. Nor do you deserve how I treated you."

"You may not think so when I tell you everything." He reached for her hand again. "I have much to say."

His face paled.

Was this too much, too soon? "Joseph, please rest. It can wait."

"No, I've waited long enough." He entwined his fingers with hers. "Too long."

◄ ♦ ►

The warmth, the intimacy of Amanda's palm pressed against his was as right as finally telling her the full truth—more right than the agreement he'd made with his aunt.

"As you know, I own the Grigg house," he began. "Or did, until the day you discovered the deed."

"You. . .you don't own it anymore?"

He shook his head. Bad idea. The dull throb beat harder, pounding against the inside of his skull. Shifting on the pillow, he pushed up a bit more, easing the ache and allowing him to continue. "I transferred the title to my colleague, Reverend Bond, in Chicago. When you first came to me about the Grigg estate, I knew you'd be successful at sleuthing out who it belonged to, for such are your keen abilities."

A pretty red flushed her cheeks, deep enough to shame a spring rose.

"So I unloaded the deed." Two beds over, a fellow patient moaned—and the sound resonated deep in his gut. How to explain this? "It's all so complicated. I hardly know where to begin."

Amanda patted his hand. "Let me help. Your friend Henry filled me in on most everything, but not all. He told me about your plan to help women escape Hannah Crow's—which, I might add, is quite a reckless and noble thing for a city attorney to do." Sunlight slanted in through the window above his bed, creating a golden halo around her head. Her smile shined even brighter. "But the thing I don't know is why? Why take on such an endeavor in the first place?"

"Elizabeth," he breathed out, then clamped his jaw. Could he do this? Of course he should, despite his aunt. But how to say the words that would blight his sister's memory in the eyes of the woman he loved and tarnish his family's reputation?

Amanda's brow puckered. "Your sister? What has she to do with this?"

He stood on the edge of a riverbank—the wild, raging river of the past. It was either step back now or jump in whole and possibly drown from the truth.

He jumped. "While it's true that Elizabeth died in California, the circumstances are not what my aunt allows everyone to believe. My sister didn't die in childbirth. She died in a brothel. Elizabeth was a woman of ill repute."

He expected the gasp. The look of horror. But when Amanda's face softened and she rested her palm against his cheek, he never predicted such tenderness in her gaze.

"I am so sorry. For you. For her. She must have been desperate, indeed."

"Desperate?" He grimaced, then winced from the pull of scalp against bandage. "That and more."

"What happened?"

"There was a man—Peter Gilford. Elizabeth loved him, yet Father would not grant his blessing. He went so far as to forbid her to ever see the man again. It was an ugly affair. Peter ran off to California. Elizabeth followed, headstrong to a fault." He deflated against the pillow, awful memories weighing heavy, wearing his spirit to the bone. "Father was right about Peter. He was a shiftless fellow, leaving my sister penniless on the streets of San Francisco."

"How awful!"

The clack of heels on tile entered the far end of the ward. Amanda glanced up at an attendant who rolled in a cart on wheels. The smell of some kind of stew spread throughout the room. "Looks like lunch. You must be famished. Finish your story later. I promise I will not leave your side."

Ahh, but that was good to hear. Aunt had said no respectable woman would have him if the truth of their family was known. For the first time ever, he wondered what other false views Aunt had convinced him to adopt, but with the attendant approaching nearer, he'd have to save that line of thought for another time.

"I am nearly finished. Elizabeth wrote, asking for money. Father refused, telling her to find her own way home. She did the only thing she could to earn her fare—and it was the death of her. She was trying to get back here, that's all. She just wanted to come home." Grief and guilt burned his throat, leaving a nasty taste at the back of his mouth. The smell of the stew turned his stomach. "If only I'd known at the time, but I was off at school. I failed her, Amanda. I failed my sister."

"Ahh, love, in your own words, you didn't know." She squeezed his fingers. "And you came up with a way to save others like her. She wouldn't think you a failure. She'd be proud of you, as am I."

The admiration heating her gaze burned straight to his heart, and he squeezed her hand right back. "You were wrong, you know."

Her nose scrunched up. "How's that?"

He lifted her knuckles to his lips. "I am the one who does not deserve you."

Epilogue

A few stubborn oak leaves let loose and skittered to the road in front of the carriage. Amanda admired the way the horse high-stepped along the cobbles, then turned her face and admired the driver even more. The bruises had faded to a faint shade of yellow around Joseph's eye, hardly distinguishable now, especially in the twilight. The cut on his chin still stood out, though, and would leave a scar, but the mark would ever remind her of how close she'd come to losing him.

"You study me as if I might vanish." Pulling his gaze from the road, he grinned down at her. "Go on. Ask me again. You know you want to."

She flattened her lips. Ought she be annoyed or thrilled that he knew her so well? She peered closer, and concern won out. "Are you certain you're up to this? Maggie will understand if we don't make her house party."

"I'm far better than Tam Nadder. That poor fellow has a long haul of it, learning to walk with crutches for the rest of his life. I've got a banger of a headache still, but that's all." Reaching his arm along the back of the cushion, he tucked her closer to his side. "And besides, we won't stay long. I don't want you turning into a pumpkin, and I promised your father I'd have you home at a decent hour. I'm surprised he allowed me to take you unchaperoned in the first place."

She leaned back, resting her head against his arm. She'd never tire of the feel of him. "I think Father's changing, in a good way. Not that convention isn't still important to him, but I'm starting to think I might be important to him, as well."

"Why the change?"

Exactly. Why? She'd turned that question over like a furrowed plot of earth these past two weeks. "While he didn't lose any close friends in that explosion, he did know some of the men who died and many who were injured. I really thought that my position as chairwoman would be the thing to impress him, but turns out my simple act of continuing to visit those men even after your release impressed him more. And in a smaller way, perhaps he realized how empty the house will be without me when we marry."

"'When we marry.' I like the sound of that."

So did she. She closed her eyes, soaking in the blessing of the man beside her. For a while they drove in the silence of naught but the wheels on the road and the occasional rattle of branches in the wind. Any time now and she'd hear the crunch of the Turners' drive—but the carriage lurched sideways onto crackling twigs and weeds.

Her eyes flew open. "Hey, this isn't the way to—what are we doing here?"

Joseph flashed her a smile as he guided the horse up the overgrown Grigg drive. "Close your eyes."

She narrowed them. "What are you up to?"

"I've got one last secret to reveal." He tapped her on the nose. "Now close your eyes."

With a frown, she obeyed. The carriage halted, then canted to the side as Joseph hopped down. His footsteps rounded the back, then stopped. A warm hand engulfed her fingers, and he guided her to the ground. What was he up to?

Ten steps later, he stopped. "All right. You may look."

She blinked open her eyes. There, in the fading light, a freshly painted sign hung on the weathered post of the Grigg front porch. Black letters spelled out: Carston Blake Academy.

Her jaw dropped, and she turned to him. "What's this?"

"Here is your building for your new school. There's no need for a safe house anymore, now that Hannah Crow's has been shut down for good. Not that other brothels can't open up, I suppose, but with Craven run out of town by the angry wives of club members, I don't think that will happen for a very long time. And besides"—he flashed her a smile—"I couldn't very well let you go to that Ladies' Aide Society meeting on Monday and take yet another beating from Lillian Warnbrough, could I?"

The tenderness in his voice, the depth of emotion in his brown eyes, the warmth of his mouth as he pressed a kiss to her brow turned the world watery. Wrapping her arms around his waist, she nuzzled her face into his chest. "You know what I love about you, Joseph Blake?"

His chuckle rumbled against her ear. "That I always do the right thing?"

"No." She shook her head, loving the strong beat of his heart. "Everything."

Michelle Griep has been writing since she first discovered blank wall space and Crayolas. She seeks to glorify God in all that she writes—except for that graffiti phase she went through as a teenager. She resides in the frozen tundra of Minnesota, where she teaches history and writing classes for a local high school co-op. An Anglophile at heart, she runs away to England every chance she gets, under the guise of research. Really, though, she's eating excessive amounts of scones while rambling around a castle. Michelle is a member of ACFW (American Christian Fiction Writers) and MCWG (Minnesota Christian Writers Guild). Keep up with her adventures at her blog "Writer off the Leash" or visit www.michellegriep.com.

Win, Place, or Show

by Erica Vetsch

Dedication

To Katie Gardner, her crew of amazing young students, and all the horses and ponies at Otteridge Farm. Your devotion to excellent horsemanship inspired this story.

And to Peter, as always.

Chapter One

Hudson River Valley, New York
June, 1899

B eryl Valentine snatched an apple from the bowl of fruit decoratively arranged on the table in the hall and hurried toward the front door, hoping to get outside before anyone stopped her. As she passed the vast mahogany pocket doors to the parlor, voices drifted through the opening.

"Beryl is twenty years old. It's time she realized her responsibility." Her father, Wallace Valentine, railroad tycoon and financial genius, had a voice better suited to a baseball stadium than a boardroom. "There's her fortune and her future at stake, and she doesn't seem to care."

Beryl stopped with her hand on the front door.

"I've got things under control." Rosemary, Beryl's mother, had a well-modulated voice ...that could still slice through the air like a razor blade. "If you'd butt out of the process, I could have her engaged before Christmas."

"*You* have things under control? With that parade of wimps you marched through the house all winter? Every one of them weak as chamomile tea and sniffing around Beryl just to get at her money. There isn't a one of them I'd give two cents for. She's our only child and heir, and she has a duty."

Beryl closed her eyes, her heart sinking to her heels. While her parents could and did argue about everything from the household help to national politics, their latest disagreements all seemed to center around one goal: finding Beryl a husband. The odd thing was that they were united in the notion that she needed a husband but definitely divided on the method and the candidates.

And neither one seemed to think Beryl should have a say in the matter. She took a calming breath.

"They weren't wimps. They were perfectly presentable young men, the sons of some of the best families in New York Society. Any one of them would make a suitable match for Beryl. I don't care how much money a man has if he has the right breeding, the right connections." Mother could put more starch in her voice than you could find in a hotel laundry.

"Not a one of them knows how to do anything useful." Something impacted wood, and Beryl knew her father had smacked his fist on a table, a familiar gesture when he warmed to a subject. "All they know how to do is inherit money and spend it. Not a man's man out of the lot."

You tell her, Father.

"I suppose those ancient cronies of yours that you bring home are better? Men more than twice her age? It's disgusting, and I won't have it."

Thank you, Mother. In that we are agreed. The wimps are bad enough, but the cronies are worse. Beryl stifled a sigh, weary of the topic and knowing they could be at it for hours.

"At least they're men, not obsequious boys. And they know how to run businesses and accumulate wealth instead of squandering it and then looking for an heiress with a healthy bank account to replenish their coffers. I don't care where a man comes from as long as he's got the brains and ambition and ability to make something of himself. I have found just the man for Beryl. He's coming over this afternoon—"

"Wallace, sometimes I think you have rocks for brains. . . ."

Beryl had heard enough, but before she could escape, the parlor maid hurried by with a tray, bobbing her head. "Good morning, Miss Beryl. Will you be joining your parents for tea?" she asked, her voice loud in the echoing foyer.

Beryl made shushing noises, but it was too late.

"Is that you, Beryl?" her mother asked. "Come in here."

The parlor maid shot her a silent apology as they entered the parlor.

The maid set the tray on the low table in front of Mother, checked that everything was in order, and dropped a curtsy. "Should I fetch another cup?" She addressed the question to Mother.

"Yes, please."

"No, thank you."

Mother and Beryl spoke at the same time.

"Mother, I can't stay. I have an appointment."

"You have time for tea." Her mother's placid voice set Beryl's teeth on edge. But she took the tea her mother handed her, blowing on it to cool it.

"Sit down."

"I'm in a hurry."

"It takes just as long to drink a cup of tea standing as it does sitting down." Mother regarded her with dark brown eyes, demanding good manners.

Beryl sat.

Father leaned on the corner of the desk, arms folded, tweed coat straining across his big shoulders. "We haven't been here twenty-four hours and you're already headed to the stables?" He raised his eyebrows. "I have someone coming to the house today whom I want you to meet."

She brushed her hand down the front of her riding habit. "I cabled ahead our arrival date, and I have a lesson scheduled this morning. I'm eager to see how Lacey traveled." Her beloved mare, Lacey, hated train travel, even for the relatively short distance from New York City. "I'm also looking forward to seeing Avila again." Avila Schmidt had been Beryl's riding instructor the past few summers, though the lessons often took the form of long rides together where Avila became more of a mentor and confidant than teacher.

"You coddle that mare. Coddling makes them soft. You might be interested to know I had another offer for her this week. Cal Brightman was looking over my stock, wanted a mount for his wife and a possible broodmare for his farm." He ran his hand down his right sideburn, pursing his lips. "I told him you'd spent a lot of time working with the mare and that he wouldn't find a gentler mount."

Fear gripped Beryl's heart, the way it did every time her father talked about possibly selling Lacey. Technically, the horse belonged to her father, but Beryl had ridden her for the past five years and had come to love her dearly. They'd competed together in a few local shows, and Lacey had been her mount every fall for fox hunting. They were a team.

"I'll never understand your fascination with horses." Mother shook her head. "I know it's fashionable for young ladies to ride in Central Park occasionally, but private lessons, horse shows, hunting. You practically live in the stables. It's unbecoming, and it certainly won't help you find a husband. You should be attending the lawn parties, picnics, and fetes like other girls your age."

"Mother, please." Beryl turned to her father. "You wouldn't sell Lacey, would you? You know I've taken a special liking to her."

"Horses aren't pets, they're assets. Assets that cost quite a bit of money to keep and train, and if a chance comes to make a profit on the sale of an asset, you take it. I bought that mare to become a broodmare, and she's more valuable on a stud farm than as your summer mount." It was a position he mentioned often, and one that made Beryl's heart hurt. He didn't seem to understand the bond she felt with her horses—not Belle, the pony he'd sold when she was ten; not Dannyboy, the chestnut gelding Beryl had ridden to her first blue ribbon when she was fourteen and whom her father had sold at that very show; and not Lacey, her sweet, kind thoroughbred hunter.

Her father wasn't cruel about it. He just didn't understand. To him, horses were objects, not individuals. They represented profit and loss. Especially those he bred and raised for racing and hunting and showing and blood stock on his stud farm up near Saratoga.

Beryl glanced at the clock on the mantel. "I must be going. My lesson starts in less than an hour, and I have to stop by and pick up Melanie. The carriage is waiting out front."

Mother picked up her needlework and poked her needle into the cloth. She never seemed interested in her projects, as if she did them only because it was expected of a lady of quality. "You will be home in time to help me with planning this week's dinner party." It wasn't a question. "I've narrowed the guest list to twenty."

Before she could answer, her father scowled. "That guest list includes the Bentleys and the Van Rissinghams, right? I'm trying to get Rutherford and Barrington to partner with me to purchase the Schmidts' young stallion, Arcturus. If we can syndicate him and stand him at stud next spring, we'll make back our investment in one season." He crossed his ankles, a calculating gleam in his eyes. "I heard Schmidt has another offer he's considering, and he's given the bidder some time to pull together his financing, but I told him I'd match any offer. Arcturus won everything there was to win at the National Horse Show last year. With a horse like that, I could name my stud fee. I've got another name for the guest list. He can partner Beryl for the evening, so the numbers are even." He shot a piercing look at Beryl, and she stifled a sigh. Another of his cronies in search of a wife.

Sighing, Mother looked at him reproachfully. "You know what will happen if the Bentleys and Van Rissinghams come to dinner. You'll talk horses all evening. It practically ruined our last dinner party. Nobody could get a word in edgewise, and you refused to change the subject. You practically recited the Stud Book from memory, and then you each took turns bragging about how one of your horses beat another at some potty little show or track somewhere."

With yet another argument brewing, Beryl took the opportunity to set down her nearly full teacup, drop a quick kiss on her mother's cheek, promise to be back to help plan the dinner, and duck out of the parlor. She hurried outside into the fresh air, nodding to the footman who held the carriage door for her.

A footman. She shook her head. Liveried and everything. That was Mother for you. Mrs. Astor and Mrs. Vanderbilt had liveried footmen at their front doors, and Mother had followed suit. Beryl thought the fad ridiculous, requiring young men to wear pantaloons and hose and braid as if they'd just stepped out of Georgian England. But to Mother, and to a certain extent, Father, too, image was everything.

At least talk of the dinner party had gotten them off the subject of finding her a husband, something she was quite capable of doing herself, thank-you-very-much. Not that Beryl wanted a husband right now. She'd get around to it when she felt like it, and not before. For now, her only love was a chestnut mare named Lacey, and that was more than enough.

------◆◆◆------

The last thing Major Gardiner Kennedy (Ret.) wanted to do for the next few months was coach twittering, giggly girls through riding lessons—females with hardly a notion of which end of a horse bit and which one kicked, taking riding lessons only because they had nothing better with which to fill their time, and because it was the "done thing" for ladies of a certain class. He'd scanned the list of students this morning, stunned that not a single male name was to be found.

Why had he allowed himself to be talked into this?

Because he needed money.

And he was helping out a friend.

And it was only for a few months.

It would all be worth it, if it helped him reach his goal. Wouldn't it?

He listed the reasons for the hundredth time in the last week since landing this job, trying to convince himself it wouldn't be so bad.

Crossing his arms on the top rail of the paddock, he studied the blood bay stallion calmly grazing in the June sunshine. Arcturus, named after the brightest star in the night sky, swished his tail, unaware of Gard's plans and dreams for him.

"I take it from your wistful stare that you're still interested?" Freeman Schmidt, Arcturus's owner and Gard's temporary employer, clapped him on the shoulder.

Gard straightened and accepted the older man's offered hand. "Very much, sir. He's just the stallion I need to get the farm started right."

"I've had two more inquiries about him just this week. I am beginning to regret setting a price and giving you until after the Deep Haven Show to meet it." Mr. Schmidt tapped his cane on the hard-packed dirt, pushing aside his tweed coat and tucking his thumb into his vest pocket. He gave a rueful smile. "You caught me in a moment of weakness, lad. Not to mention, my wife said if I didn't give you a chance, I'd be in her bad graces for ages to come." His faded, blue eyes twinkled with ever-present good humor. "Trust me, the last place you want to be is in Avila's bad graces." He propped one of his shiny, high boots on the bottom rung of the paddock fence.

Gard smothered a grin. On the one hand, Mr. Schmidt's wife could be sharp-tongued, not known for suffering fools gladly, but on the other, she was tireless in her charity work with a soft heart under all her bluster. And she had made it possible for him to get this job.

"She's a force to be reckoned with, sir, but I have a feeling that when she's on your side, you're unbeatable."

Mr. Schmidt clapped Gard on the shoulder again with a guffaw. "Then I've been unbeatable for thirty-two years now. I highly recommend the matrimonial state. Now that you're out of the army for good, will you be looking for a bride?"

Gard shook his head. "Not anytime soon, I'm afraid. Every penny I have goes back into saving for Arcturus. I'm in no position to take on a wife just yet."

"Hmph. I can appreciate wanting to be wise with your funds, but when the right girl comes along, priorities change." Mr. Schmidt pursed his lips, making his mustache jut out like walrus whiskers. "In fact, you might even consider taking on a few partners in your horse-breeding enterprise to lessen your financial burden and free up your prospects. I know I wouldn't mind buying a share of your new venture."

Shaking his head, Gard studied the stallion once more, noting how the sunlight gleamed off his red-brown coat and how glossy his black mane and tail appeared. "I appreciate the offer, sir, but I want to do this on my own. Spending my life in the military, I've lived all over the States, but I've never had a home. Now that I've inherited my grandmother's farm, I'm ready to put down some roots. I just need to earn a bit more money this summer to get the final pieces into place to make that happen."

"Well, I'm glad to have you taking over the lessons these next few months. Avila still hasn't reconciled herself to the fact that she won't be ready to resume her activities for a while yet. That was a nasty tumble she took. The doctors say she will be on crutches for at least two months, then on limited activity until perhaps Christmas. She's fortunate to have kept her limb. It was a bad break. Truth be told, I'm glad the doctor sent her to convalesce at her sister's place. Woman doesn't realize her age. She'd be out here every day in spite of the crutches if I'd have let her stay here."

I wish she were here. The military had done nothing to prepare Gard for dealing with young ladies. He knew next to nothing about girls, except that they giggled and cried a lot, both of which made him more nervous than being alone and lost in Apache country.

"I'll do my best, sir, but I've never given lessons to young ladies. I might've spent three years as an instructor at the Cavalry School at Fort Riley, out in Kansas, but the recruits and officers I was training there were all tough men. I'm pretty sure the same methods won't work with a...shall we say...more genteel clientele?" He rubbed the back of his neck, remembering the repetition, the drills, the shouting and dust and sweat of cavalry training, and trying to imagine what lady-students might be like in comparison.

"You'll do fine. Most of our pupils only want to learn to hack in the park proficiently, or perhaps compete in some of the walk/trot classes in local shows this summer. They're looking for someone to give them confidence, not ready them for the Pony Express." He chuckled. "Word's beginning to spread that we have an eligible new riding instructor. We've already had double our number of students from last year, and it's been less than a week. Twenty-seven students over last year's twelve." He rubbed his hands together.

Gard's stomach muscles clenched. "That's more than I can handle alone. Thanks for letting me bring Asa along to help. He'll be working with the greenest riders while I take on the more advanced students." Gard glanced over his shoulder toward the training ring where his former striker and friend groomed a plump white pony in preparation for his first lesson of the day. Asa's hair nearly matched the pony's, his weathered, black skin a stark contrast. He had been Gard's father's striker—sort of the military version of a valet—when Gard was a boy. Gard had no idea how old Asa was, just that he'd been a fixture in his life for as long as he could remember. And he was an excellent horseman.

Gard placed his hands on the top rail and pushed away. "I suppose I'd better stop admiring Arcturus and get back on the job." He pulled a paper from his shirt pocket and scanned the list. "I've got two lessons this morning. A Miss Melanie Turner and a Miss Beryl Valentine?"

"You're in for a treat. Beryl is one of Avila's favorite students. I don't know Miss Turner. I believe she's new."

Gard headed toward the barn, trying to think of anything he wanted less than to meet his first students.

———◆◆◆———

Beryl held her skirts aside so Melanie could sit next to her in the carriage.

"Do you like it?" Melanie waved to her new riding habit, the latest style, lovely forest green velvet trimmed in satin. "I've been dying to wear it. I have a new habit made up every year, but I've never gotten to wear one since I don't ride."

"It's beautiful." And completely impractical for more than looking good. Beryl glanced down at her own more serviceable brown tweed. Nowhere near as pretty, but it wouldn't show every bit of dust. She touched the white stock at her throat, fingering the hunting hound pin, a gift from Avila for her birthday last year.

Melanie laughed. She was always laughing, always playful. . .when she wasn't pouting, that is. "Goodness knows how this lesson will go. I haven't been on a horse since the pony rides at my sixth birthday."

"I'm anxious to see Avila. She didn't answer my last letter, but I suppose, knowing I would be coming so soon, she didn't bother." Beryl watched the trees and meadows go by, glad for warm weather and the gentle breeze after the bitter New York City winter. Sunshine filtered down on the open carriage as they turned out of Twin Oaks, the Turner family's summer estate, and headed to Schmidt Farm. The road wound near the Hudson River, and across; through the trees, Beryl could make out the gray stone buildings of West Point Military Academy.

"Oh, haven't you heard?" Melanie leaned closer, face alight at being able to relay a choice bit of gossip. "Our cook heard from the Schmidts' housekeeper that Mrs. Schmidt had a bad fall. She won't be teaching lessons. In fact, she's not even at the farm. She's gone up to Syracuse so her sister can look after her, probably for the entire summer. Mr. Schmidt hired someone to take her place, a dashing ex-Major. I hear he's gorgeous." She rolled her eyes, clasping her hands against her chest. "I just heard about it yesterday, which is the only reason I didn't beg off these lessons at the last minute."

Beryl's heart lurched. "What happened?" And how did Melanie always get news before Beryl?

"I don't know the details. A broken leg, maybe? But the rumor is that the new instructor is heart-stoppingly handsome."

Biting her lip, Beryl frowned. No wonder Avila hadn't answered her letter. And now she wouldn't even be at the farm all summer?

They turned into the Schmidt Farm drive, passing between the whitewashed brick pillars and under the wrought-iron sign. The large house and barns came into view, white-railed paddocks, closely clipped lawns, carefully raked training rings, everything orderly and familiar while chaos burst through Beryl. As they reached the south end of the riding enclosure, Melanie stopped cold.

"I told you he was gorgeous, but my, my."

"What did you say?" Beryl pulled herself from her distracted thoughts.

Melanie nudged Beryl, indicating with her chin—because it was unladylike to point—in the direction of the far side of the ring. "Pay attention." She squeezed Beryl's arm. "It's the new riding instructor, Major Kennedy. Oh my, just looking at him makes my heart flip-flop."

Beryl glanced in the direction Melanie was staring. A jolt rippled through her, but she quickly tried to quell it. Whew. Melanie was right. If that was the new riding instructor, this stable was going to be stampeded by society women wanting to learn to ride. He wore no hat on his dark curly hair, and his riding breeches and jacket fit him just right. Sunlight gleamed on his knee-high boots. Tall, thin, with high cheekbones and a straight nose, he looked like every girl's dream of a dashing cavalry officer.

He turned his head and their eyes locked. Her heart tripped and a thrill whooshed through her. Even at this distance, he had quite the impact. And yet, looking the part didn't mean he could ride, or that he could teach. What experience did he have? Did he know a cavaletti from a canter? Time would tell.

Dropping her gaze, she let out a slow breath, casually turning toward the white-railed paddock where the Schmidts' prize stallion Arcturus, grazed. This was the horse her father was trying to form a syndicate to purchase. He'd been the talk of the Deep Haven Show last fall, winning the model class as well as the open jumping class. She couldn't stop her gaze from returning to Major Kennedy, feeling a thrill go through her once more.

She turned away, disquieted by the awareness she had of the Major. No man had ever affected her this way, and they hadn't even met. Was she so shallow as to be impressed with a handsome face? She hoped not. "I wonder if Lacey has settled in. It's a long trip, even by train, and she hates to travel."

"You can't seriously be thinking about your horse at a time like this? Don't you think he's handsome?" Melanie tugged on her elbow, inclining her head toward the instructor. "No wonder your mother despairs of finding a husband for you."

Beryl winced. "Don't start. She keeps bringing home eligible men, but I don't care for any of them. They're fine but not what I want in a husband."

"Well, you *are* the heiress to a huge fortune. It's a serious decision. Wasn't there anyone you met last winter that you liked?"

"They weren't all terrible, but how can I know if they really like me, or if they just like my father's money? Almost every one of them mentioned my inheritance at one point or another. I want to marry someone who loves me for myself, not for my father's bank accounts and property. I want someone who would marry me even if I didn't have a penny to my name. And it would be awfully nice if he at least liked horses a little bit."

Melanie frowned, tilting her head as if Beryl had spoken in a foreign language. "You want to marry for love?"

The wonder and disbelief in Melanie's voice made Beryl sad. New York Society considered birth and status well above feelings and dreams, and it was the duty of all wealthy, well-born young ladies to make advantageous alliances through marriage to ensure the continuation and exclusivity of the social strata to which they had been born. This was drummed into them from their first breath, and it drove Beryl mad. Rebellion heated in her middle, and she pressed her lips together to stop the flow of words she knew Melanie wouldn't understand.

"I want to check on Lacey." She started around the ring, careful to make a wide swing that would take her away from Major Kennedy. She wasn't ready to deal with him just yet.

"Don't you want to meet the new instructor first?" Melanie trotted alongside.

"No, there will be time enough for that."

Beryl had the summer to be free, to concentrate on her horsemanship and her sweet mare. Perhaps, if she prayed hard enough, God would send the perfect husband: a man who loved God, loved her, and didn't need or want her money.

Chapter Two

B eryl entered the dusky barn and went to the third stall, the one in which her horse was always stabled. "Hey, Lace," she called.

The chestnut's head came out over the half door, her white blaze bright in the shade of the barn. The mare spied her and whickered, whiffing down her nostrils. Beryl went to her, happiness welling, and laid her cheek alongside Lacey's, breathing in the familiar scents of horse and hay and leather and dust that spelled contentment. Her fingers trailed under the crest of the mare's mane, feeling the warmth of her hide and the softness of her coat.

"Did you miss me?" She hadn't seen the mare in over a week, and while to most people that might not seem like very long, to Beryl, it had seemed forever. "Are you looking forward to blowing away the winter cobwebs as much as I am? It seems we've hardly done more than walk along the bridal paths in Central Park for ages."

Valentine's Highland Lace—to use her registered name—nudged Beryl with her muzzle, awaiting the expected treat. Beryl laughed. "Sometimes I wonder if it is me you miss or the peppermints." She placed a red-and-white candy on her palm, and Lacey lipped it up, her whiskers tickling Beryl's hand.

"You shouldn't give her that garbage."

Beryl turned and looked into a pair of deep, green eyes. Major Kennedy. A burst of hyper-awareness shot through her, and her breathing quickened. "I beg your pardon?" Up close he was even more handsome than she'd first thought, and his disapproving frown didn't detract from his good looks.

"If you want to give her a treat, make it a carrot or slice of apple at least. Candy isn't good for her. She's fat as butter now. Candy will make it worse."

Her back straightened. "She's not fat, she's just a little plump. And she loves peppermints. Surely a little piece here or there won't matter."

"No candy in my stables." Enunciating every word, he crossed his arms and gave her a stern look as if she were a child acting out in church.

Stung, she snapped back. "These aren't your stables, sir. They belong to the Schmidts. And this isn't your horse. She belongs to me. If I choose to give her a treat now and then, it's certainly none of your business."

The man scrubbed his short dark beard, tugged a folded paper from the inside pocket of his tweed hacking jacket, and studied it. "According to this list given me by the Schmidts, that horse belongs to one Wallace Valentine." He quirked his right eyebrow at her and studied her from hairline to hem. "I assume you are not Wallace?"

Heat crept up Beryl's face. "Of course I'm not. I am Miss Beryl Valentine, his daughter." What impertinence.

He shrugged and restored the paper to his pocket. "Miss Valentine, the Schmidts have put me in charge of this stable for the next three months. That includes the well-being of both their horses and all those that board here. The vet was out this morning, looking over the new arrivals, and he is concerned about this animal. Doc says she put on quite a bit of bulk this winter, and he's put her on a restricted diet to get her weight down, which means no treats that aren't approved by either him or me."

Concern scampered through Beryl's middle, and she put her hand on Lacey's neck. "What else did the vet say? Is this serious? I know she's plumped up some. . . ."

"Other than being a bit overweight, she's sound. She needs work and a proper diet." Major Kennedy pushed himself off the wall. "If you'll wait out by the ring, I'll tack her up for you, and we'll start some of that work."

"I prefer to do my own grooming and saddling."

His eyebrows rose. "Are you sure? It's hardly expected of a lady."

At this point, Melanie giggled from the doorway and edged into the barn. "Sometimes I tease Beryl that she'd make a great stable hand. She'd spend all day in the barn if she could." She held out her hand. "Melanie Turner. I'll be taking lessons from you, too, Major Kennedy." Her brightest smile lit her face. "I declare, you're even more handsome than I'd been told." Lashes fluttering, she dipped her chin.

Beryl groaned inwardly. She loved Melanie; she really did, but sometimes she wanted to smack her. Flirting, acting like a silly chit, calling Beryl a stable hand.

"A pleasure, Miss Turner. And please, call me Gard. I'm no longer a major." He took Melanie's proffered hand for a moment. "Do you have a horse of your own here that I can see saddled, or will you be using one of the Schmidt mounts?"

"Oh, I don't own a horse. I haven't ridden since I was a child." She tapped her chin with her index finger. "I'm sure I'll need *plenty* of instruction."

Mr. Kennedy raised his eyebrows, appraising her. "So, you're a beginner?" He stepped forward, ran his hand down Lacey's nose, and held it so the horse wouldn't startle, and then he shouted down the barn to the open back doors. "Hey, Asa?"

The dark-skinned man they'd seen at the training ring trotted inside. "Yes, sir?"

"Asa, it turns out that Miss Turner here is a novice rider. Please, saddle Starlight, and do an assessment of Miss Turner's abilities for me." The look he gave the older man spoke of a long relationship where much was communicated but not much needed to be said. Beryl liked the way he treated the groom with respect and dignity, saying please and asking rather than ordering him about.

Melanie, predictably, pouted. "But I thought you would be my teacher."

"Asa is better with beginning riders than I." Mr. Kennedy gave a slight bow. "He'll take good care of you."

Having no option but to go, Melanie turned, sending a perturbed look back over her shoulder at Beryl. Sighing, Beryl shook her head at her friend's theatrics but then pushed them out of her mind. She was in her happy place, and she refused to let disquieting thoughts—whether of her mother's matrimonial determination, her flirtatious, pouting friend, or her handsome new riding instructor—upset her.

Opening Lacey's stall, she led the chestnut out, clipping leads to her halter to cross-tie her in the barn aisle. She stroked her neck, looking her over from nose to tail. She seemed to have traveled well, no nicks or bumps that she could see.

Mr. Kennedy, instead of leaving her alone with her mount, leaned against the wall, crossing his arms and his ankles.

His stare unnerved her. "Is there something you wanted?"

"Just to watch how you handle a horse. To see if you need help." His tone implied that she *would* need his help.

She bristled. "I assure you, I can handle my own horse. I've been doing it for years."

"Well, you just say so. I don't have any proof, and the safety and care of the horses is my responsibility." He flicked his hand. "Go ahead. I won't step in until you need me."

Frustration at things being not as she had expected welled up. "I wish Avila hadn't gotten hurt. She never hovers."

His dark brows rose again, and she felt as if he were mocking her. Hot embarrassment chased up her cheeks.

"So what you're saying is that she pretty much let you do whatever you wanted." He sounded resigned, as if that's what he had expected all along.

Beryl took a deep breath. Better to ignore him. She picked a body brush out of the grooming toolbox on the wall and stroked it across the mare's broad back. Lacey tucked one hind leg and promptly lowered her eyelids. She loved to be groomed and would stand still all day if Beryl would indulge her. "Don't you fall asleep. I want you to give me a good ride today."

With long, brisk strokes, she brushed Lacey from neck to rump, lifting surface dust from her hide and burnishing her chestnut coat until it shone. With a damp rag, she washed Lacey's face, though the mare jerked away and snorted. It was the only part of the grooming process she fussed about. "Oh, no you don't. You're worse than a toddler about having your face cleaned."

Feeling Mr. Kennedy's eyes on her the entire time, she donned a burlap apron hanging from a nail by the grooming box to protect her riding habit and carefully lifted each of the mare's feet, cleaning them out with a hoof pick, checking for any cracks or chips, and testing that her shoes were still firmly attached. Straightening, she whisked off the apron and dropped it back over the nail.

Mr. Kennedy pushed himself off the wall. "Nicely done. I didn't expect you to do the hooves, too."

"'A horse is only as good as his feet.'" She quoted her first riding instructor, an old groom of her father's from way back who was now pensioned off at her father's stud farm upstate. "I don't shirk work when my horse's well-being is at stake." Starchy didn't begin to describe her tone.

"But you shirk work otherwise?" The corner of his mouth twitched.

Rolling her eyes, she turned on her heel and went down to the tack room. His boots crunched on the gravel behind her, but she didn't look at him.

"I'll carry your saddle for you."

"No, thank you."

His hand came out and touched her arm.

She stopped cold, staring first at his hand and then up at him. "Pardon me?"

"Look, we seem to have gotten off on the wrong lead." He removed his hand and rubbed his bearded chin. "It's clear you would prefer to be under Avila Schmidt's tutelage, and I would much prefer not to be a riding instructor this summer, but here we are. You did a nice job grooming your horse, and I'm sure you can saddle her all by yourself, but allow me to be the gentleman that I wasn't right off the bat." He tilted his head and smiled. "Surely you can be lady enough to do that?"

His eyes were the color of the jade carvings she'd seen at the Metropolitan Museum of Art, pale green, fringed with black lashes, and they held a challenge.

Relinquishing the saddle, she nodded. "Of course."

As he walked down the breezeway, she tried not to watch the slight sway of his shoulders, the lean-hipped, long stride of a lifelong horseman. He might be nice to look at, but that was where her interest ended. Melanie might flirt and giggle, but Beryl had more important things on her mind.

<hr />

Gard saddled the mare, double-checking the girth around her rotund middle before lowering the stirrup on the sidesaddle. Miss Valentine had some grit to her. When he'd questioned her horsemanship, she'd bristled like a hedgehog.

Miss Valentine was beautiful, though he chided himself for noticing such a thing. Which was why he'd jumped on her about feeding her horse sweets, acting defensive when she hadn't really done anything wrong. It wasn't like him to be distracted by a pretty woman. . .though if he was honest, he hadn't been around too many.

Her concern for her horse had been quick and real when he mentioned the vet's visit. And he'd only slightly exaggerated the situation. The horse *was* overweight, and candy wasn't good for her. But mostly Gard had baited Miss Valentine to get a reaction. She'd looked so composed and picturesque in her riding habit and hat, her hair all bound up in that net-thingy. She'd looked the epitome of the upper-crust, come-to-play-at-riding-but-not-serious-about-horsemanship debutante he had feared he'd be saddled with when taking this job in the first place.

But she'd groomed her horse by herself. And it clearly wasn't the first time. She had been calm and businesslike, and affectionate, too. What a puzzle. Had he judged her wrongly? He shrugged. Better to get on with the lesson.

"Do you want to use the mounting block, or shall I give you a leg up?" He led the chestnut out into sunshine, talking to Miss Valentine over his shoulder.

"I'll use the block, thank you."

Hmm, still a fair amount of frost in her voice. She took her time, checking his saddling job for herself, and he had a fleeting memory of his days as a new first lieutenant, straight from West Point. He'd inherited a sergeant who had ridden with General John Buford at Gettysburg and had forgotten more about military mounted tactics than Gard would ever learn. He'd checked and double-checked Gard's work for months until he was sure the green officer wouldn't harm himself or the horses through some oversight.

Good old Sergeant Barker.

Miss Valentine gathered her skirt, discreetly buttoning it up on her right hip to keep the excess out of the way while in the saddle—he'd had no idea that's how women's riding habits worked—and stepped onto the block. Gard held the chestnut's bridle as Miss Valentine settled herself into the saddle, putting her right knee into the top pommel and the dainty, black-polished toe of her riding boot into the stirrup iron.

Very tidily done.

She adjusted her skirts and gathered her reins, patting the mare on the withers.

"I'll open the gate." He went ahead of her to the training ring.

Miss Valentine waited until he was several strides ahead before following so her horse wouldn't run up his heels. Considerate.

"Go ahead and warm her up as you usually do."

He went to the center of the ring, while she walked her horse around the perimeter, letting her familiarize herself with the layout inside the fence. Gard turned slowly with their progress, taking note of her seat, her hands, her leg angle. He had set up the ring this morning with low poles on the perimeter, a clear oval path inside that, and in the middle a ring of six cross-rails, all eighteen inches or lower. Basic lesson tools.

Miss Valentine's reins were not as loose as he would like—downright snug—but he said nothing, wanting to get more information first. When she moved the horse into a trot, she posted, but she was slightly behind the rhythm. Rusty or unlearned? Her center of gravity seemed to be off a bit, putting her just behind the proper pace.

The canter was better, and she certainly didn't appear timid, but those hands. . .and her eyes were looking in the wrong place. He wondered at Avila Schmidt's riding techniques if this is how one of her most advanced students rode.

Beryl Valentine's riding was average at best. Promising but not polished. There was plenty to build on, but plenty of work to do as well.

If she was amenable to teaching. That aristocratic bearing, something he'd seen in many of the young officers who had been under his command, could prove tough to crack.

"Bring her in." Gard waved her closer. Lacey was puffing a bit, even after that short warm-up. Seriously out of shape.

"First, I'd like to know what you want to get out of these lessons. What's your aim?" He rested his hand on Lacey's neck, looking up at Miss Valentine—Beryl—he couldn't go on calling her Miss Valentine, not when they were going to be working together.

"I want to ride her in the summer training hunts with the Garrison Hunt Club. And I want to show at Deep Haven at the end of summer."

Deep Haven. Schmidt had contracted with Gard to ride Arcturus at Deep Haven, explaining that it was one of the largest shows in the state and sure to garner plenty of attention for the young stallion, who was the reigning Open Class Champion. Miss Valentine had a lofty goal considering her current riding level. "Have you shown before?"

"Of course. Since I was a child."

"And how have you fared?" Because if he'd been judging, she would have been middle of the class at best based upon what he'd seen today.

She shrugged. "Depends on the show. I've won a few ribbons. I've never ridden at Deep Haven, but I've always wanted to. Avila said this was the year."

He nodded. "If you're willing to work hard, I think we can improve on those results. But better than that, you can give your horse a better, more comfortable ride."

Her nostrils flared and her brows rose. "A better ride?"

Here was where he would find out if she had what it took or if she was all show and no stay. "That's right. You've got a promising horse here, but you've let her get into some bad habits. Her back end is weak, and she's not striding out. Probably because you're snatching at her mouth. Your hands are too firm on the reins, and she's tucking her chin. And you're about a half stride off on your post. It looks awkward and has to feel worse for the mare."

"I beg your pardon? Avila never complained about my riding, and I hold the reins exactly as she taught me."

Lacey, catching the tension, sidled and shook her head.

"I suppose she taught you to 'keep in contact with your horse's mouth at all times'?"

"Of course."

Gard refrained from rolling his eyes, not wanting to undermine Mrs. Schmidt, but her way of thinking created riders with less security in the saddle than they should have, and it also created horses with leather mouths and tentative movements. He tried to decide how to frame this so Miss Valentine wouldn't be totally offended.

"If you could watch yourself ride, you would see that you're tugging at your horse's mouth. Without meaning to, you're pulling back at the same time you're urging her forward. She's not striding easily, or confidently, because she's confused as to your signals." He ran his hand down Lacey's shoulder. "I know the last thing you want to do is confuse her or hurt her mouth."

Doubt clouded her blue eyes. She looked at the reins in her hands, her dark brows bunched.

"I'll tell you what." Gard motioned toward the gate. "My saddle is here. Let me ride her, and you watch. See if you can tell a difference."

Swapping saddles took only a couple of minutes, and Beryl stepped back, tucking a stray curl off her cheek and behind her ear. "She hasn't been ridden by anyone but me in a long time."

Gard nodded, putting his boot into the stirrup and gathering the reins. "A good horse needs to be able to be handled by more than one rider." He swung into the saddle. Lacey was broad backed and sturdy, like straddling an upholstered barrel. "Watch the difference in her stride when I use a loose rein as opposed to a tight one."

He squeezed his lower legs against Lacey's sides, and the chestnut moved forward at a walk. Keeping the reins tight, Gard could feel the hesitance in the horse's movement. Chin tucked too far under, short-strided. Half a lap at a walk, and then Gard urged her into a trot, keeping the reins snug as Beryl had done. Lacey trotted more up-and-down than forward as a result, and when they completed the lap, Gard pulled her to a stop near where Beryl stood.

"Now I want you to watch her again. It might take a few laps, but you'll notice a change in her once she realizes I'm going to leave her mouth alone."

Beryl had her arms crossed and her brows down, as if disgruntled to see someone else on her horse, but willing, barely, to go along with it.

Which was all he could ask at this point, he supposed.

He loosened the reins, letting them lie almost slack, his hands low and quiet near the pommel of his saddle. With a squeeze of his legs, he signaled Lacey to walk out. Again, the tucked chin and scratchy, too-tight steps. Halfway around the ring, the horse shook her head, making her bit jingle, and her neck lowered a fraction as if testing her newfound freedom. By the end of the circuit, she was practically sauntering, moving smoothly, head at a natural angle. When Gard urged her to trot, the tension came back; but after a lap, she was swinging along, ears twitching, balanced and easy.

Using his body weight more than the reins, Gard leaned, telegraphing a course change to the mare, guiding her toward one of the jumps on the interior of the ring. When she saw the obstacle before her, her nose went down again, and her stride shortened as if waiting for the pull-back/push-forward signals she was used to.

It was a crowhoppy jump, as was the one after. Gard eased her back to a walk, circling the ring and then lifted her to a trot and then a canter. The mare had a rocking-chair canter. It was like steering a yacht, steady, metronomic. With a loose rein, she lengthened her stride while not losing her rhythm. Gard turned her toward the jumps again, and this time she gathered herself and flew over them in stride, even changing leads fluidly as they rounded the far corner.

Gard returned Lacey to Beryl. This time, though Beryl's lip was tucked behind her teeth, she looked more thoughtful than stubborn.

"You've got yourself a nice horse here. She's willing and kind, and smart, too." Gard dismounted, patting the mare, rewarding her for a nice trip.

He didn't ask if Beryl had noticed the difference. He could see from the determined light in her eyes that she had.

"Let's get that saddle changed and try again, shall we?" He glanced at the angle of the morning sun. They had about a half hour left to her lesson. In the far ring, Asa walked in a slow circle, leading Starlight, a plodding bay mare, with Miss Turner in the saddle. Miss Turner kept looking over her shoulder at the main ring as if more concerned with what was going on with Beryl and Lacey than her own lesson. Gard sighed as he swapped saddles again and this time gave Beryl a leg up.

He took the reins from her hands and laid them on Lacey's neck. "Leave them there. Don't touch them. Walk her around the ring."

"How can I if I don't use the reins to direct her?"

"Put your heel against her side and lean forward a little. She'll move out. The reins are only a small part of communicating with your horse. Voice, weight, legs, heels, they all play a part." No doubt the mare had done many turns around this ring. She wouldn't need much guidance.

With doubts flying in her eyes, Beryl did as he said, and as he'd thought, the mare began a slow, tentative walk around the large oval. She certainly recognized the change in riders and waited for Beryl to use her mouth for balance, walking with short strides, chin tucked under. When Beryl let the reins alone, as Gard had predicted, the mare relaxed and lengthened her stride.

"Good. Keep going." He moved to the center of the ring to watch her progress. They wouldn't trot today. Both Beryl and Lacey had enough to think about right now without Gard bringing up Beryl's less-than-stellar posting skills again.

As horse and rider made yet another circuit at a walk, Miss Turner stomped to the ring fence, her face pulled into a pout. Asa remained in the smaller ring, unsaddling Starlight. A short lesson. By his design or hers?

"Mr. Kennedy," Miss Turner called, waving furiously as if he couldn't see her from the center of the large ring. He waited for Lacey to walk past again before heading her way and vaulting the fence.

"How was your lesson?" He would get a full report from Asa, but he had to ask.

"That man." She pressed her lips together. "I shall have to insist you be my instructor from now on. He said I rode like a sack of rocks, and he wouldn't even let me steer. He led me around like an infant."

Gard stifled a grin. Asa never minced words, and he refused to let green riders spoil horses.

"It's just Asa's way. In a couple more lessons, he'll let you 'steer,' as you put it. For now, he is just assessing your abilities and getting you started."

"I'm sure you are quite capable of getting me 'started' in riding. Don't you know who I am? My father is Melvin Turner, of the New Hampton Turners." She raised her eyebrows as if to say, "Even an imbecile would recognize that name."

He didn't.

She huffed. "I will not be relegated to being instructed by anyone but the best." Her hand came out to rest on his arm, a change sweeping over her from a petulant frown to a pretty pout. "And that's you, of course." Eyelashes flickering, she gave him a sweet smile.

He was in foreign territory here. What should he do? He was saved from answering by the arrival of an ornate, glossy buggy pulled by a matched pair of high-stepping grays. Three people occupied the seats, plus a driver and—Gard stared—a liveried footman. Who on earth?

The men, wearing top hats and broadcloth coats descended, and the footman leaped off his seat at the back to hold his hand up for the lady. Her broad-brimmed hat obscured her face, but then she looked up, aloof as a queen. There was something familiar about her face.

Friends of the Schmidts? Surely guests would go to the house?

As the group approached the riding ring, Beryl disobeyed Gard's instructions and tugged on the reins, bringing Lacey to an abrupt stop.

"Mother? Father? What are you doing here?"

Chapter Three

Beryl felt as if her sanctum sanctorum had been invaded. The one place she was free to be herself and not think about society or conventions or the expectations of her parents, and here they stood at Schmidt Farms. And with a stranger in tow.

No doubt this was the guest her father had alluded to this morning. A sense of foreboding invaded her chest.

"Hello, dear." Mother raised her parasol to shade her face, though her hat was doing a fine job already. Her pale pink gown should have seemed miles too young for her, but she carried the look beautifully. "We were out driving and thought we'd call in. Do come down from there and be introduced to our guest."

Gard Kennedy was back over the fence in a trice, holding Lacey so Beryl could dismount. "Thank you." She hoped her face wasn't as tight as her voice sounded.

"You did well for a first lesson. I'll take her back to the barn for you."

"Hold up there, young man." Her father's voice boomed. "We came to see that horse."

A deeper dread settled in Beryl's middle. When her father came to see a horse, it was usually to sell it. Tears pricked her eyes, and she blinked, hard, keeping Lacey between herself and her father until she had herself better under control.

"Are you all right?" Gard's voice dropped.

Her chin jerked up, and she composed her expression, calling on all her mother's teaching about what was proper in front of others. "Yes. Of course. Thank you for the lesson, Mr. Kennedy."

"Please, call me Gard. If we're going to be working together, I think a bit of informality is all right. May I call you Beryl?"

She nodded. Checking her skirts, she brushed at a bit of dust here and there, and then went to her mother, kissing the offered cheek.

"Beryl, dear, I'd like you to meet Lord Neville Springfield. He's an acquaintance of your father's and is visiting from England." Mother's voice held a touch of awe and triumph.

Warning bells went off in Beryl's head. An acquaintance of her father's, and an English lord. From the gleam in Mother's eye, Beryl knew they'd finally found a marriage candidate upon whom both of them could agree.

"Lord Springfield, this is my daughter, Beryl." She sent Beryl a behave-yourself-or-so-help-me look, confirming Beryl's suspicions that this was an eligible bachelor, a catch her mother was determined to reel in.

Mouth dry, heart hammering, Beryl extended her hand. Lord Springfield took it, removing his hat and smiling. He had thin, light hair; pale gray eyes; a long, narrow face; and a tall, lean body.

"Lord Springfield."

"A pleasure to meet you, my dear." He spoke in a well-educated, plummy accent. His hand pressed hers through her leather riding glove, and he smiled warmly, revealing straight teeth and deep creases beside his mouth. She guessed his age to be somewhere between thirty and thirty-five. About the same age as Mr. Kennedy. But nowhere near as handsome.

Beryl shoved that thought from her mind. This wasn't a competition. One had nothing to do with the other.

"Neville," Her father used his first name. "Come and see this mare."

Lord Springfield let go of her hand as if reluctantly, and as he turned to go to the fence, Melanie stepped forward.

"Ahem." She looked between Beryl and the Englishman.

"Lord Springfield, may I introduce Miss Melanie Turner?" Beryl went through the motions of being polite, though she wanted to leap onto Lacey and head for the woods, taking them both to safety.

Melanie simpered and twittered, giggling as Lord Springfield took her hand. "An English lord? My, my. What an honor to meet you, sir."

Beryl clamped her teeth down hard, as she always did when Melanie got silly. Though. . .she paused. That might be a nice diversion. If Lord Springfield focused his attention on Melanie, he would leave Beryl alone. *Go to it, Mel. Flirt away.*

"You're Kennedy, right? Schmidt told me he'd taken you on for the summer." Her father jerked his chin toward Gard. "Wallace Valentine. I own that mare, and I'd like you to put your saddle on her and give her a ride for us. Put her over a few fences while you're at it, will you?"

"Yes, sir." Gard stripped Beryl's saddle off, his movements efficient. If only he weren't such a good horseman. Lacey went so smoothly for him, she was bound to show well for Lord Springfield and her father. It galled Beryl a bit to realize Gard had been right in his assessment of her riding, and she'd had to squash down a lot of pride, but the difference in Lacey when he'd been astride had been undeniable. Beryl itched to be back in the saddle, working on improving, instead of playing the suitors game with her mother and Lord Springfield.

Father left the rail and came over. "You said you were looking for a dependable mount for fox hunting, Neville. I'll tell you, you won't find better than Valentine's Highland Lace. Lacey, as Beryl calls her." Father clapped Lord Springfield on the shoulder, drawing him away from Melanie. "She's by Highland Laird out of Lavender and Lace. She'll make a great broodmare. Not a lot of speed in that line but great jumpers. Fearless and steady."

Mel edged over to Beryl. "Wow. A lord from England. Aren't you the lucky one?" she whispered. "I take it he's here on approval?"

Beryl shrugged. "I don't know anything about him. We just met. Maybe he's just here looking for a horse." *But not hers. Please. Any horse but hers.* Did God hear prayers about horses?

Gard had Lacey saddled quickly, and with fluid grace Beryl had to admire, he mounted. He sent Beryl a look that shot a tingle through her. Gard Kennedy really had magnificent eyes. And he looked even better on a horse than on the ground.

"I've only been on the mare once, so we're still getting used to each other. She may not show to best advantage." Gard gathered his reins and spoke to her father.

"I'm sure you'll do fine. I've heard all about you from Freeman Schmidt. Only the best for his stables, eh? Go ahead and put her through her paces." Placing his big hands on the top rail, he studied the chestnut. He knew horses. Lacey had been bred on his farm, one of dozens of useful, steady hunters he'd bred over the years.

But Beryl hadn't loved any of them like she loved Lacey.

Beryl joined the men at the rail but a little apart. She studied Gard's riding. He was light in the saddle, his reins loose, hands low. When he put Lacey into a trot, he posted effortlessly, rising in the stirrups with the forward motion, dropping slightly down before rising again, in perfect rhythm with the horse. He took a diagonal through the ring at a canter, asking for and receiving a lead change before circling in the opposite direction. Without altering speed, he headed toward the first of the jumps, clearing it easily, hands quiet, eyes up. Before the next jump, he shortened Lacey's stride a bit to meet it just right. The mare landed lightly and cantered around to face the next line of jumps.

Beryl knew she was watching a master horseman at work. And Gard was getting the best out of her horse. Lacey was moving better than she'd ever seen her go. A wriggle of jealousy went through her, but she forced it down with determination. Determination to improve, to do her best, work hard, and be a better rider, not just for her own satisfaction, but because Lacey deserved it.

She dared a glance at her father and his guest, and her heart sank at the interest in Lord Springfield's eyes as he watched her horse. If the Englishman liked Lacey enough, Beryl knew her father would have no qualms about selling the mare right there. Her throat grew tight, and her hands fisted.

Then Lord Springfield's eyes moved to meet hers, and the interest there was unmistakable, too.

Gard brought Lacey to the fence and dismounted, patting the mare's neck. Lacey's sides bellowed as she breathed heavily.

"As you can see, she's a bit out of shape, but she's willing and kind." Gard ran his hand down her near foreleg. "I can give you a better assessment after I've worked with her for a while."

Father drew Lord Springfield down to the gate, entered the ring, and went to the horse. Beryl gripped the top rail, watching, but Mother ambled over, shading her face with her parasol, and Melanie came, too.

"Wallace, Lord Springfield, you gentlemen are going to talk horses." Mother smiled affectionately, as she and Father had never said a cross word to one another in their lives. "I propose I return to the house with Beryl, and you can join us there later when you've finished?"

"But, Mother," Beryl protested. "I need to tend to Lacey, and I had planned to stay a while longer."

"Nonsense. You don't need to tend that horse. There's a perfectly good groom standing right there." She tilted her parasol toward Gard Kennedy, and Beryl winced at the patronizing tone to her mother's voice.

"Mother," Beryl lowered her voice. "He isn't a groom. He's Major Kennedy, the riding instructor who is taking Avila Schmidt's place until she recovers from a broken bone. He's an excellent rider and teacher, and he's been entrusted with the stables and horses for the summer." She stopped, realizing she'd said too much, too forcefully, in defending him.

Mother flicked a glance Gard's way, as if really seeing him for the first time. "Really." Her finely arched brows rose a fraction, and the look she sent Beryl's way made an uncomfortable heat rise up Beryl's neck. "Then he's more than capable of stabling that mare when your father is finished. Come, girls." She turned toward the drive. "Wallace, Lord Springfield, we'll see you both later?"

Father nodded, waving vaguely, engrossed in his conversation. Gard handed Lacey's reins to him and vaulted the fence.

"Miss Valentine?"

"Major Kennedy," Beryl used his formal title in her mother's hearing. "I'm sorry, I have to leave. I had intended to groom Lacey and turn her out for a while."

"Don't worry. I'll see to her." He stood casually, his hands on his hips, brushing back the sides of his tweed jacket. "I'd like to work out a training routine for you and Lacey before your next lesson. I don't have the schedule fully made out yet. What is your normal interval between lessons?"

The question caught her off guard. "I'll be here tomorrow morning about the same time. I come every morning but Sunday, if I can, throughout the summer."

His eyes widened. "Every day?" He was already shaking his head. "Lacey can't handle that much work. She'll get stale."

"Avila. . .Mrs. Schmidt, let me ride some of her horses several days each week. Gloria and Rita and Bandit." If Gard didn't do the same, how would Beryl be able to justify coming to the farm every day? If she couldn't escape to the safety of the stables, how would she fill her summer? "They'll need exercise even more now that Avila is laid up."

"I see." He pressed his lips together, thinking. "Very well. I will see you in the morning, then." Sketching a bow, he turned and went back toward the ring, and Beryl breathed a small sigh of relief. She couldn't completely relax, not with her father pointing out Lacey's merits to a potential buyer. If only she had access to some of the money she would inherit when she married. She'd buy Lacey from her father and not have to worry about him selling her on a whim.

"What do you think of him?" Mother asked as they settled themselves into the carriage Beryl and Melanie had arrived in that morning. "You could've knocked me over with a gesture when Lord Springfield called at the house this morning." Smugness colored her tone.

"Why did he call? How do you know him?" Beryl looked back over her shoulder until the carriage turned out onto the road and Schmidt Farms disappeared from sight.

"Until I read his name on his calling card, I'd never heard of him. I gather your father met him when he went to England to buy bloodstock last fall." Mother crossed her wrists daintily in her lap. "Wallace issued an invitation for Lord Springfield to visit if he came to the States." She was almost purring. "His family has an estate northeast of London where they raise horses, but the family money comes from biscuits."

"Biscuits?" Melanie asked.

"Cookies. His family owns the Essex Biscuit Company. They have several factories in England, and from what I understand, his father, who is a baronet, has sent Lord

Springfield to America to investigate expanding the business." Mother took a deep breath. "And, I also understand he's single and ready to set up his nursery. Just imagine, titled, wealthy, and looking for a wife. It couldn't be more perfect." She looked like the cat that wolfed down a pet shop full of canaries. "I can't wait to show him off at one of my dinner parties."

Beryl stifled a groan.

Chapter Four

A month into being a riding instructor, Gard wished he was back in the army. At least then he would know how to dress for every occasion. Asa fussed and brushed and twitched at the new suit—a tuxedo no less—while he helped Gard dress, spending half of forever tying Gard's tie.

"Hold still." The old man swatted Gard's shoulder. "You can't be going to a fancy dinner with your tie all crooked."

"I wish I wasn't going at all. I can't believe I got roped into it." Gard studied his reflection in the mirror atop the dresser. "And I can't believe I spent money on a new suit of clothes. That money should be in the bank saving up for buying Arcturus."

Asa nodded, pursing his lips and studying the effect his ministrations had made on Gard's appearance. "Mebbe going to this little soiree will bring you more riding jobs. There are a couple of shows coming up, and you said the dinner would be full of horse people."

"That's what Wallace Valentine said, anyway." Gard picked up his hat, wishing it were his old campaigner rather than a beaver-felt top hat. He'd never worn a top hat in his life and felt like an imposter. He didn't put it on, since in his cramped, two-room apartment over the carriage house, the ceilings sloped and he had to stoop to go out the doors already. Still, having a place to live rent-free for the summer was helping with the exchequer.

"Will Miss Valentine be there?" Asa leaned against the door frame and put his hands into his pockets.

Gard stilled and then shrugged. "I suppose so. It's her parents' house." He brushed a fleck of dust off the brim of the hat. "Why?"

Another shrug. "You been giving her lessons for a month, but you ain't said much about her otherwise. You talk about all your other students but not her."

Collar growing tight, Gard rolled his neck to loosen his shoulders. Asa's dark eyes saw way too much, that's what. "What is there to say? She's coming along. And her mare's already showing a big improvement." The mare hadn't been sold yet, thankfully. He didn't know what Beryl would do if she lost that horse.

"Hmph. That's not what I meant, and you know it, Major." His striker straightened, shaking his head. "She's mighty fine lookin', and she sure loves horses. Man'd be proud to have a gal like that on his arm, I'm thinkin'."

The thought hadn't just passed through Gard's mind over the last month. It had marched in, set up camp, and stayed, hard as he tried to uproot it. But he refused to take the notion seriously. "She's not for me. Her father could buy and sell me a hundred times with his loose change. Anyway, I got the feeling her folks had picked out that English lord fellow for her."

"Ain't you always telling me that it ain't what you have but how you act that makes you who you are? You're as good as any of them, and better'n some."

Gard smiled at the chiding-yet-filled-with-affection tone. "You'd defend me no matter what. Well, I'd best get to this shindig. I imagine it will be late when I get back." He tried to tamp down some of the eagerness he felt at the thought of seeing Beryl again.

"Don't wake me up. Some of us has to get up early and feed stock. We can't all be gadding about after dark and sleeping in like a dandy." Asa spoke over his shoulder as he went to his room.

Choosing to ride over rather than bother with a carriage, Gard went to the stables and saddled up Spanky, a spring-loaded young hunter prospect Freeman Schmidt wanted Gard to show this fall at Deep Haven. Spanky had terrific breeding and athletic ability, but he needed seasoning. The ride to the Valentines' would be a good experience for him.

When Gard arrived at the Valentines' home, he took one look and wanted to turn right around. The place was bigger than the Schmidts' biggest barn. Every window blazed with light, and several carriages were pulled up on the circle drive. Spanky pawed the ground, shaking his head as Gard pulled him up at the open wrought-iron gates.

"Look at that. It's almost as huge as the new Madison Square Garden." And Beryl lived here. He'd known she was wealthy, but he hadn't known just how wealthy. She was so far above his rank, if his rank blew up she wouldn't hear the echo for a week.

He squared his shoulders and lifted his chin. He needed to stop thinking about Beryl Valentine as anything other than one of his students. Inside that house were business contacts waiting to be made, rides to negotiate on some of the best horseflesh in the country, and money to earn to fulfill his dreams.

A footman stood at the door and took Gard's hat. Another man, the butler, came to his elbow. He took the invitation Gard dug out of his breast pocket, glanced at the name, and nodded. "This way, sir."

He led the way through the massive foyer to a pair of pocket doors that had to be ten feet tall. They glided open with a mere push from the butler. "Mr. Gardiner Kennedy," he announced. Gard stood erect and walked into the room wearing his "command" face, braced to meet this new challenge, arranging his thoughts like marshalling a company of new recruits.

The room was full. Men in evening dress of black and white, women in bright gowns with glittering jewels, upswept hair and ostrich feathers. Looking from one face to another, he recognized no one, but he noted he'd at least dressed correctly.

Then someone moved on his left. He turned his head and quit breathing. Beryl rose from a gilded couch, coming toward him. She wore a red dress that rustled and showed her creamy shoulders and slender neck. A string of red stones adorned her neck and another circled her wrist. Red drops hung from her ears; white gloves covered her hands and arms; and she carried a red and white fan. Her eyes were luminous, and glints showed in her hair where two diamond combs held it back from her face.

Gone was his equestrian student in serviceable tweeds, the rider who also cleaned stalls and groomed horses and hauled feed. Before him stood a flower of society, heiress to a fortune, and more beautiful than ever.

"I'm so happy you came." Was that relief he saw in her eyes? Had she thought he might not attend? Had she been watching for him?

Then she smiled, and his heart kicked like a fractious colt at his first farrier appointment. When she offered her hand, he took it, remembering to bow.

"Miss Valentine."

"Come, say hello to my parents, and then I'll introduce you around." She threaded her hand through his arm, directing him to a group of people near the fireplace. Wallace Valentine held out his hand with a broad smile.

"Ah, Kennedy. Glad you could come. Rosemary, you remember Mr. Kennedy?"

"Of course. Welcome." Mrs. Valentine didn't appear all that glad he had come, her eyes skimming him from hair to shoes and then sliding away as if bored with his arrival. She turned to the woman on the settee beside her, a not-so-subtle snub.

Gard smothered a smile. Poor lady, having to endure the presence of a peasant at one of her parties. If he'd been surprised at the invitation from Mr. Valentine, she must've been more so.

"Kennedy, I want you to meet Rutherford Van Rissingham and Barrington Bentley." He inclined his head toward two older gentlemen, one with muttonchop sideburns, and the other with a beaky nose and narrowly spaced eyes. "They're avid horse breeders, like me. I'm sure they'd enjoy talking to a horseman such as yourself. We're working on forming a syndicate to purchase a stallion we've got our eye on. Maybe you'd like to lend us your expertise?"

"Perhaps you can discuss that later, after dinner?" Mrs. Valentine shot a sharp look at her husband, who reddened slightly but nodded.

"After dinner, then."

"I'd be happy to help," Gard said. "Though I'm sure you don't need it. Hearing you talk the other day about the bloodlines you've got going at your stud farm, I could probably learn quite a bit from you." Gard laid it on perhaps a bit thick, but it never hurt to be generous with compliments to your host.

"Lord Neville Springfield," the butler announced.

Beryl's hand tightened on Gard's arm, and he glanced down at her. Her pretty mouth was pressed into a line, and there was an annoyed tilt to her eyebrows. So, the arrival of Springfield filled her with no joy? The thought shouldn't make him so happy. It seemed Lord Springfield was always around these days. He'd leased a horse from Freeman Schmidt and kept him stabled at the farm. More often than not, he showed up when Beryl was having a lesson, though Gard had put a stop to him becoming a railbird and giving unsolicited advice.

What bothered Gard the most was when the lesson was over and Lord Springfield would invite Beryl to ride with him along the river or into Garrison for lunch. He'd never been the jealous type, but he was finding out new things about himself this summer. At least half the time, Beryl invited him to come along, and using the excuse of Spanky needing seasoning, he went. Lord Springfield seemed less than pleased about Gard playing gooseberry, but Gard didn't care. The more time he could spend with Beryl, the better. The summer was going by fast, and at its end, he'd have to say goodbye forever to his favorite pupil.

Mrs. Valentine rose and swept down the room to greet the Englishman. "Ah, Lord Springfield, so glad you've arrived. Do come in." She walked him through the clusters of people, beaming as if showing off a prized sheep at the county fair. "Let me introduce you to. . ."

"How is Lacey today?" Beryl asked.

Gard smiled. "She's fine, a little grouchy this morning. Probably a little sore from all the pole work you two did yesterday. I gave her a liniment rubdown and turned her out in the south pasture to loaf around." And he'd had to wash his hands several times to get the liniment smell out. He could just imagine Rosemary Valentine's expression if he'd come to dinner smelling like a stable.

"I never asked what you said to my father to convince him not to sell her to Lord Springfield. I know he was keen to make the deal." She let her hand slip from his elbow and opened her fan, fluttering it beneath her chin but not in a flirtatious way. More like she was warm in the crowded room.

Odd that he should miss her touch on his arm. "I told him she needed a lot of work, that she wasn't in show or hunt condition." He shrugged. "Nothing that wasn't true, mind you. She's coming on well, but another month or two, and she'll be a different animal."

"Well, whatever you said, I'm grateful. My father doesn't understand the bond that forms between a rider and horse. He sees animals as 'things' to be traded and profited from, not individuals with personalities and heart."

Gard had met men like Wallace Valentine in the army, treating their horses like equipment issued to them like their rifle or bedroll or canteen. Those men saw the cavalry as a place to earn glory, advancement, excitement. Just like Valentine saw breeding, buying, and selling horses as a way to impress his peers, make money, and exert dominance in the horse world. He feared he'd only delayed the inevitable by mentioning Lacey's conditioning. She didn't even look like the same horse now. Mrs. Valentine arrived at their side with Lord Springfield just as the butler opened the doors into the foyer once more.

"Ladies and Gentlemen, dinner is served."

"What wonderful timing. Lord Springfield"—Mrs. Valentine arched her brows and smiled at her favored guest—"would you escort Beryl into the dining room?"

"My pleasure." The Englishman inclined his head. "You look lovely tonight, Miss Valentine."

"Oh, do call her Beryl. After a month of seeing each other almost every day, you can't stand on formality. Did you know Beryl is named after the gemstone? In fact, that parure she's wearing is made of her namesake jewels." Mrs. Valentine twittered much like Melanie Turner—who was also attending the dinner and holding court near the bay window. Were all women born knowing how to flirt and simper?

Beryl stiffened beside Gard, not a batted eyelash or alluring tilt of the chin in sight. Come to think of it, he'd never seen her flirt or simper.

"Mother, you go ahead with Lord Springfield. I had a quick question for Major Kennedy." She slipped her hand through his arm once more. "We won't be a minute."

"Nonsense," her mother wouldn't be thwarted. "You will see him at one of your lessons, and you can ask him your questions then. We can't be rude to Lord Springfield." Though evidently she could be rude to a mere riding instructor.

Beryl drew a deep breath and put a smile on her face. "Of course. Perhaps we can speak after dinner, Major?"

That she called him Major in front of her family instead of mister or Gard, as she had been doing at her lessons amused him. Not that a major was anywhere near a lord in importance, but it gave him some sort of standing in that company, he supposed.

The table was long enough to seat an entire company of men. Candelabras marched down the center in ranks, and silver, crystal, and china winked in the light. Gard found his place halfway down the side of the table, away from both his host at the head and his hostess at the foot. And much too far from Beryl who sat to her father's left and next to Lord Springfield. At least he could see her down the way.

"Well, if it isn't the riding instructor." Melanie Turner came up on the arm of Mr. Van Rissingham.

Gard held her chair for her. "Miss Turner. How nice to see you again. You haven't come to the farm again. Have you forsaken riding lessons altogether?"

She waved her hand, airily. "Oh, I'm done with riding. It's much too physical a pursuit for me. I've decided to focus on my archery lessons this summer instead. That is a much more ladylike activity, I think." She leaned back as the footman spread her napkin for her.

Spread her napkin? Did the servants fork in the food, too? Did the elite really need someone to do even the simplest tasks? And what about all the cutlery laid out in front of him? He counted thirteen knives, forks, and spoons, and no less than five crystal glasses. Two coffee cups—one regular sized, one tiny—and four plates and a soup bowl.

He pitied whoever had to wash up after the meal.

And he worried that he would make a fool of himself. He had no idea which fork to use when or what all the glasses were for. He wiped his palms on his thighs under the edge of the pristine tablecloth.

Four chairs down on the opposite side, Beryl sent him a small smile. When the first course was laid, a pale green soup, he watched her. Slowly, she reached for the rounded spoon, dipping it into the soup and sipping from the side of the spoon rather than sticking the whole thing in her mouth. He watched as other guests did the same and then took up his own spoon.

Trying not to grimace, he swallowed. The soup was cold! Was the cook an idiot, or was that how rich people ate soup? No one else seemed surprised at cold soup.

Salad, fish, chicken, ham, venison—the meal went on and on. Through each course, he took his cues from Beryl, and after the third plate had been whisked away, he realized her movements were deliberate, as if she were coaching him through the dinner.

The horseshoe was on the other foot, wasn't it? He smothered a laugh. *I guess I'm lucky she isn't sitting beside me, threatening to smack my hand if I reach for the wrong fork.* He remembered her outraged face when he'd suggested riding alongside her and tapping her hand with a quirt every time she used the reins for balance or snatched at her mount's mouth.

But she'd gotten better over the past month, and her confidence on horseback had grown. Maybe, if he had to endure more of these dinners, he'd gain some confidence that he wouldn't make a glaring faux pas.

Melanie kept her shoulder turned away from him, talking to the gentleman on her right. To his left, an older woman who smelled like mints and cough syrup, clattered her silverware.

"Who are you? I don't believe we've met."

"Gardiner Kennedy, ma'am."

Her pale, blue eyes widened. "You're. . ." she raised her voice. "Irish?" She said it as if it was the worst thing she could think of being.

Conversation ceased, and Gard almost laughed, catching himself in time. "Well, my grandfather was from Ireland, it's true, but I'm an American. And you are?"

"Glorinda Claes. Of the New York Claes." She waited for a response, but he'd never heard of her or her family. "My family helped settle New Amsterdam. My great-grandfather served in the state senate."

"Oh, *those* Claes. Well, ma'am. It's an honor to meet you." Gard still had no idea who she was, but his response seemed to mollify her. He caught Beryl's eye and she let hers twinkle, setting off a burst of warmth in his chest. What was it about her that made her different from any other woman he'd ever met?

Dinner seemed to last forever, but eventually, dessert dishes were cleared and the ladies were excused. Where were they going? Would he see Beryl again tonight? Without her to guide him through this maze of rituals, how would he know what was acceptable and what wasn't?

"Come down here, Kennedy." Wallace motioned as he took his seat at the head of the table. The butler and a footman entered carrying trays and a decanter. Several men lit cigars. Gard took a chair near Valentine and declined the port and a smoke. He never indulged in either.

"Rutherford, Barrington, this is the fellow I was telling you about. He's running the show over at Schmidt Farm for the summer, so he'll have the inside information we're looking for."

Gard's brows rose. Inside information? That had a clandestine ring to it. They'd finally gotten to the reason behind his invitation, no doubt. Mrs. Valentine certainly hadn't invited him as a social coup.

"What can I help you gentlemen with?"

"Like I said, we're forming a syndicate to purchase a stallion, and since you're around him every day, you can tell us about him. Is he sound? Does he have any confirmation weaknesses you think might be passed on to his get? Does he have any bad habits?"

"Which stallion are we talking about?" A boulder settled into Gard's gut, not from the rich dinner, though he was unaccustomed to such food in such quantities. No, it was because he suspected which stallion Valentine referred to.

"Arcturus."

His heart thumped against his breastbone. Arcturus. The stallion who was destined to be the foundation sire at Gard's fledgling stud farm. Once he raised the money.

He spread his hands on his thighs, gripping hard. If Valentine and his cronies banded together and got into a bidding war, Gard would lose quicker than Spokane won the Derby. Would Freeman Schmidt honor the handshake agreement to sell Arcturus to Gard for the asking price after the Deep Haven Show? Or would he be swayed by a higher offer?

Gard couldn't lie about the horse. If the deal fell through, then he'd have to trust that God knew what He was doing, and that another stallion would come along. But he couldn't deny the disappointment that would come. Not just because Arcturus was everything he was looking for in a sire, but because, after spending time with the stallion, Gard had grown attached to him.

"Sir, Arcturus is sound. I've ridden him many times, and Mr. Schmidt has given me the ride on him at the Deep Haven Show before he retires him to stud. He's got heart, and he's smart. Learns quickly and jumps fearlessly."

"I told you boys." Valentine leaned back in his chair, smiling, his eyes narrowed as if looking ahead to a lucrative future as Arcturus's owner.

"As to his confirmation, he's well put together. No flaws." Gard had even convinced Schmidt to enter him in the model class at the show. "As to what he will pass along to his get, it's impossible to say since he's not sired any foals yet. But there are no warning flags that I know of."

"What about stable habits? Is he aggressive?" Van Rissingham tapped ash off his cigar.

"I won't have a vicious stallion." Bentley frowned, swirling the liquid in his glass. "Too dangerous."

"He's a stallion, not a lapdog. You always have to be careful with stallions, but so far he hasn't shown himself to be aggressive. He's stabled and pastured well away from any mares, so that helps. He's easy in the barn, no pawing or cribbing or biting. And he loads fairly easily and travels well. I brought him up from New York City for Mr. Schmidt last month. His only quirk that I know of is that he's reluctant to drink anything when he's away from his normal routine. He didn't drink anything on the train trip up, which wasn't terrible, because he was only on the train a couple of hours, but Mr. Schmidt says he's like that when he travels for shows, too. It's hard to keep him hydrated." Gard had a couple of things he wanted to try with Arcturus the next time they traveled, but he wouldn't mention them now. "It shouldn't matter once he's installed at a stud farm. He'll settle down."

"He sounds perfect." Bentley rubbed his narrow hands together. "The question is, where will he live? Whose farm?" He drew out a pair of pince-nez and perched them on his skinny nose.

Mr. Valentine's brows darted toward one another. "I suppose he'll stand at stud at the farm of the partner who puts up the most money toward the syndicate."

"So you're not proposing a three-way split of the cost?" Van Rissingham laid his cigar in the ash tray at his elbow and leaned forward.

"Actually, it would be a four-way split, if we decide to divide the cost equally." Valentine nodded down the table. Lord Springfield raised his glass. "Neville is interested in joining our venture."

Gard didn't miss the look Van Rissingham and Bentley shared. The other five male guests looked bored, talking among themselves at the far end of the table. "Perhaps"— Gard stood—"Lord Springfield would like my chair so you can talk it over better? I don't know that there's anything I can add to the conversation. Arcturus is an excellent prospect as a stallion."

"There is one more thing." Valentine shot his cuffs. "I heard that Schmidt had another interested buyer, that they'd agreed to a price providing the buyer could get the funds together. Do you know who that buyer is, and even more important, what the price is?"

A tingle zipped across Gard's chest, but before he had to answer that he was the buyer in question, the dining room door opened and Beryl entered a few feet. She winced at the cloud of cigar smoke, waving her hand before her face and backing up.

"Father, Mother sent me to fetch you to the drawing room. Melanie is going to play a song on the piano for us. She's just waiting for the gentlemen before she begins."

Gard followed his host into the room across the foyer, grateful for the interruption and wondering when he could decently escape this party. What was the protocol for leaving a society dinner party? But did he really want to leave if staying meant spending more time with Beryl?

"Oh, Lord Springfield, would you mind ever so much turning pages for me?" Melanie called from her place on the piano bench as they entered the drawing room.

Go, Melanie. Keep the Englishman busy and away from Beryl. Which I suppose isn't very sporting of me. Lately he'd begun to suspect that if he had the means and the social standing, he might be willing to give up his bachelor status for Beryl.

"Of course, Miss Turner." Springfield saw Beryl seated on a sofa and went to the piano.

Beryl sought Gard's eyes and tilted her head toward the empty space beside her. He didn't need to be asked twice. Easing down beside her, he couldn't look away from her face, her hair, her dress that seemed to fit her right in all the right places.

"You look so different tonight. I almost didn't recognize you."

Humor touched her eyes and she smiled. "Is that a compliment to how I look tonight or a dig at how I usually look?"

Gard knew his color was high, and he shook his head. "That didn't come out right. What I meant to say is that you look very nice." Which was insipid. She looked amazing, beautiful, gorgeous, striking. . .so many words that would've been better than just *nice*.

She leaned a bit closer and he did the same. "Truth be told, this get-up is uncomfortable and cumbersome. I'd much rather be in my riding clothes."

He knew just how she felt. His own suit was stiff and confining. He longed for one of his old hacking jackets and riding breeches and his favorite pair of boots. Looking around at the sumptuous furniture, the valuable artwork, the gilding and carving, he wondered if he would treat Beryl differently at her next lesson. Knowing she was well off and seeing the extent of that wealth were two different things.

Melanie began to play, proficiently enough, he supposed, though he was no music expert. Springfield sat at her side, close because of the shortness of the bench, and when she nodded, he turned the sheet music.

"You had a question for me before dinner that you didn't get to ask," he said. If he could get the conversation onto something riding or lesson related, perhaps he could get his equilibrium back.

"The Garrison Hunt Club is going to have a hunt trial this weekend, and I wondered if you thought Lacey was ready, and if you would like to join us?" Beryl opened the pleats on her fan one-by-one, revealing the red floral design, and then just as slowly closing it, not looking at him.

He'd noticed that when the topic really mattered to her, she avoided eye contact. He found the trait endearing.

"A hunt trial?" He'd not heard of such a thing.

"Yes. The hounds need training, so the Hunt Club holds a trial. . .a practice hunt. Usually there are only a few riders, but a couple of times each summer, they assemble a larger field."

"Do they hunt fox in the summer?"

She smiled, glancing up for the first time. "No. Someone drags a fox pelt over the route about an hour before the hunt. The hounds follow that trail. . .usually."

"How long is the course? Lacey's improving, but she isn't in top form yet."

"It depends upon how long it takes the hounds to pick up the scent, but Lacey and I have ridden in several, and I don't believe it taxed her too much. And you can drop out of a hunt at any time."

His mind galloped through the list of available mounts at Schmidt Farm. Rita or Delaney could certainly handle the going, but Spanky would benefit the most.

"Sure, let's go. Though you'll have to coach me on the etiquette. I've never done any fox hunting."

"Fox hunting?" Lord Springfield stood next to Beryl. Gard hadn't even noticed that the music had stopped. "I love a good hunt. Do tell me there are some clubs nearby?"

Wallace Valentine, overhearing, leaned back in his chair to speak over his shoulder. "Garrison Hunt is one of the best. Beryl will be happy to introduce you to the master, won't you, Beryl."

The slight look of dismay in Beryl's eyes only partially mitigated Gard's feeling of disappointment that his lordship would no doubt be joining them on the practice hunt.

Chapter Five

Beryl arrived at the Garrison Hunt Club well before the appointed start time. She wore a dark blue velvet riding habit, derby, and face net. She kept the net up and off her face for the moment. There would be plenty of time, once the hounds were released from the kennels, to adjust it.

Lord Springfield accompanied her. He'd called for her at the house, something no doubt engineered by her mother. She had been throwing them together constantly for the last month. After the dinner party, Mother had gushed and preened by turns at how much Lord Springfield had enjoyed Beryl's company, and what a catch he was, and wouldn't it be something to be known as Lady Springfield?

Beryl had said nothing. Lord Springfield was a nice man, but much like the rest of the eligible bachelors her parents had paraded through her life, she felt nothing for him beyond polite interest.

Not like what she felt for Gard Kennedy.

Which was ridiculous, since they had only met a few weeks ago, and that first meeting had not exactly been cordial, what with him pointing out every flaw he saw in her riding and doubting whether someone of her social standing could be serious about horsemanship.

But she thought she had begun to dispel his doubts. And he had been correct in his assessment of her riding, something that made her wince considering she'd thought herself quite proficient up until now. It was seeing the difference between Lacey's demeanor with Gard in the saddle as opposed to when she was riding the mare that showed he was right about her riding deficiencies.

"Is this a large kennel?" Lord Springfield looked over the early arrivals as he tugged on his gloves.

"They have a large kennel, but not all the hounds will hunt during this trial. Probably a dozen pairs will go out today."

"Good. And is the Master competent?"

The way he said it set Beryl's teeth on edge. Perhaps he didn't mean to be patronizing, but that's how it felt.

"He's an excellent Master of Hounds. Speaking of whom, we should go and greet him."

Before they could cross the grass to where the large man in the red hunting coat stood talking to his whippers-in, Beryl spied Gard and Asa approaching on horseback. Her heart rate kicked up, and she had to take a steadying breath. Gard rode Spanky and led Lacey, and Asa rode Bandit, the mount Lord Springfield had leased from the Schmidts for the summer.

Beryl changed course, going to greet them. Lacey nudged her hand for a treat, but she had to settle for some pats. Beryl had stuck to the feeding schedule Gard had set up for the mare, and it was already paying dividends. Lacey was getting fitter and leaner by the day.

She glanced at Gard's attire, thankful that he'd gotten it right. Hunt etiquette was strict, and everyone was expected to adhere to it. With his black jacket, buff breeches, and black hunt cap and boots, he would blend right into the field of riders. Except that he would be by far the handsomest.

"Looks like a good day for it." Gard slid from the saddle. He loosened Spanky's girth while Asa did the same for Bandit.

"Hello, Asa. Thank you for helping get the horses here." Beryl smiled at the old horseman. "They look to be in fine form."

"My pleasure, Miss Beryl." He bobbed his snowy head. "I'll be right here to get 'em back home when you return." He pulled a book from his pocket and went to sit in the shade of a huge pine tree away from the horses and people arriving.

Lord Springfield looked Bandit over. "I hope he gives me a good ride today. I'm wondering about switching to another horse for the rest of the summer. Do you think Schmidt would lease that stallion Arcturus to me? I imagine he'd be exhilarating over fences."

Gard ran his hand down Bandit's nose. "I don't think Schmidt is interested in leasing Arcturus. Bandit will give you a nice ride, though I've noticed he likes to lie on your left leg. He could do with some straightening going into a jump."

Lord Springfield's eyes blazed. He took Bandit's reins and led him away. Beryl almost laughed. Gard had no compunctions about giving out riding instructions, even to haughty English lords. Maybe that was what she liked most about him. The horses came first.

Taking Beryl's arm, Gard guided her to the far side of the horses, keeping his voice low. "What's the procedure here? I don't want to do something stupid. Can you run through how things will go?"

"Of course." She searched the growing group. "That tall man over by the fence is the Huntsman. He rides first and he manages the hounds. He carries the horn, and he'll signal the pack as he rides. Helping him are the Whippers-in, or the Whips. They encourage the hounds who are straying or lagging to stay on track, and they keep an eye out for the quarry. After the Whips comes the Master. He's actually in charge of the entire hunt. We'll be part of the Field, and we come after the Master."

At that moment, the handlers brought the pack around from the kennels. Beryl estimated twenty pairs—large, athletic, tricolored. Tails wagging, ears flopping, they went straight to the Huntsman, who patted and rubbed and greeted them.

Beryl took that time to introduce Gard to the Master, mentioning that Lord Springfield was also in attendance. The Master shook their hands, cordial and welcoming. "Beryl, always good to see you and meet your friends. The Field is small today, so we'll all stay together, but if either of you is a novice jumper, hang to the back."

Soon they were all mounted, and the Huntsman led them out. Beryl lowered the net on her hat brim to protect her face, and found herself neatly sandwiched between Gard and Lord Springfield.

"The Master said you'd stay together today. Is that unusual?" Gard asked as they trotted down the road.

"When the Field is large, they are divided into Flights. The First Flight goes with the Master and is made up of experienced hunters or good jumpers. The Second Flight is reserved for those who either don't jump at all or those who are visiting or those who like to pick and choose which jumps they will take. But with only twenty or so of us in the Field today, there's no need for Flights."

"I say, Beryl," Lord Springfield nudged Bandit closer. He smiled at her, brows raised. "I'm looking forward to seeing how that mare goes today. Your father has named his price, and I'm thinking it over. I would've ridden her myself, but your groom here refused." He looked down his rather long nose and sniffed. "Something about not interfering with your lesson progress?" He said it as if he suspected Gard was being deliberately obstructive.

Though her throat was tight, Beryl said, firmly, "Gard is not my groom. And he's correct. Lacey and I have been working very hard, aiming at competing at Deep Haven at the end of the summer, and today's ride is part of that training." Her father had named a price for Lacey? Without even telling her?

The Field followed the pack as they left the road and approached a covert. The Huntsman blew his horn—a short, sharp note—and the dogs spread out, noses down, casting about for the scent. They were silent, though the Huntsman's calls of encouragement could be heard well back in the Field.

Before long, one of the hounds gave a short howl, and several more joined it. A ripple went through Lacey, and she strained at the bit, ready to be off. Beryl's blood thrilled to the sound as the pack found the scent trail and crashed after it, baying in full throat. The Huntsman blew "Gone Away" and the Master and Field were off in pursuit.

The trail led through the woods and pastures, over streams and ditches. Beryl concentrated on meeting each obstacle just right, keeping her hands on Lacey's withers, reins loose as they cantered along. Lord Springfield seemed to have no trouble with Bandit, rising into a two-point stance at each jump, chin up, clearly an experienced rider.

Spanky was another story. Gard fell behind, and Beryl couldn't tell if it was deliberate or if Spanky was giving him trouble. As they came to another open hayfield, Beryl slowed Lacey, looking back. Spanky appeared over the rise, Gard firmly in the saddle, and Beryl let go the breath she'd been holding.

Gard spied her and directed Spanky alongside Lacey. "He's not sure about all this yet, so I thought it best to keep him in the back, give him plenty of time to size up the obstacles and not get jostled by the other horses."

She nodded. "The trail narrows up here, so we'll have to go single file, and we'll have to wait our turn at the next gate."

They rejoined the Field, staying near the rear, and Beryl enjoyed every minute. Though it was only a trial, she loved the speed and the sounds and the sense of partnership with her horse.

The hounds were still hot on the scent, baying and running, and the Field worked to stay close. They entered a stretch of woods, traveling on a faint bridle path. Beryl and Lacey went ahead of Gard and Spanky. Lord Springfield on Bandit rode just in front of Beryl. When they reached the next fence on the edge of an open glade, riders milled and circled, waiting their turn.

Lord Springfield circled on Bandit, who shook his head and stomped, up on the bit, eager to run. He sidled, bumping into a chestnut who wore a bright red ribbon on his tail. Without warning, the chestnut lashed out with his hind feet, startling Bandit, who charged out of the way, Lord Springfield lurching in the saddle.

Beryl, who had started her approach to the fence, leaned forward in her saddle, readying herself for Lacey's leap over the wooden bars, when she felt her horse veer in midair. Bandit, head up, barreled into Lacey from the left, throwing her off and sending Beryl flying out of the saddle.

The trees and earth and sky spun in a kaleidoscopic effect, and she tumbled hard to the ground on the far side of the fence. A searing pain shot up through her left wrist, and the air whooshed out of her lungs. Hooves lurched near her head, churning up clods of dirt, and someone shouted.

Before she could push herself upright, strong hands pressed her shoulders.

"Beryl? Are you all right? Be still. Don't try to move yet."

She turned her head to find Gard's face very near hers. His green eyes were clouded with worry, and she wanted to reach up and touch his cheek, assure him that she was fine.

"I'm all right." Sucking in a deep breath, she took stock of her situation. Her shoulder ached, and her head spun a little, but the most severe pain came from her wrist. "Help me up."

He put his arm around her shoulders and eased her to a sitting position. The whirling in her head stopped, but she rested her head against his strong shoulder. His hand came up and touched her hair, cradling her head in the crook of his neck, whispering her name. "Beryl, you scared about ten years off my life... You might've been killed."

Was she mistaken, or did his lips brush her forehead? She felt safe and sheltered and yet as if she were flying free all at the same time.

She looked up into his face, so close, so dear, and something charged into his eyes, making them darker and more intense. Was he going to kiss her? Her lashes fluttered closed....

Someone cleared their throat, and Beryl's eyes popped open. A trio of riders had dismounted and stood in an arc around them. Their horses stamped and swished their tails, eager to be back on the trail, but their riders looked on with curious expressions. Embarrassment whipped heat into Beryl's cheeks.

"Where is Lacey?" She scanned the area, hoping to see the chestnut mare.

"Lord Springfield went after her." Gard's voice was clipped and his mouth was tight, as if he, too, had just realized they had an audience. "Are you sure you're not hurt?"

She winced as he helped her stand, trying to calm the flutters in her chest and the crashing disappointment of not being kissed. "Mostly my pride." Her hair had tumbled out of its net and hung in leaf-littered tangles over her shoulders. "And my wrist hurts a bit." Actually it hurt more than a bit, but a fox hunter was tough, and she wouldn't crumble in front of her peers.

Gard kept his arm around her waist, which she had to admit was pretty nice. "You can all go ahead. I'll look after Miss Valentine and see she gets home." He spoke to the three riders who had stayed behind.

One woman lingered. "I'm so sorry. I'm afraid Clip Along started this mess. I was trying to keep him away from the other horses, but that Englishman kept circling us, in spite of the red ribbon on Clip Along's tail, and finally he just kicked out."

"It's not your fault, Eugenie." Beryl brushed her hair back with her good hand. "Perhaps the customs are different in England and he didn't know what the red ribbon meant. I should've explained it better."

Lord Springfield returned as the others were leaving, and he led Lacey behind him. He remained in the saddle. "My dear, are you injured? Where is that careless woman who caused all this?" He stared after the departing riders.

Gard's hold on her waist tightened. "Springfield, the fault is yours. That horse you were crowding had a red ribbon braided into its tail. That's the universal signal that the horse is a kicker. Everyone knows that. Your carelessness could've killed Beryl, and you could've ruined a good mare in the process."

Neville's face suffused with red and his pale eyes blazed. "Such impertinence from a hireling. You've been reaching above your station all summer, but you'll never be anything but a shanty mick. Now unhand Miss Valentine, you bog jumper."

"That's enough. Please remember that you are both gentlemen and there is a lady present. Neville, name-calling is beneath you. Gard, thank you for your assistance." Beryl slipped from his grasp and cradled her throbbing wrist with her good hand. "I seem to have injured my wrist and my pride, but I'm otherwise unharmed. I'm more concerned with Lacey."

"Here, let me." Gard unwound the stock from his neck. "Do you think you've broken your arm?"

She flexed her fingers, wincing, but shook her head. "Probably just a sprain." He took her hand, sending flutters across her skin in spite of the pain. Carefully, he wrapped the wrist from the base of her fingers to halfway up her forearm.

"Can you untie your stock? I'll make a sling."

Lord Springfield scowled. "You aren't a doctor. Shouldn't you ride for help or something?"

"You're the one still in the saddle," Gard shot back. "I suggest you ride back to the club, let Asa know what happened, and send him for a carriage."

"Fine." The Englishman jerked Bandit's head around and jabbed his sides with his heels, circling the horse and leaping the jump, disappearing down the bridle path.

Beryl managed to get her stock pin out and her stock unwound. Gard, with great gentleness, fashioned a sling and slipped her wrist into it. Would he, now that there were no spectators, perhaps kiss her?

He didn't. Finishing with his first aid, he went to Lacey to check her over. The mare had no obvious injuries, but she was skittish, tossing her head and picking up her feet. Gard approached her slowly, loosening the reins from where Lord Springfield had tied her. "Easy, girl. You're all right."

Once he had her calmed, he led her around. She moved easily, no limps or head bobbing to indicate she was in pain. "I think she's fine. Let's get you back into the saddle and headed home."

He didn't interlock his fingers to give her a leg up. Instead, he spanned her waist, lifting her easily into the saddle without jarring her wrist. "Take your foot out of the stirrup." He untied Spanky from a nearby tree where he'd been tethered, but instead of mounting the gelding, Gard poked his toe into Beryl's stirrup and mounted Lacey, seating himself behind the saddle.

Lacey, unused to riding double, sidled a bit but quieted at Gard's calm, "Whoa there, girl."

His arms went around Beryl's waist, and he picked up the reins. "We'll take it slowly, and you be sure to tell me if you need to stop."

Sheltered in his embrace, Beryl almost said what she was thinking. . .that she never wanted the journey to end.

Chapter Six

"This is getting out of hand, Beryl Valentine." She spoke to her reflection in the train window. No matter where she was or what she was doing these days, thoughts of Gardiner Kennedy invaded her mind and heart. When they were apart, she wondered what he was doing, and when they were together, she could hardly concentrate for the flutters in her chest.

She flexed her wrist, thankful that over the last week, the soreness had lessened. As she had thought, it had been sprained but not broken. The long ride back to the Hunt Club had seemed all too short to Beryl, but the ensuing week had been never-ending. Her mother had been horrified at the injury, and the doctor had prescribed rest as the only cure. At one point Mother had been on the brink of forbidding Beryl to ride ever again, but Father stepped in saying he was proud of her grit and that she would be back in the saddle soon.

Lord Springfield had called repeatedly during the week, bringing her chocolates and books and staying to keep her company. He made a couple of disparaging remarks about Gard, but Beryl reprimanded him for it and he stopped. Mother sat in on his visits, visibly charmed and doing everything she could to encourage his efforts.

Gard had not come, though he sent a note to explain his absence. Mr. Schmidt had entered Arcturus and Spanky in a show in Albany, and Gard had taken them up there. The note contained nothing personal, just an explanation of his absence from their lessons for the week, a mention that he hoped her wrist would mend quickly, and an apology for his outburst toward Lord Springfield. Beryl kept it with her constantly, reading it over and over when she was alone.

The train rocked and swayed its way toward Syracuse and an overnight visit with Avila. Beryl had tried to put everything she was feeling into a letter to her mentor, but somehow, the words wouldn't come out. She needed to see her friend face-to-face, to hear her words of wisdom.

Avila was seated in a wheeled chair on a broad front porch, her leg elevated and covered with a light afghan. Beryl almost cried as she ascended the steps and bent for an awkward hug.

"Beryl, dear, I am so glad you came. I'm about to go out of my mind with boredom. I miss my horses, and though Freeman visits every week, he never tells me anything." She kept hold of Beryl's hand, her dark eyes bright and blinking quickly. "How have you been? How are my lovely horses?"

Beryl told Avila all about the horses, how the vet was certain Rita was in foal, how Lacey was improving, and how Spanky was getting plenty of time under saddle. She mentioned the tumble she'd taken during the hunt but quickly showed that her injury had healed.

"Go on," Avila said.

"Lacey's entered at Deep Haven in the Handy Hunter and in the Ladies' Equitation. I'm nervous about showing on such a big stage, but I'm excited, too."

"Go on."

"My father has come close several times this summer to selling Lacey." Beryl straightened the fringe on Avila's afghan. "He says she's in her prime breeding years, and he can get a good price for her."

Avila squeezed her hand. "He's not wrong there, but for your sake, I wish he'd just gift you the mare so you could stop worrying. Go on. You haven't gotten to the real reason for your visit." She tugged on Beryl's hand to get her to look up. "I know you. Something's bothering you."

"I'm here because of Gardiner Kennedy." Beryl blurted out the truth, her heart bumping at just saying his name.

Her friend's brows rose. "Oh? What's he done?"

"Nothing, that's the problem." Beryl removed her hand and stood, too restless to sit still. She paced the porch. "He's been wonderful. He's kind and thoughtful and such a good horseman. He treats all the horses like his friends, and he's taught me so much. He's kind to the stable hands, he keeps the stable running smoothly, and he's the most talented rider I've ever seen."

"And he's the best looking thing in riding boots?" Avila asked, her tone dry and knowing.

Beryl flushed, staring at her hands.

"Are you in love with him?"

"I don't know!" She turned, shrugging and spreading her hands wide. "How can I tell? And what if I am? My parents will have several conniptions hand running if I waltz in and say I've fallen for my riding instructor. There would be a positive earthquake." Tears burned her eyes. "They've got a toff of an Englishman picked out for me. Lord Springfield. He and my father are partnering together to build biscuit factories in Newark and Philadelphia, and he's been underfoot all summer. I think he plans to offer for me, or maybe even skip asking me altogether and just work out an agreement with my parents."

"What are you going to do?"

"I don't know. Help me!" Beryl plopped into her chair once more. She pressed her palms to her middle. "Lately, I can't think of anything but Gard Kennedy. When I'm with him, I can hardly breathe, and when we're apart, I feel as if the most important part of me is missing. I don't care that he's a mere riding instructor. I only know that I'm happy when I'm with him and miserable when I'm not."

"That sounds like love all right." Avila frowned.

"And you know what? I realized that I cared more about him than I cared even about Lacey or any horse I ever had." She was still amazed at this realization. "I never thought anyone or anything could mean more to me than my horses, but now I know that if Gard Kennedy asked me to forsake them and marry him and never own a horse again, I'd do it."

Silence reigned on the porch as the truth of her statement sunk in. She'd never voiced it aloud, and had hardly even let herself think it.

"Has he made a declaration?" Avila finally asked.

"No." Beryl took a deep breath. "I want him to, but I don't know what to do about my parents if he does. My mother says it doesn't matter if you have money, it only matters what your family connections are. And my father says he doesn't care about connections, as long as you can make money. Gard doesn't have connections *or* money, so neither of them will be happy. I wish I was just an ordinary girl, that money and connections never came into it."

Avila reached out and touched Beryl's cheek, surprising Beryl by wiping away a tear she didn't realize had fallen. "Oh, child, even if you had no money or connections, you wouldn't be ordinary. Sometimes, as Shakespeare said, 'The course of true love never did run smooth.' If Gard Kennedy is the one you love and want to spend your life with, it might mean disappointing your parents. But losing your parents' esteem and making them unhappy isn't something you should do lightly. Consider it from all angles, trying to be objective, though I know you can't really. Try to see things from your parents' perspective. . .and keep in mind, Gard hasn't made any declaration to you. You might be laboring under a false expectation."

By the time Beryl boarded the train the next afternoon, Avila had given her much to think about. Talking with her friend had clarified things in Beryl's mind, but her heart was still in chaos. She loved Gardiner Kennedy, and she thought he might have feelings for her, too, but there seemed to be little either of them could do about it. Not unless she wanted to break her parents' hearts.

———●◆●———

Gard sat on a straw bale, resting his back against the side of the boxcar. Arcturus and Spanky stood quietly in their stalls at the far end. It had been a long week. Asa joined him on the bale, holding his back as he eased down.

"That is one persnickety horse. But it was smart of you to bring water from home." Asa spread his gnarled, dark fingers out over his knees. "Mr. Schmidt is going to be mighty happy with your results up there at that show." He motioned to the ribbons hanging on a wire strung across the opposite wall. They fluttered in the breeze created by the side door being cracked open a foot or so to let light into the car.

"I'll be lucky if he doesn't raise the asking price, what with how good Arcturus is." Gard glanced at the stallion again. Both he and Spanky had done well, and they traveled like seasoned pros. But they, and he, would be glad to get back to Schmidt Farm.

Though the trip had been good for them. And for him. He had needed the breathing room to remind himself of his situation. . .to get his focus back on what was important.

Not that it seemed to help much. Try as he might, he couldn't stop thinking about Beryl. The moment when she catapulted over that jump was frozen in his memory. . .as was the dizzying relief when he'd held her in his arms and knew she was alive.

He'd come within a gnat's eyelash of kissing her right there in the woods with a handful of spectators looking on.

"We're so close to everything we've worked for." Gard leaned forward, putting his elbows on his knees. "There's only a few more weeks of lessons, and then Deep Haven, and I'll have the money put together for Arcturus. We can take him to the farm and start booking mares for the spring. We'll spend the winter getting things ready, making sure all the fences are in good shape, doing any repairs on the barn or house. And we'll start looking for mares of our own to buy."

"Mares like Miss Beryl's Lacey? She's just the type. I think she'd drop some nice foals."

Gard shook his head. "I think she would, too, but I couldn't buy her from Mr. Valentine. She means too much to Beryl. We'll look somewhere else for hunter mares."

"What are you going to do about Miss Beryl?" Asa asked.

It was the question that had been plaguing Gard since the moment he saw her. And the answer was the same as it had always been. "Nothing. I'm going to continue to give her lessons, get her ready for Deep Haven, and then say goodbye."

Asa shook his head. "You gonna break her heart?"

"It won't break her heart. She's got an English lord all lined up."

"Her mama has an English lord lined up. Miss Beryl might have other ideas, like maybe a washed-up cavalry man who is soon to be horse rich and cash poor."

"It's the cash poor part that means I need to steer clear of any entanglements. If you had seen the Valentine house. . .just the place where they spend the summer, mind you. . .you'd know what I mean. Can you imagine someone who grew up in a palace like that coming to live in a farmhouse that's been closed up for the past six years? Can you imagine the belle of New York Society marrying a third-generation Irishman with nothing to his name but a farm and a horse?"

Asa grunted and closed his eyes, leaning back against the side of the boxcar. "If she loved you, she would. If she loved you, she'd say yes before you even finished the proposal."

"Well, she's not going to get the chance. Even if I did offer for her, her parents would laugh me right out of town. They've got higher aims for their daughter than a man like me."

Maybe if he said it often enough, he could force himself to believe it and stop trying to find a way to make Beryl his.

Chapter Seven

Gard kept things professional at Beryl's lessons leading up to Deep Haven, and he stayed busy training Spanky and Arcturus for the show. He'd managed to pick up several other rides as well and spent a lot of his time getting from one stable to the next to school those mounts.

He could tell Beryl was confused and frustrated by his aloofness, but it was for the best that he kept his distance. She would forget about him soon enough, especially with Lord Springfield hovering all the time.

Springfield had decided to enter Bandit in the Open Hunter Class at Deep Haven, which would put him up against Arcturus and Gard. And the Englishman spent quite a bit of time readying his horse for the show. He refused to speak to Gard unless absolutely necessary, something that didn't bother Gard at all.

Soon it was time to head to Deep Haven. The Deep Haven Hunt Club was one of the oldest in the Hudson River Valley with a rich tradition and excellent reputation. And its grounds just happened to border the farm Gard had inherited from his grandmother. He'd have a chance to look things over again in preparation for taking Arcturus there next week, the Good Lord willing.

Getting the horses to Deep Haven took an entire day. Bandaging legs, packing tack and supplies, water for Arcturus and feed for everyone, show clothes and barn clothes. Asa was invaluable, keeping lists and organizing. Schmidt had also hired two extra grooms for the show who needed instruction and supervision.

In addition to being the premier hunter show of the summer, Deep Haven was also known as a place to buy and sell horses. Freeman Schmidt was sending four additional horses to the sale barns, and those needed looking after as well. In all, Gard was in charge of eight horses and three stable hands. . .though he wasn't really in charge of Asa.

The show would span three days, the first day taken up with pony and youth classes, the second for model and ladies' classes, and the third culminating in the Open Hunter Class.

And hopefully in his purchasing Arcturus and starting his future.

Mr. Schmidt, as a well-known horseman and member of Deep Haven, had reserved space for his show horses in the best barn. The sale horses went to another barn, and Gard put them into the care of the new grooms. Asa would check up on them. Gard focused his attention on Arcturus, Spanky, Lacey, and Bandit.

"They traveled well then?"

Gard turned from filling a grain bucket. Beryl stood in the stall doorway, the light behind her silhouetting her form. He hadn't seen her for two days, and it felt like an eternity. He let the bucket slide back into the grain sack.

"We got everyone here safe and sound. Lacey's in the end stall." He'd put the mare in the one farthest from Arcturus so the stallion wouldn't get any frisky ideas.

"Did you get our schooling times from the show secretary?" Her voice was business-like as she stepped into the aisle. She held a pair of gloves, tapping them into her palm. But her eyes belied her professional tone. They held questions, questions he didn't want to answer. And hope, which he couldn't fulfill.

"Asa just went to pick up the times. We don't have any classes today, but Lacey goes tomorrow, so she'll need a pipe-opener schooling today."

"That's why I'm here. Is there anything else I can do? I assume we're washing and braiding tonight?"

He raised his brows. "Yes, but I don't expect you to do that."

"It's one of my favorite parts of showing, all the backstage bustle. And Lacey loves to be braided and fussed over. And you have Arcturus to do for the model class, so you'll need someone to do Spanky and Bandit."

Which meant Beryl would be in the barn most of the day. Gard's resolve to keep his feelings to himself would certainly be tested.

"Miss Beryl, just on time. We've got the use of the practice ring in half an hour." Asa came by, carrying a pitchfork over his shoulder and consulting one of his lists. "Miss Lacey is up on her toes and ready to go. You want me to saddle her for you?"

"No, Asa. Thank you. You're busy, and I can tack her up." Beryl smiled at the old man. That was something Gard loved about her, the respect and courtesy she showed to Asa. If he was going to ever marry, his bride would have to accept Asa as part of the package.

Stop thinking along those lines. You aren't in a position to marry, and even if you were, marrying Beryl isn't possible.

"I'll get Spanky tacked up and we can school them together." Gard retrieved the grain bucket and fed Arcturus before heading to Spanky's stall.

Lacey, who was in tip-top shape, took to her schooling well. Beryl was calm in the saddle, loose with the reins, and attentive to her mount. He'd instructed and trained them both to the best of his ability. Now it was up to them to carry all that work into the show ring.

Spanky, on the other hand, acted as if he had ants in his britches. He shied at figments of his imagination, bounced around, and generally skidded his way through the practice. It took all of Gard's considerable horsemanship to keep him under control.

"Hopefully he got his wiggles out." Gard dismounted at the gate to lead Spanky back to the barn and Beryl dropped to the ground, too.

"It's like he's giddy at all the newness." She shook her head. "If he acts like that during his class, he's going to get the gate right away."

"Don't I know it. And he's my first ride of the show. If he gets booted early from a class, it might mean my other rides will disappear." Gard rubbed the back of his neck. "Still, he's got a couple days to settle down. We don't go until Friday, so I can school him again before then."

They returned to the barn and began the process of getting the horses groomed and ready for their events.

Beryl spurned no job, carrying buckets of water, scrubbing Lacey from nose to tail, and walking her in the hot sunshine until she was dry. Lacey basked in the attention, leaning into

Beryl and going so far as to start snoring while she had her mane and tail braided.

Arcturus was another matter. He hated being fussed over, tossing his head, snorting, sidling, and letting Gard know he wasn't in the mood to be prettied up. He stood crosstied in the aisle of the big barn, but he shifted his weight and tugged on the lines frequently.

"Knock it off, big boy." Gard swatted him on the rump. "It's your own fault. If you weren't so good looking, you wouldn't be in the conformation class. And if you're going to go, you're going to be clean and shiny."

Beryl laughed when Arcturus knocked over the suds bucket. "Do you need some help?"

He eyed the row of tight, neat braids marching down Lacey's chestnut neck. "Where did you learn to braid like that?"

Her eyes sparkled. "Obviously you didn't play dress-up with your friends as a child. We all braided each others' hair all the time." She motioned to the coiled braid on the back of her head. "Who do you think does this every day?"

He shrugged. "I thought you had a maid or hairdresser or someone who took care of that sort of thing."

"I do have a maid who looks after my clothes and cares for my room, but I do my own hair." She picked up the mane comb and her thread. "Would you like me to braid Arcturus?"

Gard considered it. Her braids were better than his, no doubt, but stallions were unpredictable creatures. "All right, but I'm going to hold his head. If he starts acting up, you get out of the way, got it?"

Beryl nodded and got to work. Gard had the opportunity to observe her, loving the way she talked to Arcturus under her breath.

"What a lovely, thick mane you have. You'll make all the other horses jealous, that's what."

The stallion swiveled one ear around, listening to her.

"You're such a handsome fellow. I know Mr. Schmidt is going to sell you after the show, but I hope whoever buys you remembers you're more than just a bloodline. I hope they remember you're a fine individual who likes to roll in the grass right after you've had a bath, and that you like your apples cut up for you, and that it takes you a while to settle into a new place..."

She'd learned a lot about the horse. Come to think of it, she knew little things about every horse in the Schmidt barn.

Beryl had just finished and taken the equipment back to the stall they were using as a tack room when Arcturus's head came up and he whinnied, staring at someone over Gard's shoulder.

"I thought I'd find you here, Kennedy."

Wallace Valentine and his friends, Mr. Bentley and Mr. Van Rissingham.

"Mr. Valentine." Gard turned to shake hands with him, keeping hold of one of the stallion's crossties. "Gentlemen."

"How is this old boy?" Mr. Valentine stepped to the side to view the stallion in profile. "I saw Freeman Schmidt and gave him our price this morning. He said he'd consider it, especially if his mystery buyer can't come up with his financing by the weekend."

Gard nodded. He'd have his financing. With the money he would make on his extra rides, it would be just enough. Come Friday evening, Arcturus would be his. If Mr. Valentine wanted, he could book a couple of his mares to come to the farm next spring, but hopefully, that would be as close as he got to owning a piece of Arcturus.

"Beryl, dear, I didn't know you were in the stables this afternoon." She had stepped out of the tack room. Wallace held out his arms and she went into them for a brief hug and peck on the cheek. "Your mother was wondering where you'd gone. She and Neville are at the Members' Tea, and I believe she thought you would attend, too?" He gave her a skeptical look. "She's going to be more than a bit put out, you know."

"I know, but I needed to school Lacey, and then there was the grooming to do. Doesn't Arcturus look fine?"

"He does. And he'll look even better at Valentine Ridge in the stallion barn." He put his arm around Beryl's shoulders. "Oh, I have some news for you. Remember I told you a couple months ago that Cal Brightman was looking for a mare for his wife?"

Beryl's face froze and the light went out of her eyes. "Yes."

"Well, he agreed to my price on Lacey. He'll pick her up after the show, so you can still compete. I got him to agree to that. I knew it would make you happy." He beamed. "She brought a handsome price, one that will go a long way toward paying my share of Arcturus, here. Isn't that great news?"

The color went out of her face. Her eyes sought Gard's, and he could read the pleading, heartbreak, and desperation there. It cut him to the core. Her worst fear had been realized, and her blustering father had no idea he was the cause of her devastation.

— • ◆ • —

Beryl had to get out of there. She was numb everywhere except the pit of her stomach which had tightened into a knot of despair. Panic welled up, and she slipped from under her father's arm as he turned to talk to his friends. Keeping a tight hold on herself, pushing the sobs down, hardly feeling the impact of her riding boots on the dirt, she headed out of the barn and into the sunshine.

People bustled around the barns—show people, spectators, grooms. Everywhere she looked there were more people. Over to the east, the white roof of the members' tent poked up, the enclosure where her mother and Lord Springfield were drinking tea and chatting with the upper crust. To the west, the show rings were in use, ponies and youths everywhere.

Melanie Turner went by on the arm of one of her beaux, and though she called Beryl's name, Beryl didn't stop. She had to find a place to be alone.

There, she spied a copse near the edge of tomorrow's hunter course. Lifting her hem, she hurried across the open grass, entering the shade of the trees, gulping for air as the sobs she'd held back overwhelmed her.

Beryl sank to the ground, hugging the slender bole of a white birch, seeing nothing through her tears. Though she had known this day would probably come, she hadn't been prepared. Her beautiful Lacey. . .

Strong arms came around her, familiar arms. "Shhhh. . ." he whispered against her hair, rocking her gently. "Shhhh. . . ."

Gard.

She melted against him, trusting him with her pain as she had trusted him with her heart. He would understand, because he had the capacity to love horses, just as she did.

When the storm of tears finally passed, she went still, pressing her ear against his chest, listening to the thudding of his heart, strong and steady, and the sound of his breathing, feeling the warmth of his muscles through his shirt, the security of his arms around her. Having him here with her was making the loss of Lacey endurable. . .barely. She sat up, and his hands came up to cup her face. His thumbs brushed at her tears.

The wind had ruffled his dark hair, and his eyes were filled with compassion. "I'm so sorry, sweetheart."

The endearment spread balm on the raw edges of her heart. She didn't know who leaned into whom, but before she realized it was happening, his lips were on hers, and she was gathered tightly in his arms again. Pain of a new kind washed over her. Gard did love her; she could feel it in his kiss, feel it in the hunger of his embrace, and yet, what could they do about it?

She quit thinking and just felt, tunneling her fingers into his hair, saying everything through touch that she couldn't put into words. Her tears wet his face and dampened his beard. When he broke the kiss, it was by degrees, pressing his lips to her forehead and then coming back to touch her lips, her cheeks, her eyelids, brushing the tip of his nose against hers and then burying it in the hollow of her neck.

"Oh, Beryl," he groaned. "I didn't mean for this to happen." He tucked her head under his chin, wrapping her close. His chest heaved as he drew in deep breaths.

Neither of them had. The heavy weight of Lacey's sale pressed on her heart again, and she closed her eyes, savoring the comfort of his embrace. At least she had Gard.

Finally she leaned back, looking up into his face. "I don't know what my parents are going to say, but I don't care. We'll make them understand somehow."

His brows drew together. "Make them understand what?"

"That we love each other. I know they would prefer me to marry Lord Springfield, but that's impossible. I don't love him. I love you."

Gard scrambled to his feet, pulling her up with him. "Whoa, there. Who said anything about marriage? I can't get married, and I certainly can't marry you." The panic in his eyes reminded her of a horse that had just scented danger and stood ready to flee. "I have plans to see through. I won't be ready to get married for years yet."

For the second time in an hour, Beryl's world crashed to bits around her. Mortified, she spun away from him and ran, not caring who saw or what their conclusions might be. And worse, he didn't try to stop her.

Chapter Eight

Except for pain, Beryl didn't feel anything. Her mother fussed over her, asking if she was ill, and her father put her distractedness down to pre-show nerves. After a sleepless night alternately mourning for Lacey and aching for Gard, she wanted nothing more than to withdraw from the show and run away from it all.

And for the first time in her life, she avoided a stable. She couldn't face Gard. Not after humiliating herself as she had.

She sat in the stands between Lord Springfield and her father during the Model Classes, and when the Stallion Model Class was called, she took care to mask her expression. Even so, seeing Gard enter the ring with Arcturus hurt like nothing she'd ever felt before.

Sunlight gleamed off the stallion's blood-bay coat. Gard had brushed a checkerboard pattern into the horse's haunches. No false tail was needed, since Arcturus's black tail was already thick, long, and glossy. He looked impeccable.

Gard looked no less wonderful. Beryl's seat was right on the rail, and he walked by no more than ten feet away from her. His velvet hunt cap was set at the perfect angle, his breeches pristine white, and his boots glossy black. His black hunting jacket rode his shoulders perfectly, and he moved with easy grace.

The class was a large one, but nobody was surprised when Arcturus won. Gard accepted the rosette, pinned it to the stallion's bridle, and led him in a victory lap of the ring before heading back to the stables. Beryl's father was thrilled, rubbing his hands together and beaming as if he already owned Arcturus and was eager to accept congratulations.

"Your first class is right after lunch, correct?" Father consulted his program. "Ladies Hunter Equitation?"

Beryl nodded. "I had best go warm up Lacey." Even saying the mare's name hurt.

"Do us proud."

"Would you like me to walk you to the stables and saddle your mare?" Lord Springfield stood when she did and offered his arm.

"Thank you, no. Stay here and enjoy yourself."

Gard was just stabling Arcturus when she arrived at the barn. Walking past him, chin high, forbidding herself to shed so much as a single tear, she headed to Lacey's stall. The chestnut pushed her blazed nose into Beryl's chest, looking for a treat as always. With a tight throat, Beryl patted her neck instead, opening the stall and leading the mare out into the aisle.

"I polished your tack last night. Shall I saddle her up for you?" Gard asked quietly.

"No." She couldn't say anymore past the lump in her throat. Why didn't he go away?

"Beryl, please." He reached out for her.

"Just leave it." She shook off his hand on her arm.

She tacked up Lacey, used the mounting block, and went to the warm-up area without another word.

When the class was called, Beryl rode Lacey into the ring.

It was the worst showing of Beryl's career. To her mortification, she received the gate less than halfway through the event. To get the gate was to be disqualified for being subpar. And none of it was Lacey's fault. Beryl hadn't been paying attention, hadn't been listening for the changes of gait, for the changes of direction even, and had nearly caused a collision when everyone reversed their routes but her.

Gard met her at the gate, his face a thundercloud. He took Lacey's reins near the bit and frowned up at Beryl. "What do you think you're doing?"

"Leave me alone."

"No. Not when you're acting like this." He led the mare toward the stables with Beryl still in the saddle, a helpless passenger.

"And just how am I acting?"

Gard stopped and turned to look at her. "You're acting like one of those spoiled debutantes I thought you were when we first met. You didn't get your way in something, so you're taking it out on everyone around you."

Outrage stormed through Beryl, and she leaped to the ground. "Spoiled debutante?" Her voice rose, drawing attention from passersby. She lowered her tone and whispered, "Spoiled debutante?"

"That's right. You're only thinking of yourself instead of your horse, which is something I never thought you'd do. Lacey deserves better, and frankly, so do I. We've put in too much work for you to spoil it all over a tantrum. Pull yourself together and be a professional." He turned on his heel and led Lacey away, leaving Beryl standing alone.

She wanted to stomp her feet, scream, throw something. . .until she realized that's exactly what a spoiled debutante would do.

The fight drained out of her. She *had* let Lacey down. Her beloved, beautiful Lacey who deserved so much better. It wasn't the horse's fault that she had been sold, nor was it her fault that Beryl had laid her heart out before someone who didn't want it.

They had one last event together, the Ladies' Hunter Class. They might not win, but it wouldn't be because Beryl wasn't trying. Lacey deserved her best effort.

Their class went splendidly. In a large field of contestants, Beryl rode with confidence, hearing in her ear all Gard's instructions. Hands low, heel down, eyes up, weight forward. Lacey responded beautifully, meeting each jump just right, changing leads, never altering her cantering cadence.

Beryl accepted the rosette with bittersweetness in her heart. Gard waited for her as she came through the exit.

He gave her a tight smile and took the ribbon, clipping it to Lacey's bridle. "Congratulations. That was beautifully ridden."

"Thank you."

Leading them to the barn, he stopped outside the doors. "Beryl, we need to talk."

She shook her head. "No, we don't. You said everything you needed to say. I have lost everything I thought I cared about, and talking about it won't change anything." She slid from Lacey's saddle for the last time. "Now, I want to say goodbye to my horse in private, if you don't mind. Mr. Brightman will be sending a groom for her this evening, I understand."

Beryl took the reins and led Lacey into the barn. Once she had the mare unsaddled and in her stall, she wrapped her arms around the chestnut neck and gave way to tears.

••••

Gard was so proud and miserable; he didn't know what to do with himself. Beryl's ride on Lacey had been a thing of beauty, the culmination of weeks of hard work. And though he knew she was hurting, she had held herself together.

At least until she got back to the barn. The sound of her crying had shredded Gard's heart. He wanted to go to her, but his presence was the last thing she wanted.

He hadn't said anything about what had happened to Asa, but he didn't need to. His wise friend had somehow known.

"You need to take a look at what is really important in life, Mistah Gard. It is fine to be focused on a goal, but sometimes God brings something even better into your path. If all you're looking at is the good goal you have set, sometimes you miss the better thing God would like for you to have."

Asa said no more, sauntering down the barn aisle, leaving Gard to consider his words. As he cleaned stalls and fed horses, Gard prayed and thought and prayed some more. He wasn't sure what God was doing, but he was going to trust, and he was going to go with his heart. He might lose everything in the end, but at least he would've tried.

••••

If only she could get through this evening, perhaps she could start the healing process. Beryl stepped out of the family carriage onto the gravel drive of the Deep Haven Hunt Club Hall. Lights shone from every window, and music drifted out through the open French doors that marched down the side of the Hall.

Lord Springfield drew her hand through his elbow and guided her up the steps, following her parents in evening dress for the Hunt Ball to celebrate a successful show. Her mother looked back over her shoulder, an expectant gleam in her eyes. Beryl sighed.

"You look lovely, my dear. Did your father tell you we have worked out a deal to build a factory on his property in Brooklyn? It will be most advantageous for both of us, and it will mean I'll be in America for the foreseeable future." He covered her hand with his. "Your mother has asked me to stay with you all in Manhattan while I look for a suitable house. I hope that meets with your approval and that you will assist me in the search for an appropriate home."

The way he said it, leaning close, made Beryl want to yank her hand away from his grasp and step back. Staying with them in the city? Looking for houses with him? Her future closed in around her.

The ballroom was ablaze with light, both gaslight and the newfangled electric lights. A small orchestra played on the balcony, and couples were already whirling around the dance floor. Ball gowns and tuxedos flashed by. Beryl smoothed her ruby velvet gown, checking the diamond brooch at her shoulder and fingering her beryl and diamond necklace.

After being announced, Lord Springfield asked her for a dance, and she went into his arms woodenly. He was a competent dancer, and she followed his lead easily enough, though her heart wasn't in the dance. It wasn't even in the room.

They passed the trophy table where all the silver cups and trays and statues that had been won at this year's show were on display. They would be sent to the engravers to have the winners' names etched on them, then they would be placed back in the display cases in the trophy room to be admired on a cold day after a successful fox hunt.

Gard stood near the table, deep in conversation with Freeman Schmidt and Cal Brightman. She turned her head away.

At the end of their waltz, Beryl and Lord Springfield applauded politely. How could she get through this evening when her world lay in shattered pieces all around her?

"Would you like to take a stroll on the terrace?" Neville asked.

"I'd prefer a cup of punch, if you'd be so kind." She didn't really want punch, but it would get him away from her for a while so she could think.

An hour later, after dancing with several partners, Gard approached her. He looked magnificent in formal clothes, his military bearing evident. "Beryl, I know you're upset with me, but we need to talk." He waited for her assent. "Please?" Offering his arm, he motioned toward the open French doors and the terrace beyond. "It will only take a moment."

They stepped outside. Strings of electric lights lit the perimeter of the terrace, competing with the summer stars. A cool breeze touched Beryl's cheeks, and she lifted her face, turning into it, letting it blow some of the cobwebs from her mind.

"Beryl"—he took her hands, squeezing them to get her to look into his eyes—"I've been an idiot. I am so sorry for the way I hurt you. I just didn't see how it could work between us. I still don't, but right now I don't care. You deserve to know the truth, and that is that I love you more than life. I had this crazy idea that falling in love and asking someone to marry me would be putting aside my own goals. And it might mean that. In fact, it already has. . .at least it's delayed those goals, but I'm willing for that to happen. I mean, a delay isn't the same as it never happening, right? And I couldn't let this chance go." He spoke so fast, she had a hard time following. But she'd heard one thing clearly. He loved her.

"What are you talking about?"

"I'll explain everything, but first, put me out of my misery. Beryl Valentine, I love you and I want you to be my wife. I know I'm not the kind of man your parents want for you, but I promise you I'll spend my entire life providing for you and loving you. And I'll work hard to win their approval, too."

Love crashed through Beryl, washing away the hurt of the past forty-eight hours. He loved her, and he wanted to marry her. She could only nod, unable to speak.

His arms came around her, and she lifted her face for his kiss, sealing the promise and giving a hint of the joys to come.

"I say. Beryl!" Lord Springfield's voice interrupted.

Beryl would've sprung from Gard's arms, but he held her tight.

"Springfield, be the first to congratulate us. Beryl has just agreed to become my wife." Gard kept one arm around Beryl while extending the other.

"Beryl, is this true?" her mother gasped from behind Lord Springfield. "Oh, Major Kennedy." She beamed and stepped forward. "This is so sudden. Beryl, I had no idea. . ." She looked confused but not unhappy, which puzzled Beryl.

"I can see we have much to discuss." Her father's voice cut through the group. "Perhaps this conversation would be better held in a more private location. Will you excuse us, Lord Springfield? Beryl, Rosemary, come with me. You too, Kennedy."

They left the gaping Neville Springfield standing alone under the terrace lights, and

Father herded them into the Master of Hunt's office.

"Kennedy, when you said you had something to talk to me about, I didn't assume it was this." Father leaned against the desk.

Gard kept hold of Beryl's hand. "I know this is coming out of the blue, sir, but I love your daughter and she loves me. I've asked her to marry me, and she's agreed." He sent her a look filled with private messages that she treasured.

"Mother, I know you care about status more than money," Beryl jumped in. "And Father, I know you care about the ability to make money more than anything else, but I value character and integrity, and I love Gard Kennedy." She said it as firmly as she could, her heart beating fast and her breath coming quickly. If they couldn't be made to see, if they didn't give their consent, she would be crushed. "I know you would prefer me to marry Lord Springfield, but I don't love him and I never will. My heart belongs to Gard Kennedy."

"Beryl, don't you know who this man is?" her mother asked. "He's the owner of Stuyvesant Run. His grandmother was a Stuyvesant." She clasped her hands. "I only became aware of this tonight. If I had known. . ." ·

She turned to Gard. "A Stuyvesant?" Stuyvesants were the equivalent of New York royalty. And Stuyvesant Run had been one of the most successful thoroughbred breeding farms in America until there was a falling-out in the family and it had been closed up and the horses sent elsewhere.

Her father stroked his sideburns, a gleam in his eye. "So, that explains why you were the mystery buyer for Arcturus. I wormed the information out of Freeman Schmidt tonight. You could've knocked me over with a gesture."

"About that, sir. I released Mr. Schmidt from his promise to sell me Arcturus. I bought a different horse today, and didn't have enough left over for the stallion, too."

"Oh, how sad. And after you rode him so brilliantly to the championship this afternoon." Mother shook her head. "But good news for you, Wallace, since you've been so eager to buy the animal."

Beryl tugged on Gard's hand. "Wait, you were going to buy Arcturus? And you own a stud farm? And you come from one of the oldest, most respected families in New York?" She couldn't keep up with all this information.

"Yes, I was, but I didn't. Yes, I do, about a mile from where you're standing. And, yes, but they don't claim me. My grandmother had the temerity to marry a wild Irishman with a way with horses, and they had my father, who had the audacity to join the military as a cavalryman, who then had me, who also spent time in the army." He shrugged. "I'm not wealthy, not in cash terms, that is. But I do have a home and a farm, and if hard work can see it done, it will someday be restored to its former glory." He raised her hand to his lips. "With your help, we can't fail."

Her father harrumphed, and her mother clapped her hands. "My daughter, a Stuyvesant."

"I'm curious, lad. Why did you back out of the sale of Arcturus? He would make the perfect foundation sire for your new venture," her father asked.

Gard smiled and drew Beryl deeper into the crook of his arm. "Because I bought a different horse. Her name is Valentine's Highland Lace, and she's back in the show barn awaiting her new owner's pleasure. Beryl, she's my gift to you." He dug the sale papers out of his dinner jacket and handed them to her.

Through blurry eyes, she read her name on the ownership line.

"Whether you agreed to marry me or not, I wanted you to have her."

Beryl threw her arms around Gard's neck, clutching the bill of sale, hugging him as tightly as she could. "Oh, you wonderful, wonderful man."

"Beryl, really." Her mother fluttered her fan. "Sometimes I wonder if it is the man you love or his horses."

With a laugh, Gard gave Beryl a squeeze. "We're a package deal."

"Hmm, I can see that you are." Father straightened. "I expect you to spend your life making my girl happy, but I'd say you're off to a good start. And I'll add to it. Let me be the first to give you an engagement gift. Freeman gave my syndicate the option on Arcturus, but I'd rather give you the money as a wedding present to buy him yourself. I'm sure the other gentlemen in the syndicate will understand. In fact, Van Rissingham has a line on another stallion he thinks we might be able to get for a song."

Beryl transferred her hug from Gard to her father, and he staggered back. "Really, my dear." He patted her back and accepted Gard's thanks.

"Now, let's go out and make the announcement." He beamed. "About the engagement, not the horse." Father laughed at his own little joke.

"We'll be right there, sir." Gard kept Beryl from following her parents out the door, and when they were alone, he gathered her close again.

"I can't believe any of this is happening." Beryl touched his face, his hair, drinking in the countenance she knew so well. "Why didn't you say anything about your farm, about Arcturus, about. . ."

He shrugged. "Because it was all so tenuous. I was saving money like mad, living like a pauper. The farm has been closed up for years and needs a lot of work. And you were from a completely different class than me. I was focused on my own goals, and I didn't know what to do when you rode into my life. And I had no idea what your parents would say if I asked to court you properly."

She laughed, unable to believe how things had come to a head. "You ticked all their boxes. Mother cares about name and status, and Father cares about ambition and ability, and I care about heart. . .*your* heart. You swept the eligibility category—win, place, and show."

His embrace nearly squeezed the life out of her as he lifted her from the ground and kissed her.

Erica Vetsch is a transplanted Kansan now residing in Minnesota. She loves books and history, and is blessed to be able to combine the two by writing historical romances. Whenever she's not following flights of fancy in her fictional world, she's the company bookkeeper for the family lumber business, mother of two, an avid museum patron, and wife to a man who is her total opposite and soul mate. Erica loves to hear from readers. You can sign up for her quarterly newsletter at www.ericavetsch.com. And you can email her at ericavetsch@gmail.com or contact her on her author Facebook page.

The Fisherman's Nymph

by Jaime Jo Wright

Dedication

To Cap'n Hook.
The rogue who taught me the art of fly-fishing.
Who untangled a mess of my fly line without complaint,
and who tolerated me sneaking novels into my wader's pocket.
Because, let's face it,
ten hours on a river gets a little long.

Special thanks to:
My sister Sarah, who will always understand my love of the wilderness and the heart that beats deep in its shadows. And to my other sisters, Kara, Halee, Laurie, and Anne. Without you all, I would be a pile of mush. Well, I still am a pile of mush, but somehow you all put me to rights in your own unique ways. I love you—all FIVE of you.

And always, to stellar parents: Mom and Dad, you knew this book-thing would happen before I ever did, and Russ and Joanne, you shatter all in-law stereotypes. Love you all!

Finally, to Hidden Cove Resort in Phillips, WI, and dear friend, Darren Hornby, whose cabins on the lake and not far from the Flambeau River inspire all sorts of adventures!

Chapter One

Flambeau River, Wisconsin
1890

His brown eyes were cavernous pools boiling with mayhem. A lazy toothpick waved from the corner of his mouth with quite a bit of devil-may-care. Abby wasn't impressed by the twinkle in rich boy's eyes either, nor did her stomach do any twists and flips when his eyelid dropped in a flirtatious wink, daring her not to swoon. Wait. She was wrong. Her stomach *did* twist and flip, but only because she was trying to adjust to her father's new excursion trips. Taking the wealthy on fishing and canoeing tours, boarding them in the empty cabin adjacent to theirs, and creating experiences for people who ate money for breakfast. She would do anything for Papa, for his dream, to help support his livelihood. But Charles Farrington III on her beloved river? To fish her waters?

Between the toothpick, the mischievous smile, and the oozing of charm, it was more than apparent they were worlds apart. Charles Farrington III hailed from Milwaukee, which held many stark differences to her Flambeau River, tucked away in the northern woodlands of Wisconsin. Yet, here he was. Paying Papa to catch a fish, on *her* stream, that fed *her* river, that was *her* oasis. He had traveled here with his friend Jonathon, whose relations with Abby and her father went far back. Jonathon was welcome here. Abby gave Charles Farrington III a sideways glance. He was not.

"This way." Her words tossed saucily over her shoulder, emphasized by the slap of the wicker fishing basket hanging across her chest and against her hip. Abby winced at the tartness in her voice. Sour. Unfriendly. It wouldn't bode well to have Charles Farrington III go back to Milwaukee and future potential guests, complaining about the inhospitable daughter of Nessling's Northwoods Guided Tours.

She raised a disbelieving eyebrow at the tall, broad-shouldered man who stumbled over a log in his attempt to keep up. That he wasn't accustomed to the woods was more than obvious. He swiped at a fly on his shoulder. Then his face. A nice face, she admitted, but that was about the only thing nice about him.

"Where are we going?" The unwelcome guest ducked under a branch.

Abby pushed away another oak branch, laden with dew-spotted leaves. She passed by it, holding it away from her, then released the branch. The resounding *slap* and Charles Farrington III's grunt made Abby roll her lips in a smirk.

"Classy dame." His retort was laden with sarcasm mixed with flirtation. "You know. . ." Charles Farrington III's booted feet slogged in the damp earth behind her. He just wasn't going to stop chattering on like a smitten squirrel, was he? "I've never fly-fished before, however there is beautiful scenery here."

Abby ignored him, but she could feel warmth creep up her neck. Maybe he meant the scenery, but his tone insinuated he meant her.

"Of course"—the man nattered on—"some gentlemen might find it a tad embarrassing to learn from a woman, but I'm certain I am going to enjoy it. Significantly."

For all the fish in the river! Abby whirled, considering her options as her heel took its little spin. But her eyes collided with Charles Farrington III's and she was suddenly tongue-tied.

"Has anyone ever told you that your eyes are as feisty as gingersnaps on fire?" His voice dropped a notch. Abby swallowed. She ran her thumb under the leather strap that straddled her shoulder and attached to her fishing basket.

His finger darted forward and flicked her flirtatiously on the nose. Improper at least, horrifying at best. Abby staggered backward. Papa should *not* have her guiding a man alone. It was improper. But what choice did they have? Two guests required two guides if they were to have multiple outdoor experiences.

"That is quite enough, Charles Farrington the Third." His full name sputtered through her outraged lips like poetry spit at a black bear.

His dark eyebrow rose over his left eye. A quirk to his mouth and that rapscallion-like narrowing of his eyes rounded out the perfect picture of a Milwaukee playboy. "Charles. Just call me Charles."

"No." It was all she could think to say. Abby righted her insides and stiffened her shoulders. She wasn't going to make company with the long line of women he must have left behind him in Milwaukee. Women who had fallen for his cocoa-charms and hot-coffee suave. And, by glory, she *would* call him "Charles Farrington the Third" until his little recreation spree to the Northwoods was over. Anything more was too gentlemanly for this rake, and anything less was—well—it was too familiar. Familiar was *not* a place Abby wished to be when it came to Charles Farrington III.

<hr>

He had met many debutante women, but Abigail Nessling wasn't one of them. Charles followed the tiny, nymph-like girl who was all of five foot two inches and had a waist smaller than one of his legs. In fact, at first glance, he'd been convinced that she wasn't even sixteen, but his best friend and partner, Jonathon Strauss, informed him later that she was well past her marrying prime. The ripe old age of twenty-four and counting.

Now, Charles appreciated her as he followed. From her wispy, white-blond hair twisted into a fine ribbon down her back, to her delicate neck and confident pace. She owned these woods. That, and the fact she had enough fire in her to burn down the entire forest, completely intrigued him.

"*She is off limits, Charles.*"

He heard Jonathon's warning even as he considered the memory of her rosy lips pursed in bewilderment when he'd flirted just a moment before.

Charles stepped over a fallen branch. His boots were muddy, and the forest floor was a bed of moist leaves and moss. The sound of the river rolling over rocks met his ears. Abby paused in her step long enough to tip the ends of the fly rods lower to avoid tangling with a tree, then pressed on.

"*Off. Limits.*"

Jonathon had reiterated it with a hissed whisper when he'd veered off with Abby's father to go further upriver. Charles had only wagged his eyebrows, which drew a scowl. He had no investment in this trip, so he really had nothing to lose with a little flirtation.

The Strauss family apparently had connections to Abby Nessling's father, and sure, why wouldn't he jump at the chance to go on a recreational adventure in the late summer? If he were honest with himself, which was a rarity, Charles was beyond weary with life in Milwaukee. He followed in his father's shadow and the brewing industry that he was in line to inherit. It burdened him rather than drew any passion, and Charles knew his father was already braced for more disappointment from his youngest son. So why even try? His social life was all that kept things exciting, and while he wasn't the rogue that some believed him to be, he did enjoy a fun little chase.

Charles waved at a fly that dipped and buzzed at his face. A little chase never hurt anyone. Well, he didn't think it did, although Jonathon seemed to believe Charles left a trail of broken hearts in his wake.

Abby's frame was silhouetted in the clearing as the woods opened up to a rocky shoreline and the glistening waters of the Flambeau River. The blue sky haloed her hair and, as she turned, the tree line behind her made her pale skin look almost angelic.

Before Charles could react, Abby shoved a fly rod into his hand. Their fingers brushed and while she appeared completely unaffected, Charles couldn't help the frown that tipped his brows into a V. She wasn't supposed to affect *him*, *he* was supposed to affect *her*. But it appeared that if he was going to charm his way into her good graces he was going to have to work harder. Little Miss Fisherwoman was already flipping open her tin fly-box and eyeing up the flies with the tenacity of someone who wouldn't be easily deterred from her duty.

"Well, Little Miss, let's fish!" Charles didn't bother to hide his grin as she leveled him with a well-placed glare of golden-brown eyes. For sure, she would be a spot of fun. But it was the shadow that flickered quickly in her eyes that gave Charles pause. A shadow that stilled his jovial game and cautioned his senses. He adjusted his grip on the fly rod. If he knew how to read a woman, and he believed he did, this one hid something. Something from everyone. Something she had no intention of sharing and he had every intention of finding out. Someone as pretty as Abby Nessling, with her man-trousers and billowing plaid shirt tucked into the waist, did not deserve to hide shadows in her eyes. She should be filled with laughter and joy and carefree spirit. Something he was— or tried to be. If he could only forget the life he left behind in Milwaukee, his father, and, if truth be told, memories that tormented him when nighttime fell and the world became quiet.

Fine then. Maybe he and Abby Nessling shared a hidden shadow of something, but for the next two weeks, maybe they could forget it. That's what he was good at. Fun, frenzy, and forgetting. Because remembering was just too painful.

Chapter Two

T
he river is that way." Charles Farrington III pointed toward the broad river, whose blue-green waters rolled and tripped over rocks in a tempestuous whirl of white-water.

"I know." Abby wasn't going to try to explain anything to the fly-fishing novice. Their rods weren't weighted enough to hook a bass or for certain, a muskellunge. Those larger fish made for exciting catches, but if she *had* to take this interloper into her world, she may as well manage a little enjoyment in the process. Which meant she would border the river and wind parallel to it until she found her stream that fed into the Flambeau's waters and hid a special harvest of brook trout.

The rippling music of the stream met Abby's ears, and she couldn't help the slight smile that tilted her lips. She drew in a deep breath of peace as she ducked under a sweep-ing pine branch. It didn't matter that mister rich boy followed in her steps. No. At this moment, she was in her place of solitude. Every vibrant forest color reminded her of her paint palette back at the cabin that she shared with her father. Shades of rich evergreen, delightful moss, and touches of river-blue met with the glossy tones of browns and yellows that dotted and swept across the body of the trout they were about to snag.

"So, about the river. . ."

Abby waved Charles Farrington III to silence. The stream cut its delightful path through the forest, tumbled over a small rocky ledge, and wove around a corner where it would soon meet up with the river. She eyed the surface of the water, noting the undercut banks where the trout were sure to be lurking and watching for the water to be broken by the small vibration of a fly hitting its surface. Abby crouched by the water's edge, her fly rod held firmly in her left hand, and studied the water. There wasn't a hatch of flies this afternoon. She nodded. She knew what fly they would need. When she'd looked in her fly-box minutes earlier, she'd taken a guess. It was nice to know her instincts were right.

Charles Farrington III cleared his throat, and Abby stifled a retort, exchanging it for a sigh of long-suffering.

"Jonathon told me we'd be fishing the river." The man wasn't going to honor the golden wonder of silence, was he?

Abby straightened. She handed Charles Farrington III her fly rod and he reached for it to balance with his own. The tips of his fingers brushed hers and she darted a glance into his brown eyes. They sparked with life, like the forest around him, and it was all too apparent he hoped the physical touch would unnerve her.

Well, it didn't. Really. Truly. It didn't.

"My father is taking Mr. Strauss on the river today. I am taking you here."

"Wither thou goest, I shall go." His jaunty mockery of the Biblical passage from Ruth made Abby turn her attention to her fishing basket so she could hide the rolling of her eyes. The man wasn't even that fantastic at charming. He was. . .foolish. Handsome, but utterly foolish.

Abby pulled out her tin fly-box and opened it, the hinges splitting the box into two deep halves with flies hooked into the material she'd padded both sides with. Wet flies lined the case. Hooks she tied herself with thread and feathers. A small bead butted up against the eye of the hook, with thread woven around the shank and around feathers to make the soft body of the fly. She'd tied a tiny bit of feather at the bend in the hook and once again along the shank so they would imitate wings. The brown of the feathers would turn dark once wet, and the line, if properly maneuvered through the waters, would float the imitation fly directly past the waiting trout.

A waft of cologne drifted into Abby's senses. She was startled as she realized Charles Farrington III had nosed up behind her and was staring over her shoulder into her fly-box. The smell of him was rather intoxicating. Woody, citrusy, maybe even undertones of cardamom.

"Yes?" His dark eyebrow cocked quizzically, and Abby realized she'd been caught lingering on his face as she drifted away with the scent of his cologne.

Who wore cologne in the woods anyway?

"Give me the fly rod."

"Say 'please'?" His mouth titled upward in a smile.

Bother. He wasn't supposed to get under her skin. She was made of thicker stuff than this.

"Never mind." Abby snatched one of the rods he held in his grip, thankful to feel the familiar hexagonal shape of the pole. She spent the next few minutes preparing the line and tying the fly to it.

"You do know how to fly-fish, yes?" she asked as she adjusted the line with a turn of the circular reel.

Charles Farrington III crossed his arms over his chest in playful offense. "Most assuredly not."

Abby didn't try to hide her short sigh of exasperation. She pushed the rod into his hand and exchanged it for her rod which she propped against a tree. So much for fishing on her own. What rich dandy decided to travel by rail to the Northwoods to do something they had no inclination how to do?

"You'll teach me." His eyelid dropped in the fiftieth wink of the morning. He winked so often he was going to end up fishing with one eye closed!

"Do you have something in your eye?" Abby quipped as she held the fly in her fingers and smoothed back the feathers. The line swooped up to the rod Charles Farrington III held in strong, but sorely incapable hands.

He grinned, long dimples creasing both cheeks and emphasizing his square jaw. "I do. You."

Abby cast him a withering glare that only prompted a broader smirk. He waggled his eyebrows, which in turn made the toothpick in his mouth dance a jig.

"Teach me, my dear, the ways of a woman and a fly rod."

He wanted it to be all light and fluffy and silly, but Charles Farrington III was soon to find out that fly-fishing wasn't the same as tossing a worm and hook into the water with a spinning reel and winding it in. It was finesse and strategy. It was serious and contemplative. It was. . .art. Something Charles Farrington III obviously knew nothing about.

⊷ ◦◈◦ ⊶

By three o'clock in the afternoon, Charles found he'd stripped himself of his wool jacket, rolled up his shirtsleeves, and spent the better part of the last few hours attempting to avoid snagging every blasted, godforsaken tree branch that surrounded him. The smug look on Abigail Nessling's face did nothing to assuage his growing irritation. Jonathon and his fabulous idea of a woodland getaway. "*All the rage*," he'd said. "*Find oneself and one's peace with nature.*" Peace? Between the knotted fly line, hooking his hat with a brown, be-feathered fishing hook, and having absolutely no luck at all in garnering one smile from his feminine guide, Charles was ready to return to the cabin.

"Having fun?"

The bubble of humor in his pretty escort's voice helped him muster up some wit for the challenge.

"Quite!" he bantered back, while he spun and unwrapped the long line from around his shoulders.

"Mmm, hmm." Abby reached out and he willingly pushed the rod into her hands. Her eyes pierced him with the intense concentration of someone who took her sport very seriously. "I told you. Because we have all the trees around us, you can't sweep the line backward, it will tangle."

Charles watched Abby's fluid motion as she flipped the rod and somehow, the long wad of line draped through the air and rested on the water. The fly drifted just below the surface as the current carried it forward.

Abby was biting her bottom lip. Charles found himself watching that rather than the line.

"Mr. Farrington?"

He blinked. She was piercing him again with those eyes. "My apologies."

"You need to pay attention if you've any hope of fly-fishing."

He didn't have many hopes. Not really. But that was a thought he'd shove down like he always did. Hopes and dreams were flimsy creations. It was better to live in the moment until it passed by and left you searching for another momentary distraction.

"So you see where the line drapes from the tip of the rod and hits the water?"

"Yes." Fine, he'd play along.

"Make that your anchor. Hold your hand so it's about perpendicular to your mouth and then . . ." A flick of her wrist and twist of the rod and Abby had rolled the line over the stream and landed the fly back up the water, right along the edge of the shoreline. "Now, as the fly is carried down, you may need to pull the line in, just a tad. You don't want too much slack. Pull with your fingers, don't reel."

She mumbled on until Charles became quite content to watch her. She probably didn't even notice when he slouched against the base of the tree and finally, the afternoon's slog drained away. She was rather entrancing to watch. Abby didn't seem to care that he was hardly interested in fly-fishing, and instead, she engrossed herself in the study of the water.

Within a few minutes, her left hand gave a sharp pull to the line and her right yanked the rod up from the water.

"Fish on!" A smile broke over her face, something he'd been trying to coerce all day. Abby was an enigma. He could make almost any woman smile and simper and fan herself. But Abigail Nessling? No, she did that for a trout. Apparently, he needed to transform into a fish.

Charles scampered to his feet as Abby pulled in line, never bothering to drop her hand to the reel. A glistening trout flipped on the end of the line and Abby knelt on the shore, gliding her hand through the water until she grasped the trout gently.

A quick survey of the area, and Charles grabbed the fishing basket Abby had carried with them. He knelt beside her on the ground, her wispy blond hair escaping its braid and feather-brushing across his face. She ignored him as she carefully maneuvered the hook from the trout's jaw.

"Look at him," Abby breathed. Charles couldn't. She had altered from a stiff, rigid female to a woman enraptured by what she perceived to be beauty. "Look!" she urged.

Charles dropped his gaze to the fish in her hand. Its underside was golden and cream, and its back dotted with brown, black, and orange spots. It had tiger-like eyes and a gaping jaw. Okay. It was—pretty. If a fish could be called that.

Abby lowered her hand and urged the trout back into the water. With a flip of its tail, it twisted and disappeared back into the riffle.

"Hey!" Charles drew back with a quizzical frown. "That's my supper!"

Abby straightened and for the first time, cast him a brilliant smile encased with sugary-sweet mischief. "No, no, Charles Farrington *the Third*. That was *my* fish." She pushed the rod into his hands. "If you want supper, you'll need to catch your own."

She pushed herself from the creek bank and sauntered over to the tree he'd been half-dozing against, making herself comfortable by its base. She gave him a small wave of her hand. "The fish are biting. Have a go!"

Oy, that saucy little self had been hiding inside of her all along. Charles grinned and tightened his hold on the rod. Suddenly, fly-fishing held a much greater appeal. If for no other reason than to show Abigail Nessling that she wasn't the only one who was master of mischief.

Chapter Three

Campfire smoke drifted through the air and the fire crackled, making the cool, late summer night even more pleasant. Charles glanced across the clearing to the Nessling cabin. They were a fascinating pair, Abby and her father. Living in one cabin while renting out another to people like him and Jonathon. It had to be an adventurous life, if not lacking some privacy as they invited strangers into their beloved wilderness. Mr. Nessling was welcoming and very hospitable, but Abby, for certain, didn't make much attempt to hide her disdain of wealthy vacationers such as himself and Jonathon.

Speak of the devil.

Jonathon lowered himself onto a log and poked at the campfire with a stick. Contentment etched itself into every crevice of the man's face, and Charles was struck with jealousy—and not for the first time. Must be nice to be secure in one's future, doing what one loved, with a family that took you as you were.

"Well, this was a fine day!" Jonathon rested the stick in the fire and leaned his elbows on his knees. "And a fish dinner you won't find anywhere in Milwaukee."

Charles nodded. The crusty, blackened, campfire-fried bass had been good. Would've been better had he added some trout to the mix, but nope. Nope, Abby had made sure to smile cheekily as he finished out the day unwinding, unwrapping, and unhooking his way to an empty fishing basket.

Jonathon's chuckles interrupted Charles's thoughts. "I knew she'd get under your skin."

Charles frowned. "Who?"

Jonathon tipped his blond head toward the Nessling cabin. "Abby. Tried to charm your way into her good graces, didn't you?"

Charles curled his lip and tossed a pine cone into the fire. It snapped and popped, the sap boiling on one of its wooden petals. "A tad."

"Told you she was off limits."

Charles shrugged. "Never stopped me before."

Jonathon stretched his arms wide then drew them back and interlocked his fingers behind his head. "Abby has always been a fine friend."

"Then why haven't you courted her?" Charles honestly wanted to know. Courting was serious business and not something he hankered for, but Jonathon? He was the sensible, family man type, and the Strauss family might be wealthy and stand on pretense, but they were also of deep faith. Charles didn't think the financial differences between families would stop Jonathon if he were serious about Abby.

Jonathon smiled as he stared at the fire. "My father and Mr. Nessling go way back. They grew up together but had different goals. Mr. Nessling came north and worked in the logging camps. Dad always said Harry was of the earth and he was of the city. Same with

Abby and me. She'd never survive in Milwaukee, and I wouldn't ask her to. I would never survive here. It's nice for a getaway, but nothing more. Besides. . ." Jonathon dropped his arms and reached for the stick he'd placed in the fire. Its tip glowed and then crumbled into the coals. "I've only seen Abby nigh on four times in my life. While I think the world of her, we don't have that—that"—he waved the end of the stick to make his point—"spark."

Spark. That was all Charles felt when he was around Abby. This morning he'd been rather fascinated with her mouth and that little spot on her neck at the bottom of her ear. Very kissable. Now, he wanted to wring her neck for making him wrestle with that daft fly rod all afternoon and catch nothing.

The Nesslings' cabin door opened and Mr. Nessling exited, running his thumbs down the length of his suspenders. He cast them a wave and retreated around the back of the cabin.

"Mr. Nessling is a good sort," Jonathon observed. "Shame about his wife."

"His wife?" Charles watched the open door of the cabin, but Abby didn't appear.

Jonathon nodded. "She died about a year ago. Mr. Nessling had just bought this land with his earnings, my dad said. Planned to retire from logging and offer expeditions to folks like us."

"Rotten luck to work your whole life and lose your wife when you finally settle in to what you want to do," Charles muttered, trying to ignore the memories that surfaced.

"Luck? Nah." Jonathon tossed his stick onto the fire for good. "God knows we all have a designated time and place." Charles could feel his buddy give him an indirect glance. Jonathon continued, as Charles knew he would, as he always did. "Grief is hard to master though, even when that loss is nobody's fault."

Charles vaulted to his feet and kicked at a renegade coal, knocking it into the campfire. "Yeah. Sure." He steered for their cabin, for his cot, and wished he was more like his father. A drink would be nice right now. But that was just another difference between them. Charles had seen liquor do its damage in his family and distanced his father even further.

Jonathon's voice stopped him. "You need to stop blaming yourself, Charles."

Charles rammed his hands into his pockets. Stop blaming himself? That was difficult to do when it'd been made clear to him that it was his fault that David was dead. That he should have saved his brother. He had failed. Plain and simple. It was why he kept moving. To stop, to think, meant he had to relive it all again.

He spun on his heel with a jaunty smile. Flippant but weighted with meaning. "Devil knows I should've learned how to swim better."

At the stunned look on his friend's face, Charles marched into the cabin. He should have become a stronger swimmer, way back when he was fourteen instead of a handful of trouble. If he had, David would still be alive.

◆━━●◆●━━◆

Nights like tonight, Abby missed her mother more than usual. She cupped her coffee mug between her palms and stared out the window, across the way, toward the men's campfire. Mama had a way of softening Abby's edgier side. It was Mama's voice that kept Abby from uttering her snippy thoughts most of the time, but this afternoon? She had been a horrendous guide to Charles Farrington III—even if he *did* deserve it.

She took a sip of coffee and eyed Jonathon as he sat alone by the campfire. She'd watched him and Charles have some sort of tense interaction, and then Charles had disappeared inside. This couldn't be good. Not for her father. She'd be willing to bet that Charles was fed up with the defeating day and complaining about it to Jonathon.

Abby bit her bottom lip and sighed. She needed to muster every ounce of her mother's hospitality and shower it on Charles Farrington III or else it would all go awry.

The cabin door opened, and she met her father's gaze as he entered. His smile matched the warmth in his eyes. His beard was flecked with more gray since Mama had died, and the color streaked through his temples, almost clouding out his once very black eyebrows.

"Hey, teacup."

Teacup. He'd always called her his "spot of tea." As if she were his one joy in the middle of a hard afternoon.

Abby mustered an apologetic smile. She had to get it off her conscience now. "I'm so sorry, Papa."

Papa frowned, shutting the cabin door behind him.

"Mr. Farrington. I—I don't believe I did a proper job of teaching him to fly-fish today."

The *clink* of the kettle against a tin coffee cup met her ears in response. The sound of liquid pouring into her father's cup followed. He sniffed. Sipped. Swallowed.

"He's a bit of a rascal."

For sure and for certain! Abby refrained from being sidetracked from her confession. She turned and almost tripped over a furry little creature that danced around her toes. Smiling, she bent and held out her hand. The squirrel her father had rescued as a baby earlier in the spring had grown exponentially and was wholeheartedly the third member of their little cabin home. It scampered into her hand and Abby clutched it, bringing it higher so it could jump onto her shoulder. Perching on its hind legs, the squirrel looked between her and her father and back at Abby.

So be it. Even Harold the squirrel wanted her to make her confession more absolute. Harold pawed at her hair and then scuttled down her back to jump onto the windowsill. His bushy tail swung back and forth.

Papa seated himself at the table, his hands wrapped around his mug. Abby gave Harold a fast scratch on his head and moved to join her father.

"Mr. Farrington doesn't know how to fly-fish, and I didn't have much patience with him today."

"Mmm, hm." Papa gulped his coffee. Waiting. As he always did. He was a man of few words, even more so since Mama had passed.

Abby pressed on. "I don't believe Mr. Farrington was very happy with me. And if he returns to Milwaukee with a negative review, well—"

"Now wait." Papa held up his hand. "There's going to be days when our guests struggle. They're not used to the woods, to fishing or hunting. That's why they come here. To experience something new."

"But what if they don't believe they're getting the service they paid for?" Abby argued. Harold scratched at the windowpane and stole her father's attention for a moment.

"We can only do our best, teacup."

"But that's just it!" Abby remembered Charles Farrington III's teasing eyes, flirtatious and incessant winking, and his intoxicating smell. "I didn't do my best."

Silence followed her confession. Harold leapt from the windowsill, scurried across the floor, and up the leg of the chair to take his place on Abby's lap. She rubbed his back with her finger and waited. Papa took a drink of coffee, then another, and finally set his empty cup on the table.

"Well," he concluded, "there's always tomorrow."

Tomorrow. The word sank into Abby like a metal sinker on a spinning rod. Charles Farrington III was still going to be here in the morning, and the morning after, and. . .he wasn't going to be a problem that just went away.

Chapter Four

She'd hoped Papa would take Charles Farrington III and she could guide Jonathon today. It would be so much simpler. This two-week excursion was going to seem like two years if she had to spend every day with this man.

"How's the beautiful Miss Nessling this morning?" Charles Farrington III met her at the workbench on the side of her cabin. His cavalier stance put Abby on edge, not to mention he was chewing on a silly toothpick again. No, no. She couldn't be jittery already. She needed to be sweet, hospitable, welcoming . . . She met his chocolate eyes, and the twinkle in them made her look away.

Charles Farrington III moved closer to see what she was working on. She was packing a fishing basket, for goodness' sakes, it wasn't that exciting! *Back away, sir, back away.* Abby could smell his cologne. Maybe the flies and mosquitos would, too, and he'd be eaten alive, forced to retreat back to his cabin.

As she chided herself for her mean thoughts, she also tried to quell the excited twist of her stomach that his presence caused. Her body froze as she felt his hand rise and his fingers fondle a strand of her hair that escaped her braid. The back of his knuckles brushed her neck. Good heavens! He was bold, daring, attractive... She could probably write lists of adjectives to describe the indecency that was Charles Farrington III. She opened her mouth to protest but was stopped by a flurry of red.

"Mother of—*Moses!*" Charles Farrington III leapt backward, spitting out his toothpick, as Harold alighted on the tabletop, his red tail swiping across the man's hand.

Abby pressed her lips together as she attempted not to laugh at the man's quickly abbreviated curse and the incredulous look on his face as he met Harold's challenging, black-eyed stare. The squirrel chattered at him.

"You've a squirrel as a guard dog?"

Abby graced him with a stern smile. "Harold is quite protective of me, yes, Charles Farrington *the Third*, and his teeth are razor sharp."

"Charles. *Charles.* This whole 'Farrington the Third' bit is loathsome." He held out a finger toward Harold, who nattered on louder. "But he is a cute little fellow."

Abby raised her eyes to the heavens. *Lord, give me grace.* She batted Charles Farrington the–fine, *Charles's*–finger away. "He *will* bite you."

Charles withdrew but tilted his head to the side. "Does he fish with you?"

"Sometimes." Abby didn't bother to tell Charles that she was trying to break the habit of locking Harold in the cabin for fear an owl or hawk would swoop down and eat her only friend. He was meant to be free, only she didn't want him to be.

"Well. Are we to begin, your beautiful highness?"

The words. Oh, the words! He was pithy and shallow, and... Abby swallowed as he gifted her with a lazy smile.

"Yes," she responded. Graciousness. Her mother always touted graciousness in the face of distress. But most of Abby's tenacity to be amiable fled with Mama when she died. There didn't seem to be all that much to be gracious about.

"Do we get to fish the river today?"

Abby shook her head. "I was thinking the stream."

"Very well."

He was so agreeable it was sickening. Abby handed him a fly rod that leaned against the work table. "Here. While I prepare a few things, why don't you practice casting in the clearing."

Charles reached for the rod, but Abby held onto it even after he gave it a little tug. She skewered him with what she hoped wasn't too patronizing of a look. "Watch for the trees."

His grin broadened, deepening those ever-present dimples. "But it'd be delightful to watch you climb one to retrieve my hook."

Abby released the rod and Charles gave her a wink as he spun on his booted heel and marched into the clearing between the cabins with purpose in his stride. His wide shoulders made his cotton shirt taut over his upper arms as he lifted the fly rod, and dark curls teased his collar. He was completely insufferable. It was important she remember that.

<hr/>

The sharp sting, followed by the inarguable feel of the hook piercing his skin, stilled Charles's forward motion with the rod. His left eye shut, he reached up with his hand and felt. If the pinching pain wasn't enough evidence, the feel of the fly against the corner of his eye was plenty to verify the hook that was embedded in his skin.

There wasn't a manly way in the world he could explain himself out of this one. With the line swinging from the hook hinged at his eye and attached to the fly rod, only humor could save his pride now. Humor, and hopes that Abby knew how to unhook more than a trout from her fly.

"Miss Nessling?"

She didn't answer. Charles twisted and saw her petite form bent over her workbench. A tiny hook was clamped in a brace, and she wrapped thread around the hook's shank. Her silence either meant she was half-deaf, or she was ignoring him. Charles knew it was the latter. He'd had absolutely no effect on the woman but to peeve her more, and while that had bothered him even up to a few minutes ago, it was a non-existent worry now as his eye began to throb.

"Abby?"

Silence.

"Ahem!" He cleared his throat.

Another wrap of the thread.

"I believe I've caught something." Maybe that would get her attention.

It did. She raised her blonde head and turned those ginger eyes on him. They narrowed, then widened, and her face paled to a color even whiter than her hair.

"Oh my. Oh my!" She clapped her palm to her mouth.

Charles swallowed. His eye twitched and tears squeezed from it as his eye reacted to the painful proximity of the foreign object in his face.

"I could use your assistance." He couldn't deny there was a plea in his voice now.

Charles was still attached to the fly rod and it would be nice to at least cut ties with the split-cane pole.

Abby slumped onto a stool. She shook her head. "No, no. I can't. No."

"What do you mean, *you can't?*" This wasn't good. Charles took a step toward her and Abby turned even paler, swaying in her seat.

"I'm not medically inclined." Her whisper was a pathetic protest against the pain he was beginning to experience. This was not the reaction he'd expected from plucky Abigail Nessling.

"It's not surgery, Abby, it's prying a hook out of my face before I'm permanently scarred for life." An exaggeration. But neither of them seemed prone to rationality.

The tiny fly-fishing guide slipped from the stool in a graceful motion...and crumpled.

"For the love of—!" Charles bit his oath and marched toward Abby, fly rod still gripped in his hand because, well, what else was a man to do when he was attached to it?

———◦•◦———

"This is a fine kettle of fish you got yourself into." Abby's father had a twinkle in his eye. Charles would have looked away, but Mr. Nessling also had hold of the fly still embedded in Charles's skin.

"Very funny," Charles smirked. It was providential that Jonathon and Mr. Nessling had chosen to return to the cabins to retrieve one of their fly rods they'd accidentally left behind. They found Charles gently slapping Abby's face. Jonathon was quick to take over this task and let Mr. Nessling ply his hook-removal expertise.

Mr. Nessling wiggled the hook and Charles winced. Blasted thing hurt like the dickens. "I'm afraid I'm not the most talented at casting."

Mr. Nessling didn't respond. Charles waited, and decided to try again.

"But your daughter is a fine teacher."

"Mmm, hm." Mr. Nessling wiggled the hook again, and Charles wondered if there was some sadistic side to the older man that was enjoying the twinge of nerves it sent through Charles's face.

"She has quite the way about her."

"Abigail is sensitive." Mr. Nessling's response held a warning tone in it. *Don't play with her emotions*, Charles could almost hear the man say.

"Of course," Charles responded.

Mr. Nessling's finger pushed firmly against Charles's skin at the base of where the hook was embedded. Charles squinted in pain and Mr. Nessling let up. He leaned back and gave Charles a square look.

"You can't wince, Mr. Farrington. I won't be able to get the hook out if you do."

"My apologies." Charles focused on keeping his expression still as Mr. Nessling pressed again, twisted the hook, and then tugged.

"Good heavens almighty holy–" Charles searched for every acceptable almost-curse he could find. Mr. Nessling held the fly up and eyed it as he extended a clean handkerchief to Charles.

"Push that against the wound. The bleeding will stop under the pressure."

Charles held the cloth to his face.

Mr. Nessling waggled the fly in front of him. "Souvenir?"

"No thanks." Charles grimaced.

Mr. Nessling tossed the fly into a tin bucket and scratched at his peppered-gray hair before leveling a stern eye on Charles.

Nothing like feeling like an eight-year-old kid who just hit his baseball through the window. Charles waited. He could tell Mr. Nessling had something to say, and he wasn't in the mood to quip in return.

"Abigail's mama died last year. She's turned into herself since then. When she decides to break free from her grief, I need someone there to catch her. 'Cause she's going to fall hard and it isn't going to be pretty."

Charles waited. He could tell this wasn't going in his favor.

Mr. Nessling gave Charles's shoulder a decisive slap that communicated the firm protectiveness of a father. "She doesn't need to be caught by a philandering boy who pretends to be a man. She needs a true man."

The older man's words jabbed into Charles's conscience, irked his pride, and ripped into his own assessment of himself.

"Yeah," he muttered at Mr. Nessling's back as Abby's father headed toward the cabin. *A "boy."* He'd never really grown up past the age of fourteen. The day David died and time had stopped.

Chapter Five

Abby was relieved that today her father had decided to guide Charles and that Jonathon traipsed beside her to the stream. She'd done a miserable job of giving Charles any sort of a pleasant experience fishing, and the concern of him returning to Milwaukee to his adventurous cohorts with a negative review weighed on her. If he continued to skewer his eyes, catch trees, and fail at attracting her admiration, then he'd share that throughout the upper echelons of his social scale. Papa could bid farewell to any recommendations. They needed these wealthy guests to trifle away their leisure time in the great "Up-North." It was her father's and her livelihood. Jonathon would share his pleasantries, Abby was sure, but somehow she knew Charles's extra-flamboyant personality would speak far louder than Jonathon's reserved one.

"I've been looking forward to trying my hand at the smaller fish." Jonathon's quiet conversation was restful to Abby. She smiled and pointed toward a bend in the creek.

"You'll want to drop the fly about seven feet up from that bend. Let it drift down and around the crook. My guess is there are trout waiting in the undercut there."

"Perfect." With expert finesse, Jonathon followed her instruction, feeding out line so it could float down the water. A flash and disruption of the surface, and Jonathon tugged his line, snagging a trout. He pulled the line through the guides on the rod, steering the trout toward them.

Abby crouched on the bank and extended a small fishing net. Jonathon steered the trout toward it and Abby scooped it up.

This was fly-fishing guiding at its best, its most relaxing. No flirtatious undertone, no expectations, no charming comments meant to entice her, and most assuredly no winking—not that Charles could wink now. His eye had been swollen this morning. If she hadn't passed dead away at the sight of the hook hanging from his eye yesterday, she might have laughed, but as it was, she had no grounds to mock. She only hoped Charles's horrid day was being forgotten as he canoed down the Flambeau River with her father for a leisurely day of sightseeing and testing some exciting white water.

"So, how are you doing?"

Jonathon's question jerked Abby from her thoughts. The fish that she'd captured in the net was now unhooked and flopping in Jonathon's fishing basket. Goodness. Her mind had wandered far away in a very fast period of time.

"Abby?"

She shook her head more to clear her thoughts than anything. "Fine. I'm fine." She reached for Jonathon's fly rod so she could check the lure, but he pulled it back. His green eyes were searching, brotherly, caring. Sometimes Abby wished there was an attraction between them. He was kind, and everything a good man should be. Contrary to Charles.

"Abigail, you've been distracted today, and *fainting*? Since when does Abigail Nessling faint at the sight of a hook?"

"It was in his eye," Abby muttered, and busied herself with her tin fly-box. It was in perfect order, as usual, but rearranging the flies seemed like a good idea.

Jonathon crossed his arms and she could sense his gaze burning into her. "You're not fine."

Abby drew her brows together in a frown. She toyed with the brown feathered wings of a fly. "You don't know me well enough to have an opinion, Jonathon."

His warm hand closed around hers, pausing her frenetic fondling of the collection of hooks and feathers. Abby lifted her eyes and studied his. Concern etched itself in the corners of them, and he tipped his head to the side. The sound of the rippling creek danced musically in Abby's ears as she breathed deep, inhaling the scent of the woods. The moist smell of wet earth, the fresh breeze that rustled through the leaves of the trees. What could she say? There was nothing to say. She would never be fine. Not content as she had been before Mama passed away. But none of that was Jonathon's business. Nor was it Charles Farrington III's.

"Abby." Jonathon's gentle tone made her shift her gaze away to the water.

"There's fish waiting to be caught," she mumbled. She pulled her hand away.

"You're avoiding me."

"Jonathon." Abby sucked in a deep breath and decided to face him. "I'm fine. I'll be fine. I'm just—tired and concerned."

"Concerned?"

"Yes. This—this guiding business is father's livelihood now. He's too old to work in the logging camps, and this was his and Mama's dream. I need to help him make it work. *I* need to make it work."

"But you need to give yourself time to grieve, Abby."

Abby nodded. "I did. I have."

"Have you? Really?"

"Please, Jonathon. We're here to fish. Let's fish."

He cleared his throat and leaned back against a tree. It was apparent he had no intention of letting the subject rest. "I know we live in two different worlds—"

"Very different," she interrupted. She tossed her fly-box to the ground. He didn't know. He didn't understand. Mama's dying, Abby trying to fill her shoes, trying to be a woman that would make her proud, all while knowing that Papa was getting older and one day she would need to care for him, by herself. They needed money, but this crazy dream of Papa's—to let rich, devil-may-care people tromp through her sanctuary—was not going to suffice for the long term. Bitterness and hurt rose in her stomach, clutching at her heart and squeezing until for a moment, Abby thought she really might cry. But not tears of grief. Tears of frustration, of anger, and unresolved desperation.

She yanked her fly rod to her from where it leaned against a tree. Clawing at the line, she busied herself with unraveling a knot that had somehow formed.

"Talk to me, please." Jonathon's low voice ripped at her deepest frustration. It was people like him, like Charles Farrington III. If she'd had what they had . . .

"It doesn't matter anymore. Mama is dead." Abby could hear the sharp edge to her voice. An edge that belied the facade of calm she tried to portray.

"Abby?"

The sound of her name tipped her control. Abby shoved her rod away from her and it fell abandoned to the forest floor. She locked eyes with her friend.

"If people like you and—and Charles—could understand, just for one day, what it's like to watch your family die in front of you and know there is nothing you can do! But you? You have all the money in the world and you toss it our direction to catch a *fish*! A fish! If I'd had that money for Mama, to save her, to get her the medical care she needed? Our lives might be different. But fishing? Canoeing? That's what bothers me, Jonathon. It's frivolous and unimportant entertainment. People like Charles throw it away as if it's nothing to them. He acts all charming, while I'm thinking if I only had a pittance of his allowance I could have taken Mama to the city to get help. His money might have saved her life, but he's spending it to do something he doesn't even have the coordination to do! That is what is bothering me, Jonathon; that is what has me ripped up inside. I lost my mama, while people like Charles Farrington *the Third* play as if they're completely unaware of the heartache around them. Pain they could take part in assuaging if they would put their priorities into others who are hurting."

Jonathon's brows furrowed. "So you're wanting charity?"

Abby swallowed. Hard. "No one wants charity, Jonathon, but if someone with Charles's financial situation had extended any sort of assistance, I would've begged my father to take it." She knew she was also throwing her bitter spear at Jonathon's own personal wealth and his choices to spend money on leisure while others in the world suffered around him. But she had said too much now to retract it. "I would have taken anything to save Mama. I would have begged. So, it's difficult to swallow that Charles Farrington the Third can toss money on a wilderness venture and be all carefree, when money like that may have saved her life."

There wasn't much more Jonathon could say, so Abby saved him the trouble and bent to retrieve her fly rod from the ground.

— ••• —

Her words hit him in the gut like the fist of an angry opponent. Charles froze, his foot in midstride. Maybe it was an accident that Mr. Nessling had steered Charles toward the river, following the same trail he'd hiked with Abby. But it couldn't be an accident that he'd heard her words. God had an ironic sense of humor—a jaded one.

Carefree? As if he'd spent an honest carefree day in his life! If only Abigail Nessling understood. Poor people, woodsmen, logging families didn't have proprietary rights over loss!

Charles fought against the urge to storm from behind the trees that hid him to confront her. To tell her what it was like to strain through the currents to get to his brother's flailing form. To try to swim strong enough, fast enough, and still be too late. It was his fault his brother was dead. If he hadn't instigated playing hooky from school and going down by the river to toss stones, and if he hadn't mocked David for being too afraid to swim a few yards out into the river, David might still be alive.

Dying had nothing to do with money. It had to do with horrible fate, human error, and in the end, someone had to bear the blame. Either God or man. In Charles's case, he knew it wasn't God's fault. It was his.

Charles took a step, but a strong hand held him back. The fingers tightened into his bicep that was flexed with sheer tension of the moment. He swung around and Mr. Nessling's stern gaze slammed into him.

"Leave it be. You have enough to bear on your own."

How did Mr. Nessling know? How did the older man who was so protective of his precious daughter, know that Charles bore a similar agony? Jonathon. It had to have been. Charles should have known Jonathon would confide in an old family friend. The very thought that Mr. Nessling knew Charles's shame frustrated him.

"Yeah. Sure." Charles wrestled his arm away and raked his fingers through his hair. A black fly landed on his forearm and he took great pleasure in slapping it with his free hand so hard he had to wipe it off on his pants.

"That way." Mr. Nessling pointed away from the clearing and the creek, where silence had fallen between Jonathon and Abby. What could Jonathon say? He was as rich as Charles, and while he probably didn't seem as carefree and impulsive, Abby's words would have their own effect on him.

A squirrel darted across the trail and Charles wondered briefly if it was Abby's squirrel, Harold. But then he knew it wasn't. She was too protective of it. She wouldn't want another loved one to die, even if it was a squirrel.

"It's good Jonathon got Abby to talk." Mr. Nessling's words sliced through the silence as they hiked toward the river.

"Yeah." There wasn't anything else to say to that. He glanced at his guide. Mr. Nessling had a reflective expression on his face, as if coming to new realizations himself. Maybe he'd never heard Abby's turbulent opinions before?

Charles swiped a branch from his path. He could hear the river in the distance. It'd be nice to deviate from the strategic sweep of a fly line to attacking the water with an oar and slicing through it with a canoe. The whitewater would match his angst, even if water in general always conjured up images he preferred to forget.

Mr. Nessling hiked past him and onto the rocky shoreline. A canoe lay overturned, and he maneuvered it right side up and pushed the bow into the water.

Charles took advantage of the moment to take in a deep breath and steady his nerve. He rested his hands at his waist, eyeing the calm, wide waters of the Flambeau River bordered by narrow shorelines and thick, green woodland.

"No money would have saved my wife."

Charles jerked from his thoughts as Mr. Nessling pulled paddles from inside the canoe. The man strode across the rocks and handed one to Charles. Charles took it, but Mr. Nessling didn't release it. There was a stricken look behind the frankness of the man's gaze that affected Charles more than he was willing to admit.

Mr. Nessling turned away. "I know you heard what Abby said. She thinks if we'd had money that we could have gotten my wife to an institution, to treat her lungs, to help her breathe."

So Abby's mother had died of consumption? Charles grimaced. It was a dreadful way to go.

"I'm sorry," he muttered. 'Cause what did a rich man say when he was talking to a widower moments after the man's daughter claimed philanthropists' money could've saved her mother?

"Not your fault." Mr. Nessling released the paddle. He hiked back over to the canoe and straddled the stern. "Get in. I'll hold it to keep it from tipping."

Charles bit back a sigh and followed Mr. Nessling's lead. The guide clenched the narrow back of the canoe between his knees, allowing Charles to step into the boat. It still tilted in the water, and Charles dropped the paddle and clutched at the sides.

"Keep your body low," Mr. Nessling directed. "Canoes like to throw you."

Wonderful. He was an epic wilderness failure. Charles slunk along until he slouched his backside onto the seat in the front of the canoe. Mr. Nessling shoved the canoe farther into the river and then climbed in, his paddle knocking against the side. The canoe wobbled in the water and then settled as Mr. Nessling found his seating. He used his oar to push against the bottom of the river and the canoe shoved out into the water.

"If I'd only known she felt that way. . ." Mr. Nessling's voice trailed away with the swipe of his paddle through blue-green water.

Charles didn't respond. The older man continued as if lost in memories and maybe the new realization of his daughter's private angst.

"Jonathon's father telegraphed me when my wife was sick. He offered to pay for her to get the care Abby thinks she needed."

Mr. Nessling swiped through the water again, the canoe surging forward. A duck, flustered and spooked, quacking angrily as its wings beat the water and it took to flight.

"Why didn't you let him pay for it?" Charles couldn't help but ask.

Silence.

Another swipe of the paddle, another slice of the bow through the water.

"It was too late. We knew it wouldn't help. Abby's mama wanted to pass at home."

"And you never told Abby that Mr. Strauss would've helped if you'd accepted?"

"Nope. Never thought she needed to know it."

Charles twisted in his seat to look at his guide. The canoe rocked and Mr. Nessling gave him a warning glance to hold still.

"Why not?" Charles would give anything if someone could explain away the pointlessness of David's death.

"'Cause Abby never asked."

"Pardon?"

Mr. Nessling swallowed, and Charles noticed his throat bob with held-back emotion. "I've never heard her speak of my wife's death. Until today."

Charles turned to face the water. The only sound was the ripples in the water, and the strokes of Mr. Nessling's paddle. It was true, Charles had to admit to himself. When a person was bitter over the death of a loved one, no amount of talking would ever make it better. Not talking, not money, not anything.

Chapter Six

There was nothing sweeter than morning's fresh air, with the green blanket of leaves overhead dripping spots of dew on the ground. Abby took a moment to close her eyes and breathe deep. When she opened her eyes, the morning's sunlight cast sparkling rays through the branches and across her canvas. Painting. It was her other escape, here in the solitude of the forest and in the shadow of the cabins. She dotted the canvas with her brush, taking a sweep across its middle, splitting the sky from the earth. Her paintings were always landscape paintings, with different-colored skies—some sunsets, some blue, and some sunrises. Trees splitting and bordering the canvas. A river. Home. But always in the distance, she painted shadows of new lands. Hints of hope, of future, of something that was just always out of reach.

Harold skittered up to her feet and chattered, a nut held between his front paws. Abby smiled down at the squirrel, but hints of the sadness embraced her heart.

"Be safe, little one," she whispered, and Harold scampered into the forest. Could she always shut the wild creature in the cabin, refusing to let him find his way? There was something symbolic about the broken little squirrel. Broken like her spirit. But unlike her, Harold was finding his way somehow.

Abby dabbed at the canvas as a whiff of coffee greeted her senses. She heard footsteps behind her. Papa often enjoyed venturing into the morning with his coffee, before the day had fully begun.

"I know it's similar to my painting last week," she acknowledged. Papa didn't respond. Abby continued with another few taps to the canvas. "I can't seem to break out of these landscapes. It's as if I'm trapped here."

"Imprisoned in the woods? Or in your grief?"

The voice was not her father's. It rippled through her and stirred emotions she didn't welcome. She spun on her stool, paintbrush held midair, and locked eyes with Charles. For a long moment, it was as if the span between them magnetized and they came together. Spirits colliding in unlikely camaraderie. But just as quickly, Abby gave her head a slight shake and the distance returned. She was in her chair. Charles stood a few yards away, hand wrapped around his coffee cup, suspenders stretched over broad shoulders. The only difference was how different they truly were.

Or were they?

He dipped his head to take a chug of his coffee, but his dark eyes were raised over the rim of his cup. Unspoken words. A challenge? As if he dared her to be honest, as she had been with Jonathon, as she had not been with her father. For a moment, she wondered if somehow he'd overheard her conversation with Jonathon. The expression on his face was a challenge.

Yes. I'm angry. I'm bitter at people like you who hold my future, my mother's future, in your rich hands and ignore the world of pain that swirls around you.

Charles didn't answer. He couldn't. He couldn't have read her thoughts. But yet, it seemed as if he had. He reached over and rested his coffee on the workbench. She noted the bruised eye as he once again connected with her. This time he closed the distance between them, and crouched before her as she rested in her chair.

"Abby." The muttered name stirred her frayed emotions. She froze as his hand rose with hesitancy, laden with intent. Her eyes closed as his palm rested against her face. "You're not alone." His words rifled through her, and before she could even breathe, or process, or *feel*, Charles was leaning forward, his lips touching hers. Featherlight and then intense. His fingers curled into her hair and she leaned into him.

What were they sharing? This man who rankled every part of her, this man she'd only known for a few days? Whose only intent was to charm—and yet, as his mouth caressed her, she felt—no she *knew*—there was something deeper. Something more. The chasm that kept them separated by miles, bridged as the unspoken bonding of their souls brought an unspoken understanding. . .

There was grief in his kiss.

And she tasted the salt of her own tears.

———◦◦◦———

He sensed her withdraw only moments before her palms shoved against his shoulders. Charles fell backward, the taste of her and her tears still on his mouth.

"Abby . . ."

"No." She shook her head, her fingertips pressed against her mouth. "That shouldn't have happened." She swiped at the renegade tears, her face pale.

Charles knew the pain he'd awakened. Pain that he experienced every day. He'd known since yesterday, overhearing her conversation with Jonathon, and by talking to Mr. Nessling, that she needed to release it. Maybe he couldn't be free of his, but she couldn't carry this bitterness that convinced her something could have been done. There was part of him that wanted to prove to her that people like Jonathon—like *him*—wouldn't have flippantly dismissed her mother's illness. Charles didn't know why it was important to him that she knew that, but it was.

"It's no one's fault, Abby," he stated as he stood.

She whirled toward her painting. Her brush attacked the canvas in broad, erratic sweeps. Charles could see the tears that raced down her face, unwanted and invading her self-imposed guard over her heart. She spun to face him, paintbrush in midair once again.

"Stop interfering. You're here for an experience, but not with me! I'm not a plaything!"

Charles tugged a tin from his pocket and flipped it open, fumbling for a toothpick. Anything to keep his hands busy. She thought him a playboy, someone who toyed with a woman's heart and then tossed it aside when another pretty face made her appearance. Fine. Maybe she was right. He stuck a toothpick between his teeth and bit down. But not today. Not with her. She was. . .fragile. He understood Abby in ways he'd never empathized with a woman before.

She stalked toward him, the paintbrush dripping paint down its shaft and onto her fingers. "I want you to go home."

Charles blinked.

"Go home," she repeated. "Even if you tell all of Milwaukee what a horrible place we have and how pathetic our backwoods fishing and expeditions are. Ruin us if you must, but don't ever do that again!"

Her brush connected with his chest, leaving a swath of blue paint across his shirt. Charles grabbed her wrists before she could transfer her angst further.

"Abby, stop. That wasn't what I meant by that kiss."

She pulled against him, her eyes wide, like a frightened woodland creature. "Then what was your intention? Besides making me act like some wanton woman and taking advantage of me?"

What was his intention, indeed? He adjusted his grip on her wrists as she struggled. Maybe there was no intention other than some need to connect with her, to be a part of her, to share that horrific loss they both felt, but neither could forgive.

Abby stopped fighting his grip. Her eyes were huge in her pasty white face, with tears brimming. "I wish you would go home."

"Stop it, Abby. Your mother dying wasn't my fault!" He barked out the proclamation without further thought. "It wasn't Jonathon's fault! All the money in the world couldn't have saved her."

Abby tore herself from his restraints and her hand connected with his face before he could duck. The sting of her slap echoed with the sound of it. A bird fluttered from the bushes. They stared at each other. Abby's chest rose and fell with agitated breaths. Her eyes had dried, and anger emanated from every pore.

"How dare you!"

"I dare because I know what it's like to carry unresolved burdens." Charles rubbed his face where her hand had most assuredly left a red stain. He bent until he could feel her breath on his face. Their eyes were locked in a silent combat, daring the other to outdo their own personal grief. "Death doesn't belong to you."

Abby's eyes widened. Ginger pools of angst. "I never said it did."

Charles pointed back toward her cabin but never unlocked his eyes from her face. "What if your father *did* have the monetary resources offered them to get medical treatment for your mother? What if they chose, together, to decline it?"

She shook her head, blond tendrils of hair brushing her forehead.

"Because," Charles continued, uncaring now whether he hurt her worse or saved her. She needed to know and apparently no one had the courage—or maybe idiocy—to tell her. "Your mother didn't want to leave home. She wanted to die at home."

"Stop," Abby whispered.

"Jonathon's father offered to pay, Abby. Your mother refused."

"You don't know this." Abby shook her head, her arms crossing over her chest.

"I do. Your father told me yesterday." Charles watched as color leaked from Abby's face. "When we overheard you and Jonathon. When you blamed people like me for not caring."

He was angry now. Angry that she would label him shallow, uncaring, and soulless. She didn't see inside of him any more than she'd allowed her father to see inside of her. It was easy to draw conclusions about someone when you couldn't get into their soul.

"I care, Abigail Nessling." Charles backed away a step. He could almost forget that he'd kissed her. To make her release that pent-up emotion that he shared. Now, he regretted it.

He couldn't forget her kiss, the feel of her, and it made him furious. Furious that he'd allow it to affect him. The reverse had happened. The kiss had opened him up as well, and now, two bitter and sorrow-filled persons held themselves in a standoff.

But this standoff was different. They both blamed him. Abby because he represented the one hope she had believed was withheld from her when her mother died, and he, because he knew the truth of that day. The day his brother died. The day Charles killed him.

Chapter Seven

It was obvious neither Jonathon nor her father knew what had transpired in the dawn hours before they'd exited the cabins. Charles had stalked away, visibly frustrated. Had she read him wrong all this time? His kiss hadn't seemed like flirtation. It held passion and depth and...something else. Abby had thrown all her paintbrushes into a bucket and her canvas she skewered on a branch in the woods. It didn't matter what Charles's kiss felt like, or communicated, he'd had no right. No right to touch her, to play with her heart, and by no means, bring up her mother's death as if he had some garish satisfaction in seeing her cry.

Now, the two of them stood in silence as they prepared for another day of fishing. Jonathon and her father had paired to go canoeing again on the Flambeau, whose intoxicating calm waters would suddenly boil into rapids breaking over rocks and speeding the canoe through its passageways. So it was she and Charles until they swapped for the afternoon and Charles received his own ride down the river.

"I hope you tip over," she muttered as she tied a fly onto his line.

"Pardon?" Charles's voice was clipped. The irritation between them palpable.

"Nothing." Abby tightened the knot. She thrust the split-cane rod at Charles. "Go fish."

"Yes, m'lady." His dark glower could never be mistaken for charm now.

Abby winced. The morning's emotions were still rife between them, but now, pushing through her clouded mind, was reality. Regardless of her earlier proclamation that Charles could smear her father's services throughout Milwaukee and she didn't care, Abby knew it was far from the truth. She *did* care. She *had* to care! It was Papa's livelihood.

"Give me the flyline." Abby reached for the line. Charles cast a narrow-eyed look her way.

"Why?"

Abby waggled her fingers. She wasn't going to tell him what she was going to do. It probably wouldn't work anyway. She didn't need to explain it to Charles. Simply guide him. It was her job.

He tipped the rod toward her and watched with a black gaze as she removed the wet fly from the line. The tense air between them toyed with her nerves, and she paused for a moment to still the shake in her fingers.

She pulled out her tin fly-box and hooked the unused wet fly into its place. A wet fly probably wasn't going to garner any fish even if Charles could cast a gentle line. Her fingers hovered over the hook she knew she should pull forth. The fish were feeding on half-developed flies. In her studies, Abby had discovered the scientific world called them "nymphs."

There was no debating trying this fly. Somehow she had to rectify the tension between them. For Papa. For their future. Abby reached for the fly she'd tied and never used. An imitation of the semi-developed flies that floated through the water until their formation was complete and they rose to the surface to take off into the wind.

Her fingers deftly tied on the nymph as Charles held the rod. Its tiny body was nowhere near as beautiful as a wet fly, but perhaps—just maybe—Charles could catch a trout with this nymph and his opinion of his vacation might change. Because certainly, at this point, there had been no redeeming factors.

"There." She released the line. "Now cast it upstream and let it float down. The closer you can land the nymph to the bank the better. The trout will be waiting for food to float by."

Charles didn't respond, but wielded the fly rod and barely missed a branch with the line before it dropped into the water. The ripples from the rough landing reverberated through the stream, but it was far enough up the stream it hopefully wouldn't frighten the very timid and suspicious fish.

They watched the line drift down the stream. It was different not to have the fly floating on the surface where it was easy to see.

"Fish on!" Charles's proclamation grabbed Abby's attention. Sure enough. The tip of the rod bent, not dramatically, but a bend nonetheless.

Charles began to reel.

"Don't." Abby hurried to his side and put her hand over his. With her other hand she grabbed the line and tugged it through the guides on the pole. "Pull the line in. The current creates slack. We need to keep it taut."

She transferred the line to Charles's eager hand. He adjusted his footing as he pulled more line through the guides. Finally Abby knelt on the shoreline, ignoring the moist earth that wet the knees of her trousers. This was the moment. A nymph—*her* nymph—had caught a trout. *Charles Farrington III* had caught a trout!

When the brown-gold flash of the fish shone in the water, Abby leaned forward and scooped it into the net.

"Stop pulling in line!" she commanded.

"Oh!" Charles gave a nervous laugh and the line stilled, with the exception of the small trout that wriggled on the end. He rested the fly rod on the ground and knelt by Abby.

She wet her hands in the water and reached for the trout. Its black eyes stared up at them as if surprised to find itself out of the stream and in a net. The tiny nymph was lodged in the corner of its mouth. Abby flicked it out with a brief twist. An easy release with no injury to the trout.

"Let him go."

She gave Charles a sideways glance. "You don't want to keep it?"

"For supper? It's so small it would only be one bite. No, let it go."

Abby shrugged and released the trout back to its home. They both stared as it flashed in the water and disappeared. Charles fingered the line and the nymph, eyeing it with curiosity.

"Why haven't we used this before?"

Abby looked away. "It's—not the typical fly."

"What is it?"

"A nymph."

"A what?"

Abby glanced at it where it rested in Charles's palm. "It's supposed to mimic an underdeveloped fly. Sometimes the fish seem to feed on those rather than full-grown flies. I don't know why."

"You made this?" Dark brows winged up beneath Charles's combed-back curls that argued against the pomade in his hair.

"Yes." Abby struggled to her feet and moved away from his penetrating look. "Want to try it again?"

He watched her from where he crouched by the stream. "Abigail Nessling, you're an enigma."

She turned her back to him but within seconds she felt his presence behind her, his breath warm in her ear as he whispered.

"An irritating, hard-headed enigma."

The kiss he left just below her ear burned her more than his words, more than the grief that still welled just beneath the surface, and more than her traitorous heart that strained to turn and rest herself in his arms. To cry. To weep.

One didn't heal in the arms of a man who would leave and who had no filter on his words or his thoughts, and who most certainly had no rights to hers.

<hr />

Abby was never more grateful to be paired with Jonathon for the afternoon. Any more time with Charles might completely ruin her. Her nerves were frayed by the insistence of his attention, as if he were picking at old scabs that covered unhealed wounds, all the while attempting to gain her affection. She sat on the bank while Jonathon fished. He was adept at casting and required little guidance. She'd attached a wet fly to his line and this time of day the fish seemed to respond. The sun beamed overhead, birds flocked and swooped over treetops, and the sound of the Flambeau River in the distance was soothing music to her unraveling heart.

She closed her eyes. Having guests on their river was horrible enough, but having them pick their way into her personal history and unwrap moments of time she'd rather keep sequestered was sheer agony.

Had what Charles claimed that morning been true? Had Papa received an offer from Jonathon's father to pay for Mama's medical expenses and refused it? Was it Mama's choice to die at home? Abby dug her fingers into the earth, capturing moist leaves in her palms. She couldn't believe that Mama would have chosen to die were she given the opportunity to live. Charles was simply attempting to save face for the rich and spoiled. Or was he? The memory of the lingering hollow in his dark eyes haunted her. It was as if, this morning, Charles had been exposed alongside of her. But what had she seen in those depths? Pain. Unrelenting pain. She would recognize it anywhere. It reflected in her own eyes each morning when she caught a glimpse of herself in the mirror.

A shout startled Abby from her mental war. She hurried to her feet and caught Jonathon's quick glance. He leaned his fly rod against a nearby tree.

"Was that Charles?"

Abby heard a shout again. The voice was laced with urgency. Surging toward the voice that was unmistakably Charles's, she heard Jonathon charging behind her. Branches slapped her face as she tried to dodge them. Charles's frame came into view, soaking wet, curls plastered against his forehead. He directed his attention past Abby to Jonathon, pointing behind him as he ran toward them.

"You've got to hurry! There's been an accident!"

"What happened?" Jonathon edged around Abby.

"The canoe—it overturned." Charles bent over, grabbing his knees and gasping in deep breaths. "Mr. Nessling—"

"What about my father?" Abby demanded. She didn't bother to give Charles time to respond but instead, lunged past him toward the river.

"Abby!" Jonathon's cry followed her and then his footsteps, and probably Charles's, but Abby didn't care. If she lost her father, too, if something horrid happened. . .

She broke into the clearing. The shoreline was littered with rock and debris from the river. She clambered over the slippery rocks and toward her father's form, hunched in a crumpled heap half in the water and half on land.

"Papa!" Abby collapsed beside him. He was breathing, but his eyes were closed, pain etched in every crevice of his face. Blood soaked his arm from a gaping wound. "Papa!" She urged him to respond, but he was silent.

"Dear God." Jonathon dropped beside her and assessed her father, ripping at his own shirt to tear off a strip of cloth. He wrapped it around Papa's upper arm, glancing over his shoulder at Charles as he did so. "What happened, man?" Jonathon shouted over the roar of the white water rapids.

Charles heaved in deep breaths. His shirt clung to muscled arms and his broad chest. Abby couldn't help it if accusation shot from her eyes. This was his fault, she knew it. It had to be.

"The canoe tipped." Charles waved his hand at the river that coursed and rolled over rocks. "We both fell out. Mr. Nessling tried to rescue the canoe, but somehow he got trapped between it and that boulder. He couldn't get free."

Abby squeezed her eyes shut. She could see the accident in her mind. The canoe had wrapped itself around a rock and her father had been trapped between them. While they weren't the largest rapids in the region, they were still powerful, and the currents didn't always run parallel to the shore. If the canoe tipped and met the rock, there was a fine chance the current would hold the canoe there, possibly even breaking it into pieces as it folded itself around the boulder. If Papa had been caught between. . . Abby opened her eyes. Papa could be busted into pieces inside.

"What did you do?" She whirled on Charles, the words spitting at him with venom.

Charles scowled, the intensity of the situation lending itself to his own furious reply. "Nothing!"

"You tipped the canoe, didn't you!" Abby struggled to her feet.

"Abby!"

She ignored Jonathon's warning. "You did this!" She pointed back at Papa.

Charles's lip curled in a wounded snarl. His eyes narrowed and he shook his head. "You would blame me."

"Tell me you didn't do something reckless that made the canoe tip. Tell me."

"Abby." Jonathon's sharp voice pierced the tension. "We need to get your father help. Now isn't the time!"

He was right. Abby stopped, but didn't release Charles's gaze. She couldn't. Not until he admitted this was his doing. Her father wouldn't tip the canoe, and if some mishap really did happen, he wouldn't have been foolish enough to get caught between the craft and the rock.

"I know you did this," she hissed. It was obvious she was right. Charles had no color in his face and in that moment, Abby saw him for all that he was. A foolish, stupid man.

Chapter Eight

Papa's dreams were over.

Abby wanted to save them. It was her responsibility, after all, to take care of him, but she'd failed. Miserably. Jonathon and Charles were packing their luggage in their cabin, preparing for an abrupt early departure. The guided excursion was ended with Papa's incapacitation.

She gripped the windowsill and gave Harold an absentminded scratch. The squirrel's tail waved and brushed her wrist. Abby watched Charles open the cabin door and her eyes narrowed. Papa would live, but his broken ribs and bruised torso were going to take weeks to heal. Not to mention the gash in his arm that the nearby logging camp doctor had closed with twelve stitches. There would be no income generated from entertaining the wealthy. It was over, all of it. Papa's dream, their income, everything. Abby's stomach turned at the thought. They would lose it all. The cabins, their future. . .

Charles lugged two suitcases to the back of the horse and wagon hitched to the rail between the cabins. Abby grimaced at the sight. The wagon had brought the doctor and now it would take him back, along with Jonathon and Charles. They would catch the train in town and return to Milwaukee. To their lives. Leaving her here to pick up the pieces alone. That knowledge put the final stamp on her assumptions that when it came to real life, the wealthy simply up and ran, buying their way out of hardship.

Abby's breath shuddered as she inhaled. She glanced over her shoulder at the cot set up in front of the fireplace. Papa's still form sent waves of anxiety through her. He could have died! He could have drowned, or bled internally, the doctor said. She should be thankful. Thankful? She looked back out the window at Charles, who hefted the luggage into the back of the wagon. There was no doubt in her mind that the uncoordinated rich boy had done something to make the canoe tip. Papa, in his urgency to save the canoe, had become its victim.

A frown creased her brow. Why was Charles shaking hands with Jonathon?

She hurried from the cabin, shutting the door softly behind her, sequestering Harold with Papa. The logging camp doctor sat beside a logger on the wagon seat. The two men ignored them as Jonathon hoisted himself into the back of the wagon.

"What's going on?" Abby demanded. And why was Charles not getting into the wagon beside Jonathon?

Charles stepped back from the wagon, his hands jammed into his trouser pockets, suspenders stretched over his shoulders.

"I hate to leave you here, Abby." Jonathon appeared genuinely distressed. He adjusted his seat in the wagon. "But I need to get back to Milwaukee. I want to see if I can make arrangements."

"Arrangements?" The day's events kept coming so fast and unexpected that it left Abby bewildered.

Jonathon gave her an understanding smile. "For you and your father." He waved toward the cabin. "You can't stay here. There will be no income. And the winter? Your father might not even be recuperated by then, let alone prepared for the snow."

Abby swallowed the lump of shame in her throat. What could she say? The writing was on the wall. It had been even before her father's accident.

"I want to see if my father can make arrangements to assist you and your father to relocate to Milwaukee. At least until he's fully recuperated. Then, you both can make whatever decisions are necessary."

Abby gave him a short nod, but the realization of his words seeped into her wounded soul. Friendship. Kindness. She blinked her eyes against sudden emotion, and turned her face away so Jonathon couldn't read her expression or discover how sheepish she felt. She'd been so sure they were escaping; but instead, Jonathon was hurrying home to find help. To take care of them. And what about Charles?

Shaken, Abby shifted her attention to him. Regardless of Jonathon, Charles was still low on her list of favorite people. His dark eyes slammed into hers.

"And what are you doing?" She glanced at the cabin behind him with its open door and the obvious absence of his luggage in the wagon.

"Staying."

The one word made Abby's heart spiral up in an uncontrollable sense of hope and then crash almost as fast. What help would he be? And why would he choose to stay when he was so underqualified to cast a fly rod, let alone help her survive in the forest while tending her father?

"Abby." Jonathon's voice of reason penetrated through her cloud of shock and consternation. "Let Charles help. I can't leave you and your father here alone without some sort of assistance. Charles has offered, and I know how you feel, but—"

"No, you don't know how I feel." Abby interrupted her friend and sealed his mouth with a firm line.

"You're right. I don't." Jonathon's searching gaze made Abby shift her feet uncomfortably. "But we're not villains, Abby. We care. No one cares more than Charles. Please stop blaming him for things he cannot help. If anyone understands your pain. . .well, it's him."

The wagon lurched forward as the logger flicked the reins. "Talk to each other," Jonathon directed as the wagon rolled away. He lifted his hand in a wave and Charles and Abby stood in the wagon's dust.

"I've no intention of *talking*," she stated bluntly, eyes fixed on Jonathon's disappearing form.

"I didn't think so."

So. That was that. Abby marched back to her cabin, to Papa, and as far away from Charles Farrington III as she could get.

◆━●◆●━◆

Maybe she wasn't going to talk to him, maybe she was going to continue to blame him, but blast it all if he wasn't going to at least try to find some atonement. Once was awful, but twice? The horror of seeing Mr. Nessling pinned between the canoe and the boulder, white water swirling around him and his face twisted in agony. . . It was just too much.

Charles hefted the axe over his head and brought it down onto a log with force. The blade bounced off the wood and hit the stump the log was balanced on. So maybe he couldn't chop wood to save his soul, but wasn't that what all hearty American pioneering males did when angry? Chop wood? What an absolute mockery to humanity he'd turned out to be.

Lifting the axe again, he dropped it with enough force to elicit a grunt. This time it stuck in the wood, but barely, and didn't make a crack.

"What are you doing?"

The contemptuous voice behind him was of course none other than the only person in the vicinity besides himself capable of walking. He dropped the axe by his foot and swiped his hand across his sweaty forehead. "Chopping wood."

"It's August." Abby's statement of the obvious was no help.

"You'll need wood for the winter."

She eyed his rolled-up shirt sleeves and his sweaty neckline, and her expression remained impassive. "According to Jonathon, we won't be here during the winter."

Blasted woman. In the matter of a few days, Charles had gone from seeing her as conquerable, to wanting to draw her out of her grief, to now wishing he'd hightailed it back to Milwaukee with Jonathon. Penance. It's what made him stay. Some way to repay Mr. Nessling, prove that the wealthy weren't unkind and self-centered, and maybe even make up a little for David's death years ago. God had to count that all for something, right? But the censure in Abby's eyes was almost enough to convince Charles that no amount of works could beg forgiveness from anyone.

"You're not doing it right." She pointed to the axe.

Of course. There was a right way to chop wood, same as there was a right way to fling a fly line, or row a canoe, or duck under a branch. If he were honest, Charles missed the smell of the streets of Milwaukee. The breweries, the smoke from the chimneys, the fumes from the motor cars, and the pungent smell of sauerkraut over sausages. There was too much fresh air here, too much. . .Abigail Nessling.

She hiked over to him and lifted the axe from where it rested by his foot. "You're going to cut off an appendage."

Charles narrowed his eyes. She was insulting now. All gloves were off. It was war. She wanted to live in her bitter grief? Well, he wanted free of his, and he'd be flipped if he let Abby stand in the way of it.

"Give it back to me." He sounded like a petulant boy.

Abby held the axe away. She pointed at the log. "You're trying to chop against the grain. Turn the log so the grain runs vertically away from you."

Charles bit his tongue but did as she said. Once the log was positioned, she handed him the axe. "Now, when you bring the axe down, don't rely on your arm strength. Use your whole body. Like you're going to drive it straight through."

He eyed her for a moment. She didn't sound pompous, but he saw the tiny shake of her head. He exasperated her. She felt he was above living in the woods, above eking out a life here like her father had so aptly done since she was a babe. Fine. He'd show her.

Charles brought the axe down with fervor, his entire torso following through with the motion. The axe head embedded in the log and it split partway. He couldn't help but smile. *Ha! Take that, Abigail Nessling!*

He turned to see her astounded expression, but she was gone. The cabin door closing echoed through the trees. Charles blew a puff of frustrated air from his mouth. Was any amount of forgiveness worth this exasperation, this sense of being completely out of one's element? He looked down at the half-split log. His efforts would never bring back David, and they would never make Mr. Nessling heal quickly enough to stay here in his forest home. In a swift motion, Charles brought the axe around and split the log the rest of the way. It fell in two halves.

He could only hope God would see his efforts, because Abby certainly did not.

Chapter Nine

Abby positioned pillows behind her father's back. Propping him without inflicting unnecessary pain took effort. The grimace etched in the lines on his face told her all she needed to know. Pain was something he would be fighting for days to come.

"You need nourishment." She stirred the stew in the bowl as she sat next to the bed.

"I can feed myself, teacup." Papa's voice hinted of a smile, but she ignored it. She had to. Her insides were twisted in a thousand different emotions, and she couldn't decipher any of them at the moment. She couldn't add humor to the mix, or it might be her undoing.

"Here." She ignored her father and lifted the spoon to his mouth. He obeyed, but his eyes never left her face. Abby avoided his searching gaze.

"Did I hear Charles's voice outside today? And an axe?" Papa missed nothing, even stuck in his bed.

Abby nodded. For sure, Papa was seeing through Charles's foolhardy idea that he could provide any support for them at all.

"Hmm." Papa mouthed a spoonful of stew then raised his eyebrows. If he could have shrugged without affecting his broken ribs, he probably would have. "Perhaps I read the boy wrong."

The spoon stilled in midair. Abby held it aloft over Papa's chest. Read Charles wrong? The man was a sorry excuse for a man, unless one counted his kissing skills, in which case he graded off the scale. Abby felt a blush creep up her neck. Papa noticed.

"I see." He eyed the spoon. "I would recommend feeding me that before it drips. Or let me feed myself."

"Oh." Abby pushed the food into her father's waiting mouth and didn't refuse when he carefully reached for the bowl of stew. His breath caught with pain, and she stretched out her hand to reclaim the bowl.

"I'm fine." Papa was stubborn. He gave himself another bite, chewed, swallowed, and then nodded. "You like him, don't you?"

Abby was sure her eyebrows almost flew off her face. "Charles? No! Not at all. Not in the slightest. The man is a—well, he thinks he can help us by staying? It just gives me someone else I need to take care of!"

Her hand flew to cover her mouth and her eyes burned with remorse. "Papa, I'm so sorry. I didn't mean it that way. I just meant—I mean—what I was going to say was—"

"It's all right," Papa's soothing voice brought her stammering to halt. "You've carried more responsibility on your shoulders than I'd ever intended you to. And now"—he waved the empty spoon toward his bruised and broken torso—"now I've added myself to the list."

"I don't mind caring for *you*, Papa. It's Mr. Farrington I can't abide."

Papa's mouth stretched in a sad smile. He read her like Mama used to read one of her books. Clear and precise, without error, and grasping all the meanings hidden beneath the words. "Abby, Charles isn't to blame for what happened to me."

"No?" Her voice was bitter. Even she heard it. "Then what happened, Papa? Explain it to me."

Papa struggled to take a deep breath, and he closed his eyes against the pain before letting it out. "I tipped the canoe."

"You?" Absolutely not. Papa was too river-smart to tip the canoe.

Papa gave her a patronizing look of patience. "Abby, canoes tip. It happens. I miscalculated and we sideswiped a small rock. It put the canoe off balance, and while I tried to right it, Charles wasn't prepared for the lurch. We tipped. Plain and simple."

"Charles wasn't prepared. Exactly. If he had been prepared, he could have counterbalanced and the canoe wouldn't have tipped." Abby's argument filled the room and was followed by silence.

Papa looked into his bowl then handed it back to Abby, apparently having satisfied his appetite. "I still got between the canoe and that boulder. That was my error in judgment. The current pulled me, and I was too enthusiastic to save the boat."

Since they were being honest. . . "And I suppose when Mama was dying, Jonathon's father also offered to pay for her to receive medical care and you refused their generosity." Abby pressed her lips together after she blurted out her statement, delivered with a tone of disbelief.

Papa closed his eyes in resignation. His breath caught, and he winced. When he opened his eyes, Abby knew all she needed to know. Charles had been right, and now, her one escape to avoid grief was being taken from her. If she could blame someone—*anyone*—for Mama's death, it was easier than facing that it was simply her time. It was easy to transfer her sorrow into bitterness and hold accountable the wealthy who tossed away income like paper confetti, ignorant of those who suffered pain and poverty. But to know that the wealthy had actually sought to provide, to give them the assistance Abby blamed them for withholding?

"Why?" It was all Abby could ask. Her choked whisper mirrored the soreness of her throat where it constricted with emotion.

Papa leaned his head back on his pillows. "Your mama wanted to die peacefully, here at home. She knew all the money in the world wouldn't save her in the end, and to live her final days in an institution?" He shook his head, a lone tear escaping and trailing down his strong cheek. "No one is to blame for your mama's death. There are no mistakes, only God's perfect timing. You cannot hold anyone accountable for my accident either—least of all, Charles Farrington, rapscallion though he may be. Perhaps he has money, but, it appears he has heart as well. He and Jonathon are going to care for us, and as much as my pride wishes to refuse, I know we need their assistance."

Abby bit her bottom lip in an effort to still its trembling.

Papa closed his eyes, obviously exhausted and worn from fighting the pain of broken bones. "He may prove to be a help in greater ways than I imagined."

"How?" Abby whispered.

Her father took a few shallow breaths, avoiding the deep intake in exchange for avoiding the stabbing pain of his ribs. "Maybe you're not the only one who is pushing through sorrow. Some, like you, turn to bitterness—"

The sound of an axe colliding with wood outside the bedroom window stilled Papa's words. His mouth turned upward in a slight smile. "And some make their penance by blaming themselves."

———◆◆◆———

Dusk had settled over the forest. The two cabins, parallel to each other with the clearing in between, were haloed by the orange tint of a sunset that streamed through tree branches. Charles slouched in a chair outside the guest cabin. It was quiet without Jonathon, and Abby certainly wasn't giving him the time of day. She'd come in and out of the cabin numerous times, but each time it was as if he didn't exist.

No matter. He wasn't here for her. Not really. He was here for Mr. Nessling. For David. For himself, if he were honest. Had he returned home with Jonathon, he'd most likely be striding down the walkways of Milwaukee to one of the many beer gardens for some good German music. Instead, he was alone with his thoughts, a glass of water, and an ache in every muscle he'd applied to an afternoon of chopping wood. His father would sneer at him if he could see him now. Sweaty, dirty, exhausted. Not the son of a beer baron, or the future heir to the Farrington fortune. Only a week ago, Charles had attempted to escape that pressure, free himself from the memories that dogged him, and find respite near the Flambeau River. Instead, he'd almost repeated his offense and watched Mr. Nessling drown, and he'd allowed Abigail to wheedle her way into his subconscious and fuel his memories of David.

Charles flung the remaining water from his glass and leaned forward in his chair, elbows on his knees, head in his hands. He was tired. His soul was tired.

"When Papa chops wood, he usually has a stack clear up to the roof after an afternoon."

Abby's voice startled him and he lifted his head. Eyeing the miniscule woodpile he'd stacked by the side of their cabin, he was reminded again of his failures. He was beyond charming his way out of his darkness. This is where he sat, and if Abby continued to point out every place he fell short, he may as well return home and live with his father. There was no grace for someone who didn't deserve it. That much was very apparent.

"But—" Abby paused, picking nervously at her thumbnail. "You did well. For a first time."

Charles glowered at her, searching her face for a hint of cynicism, waiting for the backhanded comment that would put him in his place. His gaze fell on her mouth and he sniffed. One week in and he'd already stolen a kiss. So bent on shocking her out of her own misguided grief, he'd awakened his own instead.

Abby rocked back on her heels as Harold skittered in front of her, across the clearing, and into the woods.

"Aren't you afraid he won't come back one of these days?" Charles ventured, watching the bushy tail of the squirrel disappear beneath undergrowth.

Abby's gaze followed the squirrel as well. Sadness touched her eyes. She nodded. "I am. But he deserves to live his life again."

The injured squirrel. Healed. Loved. Being given the grace and freedom to walk away from what held him back.

336

"Do we?" Charles muttered.

Their eyes locked.

Abby didn't respond and neither did Charles. What could they say, after all? Sometimes words fell horribly, pathetically short.

Chapter Ten

Word was slow in coming from Jonathon. It would take time for him to return home, and then, even though it was almost a new century, it wasn't as if telephone lines had made their way to northern Wisconsin and the remote logging camps. They would need to rely on a telegraph delivered to the railway station in town five miles away. And that was assuming Jonathon's father was as hospitable as his son.

Abby rotated a hook and wrapped thread around the shank. Creating her nymph patterns and painting her redundant landscapes was about all she could do to calm herself. With Papa still convalescing after only a week since the accident, there wasn't much for her to do outside of sit and watch him rest. That, and muster the willpower to make the trip to town and send telegraphs to the three other excursionists who had booked stays with them to round out the summer.

Abby tightened the thread on the hook. To cancel the excursions would be detrimental to their future. It would be difficult to arrange bookings for other wealthy thrill-seekers without word-of-mouth recommendations. Jonathon would pull through for them, she knew, but it was still questionable whether Charles would.

Charles. His lurking form unnerved her in so many ways. She had to admit, he'd done a fine job of stacking wood—although they probably wouldn't need it if they weren't going to be here for the winter. But he'd also spent time reading to Papa, which she had to admit gave her a much-needed break. He'd even suggested taking a spinning rod, forgoing the more technically inclined sport of fly-fishing, and catching some fish from the river for dinner. She let him, and not surprisingly, he came back with an empty basket.

Abby smiled as she finished tying her nymph design. She had to give the man credit. He was at least trying. The last few days had worn down some of her harsh edges against him. With Papa taking the blame for the accident, she had less to hold against Charles. Well, nothing to hold against him, really, outside his brazen stolen kiss that she couldn't forget no matter how she tried.

The man of her thoughts rounded the corner. His black curls hung around his face—he'd obviously given up on the citified pomade and bay rum in exchange for one of Papa's old cotton shirts and floppy hair. She ducked her head and paid more attention to the nymph than she needed to. Was it horrid that she found him far more attractive with his four days' growth of whiskers and rugged appearance than the flirtatious charmer of barely two weeks ago?

He sidled up behind her, his breath brushing her neck. So maybe the charmer hadn't totally disappeared. "Making more of your magical nymphs?"

"Mmm, hmm." Just because she had softened toward him didn't mean she needed to let him in on her change of heart. It was better to hold him at arm's length.

"Good. If we tell other potential guests that you have a special fly to lure trout, you might have a unique angle to attract more enthusiasts."

Well, that was something she hadn't thought of before. Her nymph had always been her secret. But perhaps. . . Then the truth sank in once more. "We won't be here, so it doesn't matter."

Charles reached around her and picked up one of her completed nymphs, twisting it between thumb and index finger and studying the craftsmanship. "What do you mean by that?"

Abby turned. "Papa won't be able to lead any more excursions this summer. There will be no word of mouth to carry back to the wealthy, and so no future for us next summer."

"The wealthy." Charles set the nymph back on the fly-tying table and his chest rose in a resigned sigh. "Yes, well, we all know how you feel about the wealthy anyway. You should be relieved."

He moved to take his leave but Abby reached out and gripped his shirt sleeve. He didn't deserve her scorn. Not anymore.

"I didn't mean it like that."

Charles looked down at her fingers that brushed his skin just below his rolled-up sleeve. "How did you mean it?" His brown eyes widened and swallowed her whole.

Abby blinked. "I—I. . ."

They were a sad pair, the two of them. A wealthy city boy who obviously bore some burden he'd yet to reveal and she, the tired, sorrow-filled daughter of a dead woman. Somehow life seemed to have paused for both of them. But in this moment, Abby realized, it really wasn't anyone's fault. Nor was it God's.

"I'm sorry." Her whisper swirled around them like a caressing embrace.

Charles blinked.

"I'm sorry I ever blamed anyone for Mama." Tears crowded her throat. "I just—you would have to lose someone close to understand why I have struggled so. Needing a reason, needing an outlet, having someone to blame for something that made no sense to me."

Charles's jaw twitched and she could tell he was clenching his teeth. "Yeah."

"So I blamed the people I was jealous of. People with money, people who had the luxury to get medical care for those they loved. People like you." Now that she spoke it out loud, Abby realized how horrid and shallow she had been. She tried to justify herself. "When you're in our shoes, struggling to make ends meet, my father trying to live out his dream by starting this excursion business. . .people like—like you seem to have everything, while people like us seem to lose everything."

Abby wasn't prepared for the haunted expression that passed across Charles's face, nor for his choked cough of suppressed emotion.

"People like us, eh?" He nodded, his lips pursed as if willing to bear one more burden that somehow really wasn't his.

"But I don't see it that way now." And she didn't, Abby realized. A tear trailed down her cheek. "I just miss my mama." She bit her bottom lip, but the tears began to stream burning paths over her face. "I just miss my mama."

Charles reached out and gripped her hand. "And I miss my brother."

Only two times had Charles ever felt worse than he did right now. The first was when he failed to save his brother, the second when he failed to save Mr. Nessling from his boating accident. Now he'd failed Abby, and instead of helping her, had only awakened the raw pain of her grief.

The petite woman before him wrapped her arms around herself as breaths tore from her. It was obvious she was trying to subdue the onslaught of tears, but now that they flowed, it seemed only a miracle would stop them. Her fingers had curled around his for only a moment before she'd retreated into her protective stance. But her eyes, though drowning in salt-water tears, were fixated on his.

"What do you mean? Your brother?"

Now he'd done it. He hadn't intended on ever speaking David's name again. He didn't have to. His father did it daily and reminded him constantly how he'd failed the family and better not fail it again in the business. Charles winced.

"Never mind."

Abby shook her head, wisps of white-blond hair teasing her lips. Charles averted his eyes.

"No." Abby's fingers wrapped around his once more. "Tell me."

Charles watched the tops of the trees sway in the warm breeze. "My brother David died about twelve years ago. When I was fourteen."

He heard her small intake of breath. If he were wicked, which he wasn't, Charles would turn and say, "*Yes, see? Grief isn't limited to income brackets.*" But he didn't say the first words that came to mind. Instead, he remained silent.

Abby moved closer, her fingers linking with his, like the linking of broken hearts in the places they had come apart. "How?"

Charles shifted his attention to her face. That was a mistake. He was captured by the empathy in her expression. He coughed. Blasted emotions. "He drowned."

"Oh, Charles," Abby breathed.

"It was my fault." Fine. He'd just tell her. Might as well lay it all out for her to see. "I dared him to swim out into the river, but he wasn't a strong swimmer and. . . I couldn't save him."

Abby was merciful and didn't respond. But Charles knew what she was thinking. "Just like I couldn't save your father."

"But Papa didn't drown." Abby's protest was weak.

"No. But I ruined his livelihood."

Abby didn't answer. Exactly. If Charles wasn't such a failure, such a sad excuse for a son, a friend, a man, he would have had the wits to help Mr. Nessling instead of treading water and watching the man be crushed. He would have had the wisdom to have kept David on land by him.

"It seems. . ." Abby's body moved even closer until she embraced his arm and laid her head on his bicep. A bold move. Unexpected. More than likely, she was unconscious of the stirring the action sent through him. "It seems," she repeated, "that you and I both have mistaken views of grief."

"You weren't there, Abby. You didn't see what happened. In either scenario."

"No." Her embrace on his arm tightened. "I wasn't. But I can believe you're wrong about your perspective of your brother's death, just as you can believe I'm wrong about mine and my mother's."

Charles froze. He did believe she was wrong. Her mother's death had nothing to do with medical care, or something Abby might have done to save her, or whether Jonathon's father had wired money. It had to do with. . .fate? Destiny? But the reason for David's death, even Mr. Nessling's accident, seemed so much clearer.

"David's death wasn't fate, Abby. Neither was your father's accident. I could have prevented them both."

Silence enveloped them as they stood side by side—nymphs, hook, and fly-tying materials ignored on the workbench. Charles looked down at Abby and her eyes were closed. Light-brown lashes resting on damp cheeks blushed with emotion. Her mouth moved as she spoke so quietly, Charles had to lean toward her to hear.

"It wasn't your fault, Charles. It wasn't your fault."

For the first time, Charles heard the words he'd ached for over twelve years to have just one person say. For the first time, he thought maybe he could finally believe it was true.

Chapter Eleven

Moonlight shafted through the windowpanes and across the wooden table. Abby rested her cup of tea on it, and reached for her book. Papa rested in the bedroom just beyond, but he was alert and she could see him occasionally lift his own mug to his mouth and slurp hot coffee.

A knock rattled the cabin door. Papa turned his head and Abby stood with a soft smile. "Must be Charles." Who else would it be?

She opened the door and sure enough, Charles stood there, a sheepish look on his face.

"Sorry to bother you."

Bother? Abby realized the form of Charles Farrington III didn't bother her anymore. All that remained was a lilt of anticipation, of shared understanding, of. . . friendship.

"Come in," Abby stepped aside and tried not to dwell on the heat that flooded her face as Charles's arm brushed hers when he entered. He glanced at her. Offered a small smile, a deepened dimple, and a—oh help—his flirtatious wink had returned. And, he was chewing that pesky toothpick with its devilish tilt in the corner of his mouth. His mouth.

Abby turned away. "Are you here for Papa?"

Charles nodded. "And you," he added. "But I realize the hour is late."

"You've earned it." Papa's voice came from the bedroom.

A look of surprise stretched across Charles's face as he made his way to the bedroom. "Thank you, sir."

Abby followed but kept her distance from Charles. Just in case she'd blush again, she busied herself with straightening the painting on the wall.

Papa took a sip of coffee.

"I have something I'd like—well, I have a proposition for you both." Charles glanced between them, eagerness in his voice. It was a different Charles than the man of earlier in the day. The man who'd choked back his own blame and had held her in silent, unexpected shared grief. Maybe they had both healed a little. Even though there were still shadows of sadness lurking behind his smile, he seemed. . .more at peace.

"All right." Charles rubbed his hands together with anticipation. His eyes were earnest as they sought out hers. "I know I'm horrible at this wilderness stuff."

Papa laughed then cut it short with a wince. He crossed his arm over his chest as if to hold his broken ribs together. "Don't make me laugh again, boy."

"So sorry." Charles winced along with Papa. Paused. "Really. I am very sorry."

Papa pressed his mouth together in a firm line as he studied Charles. Finally, he answered him, and it sealed away for good any doubts or blame Abby might have still fostered. "It wasn't your fault, Charles. It was an accident."

"Accidents start somewhere, sir."

Abby noticed the guilt overtake Charles's original energy.

"Yes. They do. More often than not from a string of events that no one can control." Papa's eyes narrowed in thoughtful contemplation. "I have faith, and in that faith, I know that what seems accidental or tragic to us"—his eyes met Abby's over Charles's shoulder—"is not a mistake to God."

"Guess I'm a slow learner in the faith practice." Charles grimaced and glanced at Abby, who couldn't help but give him a slight smile in shared understanding. "But it's coming," he finished. She nodded. For her too.

"Anyway..." Charles charged ahead in the conversation. "I don't know when Jonathon will touch base with the potential for you to relocate to Milwaukee. But I know it's neither of your desires to do so."

Abby didn't respond. She didn't want to influence Papa with some manipulative sense of obligation to agree to whatever Charles was about to propose.

"I'm not fond of it, but God is obviously taking us in a different direction." Papa breathed around his broken ribs. Breaths short but controlled.

Charles held up his forefinger. "Wait. I've been thinking. If I use my connections in Milwaukee, I'm sure I can book this place out until the end of this season and well into next."

"You're quite persuasive," Abby mumbled, remembering Charles's charm and flirtation.

He cast her a wicked grin. "I am. I know."

"That's all well and good, but someone has to lead the tours, the excursions," Papa argued.

"I can't do that alone." It was difficult to admit, but Abby had to be truthful.

Charles nodded. "That's where I come in."

"You?" Abby couldn't help but raise her eyebrows incredulously. The man had just admitted he was as adept in the woods and on the river as an African lion.

"I told you not to make me laugh." Papa grimaced wryly.

Charles nodded and raised his eyebrow in a sardonic expression. "Yes, well, I'm learning."

Abby covered her mouth, but it didn't squelch the snicker that escaped.

"I am." Charles winked at her. "I'm learning what *not* to do, even if I don't yet have a grasp on what *to* do."

"I still don't see how this will work." Papa glanced between the two of them. "You're thinking you and Abby will lead the excursions?"

Charles nodded, but held up a hand just as fast. "Wait. Just hear me out. I can't lead myself, I realize that. And, frankly"—he shot a wry look at Abby—"it's not wise to split up groups and have her leading a man on her own."

She choked. She couldn't help it. Papa's smile of surprise stretched across his face.

"She guided you." Papa stated the obvious.

"Yes. Also not wise." Charles's rakish smile was brazen and, yes, Abby had to turn to straighten the painting on the wall. Again. She could tell both men noticed her blush anyway.

"I see." Papa nodded slowly.

Wonderful. It was apparent by Charles's words that something had happened between them, and now he was all but admitting it to Papa.

"So we guide together. As a team." Charles ignored the awkward emotion that circled the room. "We forgo canoeing on the river, and we simplify what we offer."

"Fishing is enough to draw folks?" Papa sounded doubtful.

Abby finished straightening the painting and composing herself. "I don't think it is."

Charles waved his hand in disagreement. "It is. Think of it, Abby." His attention turned on her full force caused her horrid blush to return. She could feel its betraying warmth. He noticed, and the corner of his mouth where his toothpick still somehow lodged as he talked, turned up in a smile. "Your nymph. The new fly. You said yourself it's unique to you. That's what we advertise. We tell folks we offer fly-fishing excursions with new, never-used fly designs."

"But the trout are in the streams, not so much in the river. People come here for the river. For the white water. For the big fish." Abby's protest seemed to resonate with her father's, for Papa nodded in agreement.

Charles shook his head. "How many fish did I catch, Abby?"

She swallowed. "One."

"And how big was it?"

"About eight inches."

"And was I upset when that's all I caught? Did I ever give up fly-fishing in the stream? Did I complain once that we weren't going after the big fish?"

"No, but I assumed it was because—" She stopped. No need to finish her thought that Charles stayed only because she was a female he wanted to charm.

He grinned. "One could say my guide was pretty."

Papa cleared his throat.

Charles hurried on. "But there's something about fly-fishing that makes a man want to keep trying. It's strategic. It's an art. Like your painting, Abby. Certain strokes, patterns, the way the brush falls on the canvas. It's the same with fly-fishing. You cannot underestimate what you have here. It's not all about conquering the large muskie or bass. A man could love the hunt of fly-fishing, the *creation* around the streams, the—the colors of the trout."

"Wait." Papa held up his hand. "So you're saying, the river is only the canvas, but the stream and the fly-fishing, they're the details to our outfitting?"

Charles nodded, light entering his eyes now that Papa seemed to be grasping the idea. "That, and Abby's flies. Home-tied patterns. You can't buy those in Milwaukee. People will pay a mint for them. I'll be along to add conversation. Abby can focus on what she does best, and I'll be the host."

"Can't argue that." Papa nodded. Then his brows furrowed. "But what about your future? In Milwaukee?"

Charles ducked his head. He drew in a breath and exhaled. "I've no desire to return to my father's business. Or the blame. The guilt." He met Abby's eyes. "There's *healing* here. Now that I'm finding it, I want to stay."

The earth was dewy; a low fog drifted through the trees, floating over the underbrush toward the river. Abby rested on a wooden stool, Harold perched on her lap, his bushy tail waving back and forth as if bidding her farewell.

"You're leaving me, aren't you?" she whispered. She could sense it. Each day Harold had returned later and later. A part of her wished she'd continued the habit of locking him in the cabin, but the restlessness in the squirrel's eyes burrowed into her heart. He had healed. He needed to be free.

She reached out her finger and Harold nudged it with his nose and then scampered off her lap. The rustle of his body through the leaves and over sticks carried for a moment and then disappeared. With that, Harold was gone. Perhaps he'd return.

"You said goodbye?" Charles crouched beside her and they both stared into the brush where Harold had hurried off in search of nuts. Charles's words held so many layers, Abby didn't reply.

Goodbye? She'd never really said goodbye to her mother. Maybe that was the next part in healing, toward her freedom.

"Have you?" she whispered.

"No," he admitted. Charles shifted his body so he sat on the ground, his knees up and his forearms resting lazily on top of them. "But I will. Someday."

Abby gave him a sideways glance. "You will?"

He shrugged. "We have to, don't we?" His eyes bored into hers. Abby didn't look away this time. What she saw was understanding, concern, and maybe hints of more.

Charles reached out and pushed a strand of hair behind her ear. "I hear there's always a time to let go."

"Like I let go of Harold?" She leaned into his hand and Charles trailed his palm down her cheek before letting go.

He nodded. "Like Harold."

They sat in silence together, both gazing deep into the woods. Their woods now. In a few short weeks, Charles had transitioned from unwelcome interloper, to charmer, to enemy, and then. . .to friend. And now?

"What's next?" Abby mumbled, half aware that she said it aloud.

Charles chewed his trademark toothpick for a moment. "Well, I'll need to get word to Jonathon that your father agreed to my plan for the fly-fishing outfitters."

"No." Abby had to be honest. "I didn't mean that." Although it was a relief to know they wouldn't be leaving this beloved haven.

Charles shifted toward her. Question furrowed his brows. "What *do* you mean?"

She couldn't ask it. Not really. It was too personal, too exposing, and too soon. She blinked to break their gazes. It didn't work.

"Abby." Charles repositioned to his knees and knelt in front of her where she sat frozen on her stool. "What's next for us is to continue on. For your mama, for David, and for. . .each other."

He leaned forward and intertwined his fingers with hers. The earnestness in his expression made all his charm and flirtation drift away to expose the sensitive soul burrowed deep inside of him.

"Together?" Abby whispered.

Charles's thumb stroked her hand in a hypnotic motion. "Together, my little nymph."

In that moment, Abby knew. Charles Farrington III would never be a world apart from her again. He would be right outside her back door, and if the gleam in his eyes told her anything as he leaned in to emphasize his point with a kiss. . .he would be hers.

Professional coffee drinker, **Jaime Jo Wright** resides in the hills of Wisconsin. She loves to write spirited turn-of-the-century romance, stained with suspense. Her day job finds her as a director of sales and development. She's wife to a rock-climbing, bow-hunting Pre-K teacher, mom to a coffee-drinking little girl and a little boy she fondly refers to as her mischievous "Peter Pan." Jaime completes her persona by being an admitted social media junkie and coffee snob. She is a member of ACFW and has the best writing sisters *ever*!

The Gardener's Daughter

by Anne Love

Dedication

To the teachers who had an impact on my journey—
Mom and Dad;
Mrs. Frazier, Mrs. Andrews, and Ms. Yoder;
Professors Marion Bontrager, Ron Gingerich, and Nancy Gillespie;
And to my husband, Ted,
who believes in me—forever thank you.

Chapter One

Bay View, Michigan
1895

Thump. *Thump.* She could plant herself in a library world such as this one forever. *Thump.* Maggie Abbott stamped the catalog card of Harriett Beecher Stowe's *Uncle Tom's Cabin* and placed the book on the stack to be shelved. Books she could read when the library of Bay View's Chautauqua wasn't humming with academy students. Books she didn't have to shelve since she had just begun a new position as the front desk attendant.

The library matron had left her to lock the door at closing, and Maggie couldn't wait to dive into the newest arrival. She placed the stack of books on the return cart then reached for H. G. Wells's *The Time Machine.*

Only for a moment before leaving. A few delicious words were all she needed.

Lifting the cover embossed with the image of a winged sphinx, she heard the creak of the stiffness of a newly opened novel. She fingered beyond the beautiful vellum pages and drank in the words of the first chapter. She ignored her stomach growling and made quick work to forget that Father would be waiting for the dinner she was responsible to prepare.

"Sorry, Miss. . . ?"

Deeply lost in the world of a time-traveling English scientist inventor, Maggie jolted at the sound of the rich baritone voice behind her. Nearly dropping the precious volume, she clutched it to her white linen bodice and twirled to face the unexpected intruder.

"I'm afraid I'm a bit overdue." The man's voice reverberated through the empty library. Dark brown, drilling eyes matched the voice. His starched white collar and a fine-threaded suit coat announced he was a Bay View summer cottager, or perhaps a lecturer from the academy?

"We're closed." Her voice squeaked. Her heart still pounded with the surprise of her reverie interrupted and by the vision of a gentleman who might just have resurrected from the pages of her novel. Maggie pinched the tender skin beneath her elbow where she still clutched the book.

Ouch. Definitely not imagining.

"Ah, but the door was open. Therefore, the library is still open." He cocked a grin and braced his hands on the desk between them.

"Yes. I suppose you have a point." Maggie sized him up. Confident. Authoritative. As if the world belonged to him. Yet something in his curious grin hinted otherwise. Whatever it was, Maggie looked intently back at him and set her novel down. "How may I assist you, sir?"

"I need. . ." He hesitated, glancing at the spine of the book she clutched. "Do you always read adventure novels?"

"This one just arrived. I admit the first pages promise an exciting story. Reading as much of the materials as I'm able is a requisite. Loving them is a privilege." Maggie grinned, still infected by the thrill of the pages she'd just finished.

"And you prefer such adventure over the latest craze of suffrage or social injustice readings?"

"Oh sir, I believe overcoming the injustices of the world requires great imagination and mystery. I should think the most vital characteristics of a woman of substance begin with her willingness to imagine adventure and her desire to understand the mystery of humanity." Maggie blurted her heart's musing without thinking how it might sound to the refined man.

His eyes studied her novel once more, silent to her reply. Perhaps she'd spoken too boldly? Nervous prickles hovered over her skin.

A twinkling sparked his eyes as he looked up, as if calculating several different options while he stared openly into her eyes. "Actually, I need more than just a little assistance. If I might request a bit more of a, say. . .collaboration?"

Maggie's wits perked to attention. "Of course. A library assistant is ready to help, is she not?"

"Oh, not just 'help.' Participation. I'll need your word, your commitment. It could take all summer—if you can do it." The curious grin returned, framed by a strong jaw and a well-trimmed mustache. Seemingly quite aware he entertained her and her alone, the gentleman glanced down at his timepiece and around the empty library before handing her the edition of the *Saturday Review* for checkout.

"Well, sir. I'm intrigued, but how am I qualified for this collaboration you speak of? I know nothing of the requirements, or of you." She stamped the date on the check-out card. What an interesting chap. She suspected Wells's time traveler was just as mysterious, and she couldn't wait to read further.

"As a lecturer of Bay View's academy, I'm in charge of the material the students study in our Reading Circle on campus. I'll need selected readings pulled, read, and ready to discuss. If it goes well, the material you help me develop will be used for the *Bay View Magazine*, which you no doubt know is read nationwide since our small community of summer cottagers compose the second most popular Chautauqua in the nation—right behind the original community in Chautauqua, New York." His eyes twinkled as he awaited her response before he hooked her with the first challenge. "Start by reading the rest of that novel you were lost in when I entered."

"Read this? How does simply reading one novel count as collaboration?"

"That"—he searched for the name plate on her desk—"Miss Magdalena Abbott, is an answer you shall learn. I assure you, it is an honorable quest."

Learning. The one thing Maggie craved, and was always yearning to do. It was her insatiable curiosity that had driven James Abbott to deposit her care into the hands of the librarians while he worked after Maggie's mama had died. The library was the one place where she could travel in her mind. How could she say no to learning?

Maggie swallowed as he waited, his stance expectant and confident. His shoulders were wide and solid looking. How could it hurt to join in his proposed adventure?

"You came here for this express purpose at five minutes after five o'clock?"

"Well, not entirely. I came for a copy of the *Saturday Review*. But then I saw you, Miss Abbott, and it was clear you're the solution for our new Literary Reading Circle success.

What do you say? Will you help me research the Reading Circle curriculum? Think carefully. I'm giving you a chance to participate in the greatest national craze of higher-level learning that the ideals of Chautauqua offer—a chance to learn about culture, religion, politics, the great outdoors, and the arts—a chance to join the movement that started two decades ago and stands to influence generations to come." Though he held out his hand for her to shake as if they were merely making a business deal, his eyes twinkled as though he believed every word of his speech.

Maggie's heart thrilled. Her hand jutted into his larger one. Her lips moved despite her doubts about her qualifications for the task. He spoke as if any man or woman were a welcome contributor to the Chautauqua movement that was sweeping the nation. He didn't have to know she was merely the uneducated daughter of a gardener. "Yes. I'll do it." Her hand in his didn't exactly bounce with the shake of a gentleman's deal.

Instead, he held her hand gently and squeezed, not letting go immediately.

"I need your name, sir."

"Wesley Graham Hill the Third. Wes or Wesley to my friends." He released her hand, swept up the copy of the *Saturday Review* he'd come for, and exited as quickly as he'd appeared.

Panic and exhilaration rushed through Maggie's every fiber. She'd just made a private agreement with none other than *the* nephew of Bay View's members-only Chautauqua founder?

Maggie's heart fluttered at the idea of a real chance for a legitimate impact in the adult educational movement that had swept the nation's resort communities, and had pressed the small cottage community of Bay View to form its own academy that was now burgeoning at the seams with over seven hundred students. Surely he realized she wasn't a member or a student. Didn't he?

"Heavens, what was I thinking?" She pinched herself once more. Whether for reality's sake or for chastisement, she wasn't entirely certain.

———◦•◦———

"I'm afraid I'm a bit overdue?" Wesley kicked a stone, sending it skidding over the boardwalk outside the library. *What kind of an idiotic line was that?* Miss Abbott must have heard that line from more than one lad lucky enough to gain her attention. The fact that she hadn't evicted him from the premises on the spot with a string of well-rehearsed words from a suffragette speech was the simple reason he'd blurted out the unplanned proposal. He guessed she possessed both brains *and* beauty—two things he could stand to live with the rest of his life.

If his friend and co-lecturer Samuel Hicks had been keeping Miss Abbott's existence a secret while snatching up all the literature acquisitions for the Reading Circle, he'd never forgive the chap. How many evenings had he endured picnics in the grove, reclined at the edge of a blanket while listening to the regurgitation of a borrowed speech? Not to mention one too many poetry recitations spoken more from pretense than conviction. Wouldn't a woman rather *live* her life of equality than *talk* about it for hours on end, having never once set her foot in the ocean of her very own adventure or self-expression? How many nights had he tried to explain to Sam that he'd know what he was looking for in a woman when he saw it?

Wesley bounded up the steps of Uncle Bernard's house. Perhaps this was the summer that wouldn't be as predictable as the squeak of the hinges on the oaken front doors of the Victorian cottage on Maple Street, where he'd spent every summer of his existing memory.

Hopeful anticipation tightened in his chest and tugged a grin into place with the thought of seeing Miss Magdalena Abbott soon. Turning the brass knob, Wesley strode over the threshold and down the hallway toward the parlor, where voices filtered and the sound of silver spoons stirring in china teacups heralded feminine company among masculine voices.

"Ah, Wesley, we thought you'd forgotten all about us." Samuel Hicks stood, teacup in hand, dressed in his finest clothes for the evening's outing. A devilish twinkle in his widened eyes, followed by a wink, told Wes he'd been set up once again.

"Of course I haven't forgotten. How could I have?" How could he forget his challenge to Sam? A pledge based more on ornery determination and sheer resolution to prove his friend wrong than on a belief that Hicks would take him up on his claim that Bay View didn't harbor the woman of his future, and that she couldn't be found even if he had tea with all the ladies of the Association one by one.

Sam had argued that Wes's requirements in a future wife were far too demanding, that there were plenty of lovely candidates flocking Bay View every summer if he'd just open his eyes. Wesley had stood his ground that God had just one perfect plan for him, and it had raised the stakes, pushing the two of them toe-to-toe in the brotherly daring they'd enjoyed all through childhood. What would have ended years ago in spit and a handshake resulted instead in Sam taking it upon himself to test Wes's theory, bringing a string of ladies by the house for tea before they strolled through the grove to watch the million-dollar sunset over the bay.

Sure as the sun would set over the waters of Little Traverse Bay on Lake Michigan, the two young ladies sitting in the Hills' parlor were proof of Sam's determination. Aunt Maud quite enjoyed the parade of young ladies since she had no children of her own. Wesley's aunt had longed for a daughter, but instead had been a marvelous mother to Wesley after the death of his parents. Watching her now, engaged in small talk, made it all the harder to stop Sam's escapades when he saw how much she loved the company of each young lady. Aunt Maud was the sort of lovely woman that lavished her heart on everyone, and he loved her for it.

It was Uncle Bernard's more hard-nosed demeanor that gripped Wesley with dread. The man was driven to make Bay View the most popular Chautauqua in the nation, one which published a widely read magazine and drew diverse, famous speakers and well-known performers, while building the first onsite accredited academy. He was obsessed with the idea of transforming Bay View from a cluster of Methodist tent meetings along the bay to an up-and-coming academic powerhouse, poised to enter the twentieth century. Some said he'd sacrifice heart and spirit for the prestige, power, and ideals of his quest. Why, he could even boast that his efforts brought the likes of the nation's vice presidents to summer in the grandest hotel overlooking the bay.

Tonight, instead of his usual distraction with the latest political column of the newspaper, Uncle Bernard's voice rose to a tone he used when clinching difficult deals with the Association board of directors or working a stump speech in a fund-raising campaign.

"Well, Wesley, I'm glad to see you value punctuality at least a little." The barbed chiding belied his uncle's smile as he turned to introduce the lady assigned Wesley's courtship for the evening. "I've been anxious for you to meet this lovely young lady, Miss Mary Reed. The two of you have many passions in common, and I should think you'd want to be on your way. I'm afraid I've quite talked you up, and you're sure to take a liking to each other."

One sideways glance at Sam confirmed friend and family alike were out to settle a match with the girl as if she were the daughter of William Jennings Bryan or the heir of General Custer. As if her social standing had anything at all to do with her substance.

Because wits or not, her appearance had nothing on the vision still fogging his mind or the spirit that was already infecting his soul—the vision and essence of the library princess Magdalena Abbott.

Chapter Two

A parcel came in the mail this morning." Miss Eloise, the library matron, peered over the wire rims of her spectacles at Maggie.

"Oh? Shall I fetch it?" Maggie stood from the chair of her library desk, ready for a walk to the post office and a bit of fresh northern air.

"No need. You may sit." Miss Eloise paused, letting the air fill with anticipation before she laid the brown-wrapped package on the desk with a quizzical look on her softly wrinkled face. "It's addressed to you, and the return address is a Mister W. G. Hill, the *Third*. Do you know this man?" Her left eyebrow rose with the motherly tone of inquisition in her voice.

Maggie slid her fingers under the sealed edge of the large envelope, her heart fluttering at the remembrance of their exchange. "I've only met him once. He's from the Literary Reading Circle." The contents of the letter spread on the desk before her, the reading assignment he'd spoken about. "I'm to pull the items he requests, read them, and be ready to discuss them." She scanned the list, aware that Miss Eloise was still peering over the rim of her glasses at the papers.

"And when might this young chap be seeing you again for this arrangement of—of academic study?"

Maggie finally looked up from the list to face the gaze of the woman who had been her surrogate mother for the last decade since her mother's passing. "I haven't a clue. He didn't say."

Miss Eloise's countenance shifted. "Got you on the string, has he?"

"Oh, Miss Eloise, it's not like that at all." Maggie stood and gathered the papers to her chest, fully aware she sounded as if she were about to beg. "It's as if I'd finally be like all the other academy girls." She sighed, shoulders sagging as she looked at the list before her then back to Miss Eloise's face again. What she hoped to find in the older woman's gaze Maggie wasn't sure, for it wasn't as if she required the woman's permission.

"But what I love most about you, dear girl, is precisely that you are not like all the other young ladies in Bay View."

"I can do the assignments and still fulfill my obligations. I promise." Maggie's heart slipped a little at the reminder of her place in society, for she had vowed not to let it define her. No matter how well rounded Bay View's popular Chautauqua ideals, Maggie was ever aware of the reality that hard work and an education were her only avenues to secure a future.

"You'll still be expected to keep your post at the checkout desk."

"Of course." Maggie held her breath, as if Miss Eloise's approval was enough to justify the indulgence of such a dream. It was what she loved most about her mentor—that she had always encouraged learning and dreaming.

"How will you find enough time to read it all? And your father—you'll be finished in time to make him dinner?"

"Yes."

"Have you explained this arrangement to him?"

"Not yet." She would tell Father, of course. "It may be just this once unless Mr. Hill deems the results good enough to publish. I won't let it interfere with my responsibilities at work or at home." But she couldn't keep a begging tone from lacing her words. Learning like the academy girls was the one dream she'd harbored forever, but it was too costly and Miss Eloise knew it. If the woman didn't give her approval, any act of defiance would be a poison between them Maggie could never abide.

"How did you meet this man, what's his name?"

"Wesley. Mister Wesley Hill." She braced inwardly for the coming reaction.

"Mr. Hill's nephew?" Miss Eloise's eyes twinkled with a gleam of pride before she cleared her voice. "Well I suppose we should accommodate his request. How did this personal arrangement come about?"

"After hours." Thinking twice about her words, Maggie stumbled onward. "I mean, I'd forgotten to lock the front door promptly, and he just appeared. I suppose I'd gotten a wee bit absorbed in a novel." Rushing on before the head librarian changed her mind, Maggie swept around the desk and continued. "Oh, but have you read *The Time Machine*? It's simply delicious. Anyone with an imagination worth having would agree."

"Yes, yes, of course, but I should think the assignment will be much more academic than such fanciful fiction. I suppose he'll return at much the same time so the two of you will have a moment to discuss your readings?"

Maggie bit her lip, feeling ridiculous that the fact that she would be alone with him hadn't occurred to her, knowing she should have a proper chaperone. She held her breath, not wanting to ask a favor from the old library matron whose once-steady feet had begun to shuffle with the limp of hip pain. Her beloved Miss Eloise had begun to look older than her seventy years but insisted upon remaining at her post. Would it be too much for her to extend her hours for the arrangement? Maggie dared not ask, but she couldn't keep the pleading from her eyes as she awaited Miss Eloise's response. She'd never wanted anything more.

"I suppose I can stay late."

"Oh, *thank you!*" Maggie's voice squeaked loud, echoing across the library hall as she engulfed Miss Eloise's squishy shoulders in an embrace and kissed her on the cheek.

"Hush now, it's not as if I've moved the stars and moon." Her voice was somewhat stern, but the twinkle in her old eyes melted Maggie.

For it seemed the stars and moon had shifted in her universe.

Maggie gathered the list of assigned reading and turned toward the bookshelves, then hesitated. "Oh, and Miss Eloise?"

Miss Eloise held her with gray eyes. When had the dear woman's hair turned such pure silver?

"Thank you."

Wesley couldn't shake the mood that had stayed with him since he'd overslept and rushed off to the office for the day. The cloudy images of his late mother's face had been so real in his dreams. She had spoken to him this time, but he couldn't make out her words. The urgency of her appearance stayed with him, reminding him that Aunt Maud's faith—much like his mother's—had taught him to listen for the still small voice of God's Spirit everywhere. Even in dreams.

What if he'd misread Miss Magdalena Abbott's character?

Breathing an unspoken prayer, Wesley pushed through the front doors of the library and into the silence of the long room. A flame of anticipation of another encounter with the mysterious library princess surged through him, dashing into a pile of ashes when he found the central desk empty and tidy, as if it had been arranged for the end of the day.

Had she forgotten? Or worse, did she lavish her vivacious spirit upon everyone who encountered her, leaving him no more unique than any other? Had he misread the immediate connection? He glanced right and left through the rows of bookshelves, but she was not to be seen.

"You'll never find the girl you're waiting for if your requirements are impossible to meet!" Sam's teasing had been good natured, but Wes refused to believe it. He rang the bell on her desk and waited. His leather satchel suddenly seemed full of bricks. His necktie choked his breath. The yearning to utter his uncertainties aloud and to hear the soft reassurances of his mother's voice recalled the dream to his mind once more.

"May I be of service?" A gray-haired woman appeared from a side door and stood before him, tipping her head back to look up at him through her spectacles.

"Mister Wesley Hill. I'm looking for a Miss Magdalena Abbott."

"She's been expecting you." The woman studied his response for a moment. "Along the south window there is a study desk. She's waiting there with the materials you requested."

Relief and exhilaration warred within—such an inner battle of breath and heart rate had never occurred with any of the ladies Sam had brought for an outing. "Thank you, ma'am."

"Yes sir. I'll be in my office nearby." She fastened eyes on him. "My door shall remain open. I trust your intentions are honorable. Academic study, I believe?"

Wesley tried to read the woman's features, but they were locked up tight. "Absolutely, ma'am. I give you my word."

Her lips pinched as she nodded. Wesley was certain a smile and slight wink flashed over her face as she turned back to her office. He made a mental note that the woman was an ally not to be crossed.

Wesley turned the corner toward the south wall where the late afternoon sunshine glowed over the alcove tucked behind a tall bookshelf of reference materials. A large oaken library table sat against the wall near the corner, books littered over it, papers and notes scattered. In the center of the studious mess, Miss Abbott sat, bent over, head on her arms. Sleeping?

He hesitated. Committing the scene to memory first, he cleared his voice.

Her soft breath fluttered a sheet of paper.

Stepping closer, he shuffled his feet a bit louder and set his leather satchel on the table across from her.

The library princess jolted upright and shot out of her chair. "Oh, Mr. Hill. I've read every last word of the assigned works you've requested. I've made notes and compiled questions for discussion points." She flitted around the table, shuffling papers into piles. "It's taken me all week, but I finished just today." Arranging notes with each book, stacking them neatly, she gathered all of them into her arms and faced him. She glanced at his satchel as if only just realizing the materials would never fit, then looked up once again.

Sleep lines crossed her cheek. Her hair was neatly arranged in a smart style that framed her heart-shaped face.

"I intended to review the work with you, did you forget?" Wesley waited. The usual silence of the library seemed full of music to him, as if she were the reason for it. Her nervous rushing words, followed by a pause when her eyes matched his, affected him like a rich mellow orchestra. He couldn't have been wrong about her. He reached to rescue the books slipping from her arms.

"Of course, you did say that." She let out a nervous breath.

"Please, show me your work." He pulled a chair out across from her and spread out the outlines she'd made. The pages were filled with her neat handwriting, arranged in perfect order. "Please, sit with me."

"Certainly. I suppose I'm a bit anxious, Mr. Hill."

"Wesley."

Her cheeks brightened. "Maggie." She smiled without pretense.

Motioning her to sit, he assisted her closer to the table before taking his seat across from her.

"What do you want to know?" She ran her fingers over the gilded design of the novel in front of her.

Everything. I want to know everything about you. Wesley swallowed. "Tell me what you loved."

"The English course study." Her shoulders relaxed. "I loved everything about it, especially the story of England, the one by Mary Parmele—the histories that traced back to Scotland and Ireland were incredible." Instead of gestures of practiced etiquette, her hands fingered through the pages of notes. Referring to her outlines, she easily poured out her thoughts and questions with hardly a pause. Her delight in the process was more than obvious—it was infectious and absorbed him effortlessly into the world of words, essays, and works of poetry. Her retelling of the review was unlike any dry lecture he'd ever given and more like she'd taken him with her on a train ride through the English countryside.

So vibrantly real was Maggie's imagination, Wesley was convinced that no matter the topic, she could never bore him. Time slid into oblivion, taking him deeper in discussion with her until the wall clock rang six o'clock. The chime broke their exchange all too soon.

"I must go." Her voice clipped as she tucked her handbag beneath her arm and all too abruptly bid him good evening. Her skirt swished as she twirled and started down the hall without another word, not even pausing for his response.

"Wait, Maggie." Wesley rushed to follow her. "I'll walk you home."

"No." The answer flipped out, erasing her earlier casual ease with a nervous exit. "I'm meeting someone."

"You have an escort then."

"Yes." She stopped and turned, anxious as a mouse caught by a tomcat. Heavens, he wasn't going to pounce at her. Yet the more he backed away from her, the more relieved she appeared until she disappeared through the front doors of the library and was gone.

Maggie Abbott. He closed his eyes as if memorizing everything about her could make her reappear.

One thing was clear.

He hadn't been wrong about her.

Chapter Three

Maggie grabbed the pole of the streetcar and jumped on board just as it eased into the street and made the all-too-familiar turn away from Bay View and up the hill toward Petoskey. Ducking between other passengers, she tossed a quick glance behind her. Nowhere did she see Wesley's tall frame and broad shoulders. Relief vied with disappointment, leaving her in a twist of emotions she couldn't sort.

Stopping at the Lewis Street Suburban station, the streetcar emptied of Petoskey travelers, mostly a mix of Bay View workers and tourists who stayed at the Cushman Hotel when attending lectures in Bay View. Maggie wound through the crowd toward the long stairway from the back end of the alley to her apartment. At the top of the steps she fumbled for the key to the rooms above Easton's Hardware Store where she and her father boarded. She quickly let herself in, the quietness telling her she'd made it home before her father but had precious little time before he would appear.

Slicing some corned beef and a piece of bread, she lit the stove and took down the cast iron skillet from its place on the shelf. No cupboard graced their kitchen. Only an old dry sink, an icebox, and a miniature four-burner stove. Turning the flame to low, she placed the beef in the pan and turned to her room to change out of her one and only good shirtwaist. She dared not get grease on it. Running her hand over the linen and lace front, she hung it on a hanger from the back of the door and slipped out of the navy skirt.

"This roast beef will be black as tar if you don't flip it soon, rosebud."

"Corned beef, Papa. It's the cheapest meat the butcher has." Meeting her father in the kitchen, she threw her arms around him.

He buried his whiskers in her neck until she giggled.

"You smell like grass."

"I clipped the lawn in front of the hotel today."

"But I thought Stafford's Place Hotel had their own lawn man and you would be left to tend the gardens. How are your knees? Did they take all that bending okay, or was it like a beating?"

"Aw, don't worry about me, rosebud. The boss promised to have me back on the gardens tomorrow. The regular lawn man didn't show up today. So I did his job and my job."

"More pay, I hope—to cover the cost of the extra laundry it'll cost us. Look at your knees, all grass stained."

"Don't you worry about money. I've been saving a little back when I can. Besides, I saw Mrs. Campbell on my way to get the streetcar and she says her roses need pruning. She'll pay me a little."

"You mean with huckleberry pie?" Maggie winked at her father, who never gave up evidence if he'd eaten wild blueberry pie from Mrs. Campbell right before the dinner hour.

He still ate as heartily as if he were starving, and she loved him in spite of the naughtiness of breaking Mama's rule of no dessert before dinner. She could still see the look of love on her mama's face long ago when she had chided him with a smile.

"Mrs. Campbell has a screen door that needs fixing as well. She'll give me some money for that, too, I expect." Her father reached for her hand once she'd sat beside him. Removing his hat, he bowed his head and said the Lord's Prayer. He lifted his head and said what he always said. "The Lord always provides our daily bread, Maggie. Too much would mold anyway."

Well, bread might mold. But she was quite certain a second dress would not. Was it such a sin to wish for one more? A pretty tea dress like the one she'd seen in the window on Lake Street. Where was the hurt in dreaming?

"You're quiet today. Saw you get on the streetcar that left just before I reached it. Miss Eloise got you tied up extra late?"

Maggie's corned beef stuck to the roof of her mouth. She nodded her head and reached for her water glass. It wasn't that she didn't want to tell him everything. A rush of warm emotion tangled her stomach. It was more that she didn't quite know how to tell it. She swallowed. It was merely a simple assignment, easy to explain. Wasn't it?

"You must be tired lifting all those old heavy volumes up over your head, climbing that library ladder up and down all day."

She nodded. Perhaps he was right, the long day was the reason for the odd emotions swirling within.

"Go on to your room and rest. I'll wash up."

Truthfully, she was tired. Though it was less from her work and more from reading when she should have been sleeping, and hurrying stacks of books back to the shelves before they were missed the next morning. Maggie was grateful for the excuse to retreat to her room and close the door behind her. She laid her shirtwaist out on a clean spot on the floorboards and spread dried rose petal sachets over it for fragrance. Papa said real roses were better than any store-bought lady's perfume. And though she loved when he brought her fresh rose cuttings from the garden where he worked at Stafford Place, she still dreamt of having real perfume someday.

Her conscience pricked her as if dreaming was akin to ungratefulness. But it wasn't. Not really or truly. Nowhere had she read in the Bible that dreaming was a sin.

But keeping a secret was nearly like a white lie, and she knew it to be the real source of her anxiety, for she had always shared everything with her father. Why she hadn't just explained herself she wasn't sure.

Folding her hands, she closed her eyes. "Heavenly Father, I thank Thee for all the bread You give us, and that it isn't moldy. I thank Thee for this dress and these rose petals, and that dreaming isn't a sin. And I promise if Papa asks, I will tell the truth about why I was late. Amen."

⸺•◆•⸺

"Look at these outlines, Sam. The work is exhaustive and comprehensive. I'm telling you, this lady is a genius. None of my academy students are half as bright. I'm going to publish her." Wesley leaned back. The squeak of his weight against the oak chair echoed in the office he shared at Loud Hall with Sam. "You're sure you've never seen Miss Abbott—you haven't been keeping her existence a secret?"

"Miss who?" Sam never looked up from the desk where he sat across from Wes, grading essays.

"Sam!" Wesley stood up to pace the small space between his side of the desk and the bookcase—the space he used to think and clear his mind of clutter.

"What?"

"Have you heard a word I've said?"

"Something about genius?" Sam shifted, waiting for the ensuing discourse Wes was about to unleash.

"Miss Abbott's work. It's genius. Perfection. She not only talked with ease about England nonstop for an hour, but this work. . .it's as if she's taken a trip to Russia herself. Look at her discussion questions for *The Geography of Russia* by Georg Brandes. Perfection, I'm telling you. This is the second discussion set she's done for me." Wesley tossed the papers in front of Sam.

His friend lifted the outlined papers and studied them quietly while Wesley looped his thumbs over his belt, waiting for the agreement he expected.

Sam lowered the papers. "Seems rather ordinary to me."

"What?" Wesley snatched the papers, ready to debate as if a line had just been drawn.

But a glint sparked in his friend's eyes as he squinted and drilled his gaze in return. "This Miss Abbott—she's probably the ugly cousin of a cottager, only here and gone. Why, I've never seen her, never heard her name before. The only feminine intelligence in the library I've ever seen is old Miss Eloise. Have you fallen for the gray-haired library matron?"

"For the love of Saint Peter." Wesley took the papers and collapsed back into his chair.

Sam's laughter broke the too-serious tension. For all the years they'd shared a wrangling sort of brotherly love and competition in all things sport and intellect, Wesley prized their close bond no matter the subject. But this friendly challenge to find a woman had pressed his friend to a new level of scrutiny.

"You think she has matched your intellect?" Sam lightened the goading, his voice lowered.

"I do."

"And good character?"

"Yes." Something told him she did. Though he couldn't name one solid reason why he thought so. Certainly nothing that would hold up to Sam's debate if he set his mind to disagree. Truthfully, he hardly knew the young lady.

Sam's face grew serious, as if realization struck him. Leaning in, he pointed at Wes. "You think she meets your impossible criteria, don't you?"

The air squeezed inside Wesley's chest. He couldn't explain why he thought so.

Scrambling to his feet, Sam pounded the desk with a victorious grin. "Blimey! You do!"

"Why do you use that word?" Wesley stood to pace again. "You aren't even a Brit."

"Don't shift the subject, old chap. I'm onto you—the man who refused to seriously court a Bay View girl if she were the last woman on earth?"

Wesley turned back to deny it. After all, how could he know after only having met her little more than once? "I—"

"I'll believe you're serious about her if you actually convince her to let you take her to the Final Fling by summer's end—that is if this hidden library goddess truly exists." Sam stuck out his hand, minus the spit of their boyhood challenges.

Wesley gripped Sam's hand and shook hard before he could think twice of the implications. If it would stop the parade of engagements his friend had imposed on him for the summer, it would be worth it even if he were wrong about Maggie Abbott.

But he wasn't wrong about her.

And he would prove it to Sam.

Chapter Four

Still amazed at how much Wesley had loved her work on England and Russia, Maggie emptied the contents of the third packet onto her desk after the last patron left for the day. The package from Wesley and the list of tasks from Miss Eloise had been side by side on her desk when she'd arrived that morning. After peeking inside to see what her next assignment was, she'd placed it in her desk drawer while she completed the tasks on Miss Eloise's list.

Maggie was certain the dear woman had practically beamed with pride, as if the exchange with Wesley were equal to a social debut. But it wasn't anything like it.

Anticipation warred with her burning conscience all day. She'd had to cut short her second meeting with Wesley to arrive home before her father. Yet, curiosity for learning fueled and mounted as she read the third assignment. She was to read parts of *Brave Little Holland* and write discussion questions. Inside the packet was a copy of the book. She could take it home and read it in her room.

It wasn't that she wanted to keep a secret from her father. It was more that she couldn't bear it if he were somehow shamed by her wanting the things he could never provide. Protective sadness for him sagged her shoulders. She would tell him, but only if he asked.

Still, she would need to stay late at the library once more. It would give her access to the atlas and other reference materials she needed to complete the work.

In a prayer, she searched her heart for any wrong motivation and found none. Surely there was no harm in helping Wesley one more time.

She opened the book to the right chapter and scanned the pages.

Glancing at the clock, Maggie calculated there was enough time to spend at least an hour on the assignment. She headed to the table along the south wall, near the atlases and other maps. She spread her materials across the table and stepped onto the lowest rung of the library ladder to reach for the large table atlas on the top shelf. It was a wide and awkward book to balance. Twisting, she stepped down as the book nearly slipped from her hands.

"Let me help with that, Maggie." Wesley relieved her of the volume and extended a hand to her.

"I didn't expect you." Maggie wavered as she stepped down, startled by his appearance and the unexpected warmth on her arm when he reached to steady her. "I only just opened the assignment you sent over. I'm afraid I've not even begun it." She stepped back toward her chair, putting the library table between them. "Perhaps you should return another day and I'll have it completed for you."

She sat down to begin her study, but realized he still held the atlas, saying nothing.

Rather, he stared at her for a moment, then, "Miss Abbott, I wonder—do you do everything so thoroughly excellently as the work I've asked of you?"

She eyed the atlas she needed to get started. He caught her distraction and slid it behind his back as if to hold her attention captive. Did real professors inspire such a case of sudden nerves in all their students? Maggie drew in a soothing breath and gave him the unspoken attention he awaited.

"Your work is near perfection. I'd wager your teachers found it a delightful pleasure to instruct you in school."

Heat shimmered across her cheeks and prickled her scalp. She told herself it was not from the directness of Wesley Graham Hill, nor the kindness in his words. It had been Miss Eloise who'd taught her everything she knew since her twelfth birthday when she'd quit school to care for Papa's broken leg. The library matron had seen to it that her education wasn't halted and had put her to work shelving returned books after hours, while church ladies took turns caring for her father.

"Thank you." Maggie averted her gaze and fidgeted with the paper that listed her assignment.

Wesley stepped closer. "Maggie, you needn't be shy about it. You've got real ability. Haven't you been told that before?"

No, she hadn't. Well, yes, by Miss Eloise. But she'd not counted that in the same way she imagined it might feel to garner a top position in the classroom. Yet, now—here, in the quietness of her domain, under the study of the handsome Wesley Hill—the compliment only served to remind her of the chasm of differences between them. Though why she should care if he knew her station simply muddled her thoughts entirely.

"Mr. Hill, please. The atlas—may I have it?" Daring to look up, Maggie found his eyes dancing with delight, one half of his mouth pulled up with mischief.

"Only if you let me join you. Work the assignment along with me. Show me how you apply your genius." He held the atlas out to her.

"Well, I suppose academic study is an acceptable reason for your time spent here."

"Quite proper, I assure you." He cracked open the atlas to the map of Holland. "Now take me on a trip to Holland through the pages of *Brave Little Holland* so I can re-create that world for my readers just as you've created worlds for me in your last two assignments."

She had created worlds for him? Maggie opened the pages of three other reference books she'd found about Holland and laid them out on the table. Turning to the chapters they were to study, she found the names of towns and leaned over the map with him to find where they were situated. "There. See how the North Sea meets the lowlands on the northwest coast?" She pulled away from where his sleeve had brushed against hers and began to read aloud. She loved the descriptions of dikes, lowlands, thatched roofs, and of villages along the River Zaan where seventeenth-century windmills dotted the riverside.

The hands of the library clock ticked as she painted verbal pictures of the land and people while Wesley scribbled on papers. After he'd filled three entire pages, Maggie launched further into a description of Dutch tulips. She halted midsentence when she noticed that Wesley had stopped taking notes. A peculiar look came over his face as he leaned back in the chair and rested his head on his fingers laced behind his head.

"Shall I stop?"

"No." He continued to keep his attention on her as she paced back and forth, book in hand, looking up now and again to expound from her imagination what it must have been like to live in Holland in 1800. Still, he said nothing.

"Oh dear, I've gone off topic too far, haven't I?"

Wesley stood, moving closer to face her. "No, Miss Maggie. For you've taken me to Holland and back with you."

The look in his eye had changed.

A nervous tremor warmed through her middle. "Did you like it?"

The wall clock began to chime six o'clock.

He closed the book she held, his hands over hers. "Very much."

Miss Eloise's voice chimed over the third gong of the wall clock. "Miss Maggie, time to close up." Her footsteps sounded in the hallway, coming closer.

Maggie startled, managing to slide her hands and the book from beneath Wesley's. "I must go."

"Please Maggie, don't rush off again."

"I mustn't be late." She scooped her papers into her folder and slid past Miss Eloise, kissing her on the cheek as she did every night. "Good night, Miss Eloise."

———•◦•———

Wesley stared at the empty hallway where Maggie had once again abruptly disappeared. He'd hoped to escort her home and ask her to attend a lecture with him the following week, but she evaporated before he had a chance.

"Like a butterfly, she is. Isn't she?" Miss Eloise looked down the hall after her, then winked at him.

"Yes, she is always flitting off just as I expect her to land." He reminded himself the matron was the ally he needed, but he wasn't sure how to gain her trust and prove his mission was honorable.

"Bright and lovely, too, yes?"

"That she is. That she is." Wesley grinned, knowing he couldn't find the right words for exactly what his intentions were. To ask her to the music festival for the Final Fling at the end of the summer, of course. But having never met her parents, how was he to gain permission to court her? Or was she of independent age, able to answer for herself? There really was nothing about her that was conventional, which intrigued him all the more.

"Mr. Hill, that butterfly should be caught by someone who can appreciate her beauty and her need to fly. She has a solid mind and a passion that no circumstances should hinder. Now help me put that atlas up on the shelf. I'm too old to climb the ladder." The silver-haired matron plunged the atlas into his hands.

Wesley reached the atlas to its place and turned to find Miss Eloise studying him with a gleam in her eye and more of a grin than he'd ever seen on her before.

"Does anyone court her, Miss Eloise?"

"No sir. You'd be the first to ask about our Maggie."

He stepped off the bottom rung. "I'll be back in one week." He dared to wink at the old woman.

"Of course you will, though I'd have you mind not to trifle with her." Blessing and threat wove through her words with the precision of a loving guardian.

"You have my word of honor." Wesley laid his hand over his heart, spurred to continue his pursuit of the lovely Miss Maggie Abbott.

Chapter Five

The fourth weekly package of assignments arrived three days ahead of schedule. The new assignment was of an entirely different nature—English royalty. The questions were more probing, more concerning the character and nature of Queen Victoria. Thrilling. Maggie could hardly wait for five o'clock. But it was the yellow rose pressed flat with an attached note in his handwriting that kept her thoughts circling back again to Wesley Graham Hill.

The fragrance of the friendship rose she knew well.

The sudden catch of her breath—quite unfamiliar.

A rush of warm emotion washed over her each time she read his words of thanks for *taking him to Holland and back.* Beneath the careful script, it was signed, *"Your Friend Always, Wesley."*

The words, the rose, said nothing more than friendship. But as she worked through the questions, Maggie found she began to cherish his way of matching her curiosity for adventure and learning. Anticipation and wonder mounted as she delved deeper into study. Would his eyes be filled once more with that knowing sense that he understood her mind?

The library was silent. Miss Eloise was tucked in her office with the door half cracked open. Once Maggie had caught the matron with eyes closed though she sat over a book, making Maggie giggle to herself.

The clock chimed the fifth time. Five o'clock.

Maggie pulled the drawer of the library desk open where she'd tucked the pressed friendship rose. Was it friendship alone that fueled the expectation she felt mounting within? Pushing the uncertain thoughts aside, she gathered her study materials, found their usual study alcove, and spread out her papers.

She'd already worked through the introductory questions about England's countryside and delved into the more interesting memoirs of Queen Victoria's younger years. Maggie admired Victoria because she'd forsaken the privilege of an isolated court life for one that brought her into daily contact with the sufferings of the poor.

She looked back to Wesley's question. *"Was Queen Victoria's life of privilege more or less, or of equal value to those of lower social standing?"* Of course, she knew the answer.

But how could she explain to Wesley Graham Hill III that even though everywhere she looked in Bay View there was the belief that riches, knowledge, and opportunity were paramount to happiness, in her own humble home in Petoskey she'd flourished under the wealth of love, faith, and trust? How could she answer his question without admitting what she knew from her own experience?

Would the unveiled truth cost her the friendship she'd just begun to prize?

━━━•◦•━━━

He was late. And it dogged him, because he loved punctuality.

Wesley's brow prickled with moisture as he entered the library and turned toward his rendezvous with Maggie Abbott. The anxiety of being late, combined with the risk he'd taken and the one he was about to take, had his heart bounding as if he were a fly-fisherman hooking a feisty brown trout on the Minnie River.

It made him feel more alive than he'd been in a lifetime of camp meetings.

What could a man ever hope to gain without risk?

Wesley prayed his plans would come together as he hoped.

True to form, he found his library princess bent over her studies, the evening light glowing about her as she looked up. The smile she gave him landed straight in his chest, settling the last of his doubts.

"Maggie, I'm late. I wanted to be earlier—I've got tickets. We should hurry."

"You've what?" Her brow wrinkled at his rushed and tumbled invitation.

"To the lecture at Evelyn Hall. Isabel Garghill Beecher is speaking. It's to be magnificent. I knew you'd not be able to resist." He grinned with the knowledge that he'd paid double the price to get Sam's extra ticket for Maggie.

"But the Reading Circle questions. . .I thought. . ."

The library clock began to herald quarter of six.

"Miss Beecher is famous on the Chautauqua speaking circuit, you'll see." He began closing books and gathering papers as Miss Eloise's footsteps sounded on cue behind him.

"Maggie Mae Abbott, I've got to leave early tonight. You'd best let Mr. Hill see you out now and lock the door behind you." Miss Eloise's directive brooked no argument from Maggie, despite the younger woman's look of astonishment.

Maggie turned to shelve a stack of books on the wooden library cart, and Miss Eloise grinned at Wesley as she winked.

"We should hurry." He reached to guide Maggie's elbow.

"But I should get back. . ."

"Oh, and Maggie, I promised your father I'd bring him some cold cuts from the butcher. He offered to fix the broken window shutters on my front porch. It's the least I can do, you know. Such a gentleman, your father is." Miss Eloise chattered on, not letting Maggie excuse herself abruptly as she was accustomed. Wesley took Maggie's satchel over his shoulder and gently guided her after Miss Eloise toward the door.

Outside the library doors Maggie flashed a look between the two of them as Miss Eloise's key turned the lock. "There you are. Now, the two of you have a lovely evening at the lecture." Patting Maggie on the arm, she turned away, leaving them alone.

"But I haven't any money with me to pay for my ticket." Maggie looked a bit ambushed.

"Already taken care of." Wesley held up the tickets, waiting for an answer.

"I'm not dressed for an evening out."

She met his gaze as he held out his hand, but still hesitated.

"Maggie, it's your company I want. You look lovely."

370

"You planned this with Miss Eloise, didn't you?"

"I'll never tell." He winked at her, and the pink that sprinkled her cheeks was worth the exorbitant price of the extra ticket.

"You won't regret it. I promise."

Chapter Six

If Miss Eloise hadn't been such a champion, Maggie would think it was time to insist she keep her nose out of. . .what? What exactly was Mr. Hill other than a library patron? A friend? Beside her, Wesley Graham Hill III hadn't stopped talking about the lectures he'd enjoyed in the Reading Circle and at the assembly hall and how her mind would swell if she could hear them all. Her arm nestled in his as they crossed the wooded campus of Bay View. Of course she'd walked beneath the summer shade of these maple trees a hundred times or more, but only as if she'd borrowed the sweet place without legitimate permission. She might believe it were hers easier if she'd jumped into it with H.G. Wells's time traveler at her side in place of Wesley Hill.

Wesley led her toward Evelyn Hall, the largest and most beautiful Queen Anne-style home near the center of campus with a large wraparound porch dotted with rocking chairs. The transom windows were cracked open to let the cool summer breeze from Lake Michigan keep the crowded room they entered from overheating while Miss Beecher spoke.

Maggie hardly noticed anyone in the audience, so enraptured was she by Miss Beecher's recitation. Wesley seated her next to another academy man, nestling her in the chair between them. Lost in the story world the woman created, the transport into imagination so glorious, Maggie was convinced her own ability to take Wesley to Holland and back with her words paled by comparison.

Outside Evelyn Hall, shadows from the setting sun cast the flowers into greater brilliance than she'd noticed before. The air from the bay had grown cooler and the scent of pine trees filled the evening air. Goose bumps traveled up her arms, the absence of her seatmates' nearness now chilled her as they walked farther away from the crowded speaker's hall. She shivered and folded her hands across her arms, the story still casting a sweet satisfaction over her soul.

"You're cold?" Wesley shifted out of his suit jacket and draped it around her shoulders as the man she'd been sandwiched beside approached them. Linked on the man's arm was a stunning brunette dressed in an evening gown Maggie had seen in a shop window. Wesley draped his arm about Maggie's shoulders, pulling her closer to his side. "Come have tea with us, Mag? Please say you'll come along, it'll be just the thing to warm you."

The young man with wire-rimmed spectacles grasped Wesley's shoulder with a squeeze. "So, you've brought your own company finally, Wes? I thought I'd have to manage your schedule forever." He winked at Wesley as he waited for an introduction.

"Aw, Sam, lay off. This is the lovely Miss Maggie Abbott I've told you about."

Maggie felt her cheeks grow pink under the compliment and scrutiny. Suddenly she felt her smart navy skirt and ivory shirtwaist represented Miss Eloise's generation more than her own. Soon she'd been introduced to Wesley's lifetime chap, Sam, and Sam's lady friend, Francine, as the four drifted away from the center of campus. Away from home. Away from the train station and the library. Away from her father and Miss Eloise. A wonderful, terrible shiver enveloped her beneath Wesley's jacket. The jacket wafted minty soap with a mix of oak moss and ferns that made her feel as if she'd just slept in one of the English gardens she'd read about. Penhaligon's English Fern cologne, was it? Maggie had noticed it at Fay's Dress Shop, remembering the ingredients of the fragrance Father had told her about.

The glory of the evening was more intoxicating than any book she'd ever read, and as with books, she couldn't tear herself away from it as they strolled through the grove and along the streets lined with cottage after cottage. Each one held its own charm, white-painted gingerbread lattice framed over lace-curtained windows. Porches lined with chairs tugged at Maggie's yearning for a porch of her own where she and Father could sit and watch the stars or drink a cup of cocoa. July cicadas had begun to sing, announcing midsummer and the coming of August warmth.

At the foot of the steps that Sam and Francine ascended before them, Maggie hesitated, overwhelmed by the formality of crossing the threshold of Wesley's family cottage linked on his arm. Something warned inside her, and it must have shown on her face.

"Mag?" Wesley turned back from the steps to face her as she looked up at the two-story luxurious summer home and wondered how formidably powerful and genteel the family's winter home surely was.

"It's so lovely."

"Come meet my aunt. She's been waiting for an introduction." He stood before her, the twilight growing dark around them, the light from the parlor window around his strong shoulders. "Don't be nervous, Mag. She'll love you. You'll love her."

"You should have told me you had this in mind." She swallowed and bit her lip, taking a deep breath before she looked up at him. "You did. . .have this in mind, didn't you?" The question blurted before she could take it back, yet she really had to know just how he'd been thinking of her.

Stepping closer, Wesley laid his hands over her arms, engulfed in his jacket sleeves.

She searched his eyes that twinkled with the rising moonlight, wanting reassurance she hadn't been foolish. Her heart skipped a beat when he slid a lock of her hair away from her face.

"Would you have come if I'd asked?" That cheeky half grin she'd come to like tugged at his mouth. "Or would you have run off like you have every other time?"

Somehow his baritone voice, their conversations about worlds far away, all their talk of the wisdom of God and humanity, his patient waiting for her as he stood close, eased the warning within. She thought to pray before resting her arm in his, unsure she could hear any heavenly directive at such a moment. How did anyone know with certainty about such things?

And how had he called her "Mag" in such a way that made her think he'd thrown convention and formality aside like a society rebel, yet still managed to treat her in such a way that made her want to follow him through the front door of the most prominent family in Bay View?

Wesley wasn't sure which was more worrisome—that the formidable wealth he lived in was overwhelming, or that facing Uncle Bernard as a woman of unknown family lineage might scare her away forever.

Hand at her back, he led her through the front doors, down the hallway, and into the parlor where Sam and Francine had taken their comfortable places. He hoped Sam might buffer the conversation and any unwelcome scrutiny from Uncle Bernard. But his uncle wasn't home. Only Aunt Maud, and she brimmed with all the sweetness that he loved her for.

Wesley breathed a sigh of relief, releasing the tension and tightness from his chest. Aunt Maud, who only saw hearts and souls, could be counted on to put Maggie at ease. He winked at her from where he stood next to Maggie.

While he made introductions to his aunt, Sam and Francine drifted to the settee where they sipped tea and paged through the day's newspaper. True to her nature, his aunt engulfed Maggie with a warm embrace that made him wish his mother could have been there for the introduction. Maggie caught his gaze for a moment as Aunt Maud engaged her attention—pouring her tea, offering her pleasantries, and drawing her in with conversation about the Reading Circle and the library.

When the teacups were emptied, he and Sam convinced Maggie and Francine to take turns reading poems aloud from the Reading Circle magazine. First Francine stood in the center of the parlor to mimic the monologue stance of the evening's reader, then Maggie. Aunt Maud sat quietly in her rocker with needlepoint work that had slid to her lap as she'd laid her head back, her eyes closed while listening to Maggie's sweet recitation of "The Brook" by Tennyson.

To have her here. To listen to her voice, the rhythm of her words, the song of the cicadas accompanying her from the open windows. To let his gaze lock with hers when she looked up from the page, the soft pink on her cheeks when she did—Wesley's heart turned in his chest with the satisfaction of enjoying her presence and the feeling that she belonged here with him. He had every confidence in her, having witnessed her twill a story and paint a scene with her words. Yet, as she had glanced at him before she'd begun, as if to bolster some insecurity, she had a look on her face not unlike the near panic when she rushed away at the end of their every meeting. A look he suspected spoke of some vulnerability he'd yet to discover—an uncertainty he yearned to guard.

Sam, Francine, and Aunt Maud applauded when she finished, and Wesley stood up to take the magazine from her. A sudden urge to kiss her cheek overcame him as his hand brushed hers. All doubt vanished from Maggie's face as she smiled under their praise for her performance, her eyes twinkling with delight as he looked down at her. But the magic moment broke with the commanding voice of Uncle Bernard interjecting into the social hour that was nearly perfect until now. "What's all this excitement?"

Wesley followed social protocol with an introduction, praying his uncle would welcome Maggie as warmly as his aunt had. "Uncle Bernard, this is Miss Magdalena Abbott, my reading assistant from the library."

"So you are." He tipped his head, his direct gaze deflected to the floor a split moment as if he might dismiss her presence and turn away altogether. Instead he leaned back his head to focus on her. "So Miss Abbott, are library sciences your training and ambition?"

Wesley wanted to rescue her. Shield her from an interrogation that was sure to end in some degree of silent disapproval if she weren't connected to a solidly established family. Aunt Maud had resurrected out of her chair and come to Maggie's side.

"Yes sir. I hope to become head librarian one day." She stood straight, shoulders confident. Though a few red blotches crept up her neck, she never flinched as she returned Uncle Bernard's gaze. "It's so gracious of your family to have shared your home with me this evening." The pulse at her throat defied the calm in her voice.

Uncle Bernard's eyes squinted. "Abbott, you say? I don't recall the surname. Have you summered here long?"

"All my life, sir." Her lip quivered.

"Here in Bay View?"

"Petoskey." She glanced to Wesley, a look of uncertainty shimmering behind her forced confidence.

Sam and Francine announced their leave and bid all good night, relieving Maggie of the inevitable study of Uncle Bernard. Wesley drew Maggie toward the door, his hand on the small of her back, wanting to protect her from any impending disapproval. He would defend her strengths to his uncle no matter the pressure and resistance, but only after he'd seen her home safely. "It's late, Uncle. Forgive the short introduction, but I must get Maggie home."

Uncle Bernard bowed slightly, ever polite. "Next time we'll visit about your family, Miss Abbott." He smiled. Wesley knew he meant well, but his mannerism still boded a thorough interrogation ahead.

"Perhaps, sir." She managed to hold a confidence as she faced him, then thanked Aunt Maud. He felt Maggie's urgency mount as she moved toward the door, holding his arm a little too tightly, as if ready to bolt.

Chapter Seven

She *had* summered here all her life. She hadn't lied. Maggie reminded God of that truth as Wesley led her down the steps of his summer home. She reminded Him, too, that she wasn't tempted to lie about her humble beginnings—she cherished her faith and roots far too deeply to betray them. Why should she have to prove herself worthy to a man who only cared about her family's name?

"Maggie, slow down." Wesley quickened his steps to catch up to where she outpaced him.

She pinched her lips between her teeth to stem the rush of emotion behind her eyes.

She'd been a fool to come.

He enveloped her shoulders with his jacket once again as they walked back through the grove toward the train station. Wesley's scent filled her senses once again, holding her in the comfort of his friendship. She didn't want to resist his kindness—but she had to.

"Mag, please. Don't run away like you always do." His confidence unrelenting, Wesley kept her pace. "Didn't you love the evening?"

She shouldn't have looked up at him, but she couldn't bear to think he believed she hadn't loved every moment of it. "Of course I did."

"Then why such a rush to escape? Come with me to the lecture again next week, will you? Don't let Uncle scare you. I promise he's not uncaring."

"I'm sure he's not. That's precisely it. He cares very much for protecting his ambition, his family name—as I suppose he should. But. . ." She didn't want to say the obvious. The things Wesley seemed not to care about.

"But what? Mag, say you'll come with me again." Wesley tugged her arm to stop, while Sam and Francine walked arm in arm far in front of them.

"Wesley, I can't." She willed him to see the truth without jeopardizing the opportunity he'd extended to her—a friendship on an equal footing. "I'm *not* a lifetime member here in Bay View like you are, with a generation before me to establish my standing." Her throat nearly choked on the words that would force him to see their difference.

"You live in Petoskey. Lots of summer folk live there and still attend all our Chautauqua activities without being Bay View members."

"Wesley, I don't have a winter mansion in Detroit or Chicago. I live here year round."

"My uncle's wealthy for sure, but it doesn't define me. It shouldn't—"

"You don't understand," Maggie blurted. Her heart felt as if it were going to tear in two. She wanted nothing more than the simple comfort of her moonlit bedroom to calm the tumult charging through her. After all, he'd introduced her only as his library assistant. The rose he'd sent spoke only of friendship. To wish for more was foolish. Risky at best. She turned away from him to pick up her pace again as they neared the train station, the gas lamps lighting the boardwalk in the distance.

Ahead of them, Sam and Francine called their evening farewells as they turned back along the street that overlooked the moonlight on Lake Michigan.

"Mag, it doesn't matter to me that you haven't been a lifetime member here in the Bay." He'd kept his stride with hers even though she'd pressed onward without him.

"But it does matter." She rushed to wait for the next train under the lamplight. Shifting out of his jacket, she handed it back to him and turned to watch down the tracks.

She couldn't look at him. Grateful that he didn't argue or stand face-to-face to defy her, she released her breath and wished to return to the simple pleasure of sharing work together at the library. Where things were simpler and the lines of friendship were clear.

Life had been simpler at the library.

The tracks vibrated as the rumbling train drew near. Maggie kept her back to Wesley, willing her heart to slow down, her eyes on the train as it neared. He was a wealthy cottager.

She was the daughter of a hired gardener.

"Everything about you matters to me, Mag." His voice was close over her shoulder. She felt his strength behind her, rivaling the train that pounded louder and closer until it halted. His warm hand enveloped her fingers.

Maggie stepped away to board, her hand slipping from his. Turning back to him, she looked into his eyes drilling hers with confidence and intensity. "I'm a simple library assistant, Wesley. I haven't even an academy diploma."

He shook his head. His eyes were pleading, and for a moment she thought he might even board the train with her. But he seemed to understand she sought some safe distance.

The train started to pull away. The silhouette of his strength in the lamplight gripped her.

"Good night, Wesley Graham Hill."

⸺•◆•⸺

Wesley turned back to follow the way home only after he could no longer see her face in the streetcar window. The more time he'd spent with Maggie Abbott, the more tormented she seemed. One moment relaxed, the words of a story or scene rolling free from her imagination. The next, she was slipping through his grasp.

It had taken sheer willpower not to rest his hands on her shoulders and turn her to face him.

It had taken every shred of determination not to run after her—not to kiss her.

She wasn't the toying kind of woman, no. The look in her eyes as she departed was a sort of agony that pressed at him not to give up his pursuit. Whatever it was that overwhelmed her, he would be gentle but unremitting. And if Uncle Bernard had scared her off. . .well, he'd have to speak his mind to the man.

Wesley reached the foot of his uncle's front steps, heart still pounding and his mind still calculating. For a moment, he wondered what his mother felt when she stood there years ago to visit her sister who'd become the wife of wealthy Mr. Bernard Hill. When his mother had suffered from tuberculosis and his father had insisted Wesley spend summers in northern Michigan's clean air, it was his uncle's wealth that had afforded him breath and a future. But Wesley could never banish the memory of the ache in his mother's eyes each summer he'd left her side. He wished that as a child he could have told her what had been in his heart—that all Uncle Bernard's affluence and opportunity would never replace the love he felt for her.

Blast it if he let Uncle Bernard's wealth—the thing that had saved him from consumption and ultimately from the typhoid that had overcome his parents—blast it if it would keep him from Maggie Abbott.

Wesley took the porch steps by two and found Uncle Bernard in the parlor. The paper in his hand dipped as he peered up at Wesley, who stood fighting for words that wouldn't sound ungrateful. Aunt Maud sat forward and stood, concern and kindness lining her face.

"Oh, Wesley, she's a lovely young lady, your Miss Abbott." Her eyes twinkled as she laid her hand on Wesley's arm as if to calm his untamed thoughts.

"Thank you, Aunt Maud. It's kind of you to say so. But. . ." He didn't want Uncle Bernard to dismiss his attention. "But it's Uncle Bernard's thoughts I need." His fingers clenched tight within his fists.

The newspaper slacked further in Uncle's hands. "If it's my approval you want, I cannot give it."

Flaming heat rushed to Wesley's cheeks. "You don't even know her. For the love of Saint Peter, you practically demanded references before she was granted the privilege of simply having tea in your parlor. When did my social calls become the focal point of your scrutiny? You say next to nothing about every young lady Sam has paraded through this house for weeks, yet when I find a worthy match, you dissect her to shreds. Why, you were. . ."

Uncle Bernard dropped the paper and stood to face him.

"You were as near to rude as one could get."

"Are you quite finished speaking your mind?" Uncle's eyes were unreadable steel. His jaw tightened.

Wesley's heart pulsed in his head. Having never spoken harsh words to his uncle, his breath squeezed in his chest. He didn't desire an argument, but he would speak the truth. He trained his silence. Forcing himself to be calm and cool, he refused to look away from the speech that was to come from Uncle Bernard.

"You are right. I don't know the young woman. Nor do you. We don't know her family, her history, her connections. She's not one of us, not of the same mind. You may think you understand her, Wesley. But a life with someone like Mary Reed would be much more secure for you. A girl like Miss Abbott, well, who's to say she's not after the wealth you'll someday inherit? Your position here would be assured with a match like Miss Reed."

"You're wrong." It tore Wesley to say it bluntly. "How could you believe that your money, this cottage, or ideas for my future hinge on such thin assumptions? Is this what you've become?" Wesley sensed Aunt Maud's gasp as she held her silence beside them.

"What could ever make you pressure me into a loveless match such as that with Miss Reed?"

"I made a promise." Uncle Bernard's voice cracked. His square shoulders slumped.

"What? To whom?" Surely he hadn't made an agreement with Miss Reed's father.

"To your father."

The admittance slammed into Wesley's heart and mind, taking the wind from his determination. "What?" He shook his head, feeling as if he might stagger. Uncle Bernard had rarely spoken of Wesley's father since he'd passed.

"Before his death. Your father made me promise to look after your future—to give you the future he couldn't give you. An education. A place in my company. I promised you'd have an inheritance, that I would guard your future."

Stunned at the truth of words spoken in haste of death, Wesley could scarcely believe that the promises that had kept him safe were the very same that pushed Maggie away.

"You were such a young lad then. Your mother had already passed. I've only tried to keep my word the best I know how. I'm not perfect, but I do know some things you could stand to learn, starting with the fact that you should be grateful for what I've given you."

"Of course." Of course he was grateful. "But I'll not accept that the faith and love my parents shared is less important than the wealth and privilege you've given me, Uncle. Perhaps you've forgotten that. Perhaps this whole community has forgotten that—so swept up with the infection of prestige that we've all forgotten the birth of faith in the simple things like the old week-long camp meetings where my mother and Aunt Maud first came to know our Lord and Savior. Wealth, this place—this little Utopia—will all vanish someday. But what I'll forever be most grateful for is the love and faith I found in those camp meetings here. Perhaps my father never meant for anything more than that."

Uncle Bernard's face softened to the kindness Wes remembered from his youth. "Wealth is a privilege and a burden, dear Wesley. I only mean to protect you and your future. Forgive me in every way I've failed as a—a father to you." The contrite words cracked in a tender way that cut to Wesley's heart. Behind the stiff businessman exterior, Uncle Bernard was a gentle soul.

"Of course I forgive you, Uncle. Only let me find my way in love—by faith."

Uncle Bernard's chin quivered, his lips slightly upturned beneath his white mustache as he held out his hand and locked his blue eyes with Wesley's. For once the man's shoulders didn't look so burdened as he gripped Wes's hand and pulled him close to pat a hand on his back before they parted for the night.

Wesley kissed Aunt Maud's cheek and sauntered down the hallway toward the stairs. He paused for a moment, his hand on the banister while he listened to the low voices in the parlor.

"How I love that boy, Maud. I only hope I've done right by him."

"Oh, Bern. I remember the look of love in his eyes for you as a young boy. You haven't lost him. But I fear you know you're about to lose him to Miss Abbott, and that's truly what's got you riled."

Wesley's heart swelled with the truth of it.

He loved Aunt Maud and Uncle Bernard.

But Maggie Abbott had claimed a place in his heart that he couldn't remove her from no matter how many times she ran away from him. Uncle Bernard would come to love her, too. If only he could convince Maggie.

Chapter Eight

She hadn't slept well. The longer she leaned over the front desk of the library, the more her back ached. Or perhaps it was her heart, she couldn't be sure. The solace she'd always found in the safety of the library escaped her reach. Only misery, like the rain that clouded the windows and dripped against the windowpane, kept pace with her aching heart.

She was grateful for the few patrons and the silence that was only somewhat comforting. Another package had arrived from Mr. W. G. Hill that morning, and she'd slid it unopened into the drawer until after lunchtime. Miss Eloise had eyed her all through lunch as Maggie had picked at her food.

Finally, she took the package from the drawer and pulled out the contents of her next assignment. A pink tea rose was pressed and laid on top. Wesley's handwritten note lacked all academic tone and she could hear his voice in her mind as she read.

> *Come with me, my dear Mag. There's an afternoon tea on Friday. A reading on the lawn at 4:00 p.m.*
>
> *Yours,*
> *Wesley*

"Oh. . ." Maggie held the flower and the note to her heart and drew in a breath, closing her eyes. "Oh Lord, tell me what to do," she whispered, treasuring his invitation.

"Tell you what?"

Maggie opened her eyes wide. "Nothing. It's nothing."

"Then what is that 'nothing' you are clutching to your chest, my dear?" A twinkle lit Miss Eloise's eyes.

"It's Wesley—Mr. Hill, I mean—he's invited me for tea." Maggie's hands shook as she thrust the invitation onto the desk, pushed her chair back, and stood. "I can't go, of course." She began to pace and think out loud while Miss Eloise watched her. "How shall I tell him I can't go?"

"Nonsense. You'll go."

"What? I'll *not* go. I *can't* go. You don't understand."

The front door sounded and Maggie looked at the clock and back to Miss Eloise, whose twinkling eyes now had a grin to match as Wesley marched toward them, staring at Maggie dead on with that confidence she loved, yet at the moment she loathed. Confidence, she had a sinking feeling, that could sway her to agree to things she knew better than to agree to. When had the clock struck five? She wasn't ready to face him.

Maggie's thoughts swirled as Wesley and Miss Eloise greeted one another with conspiratorial tones before they faced her.

"So you'll be here to fetch her at three forty-five sharp on Friday. Yes, Mr. Hill, I can release her from her duties."

Wait! What had she missed while lost in her befuddled thoughts?

"Miss Abbott." Wesley reached across the desk between them. He took her hand and touched a soft kiss on the back of it before looking up. "I shall see you on Friday. Rain, or shine."

Maggie's mouth parted, but no words came forth. She swallowed dryly as he released her hand and turned, bidding Miss Eloise good day before slipping out as quickly as he'd appeared.

The front door shut, the click of the handle snapping her back to reality.

"Miss Eloise, what have you done? Why did you do that? You knew I didn't want to go, yet there you stood, taking full advantage of my. . .my. . ."

"You most certainly did *not* say you didn't want to go." The woman's stubborn hands went to her waist. Her stance said she wasn't going to lose this argument. "You said you *couldn't* go."

"But you told him I *could*!" Serious dread filled her at the thought. She'd tried to tell him she wasn't like him, give him some sort of hint that she wasn't the girl he thought she was. "I don't even have a tea dress to wear." Tears stung her eyelids. She sat with a thump on her chair. "This is terrible."

Miss Eloise came around the desk beside her. "Oh, don't worry, I have something in mind. I'll get a dress to your place in time for you to wear it Friday. Your father will swell with pride when he sees you in it, dear."

Maggie shot up from the chair. "Oh no, you can't." Panic seized her.

A knowing look came over Miss Eloise's face. "You haven't told him about Wesley, child?"

Maggie's tears spilled over as she shook her head. Overwhelmed by desire and confusion, a sob lurched from her chest as Miss Eloise swept her close the way she'd always done from the time she'd first skinned her knees as a girl. But the warm bosom of Miss Eloise couldn't whisk away the feelings in her heart this time, and before she was ready the matron pushed her away to look her in the face.

"Oh, girl, tell me, why haven't you told your father?"

Was it the desire of Wesley's friendship she was most afraid of? Or. . . "I—I didn't want to—shame him." More sobs erupted from her chest as she threw herself in Miss Eloise's embrace once more. "He's given me everything I've ever needed. He always trusts that God gives us just enough. More is wasteful. To wish for more. . . I'm so afraid I'll hurt Father's pride—that he'll think he couldn't give me enough. . . ." She swiped away tears with some relief at the admission of truth, the weight of holding it unspoken finally free from her soul.

"Are you quite certain that is the real reason for your tears, my girl?"

Maggie looked up to see Miss Eloise's tender gaze that had a way of unveiling truth she hadn't yet seen. "Yes." But tears surged forth once more. "I think so. . . ."

"Perhaps it's less Mr. Hill's social standing with your father and more your heart's position with Mr. Hill's that's got you so upended? Do you care for Wesley, my dear?"

The admission of the truth bubbled up from Maggie's heart. "Yes." The simple word both relieved her and frightened her ridiculously.

"Your father loves you, dear girl. He wants the best for you. And if Wesley Graham Hill is the Heavenly Father's best for you, then your earthly father won't be looking at the man's social standing, and you know it. He'll be looking at the young man's standing with the Lord our Father. I happen to approve, or I wouldn't have allowed him to see you in the first place. You've never let the hard times that came to your family hold you back, and I certainly hope you won't let those trials hold you back now."

Maggie wiped the last of her tears away.

"Seems to me now that you've spoken the truth, you've got to find a way of telling it to the men in your life. Maggie-girl, you can't live the rest of your life in the library like I have."

<hr />

Dinner was finished. The dishes were dried and put away. Maggie's shoulders ached from the long day. She knew her father's knees ached from the difficult gardening he'd done on all fours, up and down all day. When she knocked on the pine frame of his bedroom door, he looked up from the book that lay closed on his lap. Maggie always thought of the small space where his chair was placed beside his bed as a parlor where she stopped in to see him before she retired.

"You look tired, Father. Is the book not good? Shall I get you something more entertaining tomorrow?"

"Just a long day, my dear magpie."

Maggie lingered, anxiety gripping her mind for how to broach what was on her heart.

"Sit down here." He moved his stocking feet aside on the tattered ottoman.

Gathering her courage, she sat beside him. "Father, I've been asked to attend tea Friday."

"That's lovely. A tea with the academy girls? Miss Eloise says there are a lot of young girls who attend."

She swallowed. "It's Mr. Hill who's asked."

He stiffened. "Bernard Hill's got a boy, does he?"

"Nephew."

"I see."

But Maggie couldn't see what thoughts marched through her father's mind, what judgments, what disappointment. Yet there was some hint in the way the lines of his forehead deepened.

"Just tea then?"

"Yes sir." What did her father know of Bernard Hill? She wanted to explain that Wesley wasn't like the old man. Instead, she waited his response.

"I suppose there's no harm in having tea. I've let bygones be bygones."

"What does that mean? You know his nephew?" She'd never known her father to hold a grudge, and the mere mention of bygones cast a foreboding over her.

"Mr. Hill the senior. Before your mother died I used to garden at the Perry where he served on the board. When the hotel burned down, there was a rumor that a lantern caught some grass cuttings on fire—in the gardener's shed. The entire staff was let go, even though no one knew for certain. When he rebuilt the hotel, he started with a whole new staff."

"But you weren't to blame."

"Of course not. But they had benefactors who needed to be appeased. It made hard times for us. That was the reason your mother had to find work. Work that eventually wore her down until she caught pneumonia the winter we lost her."

Maggie held her breath as the memories that led up to her mother's passing danced behind the look on her father's face. So much sadness and heartache he'd faced. He looked up at her with a tender smile. "I forgave him and the board. Once the Father showed me it wasn't his fault any more than that fire was mine."

Though there might have been flaws in his reasoning, she could see by the light in his eyes that the peace he'd made long ago was more important. Perhaps that's what he'd decided as well. Still, there was an old pain there she didn't want to see reopened. "It's just tea, Father." She wanted to reassure him.

"Yes. It is." But the flat way he said it made her think he knew better.

In time, he might come to hold Wesley in the esteem she'd always hoped he might for the man she would choose to share life with. For now though, it was only tea she was having, for heaven's sake.

Chapter Nine

In the days since Monday when Miss Eloise had accepted Wesley's invitation for her, Maggie's days had drifted past one by one with simple routine that contrasted the panic that was growing as Friday dawned. Surely she was building up the teatime far more than she should. It was just another day, after all. Like all the others.

It had hardly seemed real yesterday when a package waited for her outside the door to their little apartment above Easton's Hardware in Petoskey. Miss Eloise had outdone herself and purchased the promised tea gown. Maggie had risen an hour early to iron out the creases from its being folded in the box. She'd taken extra time for her hair and hurried to get her work done by the time the clock struck noon and Miss Eloise released her to go home to change into the dress.

She climbed Pine Street hoping not to break a sweat. Ducking into the general store, she found the ladies' powder and laid her coins on the counter. She rang the bell for the attendant and startled when the voice of Mr. Bernard Hill sounded in the silence behind her.

"Why, Miss Abbott, you are a fast shopper on a mission. I came to Petoskey on business and saw you at the station. I tried to greet you, but you were a few steps ahead of me. I would have given up and let you go on your way, but I feared you heard me call your name and that you would be frightened that someone had followed you. Wesley tells me that you'll be sharing tea with him this afternoon."

A warning shiver crept over Maggie's nerves. The prestigious banker seemed a bit out of place, and she wished the grocer would appear to break the strange feeling that Mr. Hill had followed her with greater intentions than just a friendly greeting. "Yes, Mr. Hill, thank you." She rolled the folds of her dress between her fingers.

"Forgive me for being so forward, but your looks are similar to someone I knew years ago and I cannot let it go. Would you be kin to a Miss Charlotte Smith? She was a laborer at one time. Married a gardener, I believe." He studied her face more intently than she felt comfortable with.

Mother's maiden name? But what sense did such a question make? Did he mean to put her in her place in some way? Trepidation held her tongue.

"I knew her long before she was on my work staff. Charlotte was a remarkable girl I used to know from summer camp—from childhood. She used to come to camp meeting with her family—farmers, I believe they were. Everyone came to the camp meeting back in those days—farm hands, businessmen, even Indians." His reminiscence in such an odd time and place, the story of her father's termination before her mother's death—all of it swirled together to give Maggie the sense that she was part of a much larger story than she had imagined.

"Well, the name—your resemblance of her is subtle, but I just thought. . ." He shook his head as if it were a ridiculous assumption. "Just a coincidence, I'm certain. Those days were long ago, but you should know. . ." He paused to make the point she felt he'd truly intersected her for, the real reason he'd come to Petoskey. "It's not that we cottagers are after a privileged summer vacation. It's that we're committed to applying as much good to our world as we can. That is, we want Wesley to use his opportunities for the betterment of himself and humanity. I'm sure you can agree, as my young friend Miss Charlotte Smith always reminded me, goodness and kindness know no social limits. It is the mind that sees limits that is a mind sure to miss opportunity." The grocer appeared from behind the storeroom curtain, breaking Mr. Hill's reverie before Maggie could reply. "Have a lovely teatime. But mind you, if you are anything like that gardener's wife from long ago, you might find that the magic of Bay View leads you to believe that anything is possible. We aim to preserve this place where common can walk alongside extraordinary and where the poor man, the laborer, and the gardener all set differences aside to share in God's grace and goodness. Good day." He turned without waiting for her response, as if he didn't care what it might have been. As if he only intended to deliver a challenge, not a greeting.

Staring after him, Maggie tried to sort out the odd interchange. The grocer took her coins and set the wrapped package on the counter in front of her. "Was that man bothering you, Miss Abbott?"

"No sir." She smiled thinly and took the package. "Thank you." Outside, she slipped along the side of the building toward the steps that led to her entryway. She'd taken the alleyway many a time, but this time couldn't shake the feeling that she'd just been challenged by a powerful man. . . .

Truly, "*goodness and kindness know no social limits.*" Yet change was never without cost. She wasn't sure whether to be encouraged, or entirely intimidated.

—◦•◦—

Every self-doubt she'd ever had seemed to chase Maggie up the steps and inside her apartment like a hound on her heels. She felt that her worst traits were transparent to all and she was about to be found an imposter.

She slammed the apartment door behind her and took a shuddering breath.

Did she truly possess the power of simple faith her mother had? Faith that transcended all division, social class, and language?

Inside her bedroom, the lace tea gown teased her heart's desires from where it hung. It was nearly like the one she'd seen in the window of Fay's Dress Shop two weeks before. She ran her hand over it then pulled the window shade down and slid from her skirt and shirtwaist. Pulling the new gown from the hanger, she lifted it over her head and let it shimmer down over her hips and to the floor. Twisting to see the buttons in the mirror behind her, she reached behind to fasten them, careful not to miss one.

Turning back to face the old mirror, she wished her reflection was as crisp as the ones in the department store. Instead, her image was dim and disjointed from the cracks in the silver paint peeling from the back of the old looking glass. Maggie tried to push down the feeling that the imperfect image was a message sent to shake her from her dreams.

She twisted a loose lock of hair that had fallen and tucked it into place.

Lacing the string of her mother's pearls around her neck, she fingered them softly. "What would Mr. Hill have known of you, Mother? How could he have known you so well, why come out of the way to say such things?" All the wonderful things that had ever been told to her about her mother filtered through her memory. How she'd been fluent in the Odawa and Ojibwa languages. How she would take Indian children to camp meetings and translate the Gospel. How she never cared about class or color more than heart and soul. It was said the Indians had named her *Words of Power*.

Standing back to get a full-length view as best she could in the short mirror, Maggie paused. Wesley had claimed she had words of power. But did she?

Did she truly believe love spanned all differences?

Putting the tea gown on hadn't dispelled the discord she'd felt after her run-in with Mr. Hill. Somehow it only made her feel worse.

The differences between them were too great.

To pretend otherwise was ridiculous. Wesley cared for her, but only for the parts she'd allowed him to see. Covering her true identity with a dress or anything else—she just couldn't do it.

Maggie sat on the chest at the foot of her bed and took a paper from her desk. She prayed she was making the right decision.

Chapter Ten

Wesley flipped the cover of his pocket watch for the sixth time. She was twenty minutes late. His emotions ranged from frustration, to disappointment, to worry. Even Miss Eloise was growing concerned.

Standing outside the library on the steps, he scanned the street as far as he could see. Throngs of people had streamed past the library steps on their way toward the tea on the lawn. Maggie was nowhere. He was ready to retrace their steps the night he'd taken her to the train station, thinking to board it and search Petoskey, when a newsboy ran up the steps.

"You Mister Hill, sir?"

"I am."

The boy shoved a note into his hand and darted back the way he'd come. Unfolding the paper, Wes read:

Dear Wesley,
I cannot attend the tea with you today. It would be dishonest of me to do so. Furthermore, I must end our academic agreement. I regret any disruption this may cause you and humbly ask for your forgiveness.

Sincerely,
Maggie

"Disruption?" Wesley rubbed his hand over his chest. Did she have no idea what it did to him, to call it only a disruption? He scanned the crowd for the messenger, hoping to catch a glimpse of the boy, thinking to chase after him and find out where she lived. The urge to declare his true feelings pounded in his chest, but he was helpless to express them.

He wavered, then ran down the street toward the train station, weaving in and out of the crowd like a fish swimming upstream. When he reached the Bay View station, the train from Petoskey had just arrived. The boy was nowhere, but Wesley got on the train anyway, fighting his way against the crowd on their way to attend Big Sunday's main lecture. Finding a window seat to watch for something, anything that might point to the direction the boy might have gone, Wesley's blood stilled as he recognized the outline of his uncle's hat and the shape of his shoulders in the midst of the crowd moving away from the train platform. The man's identity was unmistakable as he strode toward Bay View's curvy wooded streets.

Wesley stood inside the train car, straining his eyes just as Uncle Bernard turned down the street. He'd seen enough to confirm it. Uncle Bernard had been to Petoskey.

Did he have something to do with Maggie's refusal?

Surely not.

Wesley slumped to his place by the window, careful not to squash the old man beside him in the seat. The man was dressed in work overalls with grass-stained knees. In his hands he held an old handkerchief full of rose petals that he arranged one by one as if they were golden treasures. Wesley sighed and ran his hands along his thighs, praying about what to do, how to find her. His library princess, the one Sam hadn't believed existed.

Wesley heard nothing from above. No divine direction whispered in his heart or his mind. Sighing heavily, he ran his hands once more along his thighs, accidentally catching the tail of the man's kerchief, sending the petals falling to the floor.

The man gasped and lunged forward to retrieve them.

"I'm so sorry, sir." Wesley reached down and picked up the fragile petals, the waft of the roses familiar in some way.

The man handled each petal with great care, stacking them one by one back into the kerchief.

"These must be special to you." Wesley held out his hand for the man to take the last three petals.

"They are for my daughter." His eyes twinkled. "I tell her God's perfume is sweeter than any store-bought kind." He looked up with softness around his eyes and a bit of sadness. "And she believes me, but I wish I could give her more than my gardener's wages can afford."

"The smell is lovely, I'm sure she loves them because they come from your heart." Wesley thought of Maggie. It would be something she would say. He sighed again.

"You are troubled today?"

The man had shared his treasure. Wesley reached in his pocket to share his sorrow. He unfolded the letter from Maggie for the old gent to see. Somehow sharing his ache eased his pain. The man was silent for a moment after reading it.

"Seems you're a might more troubled than a missed chance for some tea or study with this lady."

"That I am."

"This Miss Abbott must be special." The man's voice cracked as he fingered the rose petal on top of the stack.

"Oh, that she is, but how I'm going to find her or tell her that before her mind is set, I don't know."

"Are you a man of faith? You trust every footstep to the Lord who provides?" The train was coasting toward a halt. The man looked directly up at him, something familiar about his eyes.

"I am. I do, sir." A peace settled into the place where tumult had churned.

"Then trust the Lord. A rose worth choosing is worth the thorn that may prick when you first reach for it." The man took a petal from the kerchief and gave it to Wesley before standing and weaving his way into the crowd exiting the train.

——— •◦• ———

Maggie knew she'd done the right thing, but she couldn't distract herself from the onslaught of questions she knew was coming. How would she face Miss Eloise? Would Father see her heart when she explained?

She tried reading, but her thoughts strayed from the page.

Of course she had refused Wesley based on honesty. Wasn't that noble? Then why couldn't she shake the feeling that she'd still not been entirely truthful somehow? But she had been, hadn't she? Maggie tossed the novel aside and went to the small kitchen to start dinner preparations. Better to be busy.

She heard the door open and close as she set the table and recognized her father's step into the room behind her.

Sometimes when he came home tired, knees hurting, he was quiet, and she understood when he went to bed early. Tonight's silence as he shuffled off his work boots and found his chair at the table meant more long hours trying to keep her thoughts busy. Normally she welcomed the chance to enjoy the evening reading, but that was ruined for the night. Maybe even ruined for a lifetime.

Maggie sat down across from her father, feeling the acuteness of her own misery as they bowed their heads to pray.

"Father who provides all, provide my lovely daughter with the wisdom to know when You've sent her the right man to spend her life with."

Tears stung Maggie's eyes and her throat grew thick. She stared at her plate, unable to look up.

He set his handkerchief of rose petals beside her plate and laid his hand across hers.

Tears slipped down her cheeks.

"Why didn't you tell me this Mr. Hill is in love with you?"

She jerked her gaze upward. "Love? He's not in love with me. It was only supposed to be tea."

"Then why are you crying? You didn't want to tell me you have feelings for him?"

"Is it so obvious to others yet not to me? You only assume he returns my affections." She shuddered, seeing the disappointment in his eyes. "Oh Father, I didn't want to hurt your pride." Maggie swiped another tear. "I didn't want you to think I wasn't happy with my life, the life you've given me." Her lip quivered.

"Well, dear girl. A father feels a great many things when he thinks his girl might be falling in love, but having my pride hurt isn't one of them." His assuredness and calm only undid her further.

"I'm *not* in love with him. It was just a schoolgirl agreement to help him with an assignment. I—I turned down the invitation to tea." Her appetite vanished. She couldn't breathe through her nose.

He still held his hand over hers. "I'm old. But I once watched your mother fall in love."

"Well if this is what it feels like, it's *terrible*." Tears and sobs matched her declaration as she pushed away from the table to escape to her room, shutting the door behind her.

Letting the torrent of tears erupt, she emptied her heart as she lay on the bed.

Why was being honest so unbelievably painful?

Wasn't cutting Wesley Graham Hill out of her life supposed to bring everything back to the way it had been before?

Chapter Eleven

Wesley climbed the rising street toward his family cottage, the disruption in his plans with Maggie making a chance for greater trust in God, as the old gardener had said. But the peace that he felt from his conversation on the train was challenged by having seen his uncle coming back from Petoskey. He knew his uncle was well intended, but couldn't shake the notion that he'd been the reason for Maggie's refusal.

Wesley was late to dinner. Aunt Maud and Uncle Bernard had already been seated, their servant busy taking trays away from the table when Wesley pulled his chair out to seat himself.

"You're late." Uncle Bernard wiped his mouth with his linen napkin.

"My apologies, Aunt Maud. I know tardiness bothers you." He didn't want to upset his aunt more to bring up what was on his mind, but it couldn't be helped. "Uncle, was that you I saw getting off the train from Petoskey this afternoon?"

Uncle Bernard popped the last of a dinner roll into his mouth and nodded.

"What took you there?"

"Had some business."

"How was your tea with Miss Abbott?" Aunt Maud's voice was cheery and eager.

"She broke the plans. I didn't go."

Uncle Bernard looked up.

"Oh dear, she's not come down with illness now, has she?" His aunt's tone ever of concern.

"No." Not unless heartache was contagious. But he could tell from her letter that Maggie clearly wasn't suffering as he'd been since receiving it. Wesley pushed his plate back, his appetite lost.

"Are you sick, too? Eat your food, Wesley."

"No, I'm not sick. I'm not hungry."

Uncle Bernard stood from the table. "Follow me to the porch, Wesley."

Wesley, sensing the seriousness in his uncle's voice, picked up his water glass and followed.

The sun was setting over the bay, a ball of scarlet over the water. Three tired young boys carried buckets of beach stones as they trailed behind their mother to the cottage next door. He could hear a barbershop quartet singing, their song lilting through the trees between the campus and his uncle's cottage.

"Wesley, I know you think you know this Miss Abbott, but—"

"I do." Wesley braced himself for the challenge about to come.

"Every young man is tempted to believe the first girl he has eyes for is the one."

"She's refused me, Uncle. Even if I want to pursue her, I doubt she'll see me even if I beg Miss Eloise for her address." But as he said it, he was ready to be at the library the next morning. "If you've brought me out here to convince me to drop her and court Mary Reed, the answer is no."

"That's not my plan."

"Good." Wesley shoved his hands into his pockets and walked along the porch railing. Reaching out, he plucked a rose petal from one of Aunt Maud's bushes. It didn't smell the same as the one the gardener had given him. "You didn't bring me out here to dissuade me then?"

"Your Aunt Maud and I only want what's best for you."

"You'll consent to my courting Miss Abbott, if she'll have me, even if she's not a cottager? I thought membership was the biggest issue you've spent your life defending for Bay View. She's of Christian persuasion. Or is it more than that you require of my wife?"

"One of my priorities is to maintain the one tenet—that members of Bay View be of Christian persuasion. Perhaps you're confusing this priority with my hesitancy for Miss Abbott. They aren't the same."

"Perhaps not. Christian persuasion as a criteria for membership is a noble tenet, Uncle, but doesn't drawing lines get messy? How is it different for Miss Abbott? She's of Christian faith, but what good does it serve her if she doesn't also meet your criteria in all other areas?"

"I only care that, if you love this girl, you should really know her. Her family, who she loves, where she comes from."

This time, Uncle Bernard's tone had changed. He sounded less like a board member and more like a father than ever before.

"Be careful, it almost sounds like you're telling me to go after her."

Uncle Bernard's eyes twinkled. "There was once a girl I met at summer camp when I was twelve. I hadn't thought of her for years until your Miss Abbott stood finishing her monologue reading in the parlor last week. She had the same charisma with words. Words that could make you believe anything. It was that simple farm girl, who'd come to camp meeting with her pa, who first explained the love of Christ our Savior to me in a way that made sense. That girl would tell the Gospel to the little Indian boys who came to meeting, too—back in those days it was just a simple tent meeting for everyone. Perhaps we've let— perhaps I've let it get too complicated. Those Indian boys were different, but she didn't see that. She saw souls and witnessed to them despite what others said or saw. One night she found me eavesdropping and we became fast friends. Then she was gone and I never saw her again that summer."

Wesley had never known his uncle to reveal much of his boyhood. The token of peace, the man's confession of sorts—Wesley was grateful for the rare exchange.

"Don't get me wrong, I fell head over heels for your Aunt Maud. But I never forgot Miss Smith or the way she could move a man's heart to deeper faith. Be discerning, Wesley. Be sure you know her well. Yet be wise to remember it's actually simpler than it seems. Perhaps I'd forgotten that until now." Uncle Bernard clapped Wesley on the back, clearly relieved that he'd accomplished his fatherly duty, and left the porch.

Wesley had wanted to take his uncle to task and ask if he'd had anything to do with Maggie's refusal. Instead his uncle had left the door open. Was he actually suggesting that he should pursue Maggie further?

What of his bet with Sam? He couldn't bear to share tea times with anyone Sam might find now.

Summer wasn't over, and there was still the music festival.

He picked one more rose petal, deciding that Maggie Abbott would be by his side if he had to check out all the books in the library to convince her. Returning the stacks of student books was just the idea he needed to get her attention.

<hr>

"You didn't go to the tea?" Miss Eloise's face crumpled.

"I couldn't." Maggie set the boxed dress on the matron's desk.

"Your eyes look terrible. Did you cry yourself to sleep? You know you can never hide that from me, dear."

Maggie bit her lip and nodded no, then yes.

"That man loves you, Miss Magdalena Abbott."

"He loves who he thinks I am, Miss Eloise. When he sees the rest of my life, where I live, where I come from—he'll know he was mistaken. I'm saving him the bother."

"You've lost your mind. That is not the Maggie Mae I know."

"But it is." Maggie shuddered a breath to stifle the return of tears.

"What are you afraid of, sweet girl?"

"That he won't be able to get past our differences—that I won't be able to be everything my mother was—bigger than all that separates..." A little sob caught in her chest as she let the last hidden truth go and looked up at Miss Eloise.

"Oh dear girl, do you love him?"

Maggie bit her lip and nodded, still afraid of what it might cost her.

"Then let him love you. If you really believe that where you live, your father's work, or how you live matter to him, then you are the one who's mistaken. You've had your head in the books on these shelves your whole life, but they can't tell you what common sense and love are when you're staring them in the face. Did you see what came in today?"

"No."

"Look behind you. A full cart of returned student books. Think and pray on some common sense while you do your regular duties. Then you'll check in and shelve that cart before you leave. Maybe that will prove something."

Maggie sighed and trudged through her day, numbly attempting to reason and pray. By late afternoon she rolled the cart of books toward her desk to check them in. She picked up the first book, noted the number on the spine, and searched through the cards in the file box. When she found the right card she opened the back cover of the book—and found that there was already something inside the pocket. A folded paper, with the words *To Maggie Abbott* written on it. Inside was a short verse and poem. The salutation read *"Yours Forever, Wesley."*

She grabbed the next book—it contained another poem. The next, and the next—they were all full of notes—all the books on the cart. Heat rushed to her cheeks as she realized what he'd done to get her attention. He hadn't given up.

How could her heart soar with each word while her mind agreed with the logic of her refusal?

Weary from the emotions of the day, Maggie bid Miss Eloise good night and made her way toward the train station. Along the way a young man was putting up posters to announce the annual summer music festival. She couldn't help wondering if Wesley would attend.

She clutched an envelope to her heart. She'd filled it with Wesley's poems.

Standing at the train station, Maggie recalled Wesley's sweet words to her, the way he'd said her name, and held her hand the night of the lecture. "*Mag, everything about you matters to me.*"

Had she truly made the right decision?

<hr>

Hoping to ride the train home with Maggie after she'd shelved all the books he'd sent back, Wesley followed her toward the train station, ready to surprise her. He watched from a distance as she stopped to read the details of the summer music festival, wanting only to rush ahead and ask her to go with him. To sit once more, no, many more evenings, listening to her voice as she twilled a story.

But as he watched her, something seemed to hold him back.

He remained at a distance, waiting until she got on the train, and then climbed into the car behind hers. He waited until the train began to move, then made his way from his car to hers, thinking of how he would surprise her and declare himself.

He spotted her near the window, the seat beside her empty. Heart surging, he was ready to open his heart right there in the train where she couldn't run away. She'd finally have to hear him out. He took a step forward, and was three seats away from her when a man in front of him to the right stood up, moved toward her seat, and sat next to her. Leaning close to her, the man planted a kiss on her cheek, and Wesley's heart sank.

He reached to steady himself as the train lurched. He squeezed his eyes shut for a moment. He'd been a fool. That was what she'd needed forgiveness for? He forced his eyes open to see once more that she belonged to someone else.

He was one step closer when a familiar voice mixed with hers and the man handed her a kerchief. Wesley's heart surged as he watched her open it and dip her nose to inhale what he knew to be rose petals.

Her father was the old gardener? She was his daughter?

He staggered back, the truth hitting him full on. All the times she'd held back, tried to explain to him that she wasn't like him. True, she'd told him she wasn't a member of Bay View, nor was she an academy student. He knew her life was different than his. But he'd never thought just how different. He hadn't listened, hadn't given her the chance to be fully honest. In fact, had he somehow given her the idea her life wasn't acceptable to him? His thoughts jetted back to her reaction at his uncle's home, their prestige.

The train braked and halted.

The people rushed and pressed past him, between him and Maggie as she moved away from him and off the train, her arm linked in her father's. Wesley recalled the old gardener's admonition to trust in the Lord.

The words her father had spoken to him that day—the man had to realize the letter of refusal was from his own daughter. And still he'd said those kind words. "*A rose worth choosing is worth the thorn that may prick when you first reach for it.*"

A plan formed in his mind as he watched them walk away.

One he was certain he could entrust to the Lord.

Chapter Twelve

No book returns for her had come for two solid weeks. With each passing day, Maggie's hopes flagged a little more despite the mirth and growing cheerfulness of Miss Eloise. She'd never seen the woman get so excited about the end of the season. For Maggie it was always a bit melancholy to see all the cottagers close up their cottages, latch their shutters, and lock their doors until the next season.

It was always a rush at the end. Most the books that had been forgotten found their way back to the check-in shelf. But none of them had been from Wesley Graham Hill.

She'd checked.

With the last cart of books to shelve, Maggie decided to pace herself and sat to rest at her desk. She pulled out the last packet Wesley had sent her. The one they'd never completed together. The dried flowers were still bright, and she laid them on the desk beside her ink set.

Three academy girls turned in their last set of study books and left, arm in arm, giggling about who would take them to the music festival.

Maggie pulled out the handwritten notes from Wesley, her melancholy growing by the moment. She reread them and slid them underneath her desk calendar, waiting for the clock to chime five so she could escape the crowds getting ready for vespers.

If Wesley Graham Hill were the only love interest she'd ever have, she would cherish the five o'clock chime for the memory of the times he slipped through the doors. The memory of that first day when he'd offered an academic proposal. She closed her eyes and held her head in her hands, letting the memory of it drift through—

The door slammed. Footsteps.

Fingers drummed on her desk.

Maggie's heart surged as she opened her eyes.

There before her stood Wesley dressed in a black suit, white shirt. His hair slicked. He held his fingers over his lips with a *shh*.

She bit her lips to hold back words. Things she wanted to say.

From behind him, he pulled a bouquet of red roses. As he did, her father appeared from the book stacks next to the door and made the *shh* sign with his finger over his lips. From behind her, she heard Miss Eloise's footsteps, a gasp, and then silence.

With the proper audience assembled, Wesley grinned and dipped into a genteel bow. Then he knelt to one knee.

"Miss Magdalena Abbott, you are but a humble gardener's daughter, I know, and I am but the orphaned nephew of a kind uncle who made a promise to be a father to me. Your smile, your words, your soul and faith, I cannot live without. I don't care that you live in a simple apartment above the hardware store. I don't care that you only have one fancy dress to your name." He winked at Miss Eloise, who winked at Maggie. "None of my uncle's wealth or prominence could make me as happy as having you in my life. Forgive me if I didn't listen, never allowing you the opportunity to be forthright about your circumstances. Please do me the honor of accompanying me to the Final Fling, for you've captured my heart and I love you. For if I know you at all, I'm certain you know in your heart that faith and love are the only bridge that can bind us together, and no difference we ever face will be too great if we trust our Heavenly Father."

With each declaration, Maggie's doubts melted away. The realization that Wesley knew her and loved her in spite of their differences settled peace over her, a peace that had been missing until now. She let his words sink deep into her heart.

"What do you say?" he said finally.

"I say that you are 'overdue,' Wesley Graham Hill." She grinned, using the line he'd first said to her.

Wesley jumped up from where he knelt, clasped both her hands in his, then leaned near and kissed her cheek. He lingered close as Miss Eloise and her father clapped and cheered.

"Don't ever make me that miserable again."

"You were miserable?"

"Terribly. I thought I didn't matter to you."

"Everything about you matters to me, Mag." The words were only for her, whispered near. "All the rest of your days matter to me."

Wesley's words of a future with her, his declaration, and the peace that had settled over her were all she needed to believe the words her mother had written inside her Bible. "*These three remain: faith, hope, and love.*" Never could wealth or the lack of it, nor hardship, ease, or difference ever destroy what faith, hope, and love could build.

Anne Love is a vintage-loving author fueled by prayer, strong black coffee, and characters of generations past—both real and fictional. By day, she's a family nurse practitioner in northern Indiana, and by night, she writes historical romance flavored with vintage rural charm, inspired by her faith and family roots. Wife of a schoolteacher and mother of two young adults and a daughter-in-law, she fills her free time with genealogy, gardening, mentoring, and music. Anne is a long-time member of American Christian Fiction Writers and cofounder of the group blog www.coffeecupsandcamisoles.blogspot.com where she contributes weekly.

Connect with her at www.facebook.com/AuthorAnneLove, and at www.anneloveauthor.com.

A Tale of Two Hearts

By Gabrielle Meyer

Dedication

To my godchildren: Caleb Gosiak, Gage VanRisseghem, Claire VanRisseghem, Tucker Skoglund, and Finley Skoglund. One of the greatest honors of my life is to lead you closer to the Lord. I love you all.

Acknowledgments

I'm grateful God has allowed me to pursue this dream, and I feel blessed to be surrounded by amazing people who cheer me on. First, I want to thank the ladies in this collection for agreeing to partner with me as we presented these stories to Barbour. I'm thrilled to see my name beside all of yours. I also want to thank my lovely agent Mary Keeley of Books and Such Literary Management; my editors at Barbour Publishing; my talented writing friends Alena Tauriainen, Lindsay Harrel, Melissa Tagg, and Susan May Warren; my priceless Street Team members; my parents George and Cathy VanRisseghem, and my husband's parents, Virgil and Carol Meyer; my sister and sisters-in-law Andrea Skoglund, Angie VanRisseghem, and Sarah VanRisseghem; my church community; our family friends; and all the citizens of Little Falls, past and present, who inspire me to write the stories of my heart. A very special thank you is always reserved for my husband David and our four children, Ellis, Maryn, Judah, and Asher. Thank you for being my biggest fans and my greatest joy.

Chapter One

T he countryside sped by as Elijah Boyer pushed the Duryea Motor Wagon to twenty-five miles an hour. Beside him, Frederick Alexander held his hat with one hand and a stopwatch with the other.

"Will you try for a personal record?" Mr. Alexander called over the rumble of the gasoline engine.

Trees, bushes, and fence posts passed at a dizzying pace as the automobile vibrated under the bench seat. Eli grinned and shifted the tiller stick up to move it into third gear. "If Camille Jenatzy can break the speed record at almost sixty-six miles an hour, surely I can go faster than twenty-eight miles an hour."

Mr. Alexander looked at Eli with the mischievous grin he was famous for. "Will the Duryea ever reach sixty-six miles an hour?"

"It isn't capable of such speed." Eli rotated the tiller handle to go faster. "But with the modifications I've made, one day we might get it to forty or fifty."

The red fence post Eli had painted a year ago when he'd first come to work for Mr. Alexander stood just ahead. From that point, until the second post five miles down the dusty country road, they would calculate his speed.

Mr. Alexander watched the post as it drew near, his stopwatch ready, while Eli gripped the tiller. The automobile became harder to keep steady on the bumpy road, but Eli had hours of experience controlling the buggy-like vehicle.

"Now." Mr. Alexander started the stopwatch.

The sun beat down and the cloudless blue sky arched overhead, though Eli concentrated on nothing but the road in front of him. He rotated the wooden tiller until it was at full speed and braced himself to stay seated as the vehicle bumped and swayed over the old wagon road.

Neither man said a word as the engine whirled, propelling the automobile forward.

The wind tugged at Eli's hair and clothes, and his feet felt numb from the constant vibration underfoot. The power beneath his hands gave him incredible energy. He couldn't imagine what it would feel like to go even faster. To think Camille Jenatzy had gone almost sixty-six miles an hour in Paris just a few weeks ago seemed unfathomable. Even with all the adjustment in the world, Mr. Alexander's Duryea would never reach such speed, but maybe Eli's customized vehicle might.

More than anything, Eli wanted to race his own automobile. He'd been working on the design for over a year, building it in his spare time. He had saved up his earnings for half the year and bought a used carriage for seventy dollars. From there, he had purchased others parts as he found them. He still needed an engine and a few other necessary components, but once he had his automobile ready, he could enter races across the country and earn thousands of dollars. Then he'd start manufacturing automobiles of his own.

The second red post was now in Eli's line of sight, with the gate to Basswood Hill, Mr. Alexander's estate, just beyond.

Mr. Alexander hollered in excitement as he shook the stopwatch. "This will be your best time yet!"

Eli bent forward and lowered his head so the wind would slide over him, still thinking of his dream to start an automobile manufacturing company. He was thankful for the job Mr. Alexander had given him, but every time he worked on Mr. Alexander's 1897 Duryea, he longed for more.

The second post was only a few yards away. They buzzed by the marker and Mr. Alexander clicked the stopwatch.

"Eight and a half minutes, on the nose!" He reached out and slapped Eli's arm in excitement. "Eight and a half minutes!"

Eli rotated the tiller to the left and the vehicle began to slow. "Thirty-five miles an hour?"

Mr. Alexander clapped Eli on the back and laughed. "Thirty-five miles an hour! Can you believe it?"

Eli's personal best. He grinned as he drove the Duryea through the gate and into Basswood Hill. But his victory was soon doused with the reality that thirty-five miles an hour still wasn't good enough to compete in some of the races he'd been eyeing this past year. One of the reasons Mr. Alexander had hired Eli—who had absolutely no training in domestic service—as his footman was that he knew Eli could modify the Duryea for racing. Which meant that, instead of racing for himself, Eli would be racing another man's automobile.

Eli turned the tiller so they would head down the hill and to the barn where he'd park the Duryea.

"You're making fine progress, Eli." Mr. Alexander put the stopwatch in his pocket. "I think you'll be pleased with some of the races I plan for you to run."

"I don't know when the Duryea will be ready."

"I have every confidence that you'll have her ready when I need her."

Eli applied the brake and the vehicle came to a stop outside the barn, though it continued to bounce and rumble.

"I'll leave you to your work." Mr. Alexander stepped out of the Duryea and looked at his watch. "Mr. Walker and I have called a meeting of both our house staff in an hour."

Eli sighed. "I suppose I'll have to dress in my footman's garb."

"It won't be so bad." Mr. Alexander laughed. "We're meeting in the Walker parlor. Don't be late."

"I'll be there," Eli said begrudgingly.

Mr. Alexander walked away with his hands in his pockets and a whistle on his lips. Until recently he had been known as one of the two White Pine bachelors, heirs to the largest lumber empire in the world and managers of the White Pine Lumber Mill in Little Falls. Now, after Mr. Walker's marriage a month ago, Mr. Alexander was the lone White Pine bachelor.

The lumber barons had built mansions side by side at Basswood Hill just a year ago. It was rumored that they had built their mansions in a sort of contest to see who could impress Miss Julia Morgan. Their friendly competition was notorious in the state, and though Mr. Walker eventually won the hand of Miss Morgan, their competitions continued in other ways.

Eli drove the Duryea into the barn next to his own automobile—which stood motionless and unfinished—yet it held a wealth of promise to Eli. Mr. Alexander had been kind enough to allow Eli to store it there, and although his employer was eager to see Eli complete it, Eli's first responsibility was to the Duryea.

Eli tinkered with the Duryea and then closed up the barn to get ready for the meeting. It was a rare occurrence to have the staff from both mansions in the same room. Usually they worked independently of one another, though Eli suspected much gossip and a couple of misguided romances had passed between the houses over the past year. One such couple had married and been forced to leave employment. It was well known that domestic servants must be unmarried to stay employed. Eli didn't know a woman who would be worth giving up the best job in town for—nay, the best job in the state.

There was little time in Eli's life for anything other than automobiles.

◆◆◆

Lucy Taylor eyed the long mahogany banister, admiring the polished gleam—and had to fight the urge to slide down to the second floor. Instead, like the proper young lady she was raised to be, she straightened her spine, lifted her chin just a notch, and placed her hand on the railing to descend.

"What are you doing?" hissed the housemaid, Pricilla Addams.

Lucy jerked her foot back and almost tumbled down the carpeted stairs. She took a step away from the stairs and put her hand over her racing heart. "I'm going down to the parlor for the meeting. What did you think I was going to do?" Surely she didn't suspect Lucy's desire to slide down the banister.

Pricilla stood with a bucket in one hand and a mop in the other. Her scowl revealed crooked teeth. "Not that way, you're not."

"Which way should I go?"

"Down the back stairs, same as the rest of us." Pricilla nodded toward the grand stairway and turned her nose in the air. "Them stairs are reserved for Mr. and Mrs. Walker and their guests—not the likes of you."

The housemaid ambled past Lucy and made her way to an inconspicuous door tucked among a dozen others in the upper hall. With an emphatic tug, she opened the door to reveal the servants' stairs. "From now on, you'll be required to skulk around like the rest o' the staff. Out o' sight, out o' mind." She paused, a self-satisfied smile on her disagreeable face. "Or had you forgotten you're a servant now?"

Lucy had only just arrived to begin her work that afternoon. Her black gown itched, her white apron reeked of starch, and the pins holding her maid's cap in place stuck into her scalp. How could she possibly forget she was now in domestic service? "Of course I haven't forgotten."

"Maybe you could use the grand stairs once upon a time," the other woman sneered, clearly aware of Lucy's sudden fall from society. "But Mrs. Walker better not catch you on them unless you're polishing that banister." She looked Lucy up and down. "Though I doubt you'd know how to use a rag if—"

"Lucy?" Mrs. Walker opened her bedroom door, a smile on her pretty face.

Pricilla clapped her mouth shut and disappeared down the servants' stairs before Lucy could draw a breath.

"Would you mind terribly?" Mrs. Walker turned her back and pointed at the top button of her gown. "My hair has caught."

"Of course not." Lucy crossed the upper hall and entered the impressive sitting room of the master suite. A door to the right led to an indoor bathroom—complete with a marble shower, the door straight ahead went into the bedchamber, and the one on the left revealed a massive dressing room.

"As soon as the meeting is over"—Mrs. Walker said while Lucy unhooked the strand of hair around the button—"would you mind organizing my things?"

"I'd be happy to." From where Lucy stood she could see the dressing room was strewn with several trunks, hat boxes, and handbags.

"It's so nice to have a competent lady's maid." Mrs. Walker regarded Lucy with a warm smile. "I've been home from my honeymoon for a week and I've been so busy with household affairs, my dressing room has gone to shambles."

One of those affairs was hiring a lady's maid. Dozens of women had applied, but for reasons unknown to Lucy, she had been hired. Her. With no experience to speak of. Applying for the job had seemed almost ridiculous at the time, yet here she stood. She suspected Mrs. Walker had hired her to save Lucy's family from complete ruin. "I'll see that you're properly taken care of from now on."

"You're a dear." Mrs. Walker looked toward the dressing room. "Noah insisted I purchase whatever caught my fancy in Europe, but now I'm afraid all your time will be devoted to caring for my wardrobe."

Lucy tried to smile at Mrs. Walker's joke, but inside she wanted to weep. She longed to see Europe, and the wardrobe Mama had commissioned for Lucy's debut season had been sold after Papa became ill and passed away. He had been one of the lawyers employed by the White Pine Mill, and had been wealthy and respectable, but during his illness their debt had mounted, and they were now destitute. On the one hand, Lucy was thankful for a job that provided a steady income to help her mother and younger sisters—and she assumed it had been given to her as a way for her father's employers to help—but on the other hand, it was a constant reminder that she no longer belonged in Julia Walker's world.

"Come." Mrs. Walker linked her arm through Lucy's. "Let us go to Noah and Freddie's meeting, and then we'll return and tackle this mess."

Lucy walked stiffly beside Mrs. Walker as they left the master suite. A month ago, she would have felt completely natural linking arms with Julia Walker—after all, they had attended many of the same social engagements before Papa died. Now, however, it didn't seem right to be so informal with her employer.

When they came to the grand stairs and Mrs. Walker began to descend, Lucy paused.

"What's wrong?" Mrs. Walker asked.

Lucy pulled her arm away and glanced at the closed door to the servants' stairs. "I will be down in a moment."

Her employer looked at the servants' stairs as well. She was a bright woman—she had been raised in the upper echelons of society in New York City before meeting Mr. Walker. Surely she knew the boundaries between them.

"Do what you think best, Lucy."

Being accepted by her employer was important—but being accepted by the staff was vital. "Thank you." Lucy dipped a slight curtsy and walked to the servants' stairway.

The stairwell was narrow and winding, with one small window to light the steps. When Lucy opened the door on the main floor, Pricilla and Mrs. Cash, the cook, were just leaving the kitchen to join the others for the meeting.

Lucy met their haughty looks with a deferential nod, then she closed the door and walked behind them.

Mrs. Walker arrived at the base of the grand stairway as they approached, and she greeted the other two ladies with a polite smile.

"Aw, there's my beautiful wife." Mr. Walker's face lit up when the women entered the parlor, and he held out his hand for his wife to join him.

Mr. Alexander stood on the other side of the impressive fireplace, now cold for the remainder of the summer, and waited until the newlyweds greeted one another before he approached. "Julia." He bent over her hand in a slight bow. "Marriage becomes you."

"It's so nice to see you again, Freddie." Julia smiled at her neighbor and then moved to her husband's side.

Mr. Alexander's staff stood at attention on one side of the parlor, while Mr. Walker's staff stood on the other side. Lucy had briefly met her coworkers, but had not met the others from the mansion next door.

She took her place beside Pricilla and clasped her hands behind her back, waiting for the meeting to begin. Before her arrival, there had been four staff members in each household, a cook, a butler, a housemaid, and a footman who also served as a driver and man-of-all-work. As the fifth member in the Walker home, she felt that she had somehow made everything unbalanced.

Mr. Alexander's staff kept their gazes low, yet she noticed a few covert glances in her direction from all but the footman. He seemed preoccupied as he stared at the floor. He was a handsome young man, with golden hair and a stubborn chin. He fidgeted and tugged at the sleeves of his black coat and ran his gloved hand around his collar.

Watching him made her wiggle in her itchy new dress—yet a smile tilted her lips as she observed his continued discomfort. It was obvious he wasn't used to his uniform and didn't care who noticed.

"Thank you all for gathering," Mr. Walker said as he stood between his wife and his business partner. "Mr. Alexander and I have an announcement that may benefit some of you. It concerns the annual community appreciation picnic in four weeks."

Lucy was familiar with the picnic, having attended it with her family every year for the past eight years, since she was a girl of ten. Most of the town was employed by the White Pine Lumber Company, which held an annual picnic in the middle of June as a way to say thank you. Food, contests, and entertainment were provided. It was a highlight for everyone who attended.

"This year we're going to do something a little different," Mr. Alexander said with a roguish smile. "Most of you know I had the distinct pleasure of witnessing the first modern Olympic Games in Athens a few years ago. I plan to attend the games in Paris next year as well. With that in mind, Mr. Walker and I have decided to hold our own version of the Olympics."

Several staff members glanced at one another, yet the footman across the way only looked at Mr. Alexander. From her vantage point, Lucy could now see the sky-blue color of his eyes. His skin was bronzed, and blond highlights streaked through his hair. He looked as if he spent a great deal of time outdoors.

"Mr. Alexander and I will compile two teams," Mr. Walker said. "Our teams will compete against each other in running, archery, wrestling, shooting, cycling, horse races, tennis and—"

"An automobile race," Mr. Alexander interrupted.

The footman looked up sharply, and for the first time since the meeting started, he looked interested in the conversation.

Until he glanced in her direction and noticed her watching him. His brow furrowed and a scowl replaced the look of interest.

What had she done now?

Chapter Two

If his confounded suit wasn't so uncomfortable and he hadn't been given the surprise about the automobile race, Eli might have noticed the new servant staring at him before now. He didn't know what he was expecting, but not the pretty young woman across the room. His disappointment over Mrs. Walker's choice of a lady's maid had caused him to assume she would be an old curmudgeon—yet she was anything but. There was not a strand of her dark red hair out of place under her cap, her brown eyes were bright and curious, and her pert little nose was much too cute on her pretty face.

It made Eli all the more frustrated.

His sister Jessie had applied for the job and been qualified. It would have been the perfect solution to one of Eli's problems. If Jessie worked at Basswood Hill, they would finally be together again, and he wouldn't have to worry about her working as a domestic servant alone in Minneapolis. But Mrs. Walker had caused tongues to wag by choosing the least likely candidate—a young woman who had recently been a socialite but had fallen on hard times with her father's untimely death—and here she stood staring at him. What did she know of being a lady's maid?

"Mr. Alexander and I will hand-select our teams from among all our employees, even our house staff, after a tryout to be held next Saturday," Mr. Walker said. "Except for the drivers. Since we assume Mr. Alexander will choose Eli as his driver, I must find someone else in the state who is qualified to beat Eli."

A wave of chuckles filled the room.

"And to make the competition even more interesting," Mr. Alexander said, "we will offer a significant cash prize to the winning team."

A cash prize? Eli's full attention was on his employer again.

"Each member of the winning team will walk away with a hundred dollars," Mr. Alexander said.

Several of the servants gasped and Eli had to work hard to keep his own surprise from showing. A hundred dollars would buy all the necessary parts he needed to finish his automobile.

"We look forward to seeing all of you on the lower lawn at nine o'clock next Saturday morning," Mr. Alexander said. "That will be all."

"Please join Mrs. Cash in the kitchen," Mrs. Walker added quickly. "She's prepared refreshments for you to enjoy before you return to your duties."

Eli followed the staff out of the parlor and down the main hall, but the last place he wanted to be was with the other staff—especially the new lady's maid.

If he had a few minutes to himself, he'd rather be in the barn working on his automobile.

A large plate of cookies and a bowl of applesauce sat on the worktable in the middle of the large Walker kitchen. The room was filled with the delicious fragrance of cinnamon, making Eli's stomach growl—but he couldn't eat right now. Not with the thought of a hundred dollars still hanging in the air. Surely he could win the automobile race, even if Mr. Walker found a worthy opponent. But it wouldn't depend on him solely. His whole team would have to win.

Conversation erupted in the room as the staff discussed the announcement. The women gathered around the worktable—all but the lady's maid. She stood off to the side, her hands clasped in front of her slender waist as she watched the others with a reserved smile.

"If you ask me," Pricilla said, "that meeting was a waste o' my time. We all know there won't be any women in those competitions."

"And rightly so," said Mrs. Cash with a decided nod. "Women don't have any business in sporting activities."

"Actually. . ." The lady's maid spoke up. "The second Olympiad will include women for the first time next year."

Everyone stopped speaking and looked at the new maid.

She tilted her chin up just a notch. "They will compete in tennis, sailing, croquet, equestrianism, and golf."

"Well, I never." Mrs. Cash crossed her arms under her ample bosom. "What woman in her right mind would want to parade about and compete in such a fashion?"

"A prideful woman, that's who," said Pricilla with a pointed glare.

"Or one who enjoys sports," the lady's maid offered. "It doesn't seem so preposterous."

"I doubt Mr. Walker and Mr. Alexander intend for any of us to enter the competition," Mrs. Cash said. "So it doesn't pay to discuss this further."

The other women nodded in agreement.

"I'm not so sure." The lady's maid addressed the cook. "Why would they have called us together if they didn't intend for us to compete?"

No one said anything for a moment and then Pricilla spoke up. "Do you plan to try out, then?"

The lady's maid stared at Pricilla without flinching. "I may."

Several eyebrows rose.

"And what does a young lass like you know about sports?" Mr. Yankton, the butler at the Alexander home, gave a pitiful shake of his head.

She lifted her chin even higher and Eli recognized the spark of determination in her eyes. It was the same way he felt when people questioned his dream to build automobiles.

"I know a great deal," she said. "Growing up I played tennis, rode a bicycle, and spent hours shooting a bow and arrow with my father."

Mr. Yankton patted her shoulder. "I'm sure you did, my dear, but I think you'll have more fun cheering from the sidelines."

She clamped her mouth closed and didn't respond, though Eli suspected she had a lot more to say—and for some reason, he wanted to know what that would be. He admired a woman with a bit of pluck. They were few and far between.

Mr. Yankton turned back to Mr. Timmons, the butler from the Walker mansion, apparently done talking to the lady's maid. "I could do a lot with an extra hundred dollars."

"We all could." Eli spoke the words before he even realized he had something to say.

The lady's maid looked in his direction and he was surprised all over again by how direct and clear her gaze was. She studied him for a moment before approaching.

He stood straighter and tried to muster the frustration he'd felt earlier. She had stolen his sister's job, hadn't she?

"I'm Lucy Taylor." She put out her hand. "I'm pleased to meet you."

He paused for a moment, unsure how to proceed with this lady. He rarely interacted with the Walker staff, especially the women. He couldn't afford any misunderstood relationships between them. But he couldn't very well turn his back to her, either.

He took her hand in his and was surprised at the confidence in her handshake. "Elijah Boyer."

"It's nice to meet you, Mr. Boyer. You're the automobile racer?"

It would be better to walk away, but something in her keen gaze made him want to stay. If nothing else, maybe he could find a crack in her facade and help Mrs. Walker see she had made a mistake. Jessie could be hired and Miss Taylor would be on her way.

"I am."

Her eyes sparkled and her cheeks took on a flush. "Are you familiar with Charles Duryea and the *Chicago Times-Herald* Race?"

"Of course." Who wasn't familiar with the first auto race in the United States? It had only been four short years ago, but it had sparked the imagination of people around the world—and been the very thing that interested Eli in motorized wagons to begin with. Yet, he'd never met a woman who had shown an interest.

"Do you race automobiles often, Mr. Boyer?"

"Not as often as I'd like." He had not intended to familiarize himself with the new lady's maid, yet he couldn't make himself walk away. "I drive Mr. Alexander's Duryea."

"I've seen it around town," she said with awe. "I've always longed for a ride."

He couldn't very well offer her a ride. What would his employer think? What would everyone else think? He couldn't take any risks getting to know this young woman.

"I must return to my work," he said.

"And I." She smiled, revealing a lone dimple in her right cheek. "I look forward to seeing you compete at the picnic."

Eli took his leave, but not before glancing at the peculiar woman one more time. For some reason, he looked forward to seeing her compete, too.

He wouldn't mind seeing that dimple again, either.

———— ••• ————

The following Saturday, Lucy looked out the window of Mrs. Walker's dressing room and stared at the lower lawn of Basswood Hill. The Mississippi River was hard to see through all the trees lining the property, but she could make out the sparkle of the water and the floating logs as they went downriver toward St. Paul.

"Lucy, have you seen my parasol?" Mrs. Walker entered the dressing room with her gloves in place and her hat secured to her dark-brown hair. She was a beautiful woman, both inside and out, and Lucy enjoyed serving her. It made her sudden drop in society less troublesome to bear.

"It's right here." Lucy picked up the parasol and handed it to her employer.

"Aren't you coming to the tryouts? They will begin in less than half an hour."

All week Lucy had planned to try out for archery, but as the days slipped by she had lost more and more of her courage. No doubt she'd be the only woman in the competitions and she'd probably embarrass herself. Any time she spoke about it around the Walker staff, she'd been ridiculed by Mrs. Cash and Pricilla. They had all but ostracized her from their company, and she had spent her spare time by herself.

"I don't think I will."

Mrs. Walker set the tip of the parasol on the ground and leaned onto the handle. "Why ever not? I heard you had contemplated trying out for the archery competition."

Lucy bit her lip and turned to the dressing table.

"Just think what you could do with an extra hundred dollars." Mrs. Walker smiled. "Maybe buy a few pretty dresses."

If Lucy had a hundred dollars she wouldn't fling it away on frivolity. She would give the money to her mama so her younger sister Margaret could have the surgery she needed. She'd broken both her legs when she fell out of a tree a couple of months before Papa died, and the doctor had not set the bones properly. Poor Margaret could not walk and was forced to spend her days in a chair. If she didn't have the surgery in St. Paul, she would be crippled for the rest of her life. There was no extra cash to pay for such a procedure, not when there were six mouths to feed and little more than Lucy's income.

"Do you think it would be unseemly for me to try out?" Lucy asked.

"It would be unseemly if you didn't try."

"Truly?"

Mrs. Walker put her hand on Lucy's arm. "Go get ready and meet me downstairs in ten minutes. We'll walk outside together."

"Do you think Mr. Walker and Mr. Alexander will be upset if a female enters the tryouts?"

Mrs. Walker lifted her chin and took on a regal air. "If they do, they'll have me to contend with." She laughed. "Now run along."

Lucy's heart pumped with excitement as she raced up the servants' stairs to the third floor where her little room was tucked under the charming eaves of the Walker mansion. It wasn't much to speak of, but it was warm and clean and all hers.

She quickly removed her maid's uniform and put on a serviceable calico gown she had brought from home. It wasn't fancy and neither was it plain. It was perfect to wear for archery. Next, she grabbed her simple straw boater and pinned it snugly in place.

Mrs. Walker waited for Lucy in the main hall and together they left the mansion.

"I'll be cheering the loudest for you." Mrs. Walker squeezed Lucy's hand. "You'll show all those men what a woman can do."

Lucy hoped and prayed Mrs. Walker was right—because if she wasn't, then Lucy would embarrass both of them today.

Word had spread around the mill and throughout town that there would be a competition. Over a hundred people gathered on the lower lawn of the estate for the tryouts, including Mr. Boyer, who stood with a group of men.

As Lucy and Mrs. Walker approached, Mr. Boyer looked up and caught Lucy's gaze.

Lucy dipped her head in greeting and he did the same.

She had noticed him several times throughout the week, though from what she could tell, he spent most of his time in the barn at the bottom of the hill. Once, she and Mrs. Walker were on a stroll around the estate and they had come across him working on an automobile. Lucy had been fascinated and he had answered all her questions with patience.

But today she didn't have the luxury of thinking about pleasant things. Perspiration began to run down her back as she surveyed her competition. Men of all sizes and shapes stood around. Very few wore their coats, and most had their sleeves rolled up their muscular forearms. The air had a festive quality about it as people laughed and joked with one another.

Everyone seemed so confident.

Everyone but Lucy.

The Walker and Alexander mansions loomed on the hill behind everyone and suddenly Lucy longed to be back in her cozy fortress. Why had she agreed to do this thing?

"Gather round," Mr. Walker said from where he stood on a box at the south end of the lawn.

Lucy closed her eyes for a brief moment and pictured Margaret. No matter how nervous she was, she would compete for her sister's chance to walk again.

When all had congregated near Mr. Walker, he lifted his hands to silence them. "We will have two teams compete in eight events at the picnic. Anyone employed by Mr. Walker or me is eligible to try out for as many events as he'd like." He looked around the crowd. "We will only choose the best of the best today, so show us what you're made of."

Lucy swallowed hard as she looked around at the dozens of men who were getting ready to compete. "How will I measure up? And what if I don't qualify for the archery event?"

Mrs. Walker patted her arm. "I assume you have good aim."

"I suppose."

"Then try shooting, as well."

"Shooting?" Lucy put her hand to her throat. "I've only shot a pistol half a dozen times."

"That's half a dozen more than some."

Lucy groaned and Mrs. Walker laughed.

"What do you have to lose, Lucy? Give it a try."

Mrs. Walker was right. How would she know if she didn't try?

The sun shimmered through the branches of the basswood trees as Lucy walked up to the registration table and waited in line. Several men looked in her direction and some joked loud enough for her to hear.

"I see you're still planning to compete." Mr. Boyer appeared beside her.

"I am."

"And what sport do you think you can win?"

Lucy took a step forward to stay in line. She was afraid she wouldn't win at anything, but she couldn't show him, or anyone else, her trepidation. "Archery and shooting."

Mr. Boyer lifted his eyebrows. "Two sports?"

"What about you?" she asked quickly. "Do you plan to try out for anything besides auto racing?"

He stepped forward. "I hadn't thought about it until now. But maybe I will, after all."

Children ran around the lawn as women stood in small groups and conversed. Mrs. Walker had been joined by several women Lucy had been friends with since she was a child. It hurt that they would now look down upon her—but there was little she could do about her circumstances. God had chosen for her to be the oldest child in her family, so the responsibility to provide fell on her shoulders.

"Are you good at anything besides racing automobiles?" Lucy allowed her eyes to assess his physique. He was tall and well built. "Surely you could best any man here at wrestling."

Mr. Boyer lifted one brow. "And what makes you think that?"

Lucy's cheeks grew warm as she advanced in line. "Don't all men wrestle?"

He shook his head.

The man in front of them moved away and Lucy found herself staring at Mr. Walker.

"Why, Lucy!" Mr. Walker smiled. "I didn't know you planned to try out."

"Do you have any objections, sir?"

Mr. Walker glanced at Mr. Alexander, who shrugged and shook his head.

"I don't see why you can't compete." Mr. Walker put his pen to the paper and wrote Lucy's name. "What sport would you like to try?"

"Archery and shooting."

"Two events?"

Lucy nodded. "I'd thought I'd double my chances."

Mr. Walker laughed and handed her two slips of paper. "Sounds reasonable to me. Give these to the referee for each event."

Lucy curtsied and stepped aside for Mr. Boyer.

"And what about you, Boyer?" Mr. Walker folded his arms on the table. "Tennis and cycling, perhaps?"

"Put the man down for the auto race," Mr. Alexander scowled. "He's on my team."

Mr. Walker gave his friend a sideways glance. "Of course he is."

"I'll also sign up for archery," Mr. Boyer said.

It was Lucy's turn to raise her eyebrows in surprise. "Are you any good?"

Mr. Boyer looked at her and grinned. "Now that I know you're the competition, you'll have to wait and see."

"Just what I had hoped," Mr. Alexander said. "Some friendly rivalry between the two houses."

By the looks of Mr. Boyer's satisfied smile, he would be a formidable competitor, though she had no desire for a rival.

Chapter Three

The sun beat down on Eli's shoulders as he pulled the bowstring back, aimed the arrow, and let it fly. It sailed through the air with a whistle and hit the target on the right edge of the bull's-eye.

A round of applause met his ears as he lowered the bow with a bit of self-satisfaction. So far, his three arrows had garnered more points than the other fifteen men who had competed.

"Very nice." Lucy Taylor, the last competitor to take a turn, stood behind Eli and clapped with the others. "It looks like you're the person to beat."

Eli offered a slight bow and stepped out of the way for her to take his place. They stood in the driveway of the green barn where a target had been set up. On either side of the drive, two massive gardens were just sprouting to life, so the spectators had been forced to stand on the edges of the gardens or behind the archers.

Other competitions took place on the lower grounds of the Walker and Alexander estate, dispersing the competitors and spectators throughout the property. Slowly, as Miss Taylor had moved to the front of the line, people had begun to wander over to the archery competition. No doubt they wanted to know if the sole female at the tryouts would be any good.

Eli was pretty curious too.

Miss Taylor handed her slip of paper to the referee and was given a bow and three arrows. She wore a pretty green dress that complimented her red hair, and when she glanced at Eli, she smiled—yet he could see a hint of nerves behind her brown-eyed gaze.

He was impressed she'd even try to compete against all these men, especially with so much opposition from the female staff. What drove her to want to participate? She didn't appear prideful or out to prove a point.

Miss Taylor took her position on the line marker and placed the arrow on the bowstring. She lifted the bow, pulled back the string, and aimed toward the target. After a split-second hesitation, she let the arrow go and it landed dead center on the target.

There was a slight pause and then the crowd went wild.

Eli clapped with the rest of them, wondering if it had been luck or if she was a skilled archer after all.

Miss Taylor smiled at her audience and then repeated each step with a second arrow.

Again, the second arrow landed in the middle of the bull's-eye, just to the right of the first one.

The onlookers cheered again and Eli glanced around to see how the naysayers would respond. Mrs. Cash stood beside Pricilla, but neither smiled at their fellow employee's achievement. Instead, they crossed their arms and scowled.

Miss Taylor shot the third arrow and it landed on the left edge of the bull's-eye. She had easily beaten her competitors.

"We have a winner!" the referee called. "Miss Lucy Taylor."

More cheers and a few whistles filled the air. The pretty lady's maid blushed and her eyes shone with delight. Gone were the nerves she'd had earlier. Now she looked completely happy.

"Our second competitor during the picnic will be Mr. Boyer," the referee went on. "Congratulations to our winners, and thank you to everyone who participated."

The crowd began to break up and Eli approached Miss Taylor. "Congratulations. I'm impressed with your skill."

She dipped her head. "Thank you. The same to you."

"I definitely have some practicing to do if I want to win."

The referee moved the archery target to the side and began to set up the targets for the shooting competition.

"Will you still try out for the shooting event?" Eli asked.

Miss Taylor looked over her shoulder at the new targets. "I don't see why not."

If her shooting was anything like her archery, she might very well win that as well, and then what would the naysayers think?

"Eli." Mr. Alexander walked down the gravel driveway. "May I have a word with you?"

Eli glanced back at Miss Taylor, but she waved him away. "I need to go familiarize myself with a pistol again."

He chuckled and she walked toward the table where the pistols were waiting.

"What can I do for you?" Eli asked Mr. Alexander.

"I just received some promising news and I wanted to share it right away."

"Yes?"

"You know I've been in contact with a group of men from Minneapolis and Chicago who are interested in investing in automobile racing."

Eli was very familiar with Mr. Alexander's desire to find investors. His employer was capable of laying down the money, but investors were valuable for networking and connections as much as they were for finances. "Yes, of course."

"I've been trying to get them to Little Falls to meet with us for months now, and I just received word that they will arrive next week."

It was wonderful news—exactly what they'd been hoping for.

"There will be five men coming along with their wives," Mr. Alexander explained. "Noah and Julia have agreed to host three of the couples and I will host two. They will stay for three days. We will show them around Little Falls, take them through the lumber mill, and entertain them with various activities. But the most important part of their visit will be to meet with you and watch you race." He grinned. "If they like what they see, I believe we will have enough support to go into racing full time. What do you think of that?"

The idea of racing full time, and no longer acting the part of footman, was an appealing thought. "I couldn't be more pleased."

Mr. Alexander's smile dimmed. "There will be one aspect of the visit you probably won't care for."

"What's that?"

"We'll need you to fulfill your duties as footman while they are here. Mrs. Walker is hosting a formal dinner to welcome all our guests, and staff from both houses will be needed to serve."

Eli wanted to groan.

"It will take a lot of work to prepare for their arrival and see to their needs while they're here," Mr. Alexander continued. "You'll need to speak to the footman at the Walker home to learn the particulars of your duties before next week."

Eli hated the prospect of wearing his footman garb for three solids days—but if it meant they might find investors, and that he could be done with domestic service for good, he would do whatever it would take. "I'll see to it right away."

"Good." Mr. Alexander glanced at Miss Taylor, who was taking her place in line for the shooting competition. "For now, I think we should cheer Miss Taylor on to victory. I hear she bested you at archery."

"That she did."

"Then it looks like you might need to take some archery lessons from her, too." Mr. Alexander laughed as he clapped Eli on the back.

Eli didn't need a second invitation to watch Miss Taylor compete in the shooting competition. He walked to the sidelines as she waited to take her turn. She noticed his arrival and sent him a warm smile.

Something about the way she carried herself drew his attention over and over. He admired her determination and courage, and he was captivated by her unassuming beauty, but it was her sweet and gentle countenance that really attracted him.

If he wasn't careful, he might grow to like her more than he should, and that wouldn't serve either one of them well.

The first two men shot at the target and received a polite response, but then Lucy went to the line, and before she even shot the pistol, an uproarious applause filled the air.

With her left eye closed and her right arm extended, she raised the pistol and aimed at the target. The gun went off with a bang and the bullet landed in dead center, just as the arrow had.

The crowd cheered even louder and Miss Taylor's eyebrows rose in surprise. She looked baffled by her accuracy and Eli couldn't help but laugh. Two more times she aimed and fired, and two more times she hit the center of the target.

With a bit of a stunned expression, she moved to the side to wait until the others took their turns. From time to time, she looked in Eli's direction and shook her head in amazement.

By the end of the competition, no one had come close to beating Miss Taylor.

"First place goes to Miss Lucy Taylor," the referee called.

More applause rose in the air and she curtsied, then came to stand beside Eli and Mr. Alexander.

"I'm still amazed," she said.

"It appears we have a markswoman in our midst." Mr. Alexander offered a gentlemanly bow. "You will be an asset to Noah's team in both events."

"It doesn't seem possible." She shook her head. "But I'll do all I can to help my team win."

If Miss Taylor's team won, that meant Eli's would lose—and he couldn't let that happen, not with a hundred dollars at stake.

Suddenly, he wasn't quite so pleased to witness the pretty maid's accomplishments. After all, she was now the competition.

◄━━━●◦●━━━►

Lucy hummed as she stood in the butler's pantry arranging fresh-cut flowers. Sunshine filtered through the lead-glass window and made the crystal vase sparkle. The scent of irises and gladioli filled the room with their heady perfume. Lucy stepped back and admired her bouquet, feeling a bit guilty that her days were filled with such things as styling Mrs. Walker's hair and arranging flowers, while her mother and sisters spent their days in the drudgery of washing and mending clothes. Before Father's death, Mama had been preparing her daughters to be the ladies of fine homes. Lucy had all the skills necessary—she just never imagined she'd put them to use as a lady's maid.

It didn't pay to think about what would never be. Instead, she'd concentrate on what she could do. It had been a week since the tryout and she was still amazed she had made Mr. Walker's team. Since she was competing in two events, there were six men and her on the team. She'd met her teammates briefly, and she'd been given a frosty welcome. Clearly, they saw her as a liability and not an advantage. But she would do her best to win. Margaret's future depended on her success.

With a sigh that left her feeling a bit deflated, Lucy exited the butler's pantry and entered the dining room. Dark walnut paneling covered the walls and a crystal chandelier hung over the long table. Last-minute details, like the flowers, were being added to the house in preparation for the arrival of their guests in the morning. After she placed the flowers, she would need to press the linen, polish the silver, and write out the place cards.

She bent forward and set the vase in the center of the table, adjusting it to the left.

The floorboards creaked and she looked up to find Mr. Boyer standing in the doorway, hat in hand. He wore his everyday clothes, which were stained with grease and looked a bit rumpled. His blond hair fell over his forehead and he pushed it away, revealing his stunning blue eyes.

She stood straight, her pulse ticking a little faster at his unexpected presence. "May I help you, Mr. Boyer?"

Something about the way he stood made her suspect he was embarrassed—but why?

"Is Jack here?" he asked.

"I believe he's somewhere in the house." She tried to recall the last time she'd seen the footman. "He's been very busy today. Is there something I can do for you?"

He looked away from her as he clutched his hat. "I don't believe so."

She moved around the table and stood before him. "I can always try."

He finally looked back at her and let his arms fall to his sides. "I need some help, and I've run out of time."

"What kind of help?"

He looked out into the hall and then leaned forward and whispered, "I don't know how to serve at the table."

Lucy leaned forward and also whispered. "But aren't you a footman?"

"Yes." He didn't meet her gaze. "But I've never been required to fulfill that particular duty."

She straightened. "How is that possible?"

He shrugged. "Mr. Alexander rarely entertains, and when he does Mr. Yankton is all that's needed. I was hired to work on automobiles—not serve supper."

Lucy studied the young man before her, puzzled by so many things. "Surely you found out before today that you'd be required to serve. Why did you wait so long to consult Jack?"

"The men coming to visit are possible investors and are more concerned about the automobile and my skills as a driver. I've spent all week working on Mr. Alexander's Duryea."

"You do realize it will be impossible to learn everything you'll need to know by tomorrow."

"How hard can it be?"

"How hard—?" She shook her head in amazement. "The formal meal is a time-honored tradition that has been revered throughout the centuries. It has taken me my whole life to observe the proper etiquette and learn the customs."

He stared at her. "Isn't the point of a meal to simply fill your stomach?"

"A dinner party is the height of a lady's social accomplishment." Lucy's mother had given some of the most magnificent dinner parties in town before they were forced into poverty. "This will be Mrs. Walker's first opportunity to play hostess since becoming a married lady and she's planned each course in great detail. A formal dinner is meant to not only fill a stomach, but to provide a setting for conversation, relaxation, and entertainment."

"Fine." He let out a frustrated breath. "Will you just show me the basics?"

The basics? She wanted to scoff at such a notion. "I wouldn't know where to begin."

"Lucy, please." It was the first time he had used her given name, and it brought her thoughts to a sudden halt. "I need some help."

She ran her hand down the front of her spotless apron, wishing she wasn't so aware of this man and the effect he had on her. "Why haven't you asked Mr. Yankton or one of the other staff from Mr. Alexander's house?"

"They're just as busy as everyone else." He sounded desperate. "I need to impress these investors and I want them to think me capable. Do you have the time to teach me?"

"I'm very busy, as well. . ." Yet, if Eli—yes, Eli—hadn't he just called her Lucy?—didn't know how to serve Mrs. Walker's guests, her employer would be mortified and all the hard work she'd put into planning her house party would be wasted. "I'll do what I can to help, but it will be impossible to teach you everything."

He let out a relieved sigh and spoke gently. "Thank you. I just need to know enough to get by."

He set his hat on a chair near the door and followed her to the sideboard where the silverware, dishes, and linen were stored. Piece by piece, she took out a full service and showed him where to place each item on the table. "Each place setting should include a plate, two large knives, a small knife and fork for fish, three large forks, a tablespoon for soup, a small oyster fork for raw oysters, and a water goblet. Mr. and Mrs. Walker do not drink or serve alcohol, so we will not need to worry about wine glasses." She watched him carefully as he nodded. "The knives and oyster fork should be placed on the right side of the plate, the other forks on the left. Can you remember all that?"

He looked up, his eyes already glazed over.

"The bread will be sliced into thin pieces, and you will need to lay them on a napkin to the left of each plate." She pointed to the location. "Place glasses to the right of each plate." She went to the head chair where Mr. Walker would sit. "The service will move in a single direction to the right, counterclockwise, starting with the guest of honor at Mr. Walker's right hand. Beverage service progresses to the left, clockwise."

Eli ran his hand over his forehead. "Right. Left."

"You must always make sure the traffic level in the dining room is kept at a minimum so you don't disrupt the conversation. Ideally, a footman will exit and reenter the dining room not more than four to six times per course." She moved to the opposite side of the table from him. "The only time you should leave the dining room is when you go to the kitchen to perform four tasks: retrieve the plates for each course, provide a sauce if it's needed, replenish water, and clear the plates."

"To serve, to sauce, to water, to clear." He tapped each step on his fingers.

Lucy couldn't help but smile. "If you have trouble, just remember that Mr. Yankton will be in charge and you should follow his lead. He will speak as little as possible, so be sure to watch him at all times to make sure he is able to communicate without speaking."

"Communicate without speaking?" Eli's handsome brow crinkled.

She went to the hutch and removed a large platter. Coming around the table, she stood before him. "You must hold the serving platter one inch above the guest's plate to allow him to serve himself comfortably." She handed the platter to him and their fingers brushed.

For the first time since she began to teach, he seemed to come to his senses, and he searched her face.

"After you serve the guest"—she said quickly, putting space between them—"lift the platter above the guest's shoulder instead of over his head." She pulled a chair out and took a seat. "You should practice."

He took a deep breath and put the platter near her, just as she had instructed.

"Very good," she said.

"What if they want a second helping?"

"There are no second helpings at a formal dinner."

He sighed. "All of this is more than I ever thought I'd need to know. My father was a mill worker and my mother a laundress. The fanciest we got was on Sundays when we went to church." He moved the platter away from her and didn't meet her gaze. "I never thought I'd be serving a formal meal."

She studied him for a moment, appreciating his candor. She'd never met anyone quite like him and found it refreshing.

He caught her staring and she felt her cheeks growing warm.

She stood to demonstrate the next step and shake off the strange tension that was beginning to form between them. "At a formal dinner, plates are served from the right and cleared from the left. The moment you clear a plate, put a fresh plate in its place." She clasped her hands and smiled. "This way, there will never be an empty space in front of the guest."

"Why?"

Her smile fell. "Why, what?"

"Why can't there be an empty space in front of the guest?"

Lucy blinked. "I don't know. It's just customary."

He rubbed his face and groaned. "This whole thing is absurd."

"Whether it's absurd or not, it's proper etiquette to follow all the rules." Lucy became very serious. "Mrs. Walker is counting on all of us to make her party a seamless affair. If you do your job right, you'll be invisible and the guests won't even know you're in the room."

"Are we done?"

She sighed. "We've only just begun, but I'm afraid you won't remember anything else if we continue."

He met her eyes, something akin to hope or desperation simmering in his gaze. "Will you be here?"

She couldn't stop herself from smiling. "I'll be helping in the kitchen, yes."

"Good." He picked up his hat and clutched it again. He looked as if he might say something more, but then turned to leave. "Thank you."

With that, he left the dining room.

Lucy stood for a moment, feeling his sudden absence more keenly than she would like.

Chapter Four

T he next evening, Eli stood at attention in the dining room of the Walker mansion with Jack, the Walker's footman. Mr. Timmons had gone to the parlor to announce dinner, and any moment the guests would enter.

Eli took a couple of steady breaths and tried to remember all the details Lucy had given him yesterday. He had hoped to see her before the meal started, but he hadn't caught a single glimpse of her all day.

Out of the corner of his eye he watched Jack. The man was as cool and composed as ever, but then, why wouldn't he be? Eli was the only person in the mansion who was out of his element. He hadn't even met the investors yet, and part of him was disappointed that he'd be meeting them as their servant, instead of their equal. But then, even if he became a successful racer or automobile manufacturer, would he ever reach their level?

The investors and their wives had arrived that morning and been invited to rest and then have a leisurely luncheon that Mr. Timmons and Jack had been able to handle without help. The afternoon had been spent taking a tour of the White Pine Lumber Mill.

Voices drifted down the hall and Eli took in another deep breath. He tried to appear calm, yet his insides were a mess of nerves. He prided himself on being in control of his thoughts and emotions at all times—yet right now he felt like a skittish horse next to an automobile, ready to jump at the slightest provocation.

The dining room was resplendent with crystal, silver, and fresh flowers. Gone was the iris bouquet Lucy had arranged the day before. On the white linen cloth a low-lying centerpiece of delicate flowers and shiny fruit trailed the length of the table. Candles had been lit and they flickered and waved in the still room.

Mr. Walker appeared first with an older woman on his arm. She was tall and slender with a crown of silver hair above a stately face. No doubt she was Mrs. Caruthers, the wife of the most influential and wealthiest man in the group. As such, she would be treated as the guest of honor and her husband would walk in at the back of the group with Mrs. Walker.

The others filed into the room, laughing and chatting about people and places Eli had never heard of. The only person who seemed to notice him at all was Mr. Alexander, who nodded briefly at him and then moved on. No doubt he would wait to introduce Eli later when they were with the Duryea.

Mr. Timmons was the last to enter the room, and his appearance meant that the meal would begin. After everyone found their place cards, Eli left the dining room to bring in the first course.

Lucy entered the butler's pantry at the same moment, holding a soup tureen, and looked him up and down, approval in her pretty brown eyes. "You clean up very nicely, Mr. Boyer."

Despite his nerves, he smiled. "Thank you."

"How are you holding up?" She placed the tureen on the counter and took a ladle out of a drawer.

"We've only just begun."

She smiled, making her lone dimple appear, and opened the lid of the tureen. "Just follow Mr. Timmons's lead and you'll be fine." Steam billowed out as she placed the ladle inside the soup.

Eli picked up the tureen and was about to turn, but Lucy reached out and touched his arm to stop him.

"Here." She adjusted his bow tie.

He looked down and noticed the charming sprinkle of freckles across her nose.

She glanced up and her cheeks colored as she took a step back. "You're all set."

He felt more unsteady now than he had before, but he couldn't dwell on the feelings Lucy stirred. Mr. Timmons would be furious if he kept their guests waiting.

The meal progressed with little trouble, though Eli made several mistakes. Thankfully, Mr. Timmons and Jack were quick to cover his blunders, and Lucy stood in the butler's pantry throughout the whole meal to give words of encouragement or instruction.

When the dessert had been served, and Mrs. Walker had risen from the table to invite the ladies into the parlor, Eli felt his first wave of relief. He'd made it through the meal without embarrassing himself or Mrs. Walker.

He entered the dining room after bringing the dessert plates to the butler's pantry, and the men were sitting around the table in a much more leisurely fashion.

"Ah, Eli." Mr. Alexander rose and put his hand on Eli's shoulder. "I'd like to introduce you to our guests. They've been eager to meet you."

So he would be introduced as the fumbling footman, instead of the competent automobile mechanic. No matter. He'd make the best of the situation.

Five gentlemen were seated around the table with Mr. Walker and Mr. Alexander. All of them looked in Eli's direction with keen gazes and calculating observation.

"Mr. Caruthers," Mr. Alexander said, "I'd like you to meet Elijah Boyer, the young man I've been telling you about."

Mr. Caruthers rose from his chair and offered Eli his hand. "It's a pleasure to meet you. Mr. Alexander has been singing your praises for over a year. He seems to think you're the man we should be investing our hard-earned money into."

Eli wanted to look confident, but it was hard to feel like an equal standing in his footman's uniform. "I'm pleased to meet you, sir."

Mr. Alexander introduced Eli to the other men, and they all seemed cordial and interested in his driving skills.

"We plan to go out tomorrow and show you what Eli is capable of," Mr. Alexander said. "He'll race the Duryea and hopefully beat his personal record, and then he'll give each of you a ride. Afterward, he'll show you the improvements he's made to the original design, as well as the drawings he's made for his own automobile."

"I'm most eager to speak with you," Mr. Caruthers said. "I've been looking for a competent man to partner with. I want to invest in automobiles while they're still young."

The others nodded in agreement.

"Tomorrow then." Mr. Walker stood and motioned toward the door. "Shall we join the ladies?"

The others rose and left the dining room, while Eli stayed behind to help clean up.

As soon as they were gone, the pantry door opened and Lucy poked her head into the room. "That was exciting."

"Either in or out, Miss Taylor." Mr. Timmons stood with a large platter in hand.

Lucy opened the door all the way and allowed Mr. Timmons to leave the dining room.

"Mrs. Walker said I'm invited to come out and watch you race tomorrow." She began to clear the silverware from the table. "I've never seen an automobile race."

For some reason, the thought of Lucy being there made Eli more nervous than knowing the five possible investors would be there.

"Do you think I could have a ride someday?" she asked, following him around the table, picking up more silverware.

"It's not my automobile."

"If Mr. Alexander doesn't mind?"

He didn't think Mr. Alexander would mind—but Eli had no wish to be alone with Lucy. It was hard enough to keep his mind off her when she was in a room full of people. Yet, he couldn't deny that he wanted to take her on a ride. He saw the way her eyes lit up when she spoke about automobiles. It reminded him of his own passion. Why would he deny her the pleasure of a ride? If he tried hard enough, he could control his growing attraction to her—couldn't he?

"If Mr. Alexander doesn't mind, I'd be happy to give you a ride after the investors leave."

Her eyes sparkled and she clutched the silverware. "Do you think you could take me to my mama's house? I'd love to show the automobile to my sisters."

He couldn't take his eyes off her. She was so beautiful, it hurt. At the moment, he'd say yes to anything she requested. "Of course. I'll even give them a ride, if your mother approves."

Her lips parted and she slowly smiled. "You will?"

His voice refused to work properly, so he simply nodded.

"They'll be so excited." She picked up the rest of the silverware, her footsteps light and her face shining. "Thank you, Eli. You've made me very happy."

Her happiness meant more to him than he knew it should.

———— ••• ————

Lucy held a lacy white parasol overhead, yet she still needed to squint to keep the bright sunshine from hurting her eyes. The day could not be better for Eli's exhibition. The cloudless blue sky was striking against the thick green foliage of the countryside, and the air was warm, yet not too hot to be uncomfortable.

Mrs. Walker sat next to her on the picnic blanket, while the other wives either stood or sat with them, their pleasant conversation filling Lucy with a sense of well-being. It felt good to be among women she had always considered peers—even if she was there as Mrs. Walker's lady's maid.

"Mr. Boyer looks much more comfortable near an automobile than he does at a dinner party," Mrs. Walker said with a smile in her voice.

Lucy watched Eli, who stood a little ways off with all the gentlemen as they inspected the Duryea. The motor puttered and jumped, causing the vehicle to bounce as Eli pointed out various parts of the contraption. He had driven it out after the picnic ended. Lucy hadn't had a chance to talk to him, but he'd glanced her way when he'd first arrived, and the butterflies that had filled her stomach made her realize she needed to stay as far away from him as possible. She couldn't risk falling in love and losing her position with Mrs. Walker. Her job was the most envied position in Little Falls and she couldn't give it up, especially when her mother and sisters depended on her income.

Eli stepped into the automobile and the other men backed away. After a few moments, it started to roll, and Eli turned it around and drove it down the country road, farther and farther away.

Lucy's stomach began to fill with nerves as she watched it pick up speed. The landscape all around was flat, with few trees, and it was easy to see the vehicle, even as it grew smaller.

He turned it around again, and this time it went faster and faster as it came near. Lucy stood, speechless, as the car kicked up dust. She'd never seen anything like it. Everyone had become quiet as they watched, but the tension had built up in Lucy's chest until she wanted to cheer or shout for joy.

The automobile sped by in the blink of an eye, throwing dust in the air, and everyone clapped as Eli slowed and turned back around. He pulled to a stop near the gentlemen again, but this time, the ladies went out to join them.

"Well done, Mr. Boyer." Mr. Caruthers reached out and shook Eli's hand. "Your speed was remarkable."

"It was a new record," Mr. Alexander said, holding up a stopwatch. "Forty-two miles an hour."

"Unbelievable," said another man. "Most automobiles average around twenty-eight in long races." He drew closer to Eli, his face serious. "Do you think you could maintain your speed over a fifty-mile course?"

Eli's eyes were shadowed under his bowler as he looked over the Duryea. "I believe I could keep it somewhere in the midthirties over a longer course, but pushing it to the forties probably wouldn't be wise."

The men began to talk among themselves. Eli looked up and caught Lucy's eye.

She couldn't stop herself from grinning—or walking toward him.

He smiled back, his blue eyes as bright and brilliant as ever. His face shone with joy and the passion he felt for automobiles was palpable.

"That was wonderful." She felt breathless as she stopped near the vehicle, though whether it was from the excitement of the race, or seeing him look so handsome, she wasn't sure.

"Thank you."

"Mr. Boyer will now give all of you rides," Mr. Alexander said to his guests, drawing Eli's attention away from Lucy. "Mr. and Mrs. Caruthers, would you like to be first?"

Mr. Caruthers grinned and nodded, but Mrs. Caruthers put her hand to her chest and looked at the Duryea with a bit of fear. "Is it safe?"

"Perfectly safe," Mr. Alexander said. "I've spent hours in this vehicle and have not suffered a single scratch or bruise."

She straightened her spine. "Very well."

Mr. Alexander helped them inside and Eli turned to Lucy again. "Mr. Alexander has said I may take you riding on our next day off. Would you like that?"

Lucy held her breath, the excitement more than she'd anticipated, yet she felt a catch in her conscience. She couldn't deny her attraction to Eli, and feared it would only grow stronger if she spent time with him. But she wanted a ride more than anything. "I would like that."

He tipped the brim of his hat. "So would I."

"All set, Eli." Mr. Alexander nodded at Mr. and Mrs. Caruthers, who were crammed onto the bench seat beside Eli.

Lucy stepped back, her heart pumping wildly as she watched Eli pull away with his passengers. To think that she'd sit beside him and have his undivided attention as he drove her in an automobile seemed too good to be true.

The women congregated as they watched Eli give Mr. and Mrs. Caruthers a ride.

"Your young man is very handsome," Mrs. Powell said to Lucy with a kind smile. "I'm eager to take a ride in his motorized carriage."

Heat filled Lucy's cheeks and she glanced at Mrs. Walker to see if her employer had heard the other lady. "Mr. Boyer is not my young man."

Mrs. Powell was a pretty woman, not much older than Lucy. She lifted her eyebrows now. "He's not? I'm so sorry. I just assumed, with the way I've seen you two look at one another."

It was Lucy's turn to lift her eyebrows. Were her feelings that plain? "Mr. Boyer and I have only recently met," she said quickly, drawing Mrs. Walker's attention. "The admiration you see on my face is for his automobile and nothing else."

Mrs. Walker was now listening intently. "What's this?"

"I made a mistake," Mrs. Powell quickly told Mrs. Walker. "That's all. Please forgive me, Miss Taylor."

"Of course."

Mrs. Walker studied Lucy for a moment, though there was no censure in her gaze—just curiosity.

"I hear you're participating in a sporting competition," Mrs. Powell said to Lucy, clearly trying to change the subject. "How interesting."

The ladies turned their gazes on Lucy. A month ago, she would have been completely comfortable with all of them—yet now she wasn't sure how to behave. Mrs. Walker had been kind and gracious, treating her more like a friend than an employee, and the others had followed her behavior, but it didn't seem quite right. She wasn't their equal any longer—at least not socially—and she would be wise to remember that.

Chapter Five

Eli ran the rag over the dashboard of the Duryea until it shone. He cared more than he should what Lucy thought of the automobile. Even though it wasn't his, it still reflected him and his work in every way. In a few minutes, he'd pick her up at the Walker mansion and take her for her first ride. He said a quick prayer, hoping they wouldn't break down—though the thought of a few extra hours in her company was entirely too pleasant to wish away altogether.

He had put on his best suit of summer clothes and made sure his hair was combed. While cleaning the Duryea, he took care not to get any grease or dirt on his light-colored suit. It was the one thing he owned that hadn't been ruined by automobile grime.

He gave the hood one more swipe, chiding himself for putting more effort into the vehicle today than he had before the investors came.

"I thought I'd find you here." Mr. Alexander entered the barn, his hands in his pockets, his face serious.

"Where else would I be?" Eli tried to smile, but he sensed Mr. Alexander hadn't come for pleasantries—especially not in the middle of the morning when he was usually at work.

"On your day off, I thought you'd be with Miss Taylor." Mr. Alexander went to the Duryea and ran his hand along the fender.

Eli chose not to comment. They'd been given permission by both their employers to go driving, but he didn't want Mr. Alexander or Mrs. Walker to think it was a romantic rendezvous. Not only to protect his own job, but to protect Lucy's. He couldn't let anything jeopardize her position. He smiled to himself, realizing he'd given up on the idea of his sister becoming the lady's maid. Someday, he'd find a way for Jessie to leave domestic service.

"You're probably wondering why I'm home." Mr. Alexander leaned against the workbench and crossed his arms. "I had a phone call from Mr. Caruthers."

"You don't sound too happy." Eli stood motionless, afraid of what Mr. Alexander had to say.

"The group has come to a decision—more or less."

Eli's heart pounded, though he tried to act calm. "What does that mean?"

"They were very impressed with you and the Duryea—as well as your designs for manufacturing an automobile. Mr. Caruthers said if you were the only man they were considering, they wouldn't hesitate."

"They're considering someone else?"

"Apparently they wanted to keep that bit of information to themselves."

"May I ask who?"

"His name is Edmond Lerke. You'll meet him in two weeks."

"Two weeks?"

"At the company picnic."

Eli was confused. He tossed the rag onto the workbench and faced Mr. Alexander.

"The investors are trying to decide between you and Mr. Lerke. They want to see you two race side by side. Since Noah and I already have the company picnic race advertised and marked out, I invited all the investors back to Little Falls with Mr. Lerke. Noah has agreed to let Mr. Lerke race on his team, since he couldn't find anyone else who could actually beat you."

"I'll be racing against Mr. Lerke?"

"Yes. He'll bring his own custom-made automobile—the one he'd like to manufacture." Mr. Alexander took a deep breath. "If Mr. Lerke wins the race, they will make him a partner in their venture. If you win, then they'll pick you, with one condition."

"What?"

"They believe, as do I, that if we're going to partner with you, we want you to invest some of your own money in the venture. That way, you'll have a stake in the company."

"My own money?"

"You don't need to worry. If you win, you'll have the hundred dollars in prize money to put forth."

"And if I lose?"

Mr. Alexander looked at his feet for a moment. "I've spent several years working with these men, and I believe that they are capable of building a promising automobile company. I will go along with whatever they decide, either way."

The air filled with the weight of his declaration. "If I win, I'll have it all—but if I lose?"

"You can remain as my footman—though I don't believe you'd enjoy serving in that capacity for much longer."

Mr. Alexander was right. If Eli lost, he would be forced to look for employment elsewhere, which meant he'd probably have to leave Little Falls altogether.

"I don't think I need to tell you that this is the opportunity of a lifetime," Mr. Alexander said. "There will be a lot riding on that race now, but I know you can do it, Eli."

He hoped so.

"Now." Mr. Alexander moved away from the workbench, his voice less austere. "I imagine you have better things to do with your time. Go take Miss Taylor on a ride and try to forget about all this for the afternoon."

Without another word, Mr. Alexander left the barn.

Eli stood for a moment absorbing all the information he'd just been given. It was vital that he win the race. His entire future depended on his performance.

He went to the large barn door and opened it wide, then he turned the crank several times before the Duryea began to run. He climbed into the automobile and backed it out of the barn.

The day was overcast and windier than he'd like, but it would still be pleasant enough to ride with the top down. Just thinking about Lucy sitting beside him, the wind blowing through her dark red hair, brought a strange warmth to his gut.

He tried to push aside any romantic notions he had for the attractive lady's maid and drove the Duryea up the hill, backward. If he drove up the hill front first, the gravity-fed engine would not allow gasoline to flow properly and would sputter out.

As he pulled up to the Walker mansion, Lucy stood at the servants' entrance, a warm smile on her pretty face. The moment he came within sight, she stepped out and walked toward the circular drive in front of the two homes.

Today she wore a green skirt and a white blouse. A matching green bonnet sat on her curls. Her dimple appeared as he jumped out of the vehicle and met her halfway.

"Are you ready?"

"I've been counting down the hours."

"Here." He offered his hand, just as he would if helping her into a buggy. In all truth, the Duryea looked like a buggy, without the horses attached.

She slipped one gloved hand inside his and lifted her hem with her other. With a glance of excitement in his direction, she stepped into the vehicle and let go. As she arranged her skirts, he went around and climbed in beside her. The tiller came up over the dashboard and stuck out between them. Eli rotated the tiller handle and the Duryea went into motion.

"Oh, my." Lucy grabbed his arm as the automobile jerked forward.

He grinned as he watched her face.

Several emotions played over her features as they rolled out of Basswood Hill and onto Highland Avenue. Surprise, apprehension, and then pure joy. She shook her head as she smiled at him. "I can hardly believe I'm in a horseless carriage. Can you go faster?"

He laughed and lifted the tiller into second gear, allowing it to go about ten miles an hour.

They left Basswood Hill and followed the road out to the countryside where Eli usually raced. He rotated the tiller handle again, letting the Duryea go even faster.

Lucy's gaze swept over the landscape, her eyes shining as she laughed in amazement. "This is incredible."

He could watch her all day.

"Can we show my sisters?"

"Of course."

She directed him to turn around and they went back toward town. Her childhood home wasn't too far away from Basswood Hill, and they were soon on the street where she had grown up.

"My mother was able to keep the house," Lucy said with a sigh. "But she had to sell almost everything of value to hold on to it."

"I'm sorry about your loss." He glanced at her and recognized the sadness in her countenance. "I lost both my parents at the same time. They died in a carriage accident."

"Truly?" She looked at him, concern wedging her brows together. "What happened?"

He was quiet for a moment as he thought back to that horrible day. He rarely spoke about the accident, but he sensed she was someone he could trust with his darkest memory. "They liked to ride together on Saturday evenings, just the two of them. I was home with my sister, Jessie. I was fifteen at the time. A constable came to tell us there had been an accident. My father often raced with a neighbor and his wife when they were out. That night, my father's horse spooked and became tangled with the neighbor's horse, causing both buggies to overturn. Neither couple survived."

She put her hand on his arm. "How horrible, Eli. Doesn't their death make you afraid to drive so fast?"

He loved the feel of her touch and hated when she pulled away. "On the contrary. I believe automobiles will be much safer." He wanted her to understand. He rarely shared the reason behind his passion with anyone. "That's why I'm working hard to improve them. A horse is easily spooked and unpredictable. An automobile can be controlled at all times."

She nodded slowly, as if she understood his reasoning—and perhaps she did.

"Their deaths were the hardest thing I've ever endured," he continued. "I want to use it for good."

They were both quiet for a few moments.

"That's my home." She pointed to a large Victorian house. It was set off from the street, with similar houses on either side. A wide front porch, deep gables, and bay windows completed its charm. It looked nothing like the humble home Eli had grown up in, but it wasn't as fine as the Walker or Alexander mansions, either.

"I phoned my mama and told her we might be coming."

Eli pulled up to the curb and three young girls rushed out of the house. All of them had the same ginger-colored hair as Lucy, and looked remarkably similar to their oldest sister. They stood on the porch and waved, but none ventured toward the automobile.

"Three sisters?"

"Four. My sister Margaret is inside." She smiled sadly. "She'd be out here with the rest of them, but she can't walk."

"Is she a baby?"

Lucy shook her head. "She's fifteen. She broke her legs a few months ago, and they didn't heal properly."

Eli turned off the engine and stepped out of the Duryea to help Lucy. "Will she ever walk again?"

"Only if she has surgery, but it's very expensive, and Mama doesn't have the money."

An older woman appeared at the door and stood with the girls.

Lucy walked up to the house and Eli followed behind. She kissed each of her sisters and then embraced her mother.

Mrs. Taylor hugged her daughter tight, and then she pulled back to place her hands on either side of Lucy's face. "My girl. You look well."

"I feel well."

"Good." Mrs. Taylor looked to Eli, her brown eyes taking him in. "And this is Mr. Boyer?"

"Yes. Eli, this is my mama."

Eli shook Mrs. Taylor's hand. "It's a pleasure to meet you."

Mrs. Taylor squeezed his hand and held it a moment longer than he expected. "Welcome to our home."

Her touch was warm and affectionate and she made him feel comfortable with a simple smile.

A knock at a window made Eli turn. He saw an older girl smiling and waving inside the house.

"Margaret!" Lucy grabbed Eli's hand and tugged him to the front door. "Will you come and meet Margaret?"

He didn't know if she realized she was holding his hand—but he didn't mind. He enjoyed seeing her with her family. "Of course."

She pulled him through the front door, across a wide foyer, and into a cozy sitting room.

"Lucy!" Margaret reached out to her sister from her chair.

Lucy went to her and hugged her, then bent down and looked her in the eyes. "Would you like to go for a drive?"

Margaret looked up at Eli, a bit bashful, and nodded. She reminded Eli so much of Lucy, it was uncanny. He'd never met a family that looked so much alike. "May I?" she asked.

"It would be my pleasure," he said.

Lucy glanced from her sister back to Eli. "Would you mind carrying her to the automobile?"

Margaret's cheeks turned pink and she lowered her eyes, clearly embarrassed by her need for help. She was so young, with her life yet to be lived. It was a travesty that she could not walk.

"Of course." He went to Margaret and lifted her out of her chair. She weighed practically nothing.

He carried her out to his automobile and set her inside. Her eyes lit up as she looked around the Duryea.

"Can you show me how to start the automobile?" Lucy asked.

Eli nodded and brought her to the back of the vehicle. "I can tell you're close to your family," he said as he inserted the crank into the hole.

"Yes. It's been very hard since Papa died."

Eli glanced at Lucy's mother and sisters as they stood near Margaret, exclaiming over the automobile.

Lucy put her hand on Eli's arm and made him pause.

"You've probably guessed why I'm competing during the community picnic." She looked up at him as she whispered. "If I win, I plan to use the money to pay for Margaret's surgery—but I don't want her to know yet. I wouldn't want to get her hopes up. If she could walk, she could work and help Mama with expenses. As it is, she feels so helpless and dependent." Lucy's countenance grew heavy. "I just hope I win."

Eli's chest felt heavy and the day suddenly took on a dark pall. If Lucy's team won, her sister would walk again. If his team won, her sister would be forced to remain in her chair.

Could he win the race, and the rest of the team still lose the competition? That would be ideal. But would it play out that way? He prayed they would all get what they needed, though he was well aware that they might all fail to reach their goals.

<hr>

The evening before the community picnic, Lucy finally found time to practice her shooting and archery. Mrs. Walker had given her the night off, and Mr. Walker had set up a shooting range near the barn, complete with bow and arrows, as well as a pistol with ammunition. She had been practicing for an hour, but she wasn't quite ready to go inside.

Eli was at the fairgrounds with the Duryea making last-minute preparations for the picnic and she expected him home any minute. She didn't want him to think she was waiting for him, so she lingered near the target, pulling out her arrows with deliberate care, and watched the driveway for any sign of the handsome footman.

A low rumble filled the air and she glanced up at the sky, aware of the storm clouds building in the west.

Everything was still. There were no squirrels jumping through the basswood trees, no birds twittering from the branches, and no ducks splashing on the Mississippi. A wall of dark clouds appeared on the horizon and lightning jumped within the thunderclouds, promising a wild storm. If Eli didn't return soon, she'd be forced to go inside without seeing him. The very thought filled her with disappointment.

She heard the putter of the Duryea before she glimpsed it, and she smiled, despite the sudden nerves jumping inside. After four weeks at Basswood Hill, she had grown to care for Eli more than she realized possible. Ever since he'd taken her out in the Duryea, there had been a quiet bond between them. Mama and the girls had loved him, and every time she called or went home for a visit, they asked about him and the automobile. He hadn't taken her out driving again, but she'd relived that day in her mind and heart several times since then.

He appeared at the top of the hill and turned the vehicle toward the barn. She pretended not to notice and took her arrows back to the line she'd drawn in the dirt. With practiced ease, she put the arrow on the bowstring and aimed it at the target.

With a ping, she let the arrow go. It hit to the right of her intended mark.

Eli pulled the Duryea up to the barn and turned off the engine. "I imagine you think you're going to beat me tomorrow."

She grinned without even looking at him and placed another arrow on her bowstring. "I know I'm going to beat you. You haven't even practiced."

He sauntered over to where she stood and she glanced at him out of the corner of her eye. Joy settled deep within her heart at the sight of his smile. Just knowing he was near made her mood lighten.

A crack of thunder reverberated through the air and they both looked up. Lucy prayed the storm would pass quickly and things would dry up before the picnic in the morning.

"If we have enough time before the storm breaks, would it be possible to give the competition a quick lesson?" He stopped beside her, and she had no desire to move away.

"It would be quite magnanimous to offer a lesson." She gave him her full attention and realized he was even closer than she thought. Her breath caught as she came face to face with him.

His smile slowly gave way to a deeper, more serious look—one that turned her stomach of nerves into a chorus of warmth running up and down her body.

"Here." She swallowed and handed over the bow and arrow. "Why don't you start by showing me your form?"

He placed his hand over hers on the bow and she thought she might melt from the pure pleasure of his touch. She forced herself to let go and then stepped back to allow him to get into position.

Eli put the arrow in place and lifted the bow, pulling back on the string. "Like this?"

"No." She stepped up to him, putting her arms around him from behind to show him how to stand properly. He was much taller than she was, and much broader, but she was able to reach his hands.

His shoulders stiffened and his breath became shallow as she placed her hands over his. "Like this," she said quietly, and moved his hands until they were positioned correctly.

"Lucy." He said her name gently, yet there was depth and meaning in his voice.

He lowered his hands and turned until he was face to face with her again.

Rain began to fall, yet neither moved or said a word.

The air was cool on her wet skin and she began to tremble, but all she could think about was how much bluer his eyes were with the gray sky overhead.

Did he feel what she was feeling? If the answer was yes, she shouldn't let it continue, though she couldn't force herself to step away, either.

"You're cold." He took off his coat and placed it around her shoulders. "Let me get you inside."

He took her hand and they sprinted along the bottom of Basswood Hill. Rain fell through the leaves and mixed with the soil, making the air full with the earthy smells of summer. A set of steps rose from the bottom of the hill to the back door of the Walker mansion. Eli brought her up the steps and onto the back screened porch facing the river.

If Mrs. Walker or one of the other staff caught them holding hands, she would surely be rebuked—if not let go. She should release her hold—yet she couldn't.

His coat was warm and smelled of the cologne he wore. She wanted to stay nestled in it, but she needed to hand it over before someone saw her. She finally did what she knew she must, and pulled away. "You'll want your coat."

He watched her, not saying a word, and took it when she handed it to him.

They looked at one another for a moment and then she let out a sad sigh. "Eli."

"Don't say it, Lucy."

"I must."

He shook his head. "Let's leave things as they are. I want to always remember you just as you are in this moment."

In the month she'd known him, she'd grown to admire him more than she had ever admired anyone. She'd never met someone with such deep and passionate dedication. He was thoughtful, hardworking, and highly respected. He didn't feel the need to impress anyone or put on airs, and that was something she was coming to appreciate more and more. He had told her about his desire to manufacture automobiles and she was excited to see where it would take him. He was the kind of man who drew others to him because of his quiet confidence and vision, her especially.

The rain continued to fall, growing stronger by the moment, and still he did not leave. She didn't ask him to because the truth was that she didn't want him to go yet.

She walked to the screen and allowed the cool rain to blow against her warm face. If he didn't want her to say what she felt she must, then they'd be reduced to mere pleasantries. "I hope the rain doesn't interfere with tomorrow's plans. Will you race if it's raining?"

He was quiet for a moment and then he walked over and stood beside her. "We'll have to see what the conditions are like before I decide."

They watched the rain for a little while and then Eli spoke again. "Regardless of how things turn out tomorrow, I want you to know that I hope Margaret can have the surgery."

"Thank you," she said softly.

"I'll do whatever I can to help you make it happen." He gently took her hand. "You have my word, Lucy."

Tears stung her eyes and she squeezed his hand. "I appreciate your offer very much."

He lifted his free hand to wipe a tear off her cheek. "You're a good sister. I could see how much your family loves you."

She wanted to lean into his touch. "I love them, too."

"What you're doing for them is admirable."

"I'm only doing what I can."

He caressed her face with his gaze and took a step closer to her.

Suddenly, the desire to feel his lips upon hers was so strong, and so swift, she gasped. He must leave. Now. Because if he kissed her, she was afraid she'd want another kiss and another, and soon she'd want more. A home, a family, a future—things she had denied herself when she'd agreed to take the job with Mrs. Walker. If she married, she would have to leave her job, and her mother would have no income. She couldn't very well ask Eli to support her mother and four sisters, especially when he'd also be let go.

Lucy took a step back and pulled away from his grasp. "I think you should leave, Eli."

He stood for a moment, so many questions in his beautiful eyes. "Good night, Lucy. I wish you all the best tomorrow."

"You too."

He put his hat on and left the porch.

Lucy watched him walk through the rain, down the hill, and back to the barn where he started the Duryea and drove it into the building.

She leaned against the porch rail and tried not to cry. It wouldn't pay. As the oldest daughter, it was her job to provide for her family. She didn't have the luxury of falling in love.

Chapter Six

Late the next morning, Lucy stood at the fairgrounds and watched the last raincloud drift toward the east. It had poured all night and into the early morning hours. Mud oozed under her feet and puddles gathered in all the low places, making a mess for those who had gathered for the picnic.

The sound of laughter mingled with conversation as hundreds of people milled about the fairgrounds, not letting the weather deter them. Humidity lingered in the air and the sun promised to bring warmth to the earth again—but would it dry the roads in time for the race?

Several competitions had already been completed, including her shooting. She had earned the highest points that day, pushing her team into the lead. Soon she would have to compete in the archery contest and she would have to face Eli again. She hadn't seen him since he left the porch the night before, and she was nervous that things would be awkward between them.

"Next up is the archery contest," Mr. Walker called from his platform on the grand-stand stage. A thousand people could fill the stands, but only two hundred or so had come to watch. Other contests and events continued throughout the fairgrounds, drawing spectators to one booth or the other. Children waited in line for balloons, a lemonade stand was surrounded by young and old alike, and spectators cheered as a baseball game wrapped up in a nearby field.

"Good luck, Lucy." Mama kissed her cheek. "You'll win this one, too."

Mrs. Walker sat nearby and she offered Lucy an encouraging grin.

Eli appeared in the crowd and walked toward the stage. They met at the bottom of the stairs and he stopped to allow her to go up first.

"Hello," he said.

"Hello."

The tension she feared was not there. Thankfully, he acted as if nothing had passed between them, which was what she had hoped.

Lucy walked up the steps and joined Mr. Walker, Eli beside her.

"Playing for the Walker team is Miss Lucy Taylor." Mr. Walker indicated Lucy and she waved at the crowd. They clapped and cheered, many having seen her win the sharp-shooting competition already.

"Playing for the Alexander team is Mr. Elijah Boyer." Again, the crowd cheered, and Eli waved.

"Please take your places," Mr. Walker said as he indicated the line where they would stand. "You will each be given three arrows. The archer with the best cumulative score will win the points for their team."

Lucy took a deep breath and picked up her bow and arrow. Eli did the same, working silently beside her.

They went to the line and Eli gave her a slight bow. "Ladies first."

She straightened her shoulders and put her arrow on the string. Her hands shook slightly and she forced herself not to look at the crowd. It was hard enough to perform in front of an audience, but with Eli standing so close, it was almost impossible to concentrate on the target.

With as much grace and focus as she could muster, she lifted the bow and pulled back on the string. After a moment's hesitation, she let the arrow fly. It landed on the right edge of the bull's-eye.

The crowd clapped and she let out a breath. She smiled at the audience and then stepped back for Eli to take a shot.

His face was serious and his shoulders tight as he lifted the bow and pulled back on the string. Memories from the night before, when she'd put her arms around him to show him how to stand, came flying back to her. Her cheeks filled with heat and she glanced around to see if anyone suspected her wayward thoughts and actions, but everyone had their eyes on Eli.

He cut a dashing figure in his summer suit as he poised to shoot and then released the arrow.

It landed on the left edge of the bull's-eye, equidistant from the center as hers.

"After the first round, it looks as if we have a tie," Mr. Walker said with a smile. "Come on, Miss Taylor. Show the competition what you're made of."

The crowd chuckled and Lucy took another deep breath. She had to forget about the audience and Eli, and just focus on what she was good at.

She aimed once again, and this time the arrow landed closer to the center of the bull's-eye.

"Well done!" Mr. Walker said as the audience cheered.

"See if you can beat that, Boyer," a young man heckled from the crowd.

Eli glanced at Lucy, and though he didn't smile, his eyes suggested he was proud of her, too.

His second shot landed just outside the bull's-eye, giving her the clear lead.

"One more shot," Mr. Walker called out. "Make it count."

Lucy felt more confident as she raised her third arrow and aimed it at the center of the bull's-eye. The tension on the string pulled at her muscles, begging to be let go, so she did what the arrow desired, and released the string. The arrow landed with a thud on the outside of the bull's-eye, close to Eli's second shot.

The crowd was silent and Lucy blinked several times, shocked that it had not gone where she'd aimed.

"Well done, Miss Taylor," Mr. Walker said. He offered congratulatory applause, and the crowd soon followed, though they didn't cheer as loudly as before.

"One shot left," Mr. Walker said to Eli. "Let's see what you can do."

Eli put his toe on the line and placed his arrow on the string. With beautiful form—suggesting that he didn't need her help yesterday, after all—he lifted the bow and pulled back on the string. He closed one eye and let the arrow sail toward the target. It landed with a thud beside his second arrow—making Lucy the winner of the archery contest.

"Congratulations, Miss Taylor!" Mr. Walker said. "The archery points are awarded to your team."

"Hip, hip, hooray!" the crowd chanted. "Hip, hip, hooray!"

Eli lowered the bow and turned to face Lucy. He extended his hand. "Congratulations, Lucy."

"You were a formidable contender." She took his hand and loved the feel of his touch.

"I had a good teacher." He winked and then moved away, allowing the crowd to get a full view of her. She hoped her cheeks weren't flaming with embarrassment as she smiled and accepted their well-wishes.

"The last competition of the day will take place in thirty minutes," Mr. Walker called over the cheers of the crowd. "The automobile race."

The audience only cheered louder and Lucy glanced at Eli. His face had grown very serious.

"Mr. Boyer will be competing against Mr. Lerke of Minneapolis," Mr. Walker continued as the crowd quieted. "The race will start just outside the fairground entrance and continue for ten miles, ending back here."

A young man raced up the steps onto the stage and gave Mr. Walker a piece of paper.

Mr. Walker looked at it for a moment and then lifted his hands to quiet the crowd. "It appears that the Alexander team has won the equestrian points. According to my calculations, the competition will come down to the race. If Eli wins, the Alexander team will walk away with the prize. If he loses, the Walker team wins the money."

Lucy frowned, her heart sinking at the news. More than anything, she wanted the money for Margaret's surgery—yet she also wanted Eli to win.

"May the best man win," Mr. Walker said.

Eli offered Lucy a sad smile and then turned and left the stage.

Her shoulders sank and her excitement over winning the archery contest faded.

———◆◈◆———

Eli walked across the fairgrounds as fast as he could. He'd only left the Duryea to compete in the archery contest. Other than that, he'd been with the automobile since he pulled it out of the barn early that morning.

Mr. Alexander stood by an unfamiliar automobile as he spoke with Mr. Caruthers and two of the other investors who had visited Little Falls before. A fifth gentleman, one Eli had not met, stood beside them, pointing out various aspects of the new vehicle.

"Ah, Mr. Boyer. So nice of you to join us again," Mr. Caruthers said as Eli approached. "I'd like to introduce you to Mr. Lerke of Minneapolis. He's only just arrived."

The other man was about the same age as Eli, though he was much shorter. His black hair and eyes were his dominant features as he surveyed Eli from under his derby. "The roads were almost impossible to pass," he said, extending his hand to Eli. "I didn't think I'd make it."

Eli shook his hand. "Is this your automobile?"

Lerke nodded, his eyes filled with pride. "Aye, it is," he said with an Irish accent.

The body of the motor wagon was an old buggy, which Lerke had customized into a self-propelled vehicle. "I usually average about twenty-five miles an hour on long trips like the one I just made from Minneapolis—but I don't think I went over ten miles an hour today."

Eli lifted his boot, the mud sticking to it like clay. "These conditions are less than ideal, to be sure."

"We've cleaned the wheels of me Lerkemobile as best as we can," Lerke said, "but I'll be hard-pressed to race her like I wanted today."

"We understand these are difficult circumstances," Mr. Caruthers said. "But we are confident that the man who wins today will be just the man we need to invest in."

The other investors nodded in agreement.

Eli glanced at Lerke, who was also eying him.

"Good luck, gentlemen." Mr. Caruthers shook their hands and then Eli left them to look over the Duryea one more time.

"Do you think you'll be able to win?" Mr. Alexander asked quietly as he walked with Eli.

"As long as I don't get stuck in the mud, I think I have a good chance."

Mr. Alexander nodded. "I looked over the Lerkemobile and it's a fine machine. He'll be real competition for you."

"Thank you for letting me use your automobile today." He hated to admit he was envious that Lerke had already built his own vehicle.

"You're welcome."

"Have you changed your mind about placing your investment in Mr. Lerke should he win?"

Mr. Alexander shoved his hands in his pockets and shook his head. "Unfortunately, as much as I like you, Eli, it would be foolish of me not to pool my resources with the others, though I feel I have a lot invested in you already and I don't want to see that wasted."

"I appreciate the opportunities you've given me, sir."

"I believe in you, Eli."

The words, coming from a mentor like Mr. Alexander, meant a great deal to Eli. "Then I'll do my best to win, so you don't have to make such a hard choice."

Mr. Alexander grinned and slapped Eli's shoulder. "I appreciate that. I'll crank the engine."

Lerke started his engine and it purred like a lion cub.

"Don't let him get under your skin," Mr. Alexander said as he turned the crank and the Duryea came to life. "Show him what you're made of."

Almost everyone at the picnic had moved to the starting line. The crowd was thick with bowler caps and bonnets—yet Eli located Lucy's hair immediately. She stood with her mother and sisters, though Margaret was nowhere to be seen. He hoped she hadn't been forced to stay home because of her legs, though he suspected she had.

He caught Lucy's eye and she smiled at him. She looked beautiful in a green summer gown, with the green bonnet she'd worn on their drive in the Duryea a couple of weeks ago. It had been fun to watch her shine during the archery competition and accept the praise from the audience. She had done her best, and he suspected she would want him to do his best, too, even if it meant winning the prize money. He just wished there was some way he could win and still help Margaret, though it seemed impossible.

Mr. Alexander moved away from the Duryea and Eli rotated the tiller handle to the right to put it in motion. The mud was slippery, and as he tried to turn the vehicle around to face the starting line, the wheels slid. He let up on the tiller and the vehicle came to a stop. His heart pounded a little harder, and he had to remind himself that these were not normal driving conditions.

Thoughts of his parents' horrific accident suddenly blinded his view and he had to shake off the reminder. They had died because they couldn't control their horse. He was driving an automobile. If he was smart, he could keep control of the Duryea at all times. The two were not the same.

Eli inched up to the starting line and glanced over at Lerke, who sat in his horseless carriage. The engines putted and the crowd cheered.

Mr. Alexander stood near the starting line and held his hand in the air. He looked at his stopwatch, his face serious, and then he quickly lowered his hand.

Both vehicles lurched over the starting line and Eli glimpsed Lucy out of the corner of his eye as he moved past. She waved a handkerchief and he knew she was cheering him on to the finish line.

Mr. Alexander and Mr. Walker had marked out the course the day before and Eli had been told not to inspect it, so he wouldn't have an unfair advantage. Both drivers had to follow the signs and markings to know which way to go. The only thing Eli knew was that it was a ten-mile course, which would take them out of town on a country road he was not familiar with.

He lifted the tiller to put the motor into second gear as the Duryea picked up speed. The road was as bad as he had anticipated, and he wasn't going nearly as fast as he knew he could. Lerke stayed close beside him, though Eli tried not to pay him too much attention. He'd rather focus on what he needed to do to win the race.

They came to the outskirts of town and the road opened up before him. It was a long, narrow road that led to a small town called Pierz. Eli had only driven it once the summer before. Deep wagon ruts were dug into the mud, and Eli's back wheels spun more than usual. He could only be going ten or twelve miles an hour.

He rotated the tiller, hoping to make the vehicle move faster. It inched ahead of Lerke, but not by much. Before long, they came to a red stake, which indicated they had reached the halfway mark. An arrow pointed at another country road that would take them south.

Eli turned right, just ahead of Lerke, and faced an even more treacherous road. Deep mud puddles caused the Duryea to bump and lurch, threatening to throw him off his seat.

Just up ahead it looked as if the road had been partially washed out. He let up on the tiller and the Duryea slowed as he approached. Lerke didn't slow down. He moved past Eli and tipped his hat.

The Lerkemobile made it across the washed-out road with ease. Frustration burned deep in Eli's chest as he watched his competitor move ahead. He couldn't let the other man win. If he did, all his dreams would be gone.

Eli twisted the tiller and the Duryea jerked ahead at a much faster clip. He couldn't play it safe anymore. The road looked dangerous, but not as dangerous as a future without his dream. He hit the washed-out portion of the road and, for a moment, he believed he would sail over it like Lerke had—but the Duryea spun out, and in that instant, Eli lost all control.

The automobile turned in a circle and Eli held on to the dashboard. He didn't have time to think as the vehicle began to tip on its side.

"No." He shook his head as he grabbed the tiller. "Please, God. No." This couldn't be happening. If he tipped, he would be out of the race for sure—and more than likely hurt.

At the last second, the Duryea righted itself and faced the way he had come.

His heart pounded and his hands shook. He briefly closed his eyes and whispered a prayer of thanks.

As fast as he could, he got the Duryea in motion again and turned around, facing the back of the Lerkemobile.

Lerke was two or three vehicle lengths ahead of him. Eli turned the tiller as fast as it would go.

Slowly, he gained speed and was soon right behind Lerke. Before too long, the fairgrounds were in sight and the crowd began to cheer. Eli was still behind Lerke. His pulse was racing so fast, he was afraid his heart would climb up his throat.

Putting the Duryea into third gear, the highest it had been during the entire race, Eli was able to pick up enough speed to come beside the Lerkemobile.

The man's black eyes grew round when he saw Eli, and he also turned the tiller of his automobile.

Eli focused on the road ahead and pushed the Duryea as fast as it could go. All the weeks and months of racing with Mr. Alexander were beginning to pay off, and he found the confidence he needed to maneuver through the dense mud.

The crowd jumped and waved as Eli pulled ahead of Lerke by an inch, and then a foot, and then he was a whole vehicle length ahead when he crossed the finish line.

The crowd cheered.

Exhilaration like nothing he'd ever felt rushed through Eli's veins. He hollered out a victory cry as he brought the Duryea to a stop. As soon as the engine died, he jumped out and was met with a mass of people surging toward him chanting, "Boyer! Boyer!"

Before he knew what was happening, he was lifted onto the shoulders of several mill workers and they were bringing him back to the finish line where Mr. Alexander stood waiting with the other investors.

"We have a clear winner!" Mr. Alexander yelled over the shouts and cheers of the crowd.

They let Eli down in front of Mr. Alexander and the man reached out and shook his hand. "Well, done, Eli. Congratulations."

The other investors offered their hands and their congratulations as well. Each one beamed with the same excitement and energy Eli felt.

In one moment, his entire life had changed—yet it could have ended so differently if the Duryea had turned over. It had been a miracle that the vehicle had stayed upright.

The realization that he couldn't control an automobile at all times hit him hard. His smile slipped and, at that moment, he caught sight of Lucy. She stood back with her mother and sisters, a sad smile on her face.

And then he realized there were other things, more important things, out of his control, as well. One was a future with Lucy.

Chapter Seven

A few hours later, Eli drove the Duryea back to Basswood Hill with Mr. Alexander on the seat beside him. Just behind them, Lerke drove Mr. Caruthers. The others came in a surrey with Mr. Walker. Since it was getting late, and the roads were still not ideal, Mrs. Walker had graciously invited all of them to stay the night.

Though Mr. Lerke was disappointed, and would have probably preferred to go home immediately after his defeat, he agreed to stay.

The thrill of victory was still fresh as Eli turned the Duryea into Basswood Hill and pulled up to the Walker mansion.

"Thank you again," Eli said as Mr. Alexander exited the vehicle. "I look forward to discussing the details at your earliest convenience."

Mr. Alexander stood near the Duryea and frowned. "Aren't you coming in to join us?"

"I'll be there after I put the Duryea in the barn and change into my footman's garb."

"Whatever for?" Mr. Alexander laughed. "Eli, consider yourself officially done with your position as footman. From this day forward, you are my business partner in racing and automobile manufacturing." He motioned toward the Walker mansion. "Come inside and join us for supper. We have much to discuss."

Eli swallowed hard and looked from the mansion to Mr. Alexander. Was he serious?

Mr. Caruthers and the other investors stood watching Eli and he knew that he had a choice to make. If he saw himself as their equal, they would view him that way. If he considered himself inferior to them, then that's how they'd treat him.

"Thank you. I will," he said.

"Good. Now leave the Duryea here for the time being and come inside to celebrate." Mr. Alexander motioned for the others to follow and started toward the house.

Eli stalled the engine and sat for a moment. All his dreams were coming true, yet sadness niggled at his happiness. He had been so single-minded in his pursuit to build and race automobiles, he'd never paused to think about other things he wanted in life, like a home and family. Since meeting Lucy, those things were all he seemed to think about.

Now, the idea of pursuing his automobile dreams felt almost pointless without someone to share them with. He liked the idea of having Lucy by his side, sharing his joys and sorrows, his hopes and dreams. She was just as passionate and excited about his automobile as he was. In the four short weeks he'd known her, he had come to recognize that she was intelligent, kind, and witty. Life had thrown a few unexpected surprises her way, yet she had responded with honor and dignity. Her courage to participate in the picnic games in order to pay for her sister's surgery was the most admirable thing he'd ever witnessed.

He sat back and shook his head in amazement. Somehow, in just a month's time, he had fallen in love with Lucy Taylor.

"Are you coming, Eli?" Mr. Alexander held the door open and grinned. "We have some pretty important things we'd like to discuss with you."

Eli stepped out of the Duryea and walked up to the front door, but his mind was not on the investors. His mind was on Lucy and all he wanted to tell her.

"Mr. Lerke has gone to his room until supper," Mr. Alexander said to Eli as they walked onto the front porch and into the foyer. "I don't blame him. It's a difficult situation to be in."

Eli had been working at Basswood Hill for over a year, and not once had he entered either mansion through the front door. He felt underdressed as they walked into the parlor. Mr. Walker was there already, sitting in his chair near the hearth. Mr. Caruthers and the others had also found seats.

Jack stood at attention near the door. He didn't meet Eli's eyes when they entered the room.

Mr. Alexander took a chair, but Eli still stood, holding his cap.

"Have a seat, Eli." Mr. Walker pointed at a chair on the other side of the hearth. "Do you need anything? How about a drink? Jack, please get Mr. Boyer something to drink."

Jack nodded and turned to leave the room.

"That won't be necessary," Eli said quickly.

"Nonsense," Mr. Walker said. "We need to celebrate your victory."

Eli took a deep breath and forced himself to relax as he lowered into a chair. This new lifestyle would take some getting used to.

"Now," Mr. Alexander said as he leaned forward and put his elbows on his knees. "We have a few things we'd like to discuss."

"Mr. Alexander is right," Mr. Caruthers said. "He's told us that he shared the basic plans for our partnership, but until we knew which man would win, there were a few other details we couldn't solidify."

"Like where we would manufacture the automobiles," Mr. Alexander added.

"Since you're the winner," Mr. Caruthers said, "we have decided the best place to establish the company is right here in Little Falls. Mr. Alexander and Mr. Walker have an empty building on the east side of the river, so we will rent that space and set everything up there."

Mr. Caruthers went through some of the logistics of the company and Eli listened attentively. He had a few ideas of his own and shared them freely, though he kept one eye on the front window, watching for Lucy's arrival.

"Now, for the most important part," Mr. Alexander said. "We have all agreed that you will be a full partner in this venture and will be the manager and main representative of the company. As such, you will earn a handsome income and will be required to travel around the country, taking our automobiles to races, fairs, and exhibitions." He grinned. "We plan to take our auto to Paris for the World's Fair and you will come with us."

Paris? The World's Fair? It sounded too good to be true.

"There are several races already planned"—Mr. Alexander continued, forcing Eli to keep up with the conversation—"and I've entered you in many of them. You will begin work immediately on the first prototype. We hope to have the manufacturing company in full force by the end of this year."

Eli's mind spun with all the possibilities. He'd finally be able to provide for Jessie and she could leave domestic service in Minneapolis. He couldn't wait to tell her.

"For now, you are more than welcome to stay in your old room," Mr. Alexander said. "But I'm sure you'll be anxious to find a home of your own as soon as possible."

A home. The thought of looking for a home filled him with eager anticipation, but he couldn't imagine having a home without a wife to share it with—without Lucy. Would she even consider his proposal? They hadn't known each other long, yet he sensed that she cared for him as much as he cared for her. Would she have him?

"So?" Mr. Caruthers asked. "What do you think of all that, Mr. Boyer?"

Eli looked around the room at the eager faces, and nodded. "I think we're onto something big, gentlemen."

The room erupted with laughter and good-natured excitement.

They were onto something big, but Eli had something even bigger in mind.

❖

Late afternoon sunshine filtered through the shiny green leaves, making patches of light dance on the street as Lucy walked back to Basswood Hill. She had taken her mother and sisters home after the picnic and stayed for a couple of hours to visit with Margaret. They had filled her sister in on all the activities and Mama had shared Lucy's victories. Margaret's eyes had shone with pride over Lucy's accomplishments, but a deep sadness lingered there at having missed all the fun.

Lucy lifted her hand and ran it along the bottom of a tree branch, allowing the leaves to tickle her fingers. A deep melancholy had settled over her and she couldn't make herself move any faster. She was thankful she hadn't told her mother or sisters that she had hoped to win the money for Margaret's surgery. Her loss would have been even harder if her family's hope had been dashed, just as her own had been.

She turned into Basswood Hill and faced the long, winding drive that would take her back to her servant's life. She didn't mind the work and was thankful she had a job, but she wished she could do more for her family. Where would she get the extra money for Margaret's surgery now? Every penny she made went for daily expenses.

The Duryea and the Lerkemobile were parked in front of the Walker mansion, just as Lucy had expected. There would be a fine supper that evening for their guests, and Lucy would be expected to help Mrs. Walker dress for the meal, but that was still an hour off. She wasn't expected back yet, but had wanted some time to herself after her disappointment.

Sunlight sparkled off the Mississippi like a million little diamonds, beckoning Lucy to come and sit a while. She skirted the mansion and took the drive down the hill to the lower grounds. Mr. Walker had built a beautiful gazebo there for Mrs. Walker. It was an octagon-shaped structure with thick pillars painted the same dark green as the mansion. A bench ran along the perimeter inside, a perfect place to sit and contemplate what she could do to help Margaret.

She stepped into the gazebo and let the screen door close behind her. The Mississippi was not too far away, with the large paper mill across the river on the opposite bank. A train trestle stood off in the distance and a train rushed by, blowing its whistle and puffing steam into the clear blue sky.

Lucy let out a long, weary sigh as she sank to the bench and stared at the Mississippi. She hated knowing that she had failed Margaret, and her sister would continue to suffer.

"Care if I join you?" Eli stood outside the screen door, his dear face filled with a mixture of excitement and apprehension.

She hadn't expected him, and found her emotions in turmoil at his appearance. His win had prevented her from her goal, but she couldn't fault him for doing his best. More than anything, she didn't want this to come between them. "If you'd like."

He opened the door and took a seat on the bench across the way from her. "I was in the middle of a meeting when I saw you walk down the drive."

She tore her gaze off him and watched the train rattle by. "Won't the others be upset that you left?"

"I don't think so. We have more to discuss, but I told them it needed to wait."

She looked back at him and loved the way the sunlight made his blue eyes sparkle. "I didn't get a chance to congratulate you after the race. I'm happy you won."

"Are you?"

"Very much."

He was quiet for a minute. "I'm sorry your team didn't win. You did a fine job today."

"Thank you."

Eli stood and walked across the gazebo to stare out at the river. "The investors have made an offer I can't refuse."

"Oh?"

"They want to make me a partner and begin manufacturing my automobile immediately."

Lucy stood. "Eli! That's wonderful."

He turned, but there was no smile on his face.

"What's wrong? Aren't you happy with the offer?"

"I would be." He took a tentative step toward her. "If I knew you were happy."

She smiled and shook her head. "You don't need to worry about me. I'll find some way to help Margaret. Mama and I will save enough money, somehow."

"That's not what I mean."

She looked up into his beautiful eyes. No one had ever looked at her the way he did right now. "Wh—what do you mean?"

Ever so gently, he reached out and took her hand in his. "I mean I want to know you're going to be happy every day, for the rest of your life."

Lucy swallowed. "No one knows that for sure."

He lifted her hand to his lips and placed a kiss on her knuckles.

She caught her breath at the touch.

"You're right," he said, "but if you'd allow me the honor, I'd like to try."

Her lips parted. "What are you saying, Eli?"

"I love you, Lucy. I've never met a woman I respect and admire as much as I do you." He smiled and the skin around the edges of his eyes crinkled. "I'm excited for the future, but only if you're by my side as we pursue our dreams together."

He loved her? Tears gathered at the back of her eyes. A part of her had hoped—yet she hadn't wanted to believe it was possible. "I love you, too, Eli. I think I fell in love with you the moment I saw you fidgeting in your footman's attire. I knew then that you weren't made like anyone else."

Eli laughed. "And I think I fell in love with you the moment you stood up to the other staff and defended a woman's right to compete in the Olympics." He pulled her closer and wrapped his arms around her waist. "Speaking of the Olympics, how would you like to see them in Paris on our honeymoon?"

Olympics? Paris? Honeymoon? She could barely wrap her mind around what he was saying.

"What do you think?" he asked.

"What do I think?" She laughed. "I don't know what to think."

"Will you marry me, Lucy? And spend the rest of our lives on the greatest adventure God offers in this lifetime?"

Hope and joy filled her chest—but then it felt as if a bucket of water was tossed against her and she came fully awake. "What about Mama and my sisters? I can't go off and leave them to fend for themselves. What about Margaret and her surgery? If I'm not working, who will provide—?"

"We will. Together."

"How?"

"With my income. And we will live here in Little Falls, so you can care for all of them, as much as you'd like."

The thought of having another person to help her carry the burden was more than she could have ever hoped for. "Truly?"

"Truly."

She bit her bottom lip and forced back the tears of happiness that wanted to flow. She wrapped her arms around him and leaned into his strength.

Eli lowered his head and captured her mouth in a beautiful kiss. His lips were tender and his passion evident. She melted into his embrace and thrilled at the love in his touch.

When he pulled away, her mind swam with all the things that had just happened—but one question remained. "What did you mean when you asked if I'd like to see the Olympics in Paris?"

He smiled as he ran his thumb over her cheek. "I will be taking our automobile to the World's Fair in Paris next year. It's being held at the same time as the Olympics. I was wondering if you'd like to join me."

It was Lucy's turn to smile. "I would be honored."

Eli grinned and then he kissed her again, offering her more than a lifetime of happiness. He had given her back her hopes and dreams, and made her family his own. But more than that, he had given her his heart, a priceless gift she would cherish for the rest of her life.

Gabrielle Meyer lives in central Minnesota on the banks of the Mississippi River with her husband and four young children. As an employee of the Minnesota Historical Society, she fell in love with the rich history of her state and enjoys writing fictional stories inspired by real people and events. Gabrielle can be found at www.gabriellemeyer.com where she writes about her passion for history, Minnesota, and her faith.